MONSTER Friends

ALSO BY KAETI VANDORN

Crabapple Trouble

Kaeti Vandorn

MONSTER Friends

RH
GRAPHIC

New York

MONSTER FRIENDS WAS DRAWN WITH CUSTOMIZED BRUSHES IN ADOBE PHOTOSHOP USING A WACOM CINTIQ. THIS BOOK WAS LETTERED DIGITALLY WITH A FONT CALLED MILK MUSTACHE.

Text, cover art, and interior illustrations copyright © 2021 by Kaeti Vandorn

All rights reserved. Published in the United States by RH Graphic, an imprint of Random House Children's Books, a division of Penguin Random House LLC, New York.

RH Graphic with the book design is a trademark of Penguin Random House LLC.

Visit us on the web and sign up for our newsletter! RHKidsGraphic.com • @RHKidsGraphic

Educators and librarians, for a variety of teaching tools, visit us at RHTeachersLibrarians.com

Library of Congress Cataloging-in-Publication Data is available upon request.
ISBN 978-1-9848-9682-7 (hardcover) — ISBN 978-0-593-12539-7 (lib. bdg.)
ISBN 978-1-9848-9683-4 (ebk)
Designed by Patrick Crotty

MANUFACTURED IN CHINA
10 9 8 7 6 5 4 3 2 1
First Edition

A comic on every bookshelf.

FOR MY BROTHERS,
BEN, JACOB, AND COLIN

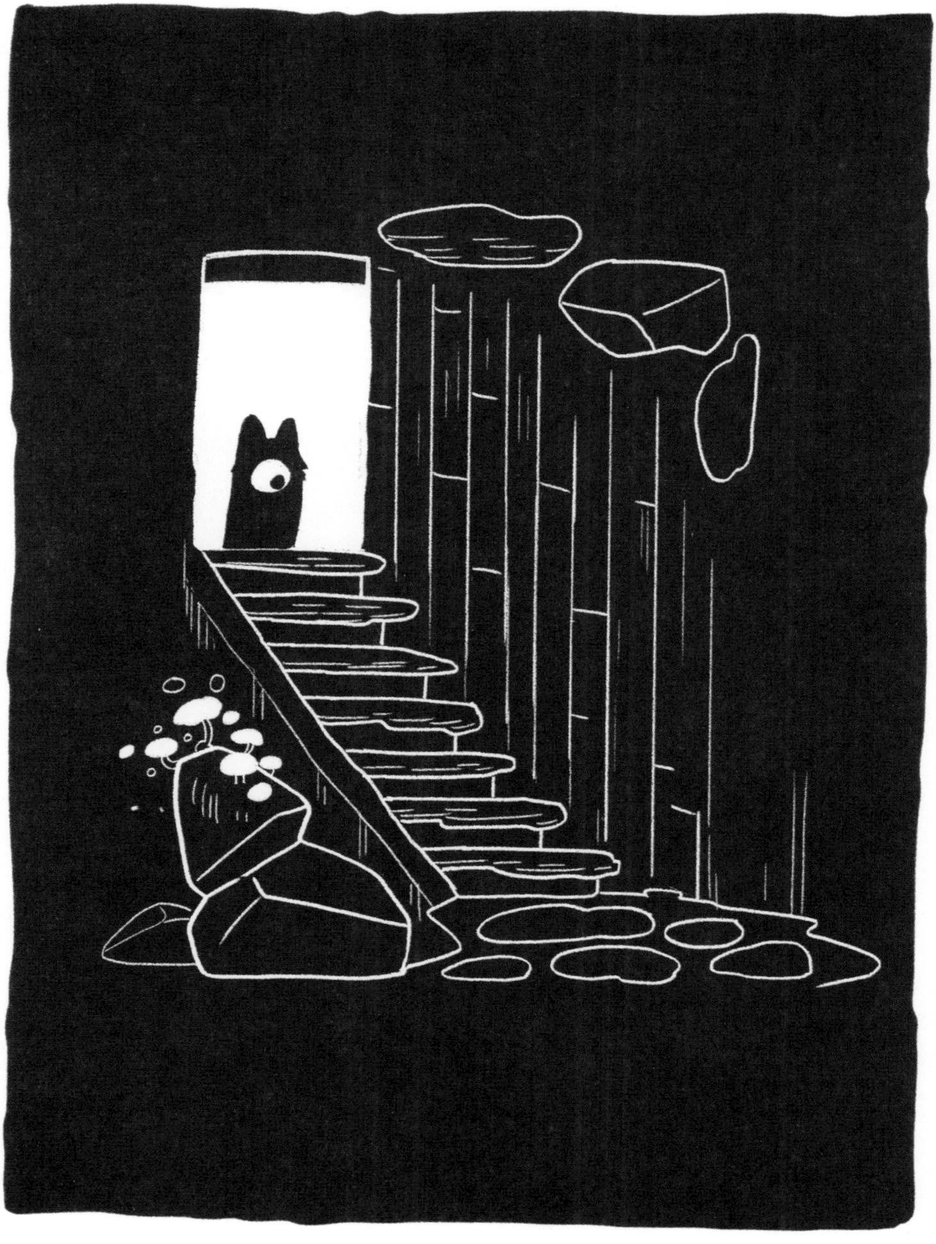

chapter 1

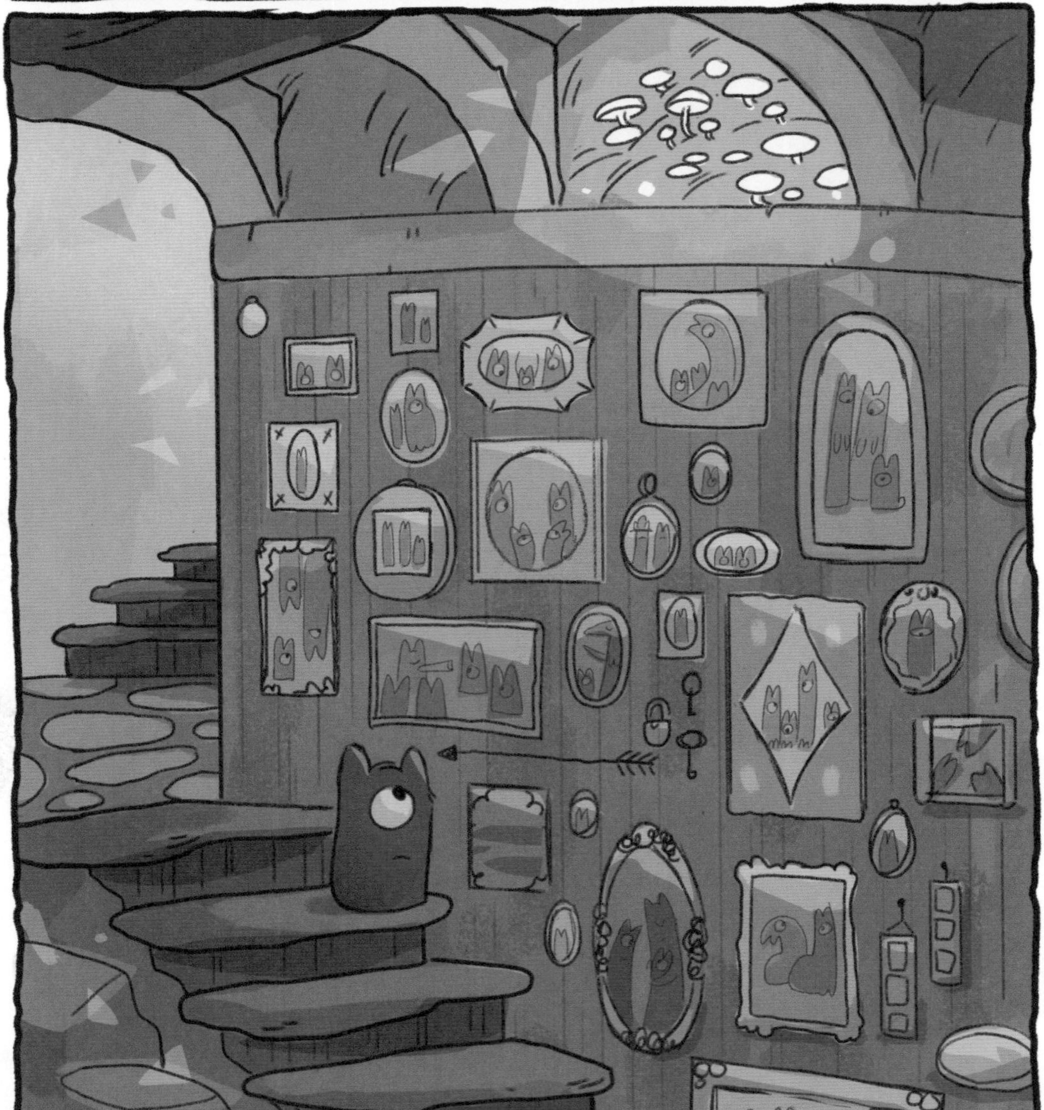

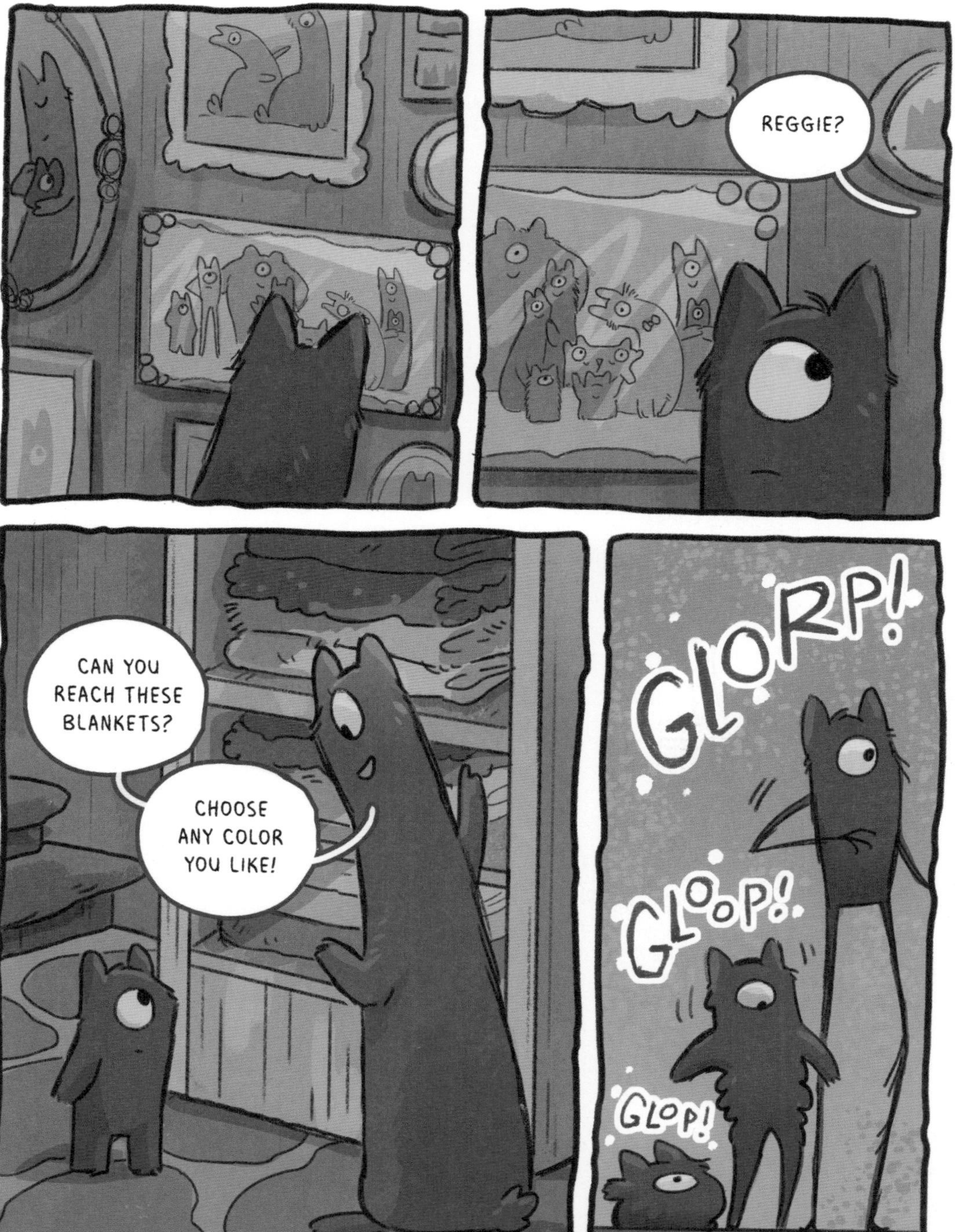
REGGIE?
CAN YOU REACH THESE BLANKETS?
CHOOSE ANY COLOR YOU LIKE!
GLORP!
GLOOP!
GLOP!

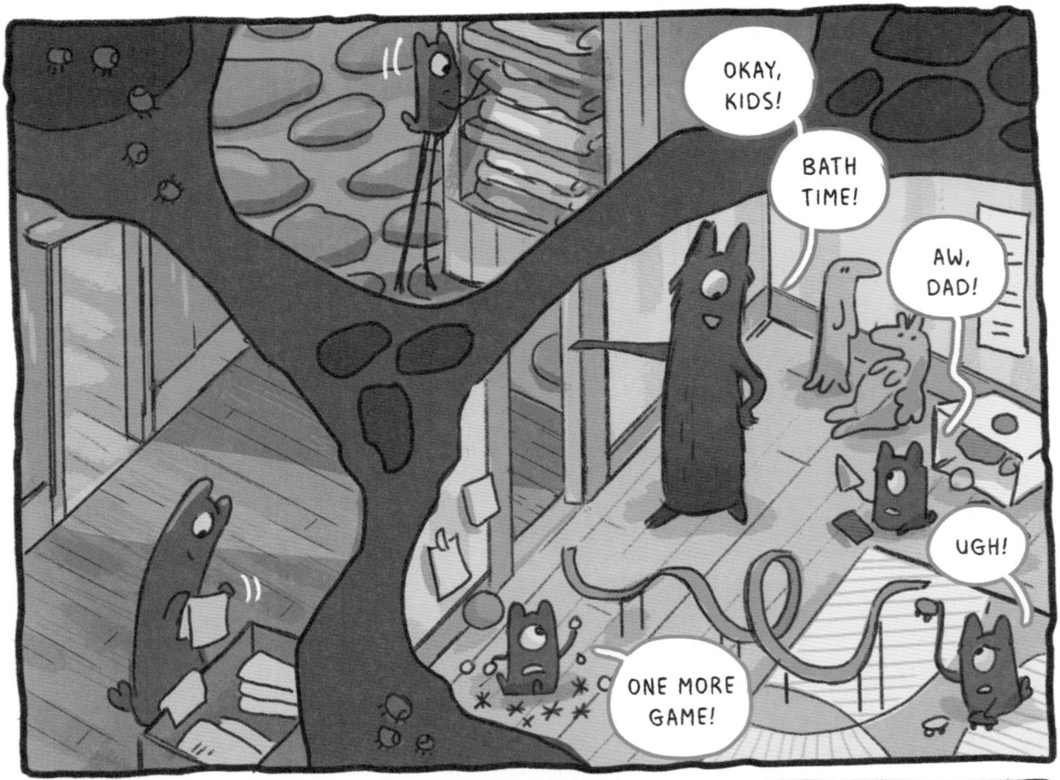
OKAY, KIDS!
BATH TIME!
AW, DAD!
UGH!
ONE MORE GAME!

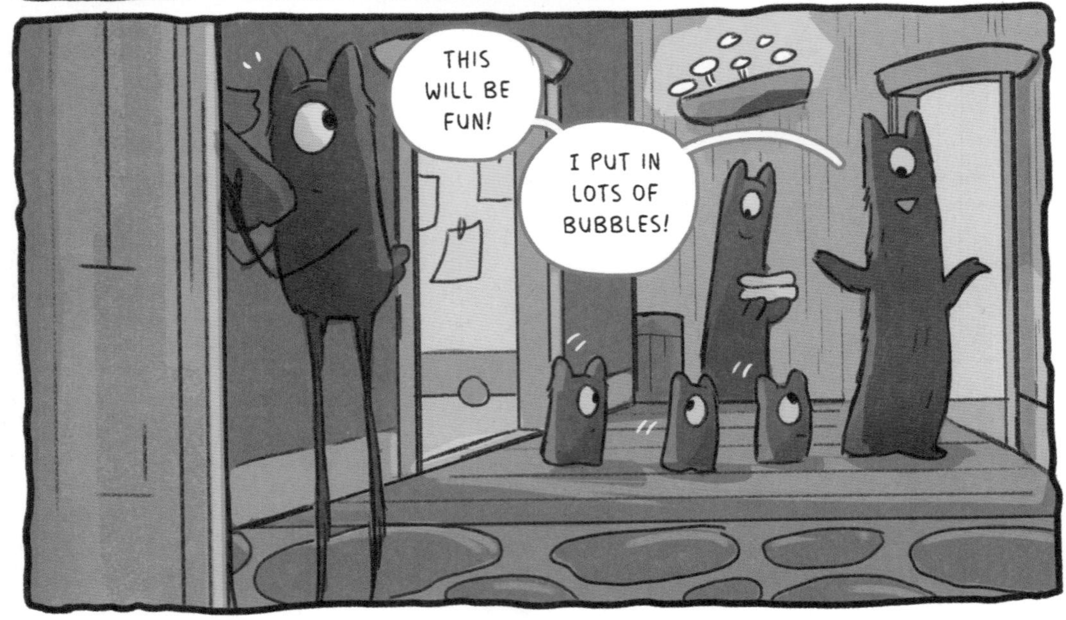
THIS WILL BE FUN!
I PUT IN LOTS OF BUBBLES!

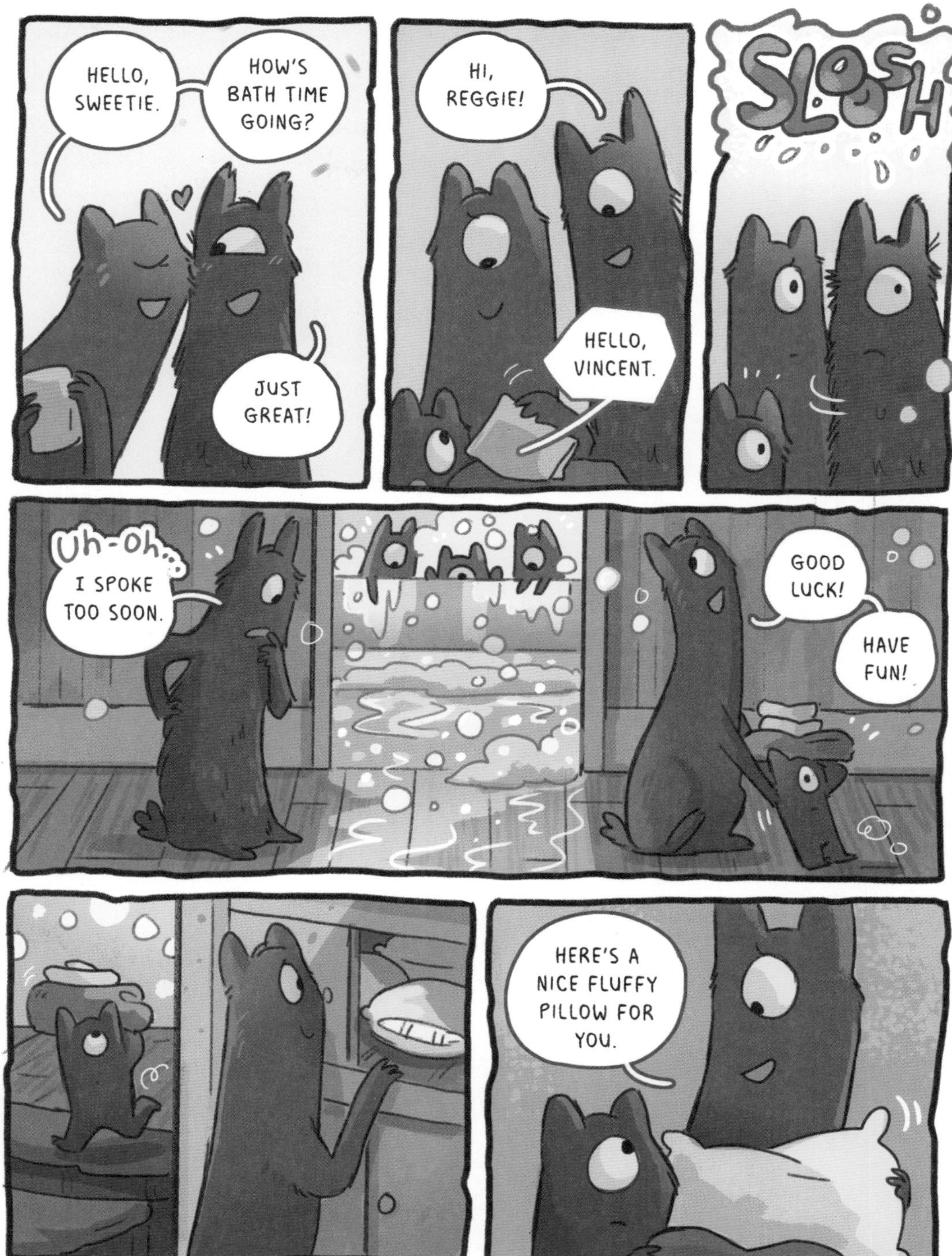
HELLO, SWEETIE.
HOW'S BATH TIME GOING?
JUST GREAT!
HI, REGGIE!
HELLO, VINCENT.
SLOSH
Uh-Oh...
I SPOKE TOO SOON.
GOOD LUCK!
HAVE FUN!
HERE'S A NICE FLUFFY PILLOW FOR YOU.

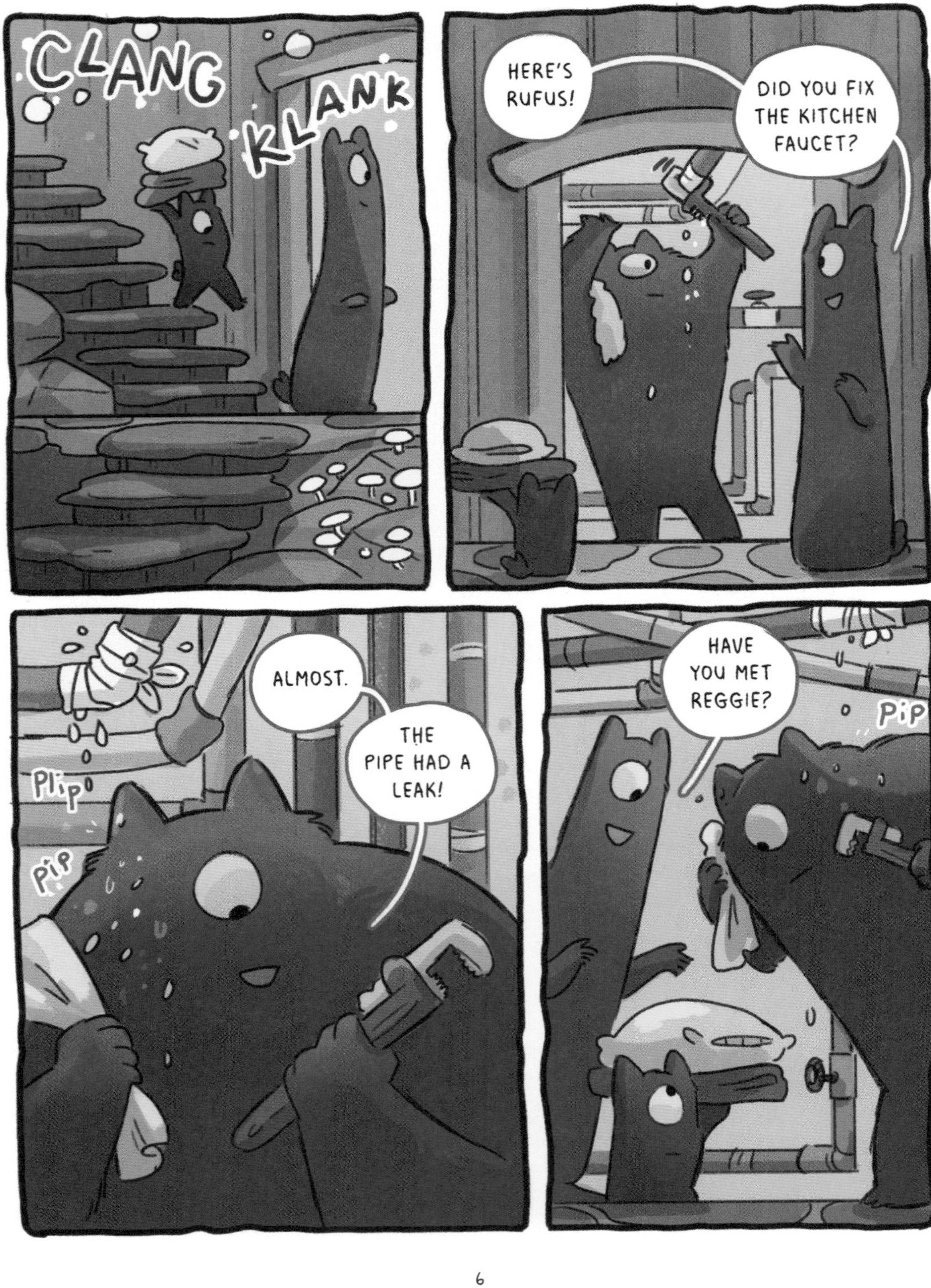
CLANG
KLANK
HERE'S RUFUS!
DID YOU FIX THE KITCHEN FAUCET?
Plip
pip
ALMOST.
THE PIPE HAD A LEAK!
HAVE YOU MET REGGIE?
Pip

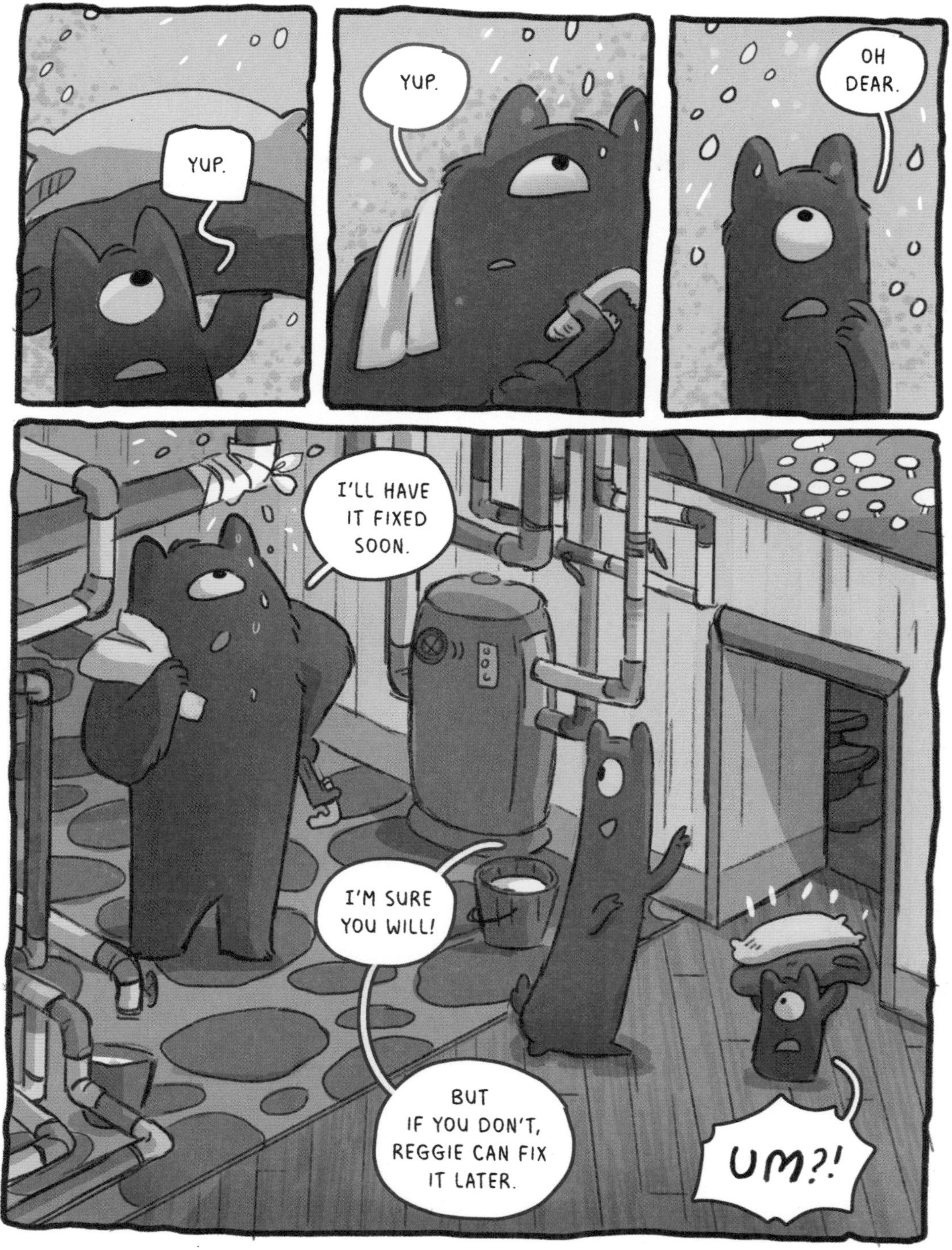
YUP.
YUP.
OH DEAR.
I'LL HAVE IT FIXED SOON.
I'M SURE YOU WILL!
BUT IF YOU DON'T, REGGIE CAN FIX IT LATER.
UM?!

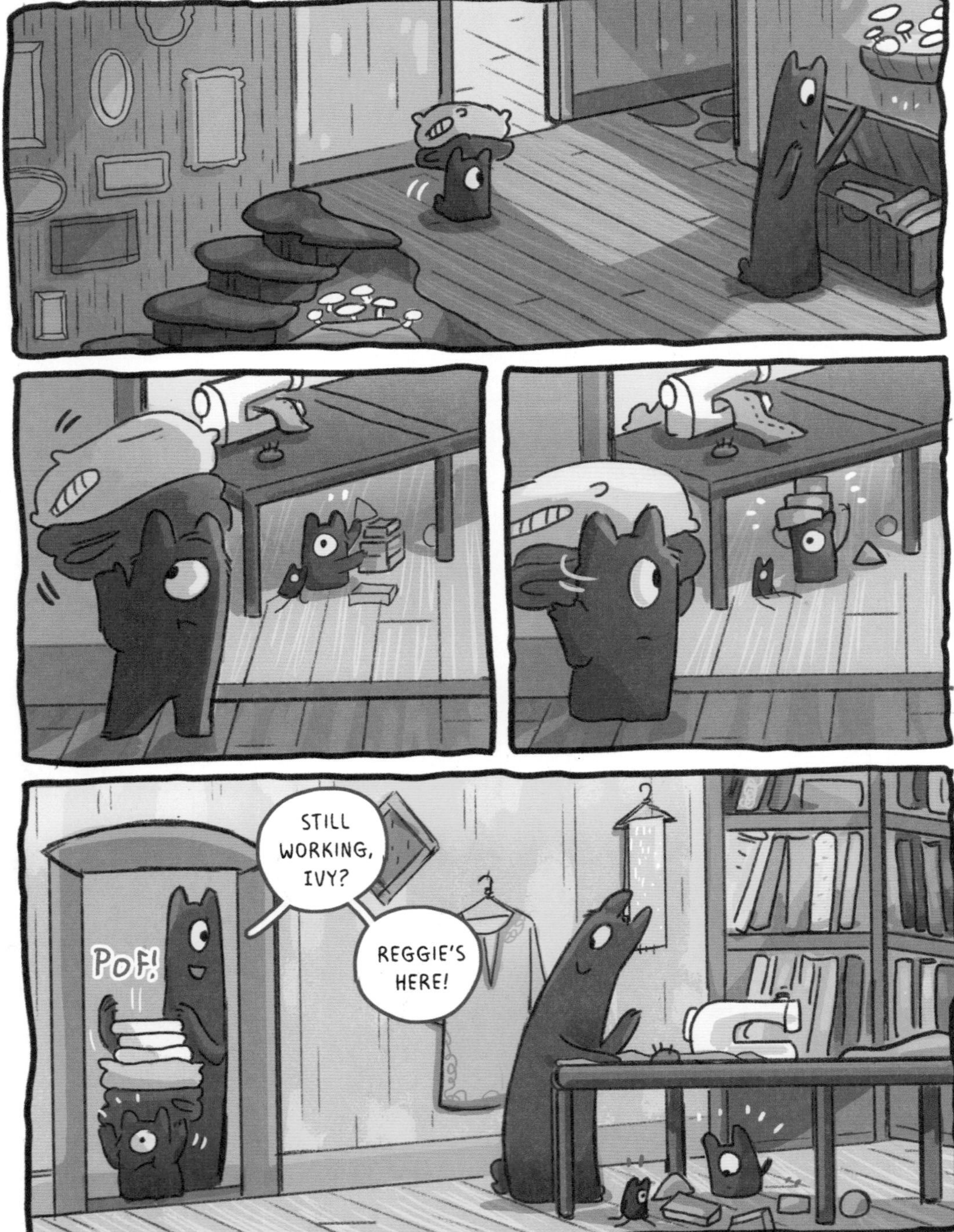
STILL WORKING, IVY?
REGGIE'S HERE!
POF!

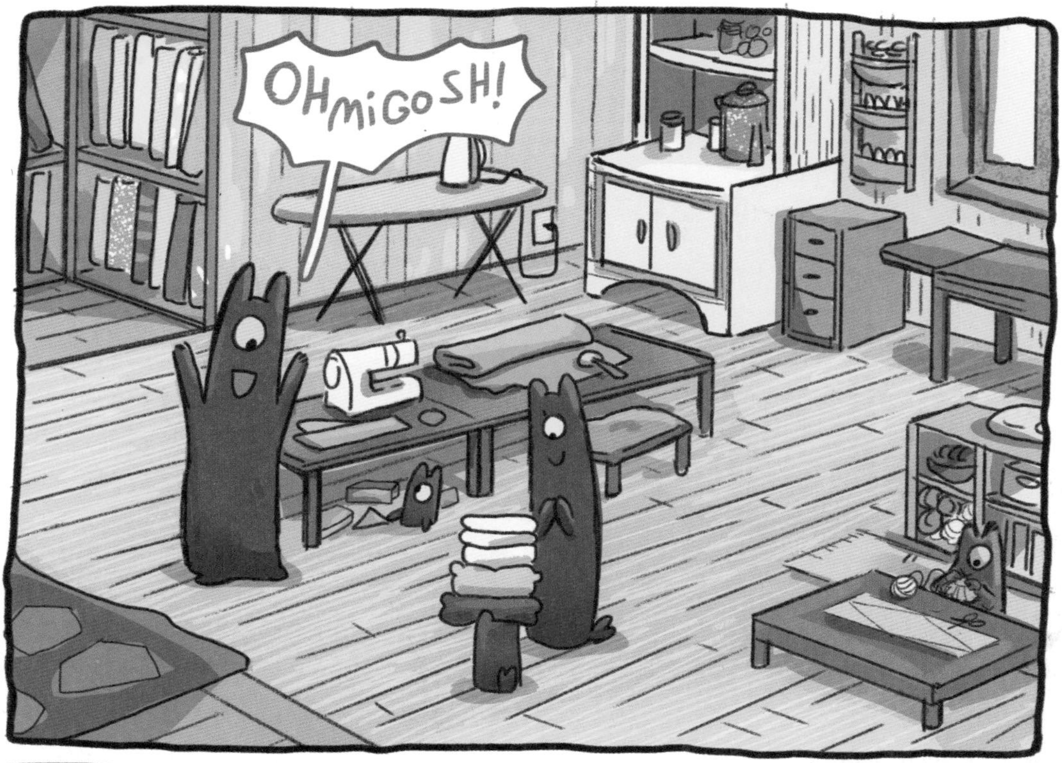
OHMIGOSH!

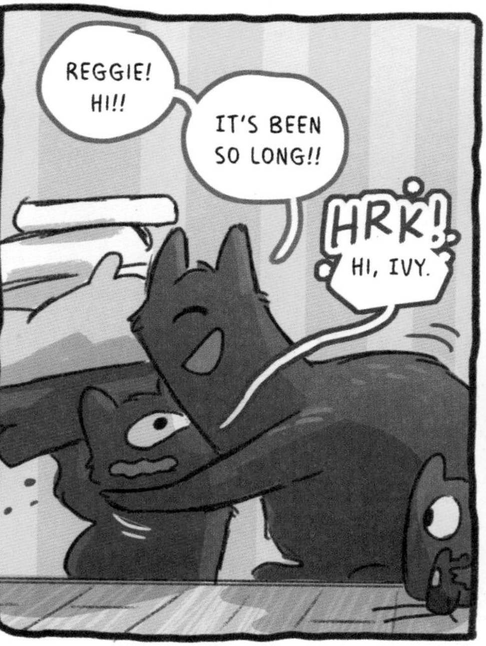
REGGIE! HI!!
IT'S BEEN SO LONG!!
HRK!
HI, IVY.

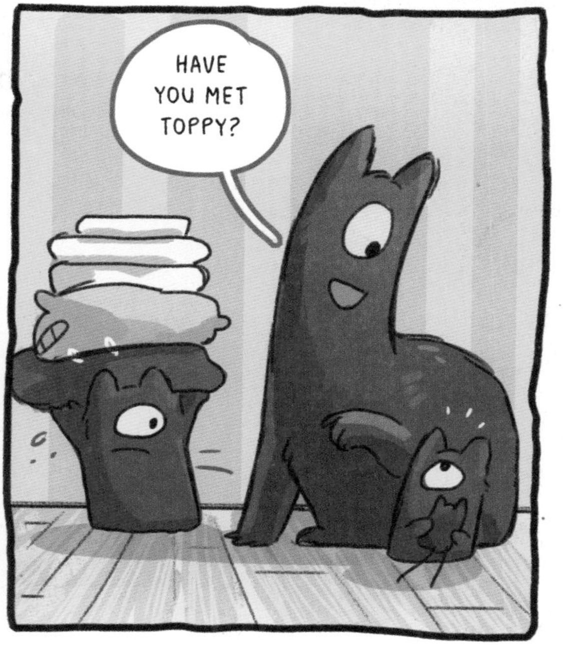
HAVE YOU MET TOPPY?

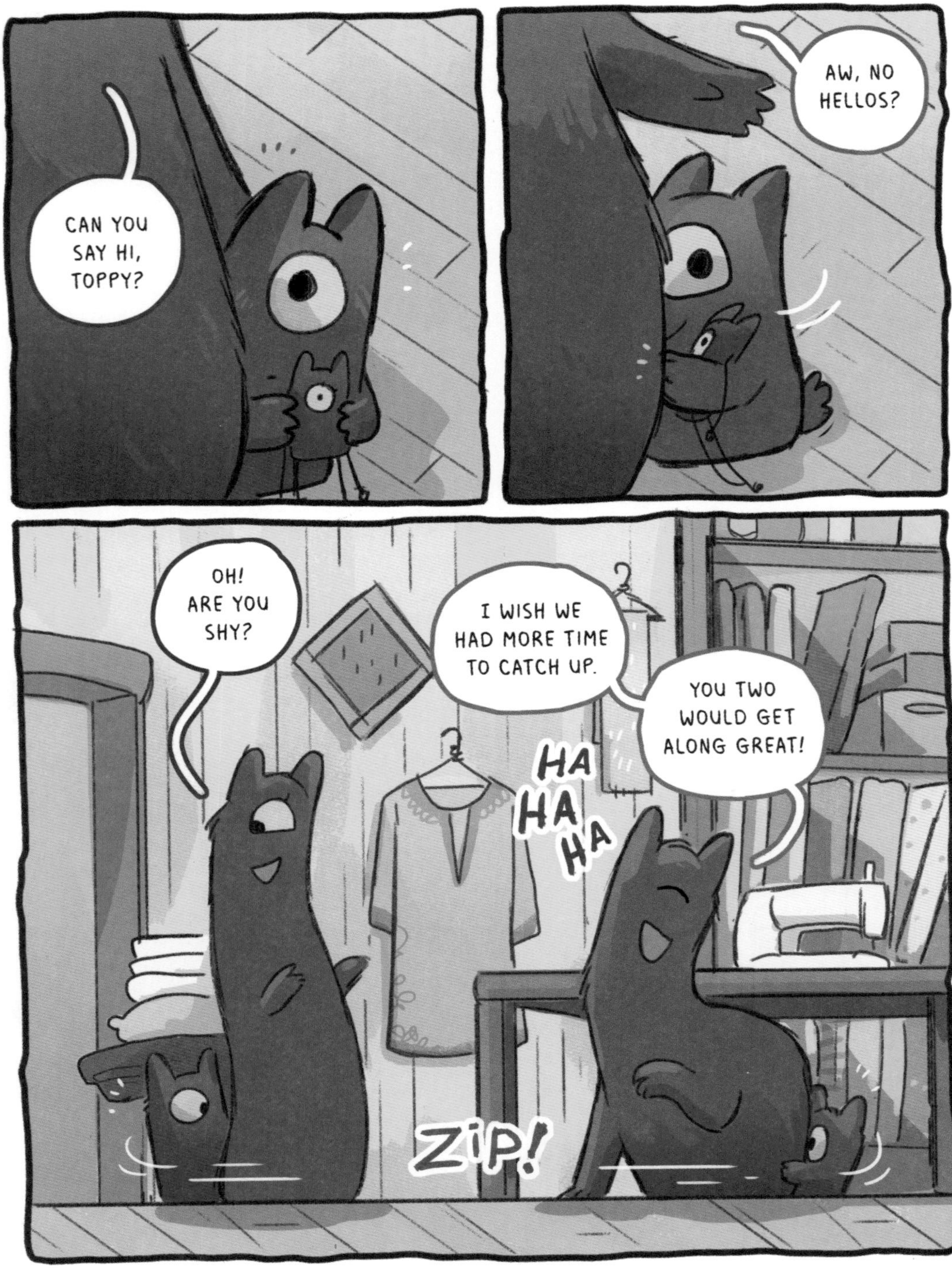
CAN YOU SAY HI, TOPPY?
AW, NO HELLOS?
OH! ARE YOU SHY?
I WISH WE HAD MORE TIME TO CATCH UP.
YOU TWO WOULD GET ALONG GREAT!
HA HA HA
ZIP!

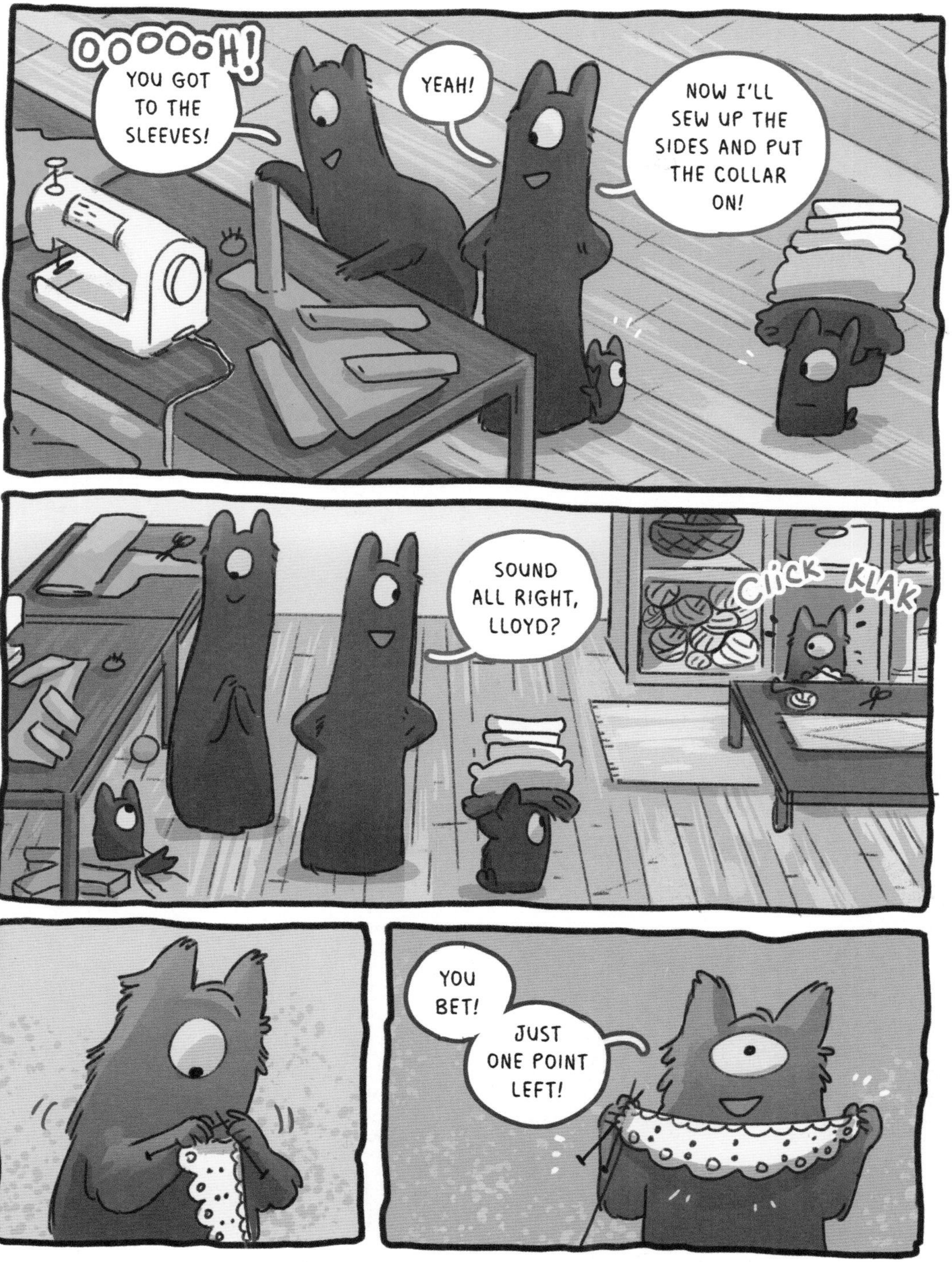
OOOOOOH!
YOU GOT TO THE SLEEVES!
YEAH!
NOW I'LL SEW UP THE SIDES AND PUT THE COLLAR ON!
SOUND ALL RIGHT, LLOYD?
CLICK KLAK
YOU BET!
JUST ONE POINT LEFT!

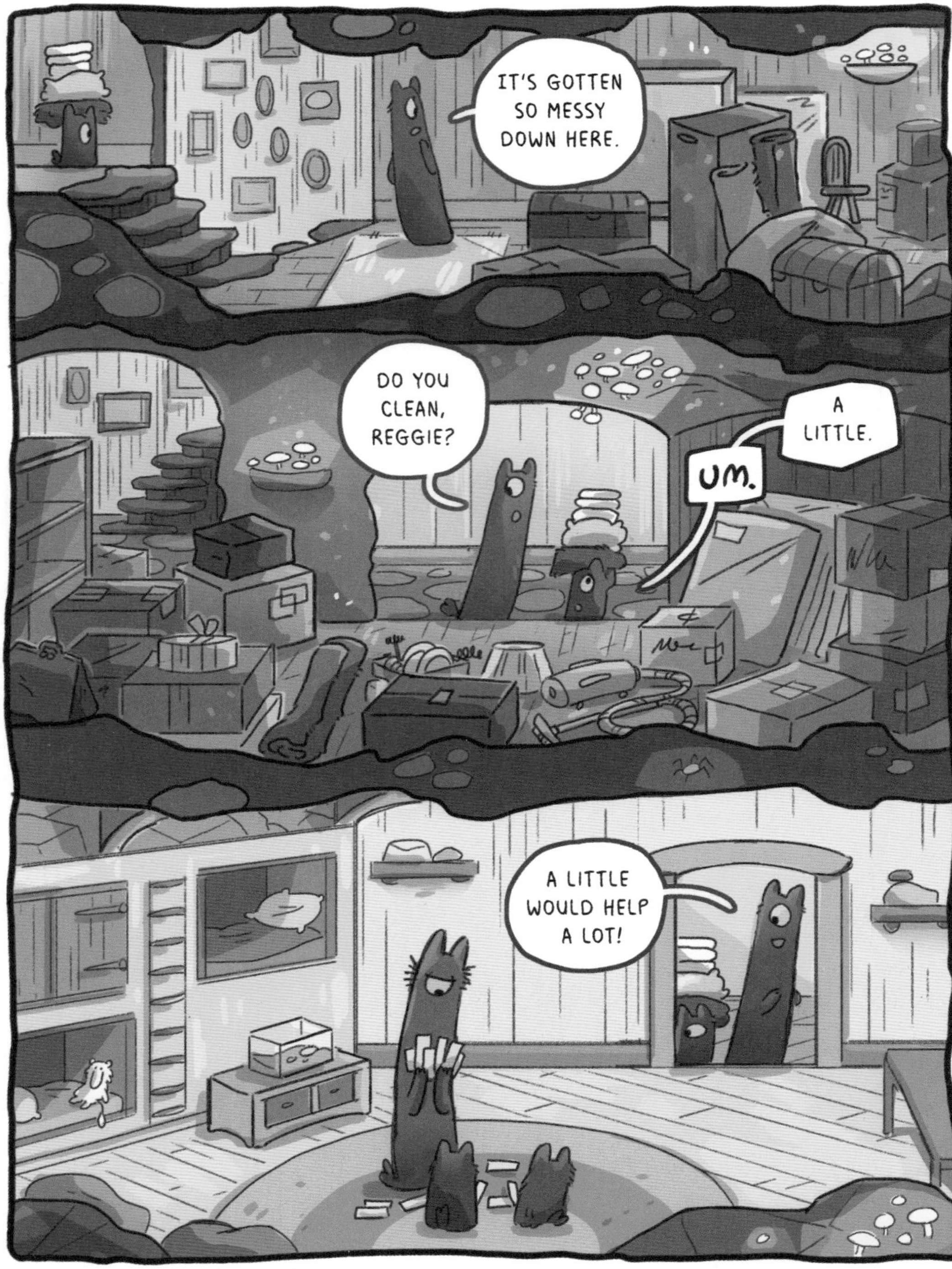
IT'S GOTTEN SO MESSY DOWN HERE.
DO YOU CLEAN, REGGIE?
UM.
A LITTLE.
A LITTLE WOULD HELP A LOT!

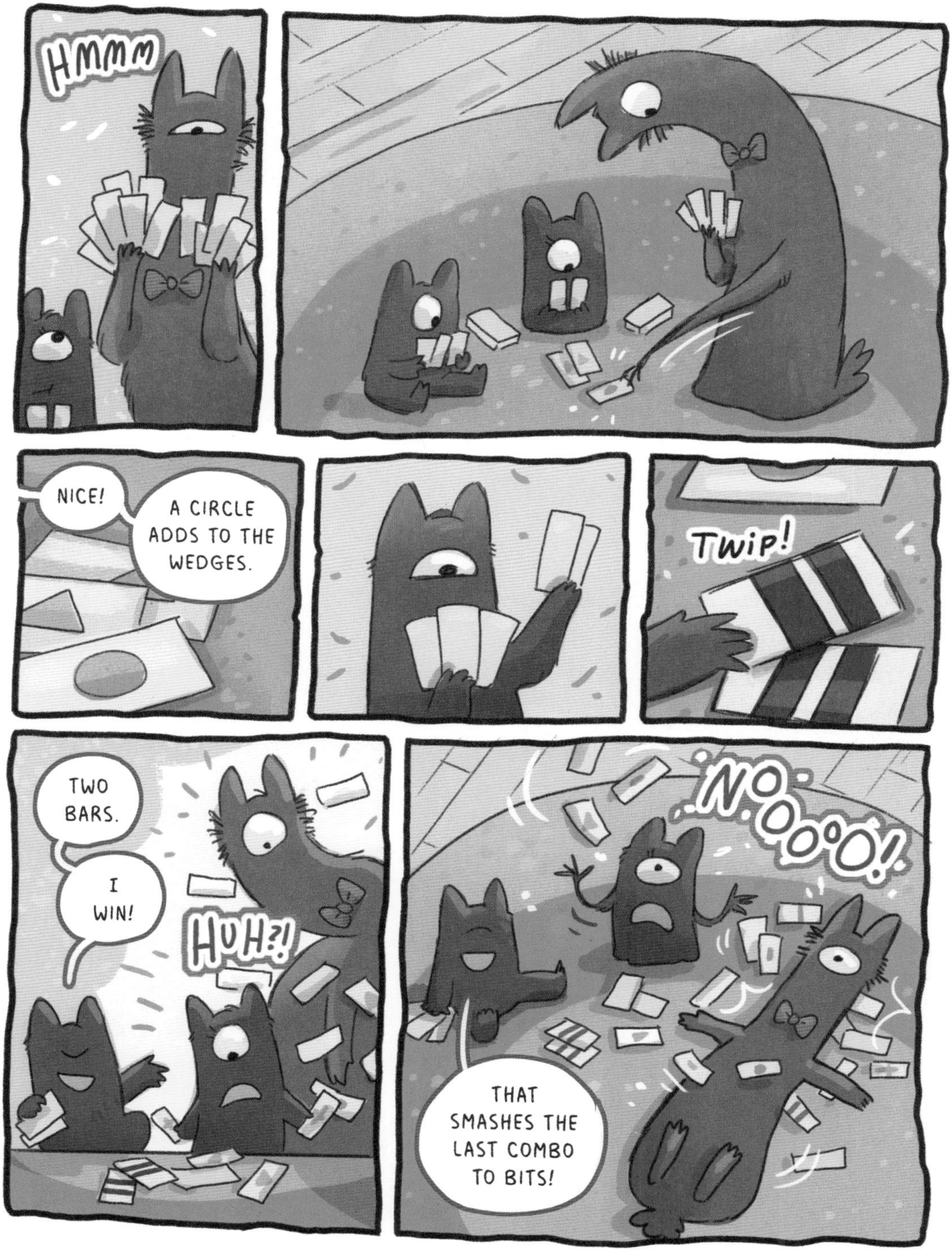
HMMM
NICE!
A CIRCLE ADDS TO THE WEDGES.
TWIP!
TWO BARS.
I WIN!
HUH?!
NOOOOO!
THAT SMASHES THE LAST COMBO TO BITS!

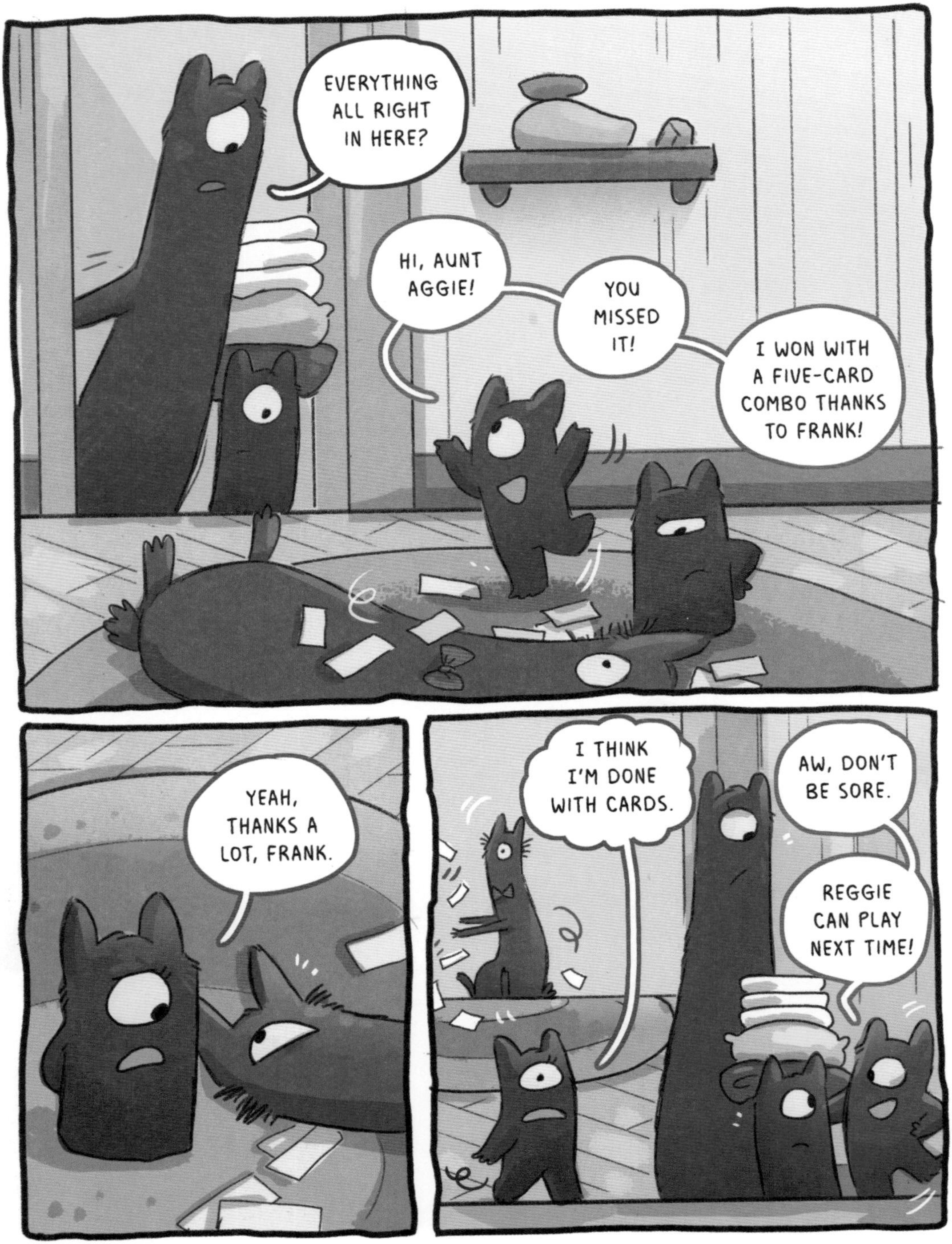
EVERYTHING ALL RIGHT IN HERE?
HI, AUNT AGGIE!
YOU MISSED IT!
I WON WITH A FIVE-CARD COMBO THANKS TO FRANK!
YEAH, THANKS A LOT, FRANK.
I THINK I'M DONE WITH CARDS.
AW, DON'T BE SORE.
REGGIE CAN PLAY NEXT TIME!

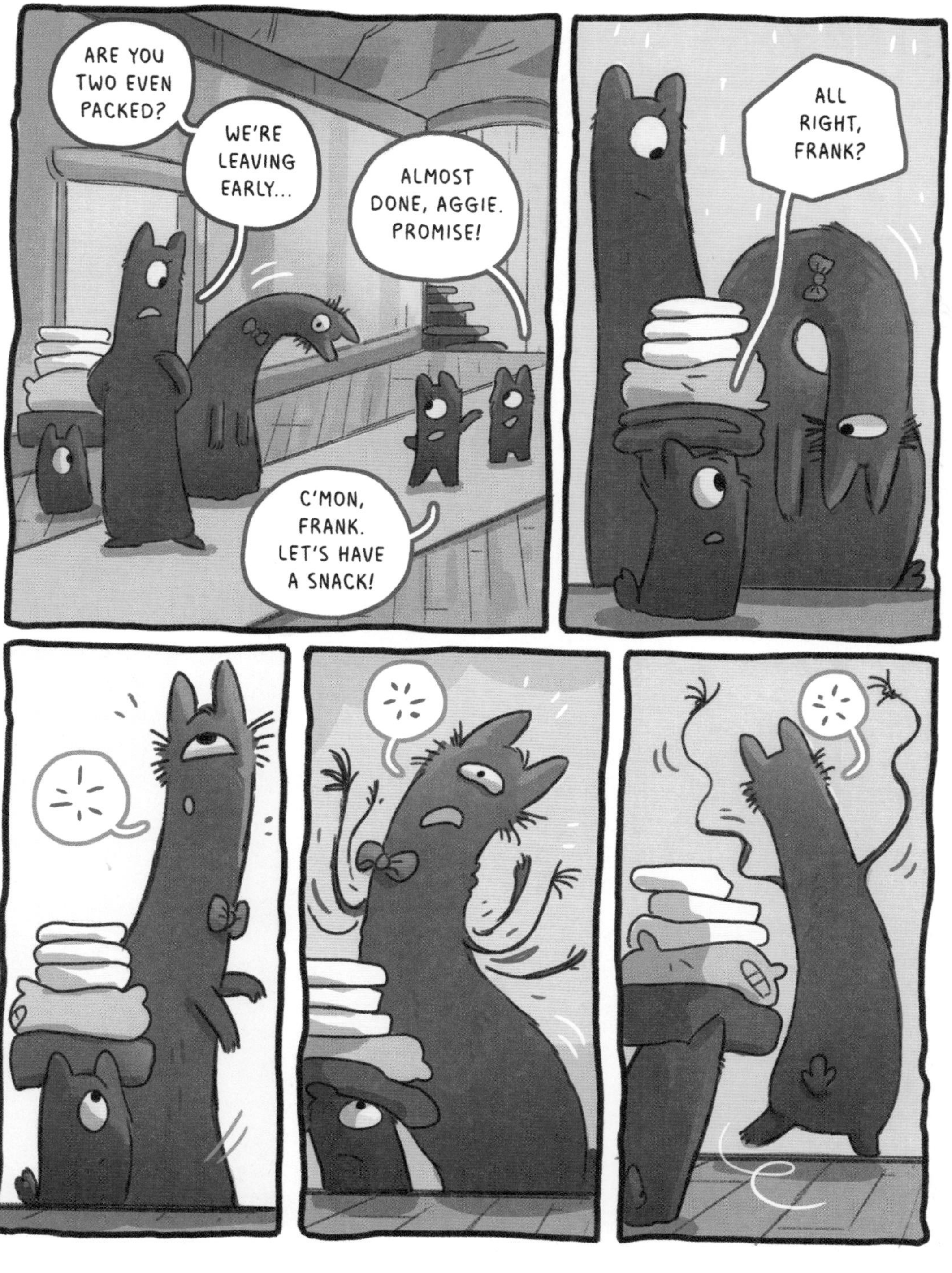
ARE YOU TWO EVEN PACKED?
WE'RE LEAVING EARLY...
ALMOST DONE, AGGIE. PROMISE!
C'MON, FRANK. LET'S HAVE A SNACK!
ALL RIGHT, FRANK?

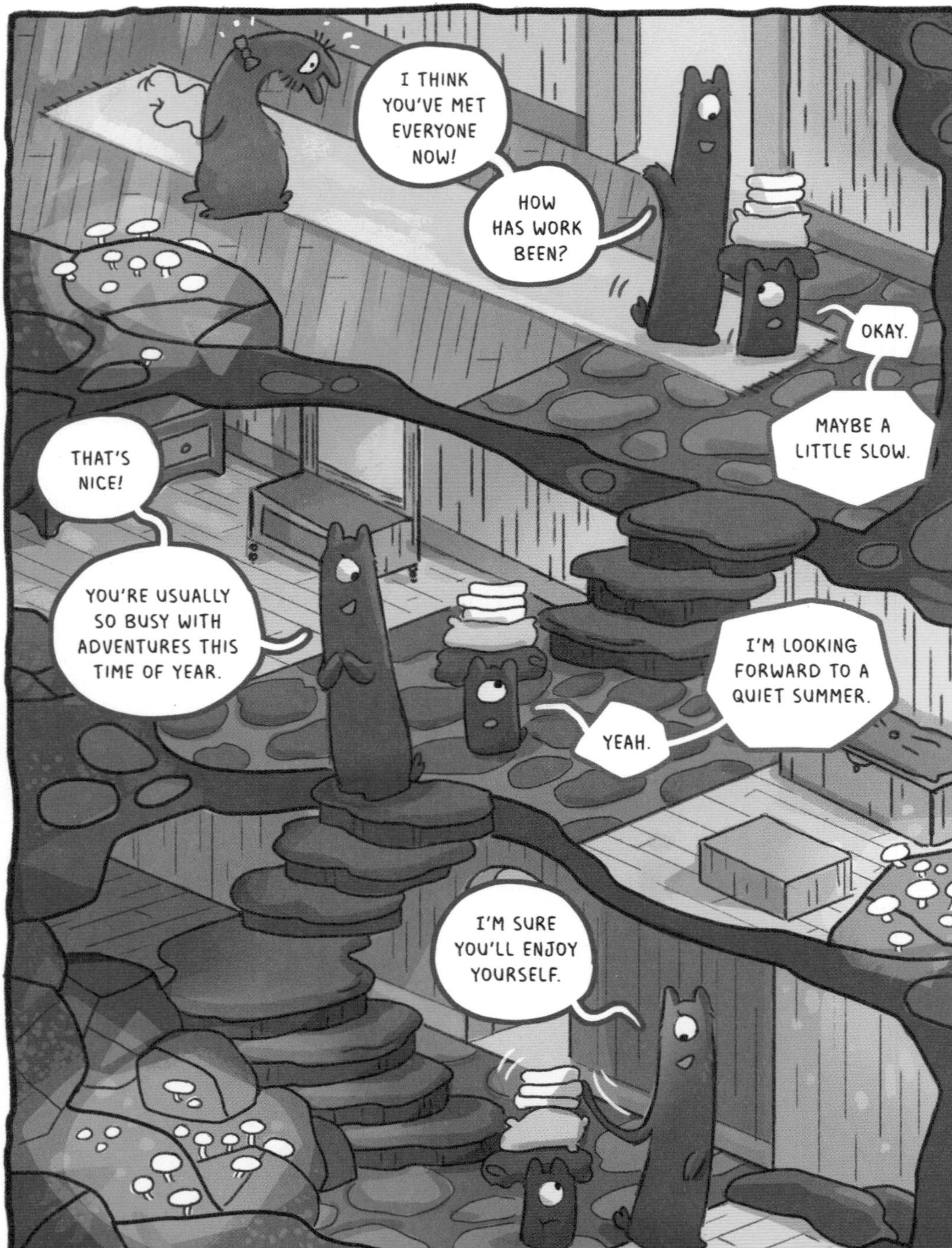
I THINK YOU'VE MET EVERYONE NOW!
HOW HAS WORK BEEN?
OKAY.
MAYBE A LITTLE SLOW.
THAT'S NICE!
YOU'RE USUALLY SO BUSY WITH ADVENTURES THIS TIME OF YEAR.
YEAH.
I'M LOOKING FORWARD TO A QUIET SUMMER.
I'M SURE YOU'LL ENJOY YOURSELF.

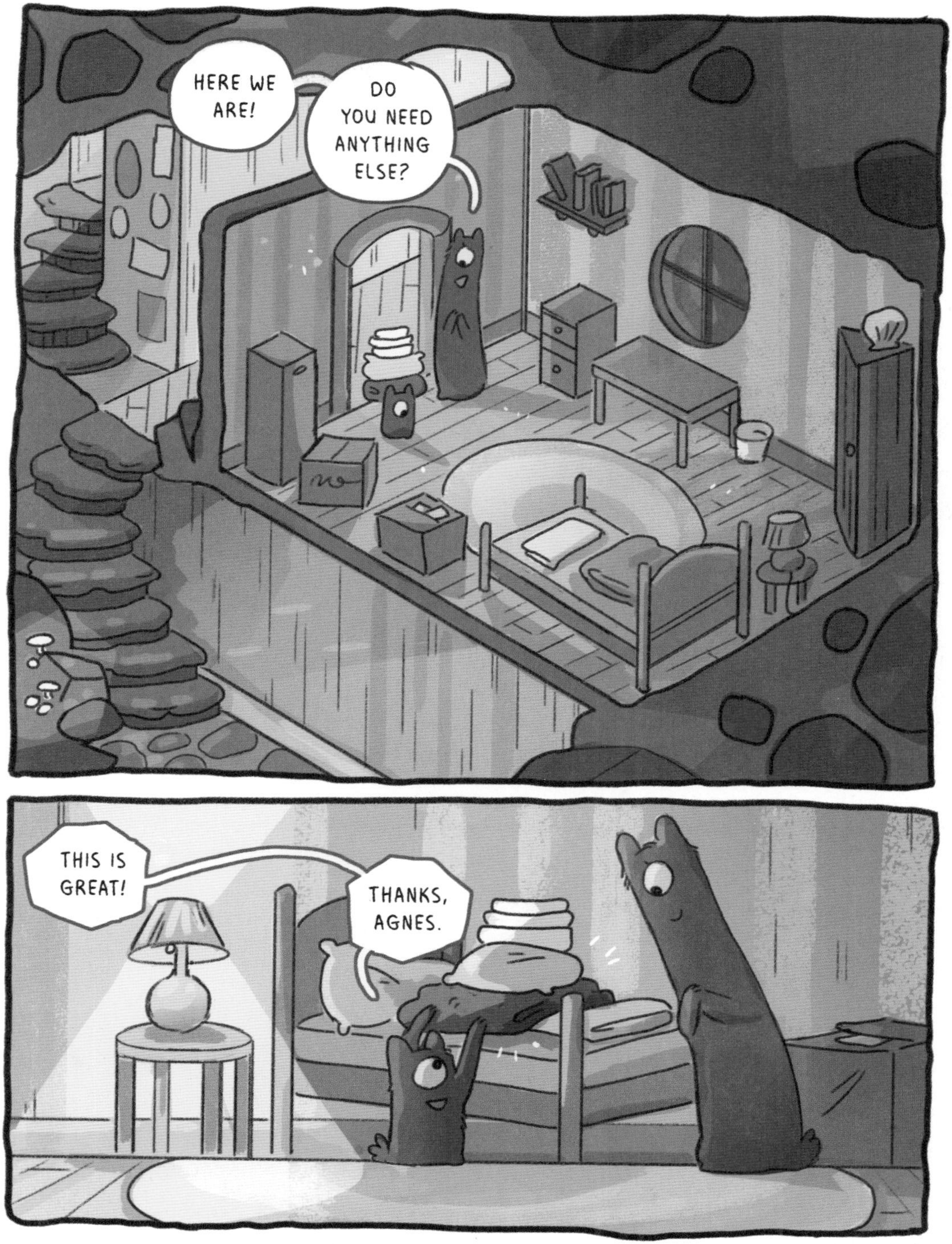
HERE WE ARE!
DO YOU NEED ANYTHING ELSE?
THIS IS GREAT!
THANKS, AGNES.

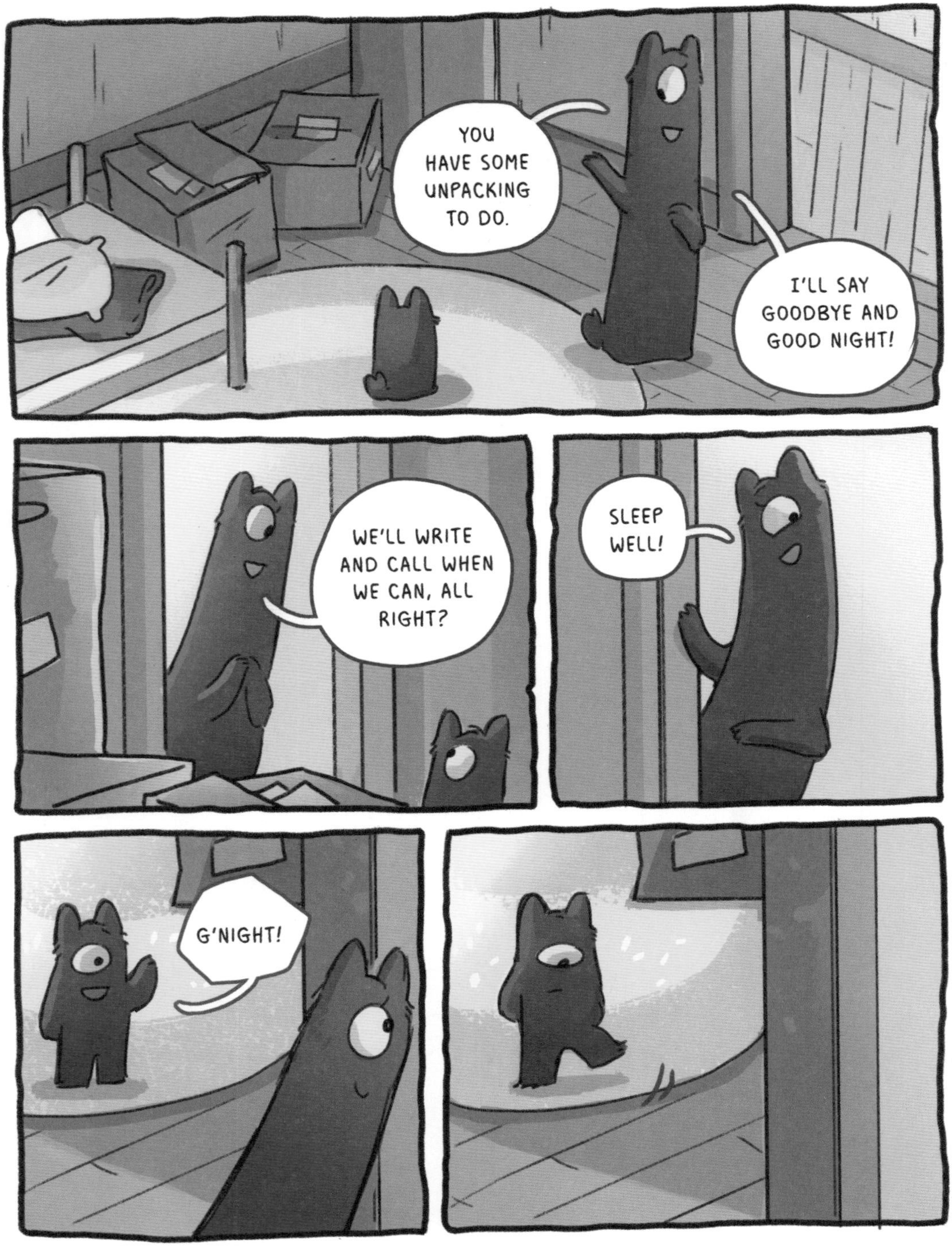
YOU HAVE SOME UNPACKING TO DO.
I'LL SAY GOODBYE AND GOOD NIGHT!
WE'LL WRITE AND CALL WHEN WE CAN, ALL RIGHT?
SLEEP WELL!
G'NIGHT!

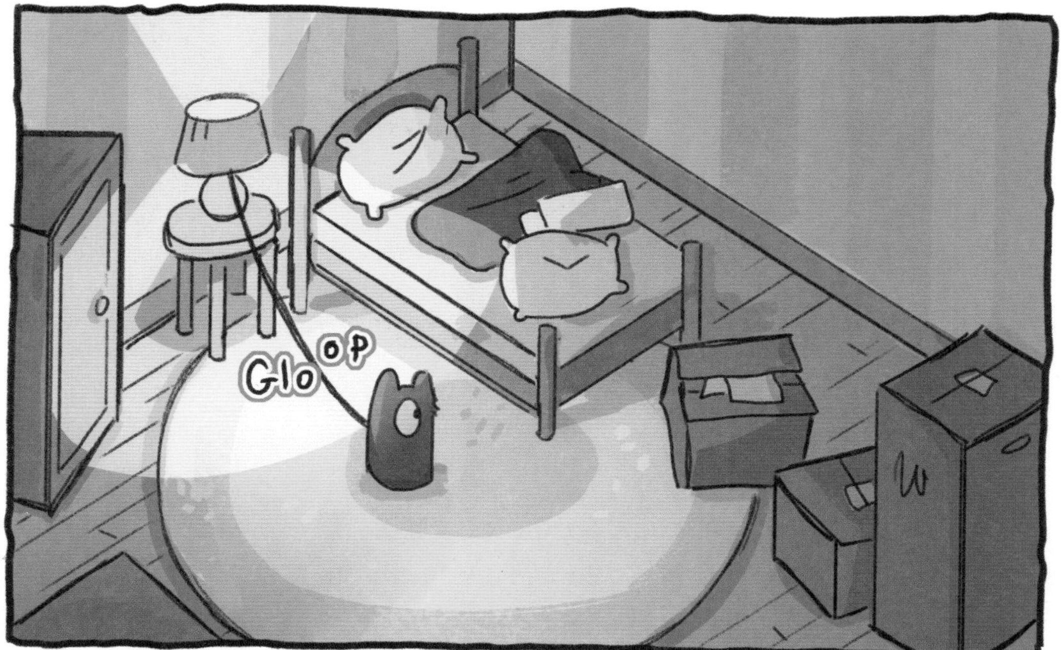
GlooP

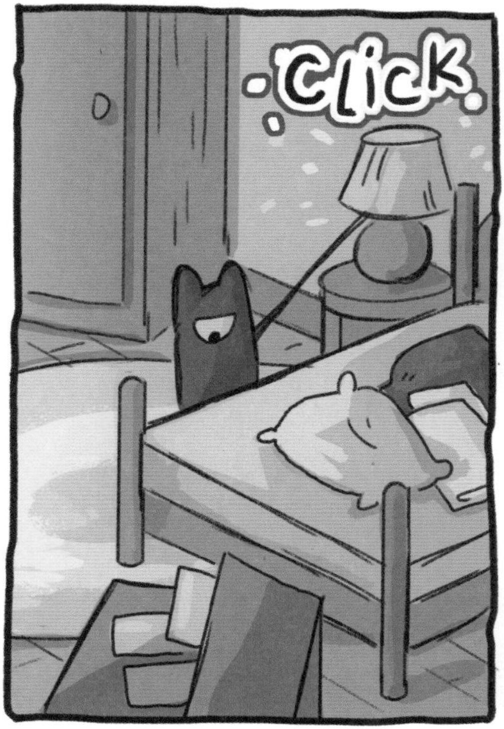
Click

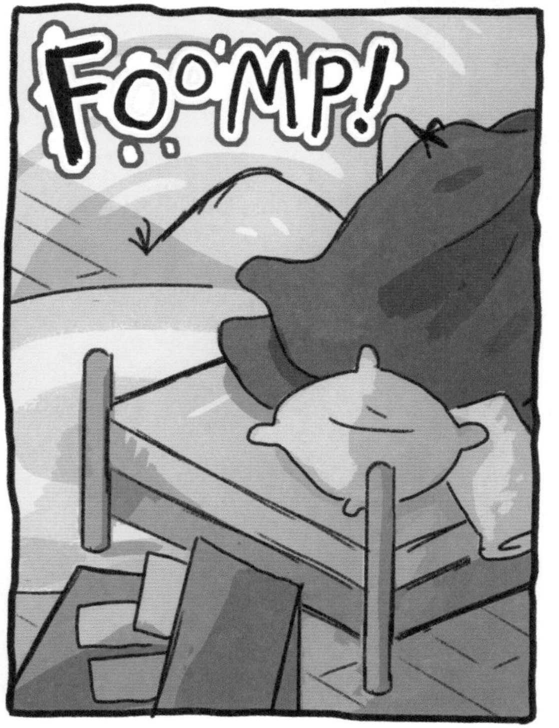
FOOMP!

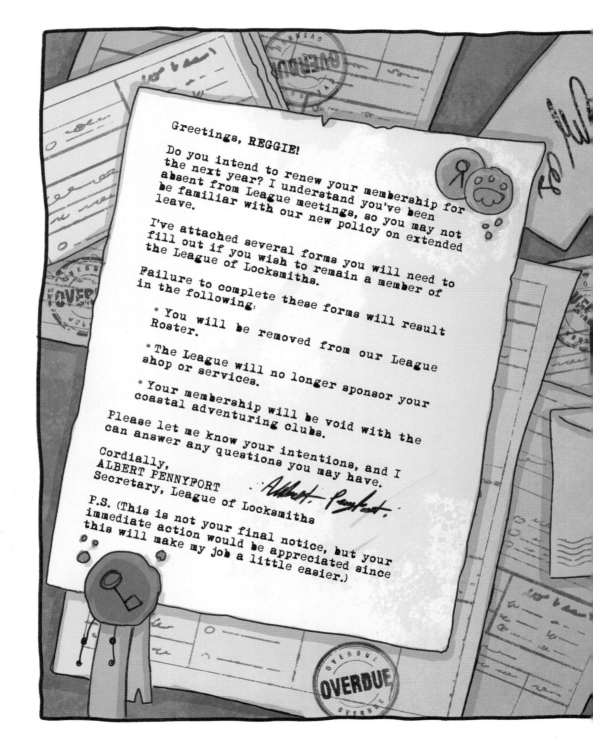

Greetings, REGGIE!

Do you intend to renew your membership for the next year? I understand you've been absent from League meetings, so you may not be familiar with our new policy on extended leave.

I've attached several forms you will need to fill out if you wish to remain a member of the League of Locksmiths.

Failure to complete these forms will result in the following:

* You will be removed from our League Roster.

* The League will no longer sponsor your shop or services.

* Your membership will be void with the coastal adventuring clubs.

Please let me know your intentions, and I can answer any questions you may have.

Cordially,
ALBERT PENNYFORT
Secretary, League of Locksmiths

P.S. (This is not your final notice, but your immediate action would be appreciated since this will make my job a little easier.)

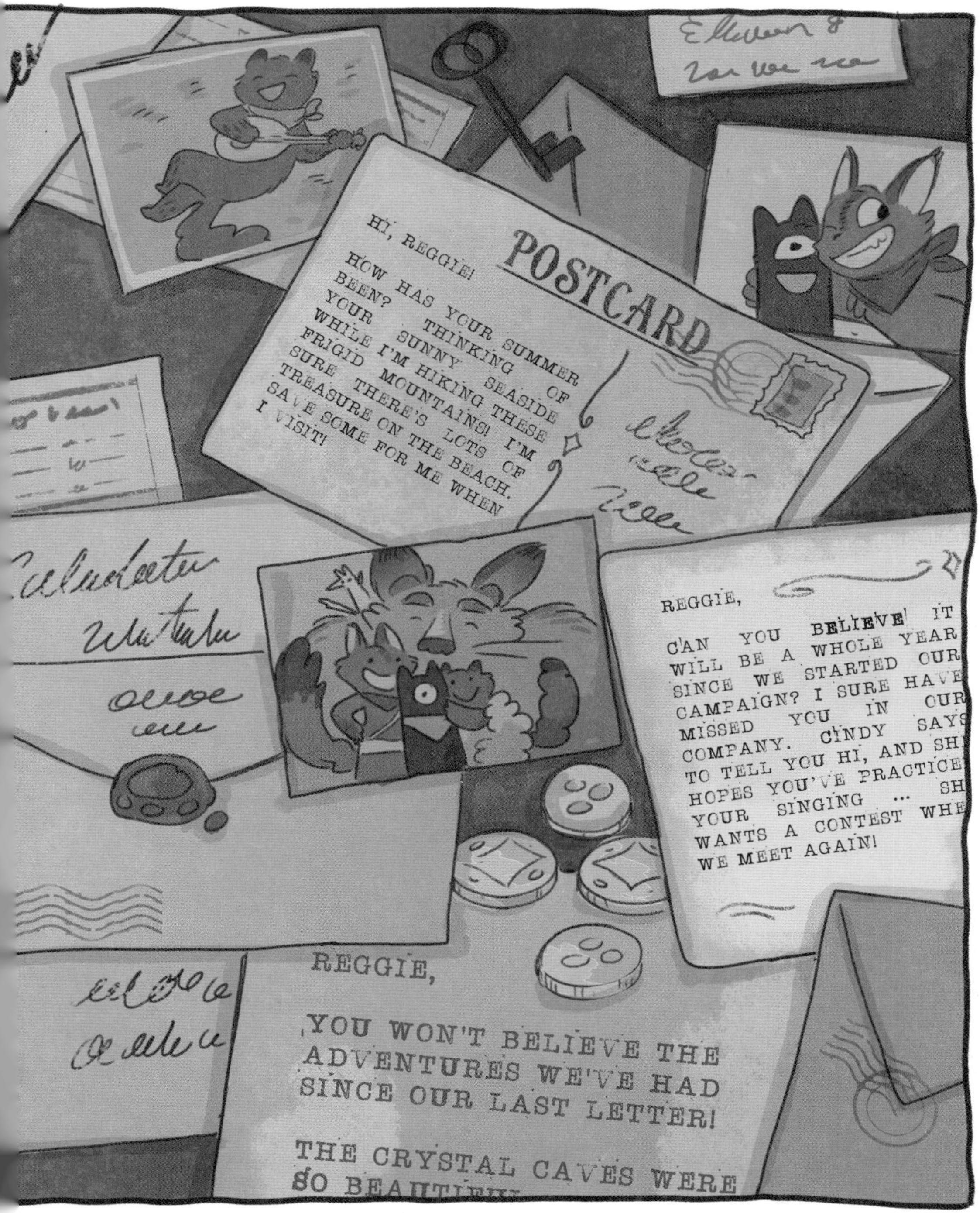
POSTCARD
HI, REGGIE!
HOW HAS YOUR SUMMER BEEN? THINKING OF YOUR SUNNY SEASIDE WHILE I'M HIKING THESE FRIGID MOUNTAINS! I'M SURE THERE'S LOTS OF TREASURE ON THE BEACH. SAVE SOME FOR ME WHEN I VISIT!
REGGIE,
CAN YOU BELIEVE IT WILL BE A WHOLE YEAR SINCE WE STARTED OUR CAMPAIGN? I SURE HAVE MISSED YOU IN OUR COMPANY. CINDY SAYS TO TELL YOU HI, AND SHE HOPES YOU'VE PRACTICED YOUR SINGING ... SHE WANTS A CONTEST WHEN WE MEET AGAIN!
REGGIE,
YOU WON'T BELIEVE THE ADVENTURES WE'VE HAD SINCE OUR LAST LETTER!
THE CRYSTAL CAVES WERE SO BEAUTIFUL

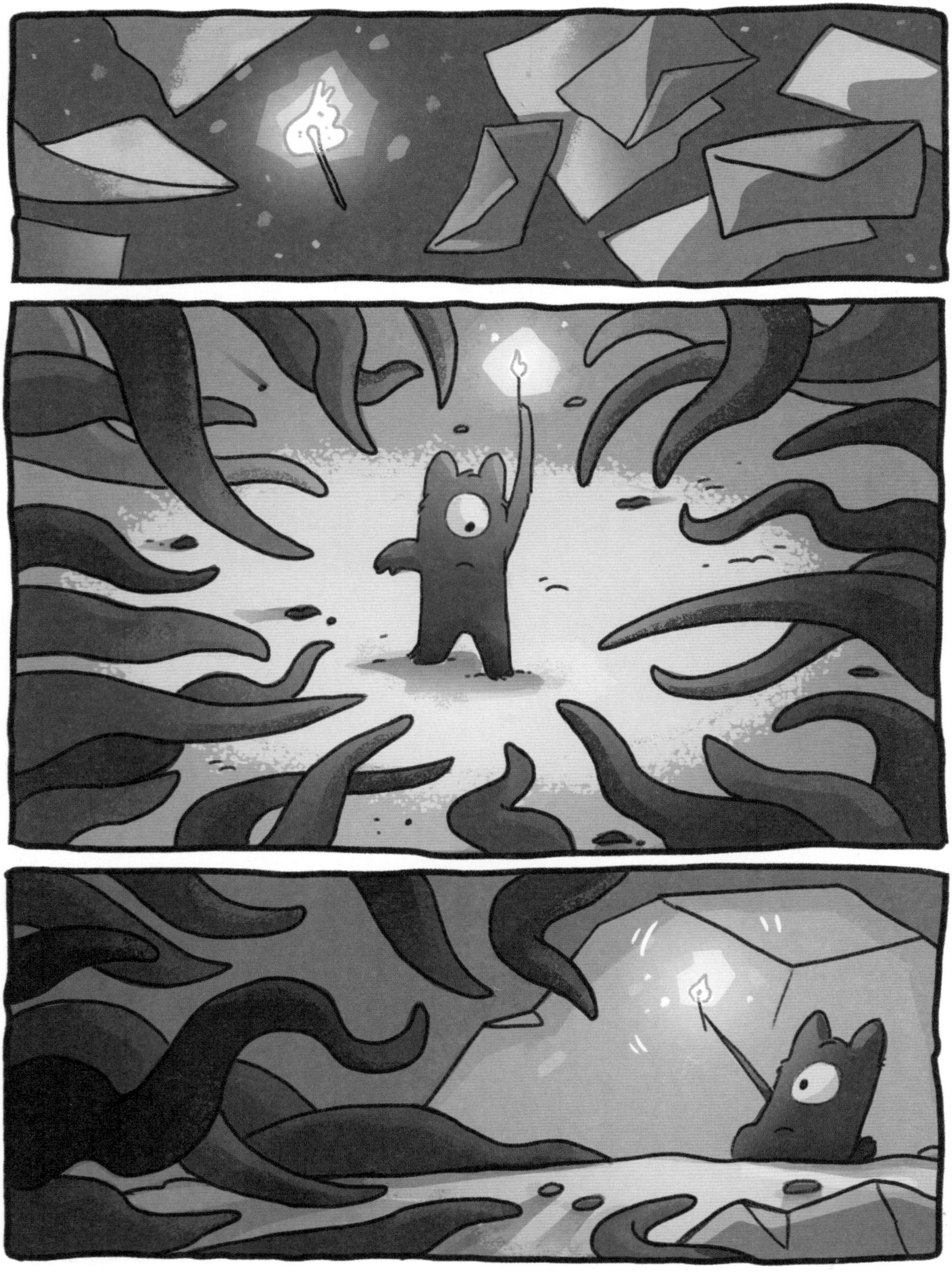

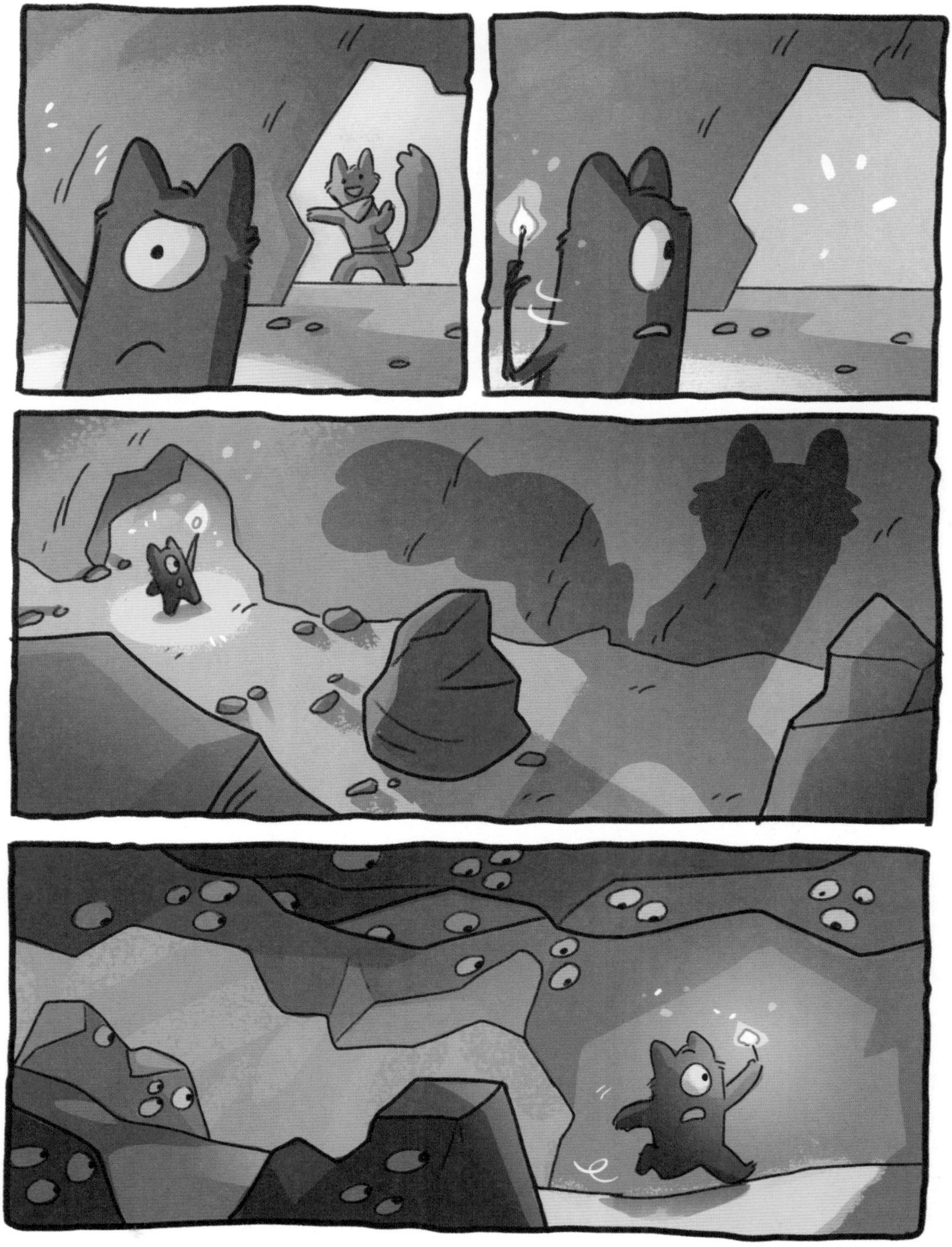

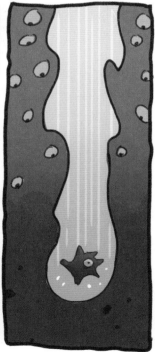

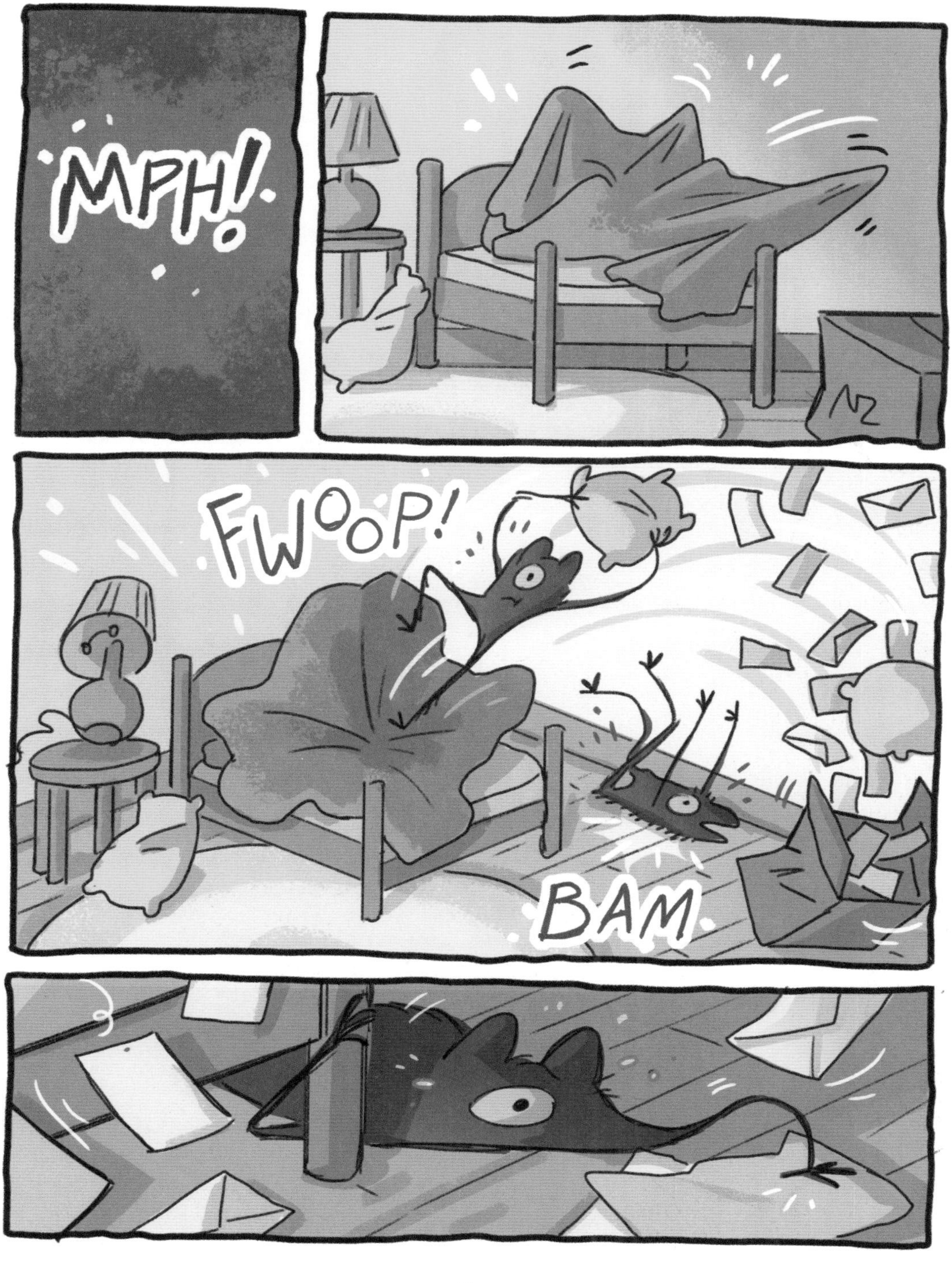
MPH!
FWOOP!
BAM

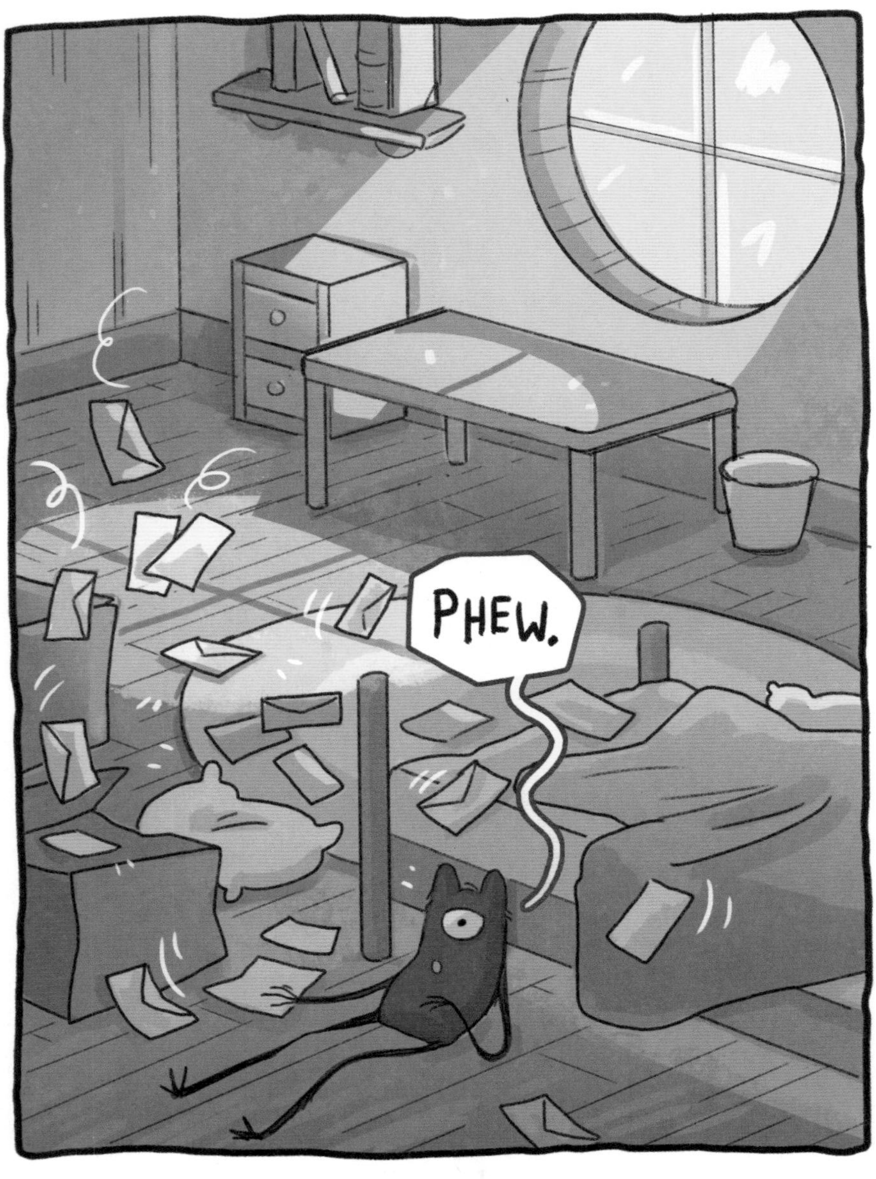
PHEW.

chapter 2

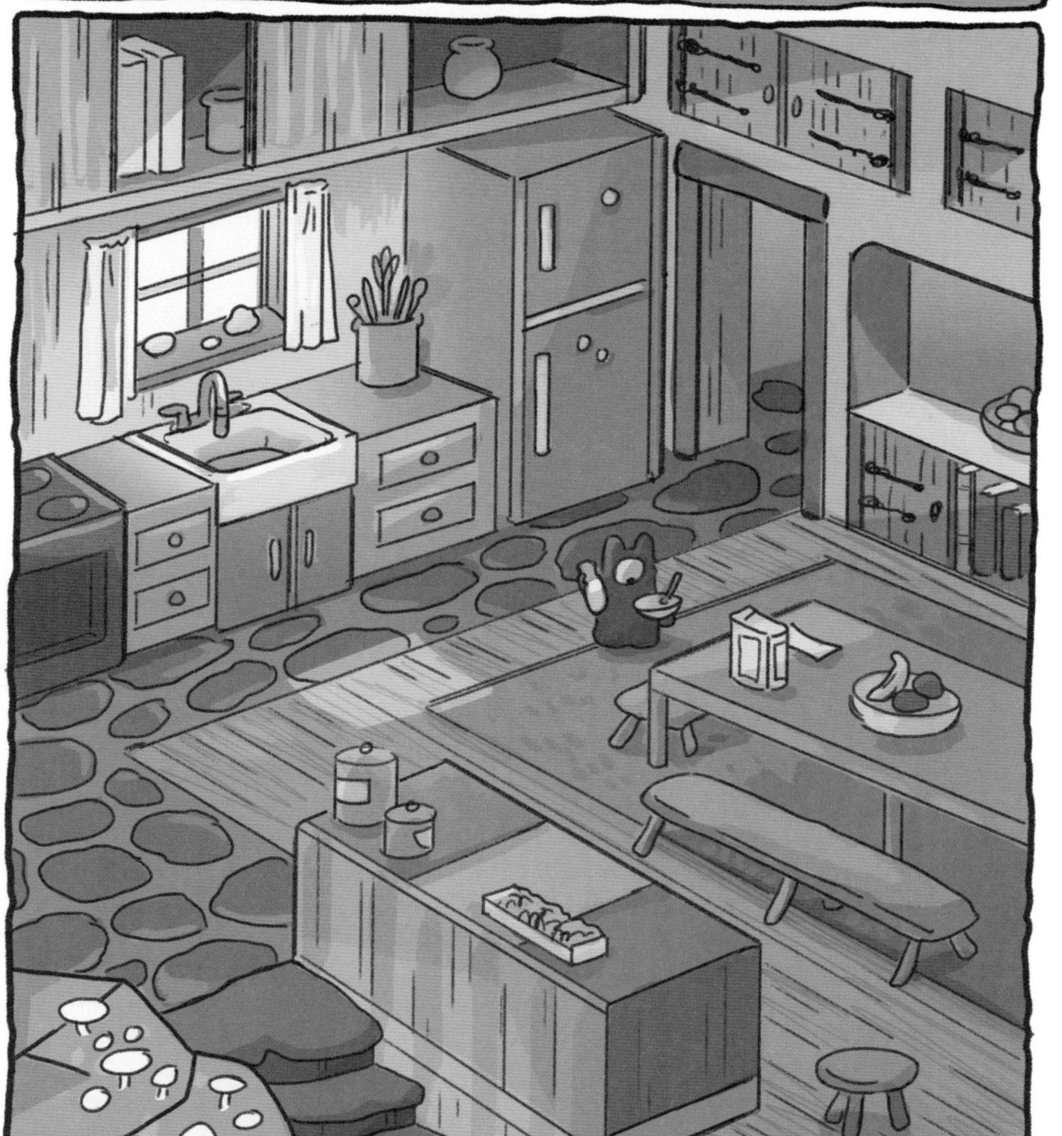

Hi, Reggie!

We will be traveling from July 10th to August 10th for our vacation.

Our contact info is by the telephone if you need to call us.

Summer Events

Summer picnic July 12th.

Beach days are every weekend.

Summer concerts are Tuesdays and Thursdays at city hall.

Weekly Chores

Dust, tidy, and sweep floors twice a week.

Water indoor plants and mushrooms on Mondays.

Weed and water garden three times a week.

Garden Stuff

Help yourself to the garden! And please share produce with the neighbors when ready to harvest.

For more pantry items, please call Marvin. His number is also by the telephone!

For more pantry items, pl call Marvin. Hi also by the te

* Write Letters

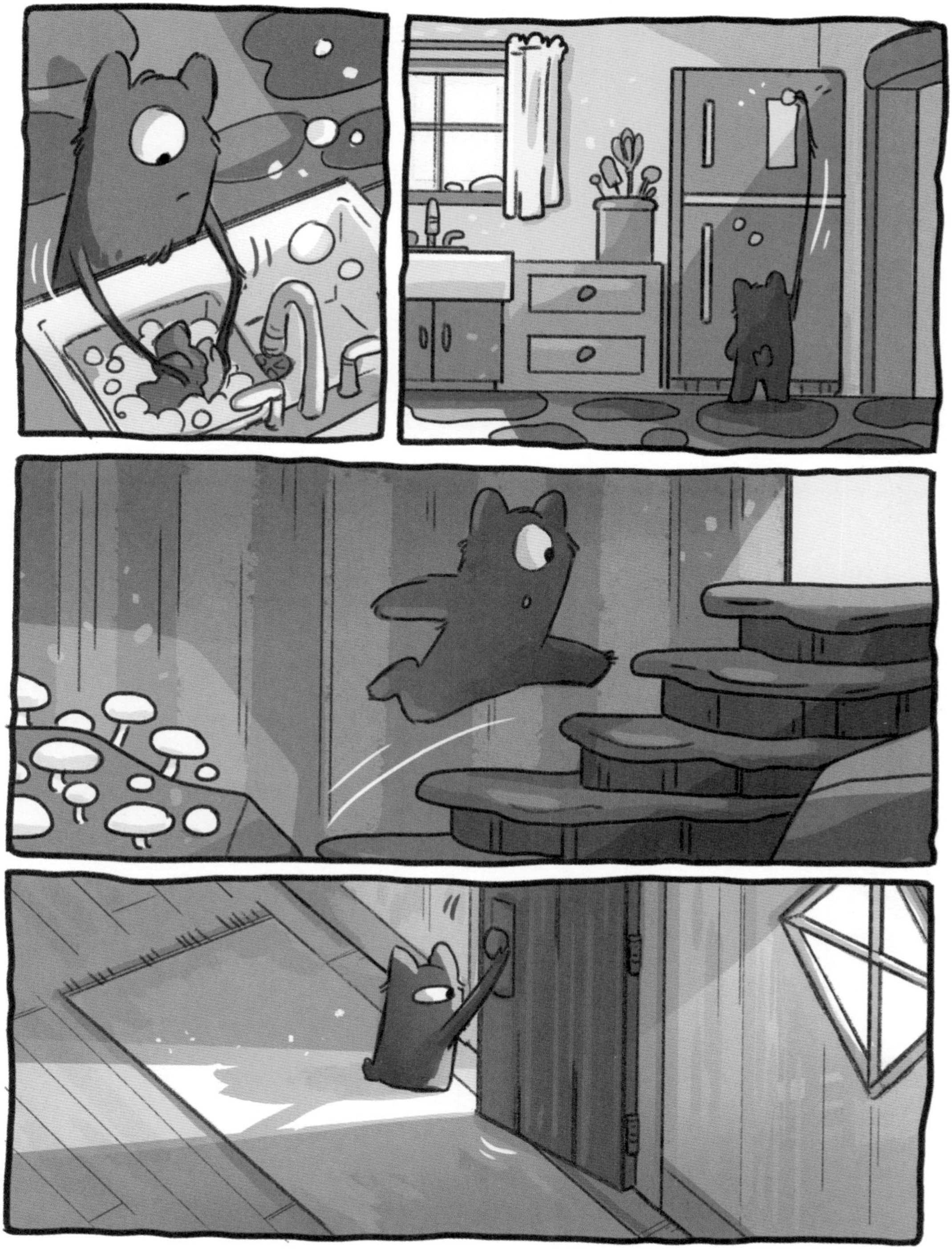

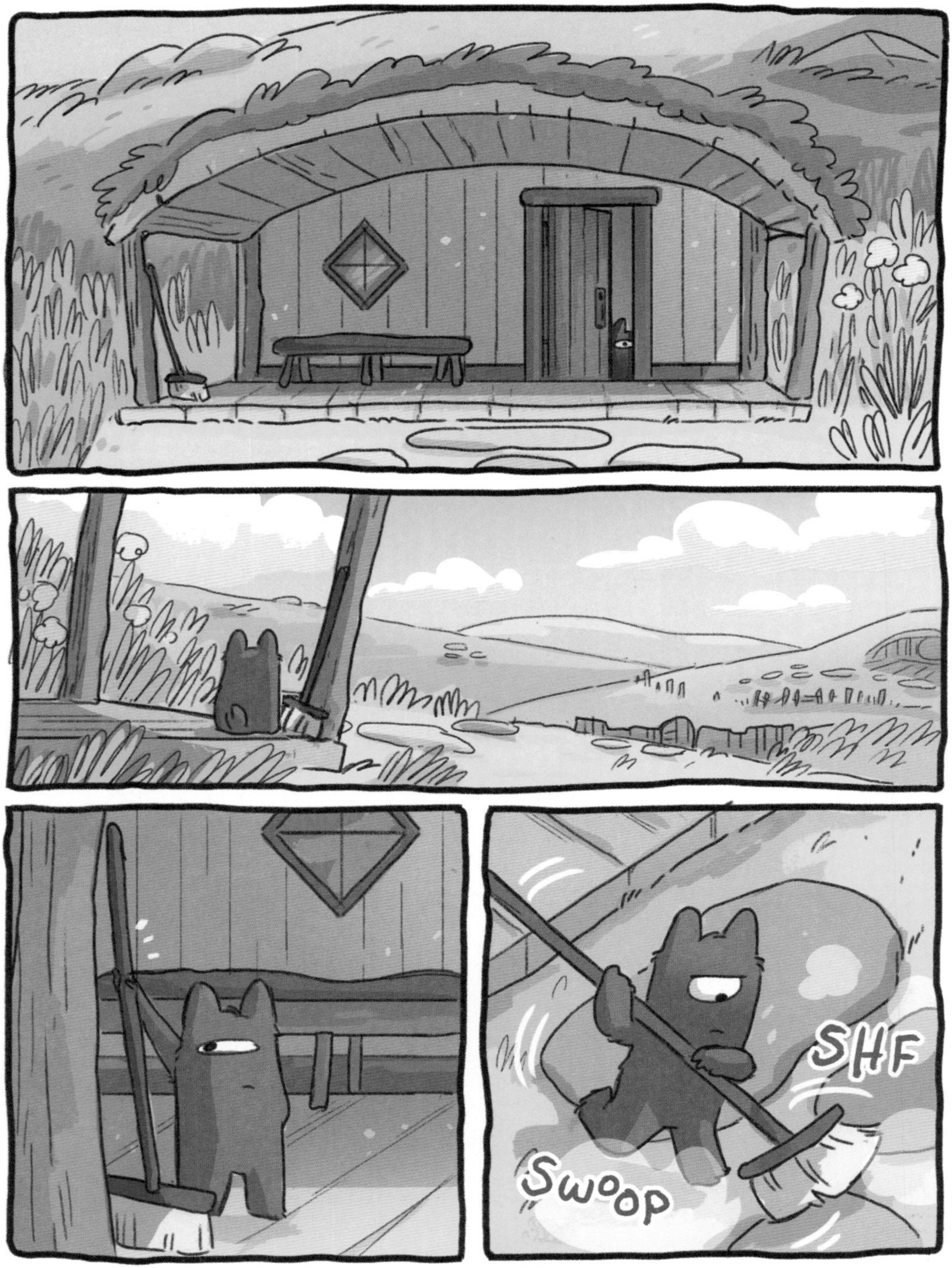
SHF
SWOOP

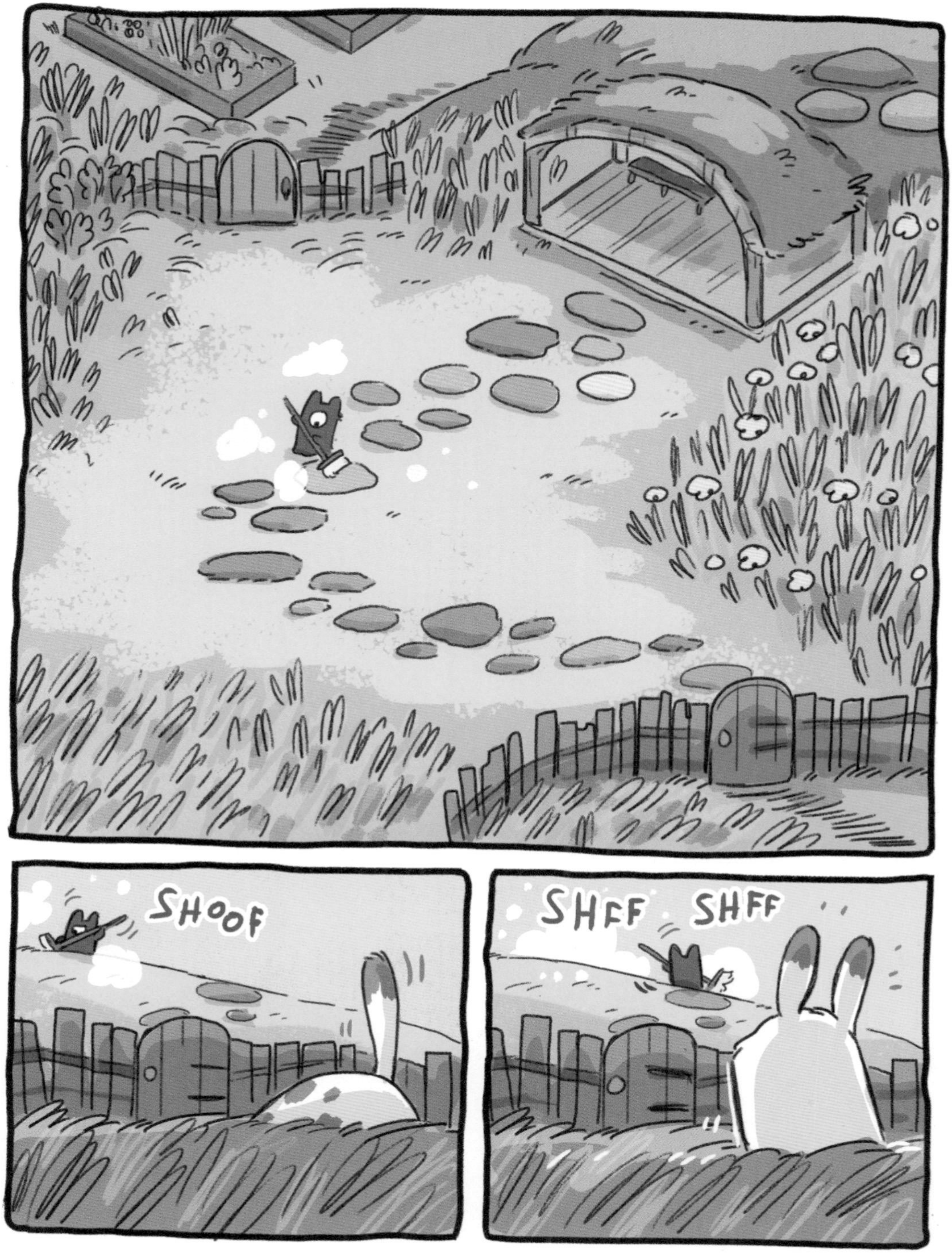
SHOOF
SHFF SHFF

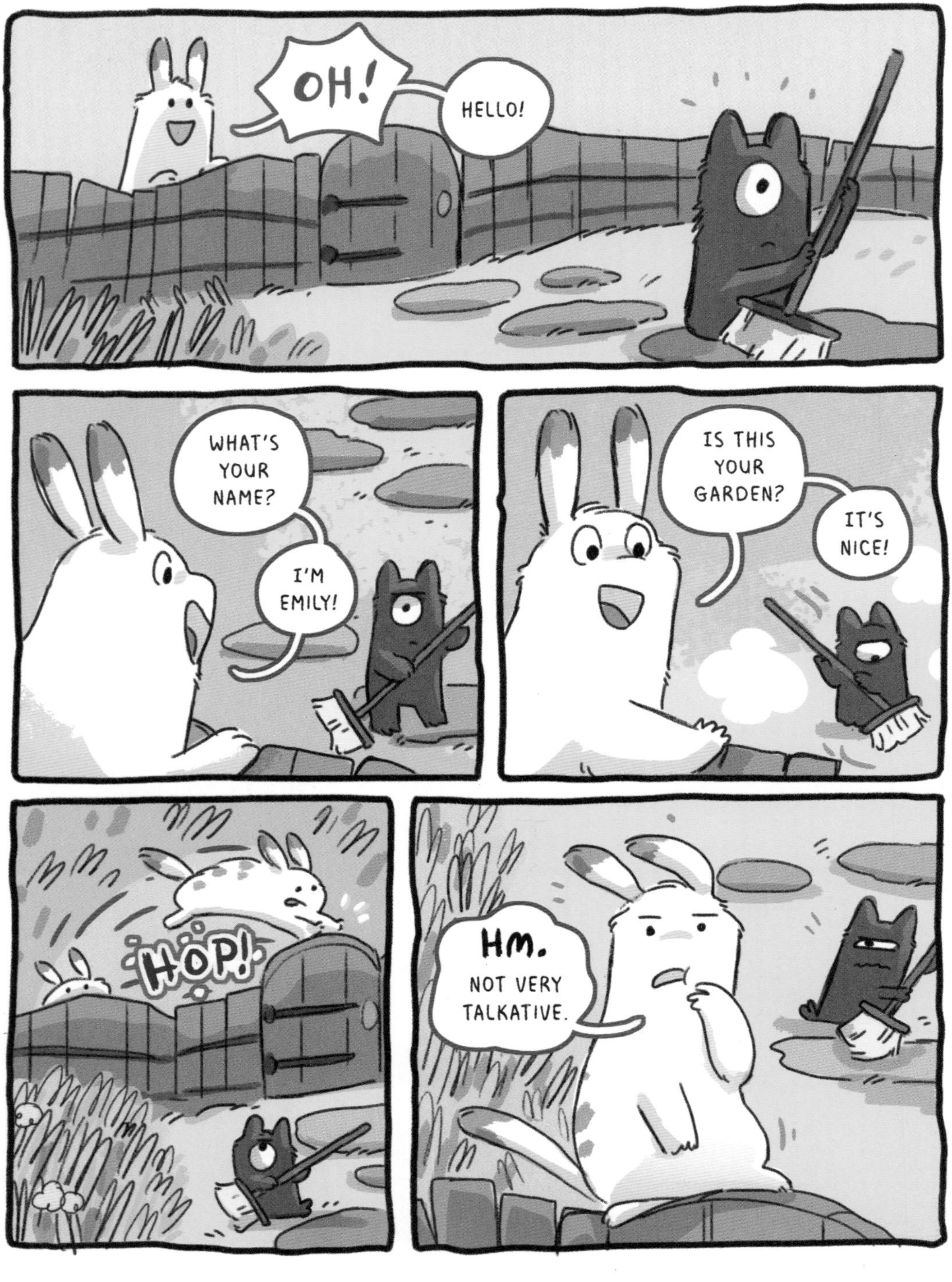
OH!
HELLO!
WHAT'S YOUR NAME?
I'M EMILY!
IS THIS YOUR GARDEN?
IT'S NICE!
HOP!
HM.
NOT VERY TALKATIVE.

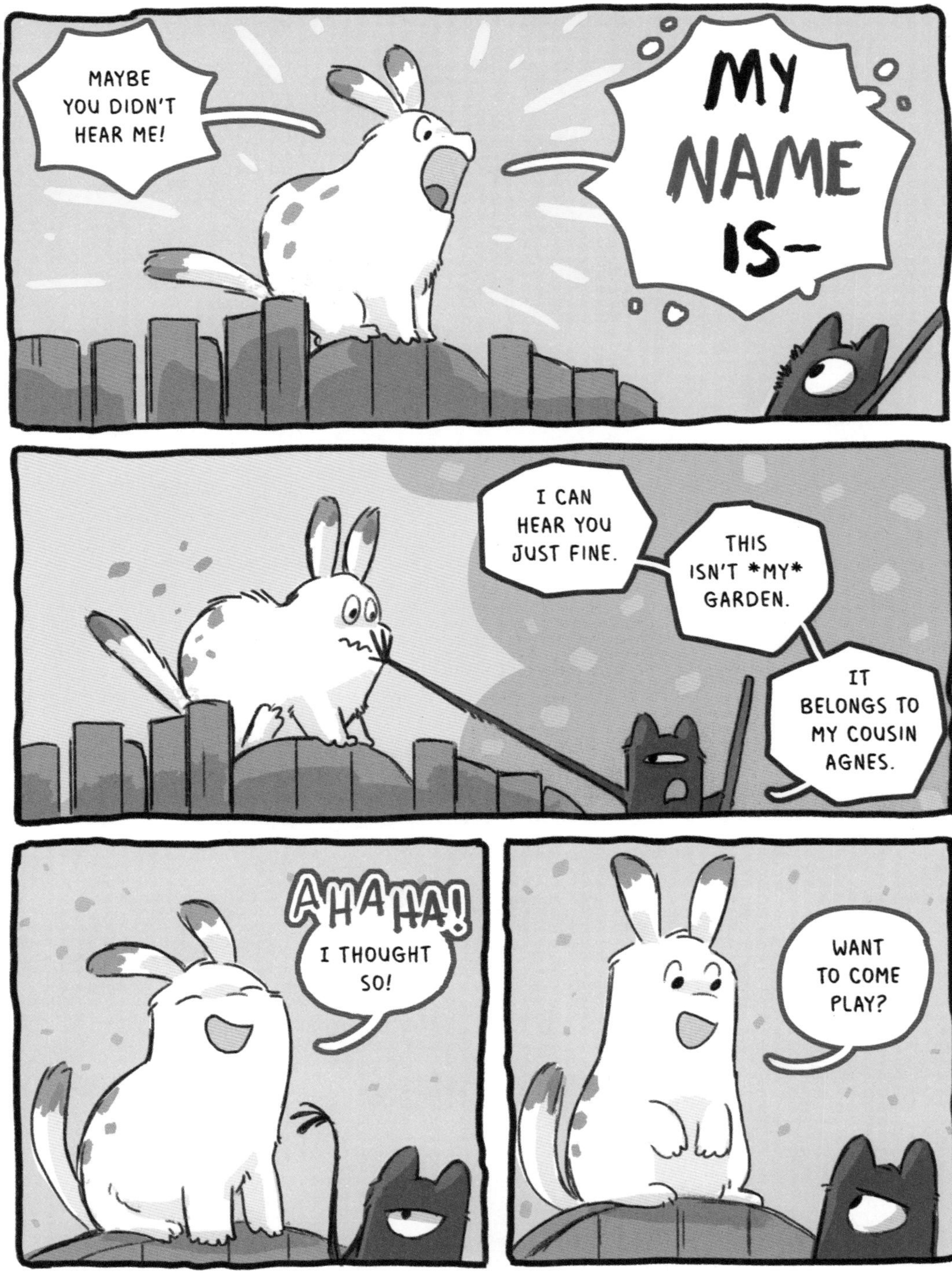
MAYBE YOU DIDN'T HEAR ME!
MY NAME IS-
I CAN HEAR YOU JUST FINE.
THIS ISN'T *MY* GARDEN.
IT BELONGS TO MY COUSIN AGNES.
AHAHA!
I THOUGHT SO!
WANT TO COME PLAY?

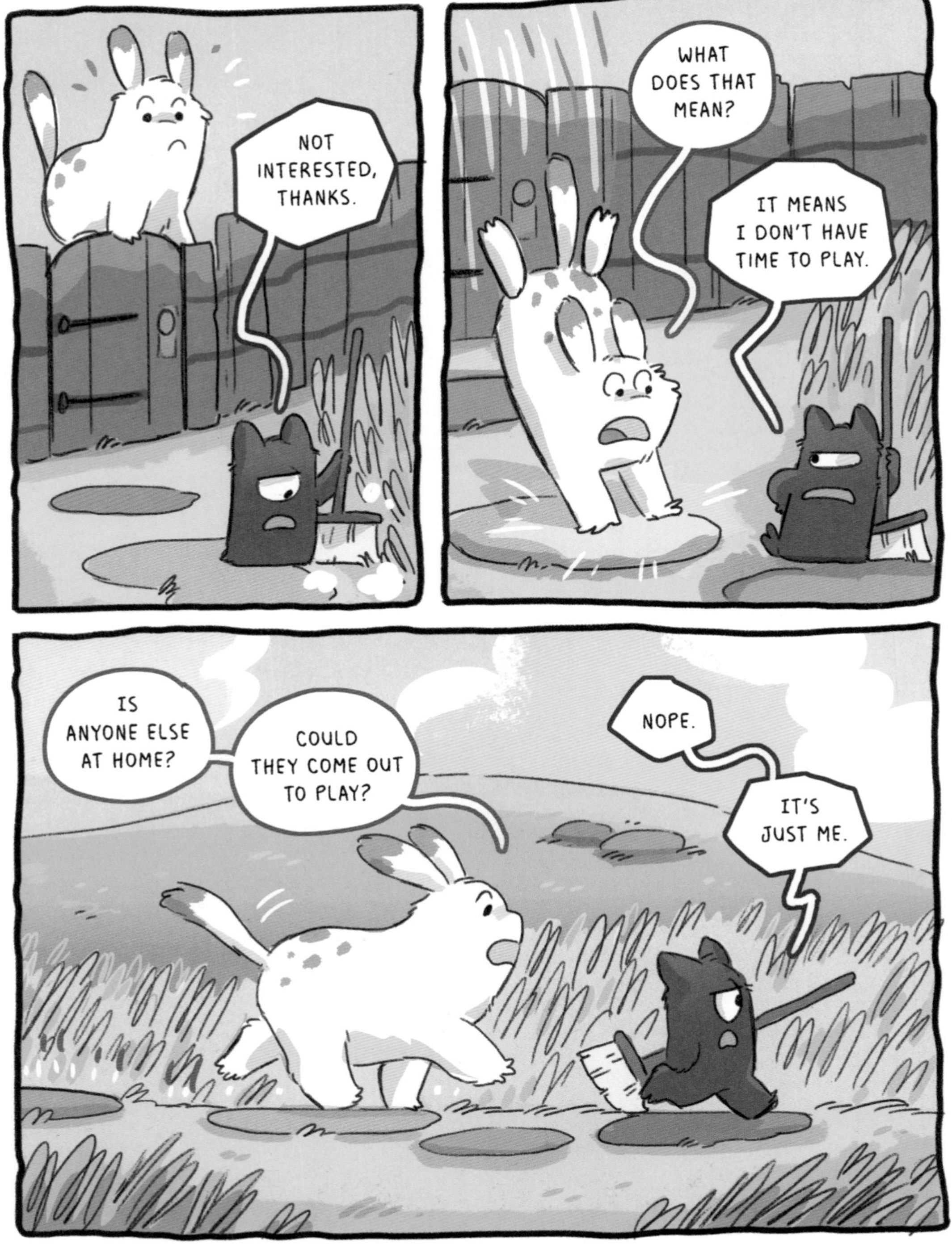
NOT INTERESTED, THANKS.
WHAT DOES THAT MEAN?
IT MEANS I DON'T HAVE TIME TO PLAY.
IS ANYONE ELSE AT HOME?
COULD THEY COME OUT TO PLAY?
NOPE.
IT'S JUST ME.

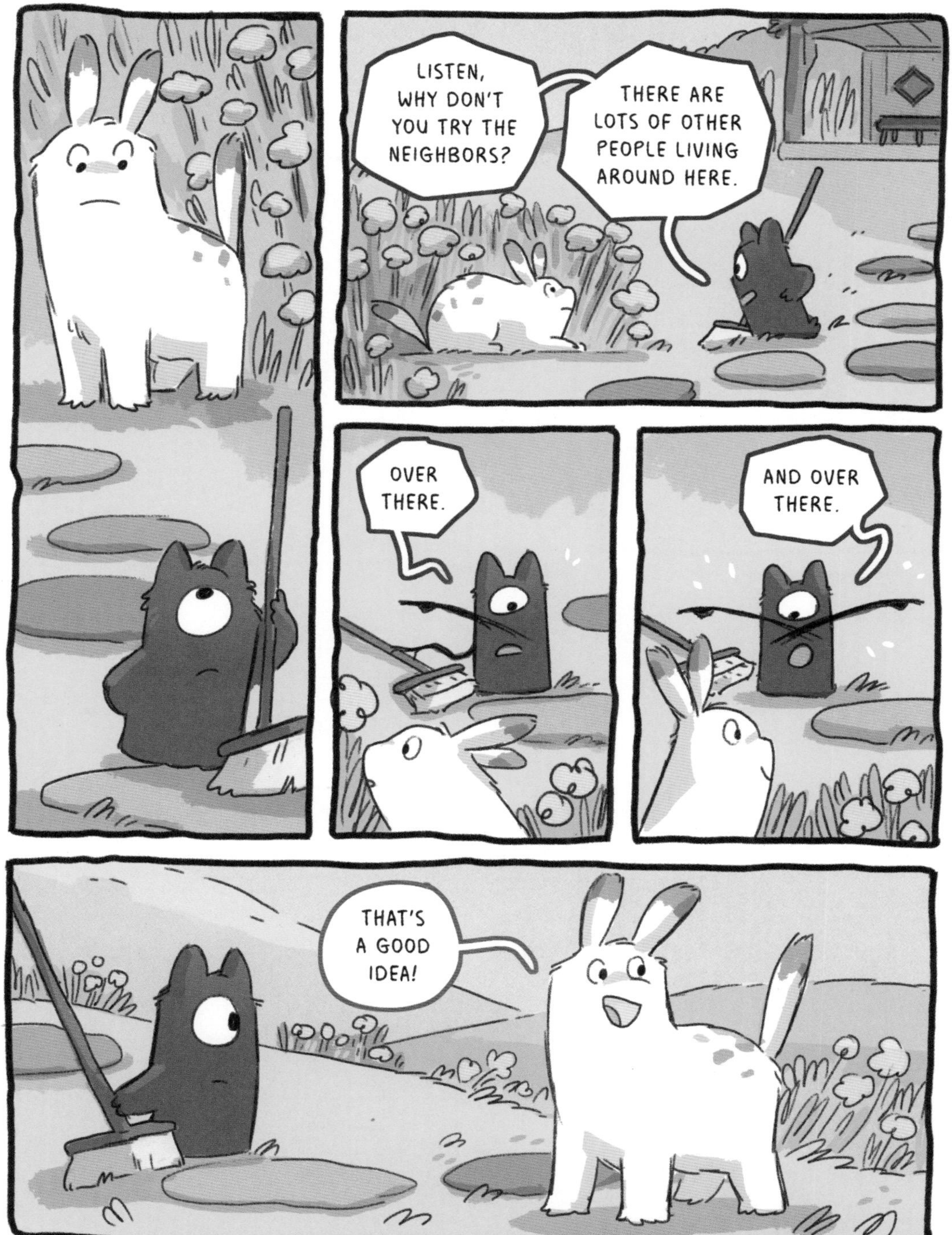
LISTEN, WHY DON'T YOU TRY THE NEIGHBORS?
THERE ARE LOTS OF OTHER PEOPLE LIVING AROUND HERE.
OVER THERE.
AND OVER THERE.
THAT'S A GOOD IDEA!

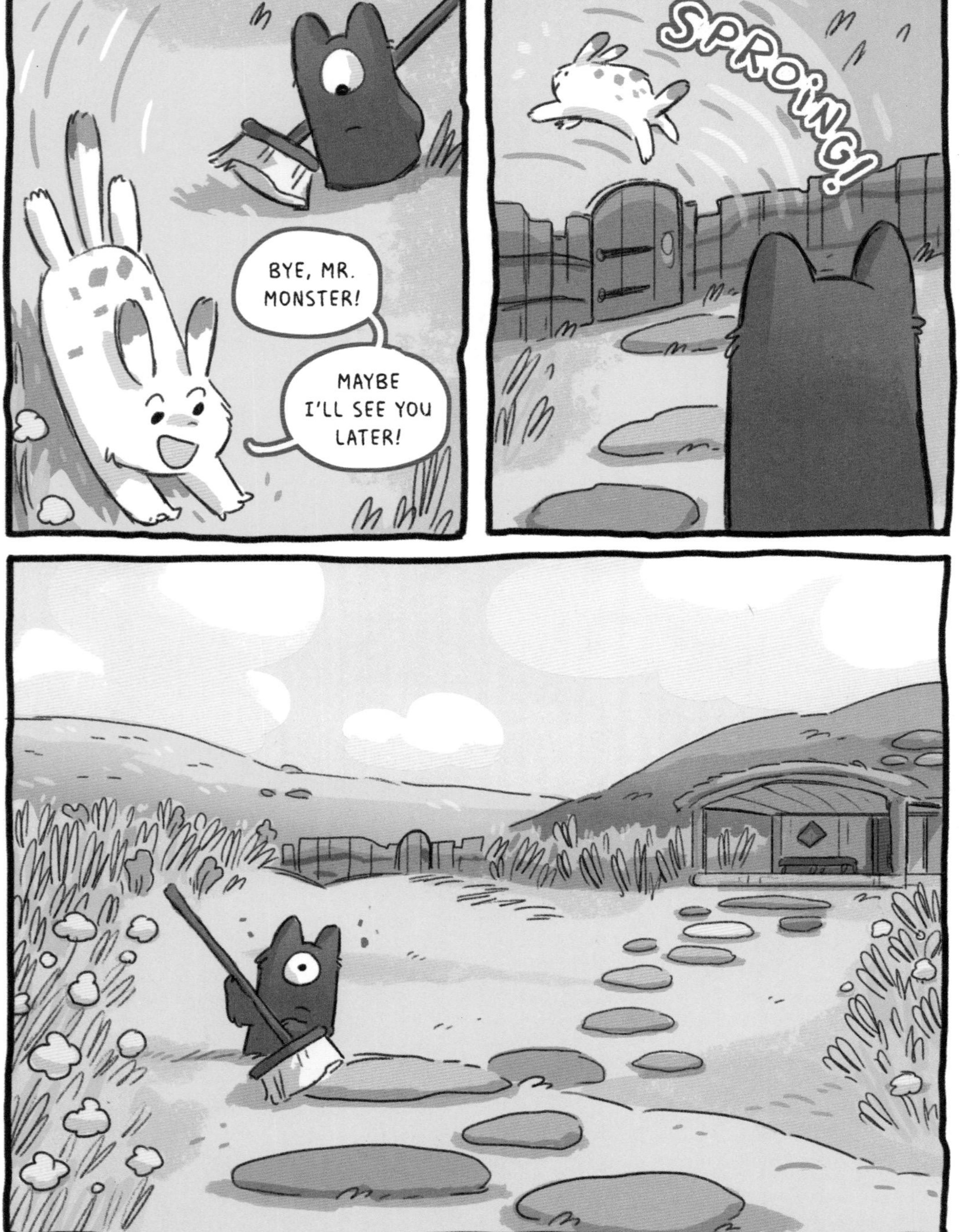
BYE, MR. MONSTER!
MAYBE I'LL SEE YOU LATER!
SPROING!

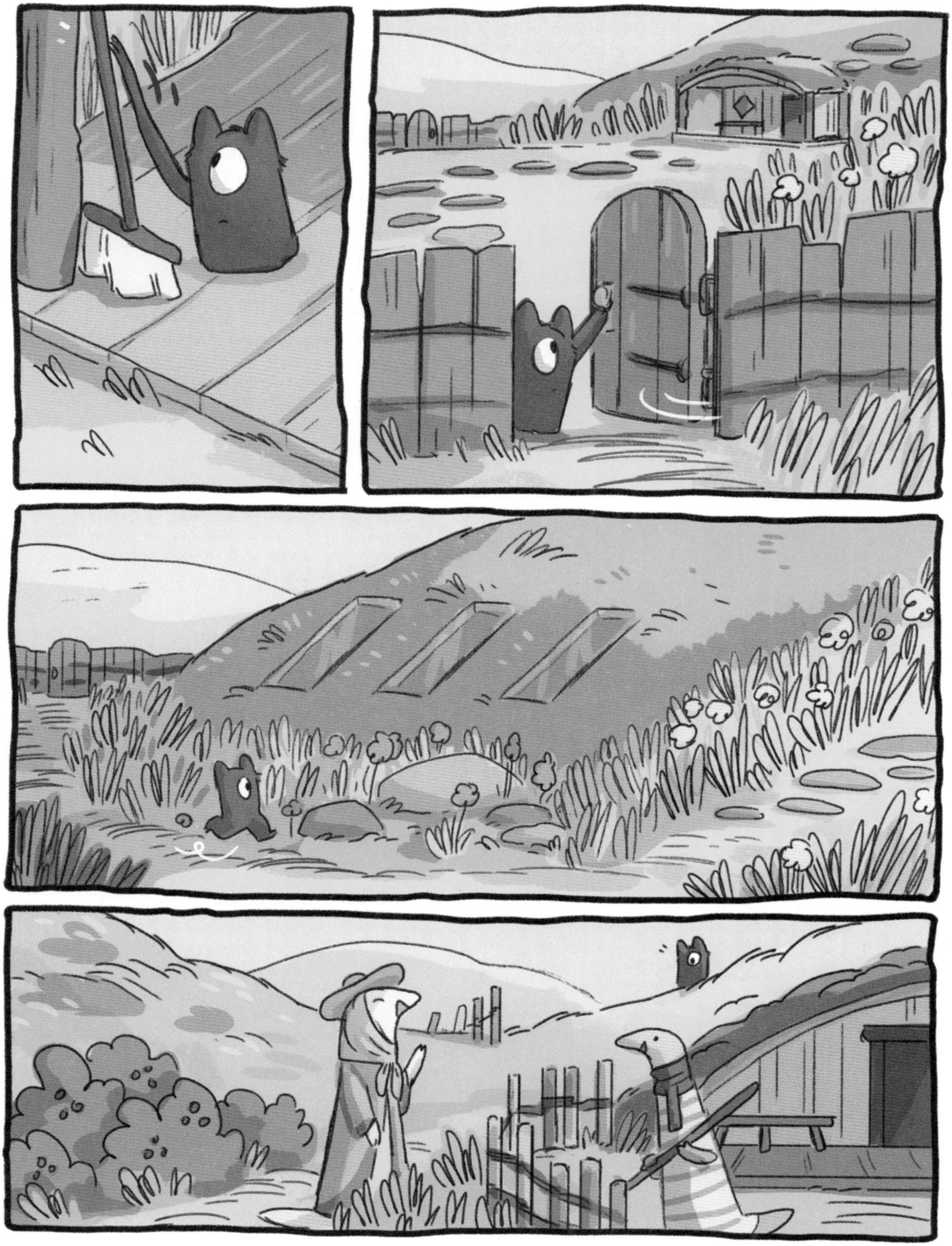

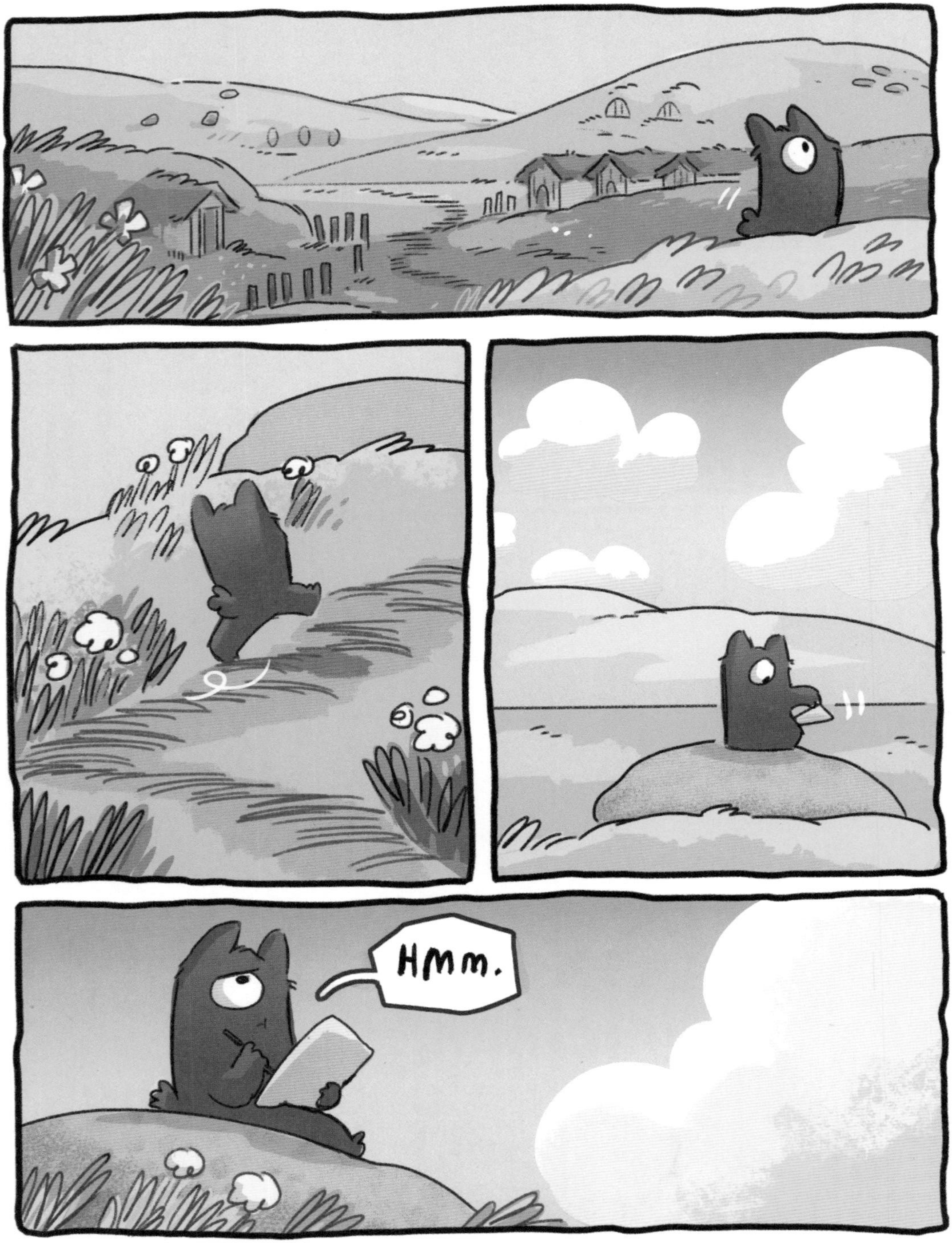
HMM.

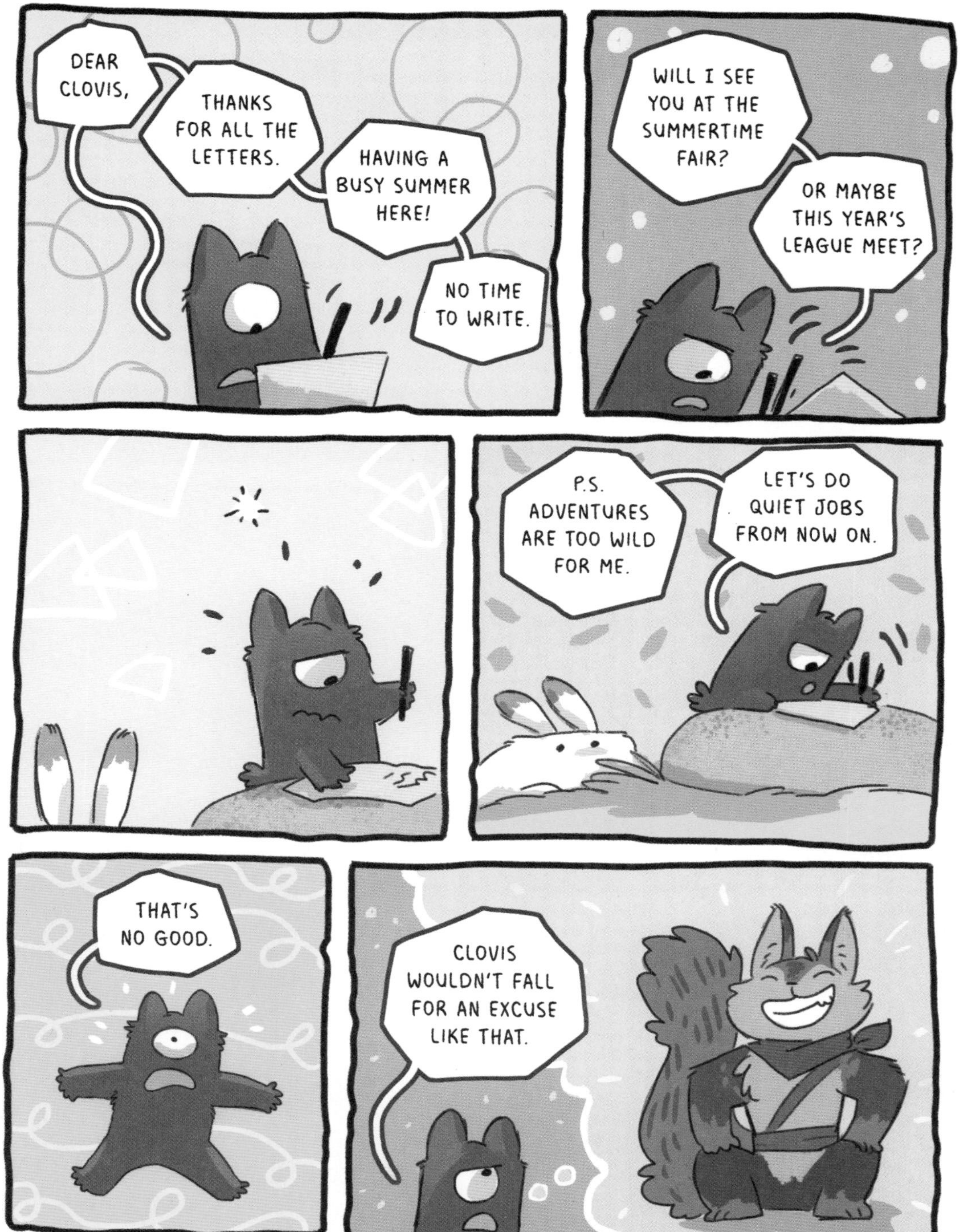
DEAR CLOVIS,
THANKS FOR ALL THE LETTERS.
HAVING A BUSY SUMMER HERE!
NO TIME TO WRITE.
WILL I SEE YOU AT THE SUMMERTIME FAIR?
OR MAYBE THIS YEAR'S LEAGUE MEET?
P.S. ADVENTURES ARE TOO WILD FOR ME.
LET'S DO QUIET JOBS FROM NOW ON.
THAT'S NO GOOD.
CLOVIS WOULDN'T FALL FOR AN EXCUSE LIKE THAT.

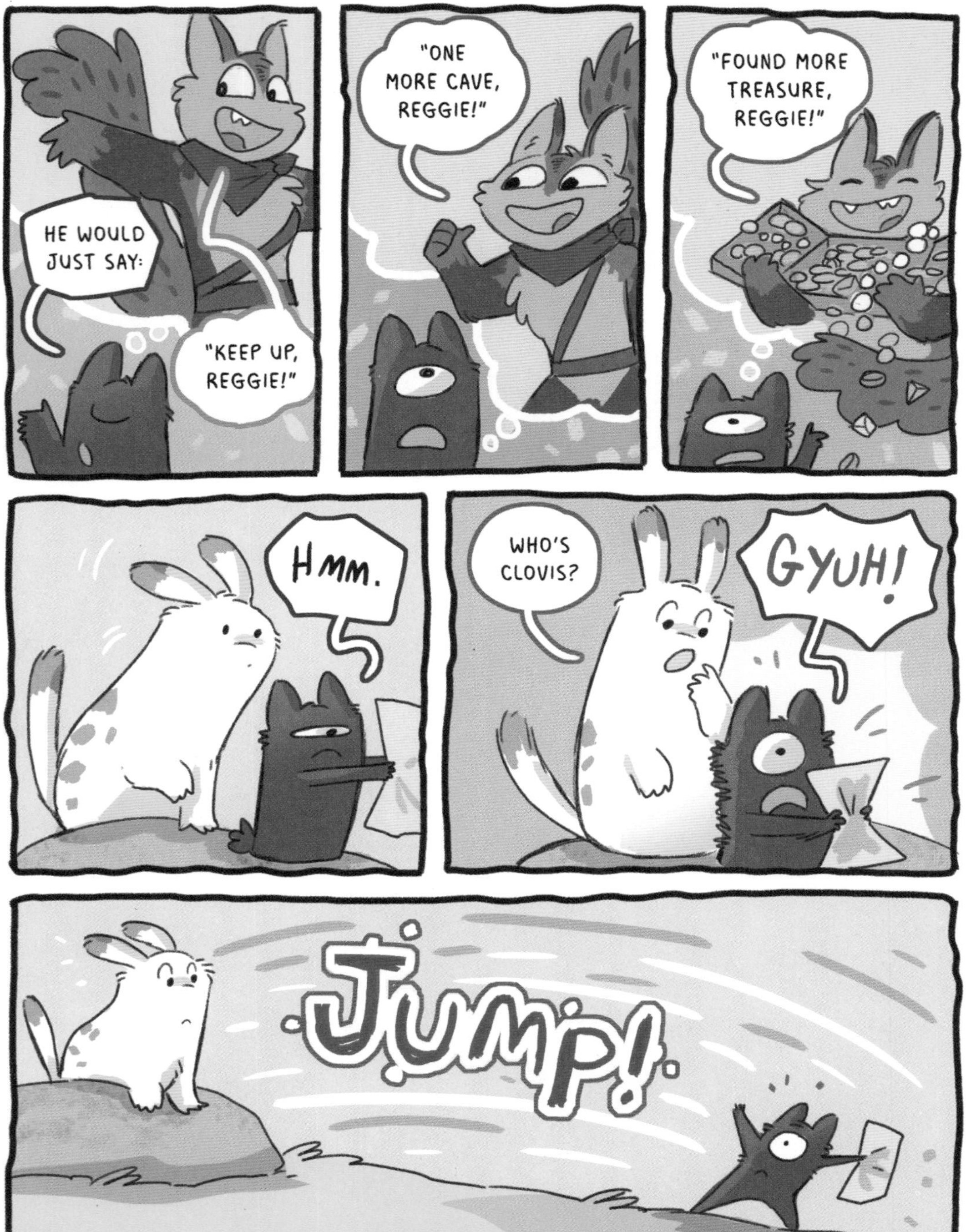
HE WOULD JUST SAY:
"KEEP UP, REGGIE!"
"ONE MORE CAVE, REGGIE!"
"FOUND MORE TREASURE, REGGIE!"
HMM.
WHO'S CLOVIS?
GYUH!
JUMP!

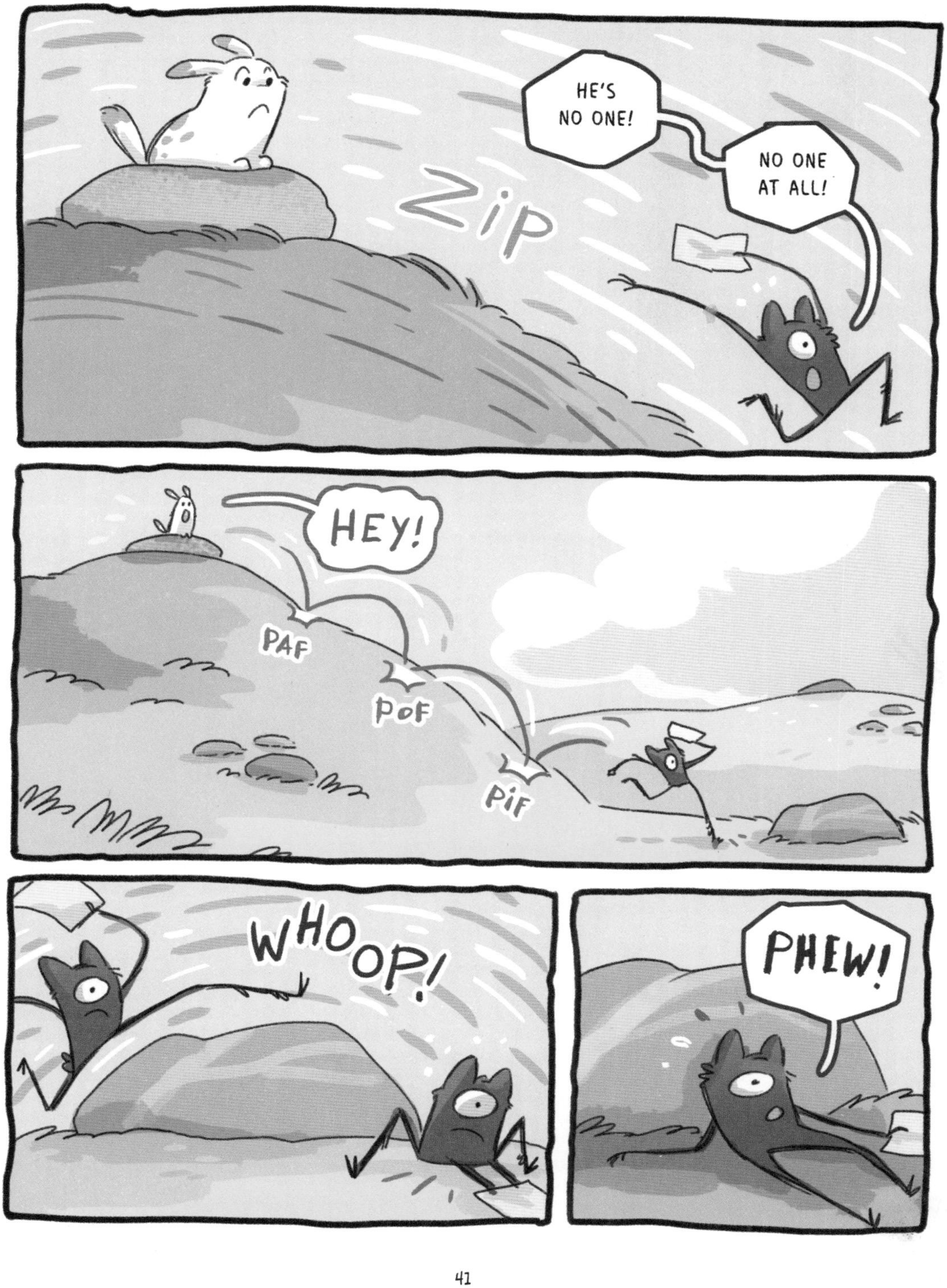
HE'S NO ONE!
NO ONE AT ALL!
ZIP
HEY!
PAF
POF
PIF
WHOOP!
PHEW!

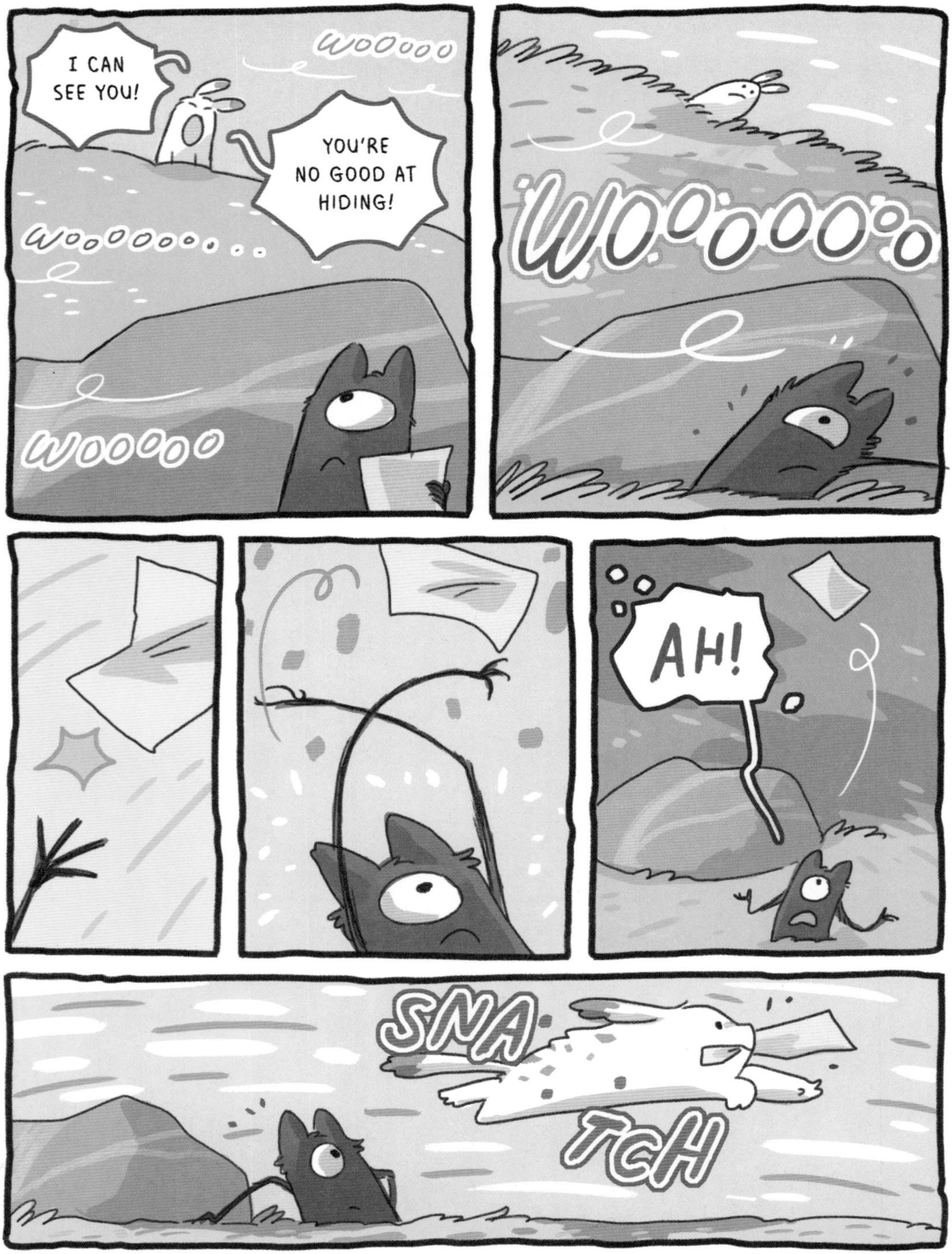
WOOOOO
I CAN SEE YOU!
YOU'RE NO GOOD AT HIDING!
WOOOOOOO...
WOOOOO
WOOOOOOOO
AH!
SNATCH

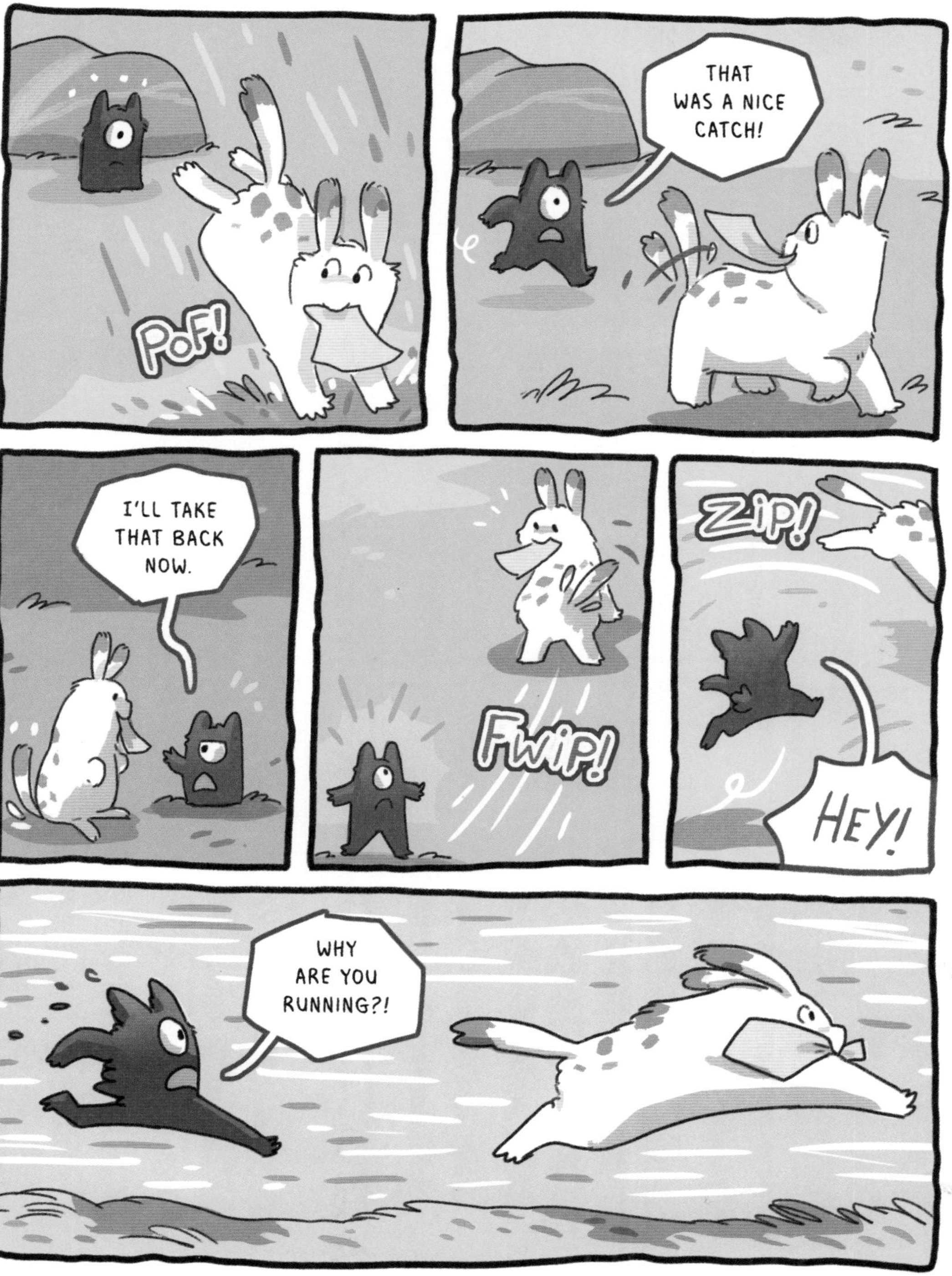
POF!
THAT WAS A NICE CATCH!
I'LL TAKE THAT BACK NOW.
FWIP!
ZIP!
HEY!
WHY ARE YOU RUNNING?!

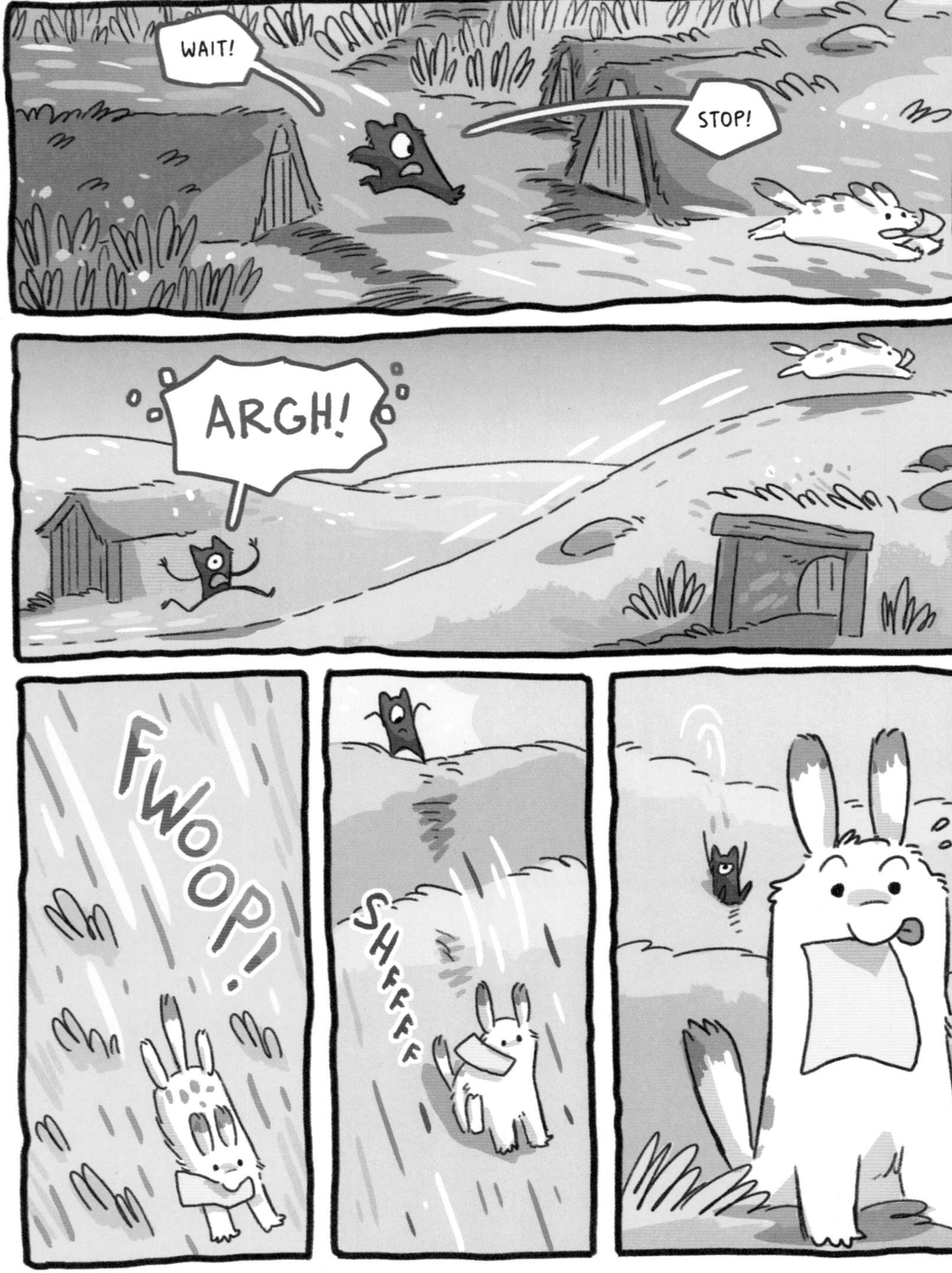
WAIT!
STOP!
ARGH!
FWOOP!
SHFFFF

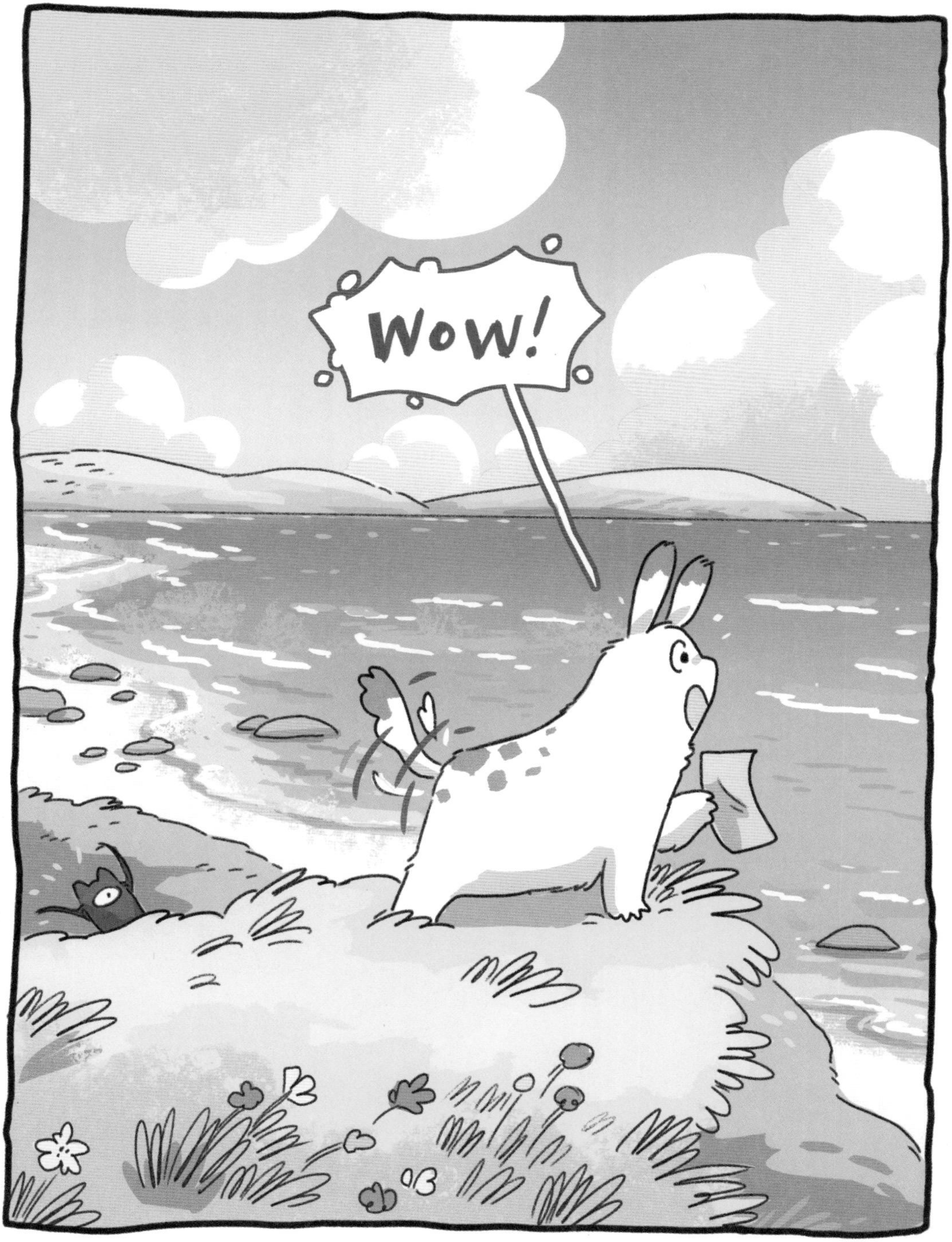
WOW!

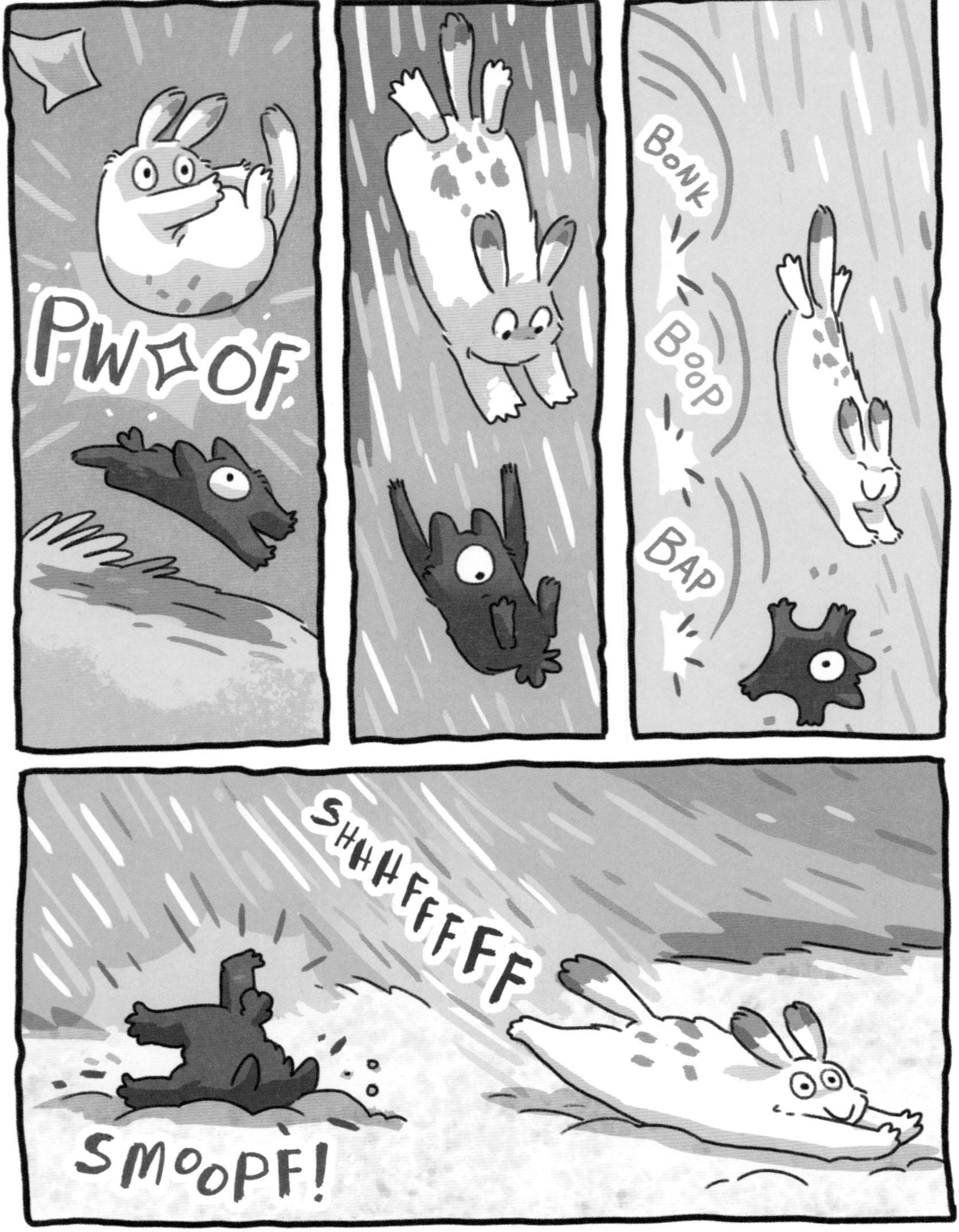
PWOOF
BONK
BOOP
BAP
SHHHFFFFFF
SMOOPF!

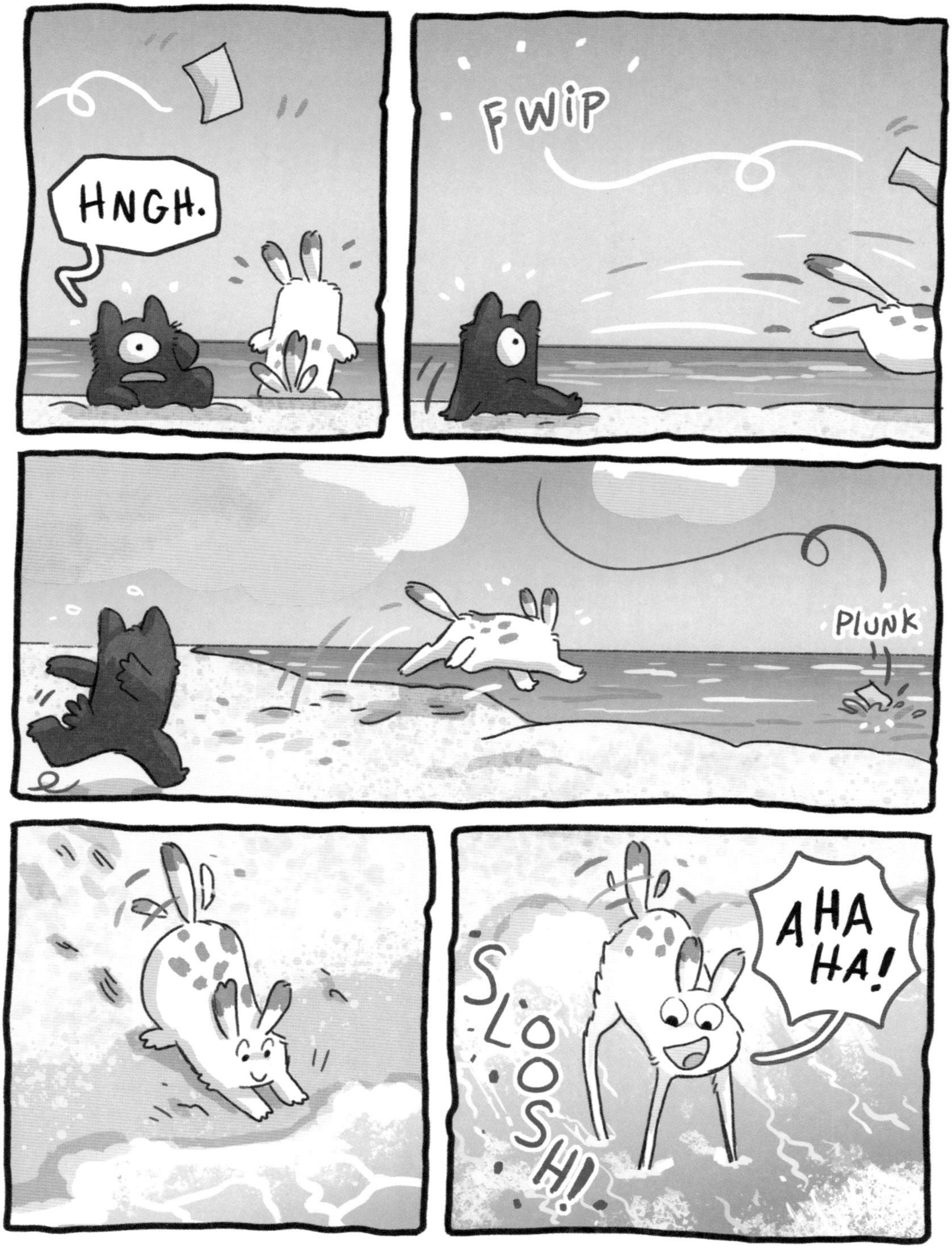
HNGH.
FWIP
PLUNK
SLOOSH!
AHA HA!

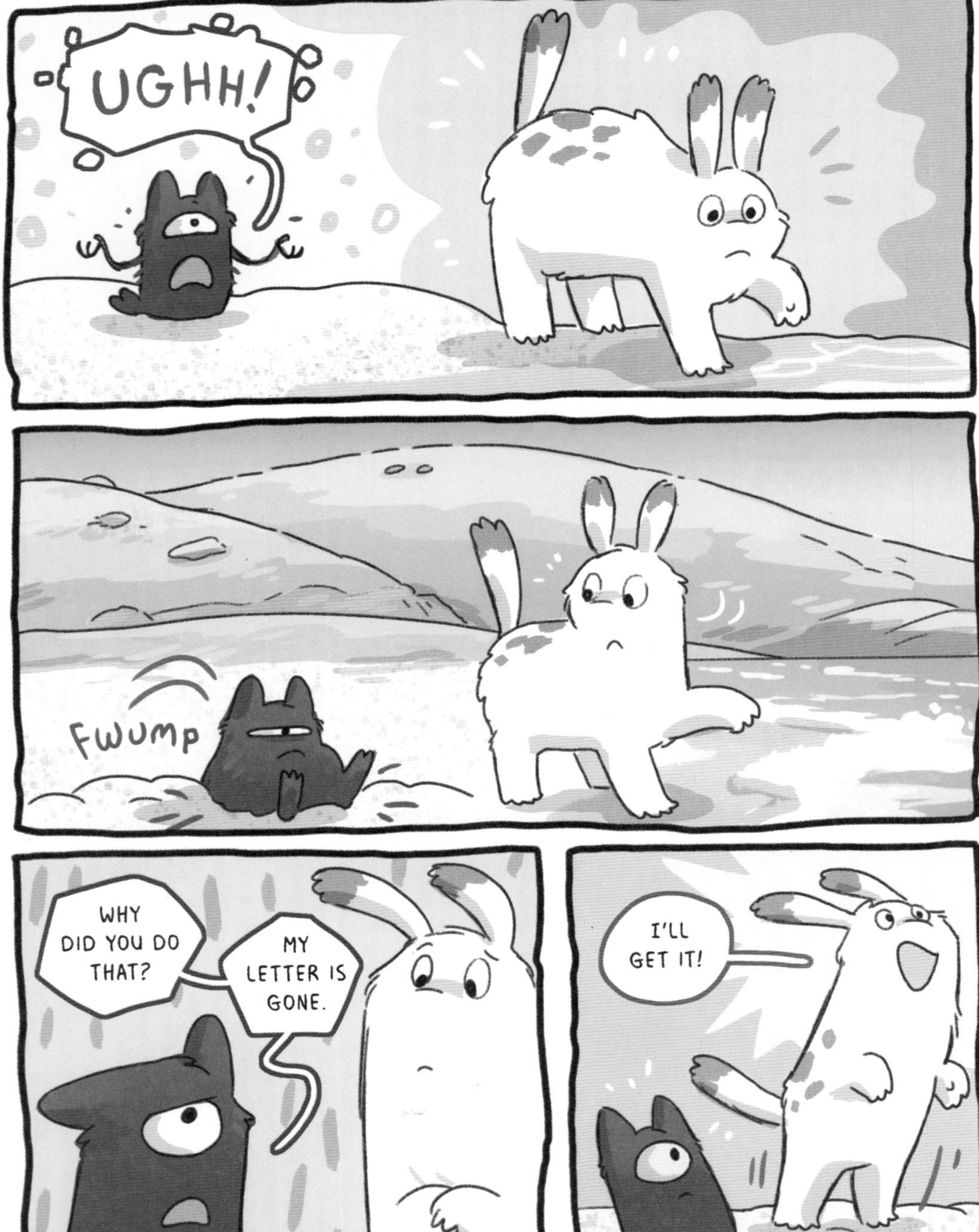
UGHH!
FWUMP
WHY DID YOU DO THAT?
MY LETTER IS GONE.
I'LL GET IT!

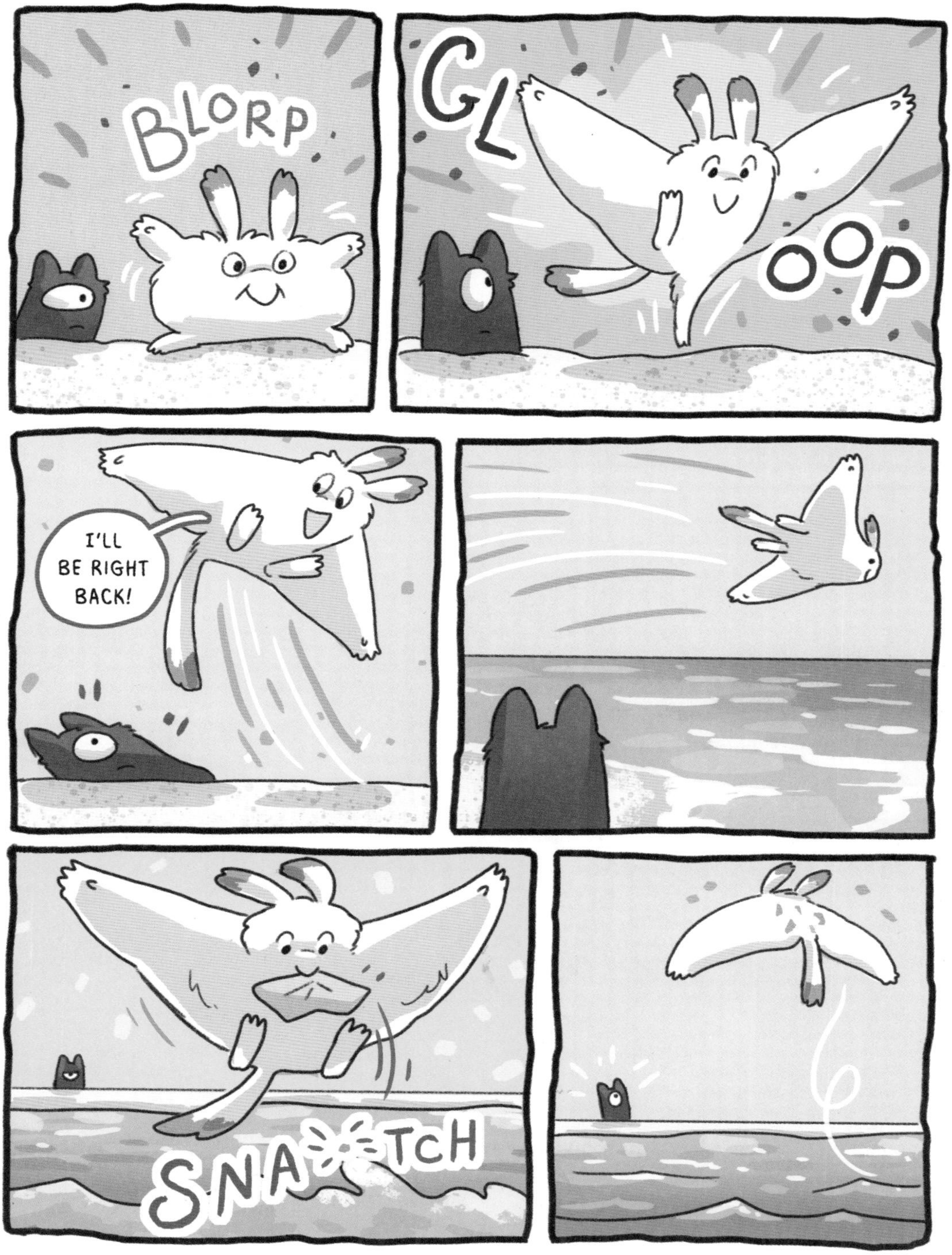
BLORP
GL
OOP
I'LL BE RIGHT BACK!
SNA TCH

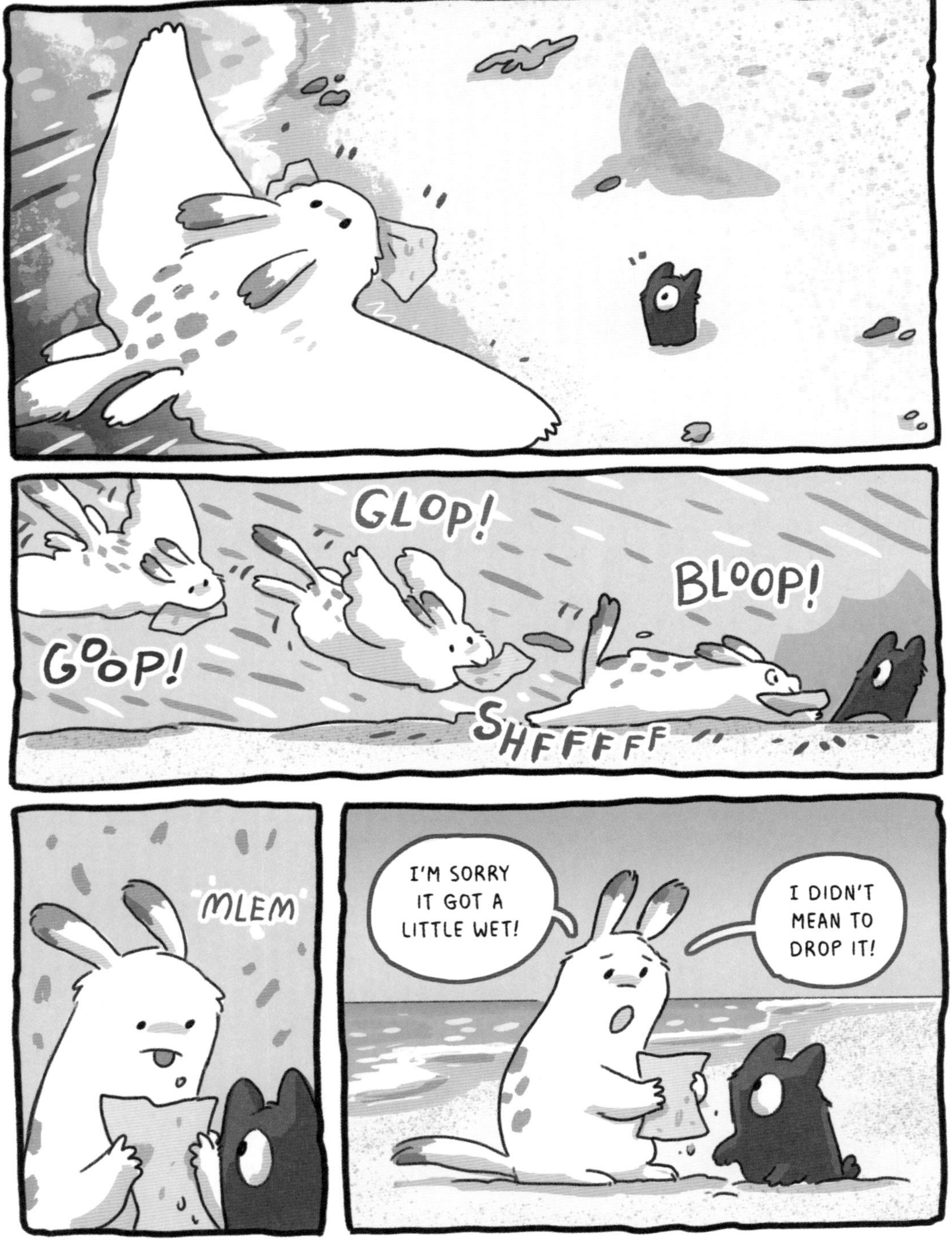
GLOP!
GOOP!
BLOOP!
SHFFFFF
MLEM
I'M SORRY IT GOT A LITTLE WET!
I DIDN'T MEAN TO DROP IT!

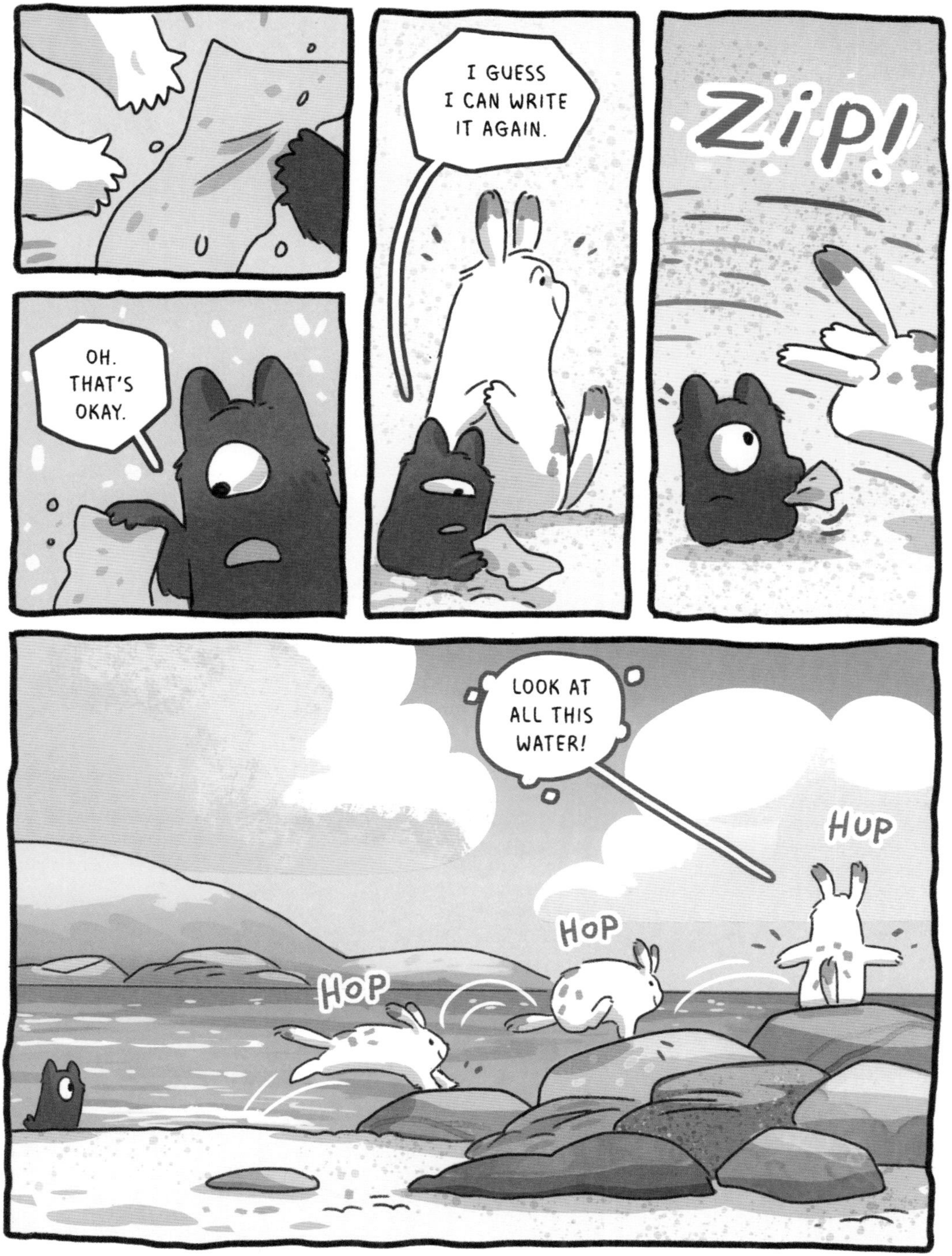
OH.
THAT'S
OKAY.
I GUESS
I CAN WRITE
IT AGAIN.
ZIP!
LOOK AT
ALL THIS
WATER!
HUP
HOP
HOP

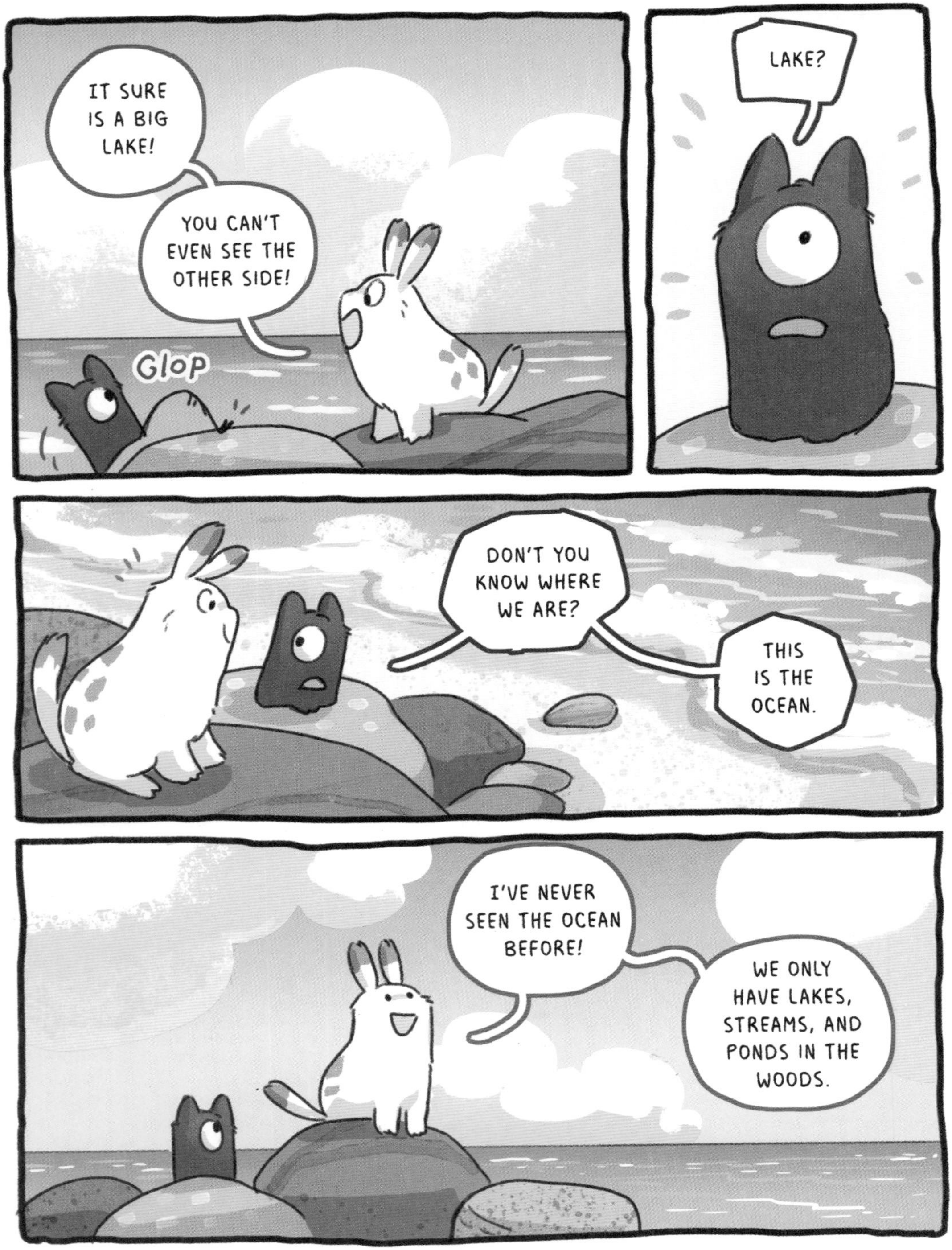
IT SURE IS A BIG LAKE!
YOU CAN'T EVEN SEE THE OTHER SIDE!
GLOP
LAKE?
DON'T YOU KNOW WHERE WE ARE?
THIS IS THE OCEAN.
I'VE NEVER SEEN THE OCEAN BEFORE!
WE ONLY HAVE LAKES, STREAMS, AND PONDS IN THE WOODS.

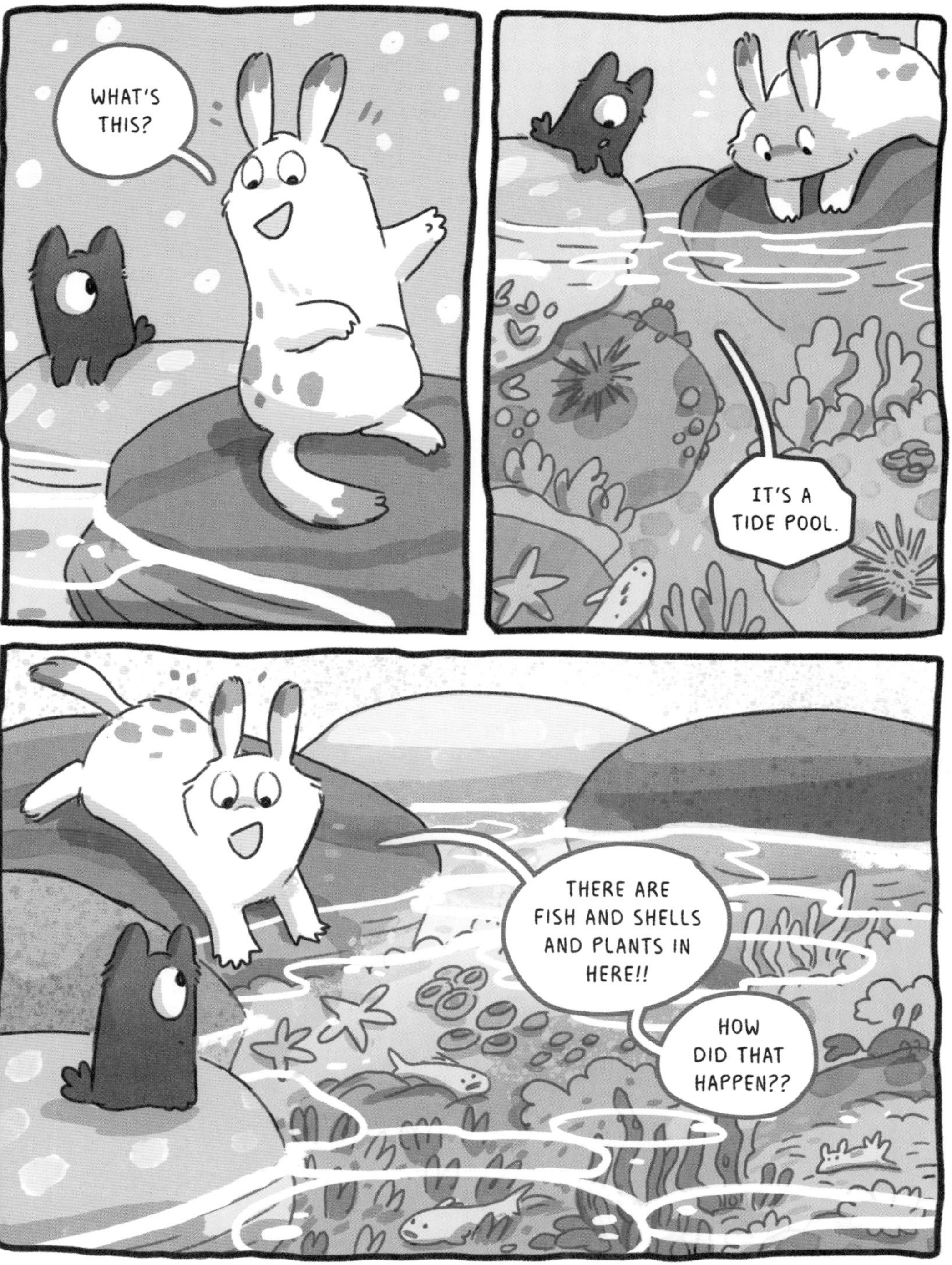
WHAT'S THIS?
IT'S A TIDE POOL.
THERE ARE FISH AND SHELLS AND PLANTS IN HERE!!
HOW DID THAT HAPPEN??

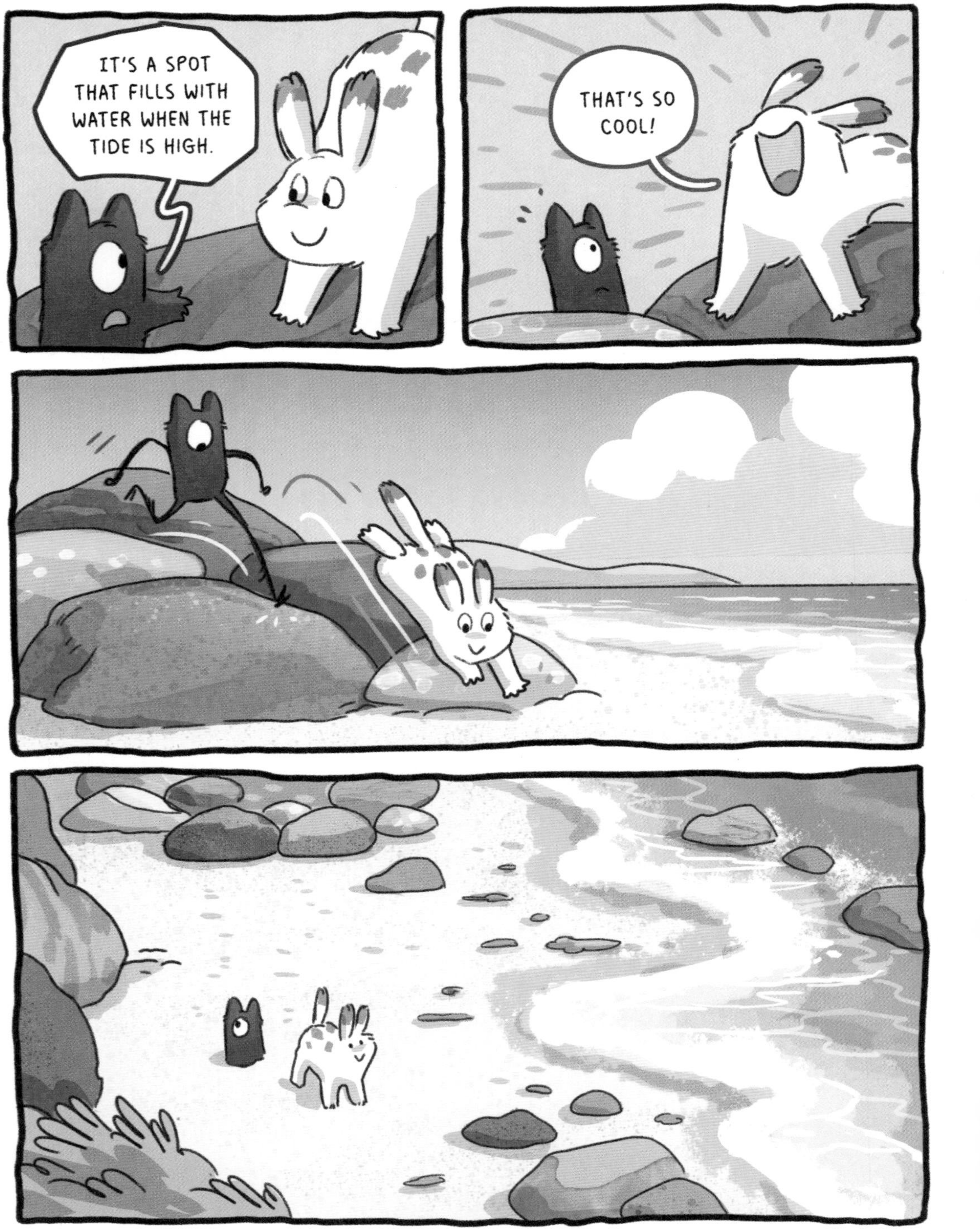
IT'S A SPOT THAT FILLS WITH WATER WHEN THE TIDE IS HIGH.
THAT'S SO COOL!

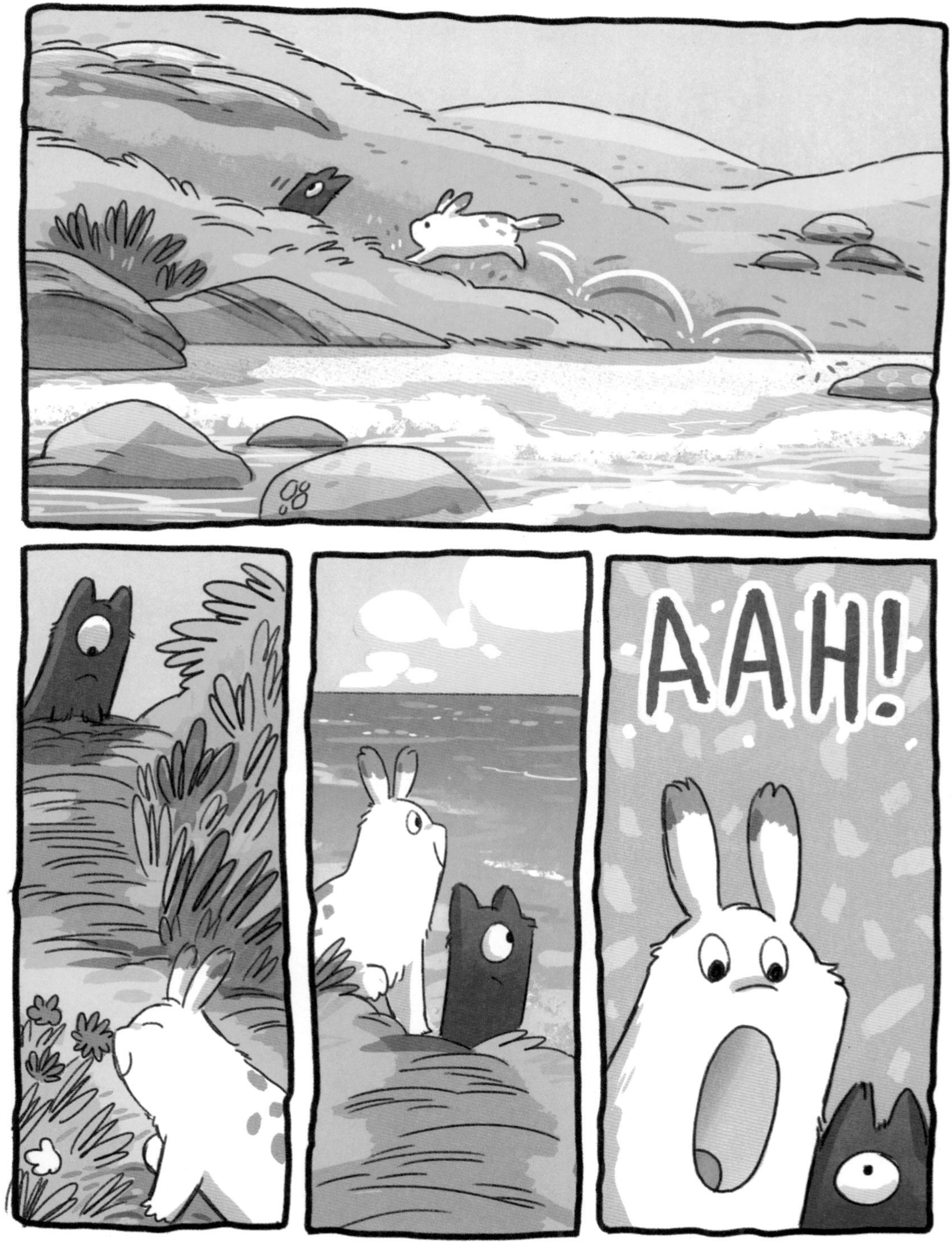
AAH!

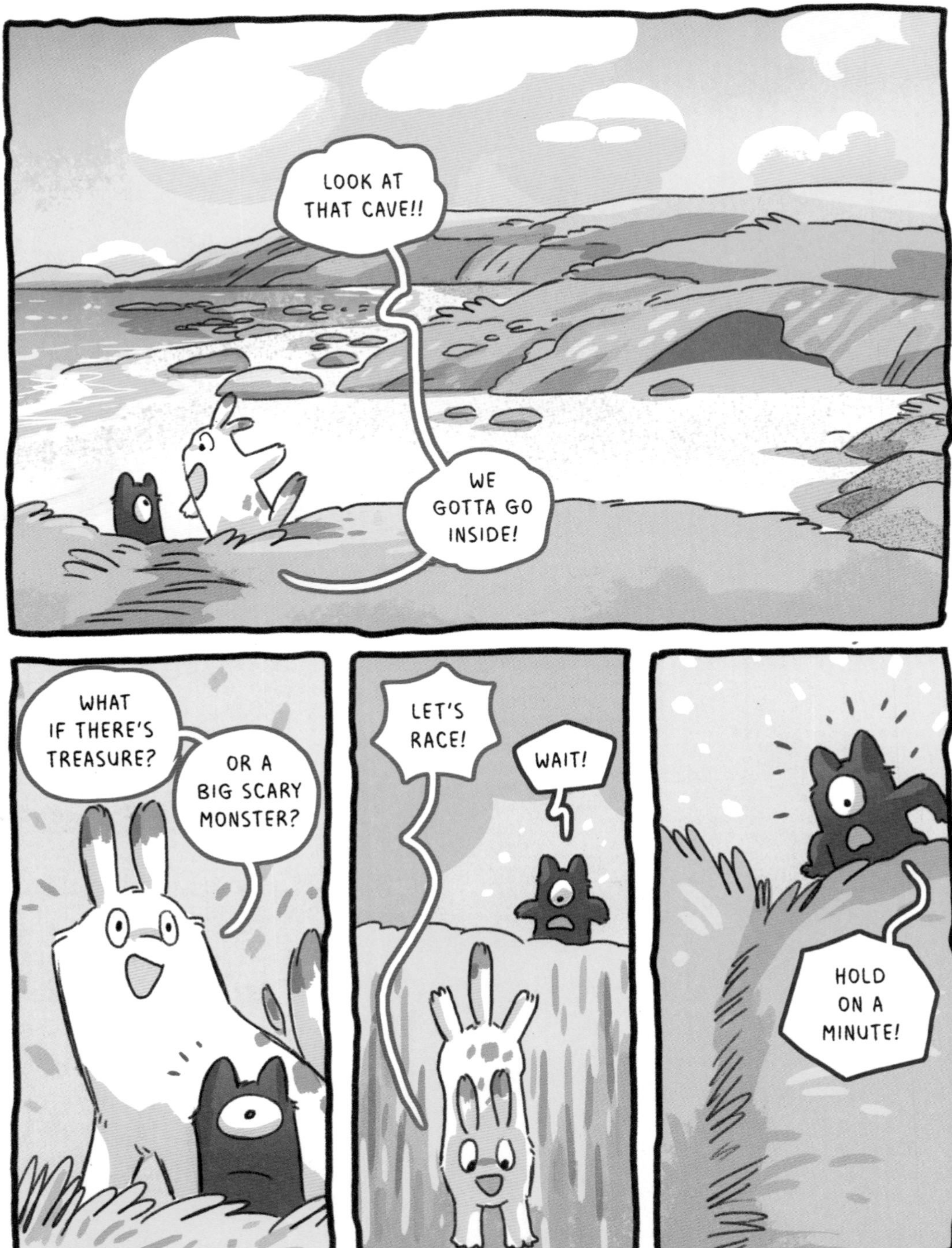
LOOK AT THAT CAVE!!
WE GOTTA GO INSIDE!
WHAT IF THERE'S TREASURE?
OR A BIG SCARY MONSTER?
LET'S RACE!
WAIT!
HOLD ON A MINUTE!

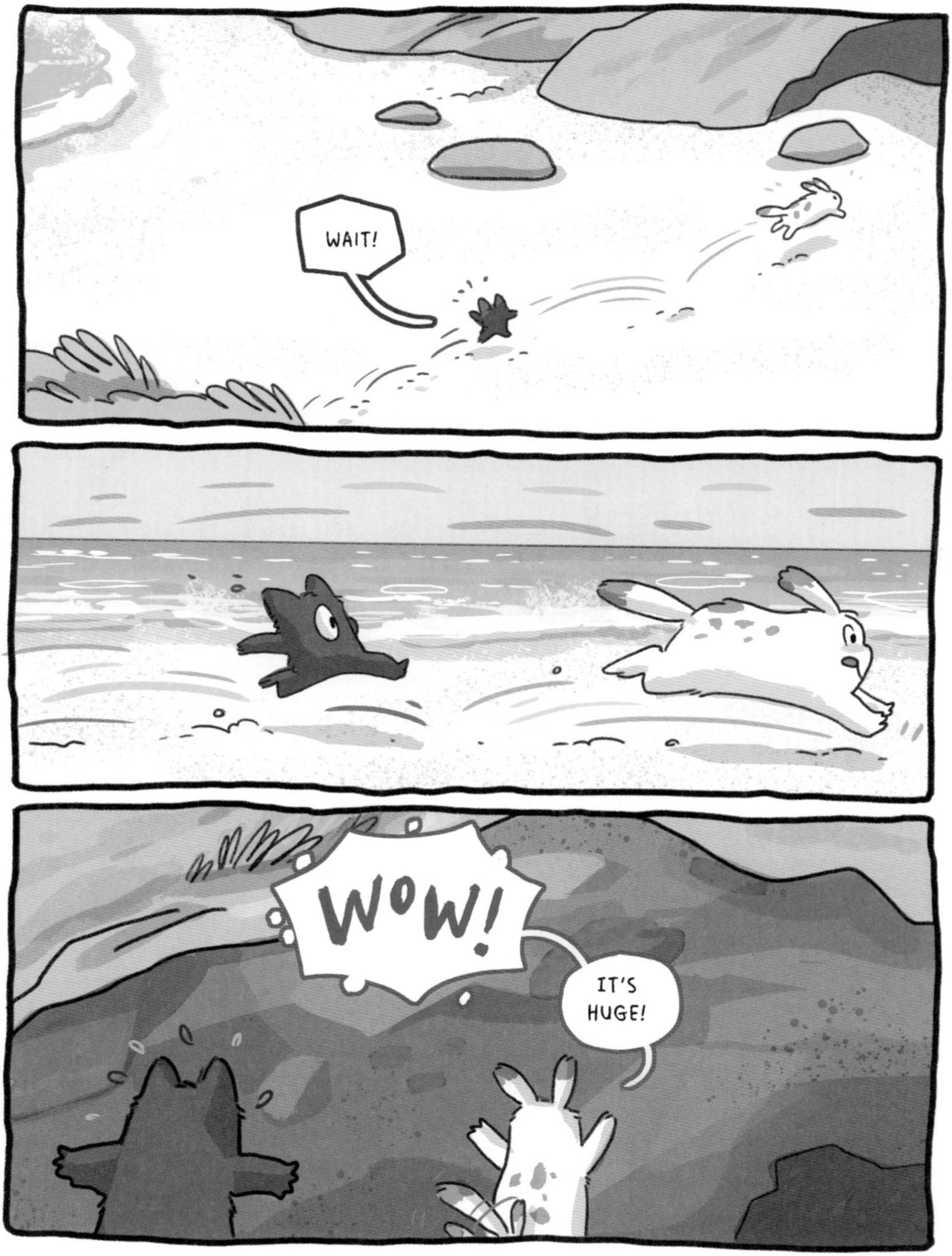
WAIT!
WOW!
IT'S HUGE!

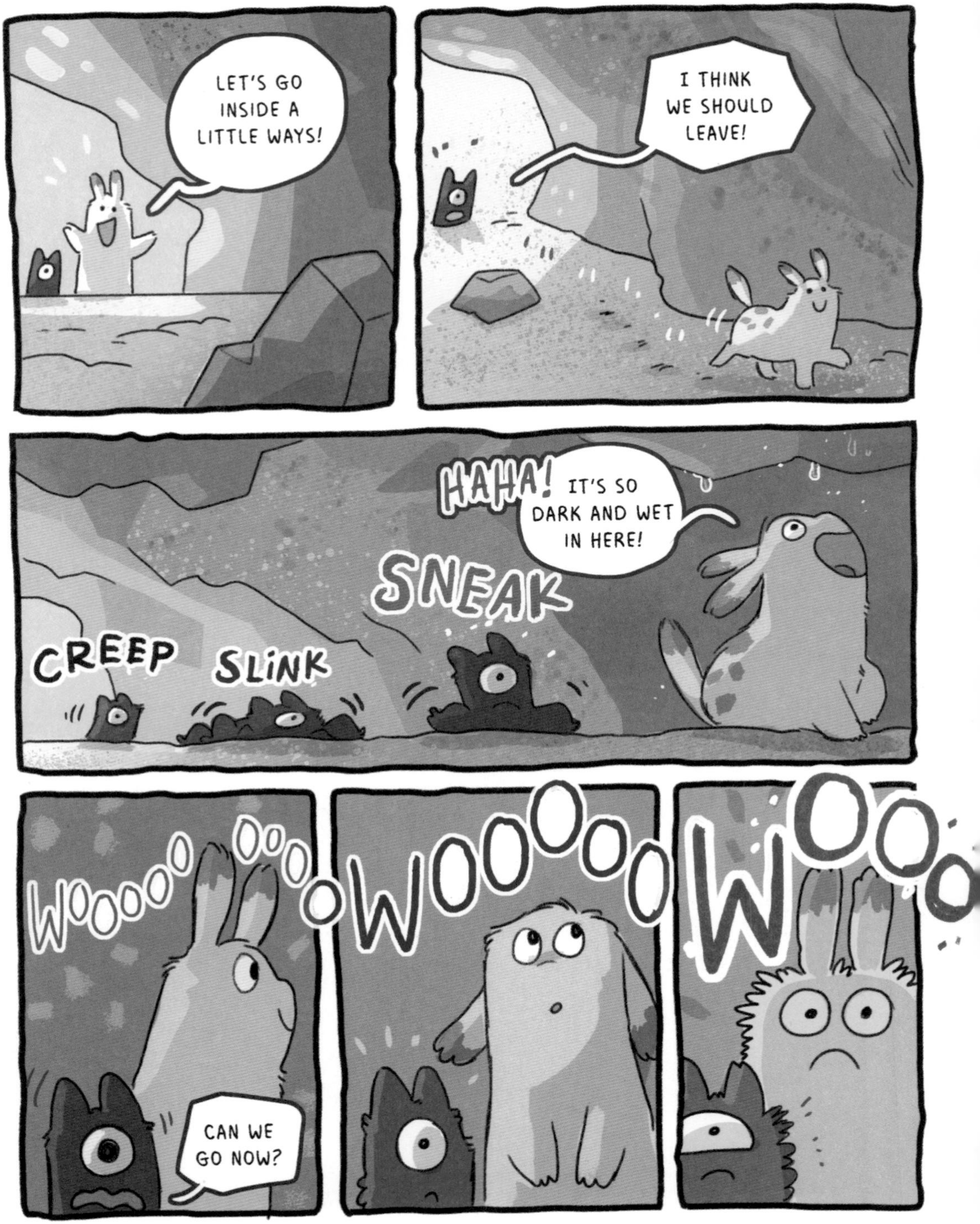
LET'S GO INSIDE A LITTLE WAYS!
I THINK WE SHOULD LEAVE!
CREEP
SLINK
SNEAK
HAHA! IT'S SO DARK AND WET IN HERE!
WOOOOOOOOWOOOOOOOWOOOO
CAN WE GO NOW?

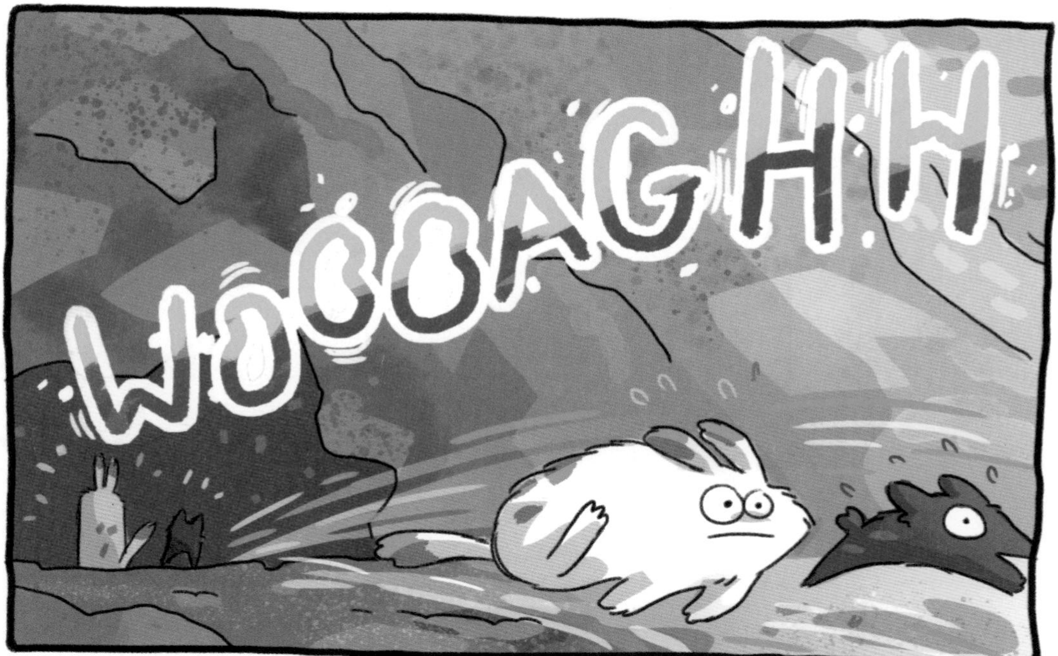
WOOOAGHH

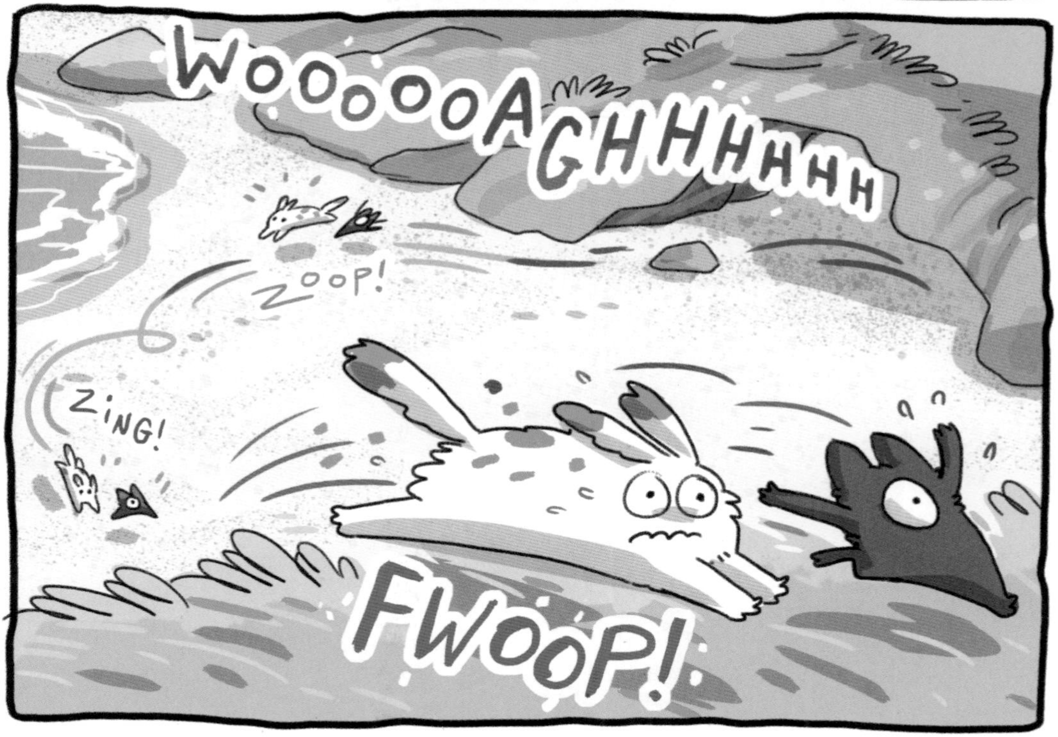
WOOOOOOAGHHHHHHH
ZOOP!
ZING!
FWOOP!

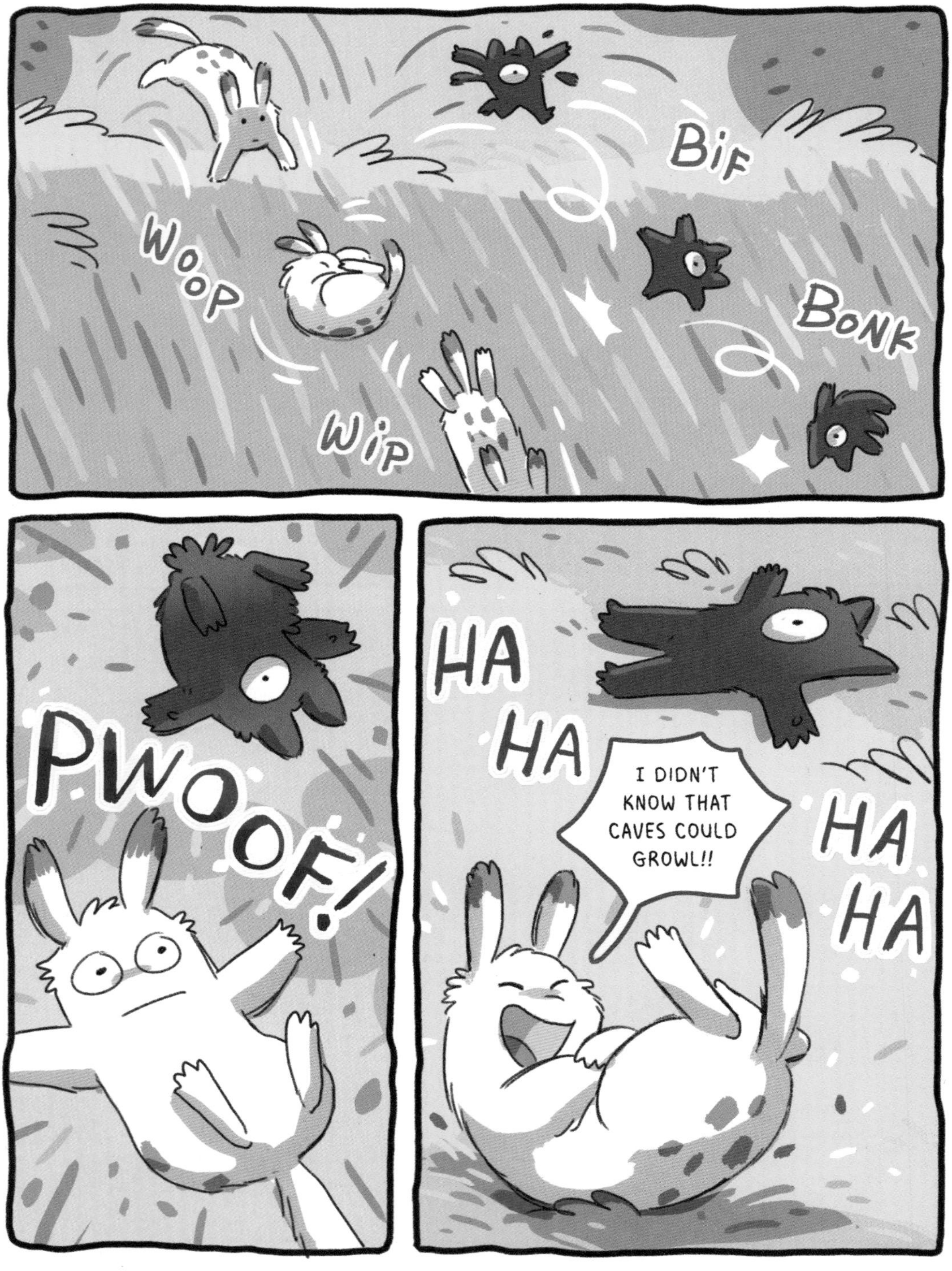

BiF
WooP
BoNK
WiP
PWOOF!
HA
HA
I DIDN'T KNOW THAT CAVES COULD GROWL!!
HA
HA

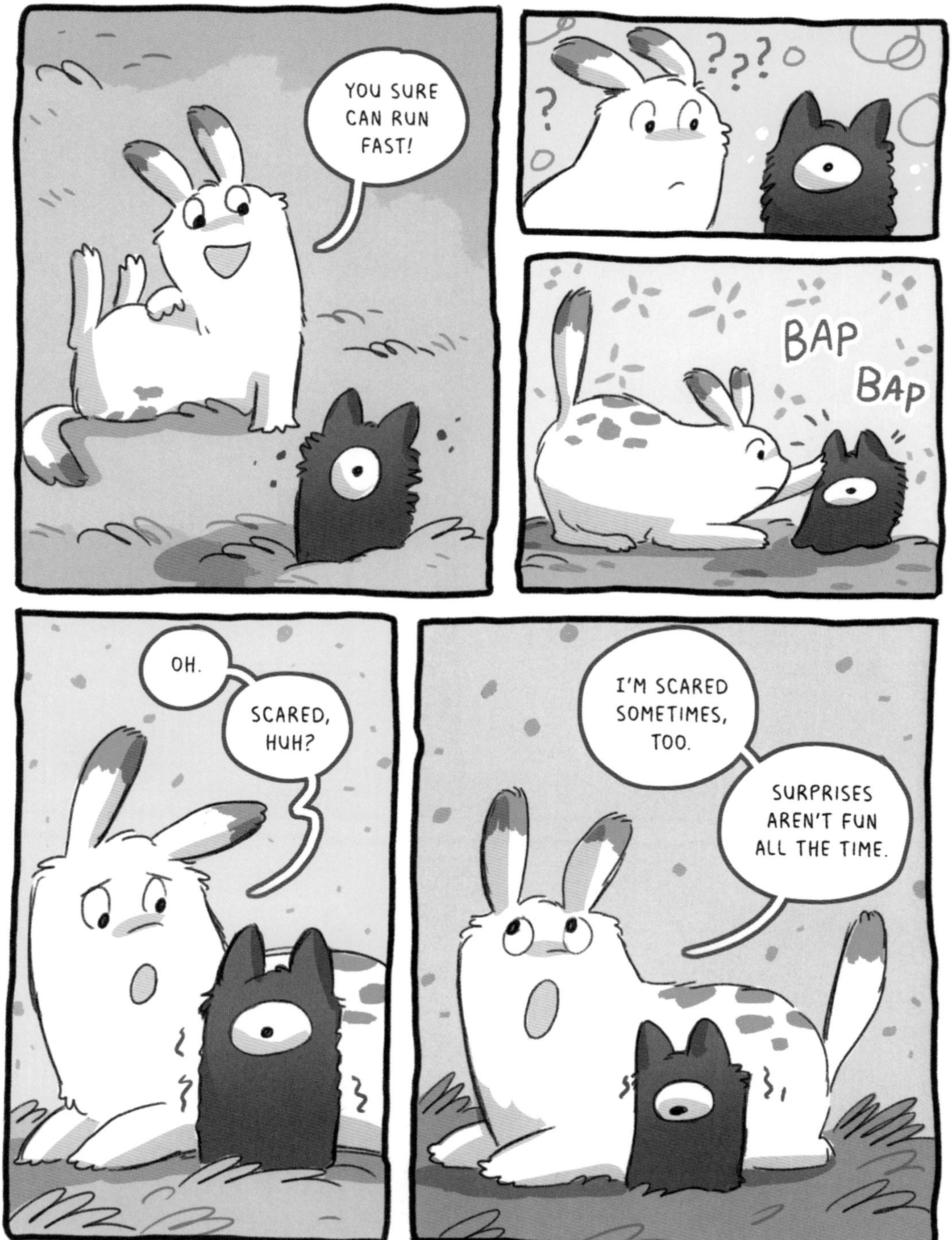
YOU SURE CAN RUN FAST!
???
BAP
BAP
OH.
SCARED, HUH?
I'M SCARED SOMETIMES, TOO.
SURPRISES AREN'T FUN ALL THE TIME.

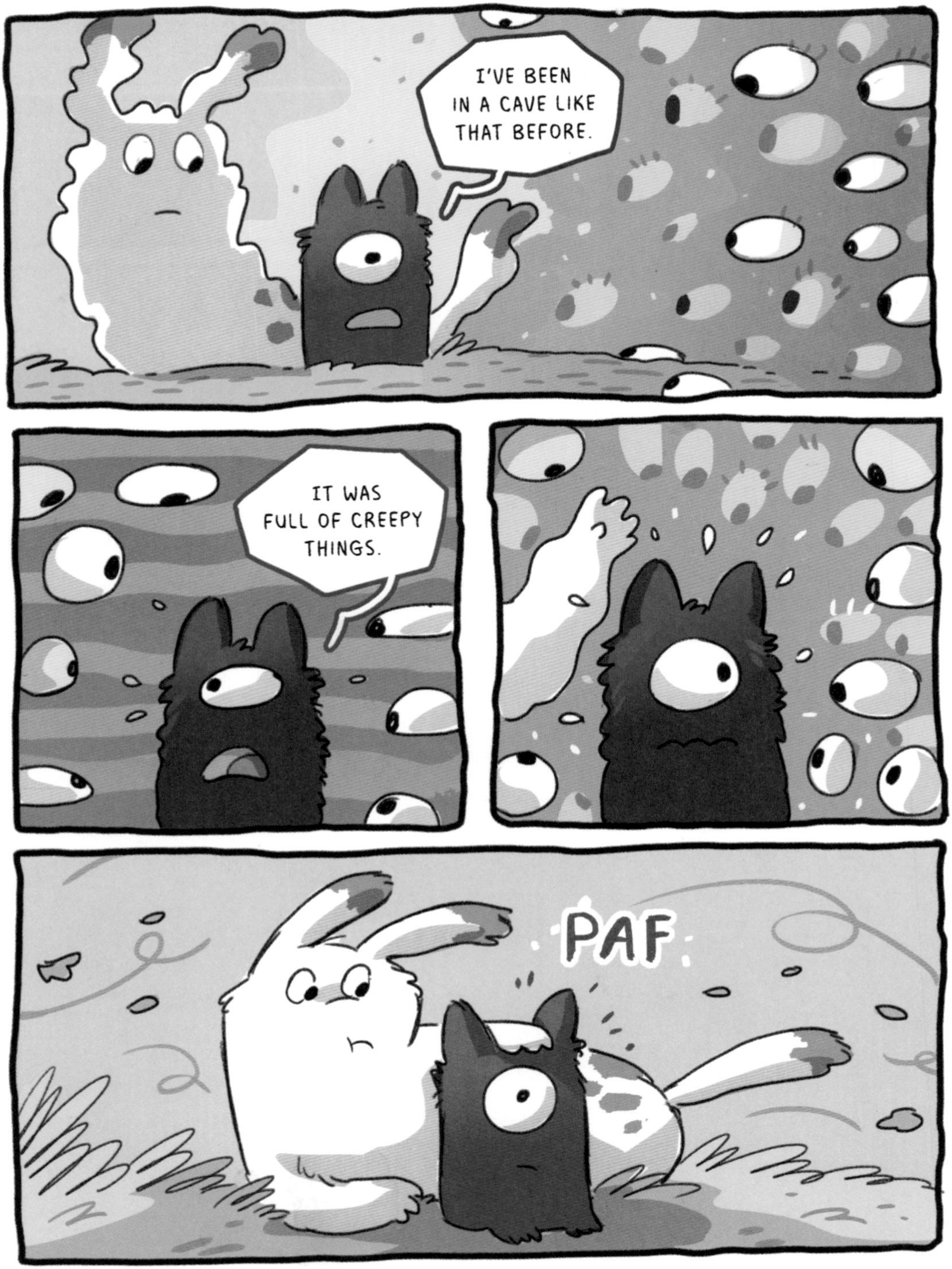
I'VE BEEN IN A CAVE LIKE THAT BEFORE.
IT WAS FULL OF CREEPY THINGS.
PAF

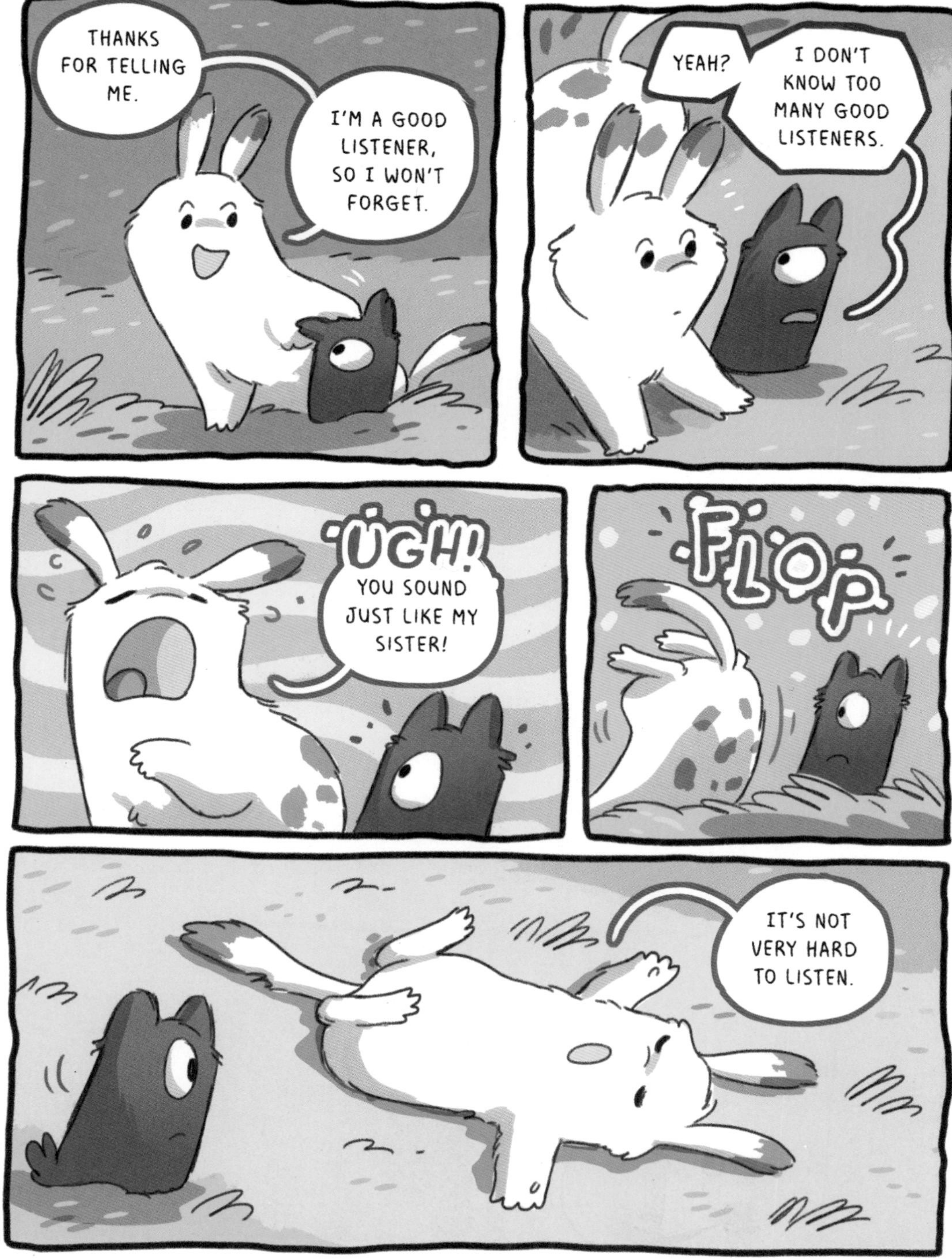
THANKS FOR TELLING ME.
I'M A GOOD LISTENER, SO I WON'T FORGET.
YEAH?
I DON'T KNOW TOO MANY GOOD LISTENERS.
UGH!
YOU SOUND JUST LIKE MY SISTER!
FLOP
IT'S NOT VERY HARD TO LISTEN.

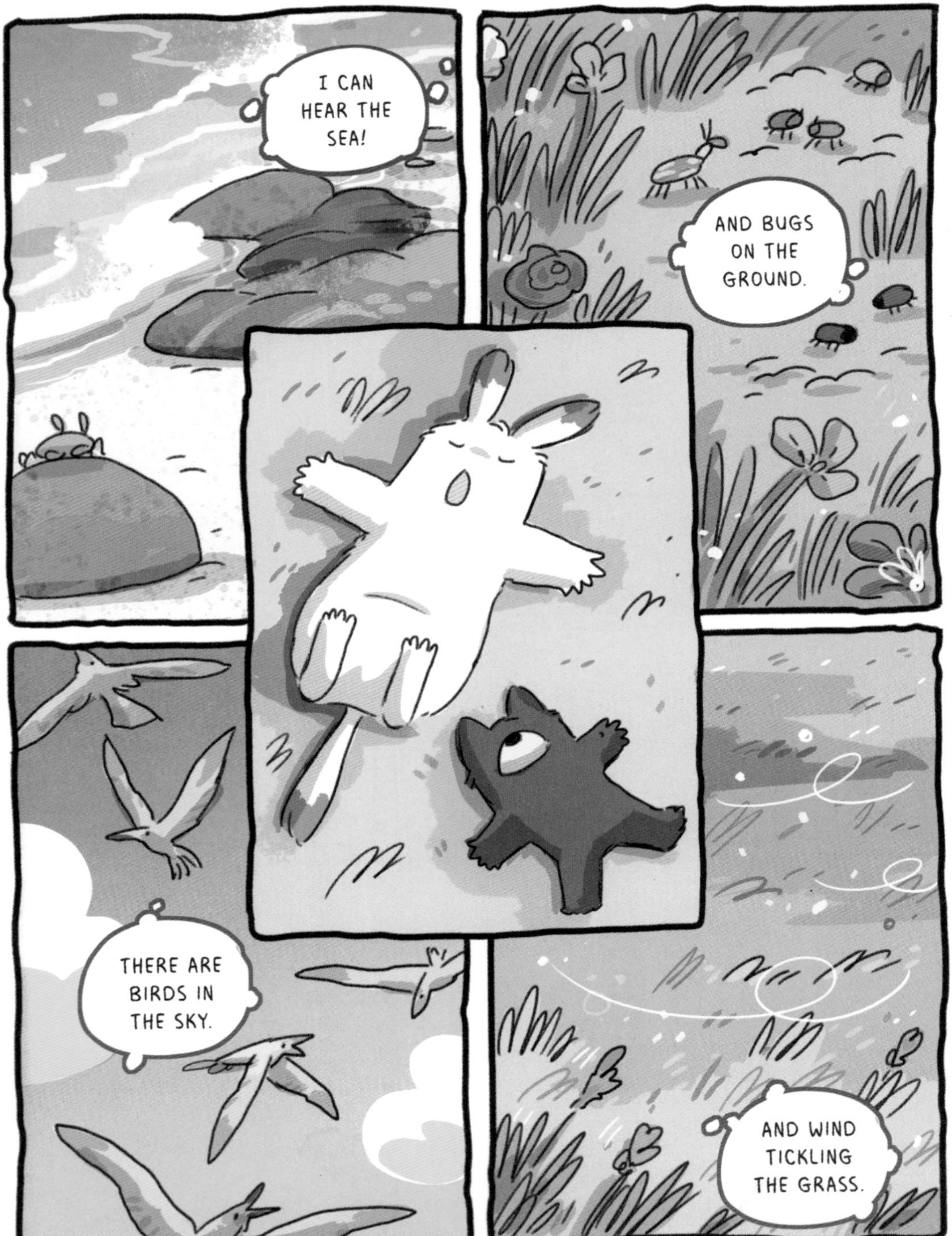
I CAN HEAR THE SEA!
AND BUGS ON THE GROUND.
THERE ARE BIRDS IN THE SKY.
AND WIND TICKLING THE GRASS.

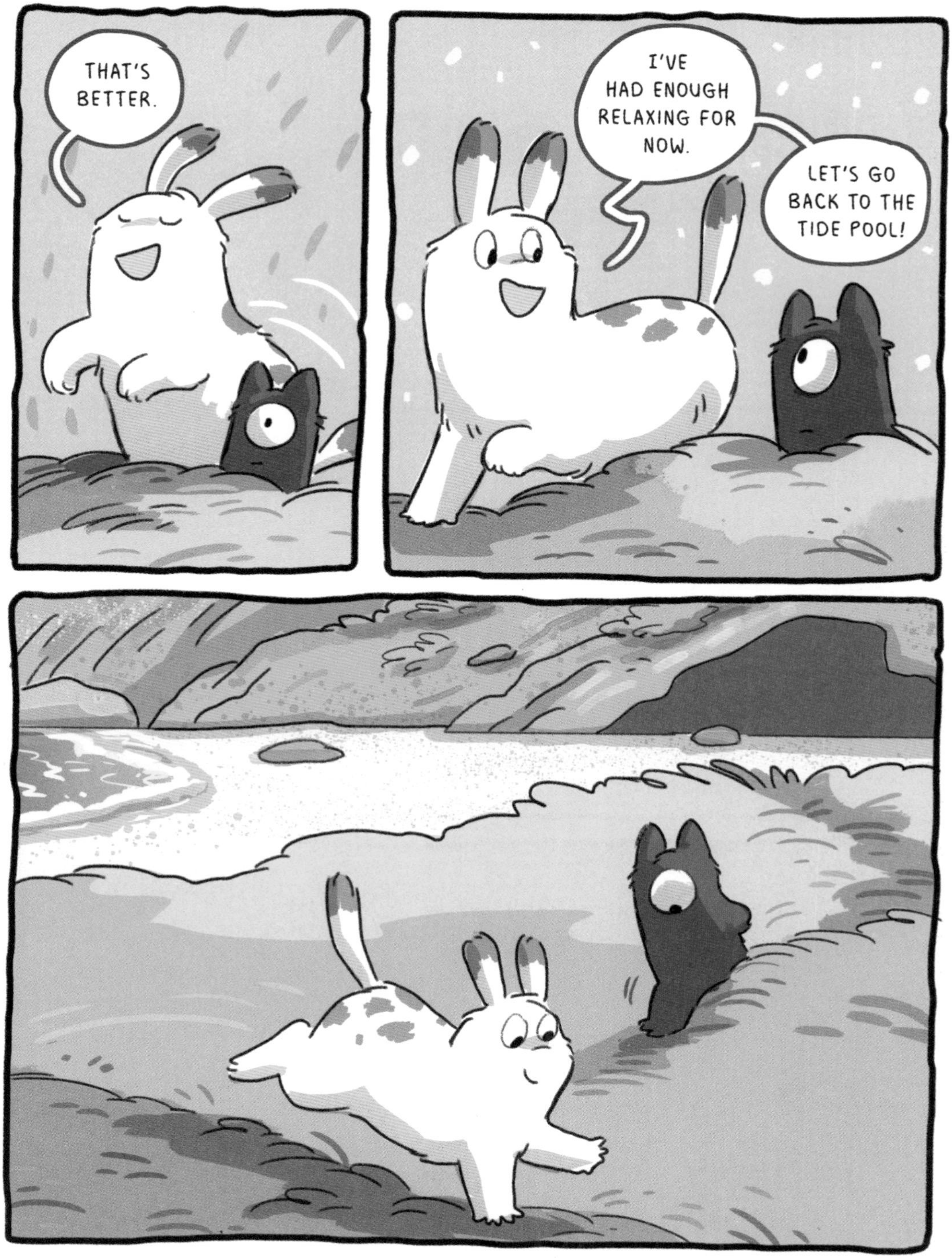
THAT'S BETTER.
I'VE HAD ENOUGH RELAXING FOR NOW.
LET'S GO BACK TO THE TIDE POOL!

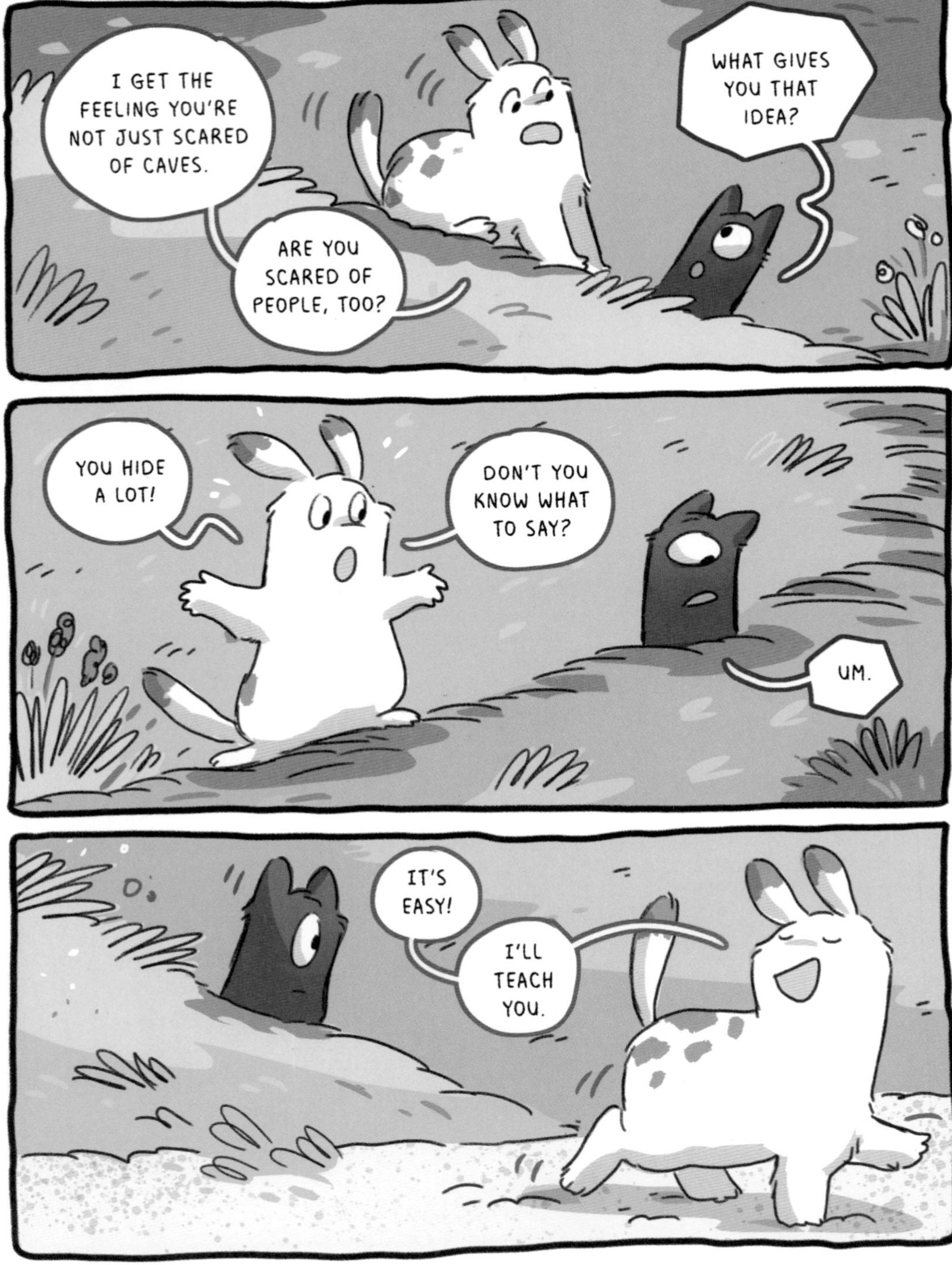
I GET THE FEELING YOU'RE NOT JUST SCARED OF CAVES.
ARE YOU SCARED OF PEOPLE, TOO?
WHAT GIVES YOU THAT IDEA?
YOU HIDE A LOT!
DON'T YOU KNOW WHAT TO SAY?
UM.
IT'S EASY!
I'LL TEACH YOU.

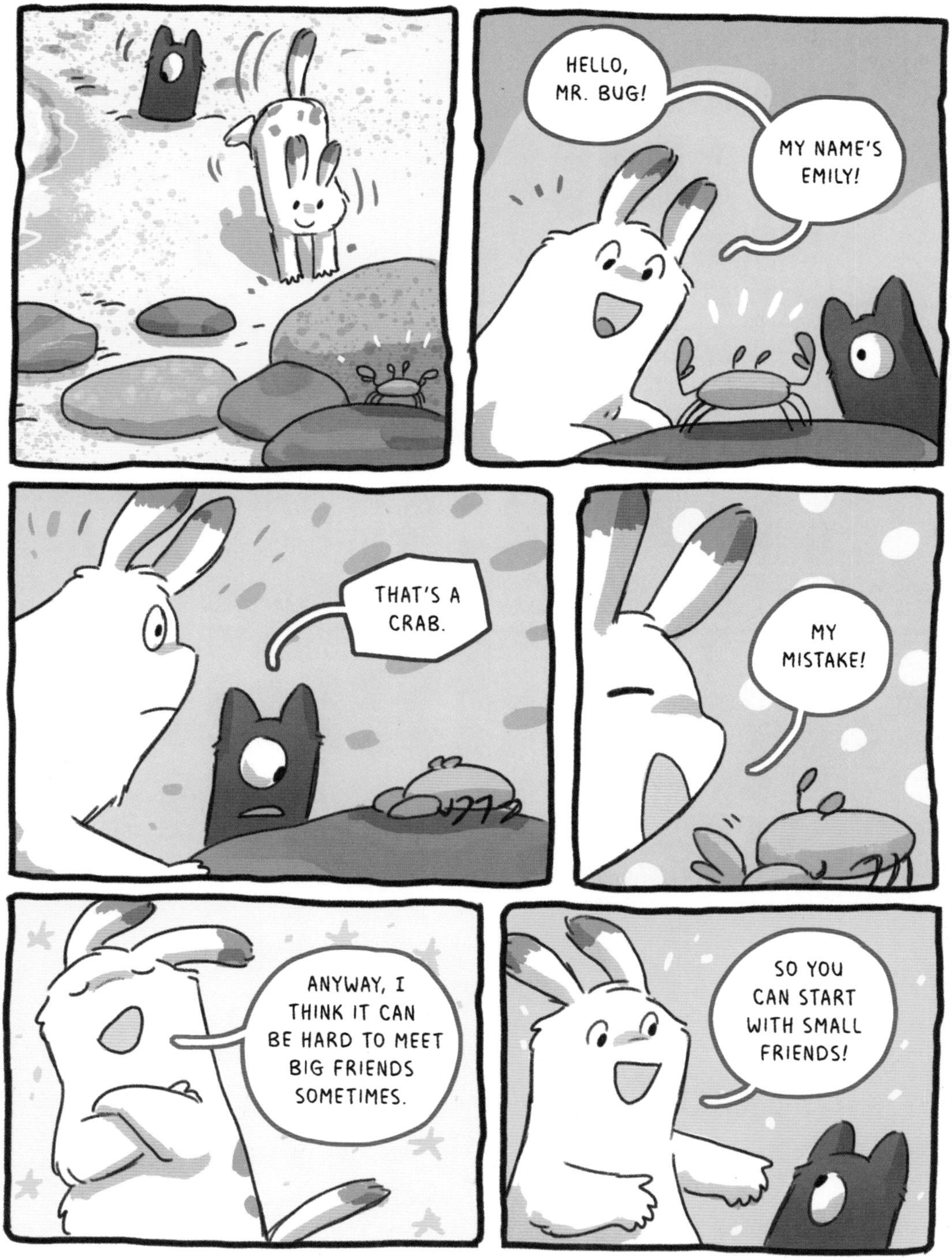
HELLO, MR. BUG!
MY NAME'S EMILY!
THAT'S A CRAB.
MY MISTAKE!
ANYWAY, I THINK IT CAN BE HARD TO MEET BIG FRIENDS SOMETIMES.
SO YOU CAN START WITH SMALL FRIENDS!

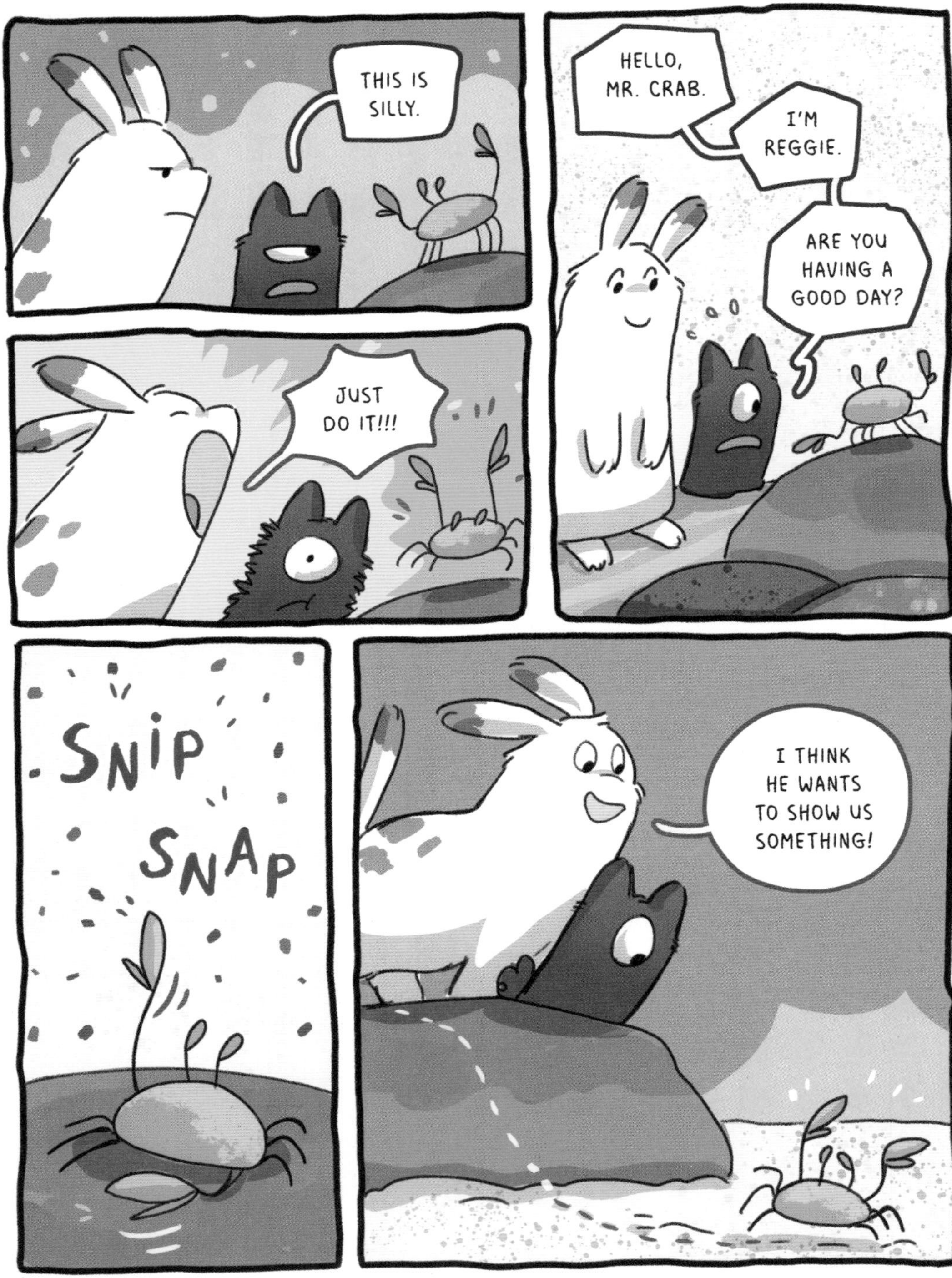
THIS IS SILLY.
HELLO, MR. CRAB.
I'M REGGIE.
ARE YOU HAVING A GOOD DAY?
JUST DO IT!!!
SNIP
SNAP
I THINK HE WANTS TO SHOW US SOMETHING!

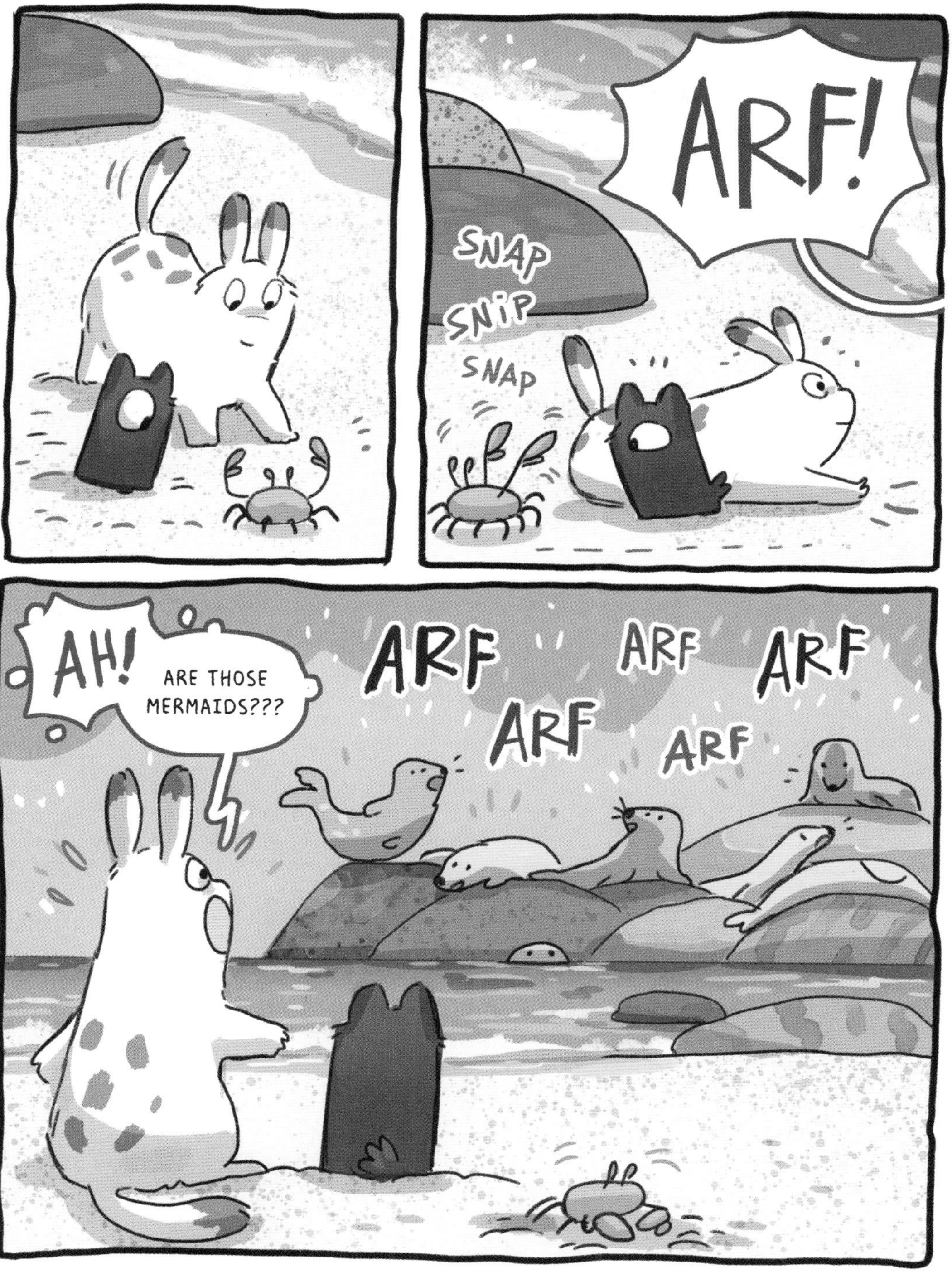
ARF!
SNAP
SNIP
SNAP
AH!
ARE THOSE MERMAIDS???
ARF
ARF
ARF
ARF
ARF

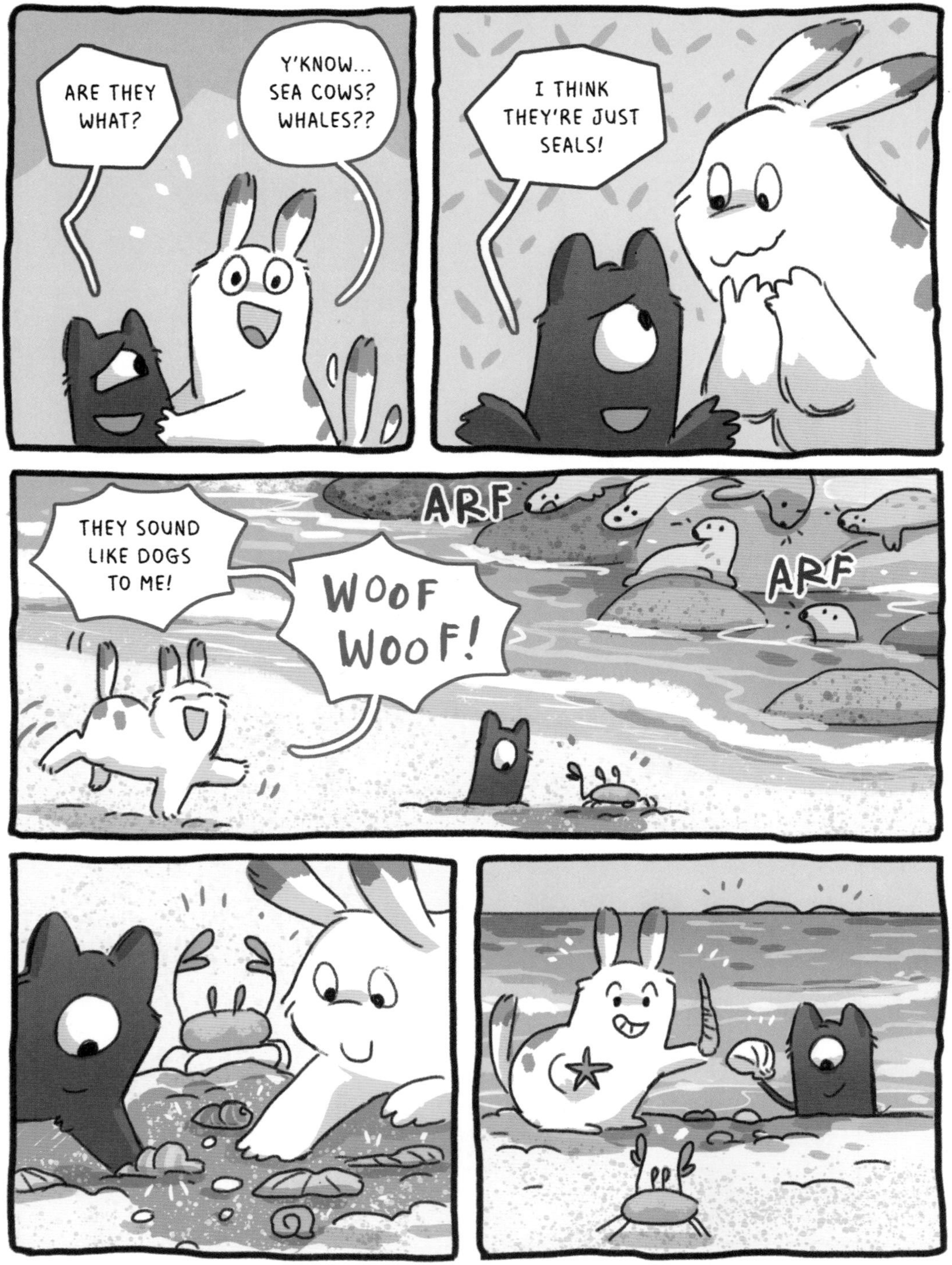
ARE THEY WHAT?
Y'KNOW... SEA COWS? WHALES??
I THINK THEY'RE JUST SEALS!
ARF
ARF
THEY SOUND LIKE DOGS TO ME!
WOOF WOOF!

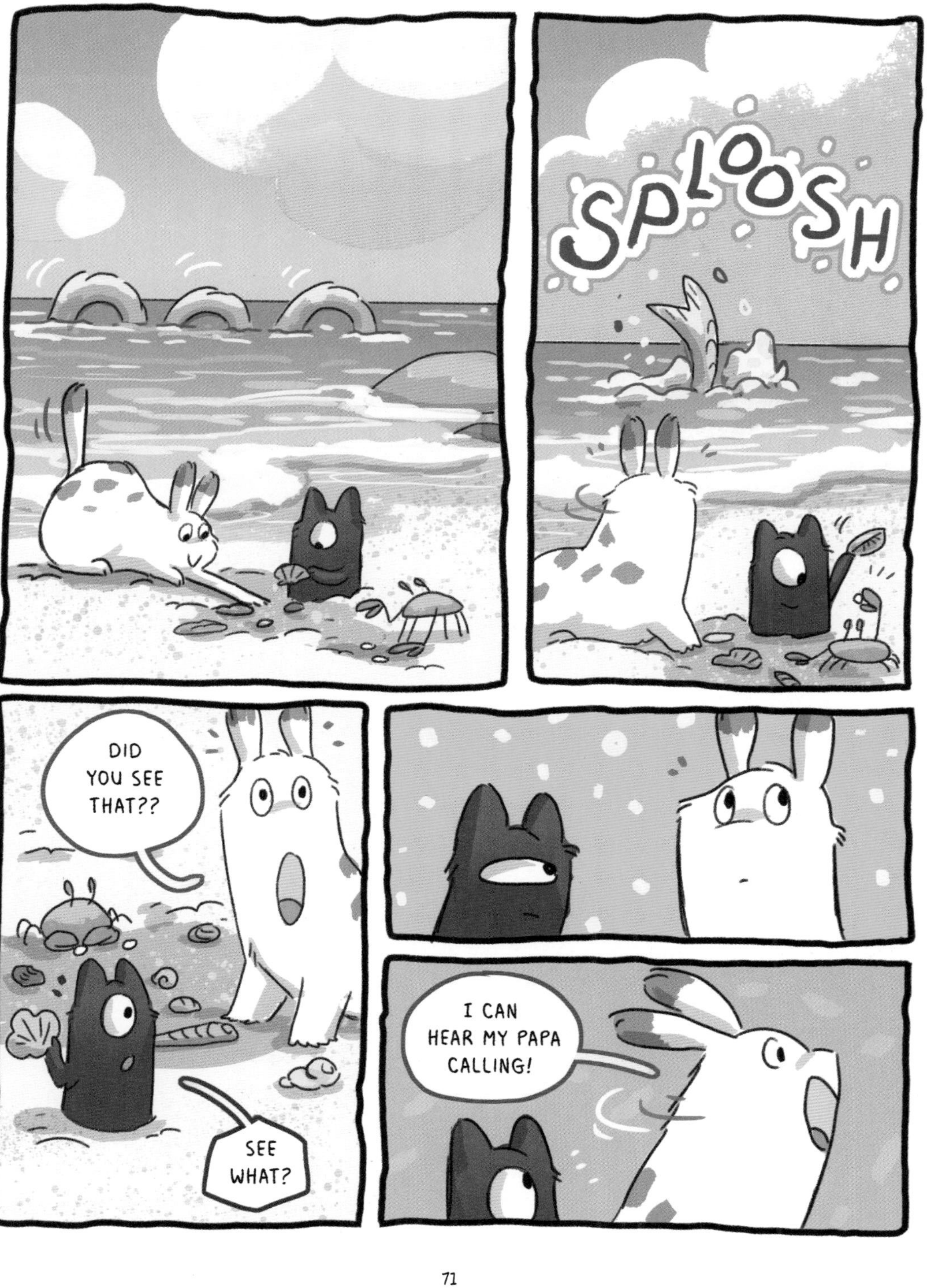
SPLOOSH
DID YOU SEE THAT??
SEE WHAT?
I CAN HEAR MY PAPA CALLING!

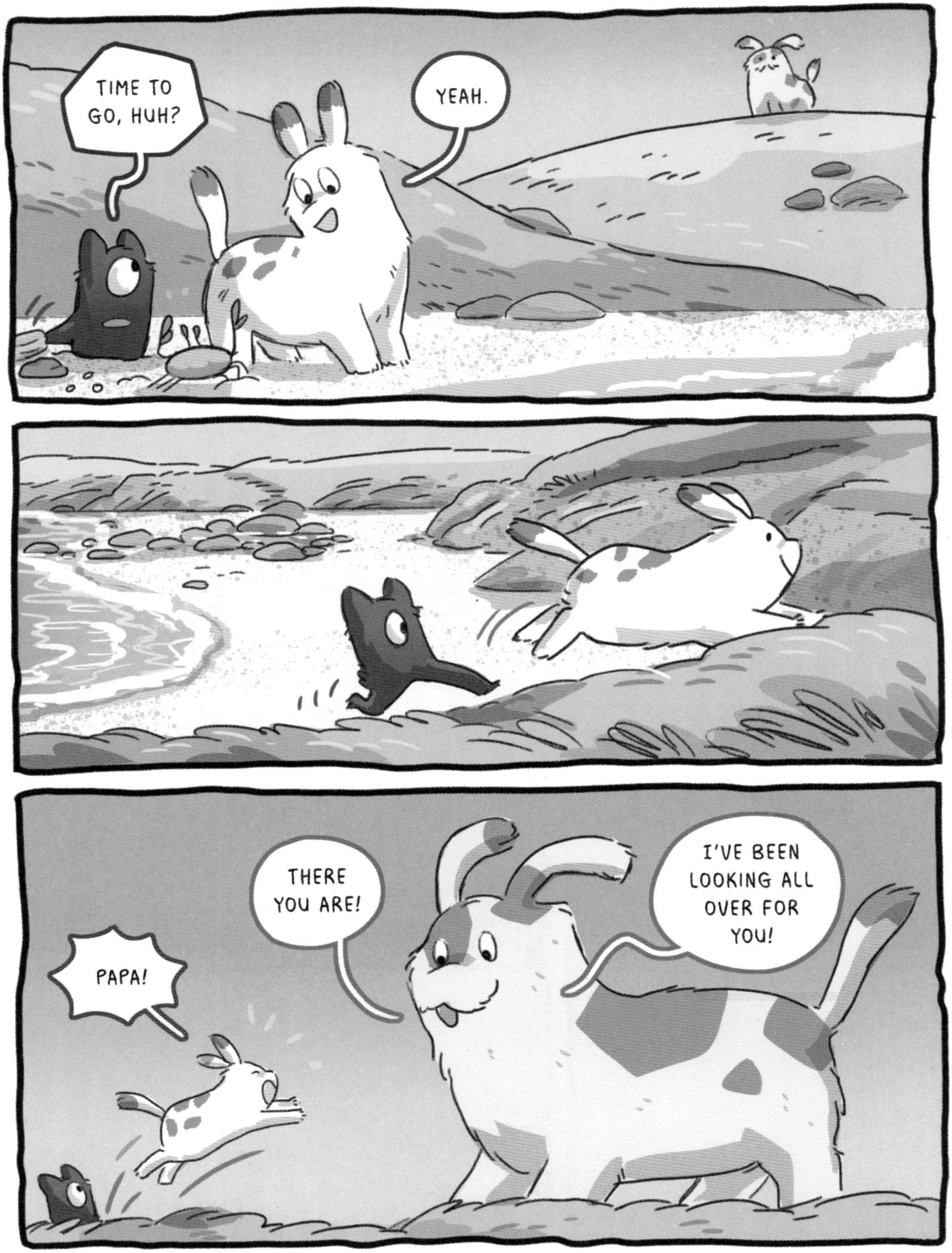
TIME TO GO, HUH?
YEAH.
THERE YOU ARE!
I'VE BEEN LOOKING ALL OVER FOR YOU!
PAPA!

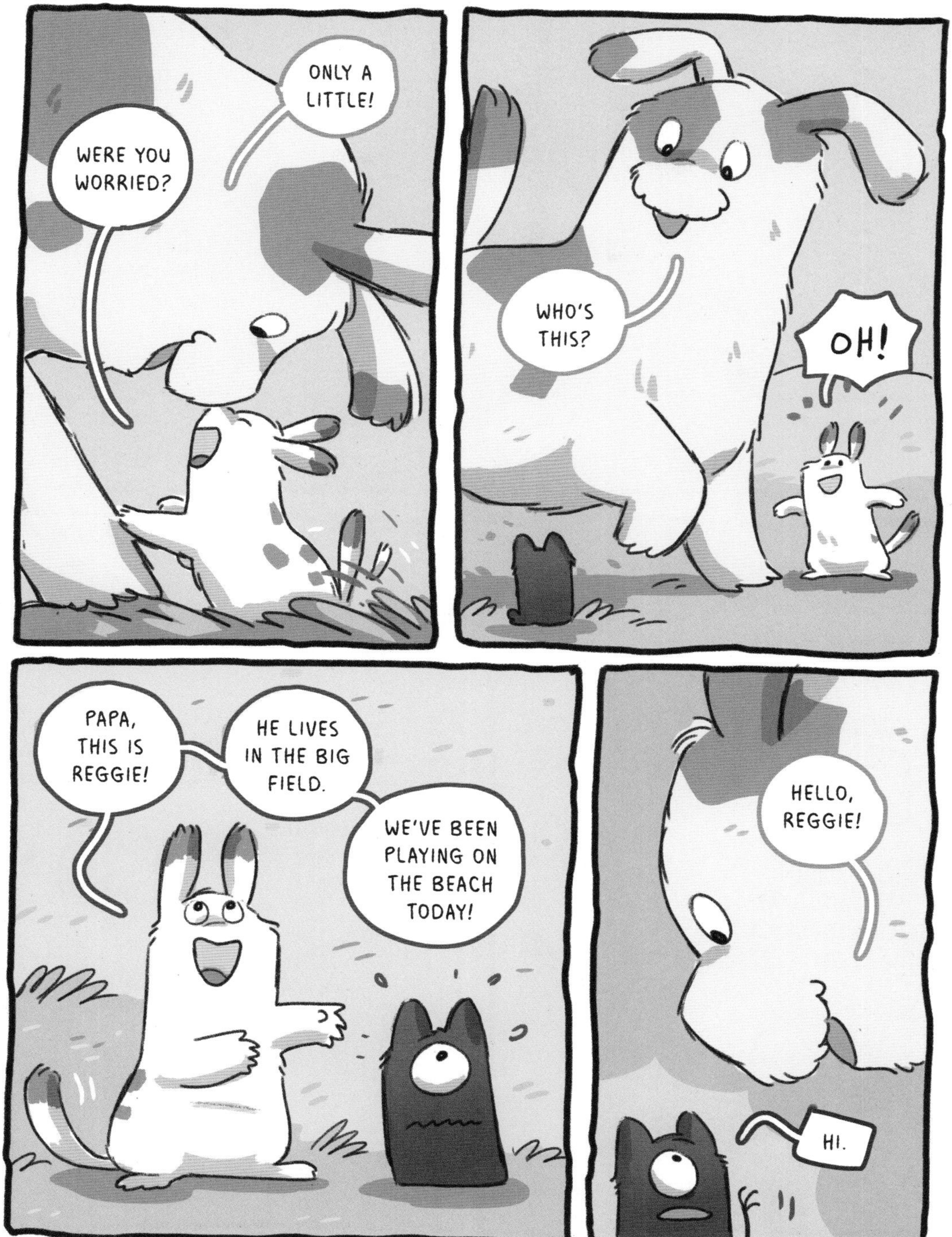
WERE YOU WORRIED?
ONLY A LITTLE!
WHO'S THIS?
OH!
PAPA, THIS IS REGGIE!
HE LIVES IN THE BIG FIELD.
WE'VE BEEN PLAYING ON THE BEACH TODAY!
HELLO, REGGIE!
HI.

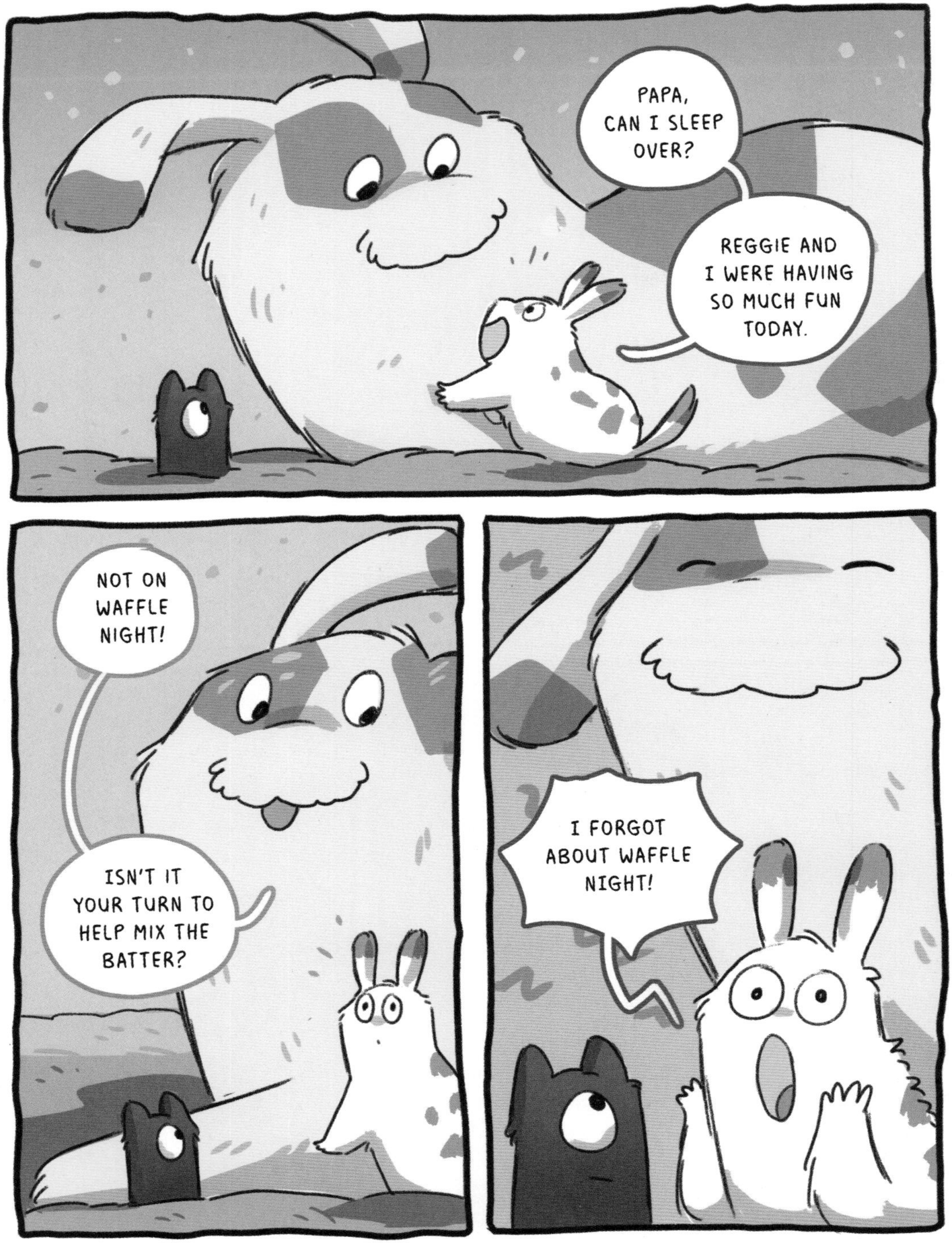
PAPA, CAN I SLEEP OVER?
REGGIE AND I WERE HAVING SO MUCH FUN TODAY.
NOT ON WAFFLE NIGHT!
ISN'T IT YOUR TURN TO HELP MIX THE BATTER?
I FORGOT ABOUT WAFFLE NIGHT!

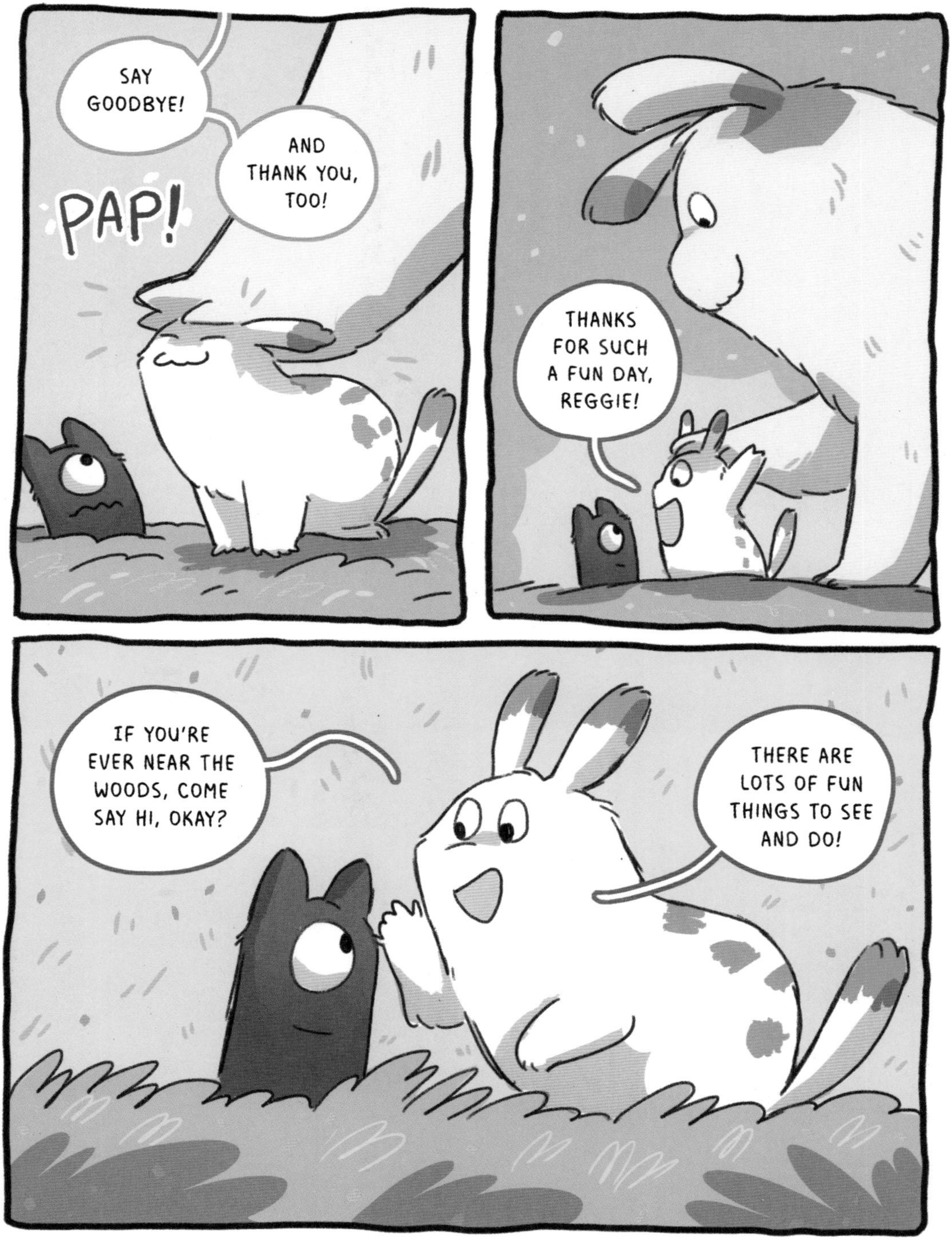
SAY GOODBYE!
AND THANK YOU, TOO!
PAP!
THANKS FOR SUCH A FUN DAY, REGGIE!
IF YOU'RE EVER NEAR THE WOODS, COME SAY HI, OKAY?
THERE ARE LOTS OF FUN THINGS TO SEE AND DO!

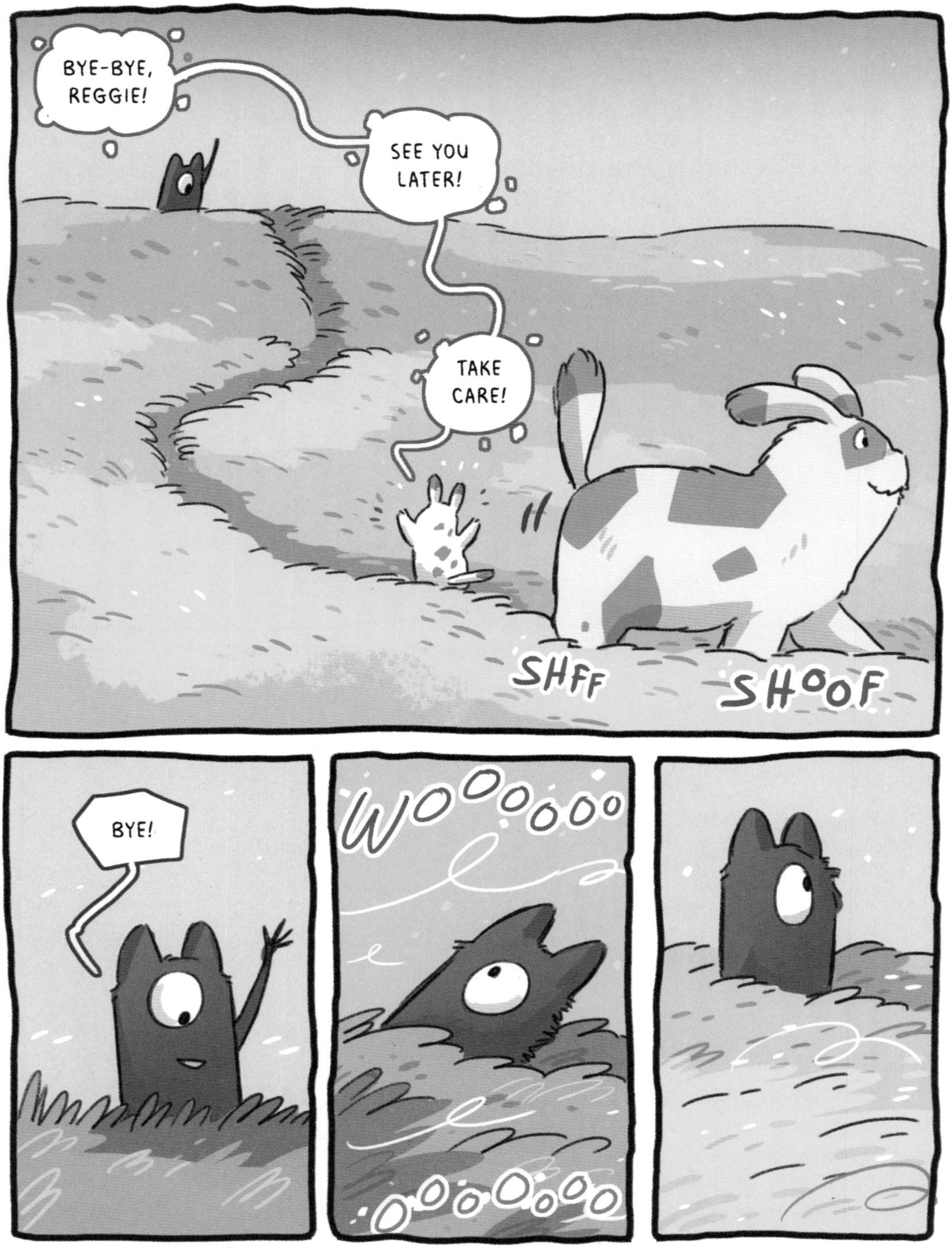
BYE-BYE, REGGIE!
SEE YOU LATER!
TAKE CARE!
SHFF
SHOOF
BYE!
WOOOOOOO
OOOOOOOO

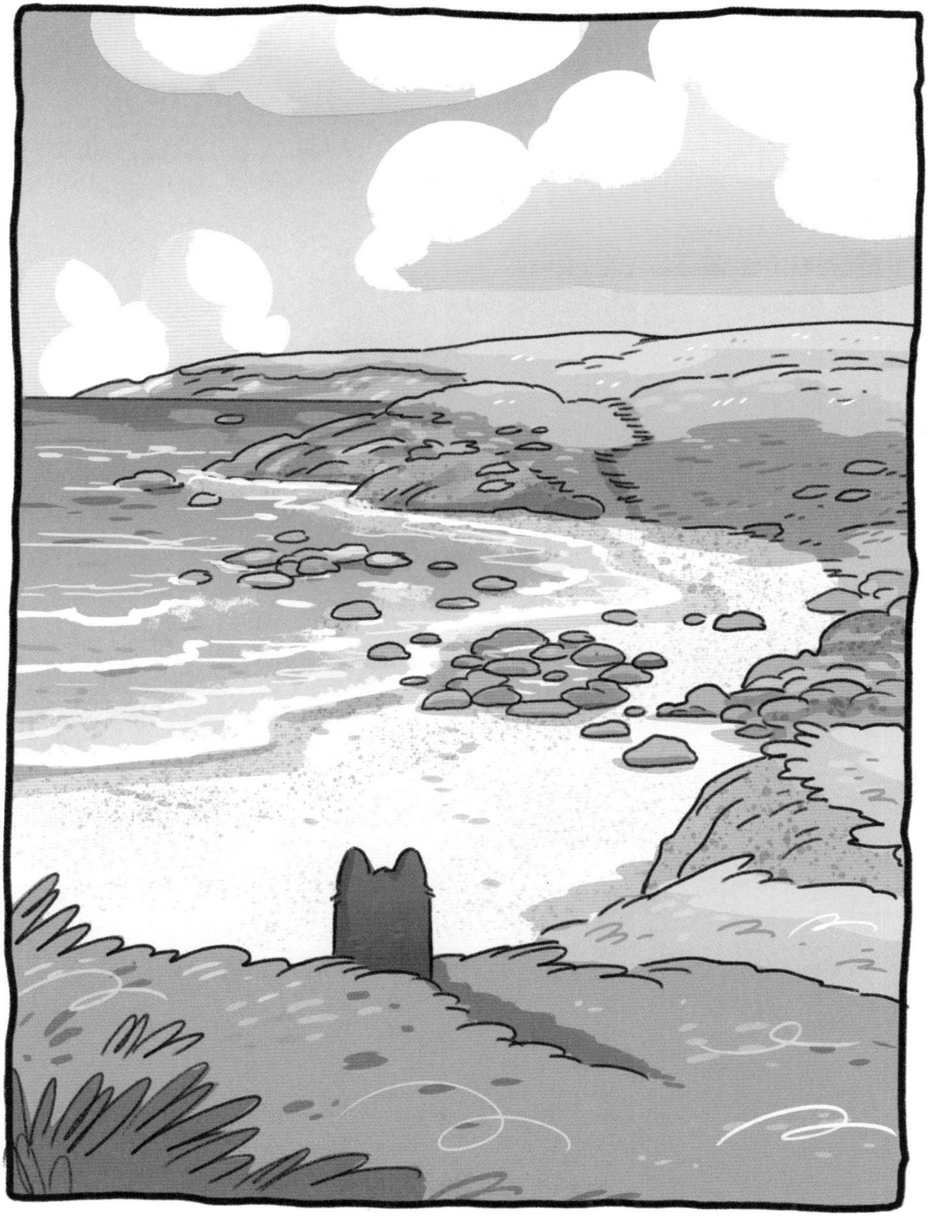

Chapter 3

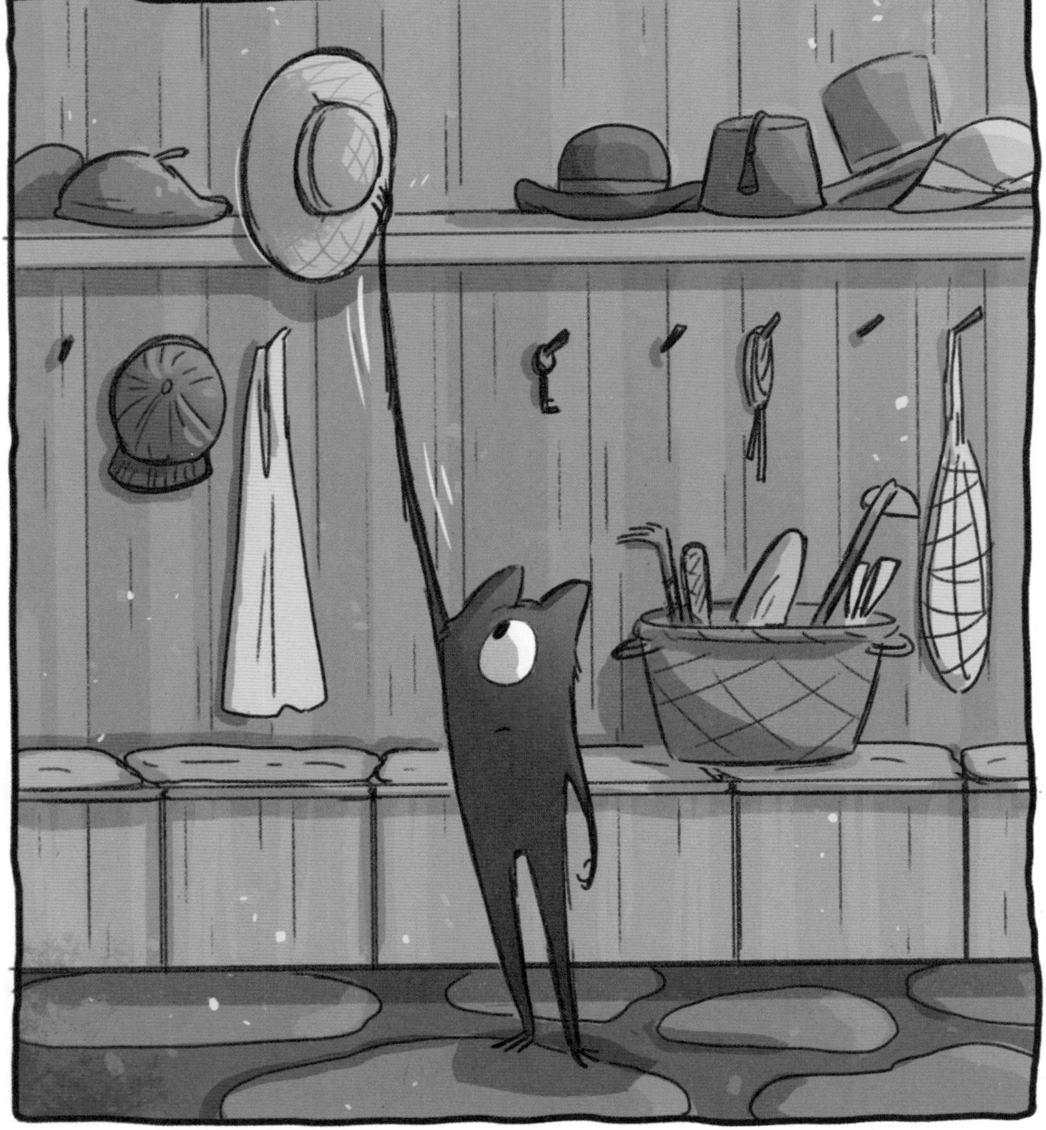

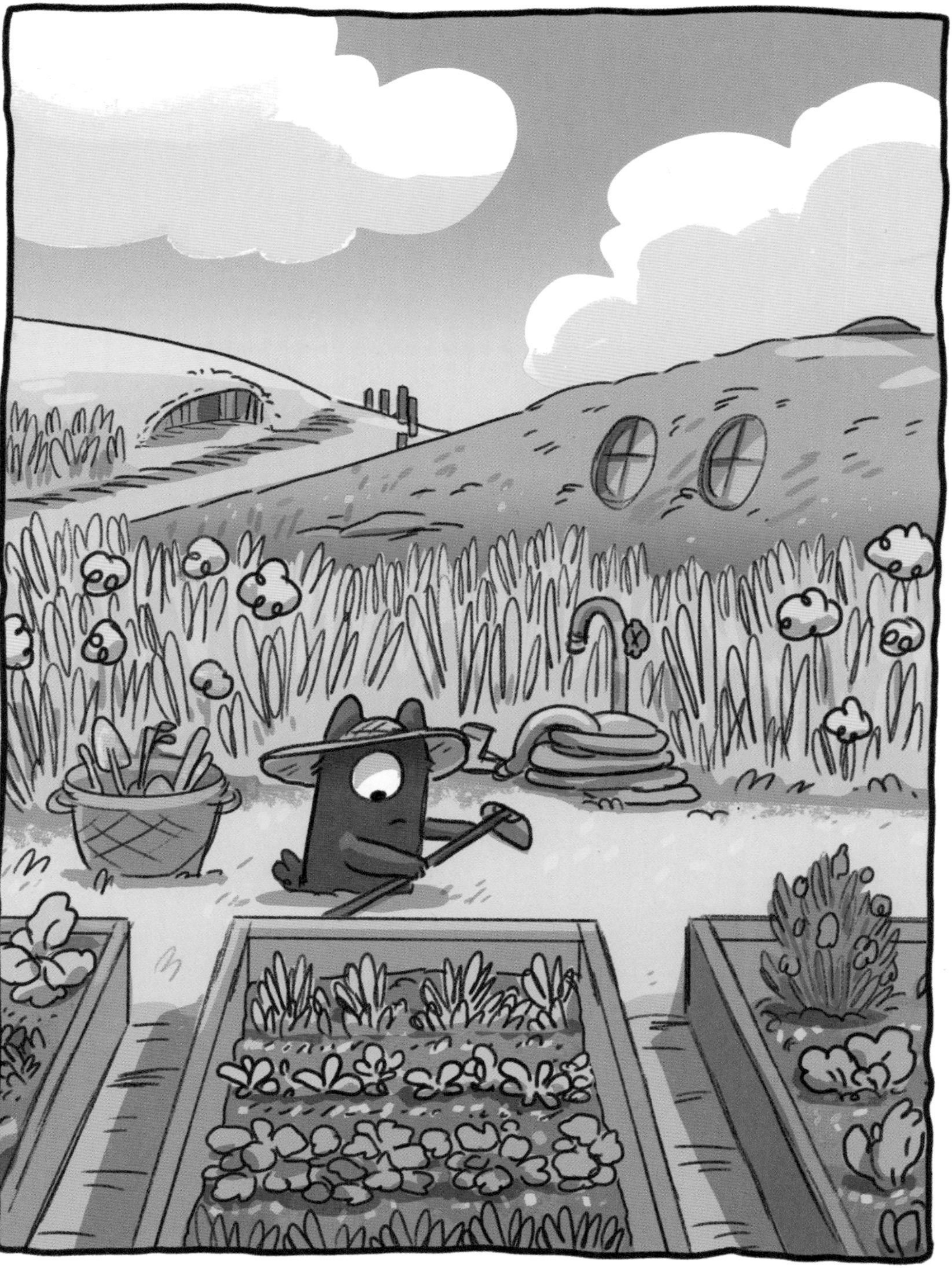

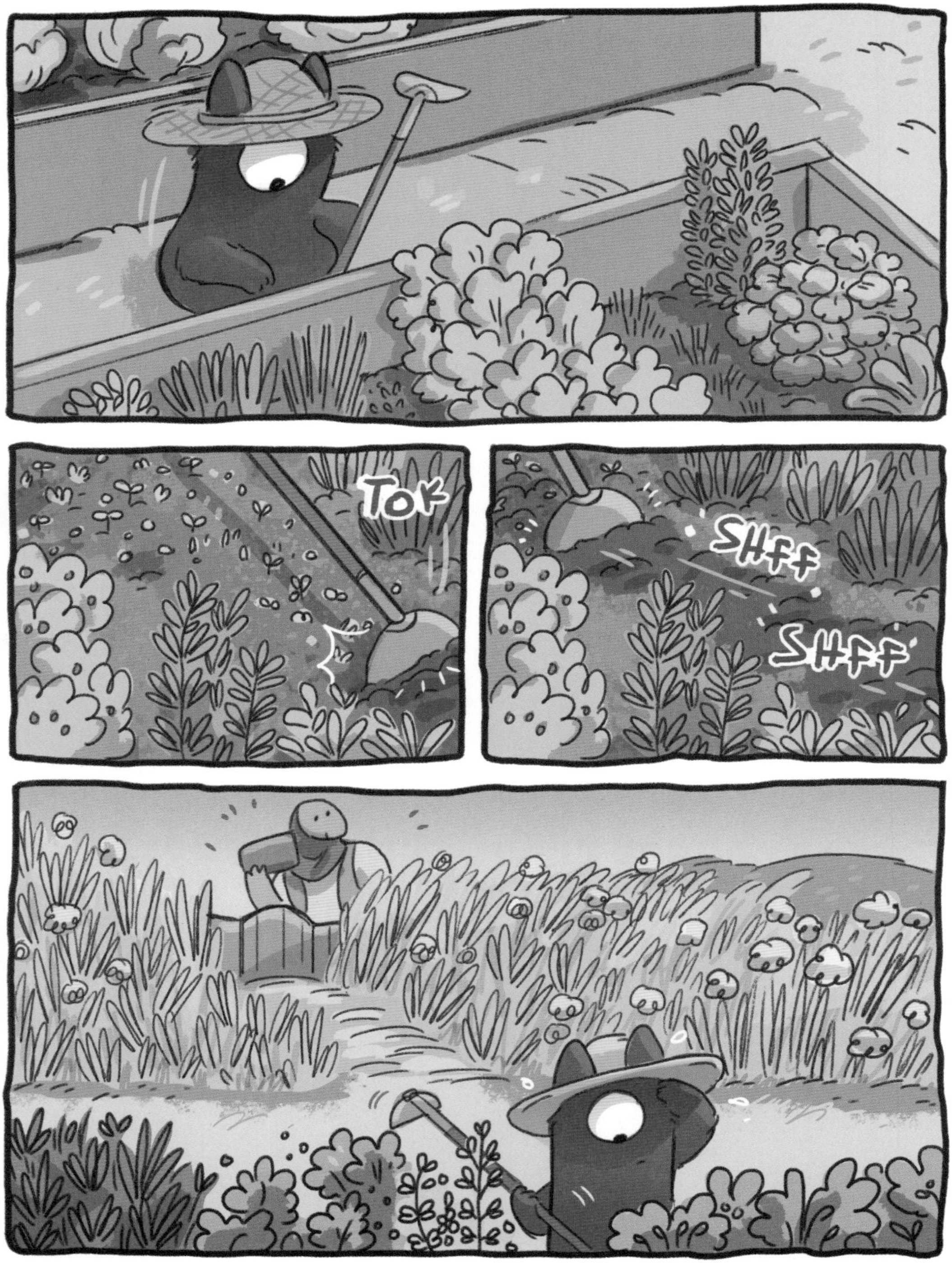
TOK
SHFF
SHFF

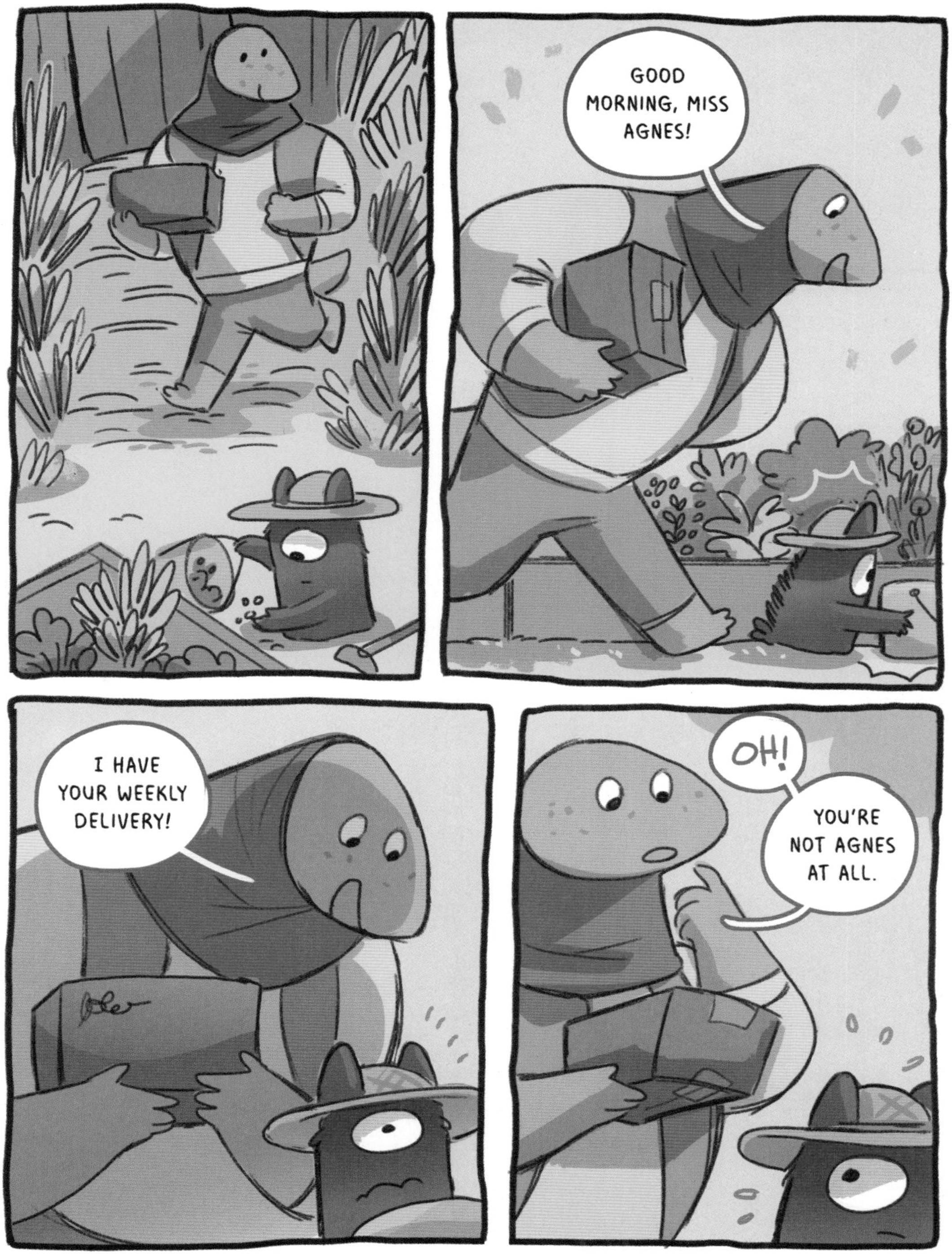
GOOD MORNING, MISS AGNES!
I HAVE YOUR WEEKLY DELIVERY!
OH!
YOU'RE NOT AGNES AT ALL.

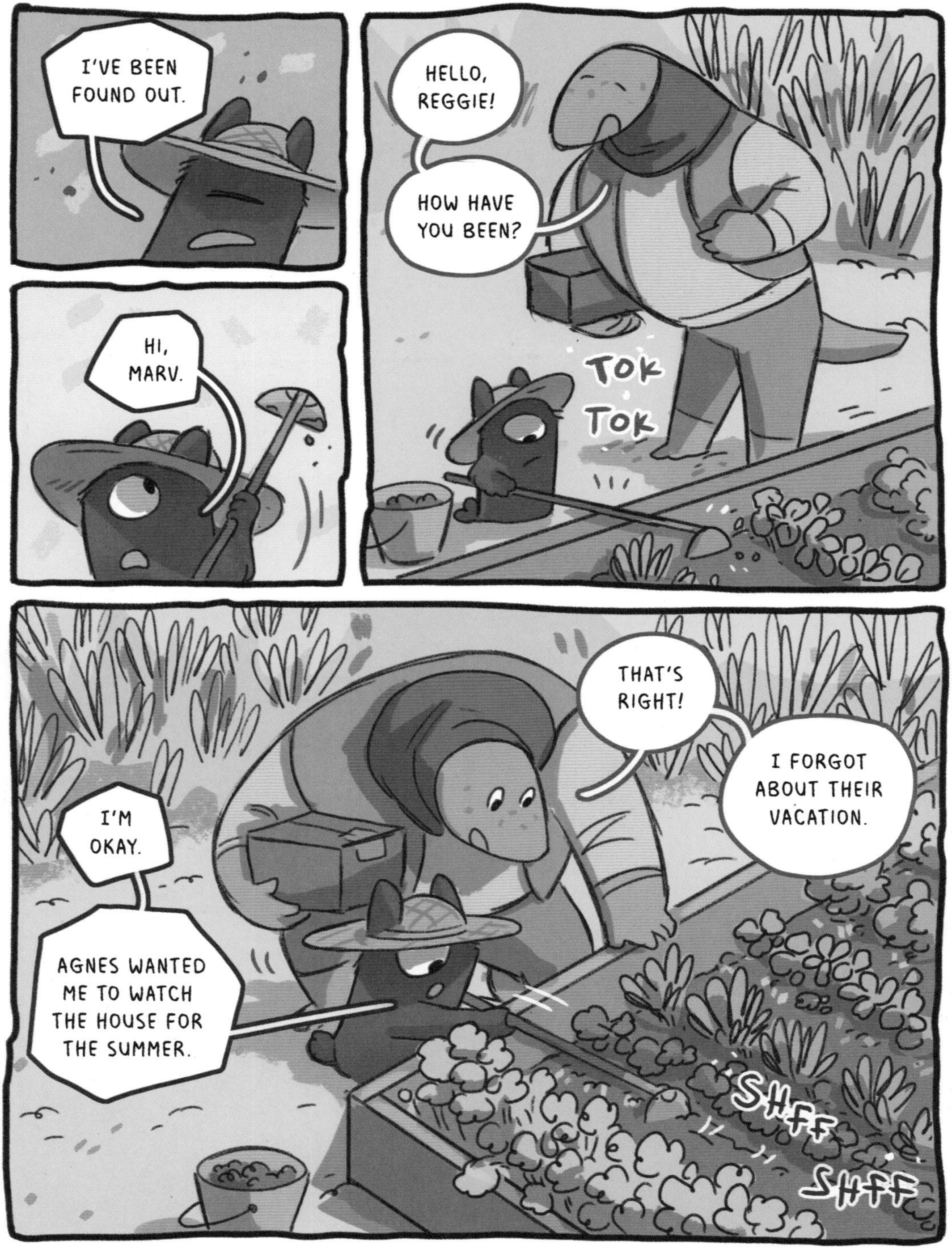
I'VE BEEN FOUND OUT.
HI, MARV.
HELLO, REGGIE!
HOW HAVE YOU BEEN?
TOK TOK
I'M OKAY.
AGNES WANTED ME TO WATCH THE HOUSE FOR THE SUMMER.
THAT'S RIGHT!
I FORGOT ABOUT THEIR VACATION.
SHFF SHFF

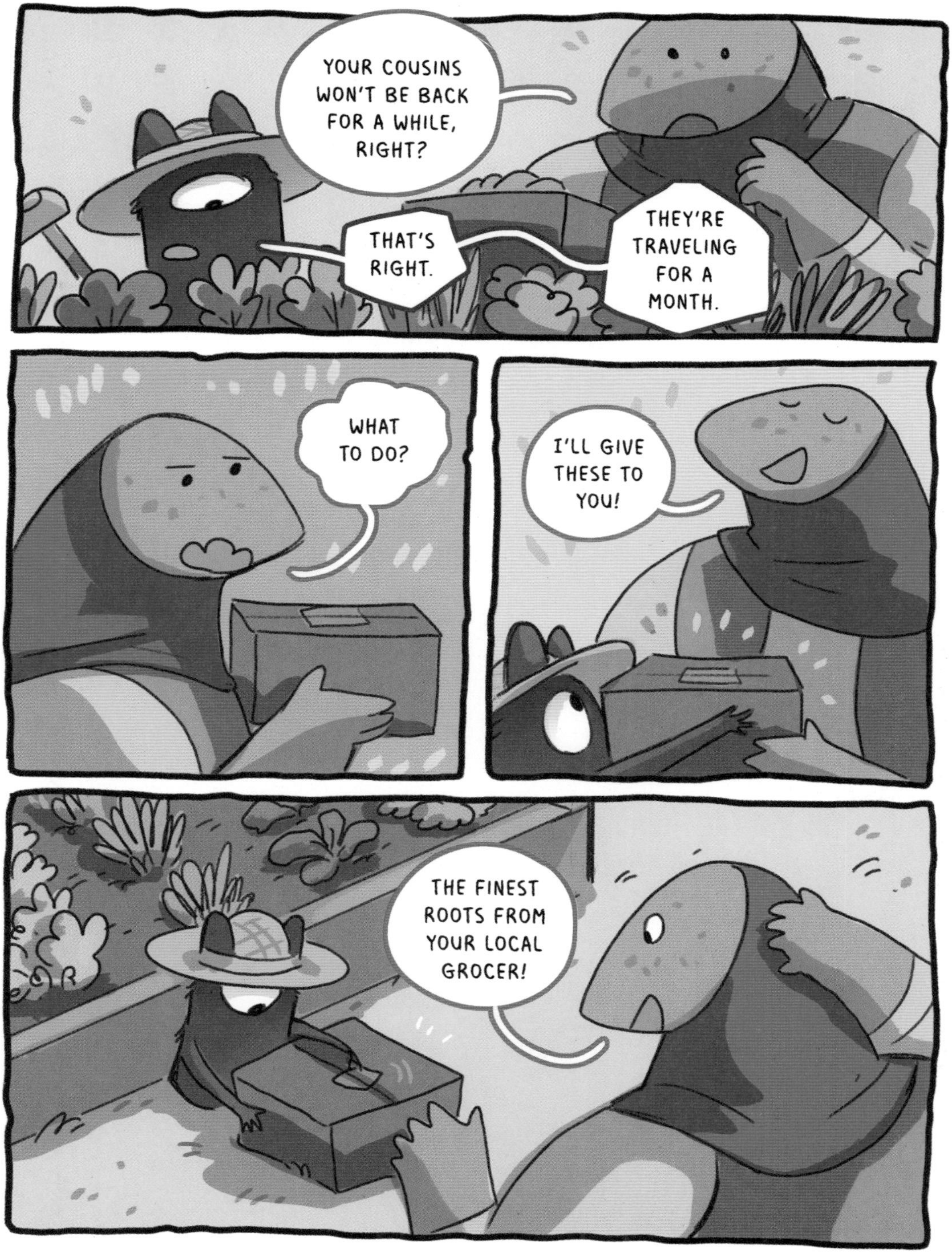
YOUR COUSINS WON'T BE BACK FOR A WHILE, RIGHT?
THAT'S RIGHT.
THEY'RE TRAVELING FOR A MONTH.
WHAT TO DO?
I'LL GIVE THESE TO YOU!
THE FINEST ROOTS FROM YOUR LOCAL GROCER!

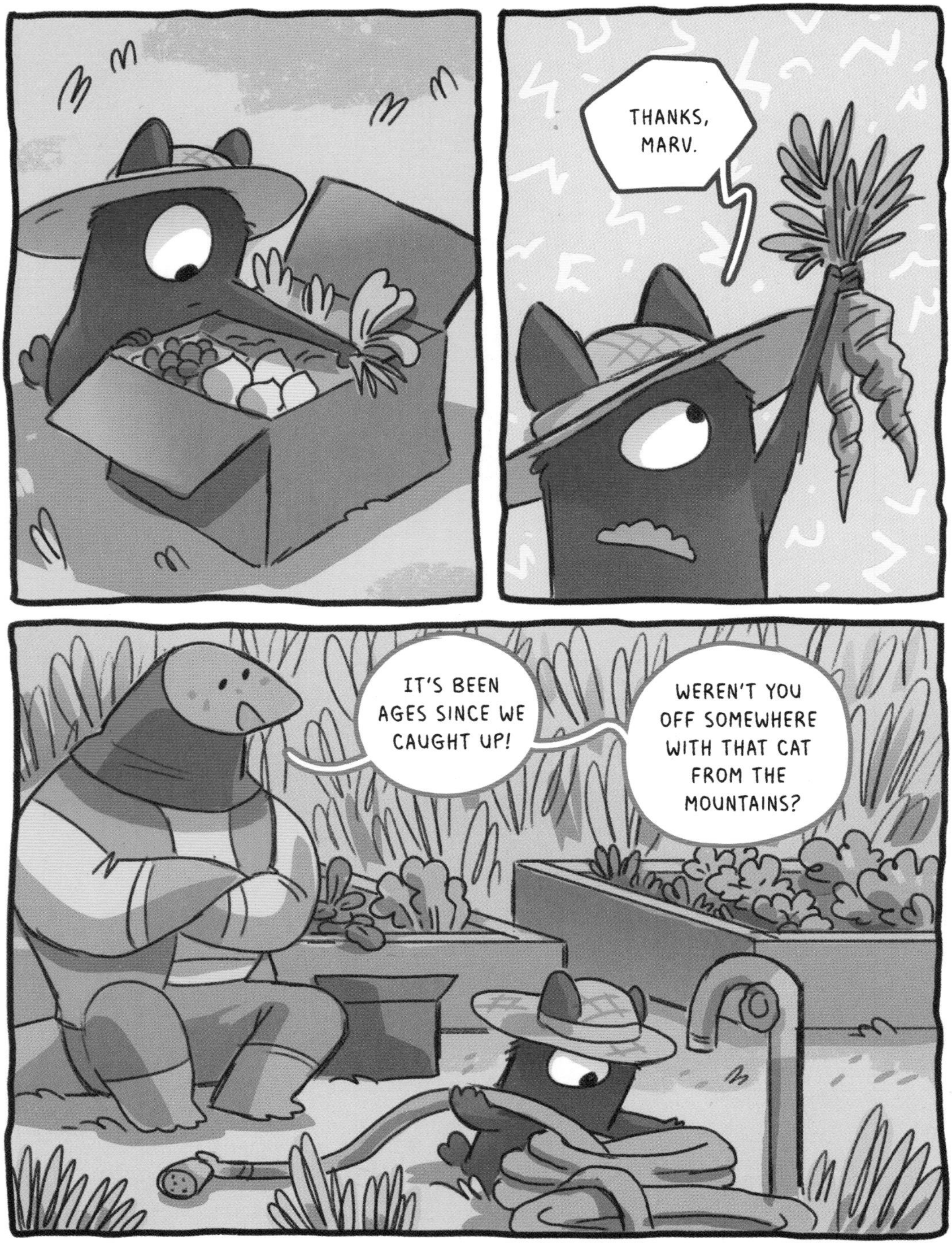
THANKS, MARV.
IT'S BEEN AGES SINCE WE CAUGHT UP!
WEREN'T YOU OFF SOMEWHERE WITH THAT CAT FROM THE MOUNTAINS?

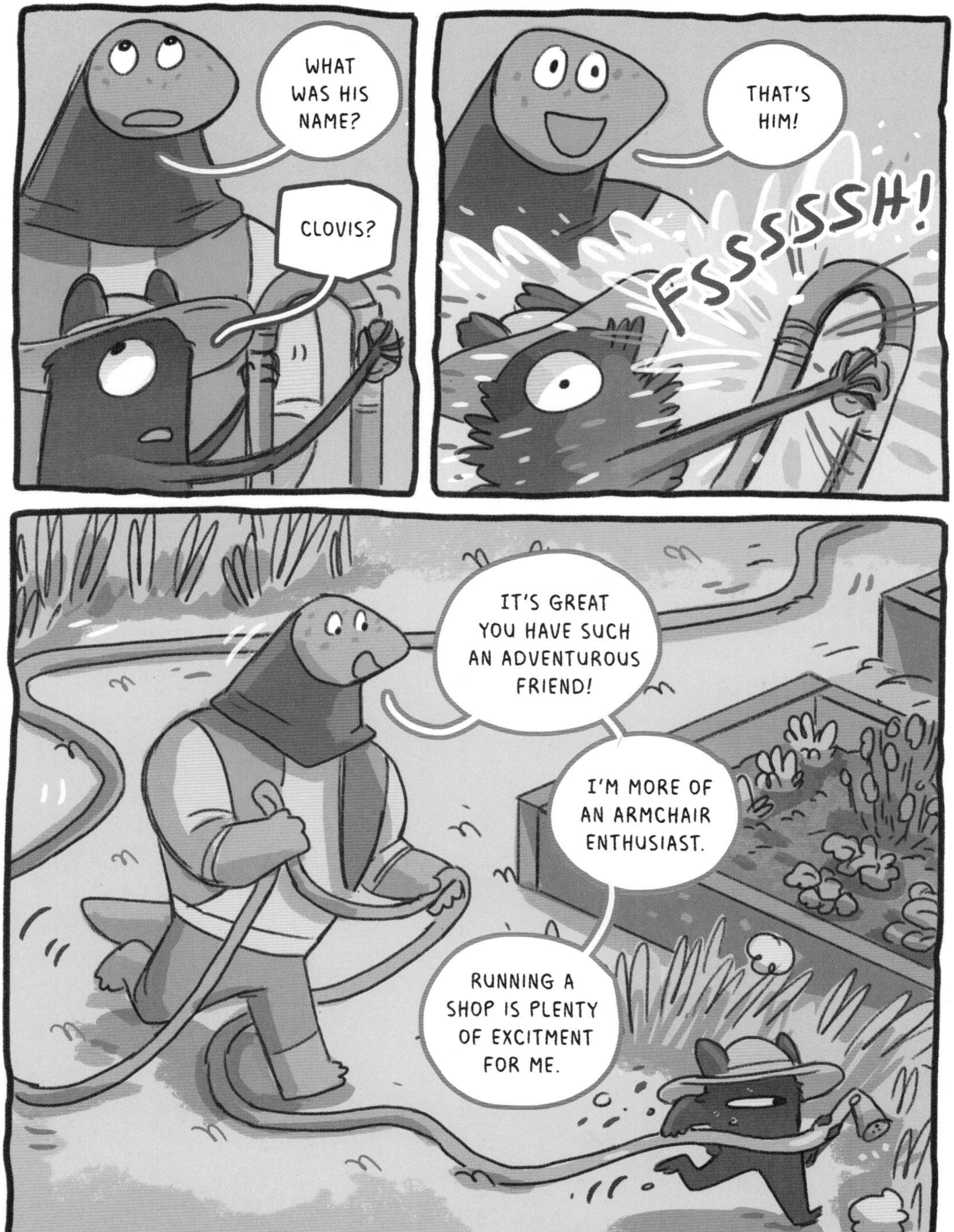
WHAT WAS HIS NAME?
CLOVIS?
THAT'S HIM!
FSSSSSH!
IT'S GREAT YOU HAVE SUCH AN ADVENTUROUS FRIEND!
I'M MORE OF AN ARMCHAIR ENTHUSIAST.
RUNNING A SHOP IS PLENTY OF EXCITMENT FOR ME.

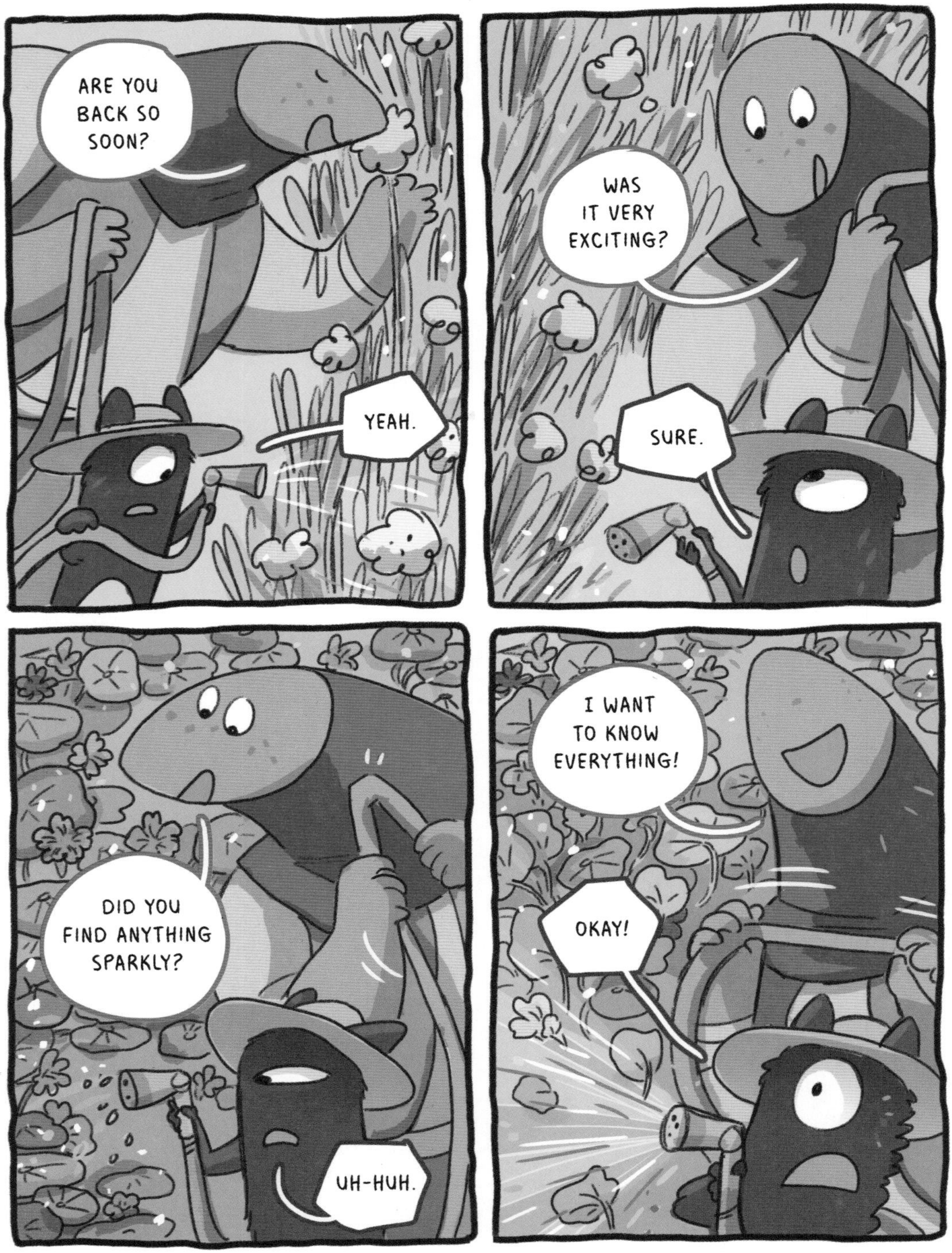
ARE YOU BACK SO SOON?
YEAH.
WAS IT VERY EXCITING?
SURE.
DID YOU FIND ANYTHING SPARKLY?
UH-HUH.
I WANT TO KNOW EVERYTHING!
OKAY!

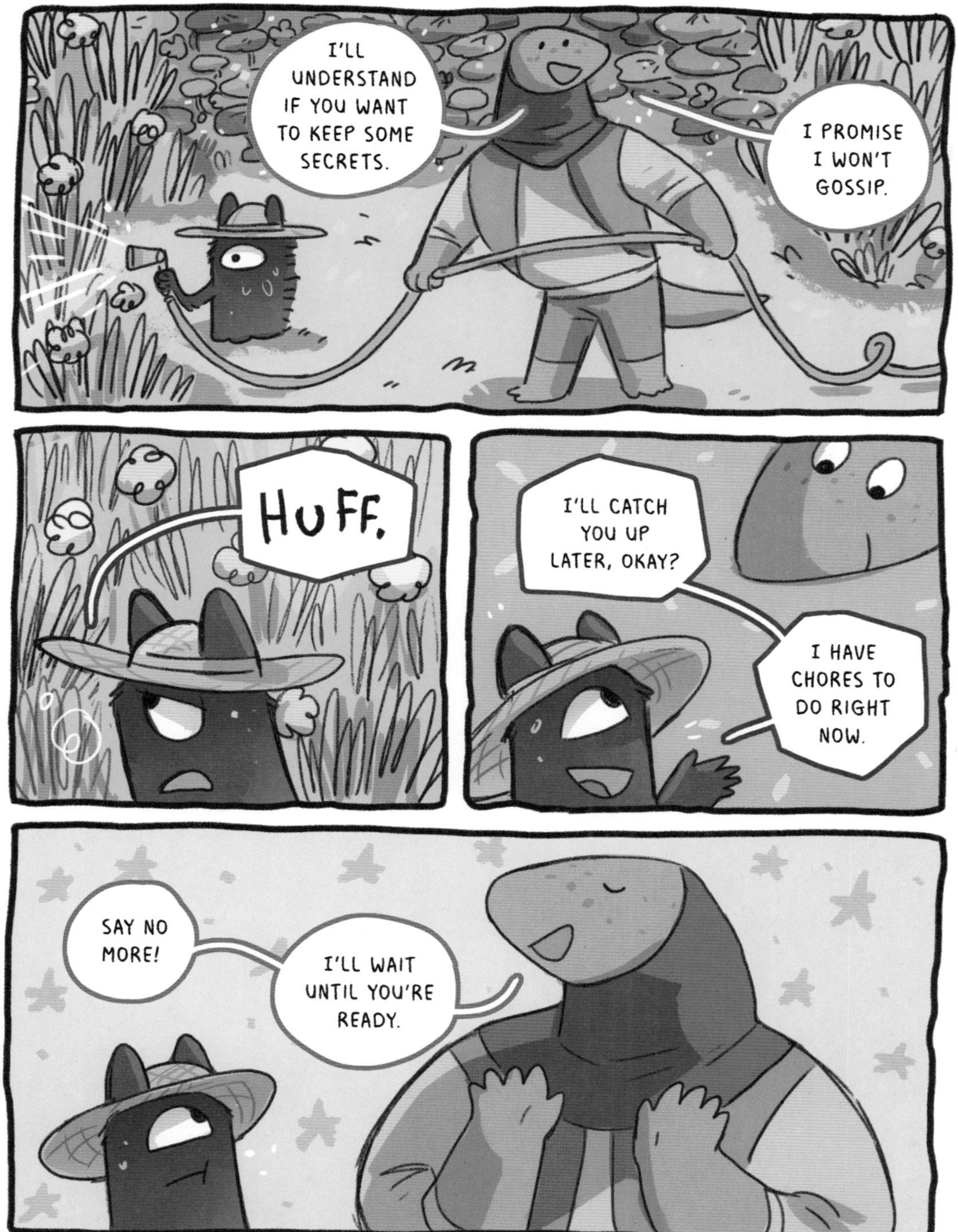
I'LL UNDERSTAND IF YOU WANT TO KEEP SOME SECRETS.
I PROMISE I WON'T GOSSIP.
HUFF.
I'LL CATCH YOU UP LATER, OKAY?
I HAVE CHORES TO DO RIGHT NOW.
SAY NO MORE!
I'LL WAIT UNTIL YOU'RE READY.

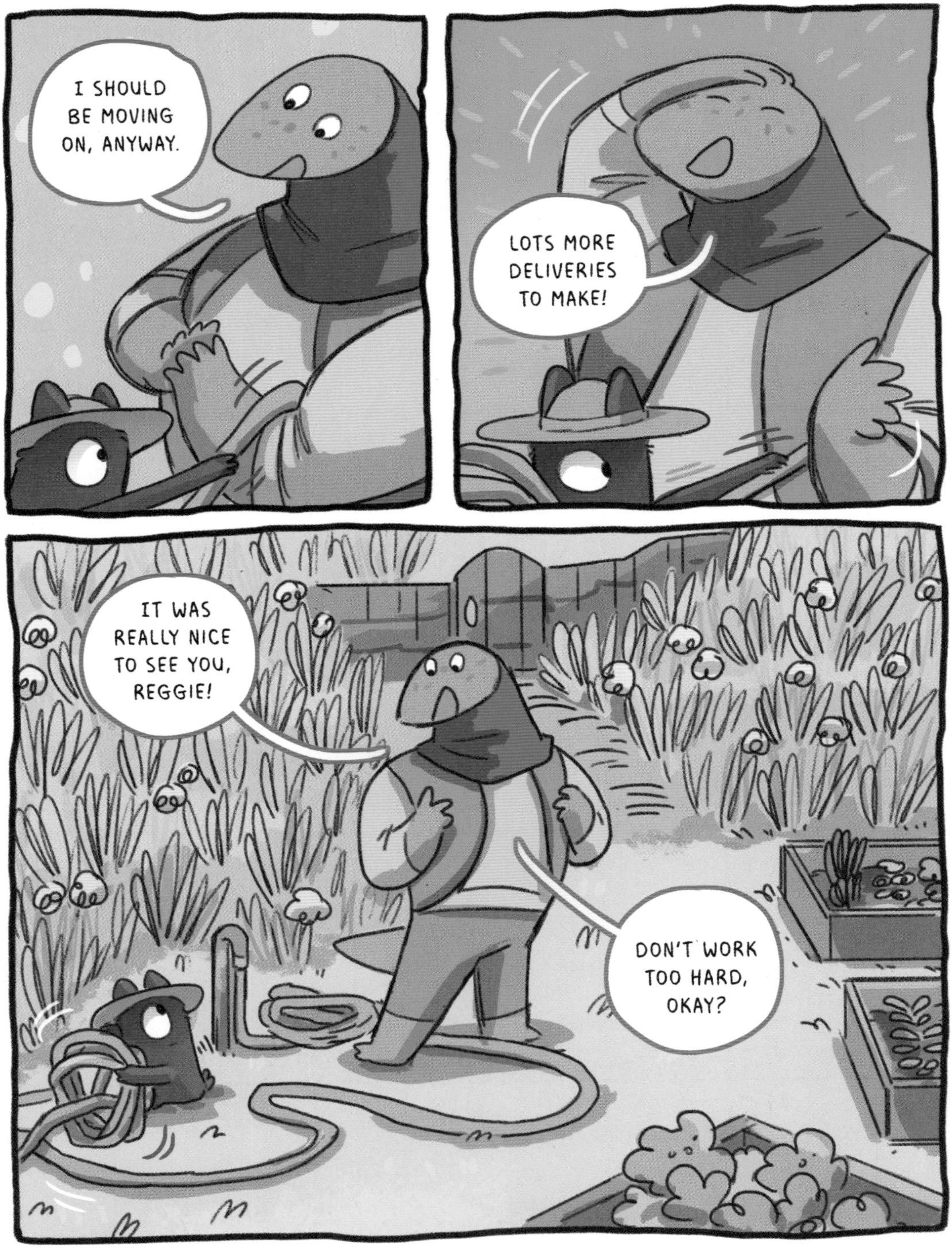
I SHOULD BE MOVING ON, ANYWAY.
LOTS MORE DELIVERIES TO MAKE!
IT WAS REALLY NICE TO SEE YOU, REGGIE!
DON'T WORK TOO HARD, OKAY?

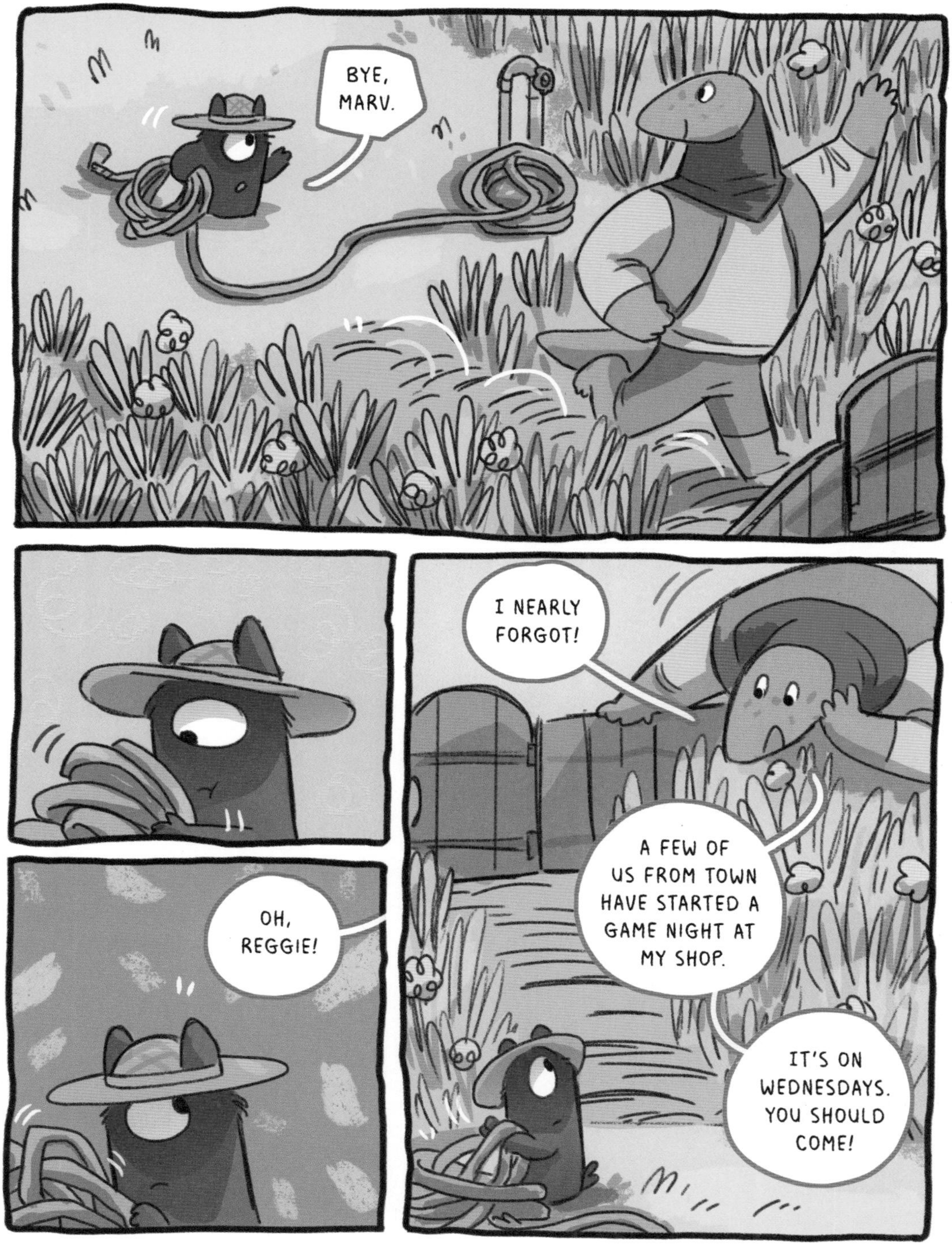

BYE, MARV.
OH, REGGIE!
I NEARLY FORGOT!
A FEW OF US FROM TOWN HAVE STARTED A GAME NIGHT AT MY SHOP.
IT'S ON WEDNESDAYS. YOU SHOULD COME!

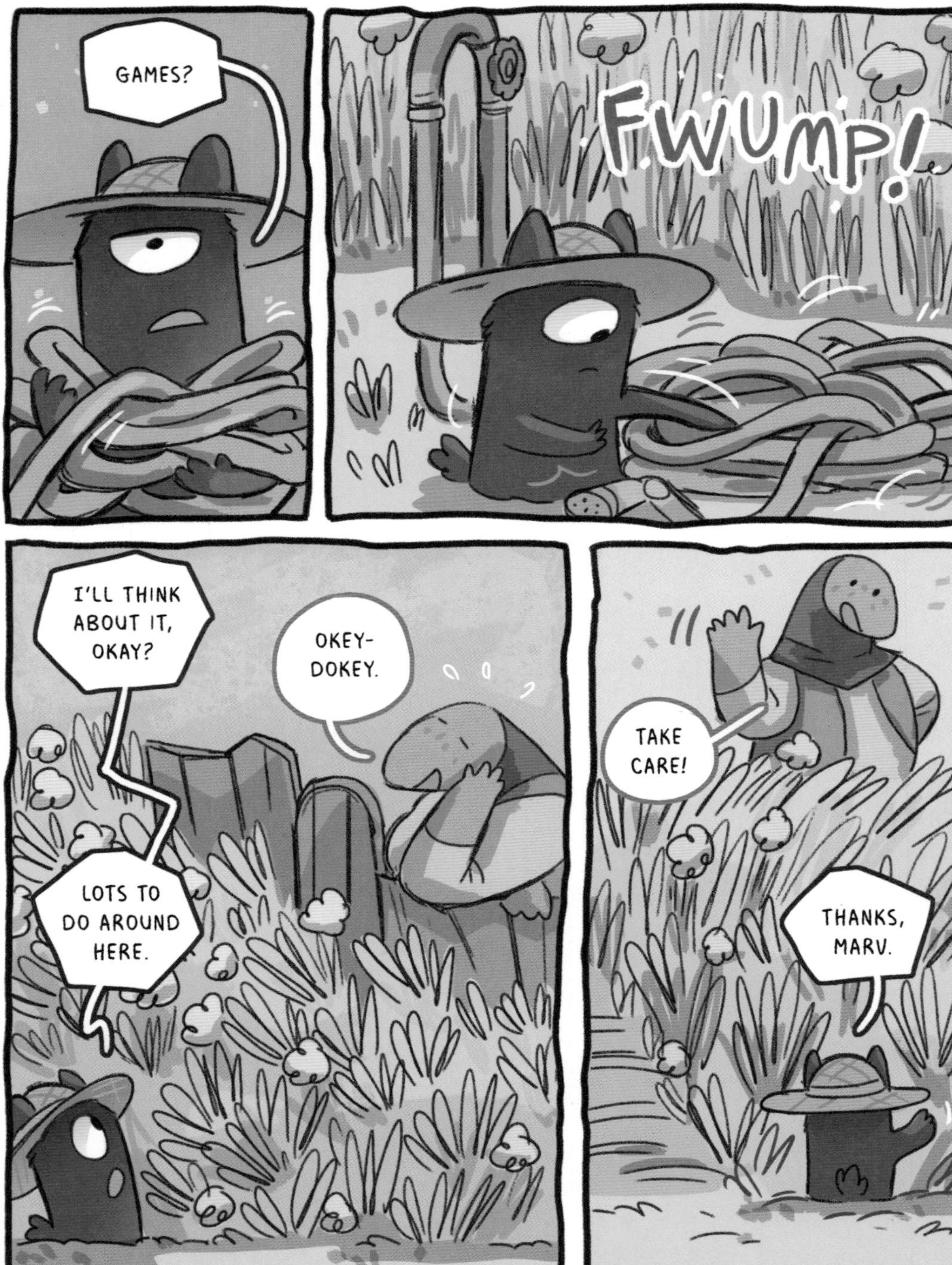
GAMES?
FWUMP!
I'LL THINK ABOUT IT, OKAY?
OKEY-DOKEY.
LOTS TO DO AROUND HERE.
TAKE CARE!
THANKS, MARV.

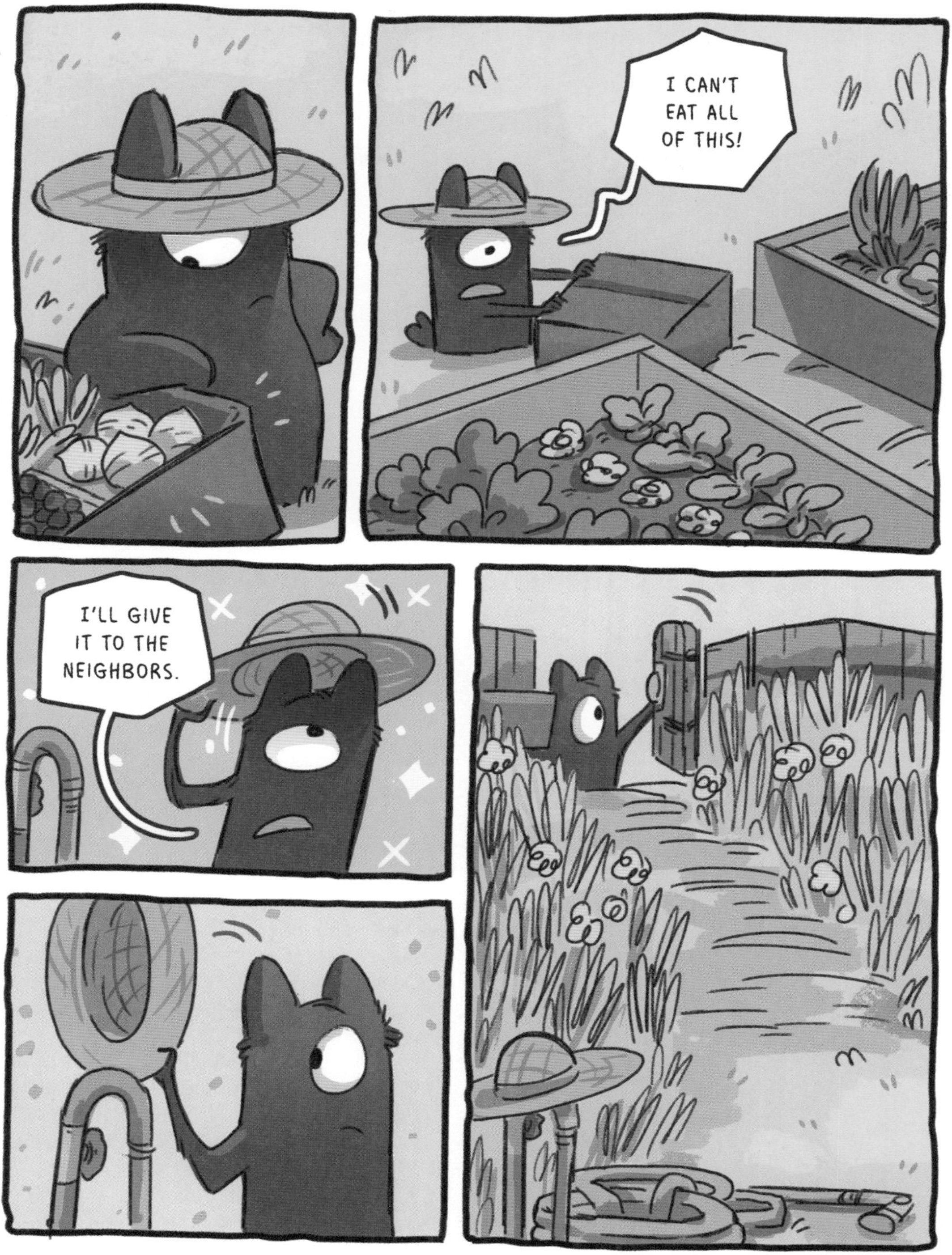
I CAN'T EAT ALL OF THIS!
I'LL GIVE IT TO THE NEIGHBORS.

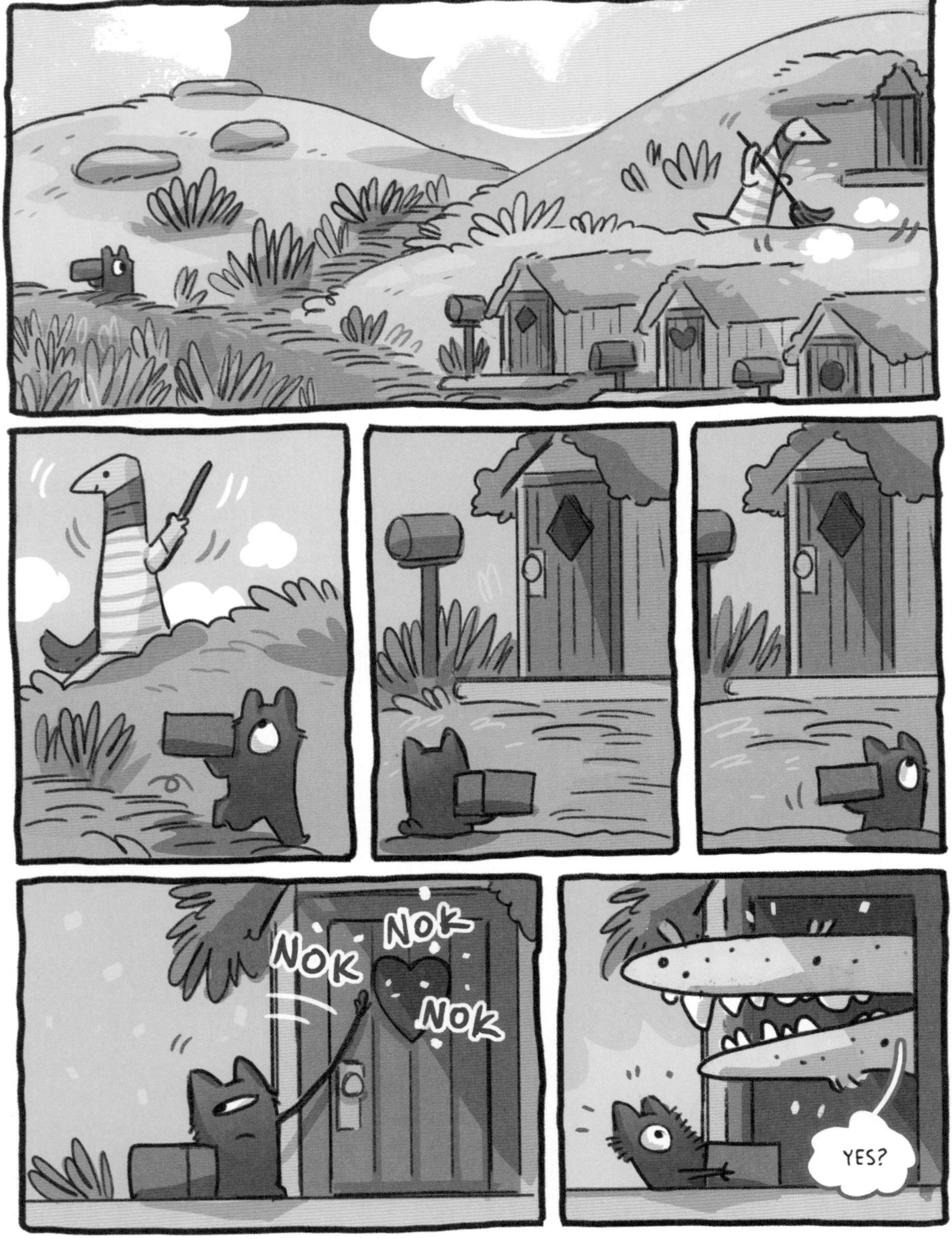
NOK
NOK
NOK
YES?

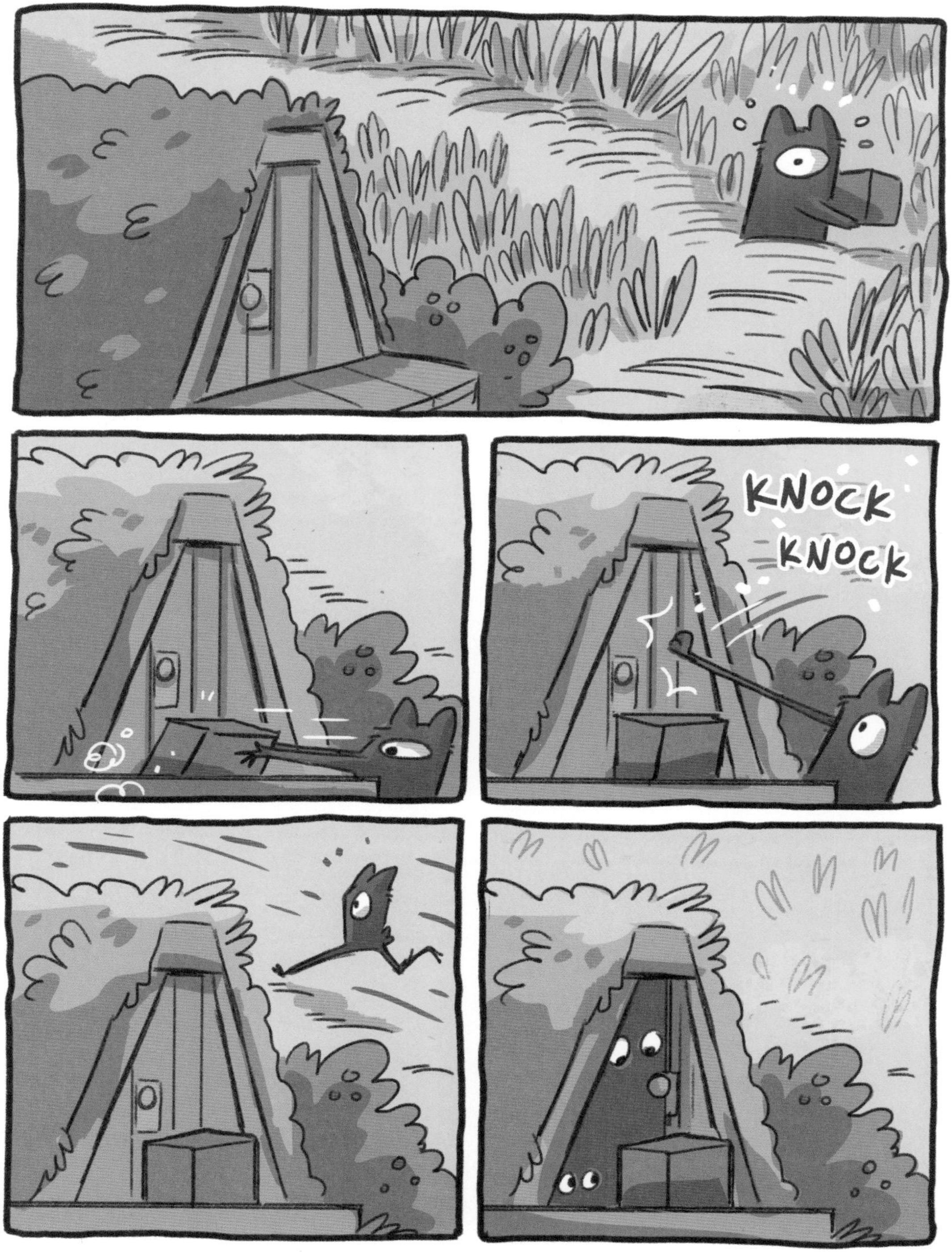
KNOCK
KNOCK

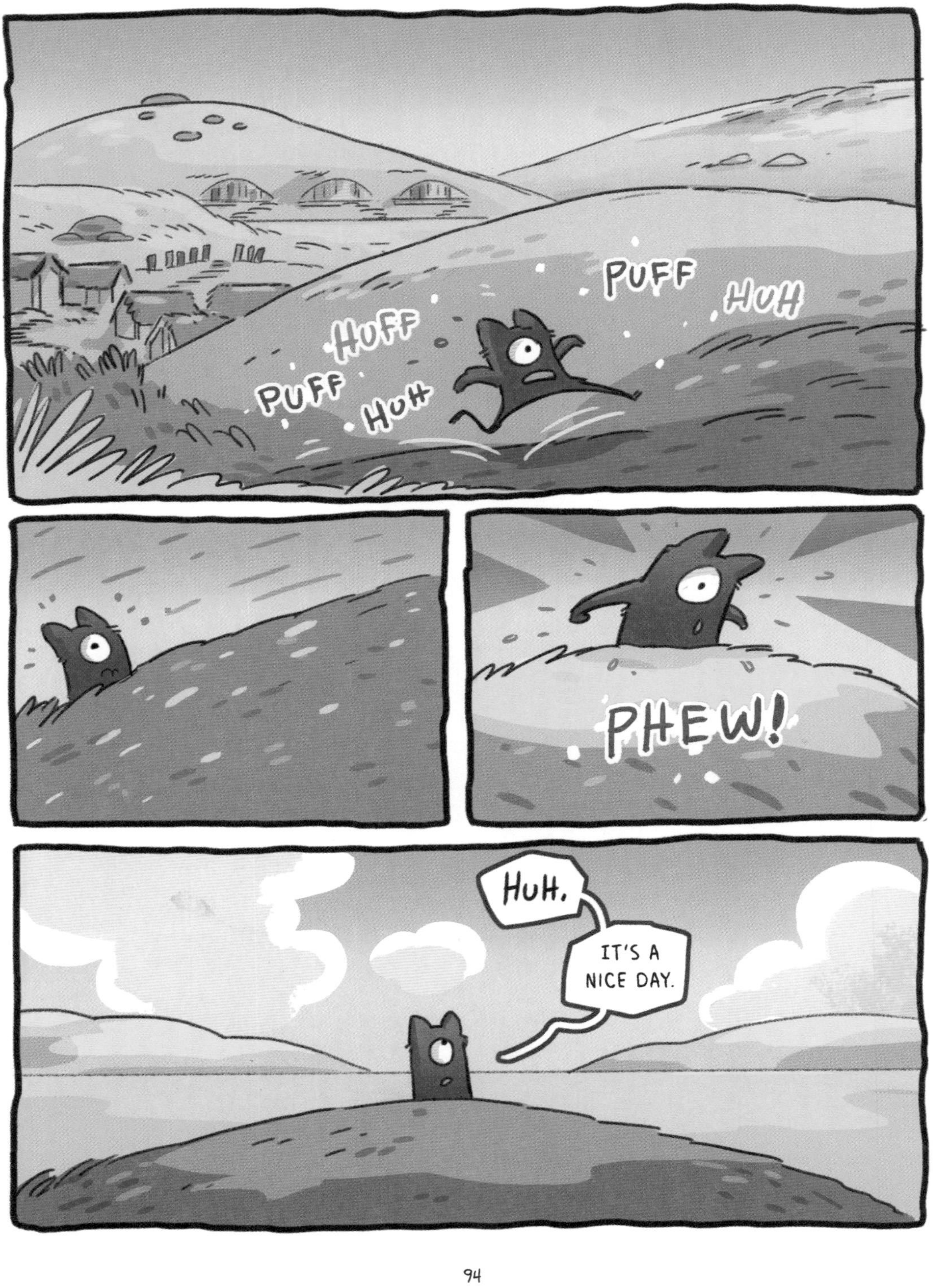
PUFF
HUFF
PUFF
HUH
HUH
PHEW!
HUH.
IT'S A NICE DAY.

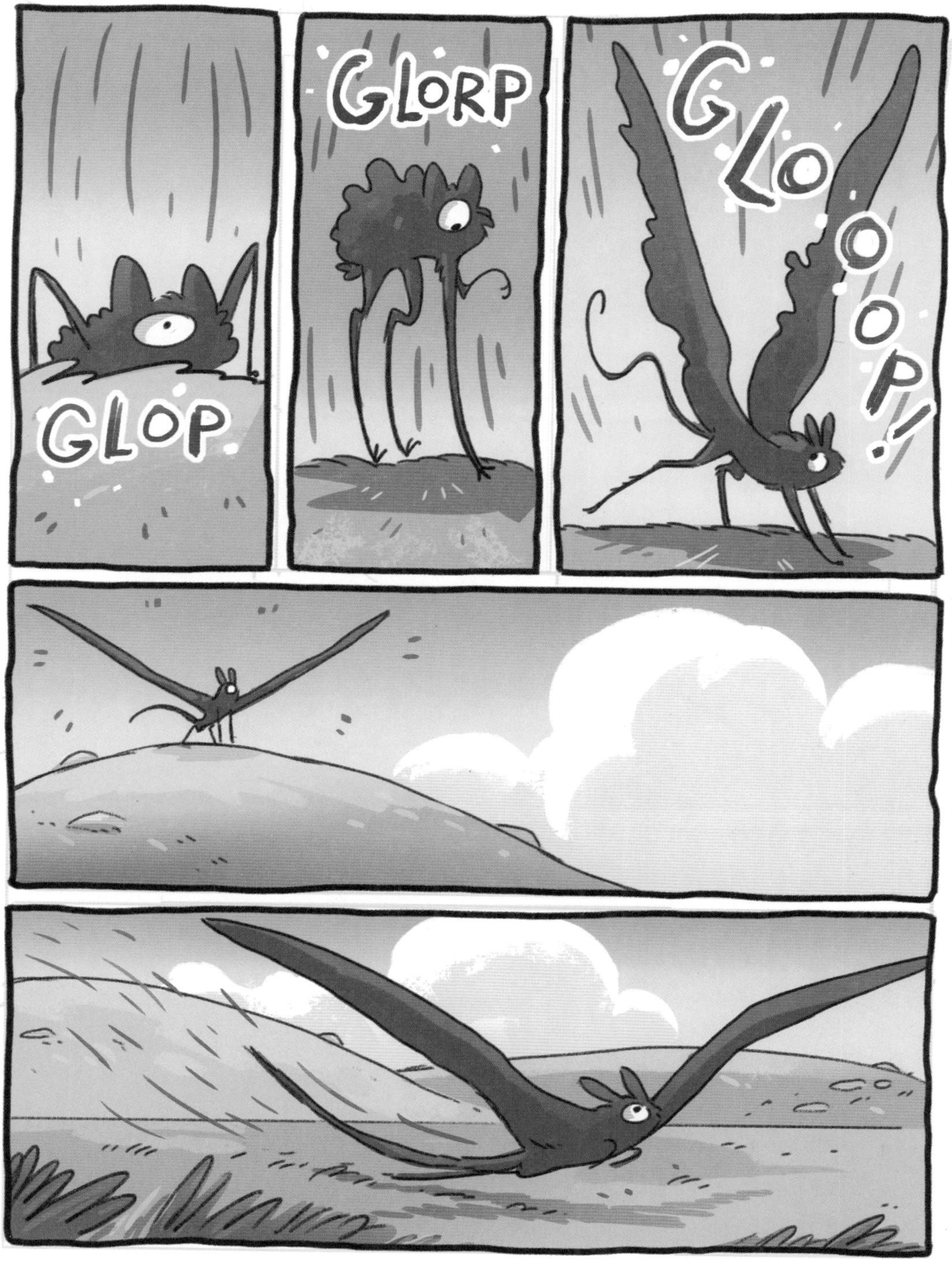
GLOP
GLORP
GLOOOOP!

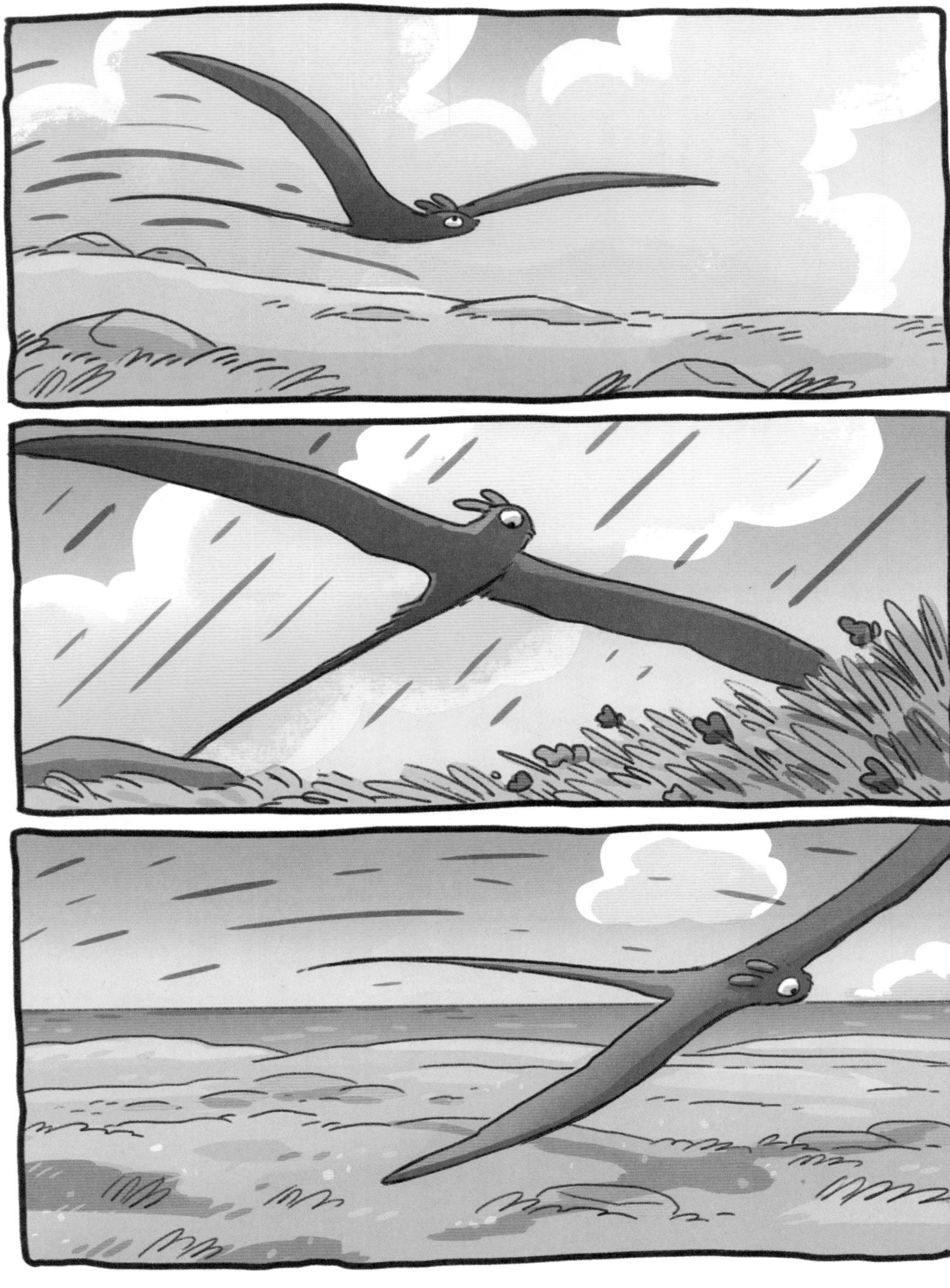

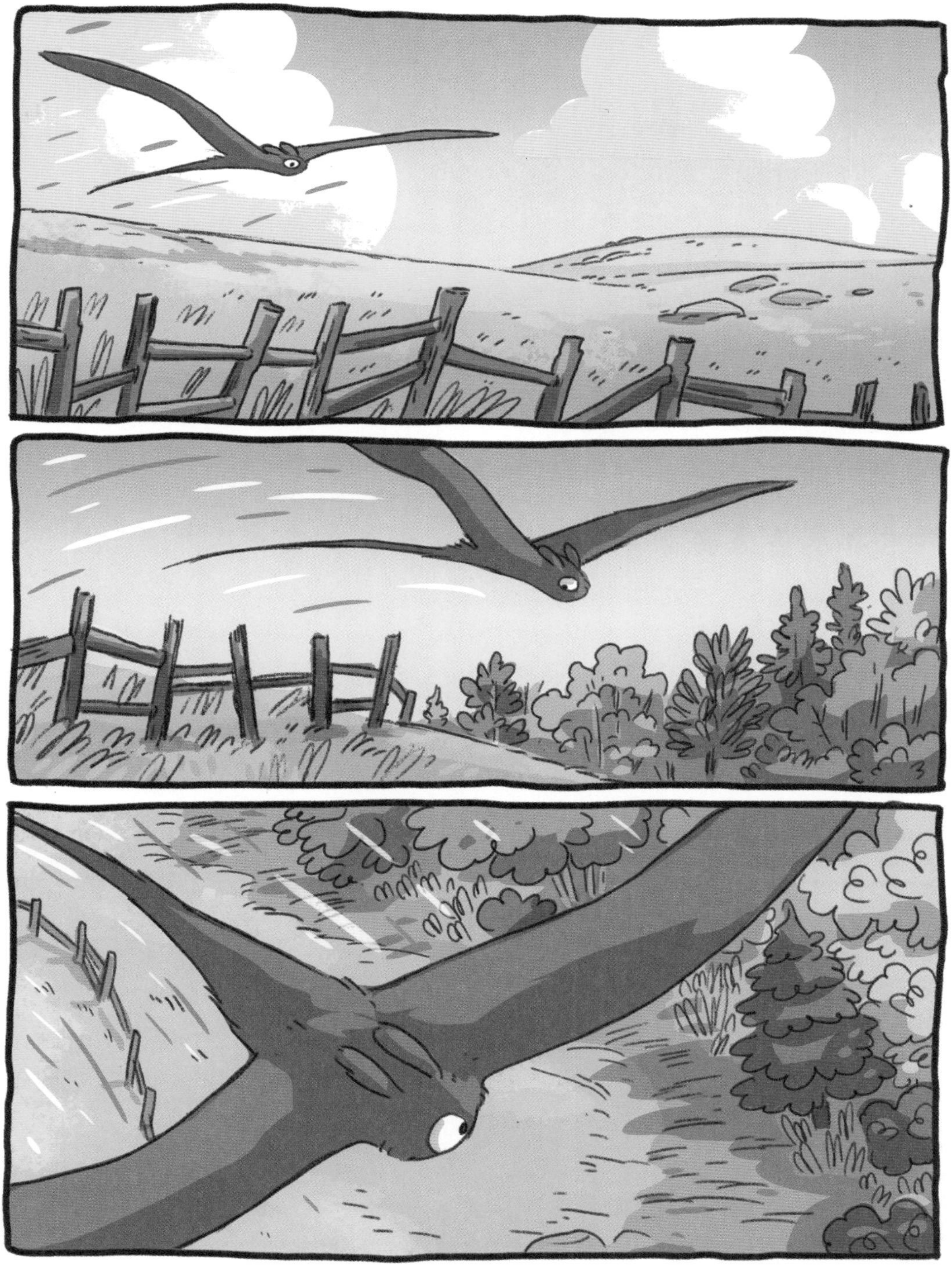

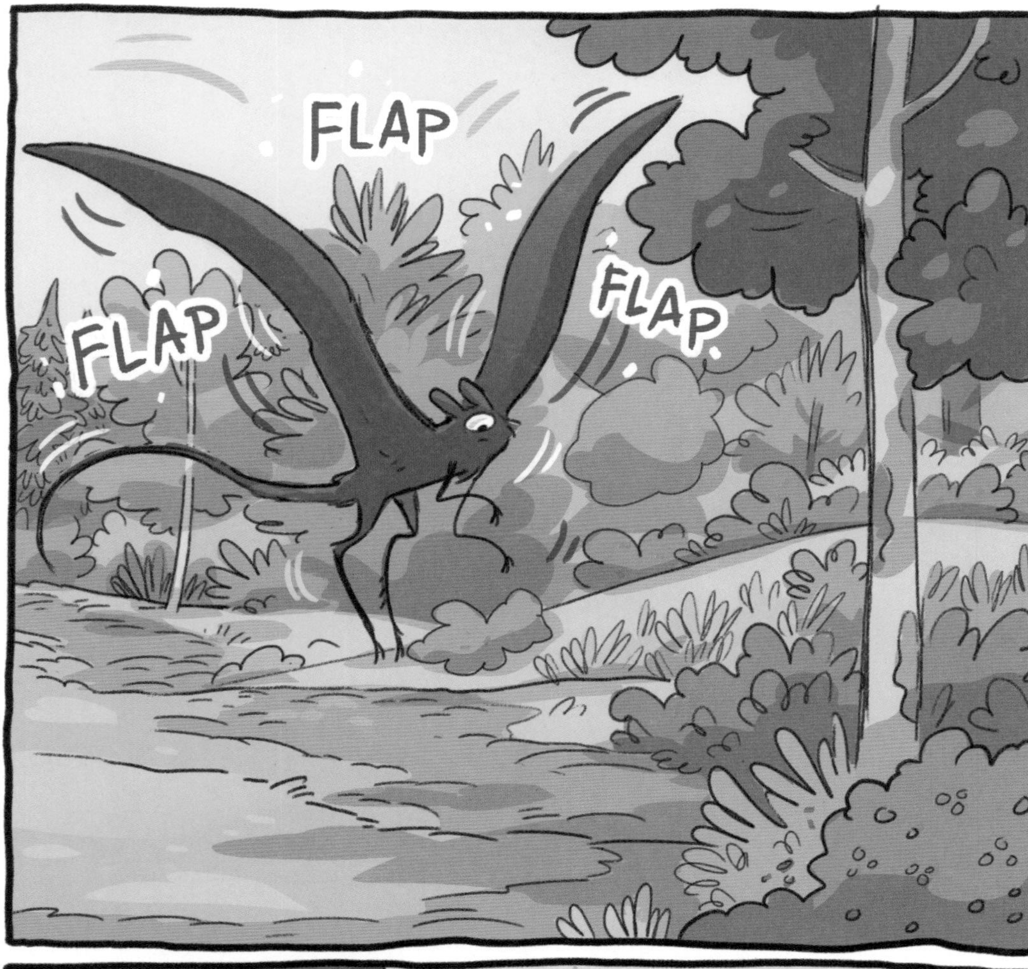
FLAP
FLAP
FLAP

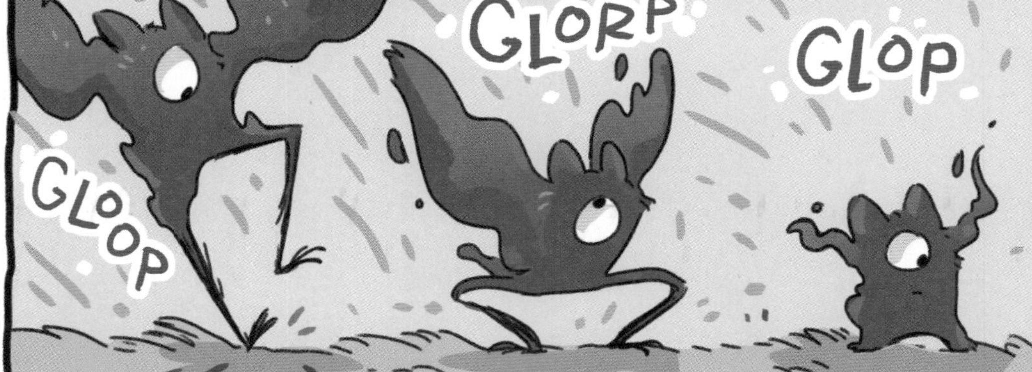
GLORP
GLOP
GLOOP

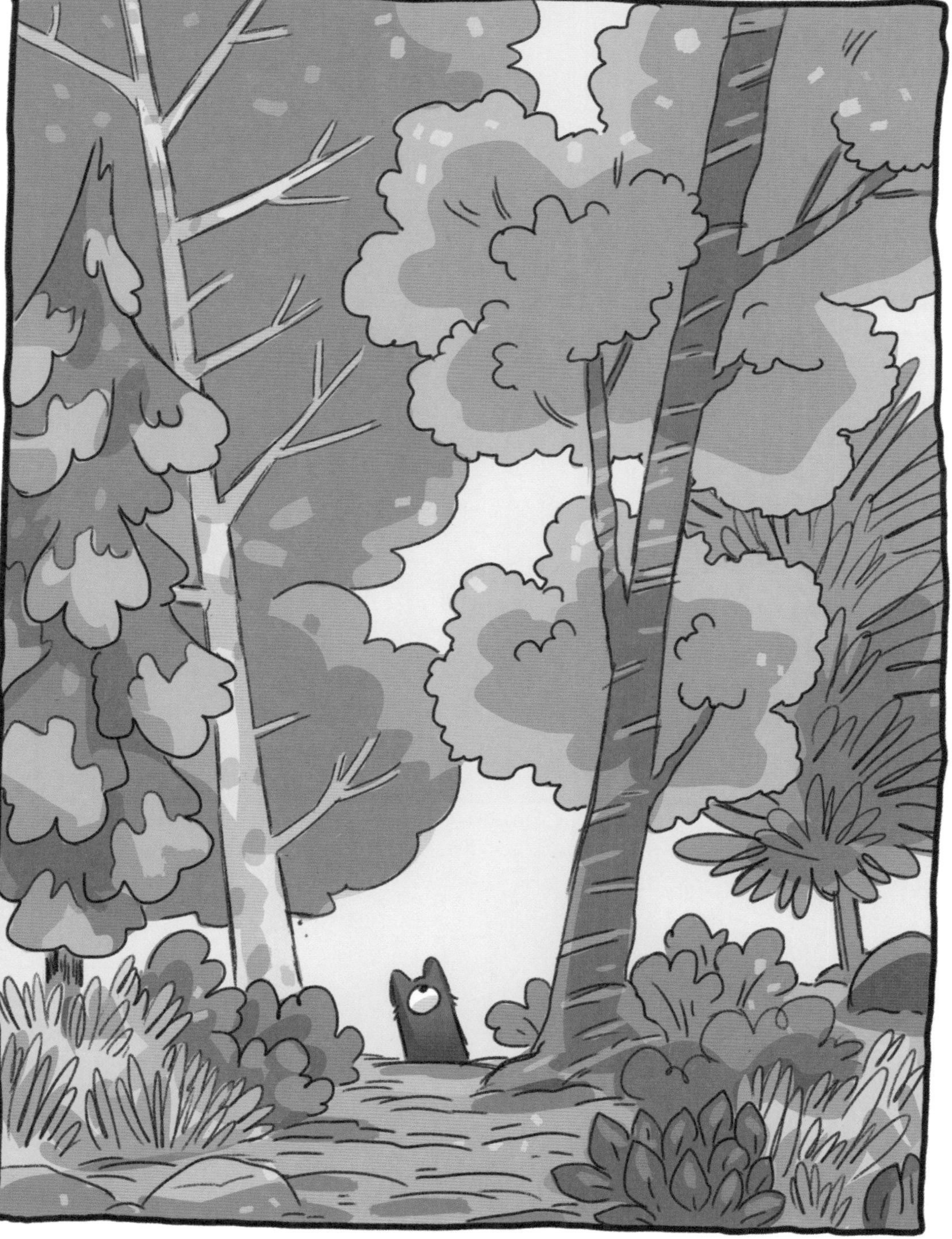

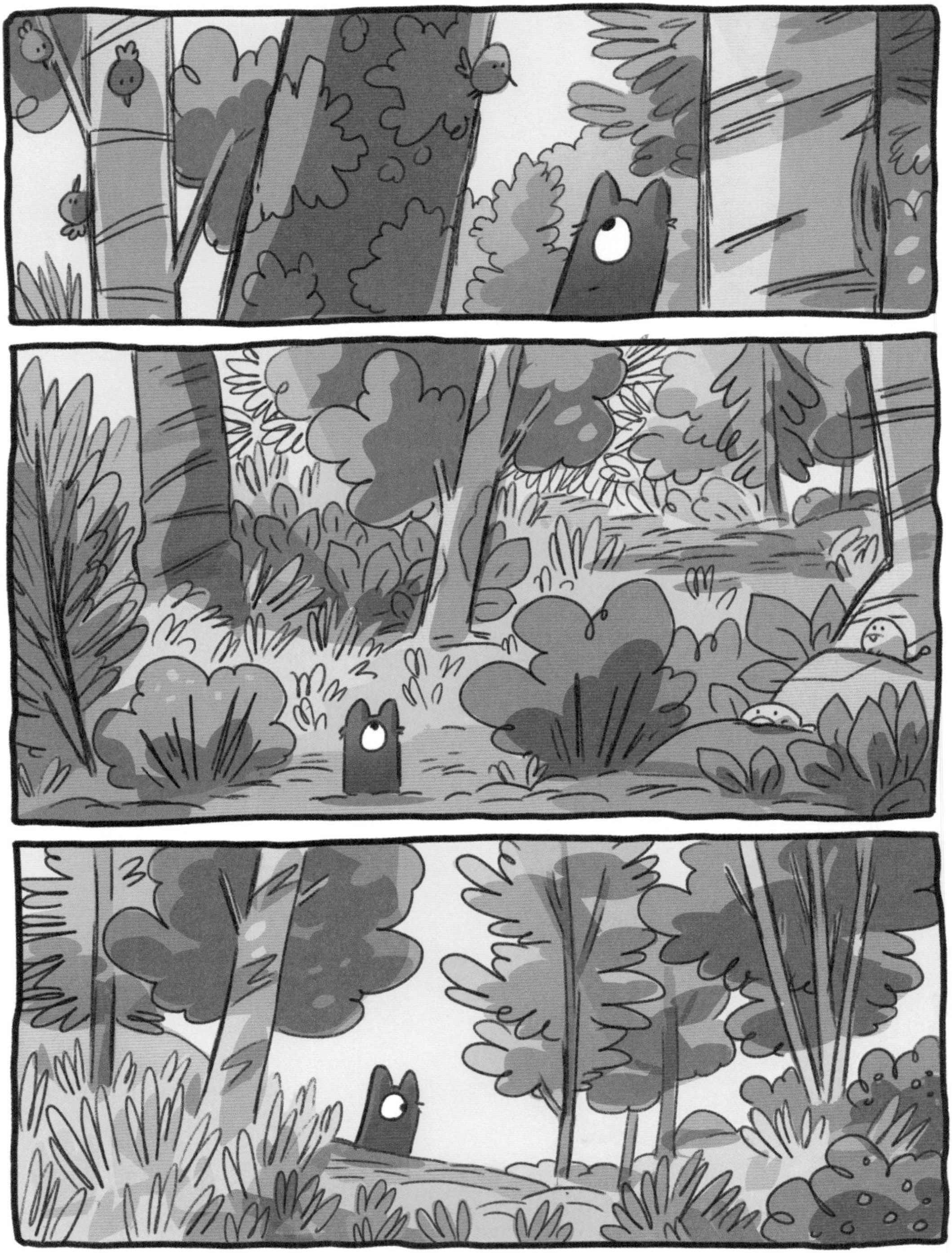

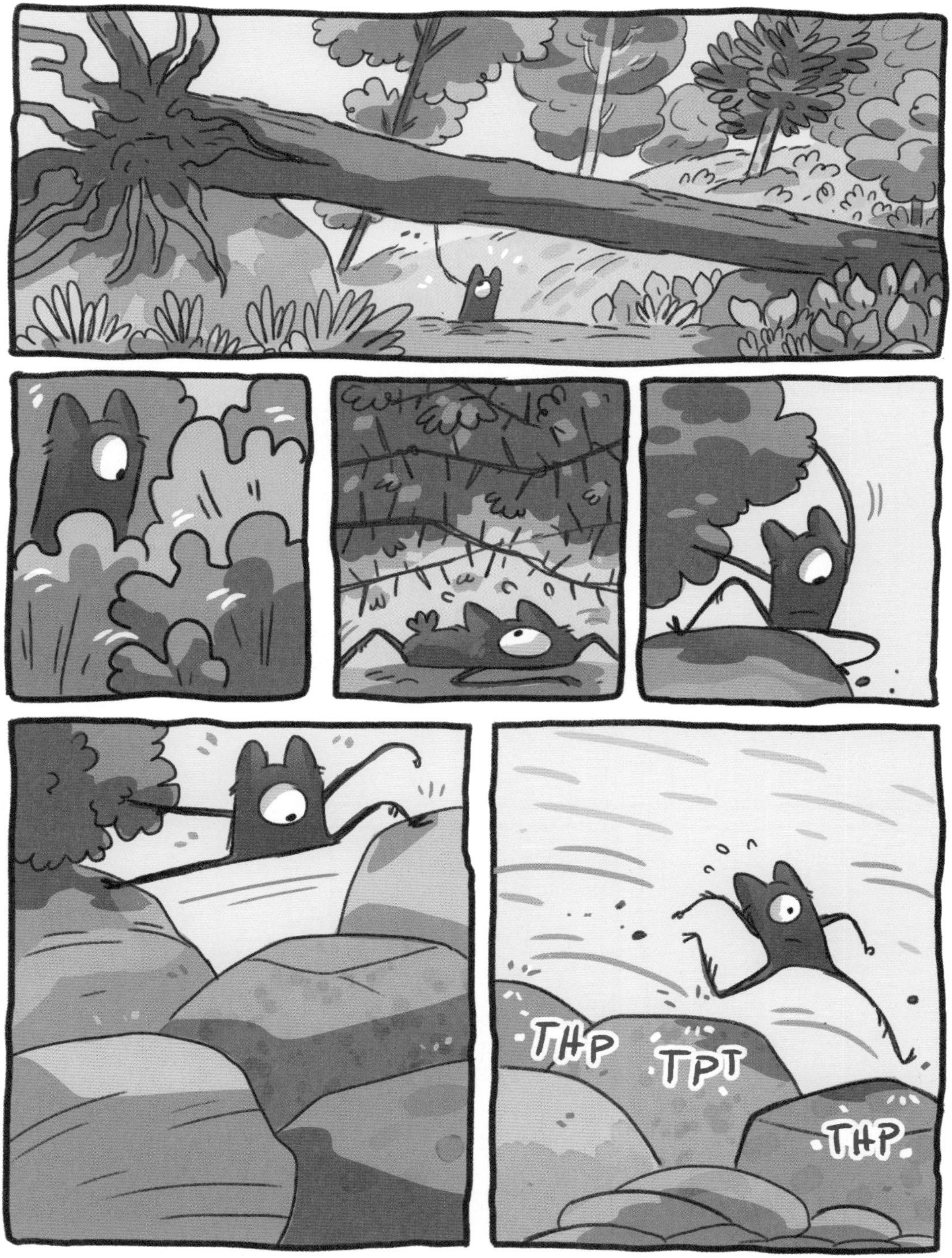
THP
TPT
THP

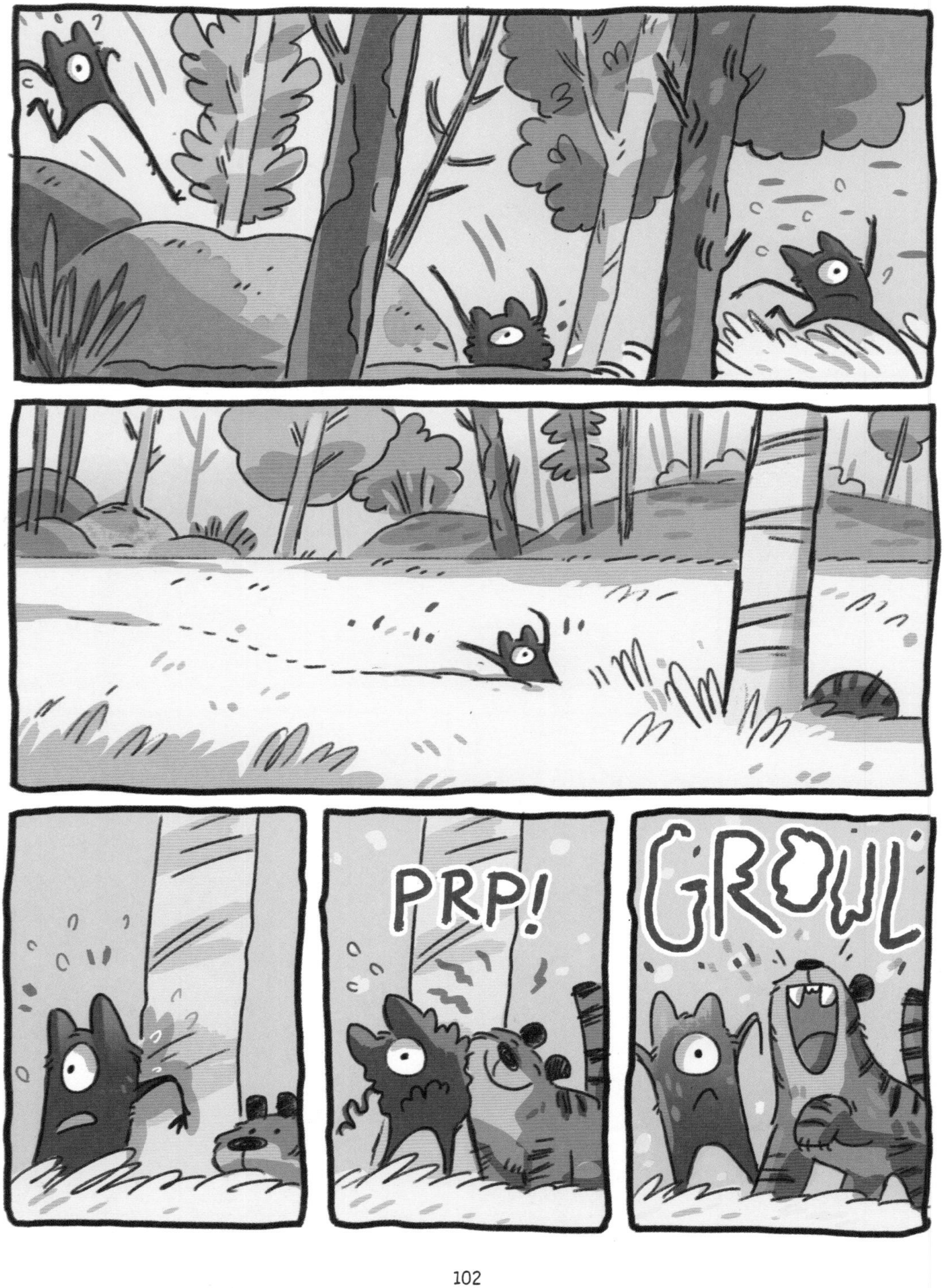
PRP!
GROWL

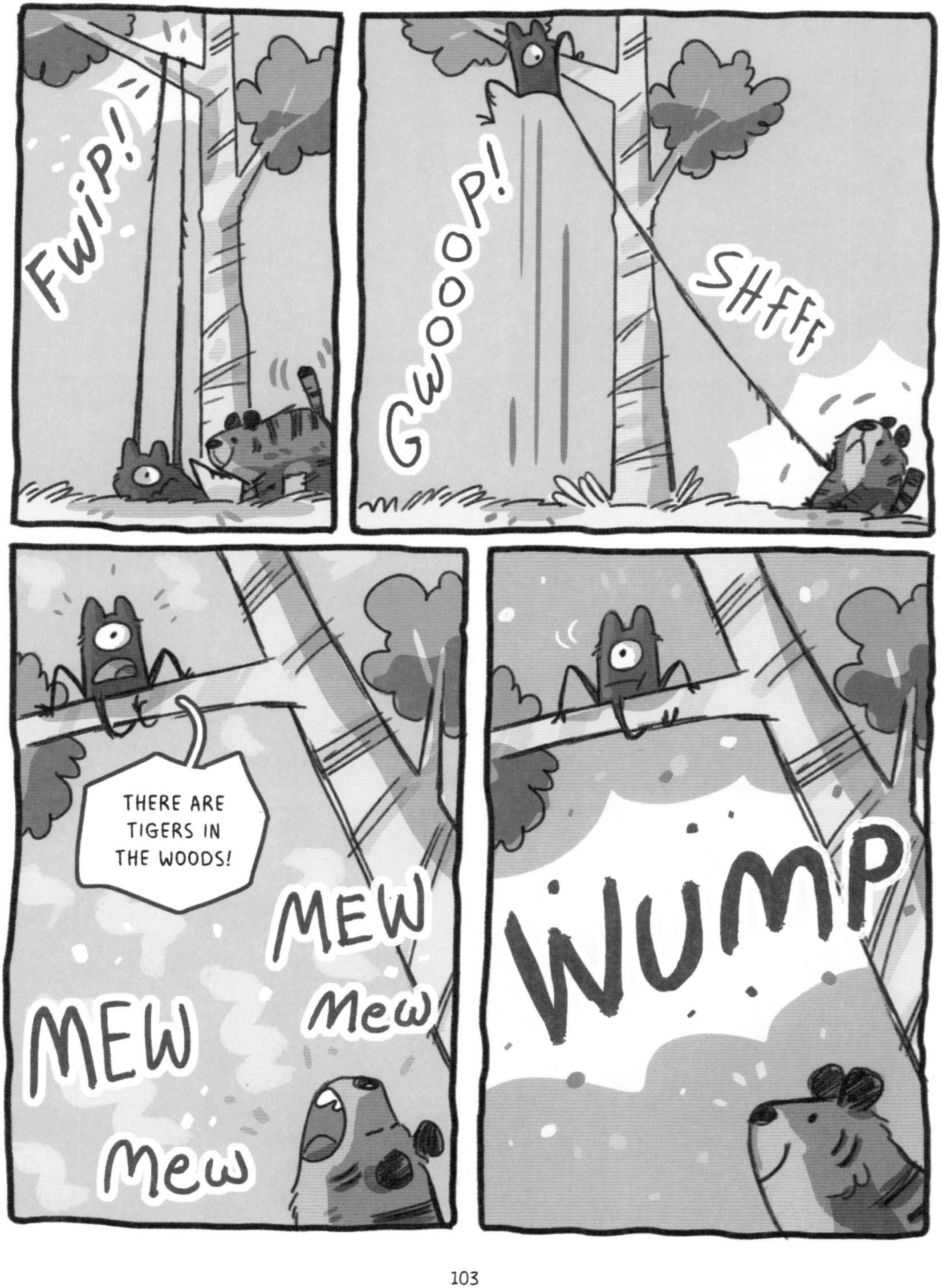
FWIP!
GWOOOP!
SHFFF
THERE ARE TIGERS IN THE WOODS!
MEW
Mew
MEW
Mew
WUMP

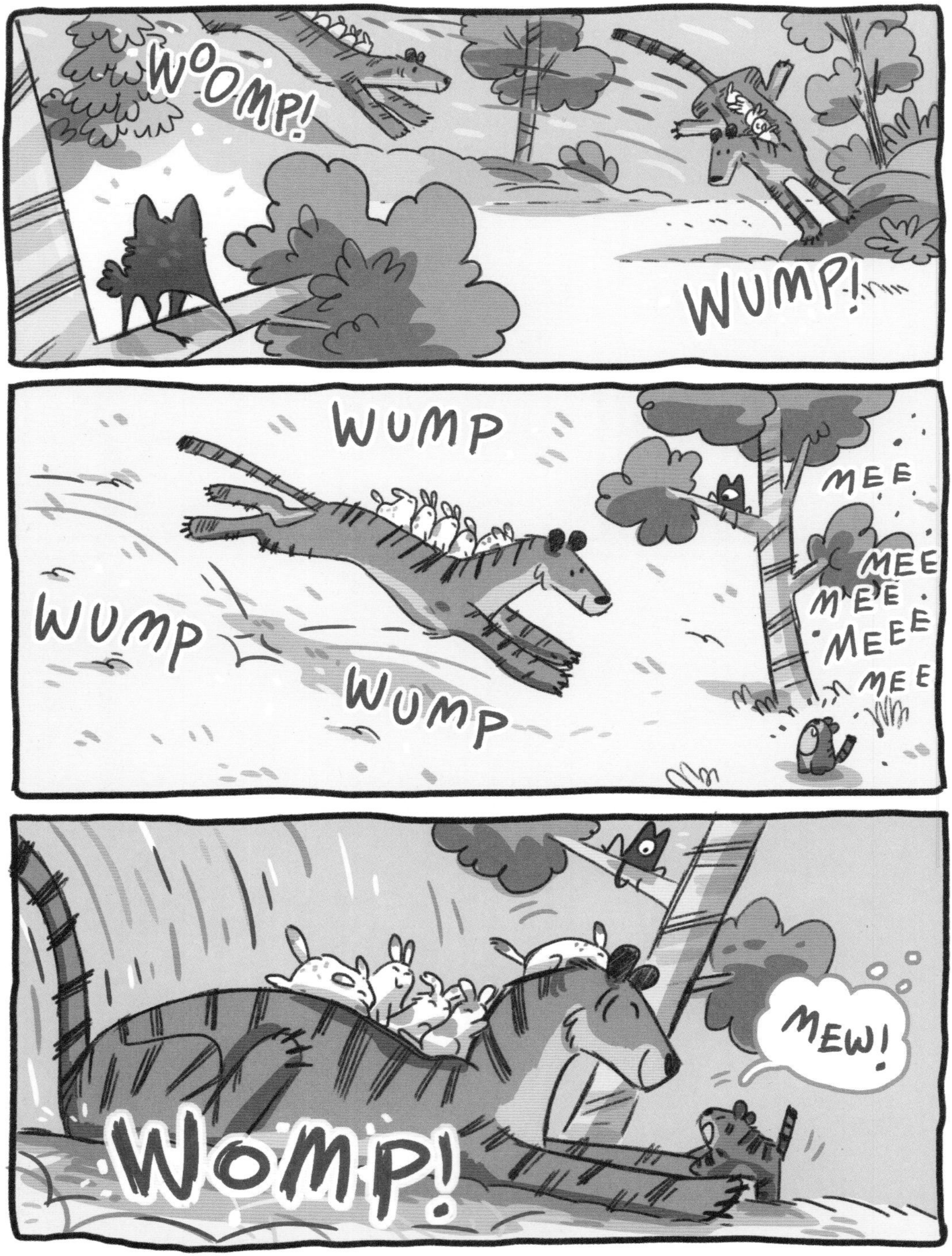
WOOMP!
WUMP!
WUMP
MEE
MEE
MEE
MEEE
MEE
WUMP
WUMP
MEW!
WOMP!

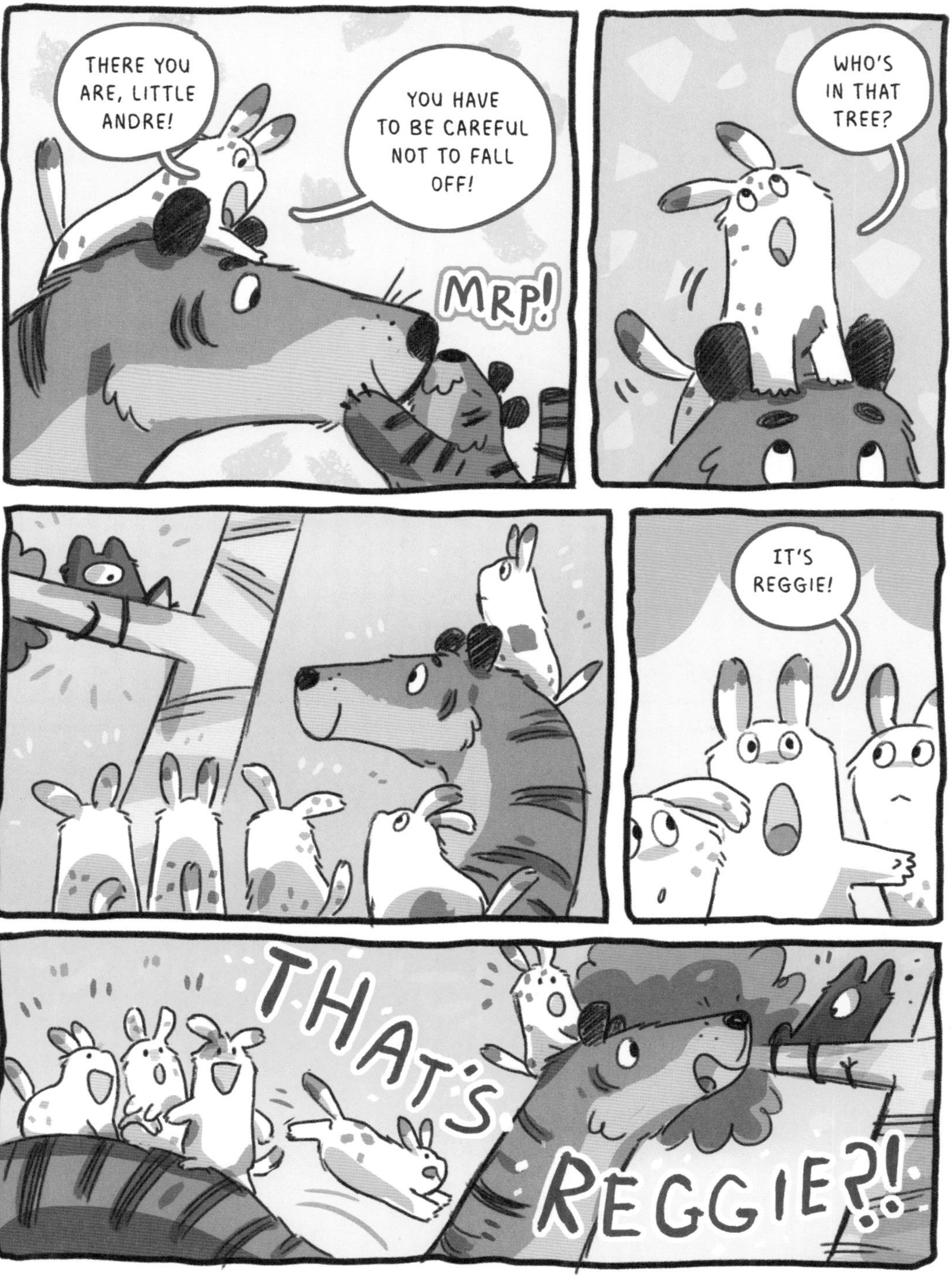
THERE YOU ARE, LITTLE ANDRE!
YOU HAVE TO BE CAREFUL NOT TO FALL OFF!
MRP!
WHO'S IN THAT TREE?
IT'S REGGIE!
THAT'S REGGIE?!

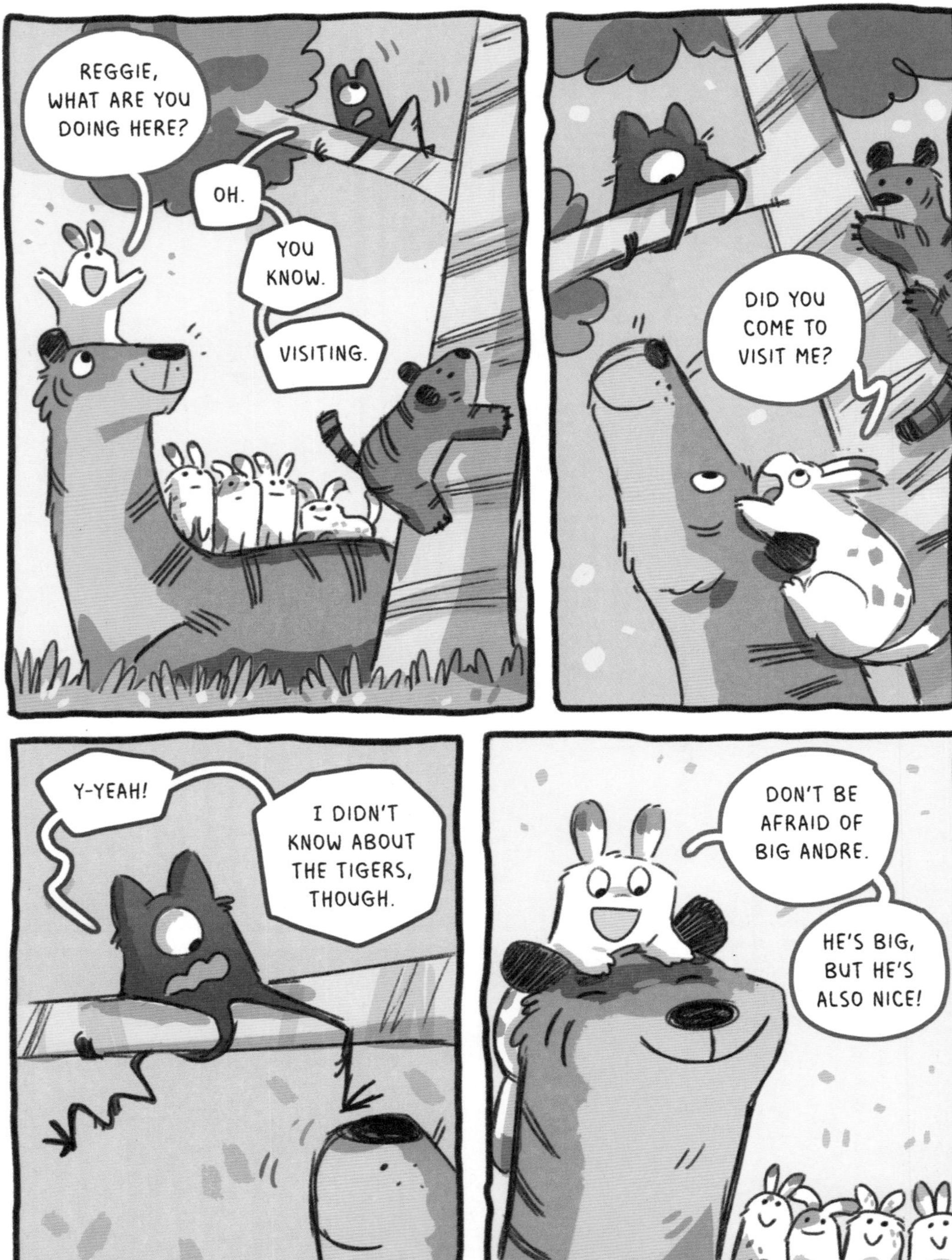
REGGIE, WHAT ARE YOU DOING HERE?
OH.
YOU KNOW.
VISITING.
DID YOU COME TO VISIT ME?
Y-YEAH!
I DIDN'T KNOW ABOUT THE TIGERS, THOUGH.
DON'T BE AFRAID OF BIG ANDRE.
HE'S BIG, BUT HE'S ALSO NICE!

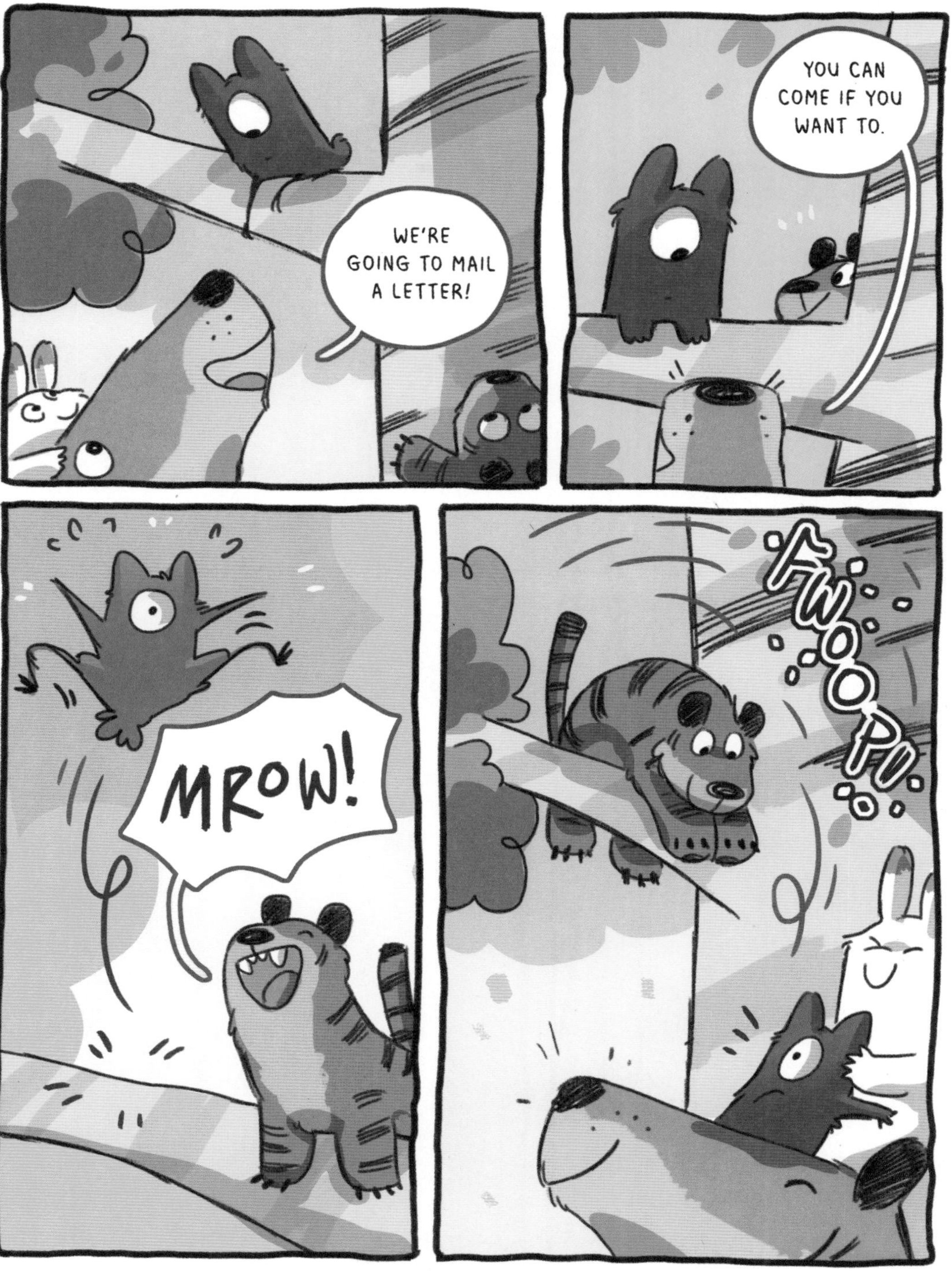
WE'RE GOING TO MAIL A LETTER!
YOU CAN COME IF YOU WANT TO.
MROW!
FWOOP!

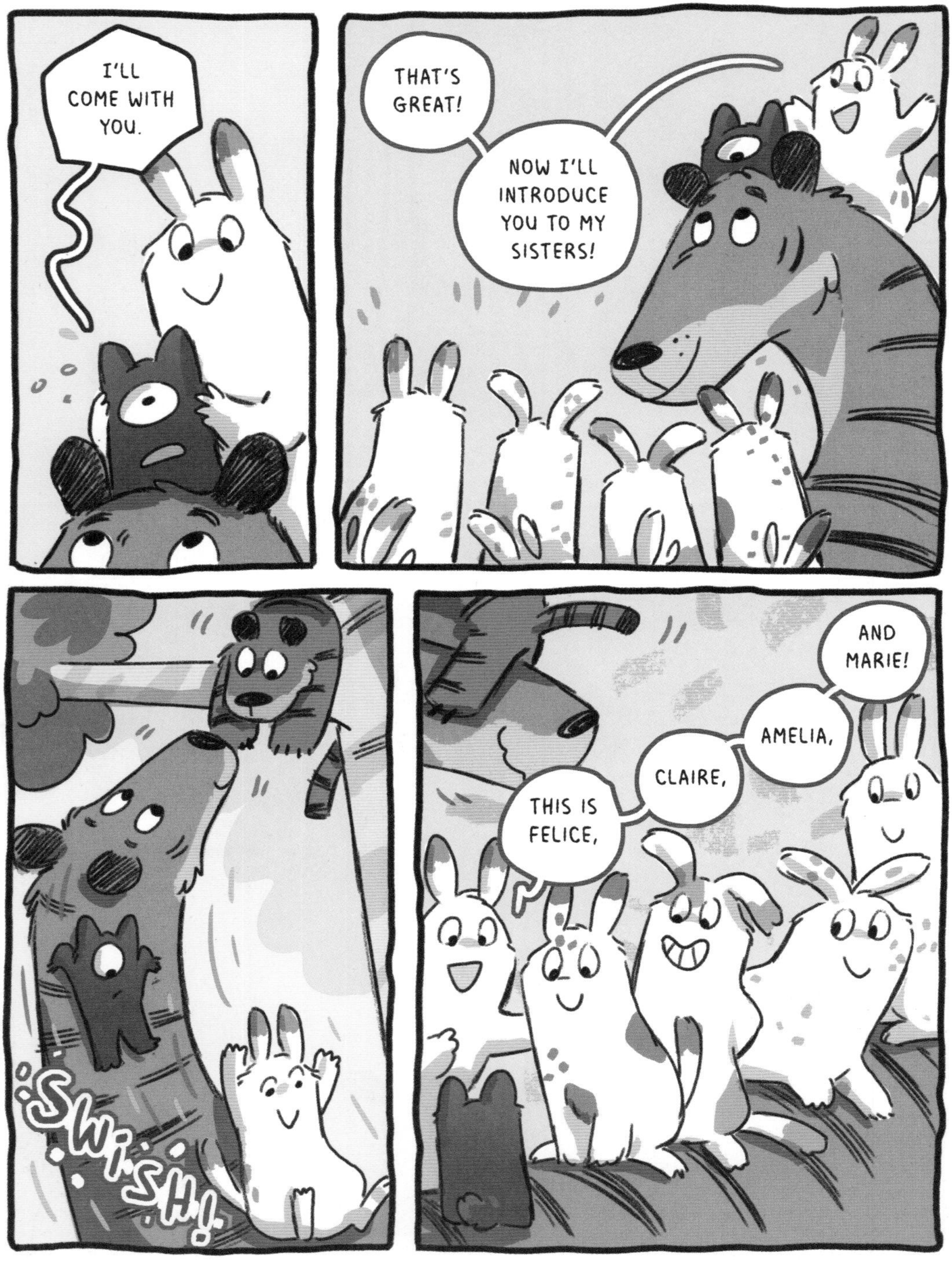
I'LL COME WITH YOU.
THAT'S GREAT!
NOW I'LL INTRODUCE YOU TO MY SISTERS!
SWISH!
THIS IS FELICE,
CLAIRE,
AMELIA,
AND MARIE!

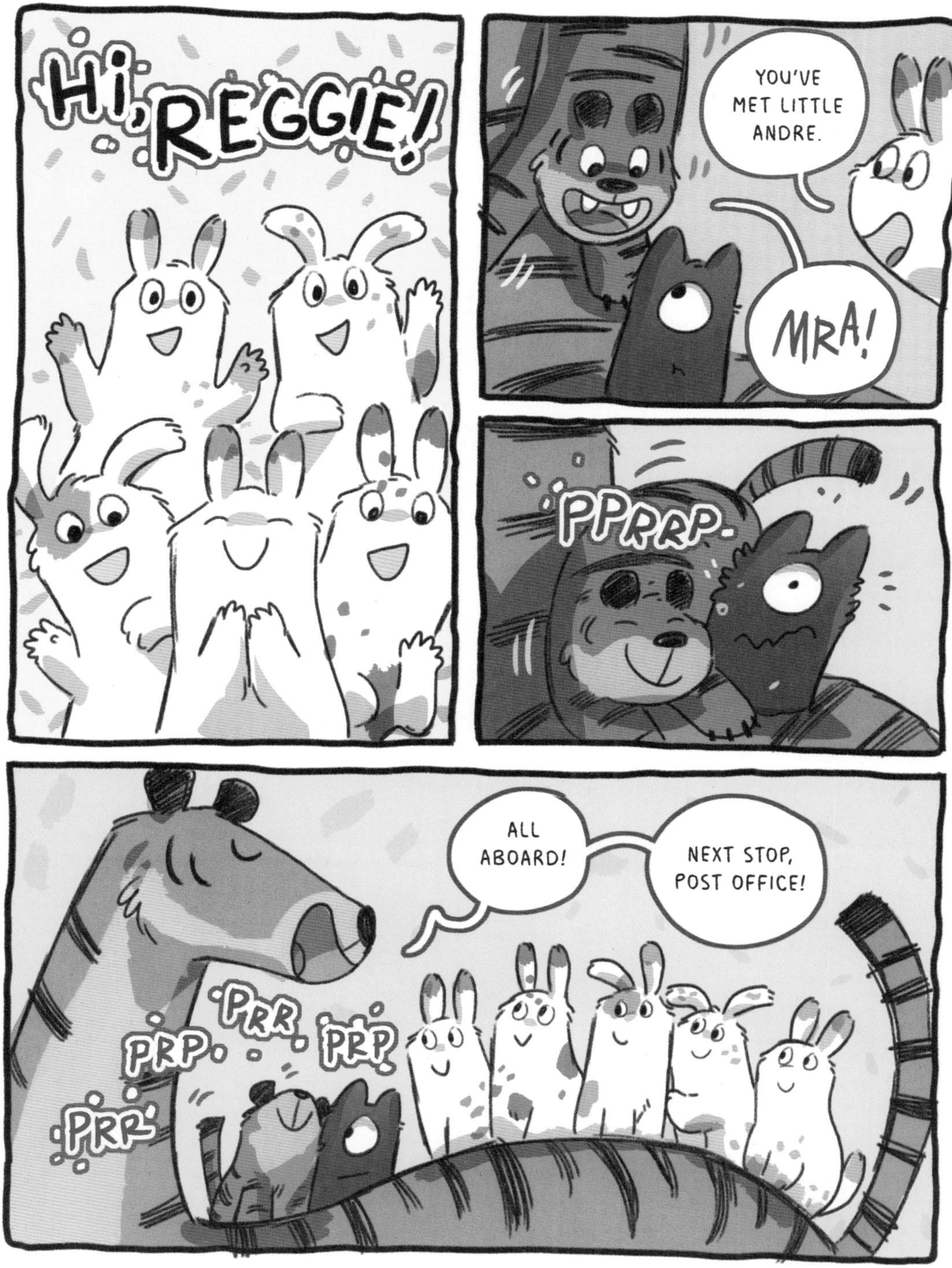
HI, REGGIE!
YOU'VE MET LITTLE ANDRE.
MRA!
PPRRRP
ALL ABOARD!
NEXT STOP, POST OFFICE!
PRR
PRP
PRR
PRP
PRR

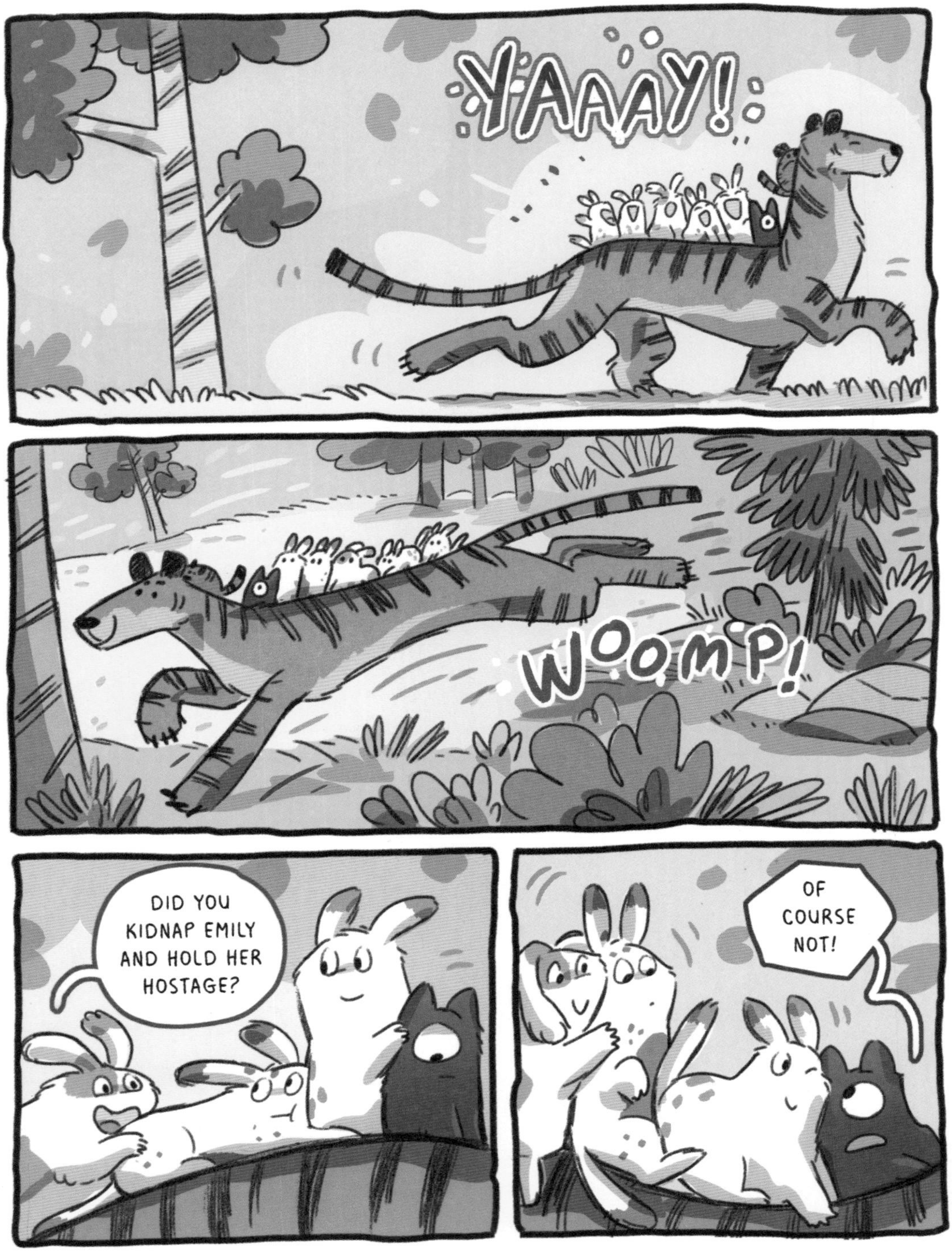
YAAAY!
WOOMP!
DID YOU KIDNAP EMILY AND HOLD HER HOSTAGE?
OF COURSE NOT!

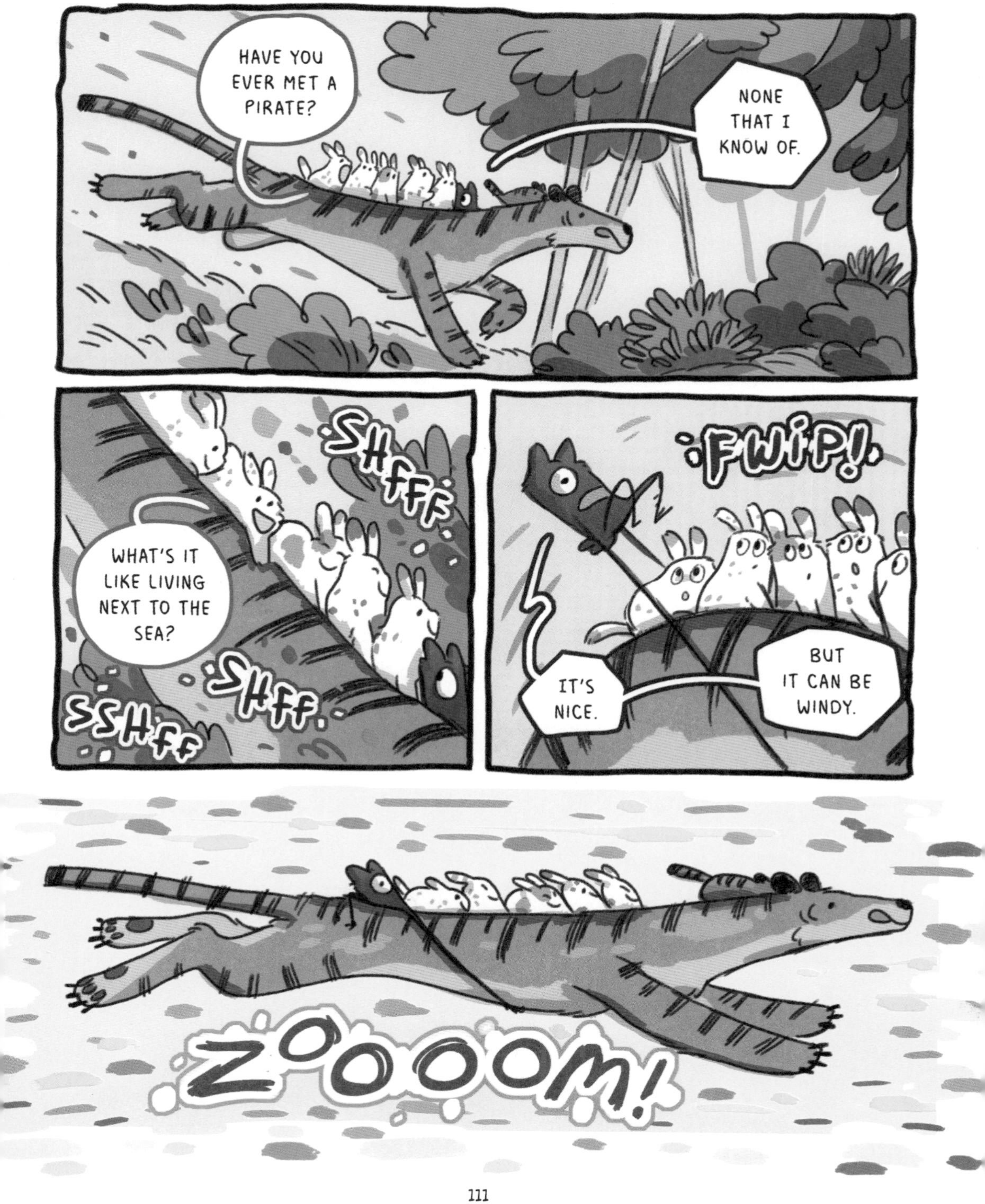
HAVE YOU EVER MET A PIRATE?
NONE THAT I KNOW OF.
SHFFF
WHAT'S IT LIKE LIVING NEXT TO THE SEA?
SHFF
SSHFF
FWIP!
IT'S NICE.
BUT IT CAN BE WINDY.
ZOOOOM!

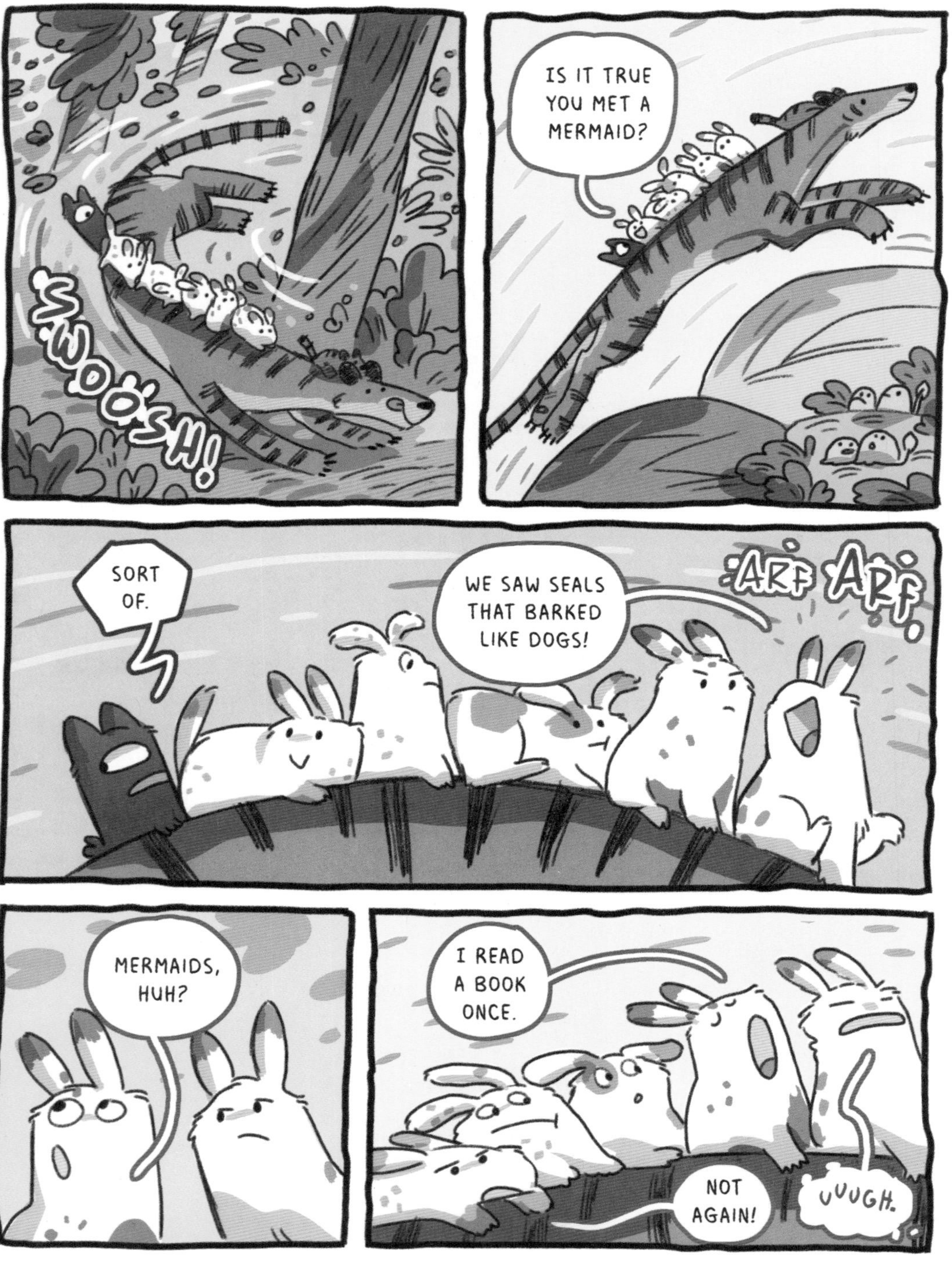
SWOOSH!
IS IT TRUE YOU MET A MERMAID?
SORT OF.
WE SAW SEALS THAT BARKED LIKE DOGS!
ARF ARF
MERMAIDS, HUH?
I READ A BOOK ONCE.
NOT AGAIN!
UUUGH.

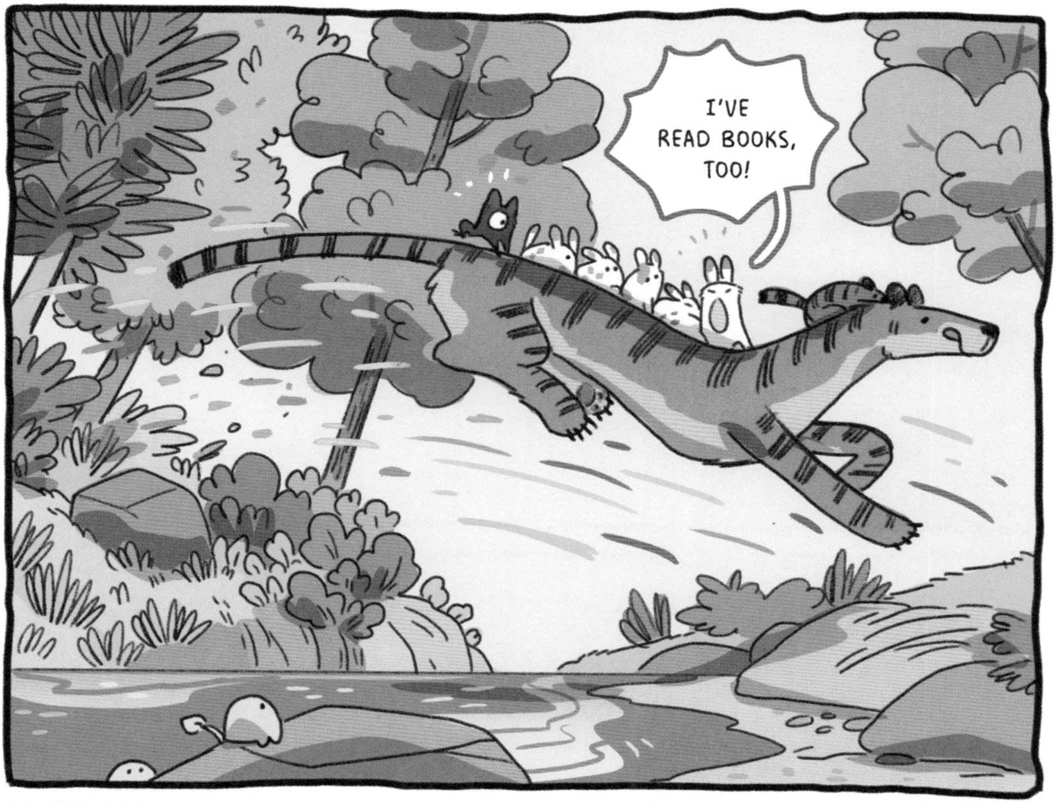
I'VE READ BOOKS, TOO!

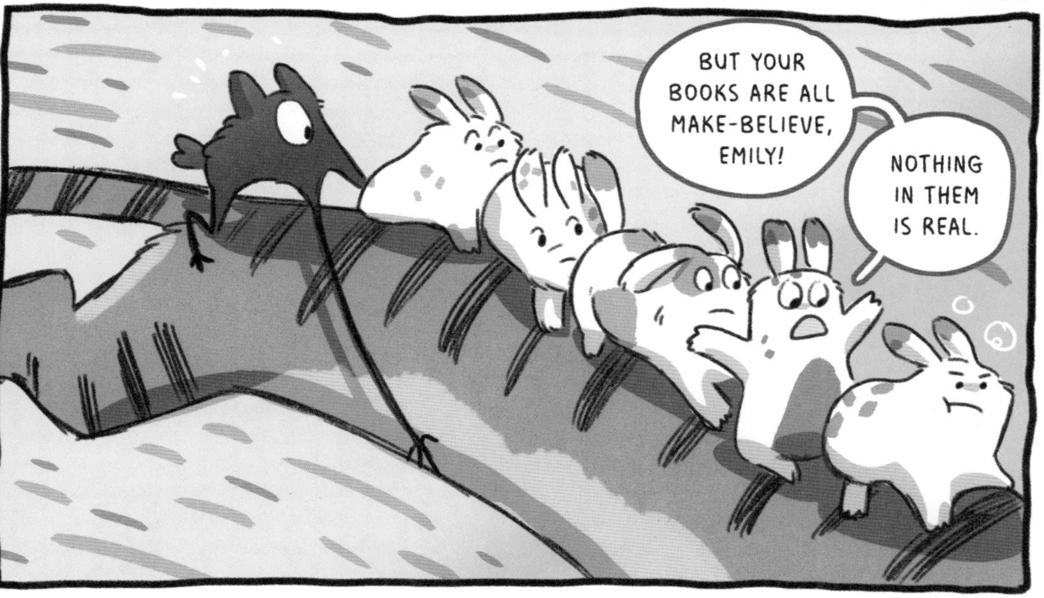
BUT YOUR BOOKS ARE ALL MAKE-BELIEVE, EMILY!
NOTHING IN THEM IS REAL.

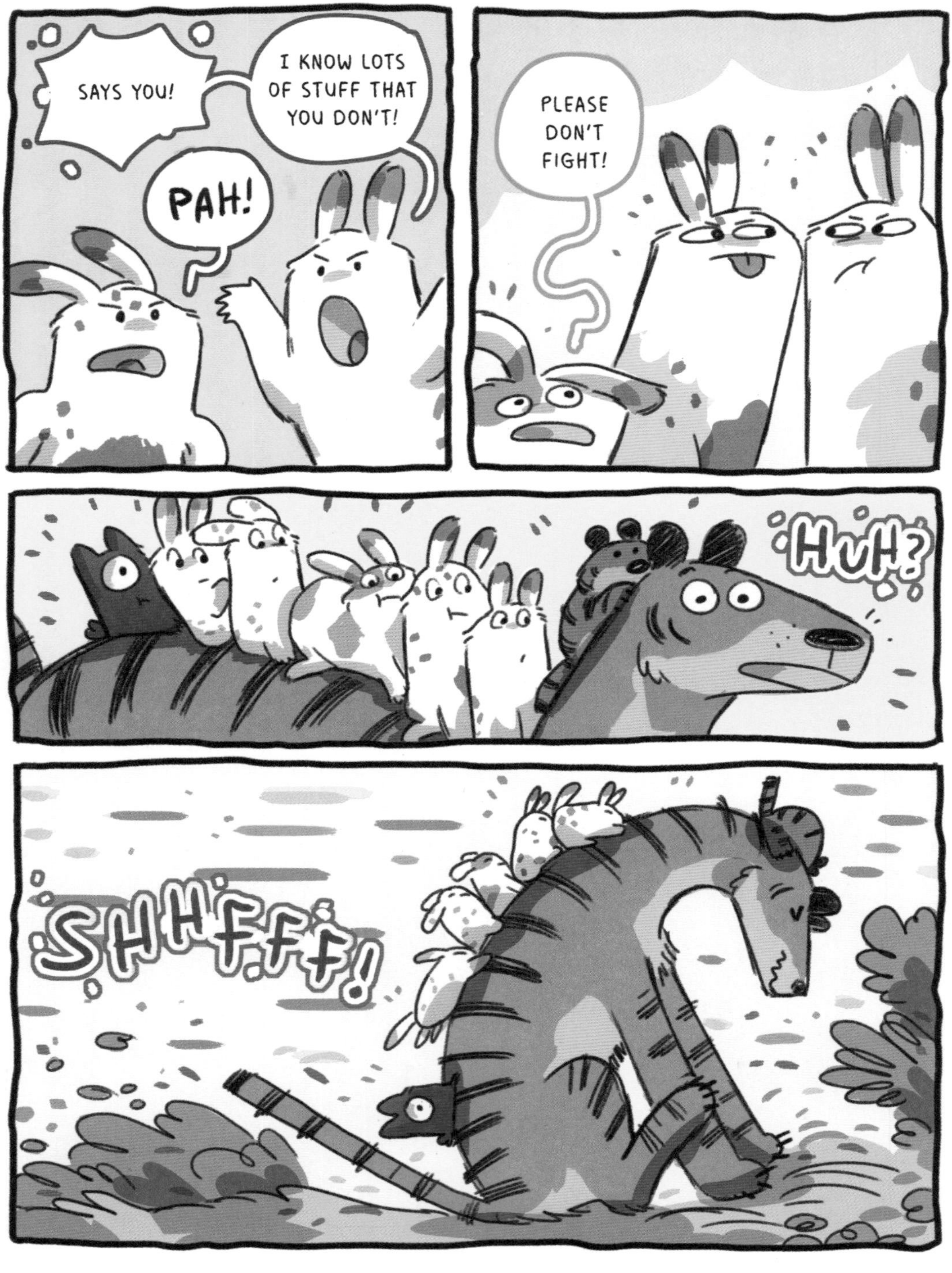

SAYS YOU!
I KNOW LOTS OF STUFF THAT YOU DON'T!
PAH!
PLEASE DON'T FIGHT!
HUH?
SHHFFF!

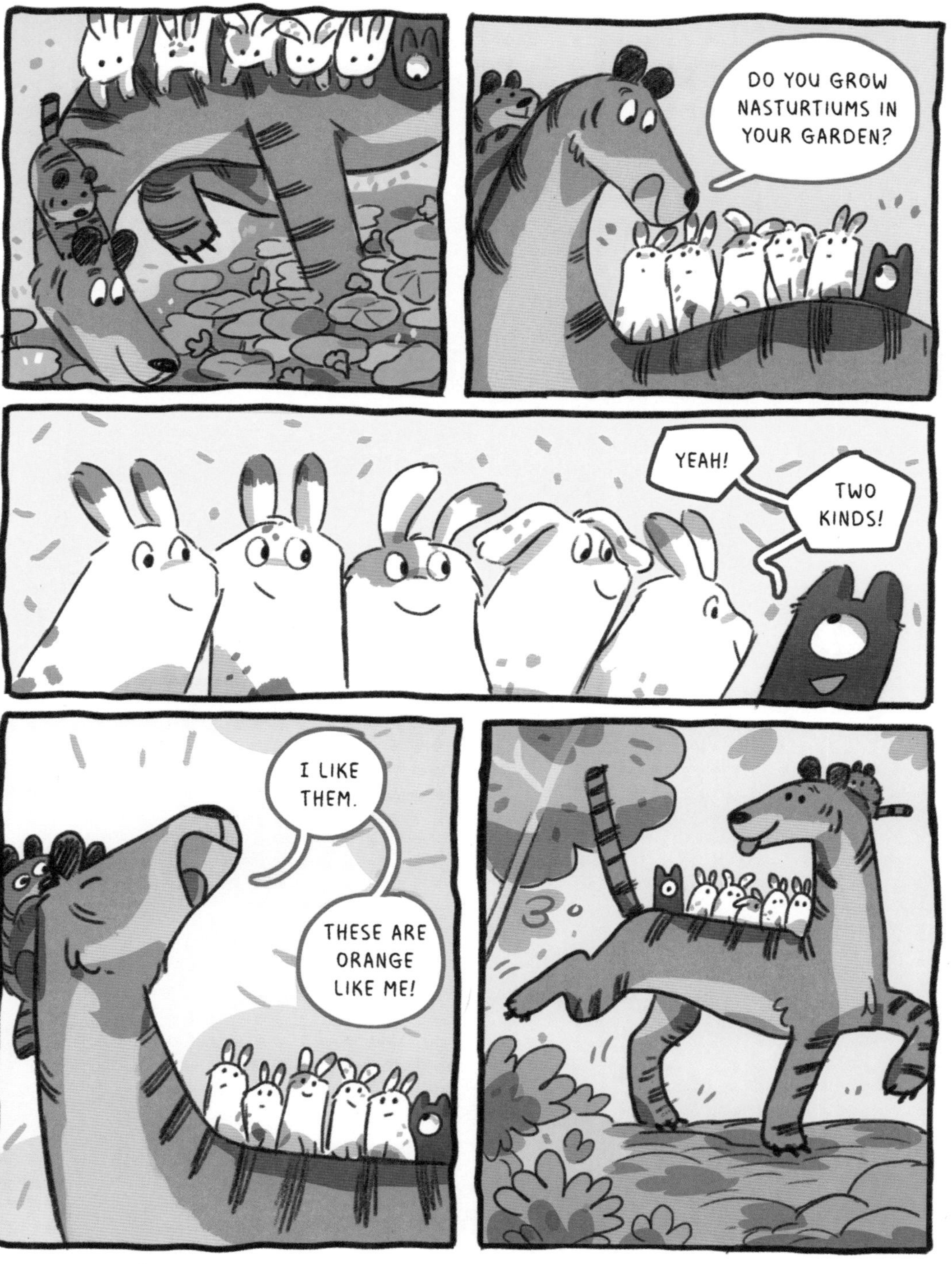
DO YOU GROW NASTURTIUMS IN YOUR GARDEN?
YEAH!
TWO KINDS!
I LIKE THEM.
THESE ARE ORANGE LIKE ME!

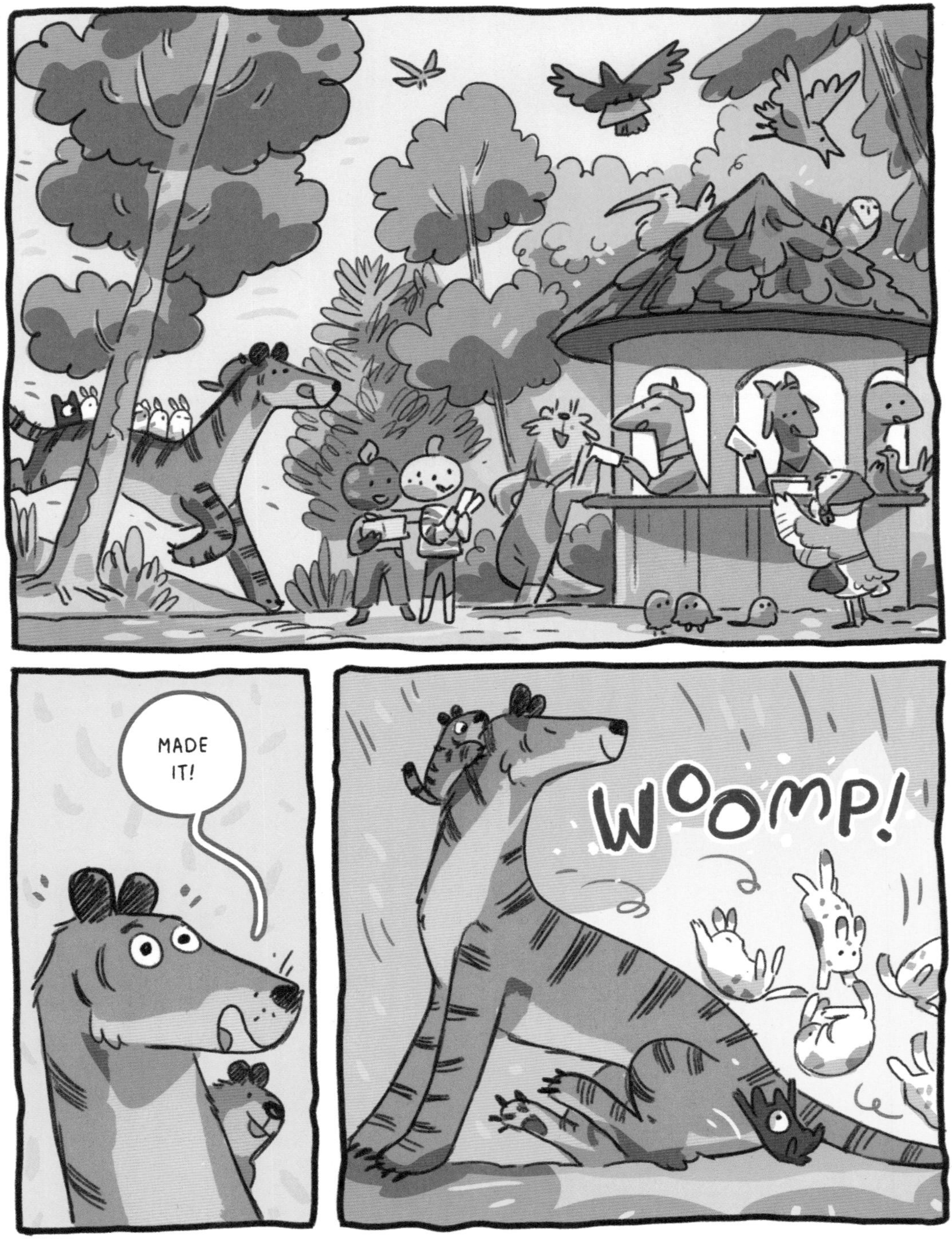
MADE IT!
WOOMP!

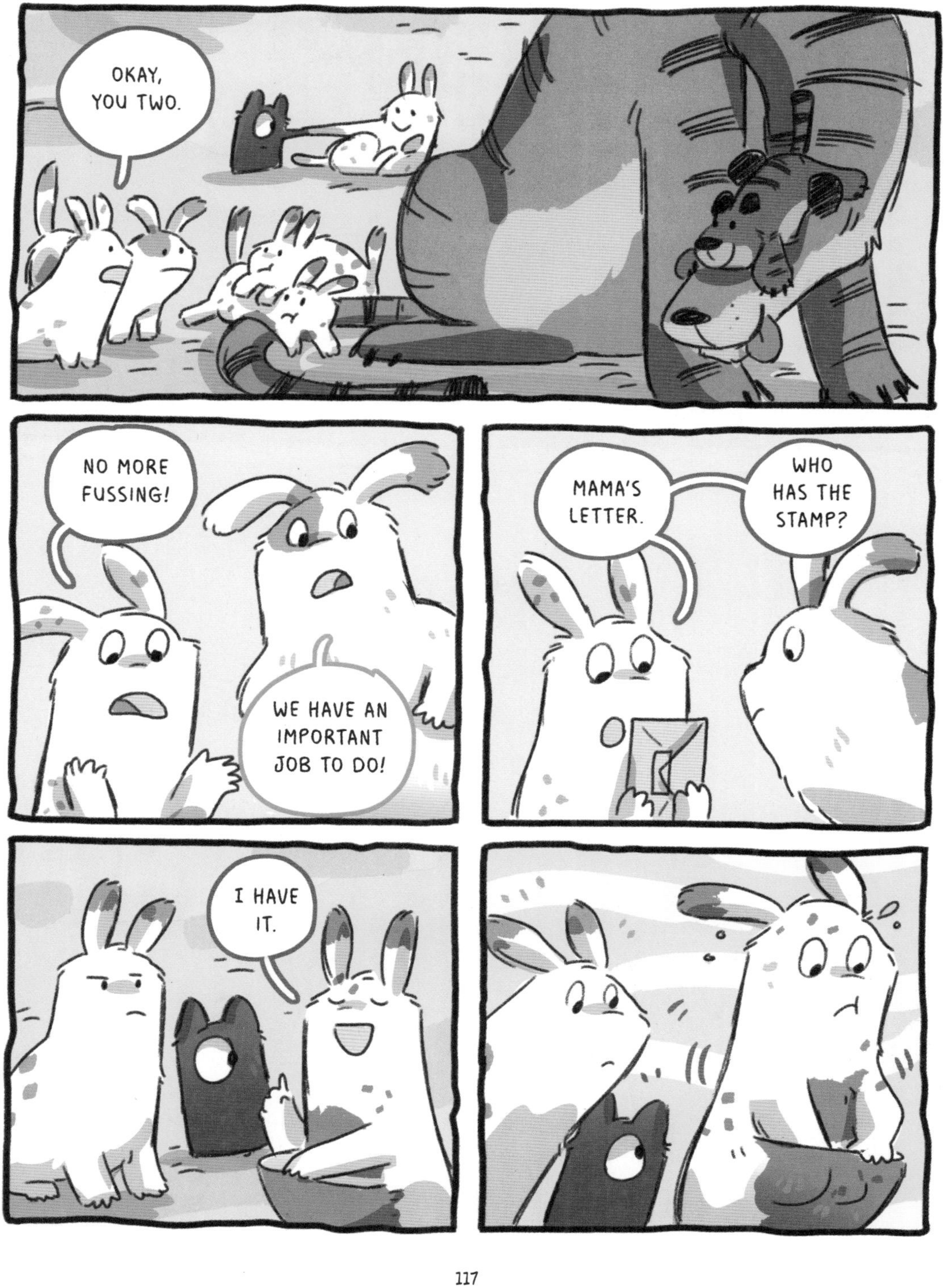
OKAY, YOU TWO.
NO MORE FUSSING!
WE HAVE AN IMPORTANT JOB TO DO!
MAMA'S LETTER.
WHO HAS THE STAMP?
I HAVE IT.

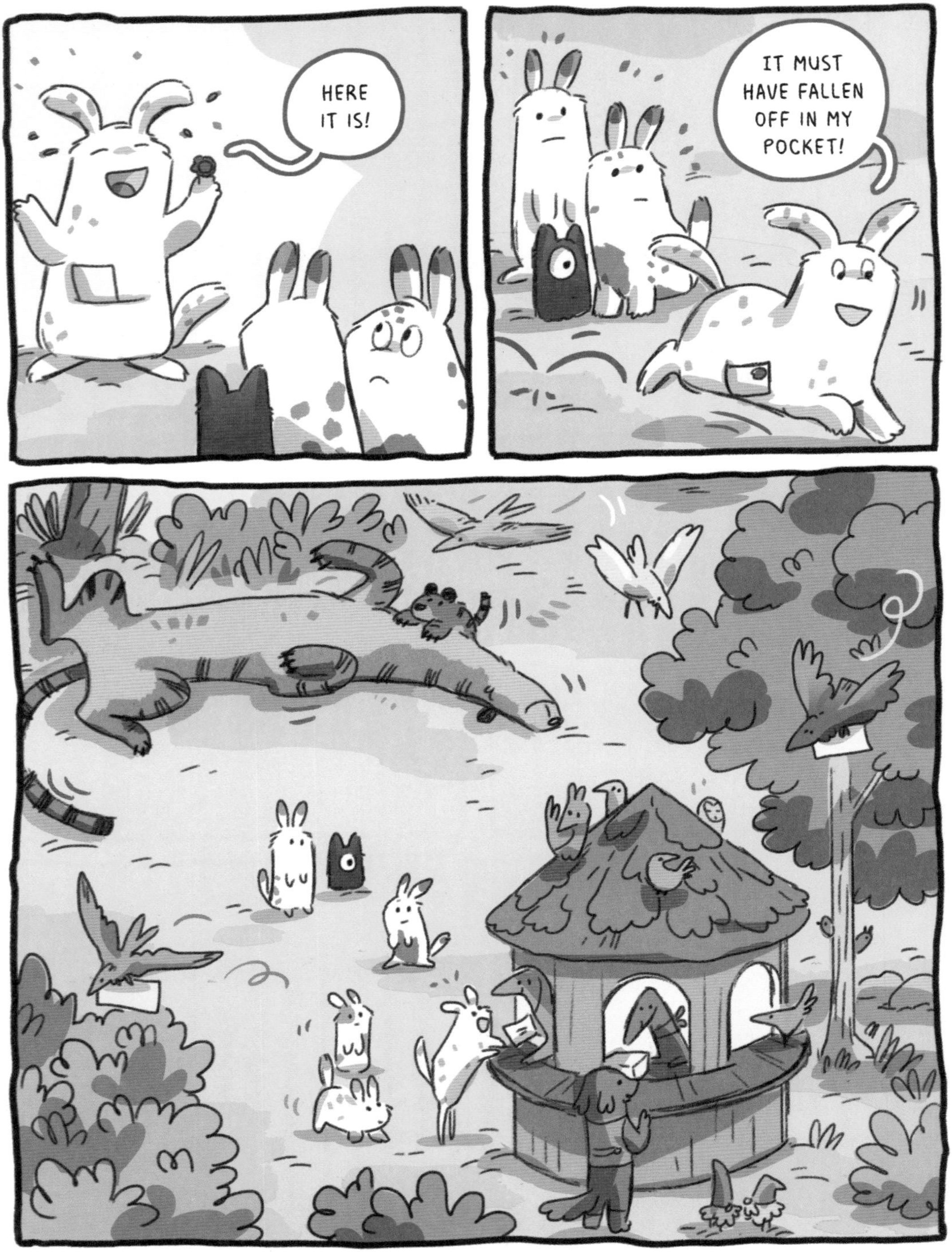
HERE IT IS!
IT MUST HAVE FALLEN OFF IN MY POCKET!

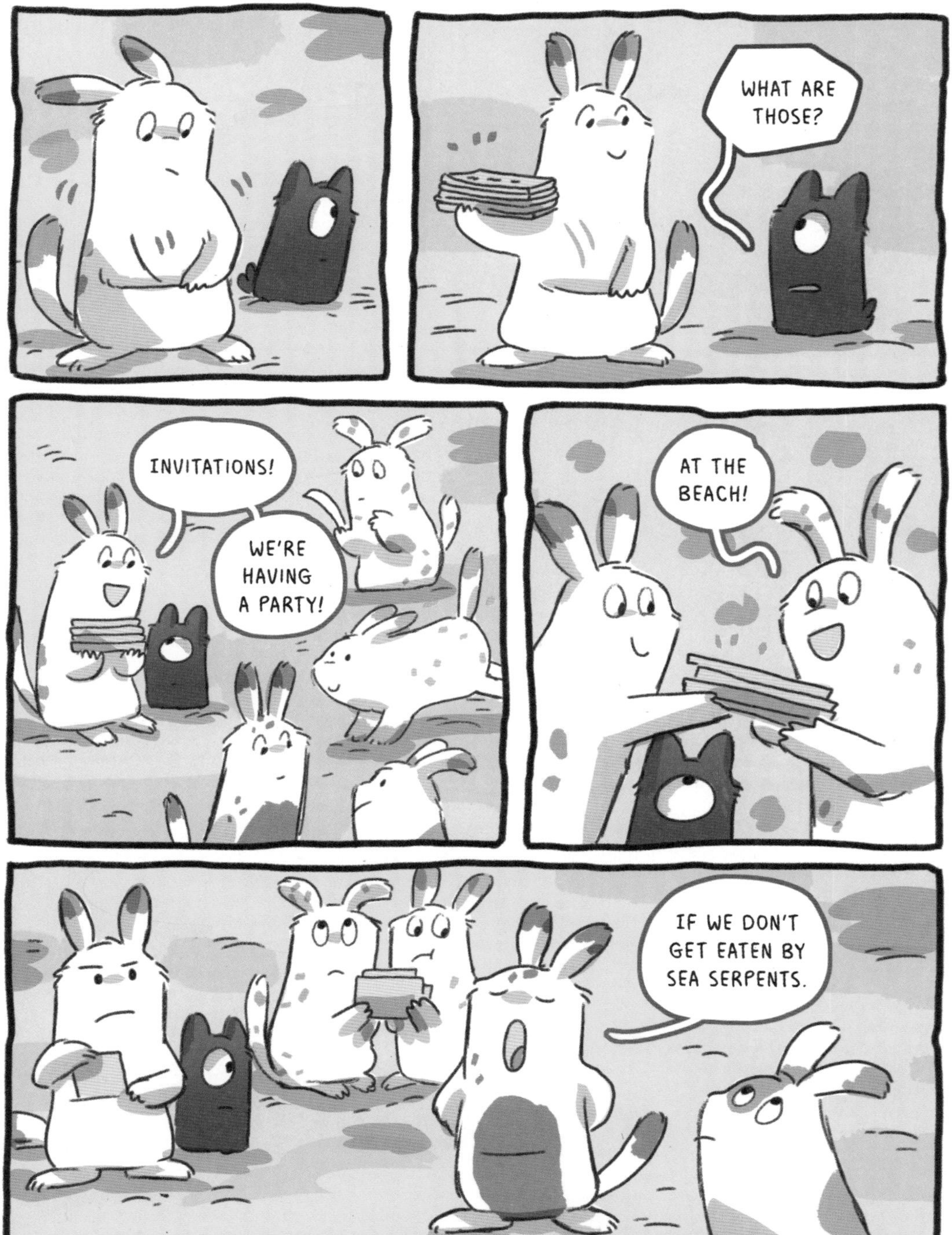
WHAT ARE THOSE?
INVITATIONS!
WE'RE HAVING A PARTY!
AT THE BEACH!
IF WE DON'T GET EATEN BY SEA SERPENTS.

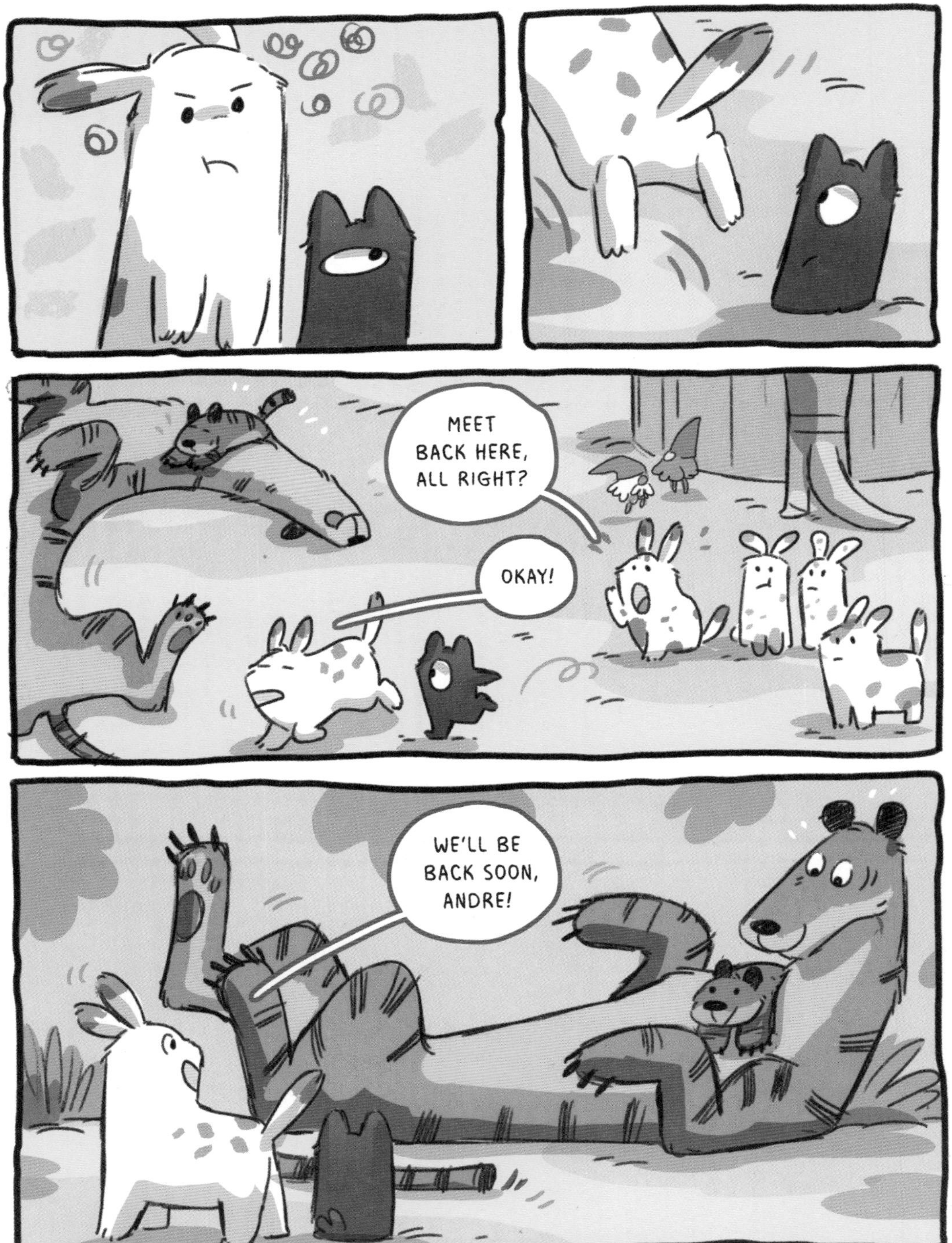
MEET BACK HERE, ALL RIGHT?
OKAY!
WE'LL BE BACK SOON, ANDRE!

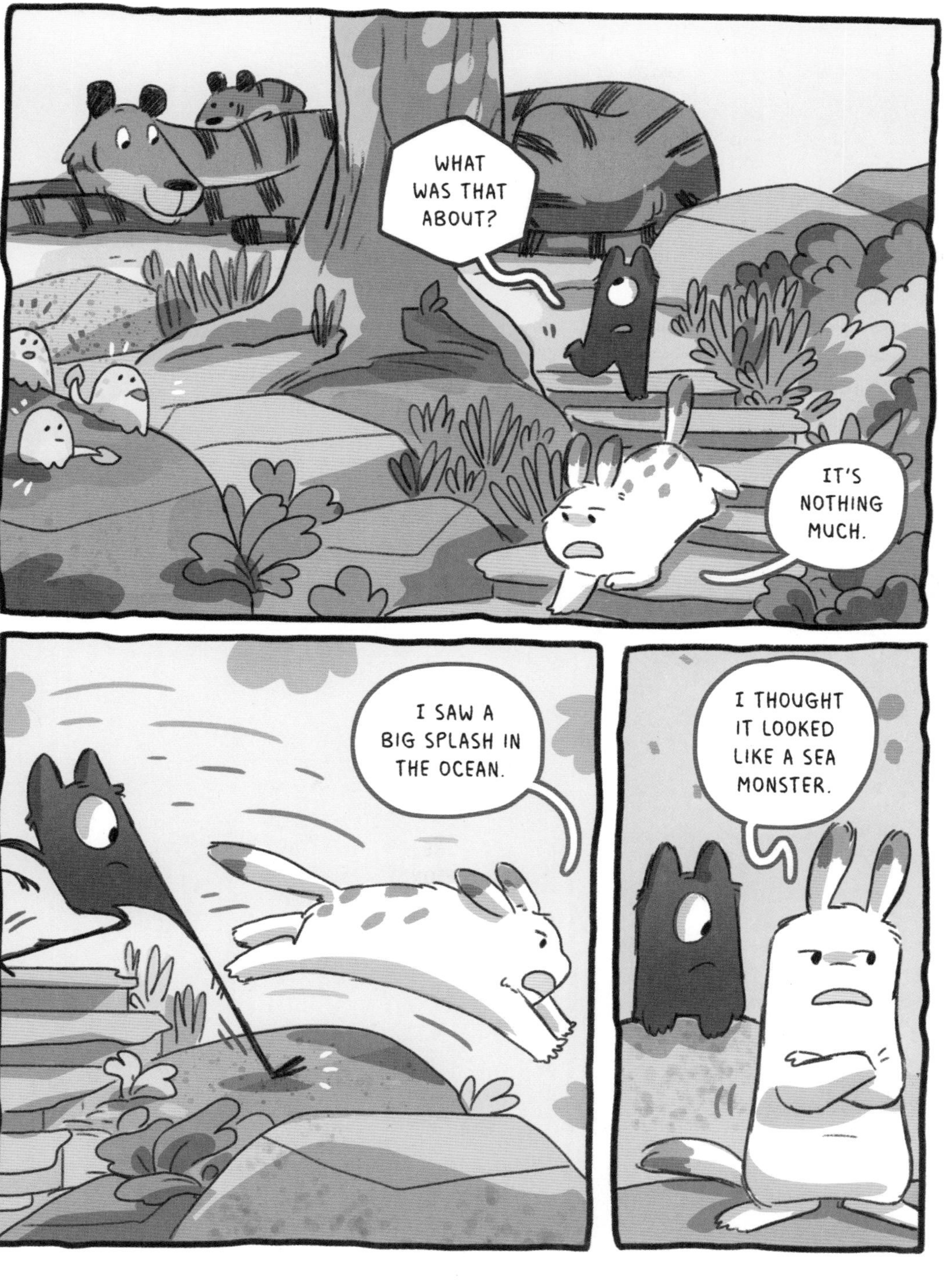
WHAT WAS THAT ABOUT?
IT'S NOTHING MUCH.
I SAW A BIG SPLASH IN THE OCEAN.
I THOUGHT IT LOOKED LIKE A SEA MONSTER.

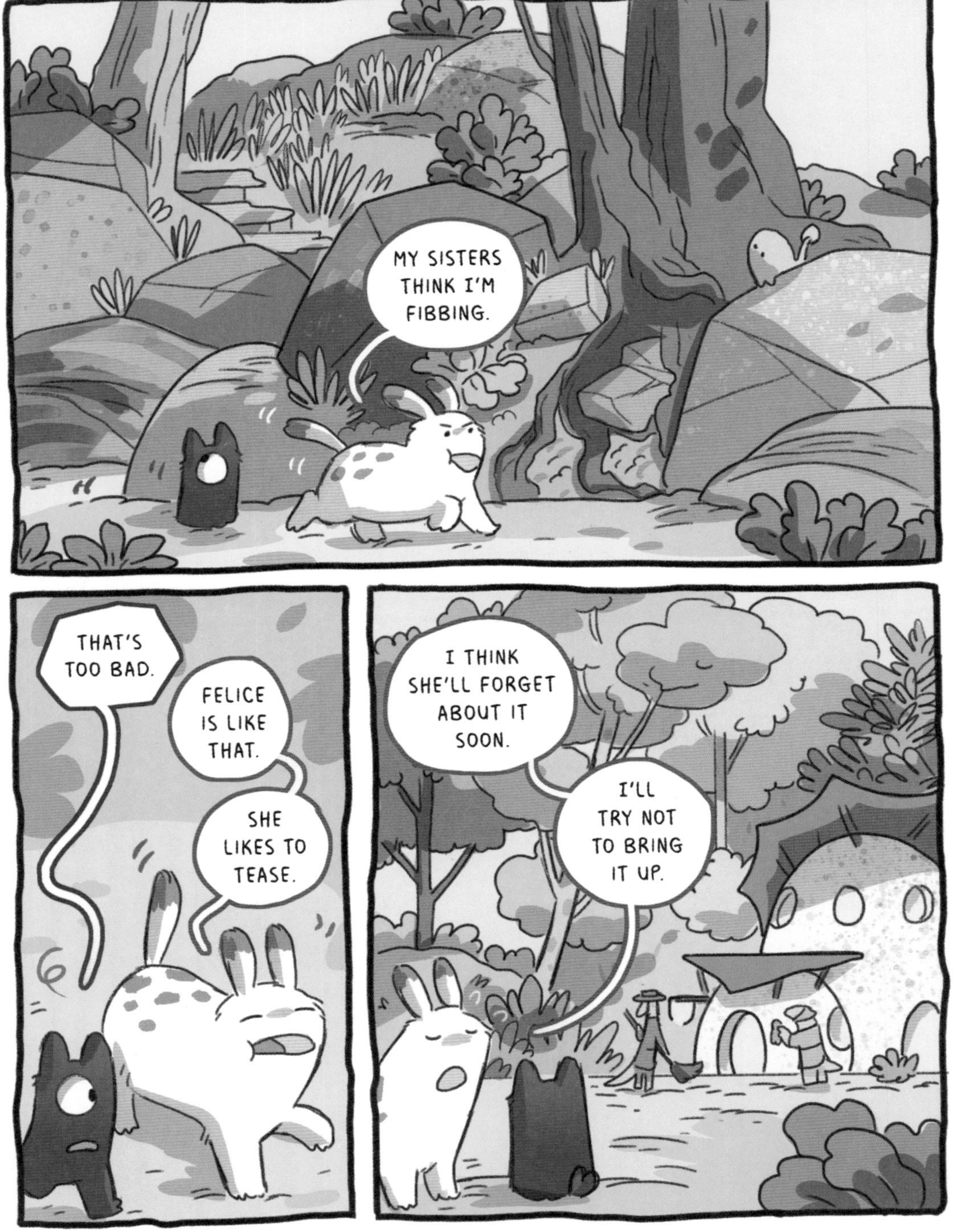
MY SISTERS THINK I'M FIBBING.
THAT'S TOO BAD.
FELICE IS LIKE THAT.
SHE LIKES TO TEASE.
I THINK SHE'LL FORGET ABOUT IT SOON.
I'LL TRY NOT TO BRING IT UP.

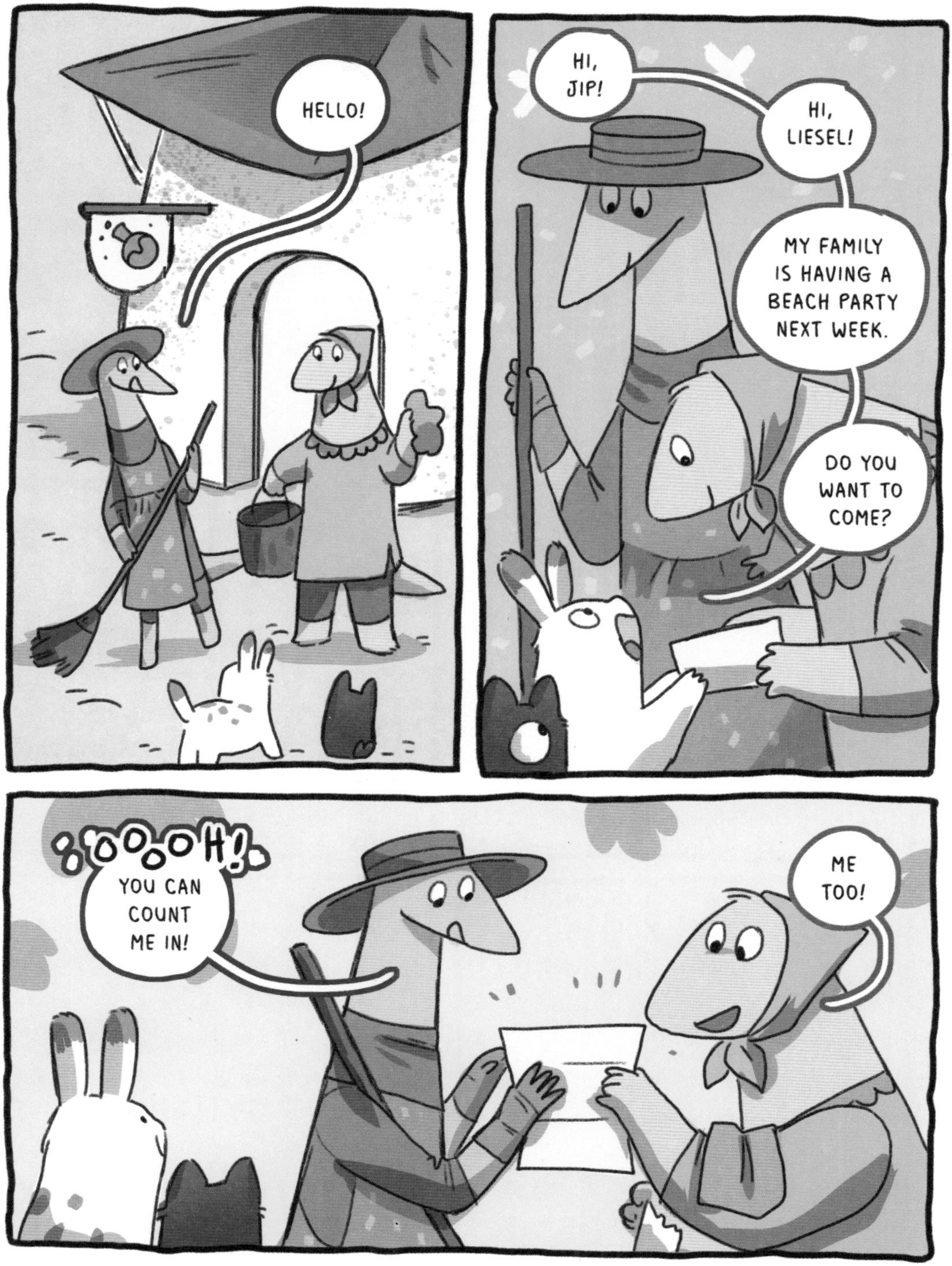
HELLO!
HI, JIP!
HI, LIESEL!
MY FAMILY IS HAVING A BEACH PARTY NEXT WEEK.
DO YOU WANT TO COME?
OOOOH!
YOU CAN COUNT ME IN!
ME TOO!

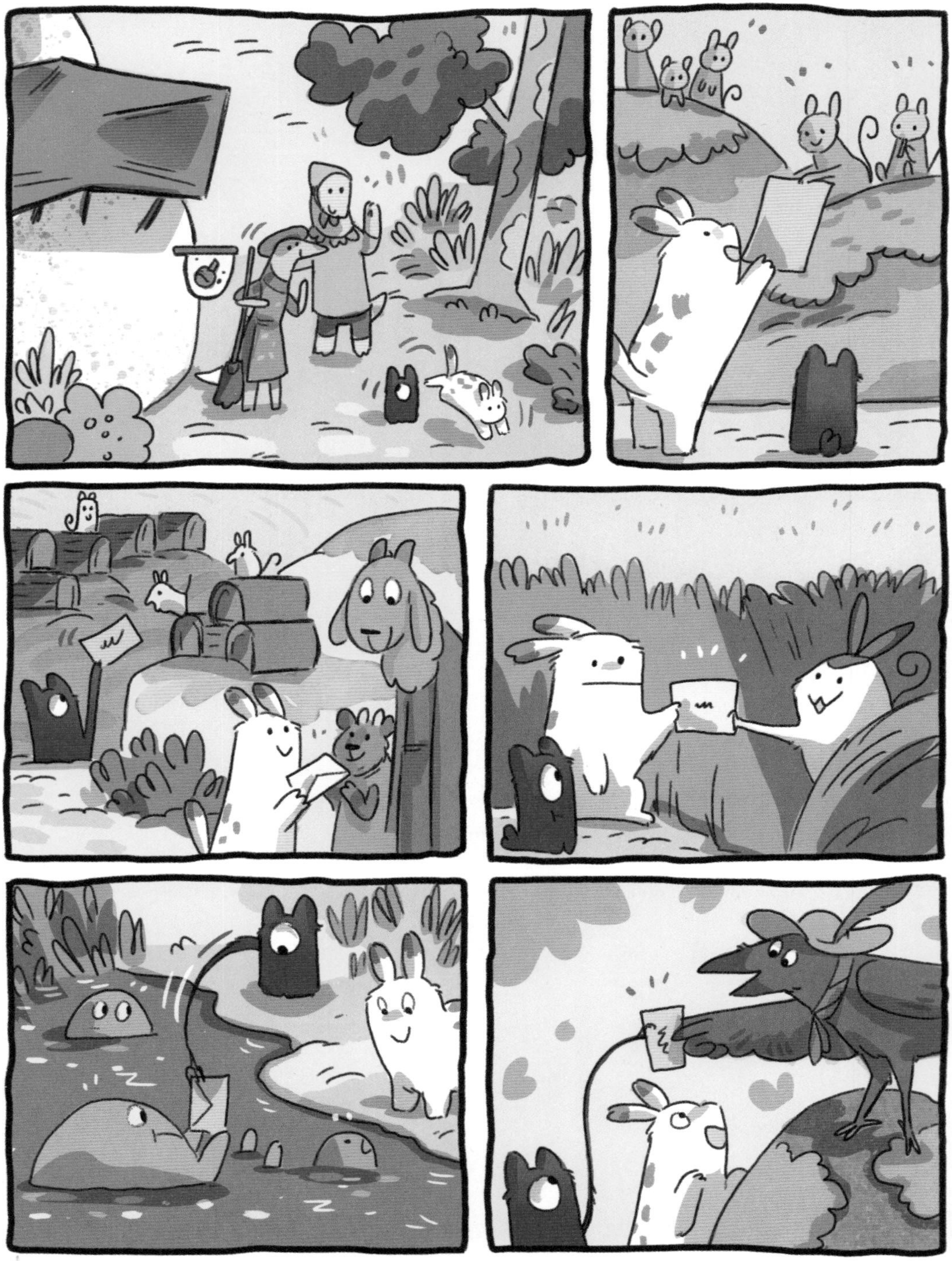

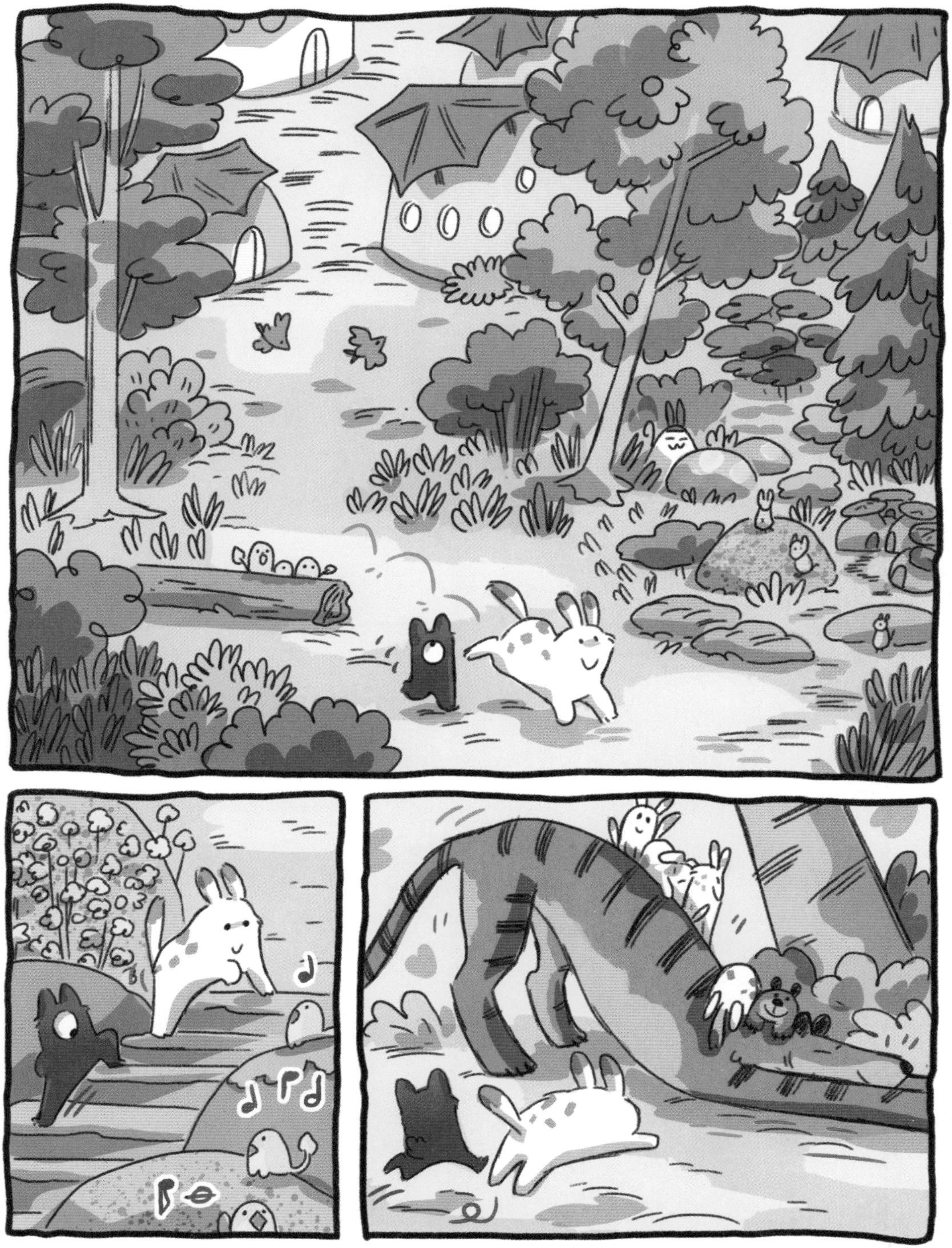

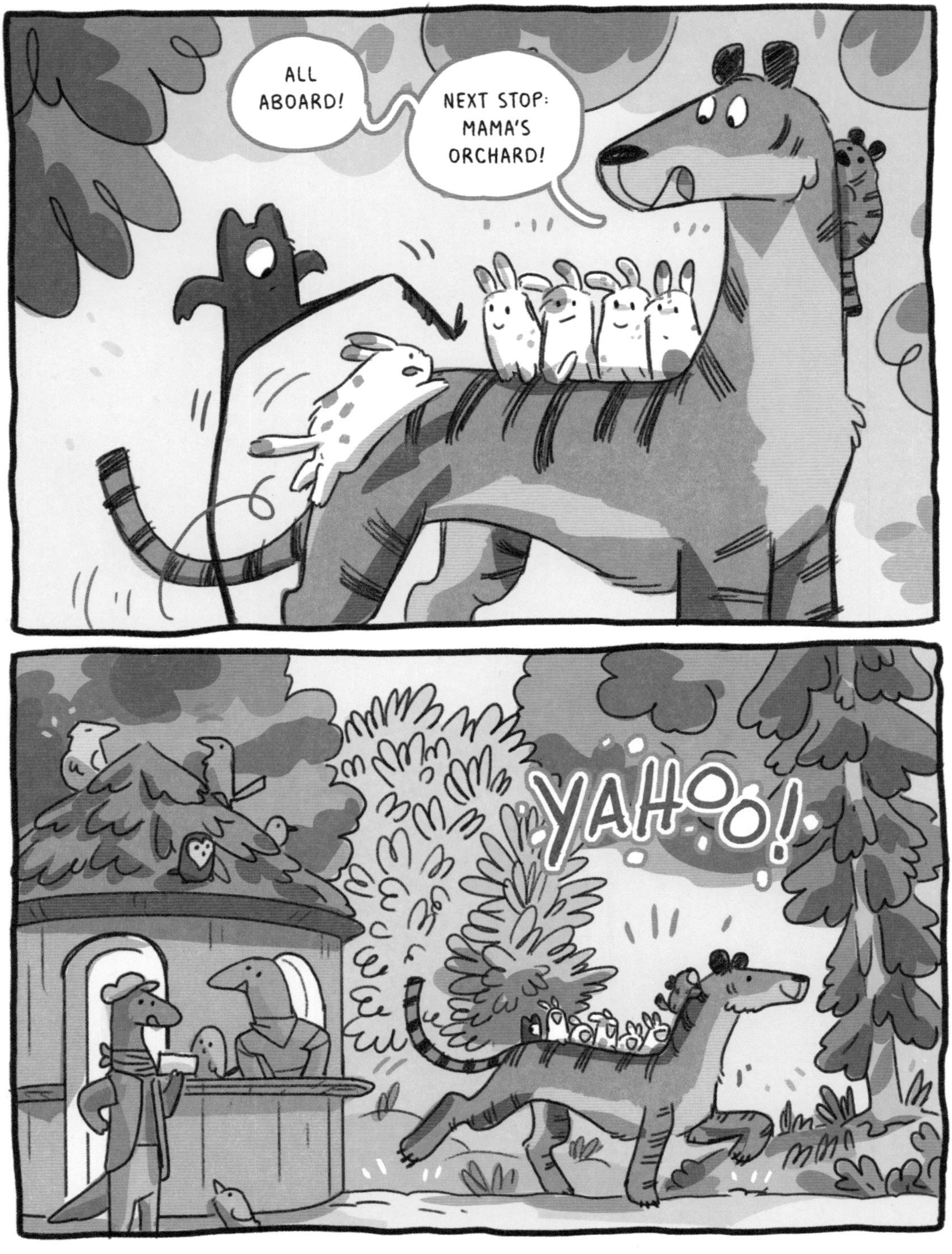
ALL ABOARD!
NEXT STOP: MAMA'S ORCHARD!
YAHOO!

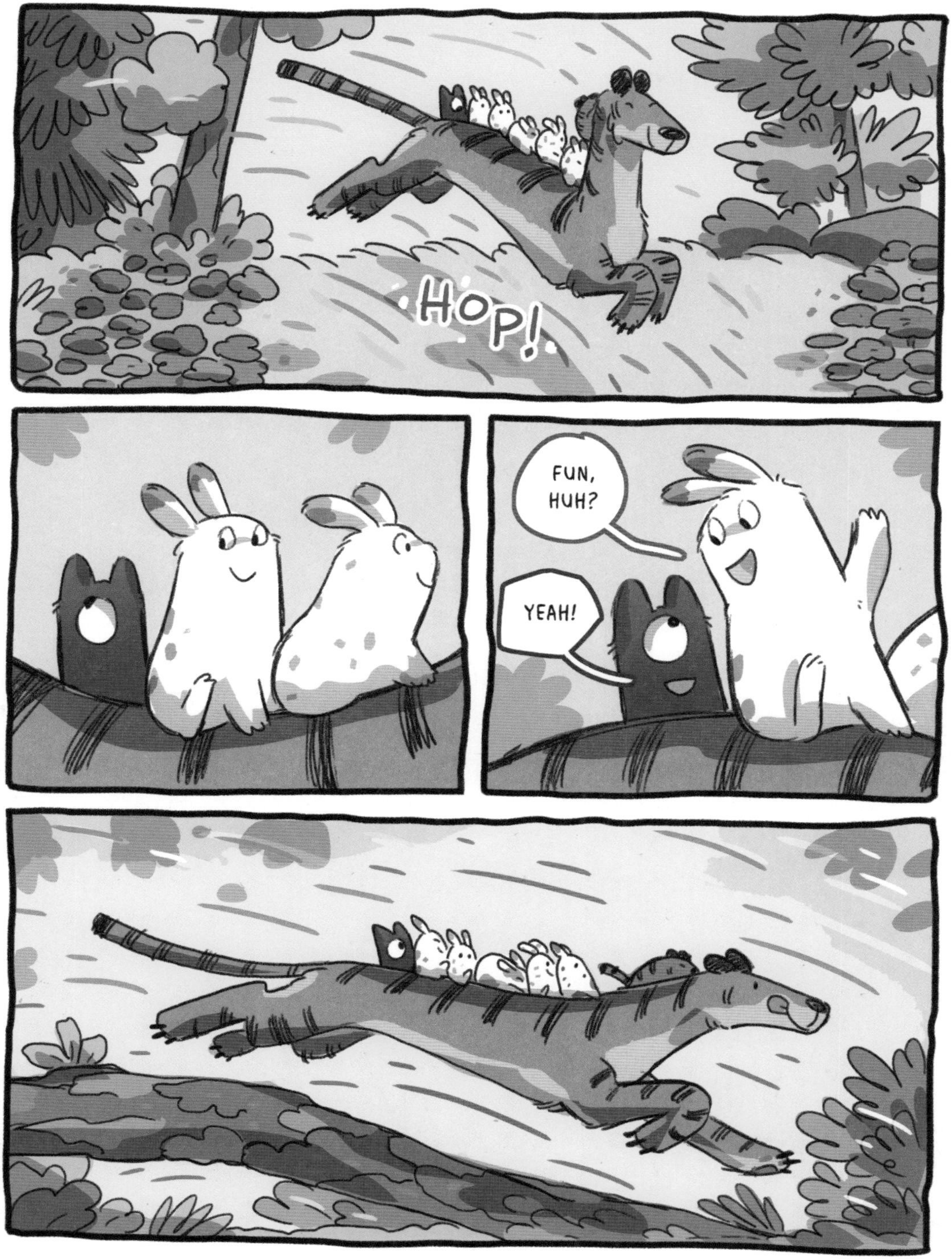
HOP!
FUN, HUH?
YEAH!

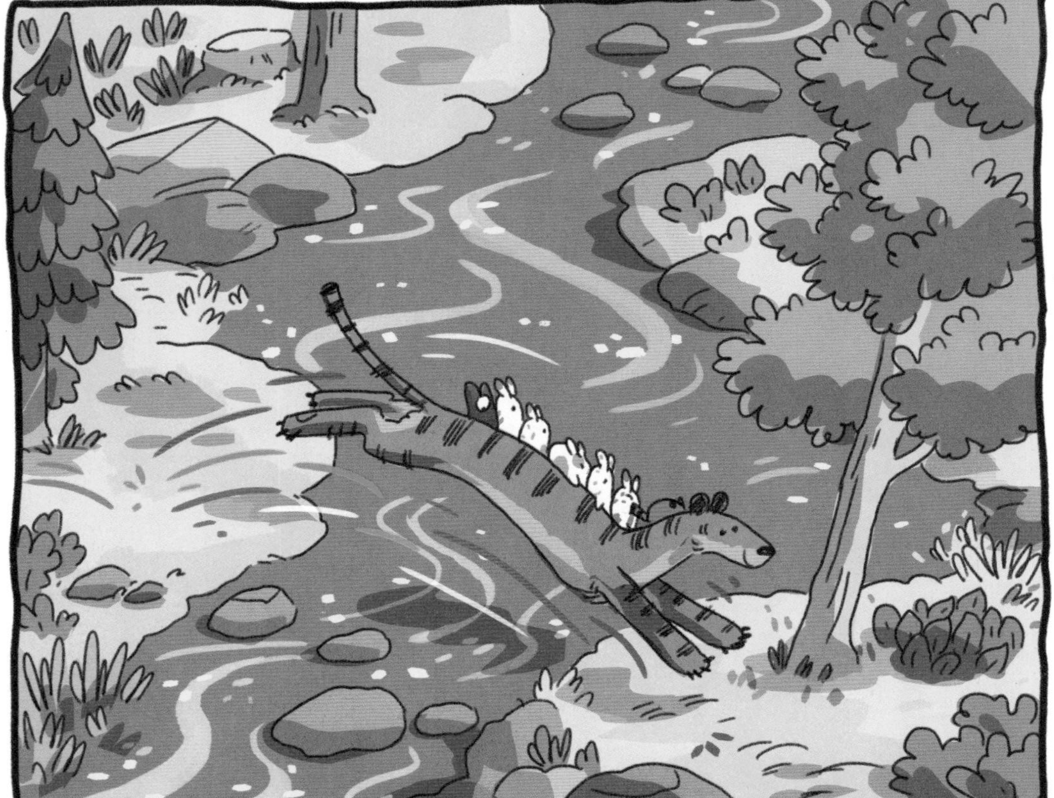

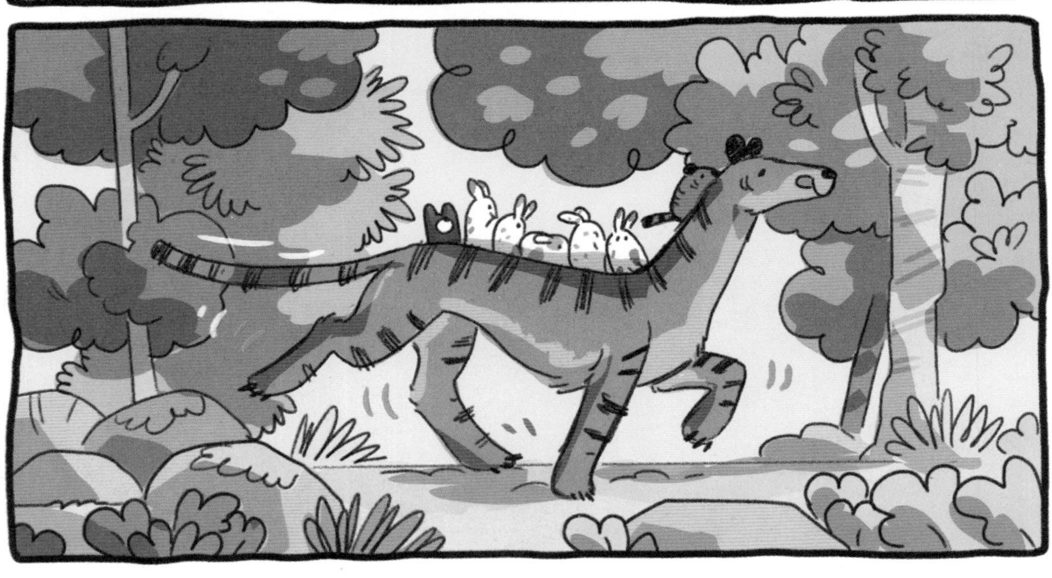

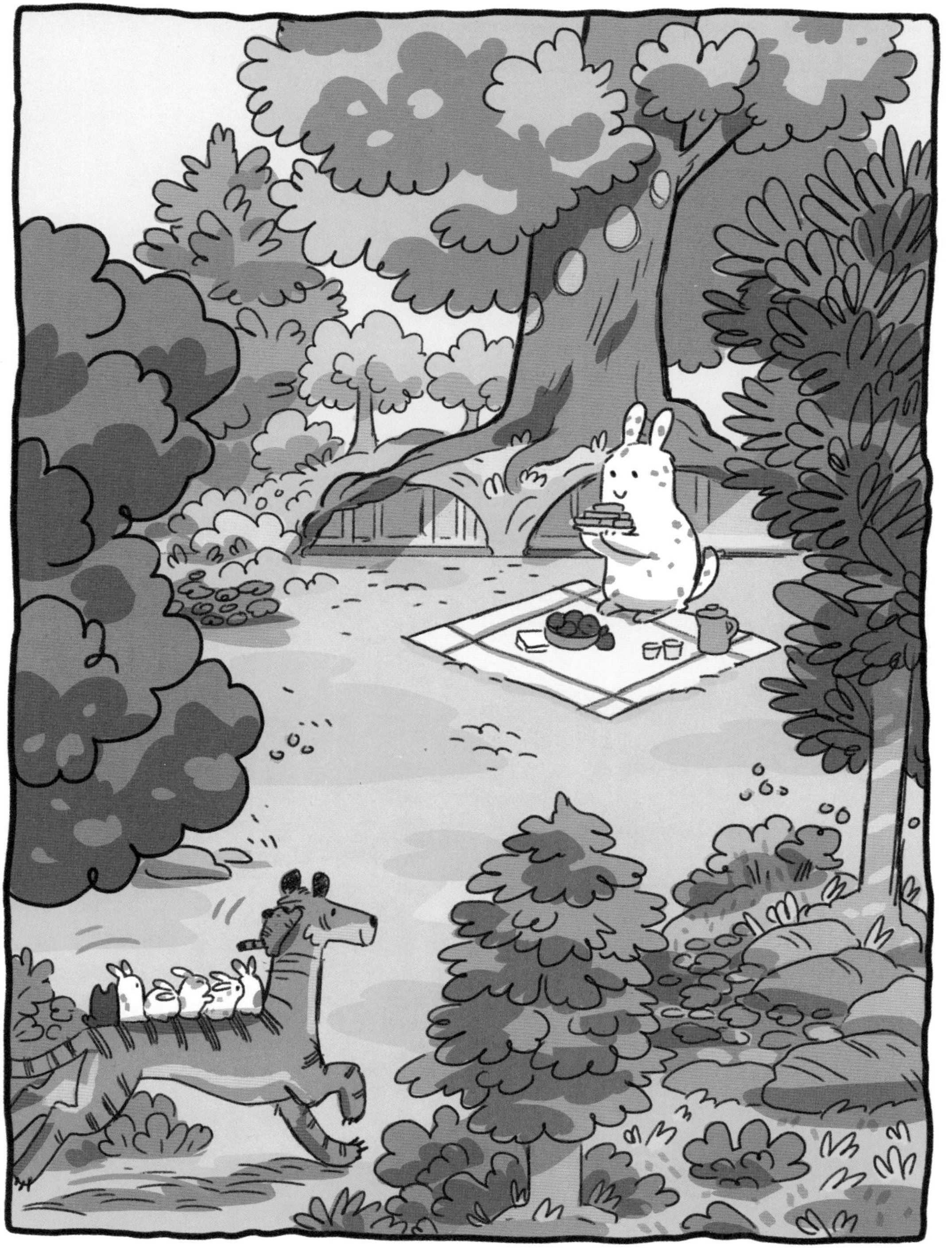

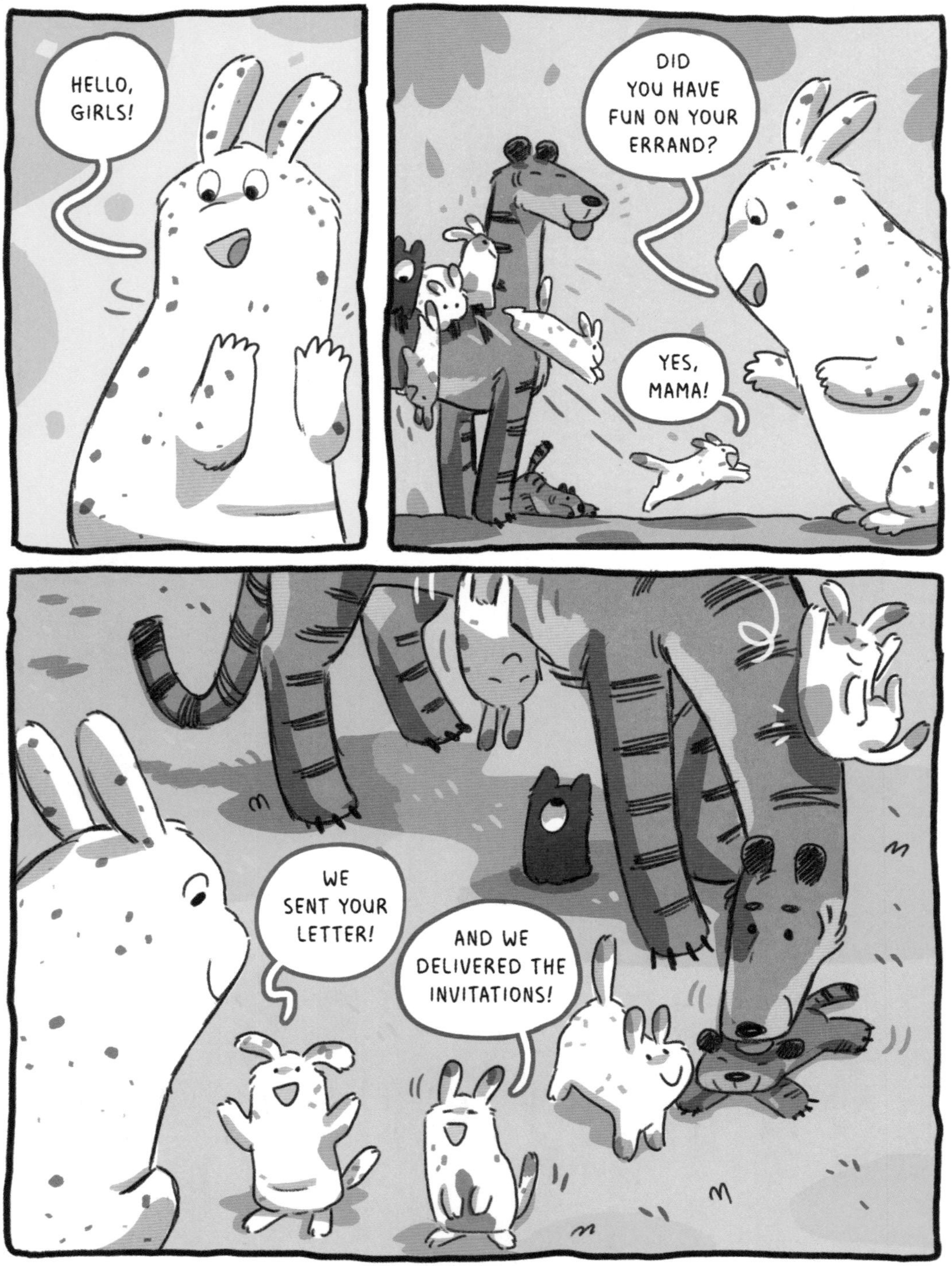
HELLO, GIRLS!
DID YOU HAVE FUN ON YOUR ERRAND?
YES, MAMA!
WE SENT YOUR LETTER!
AND WE DELIVERED THE INVITATIONS!

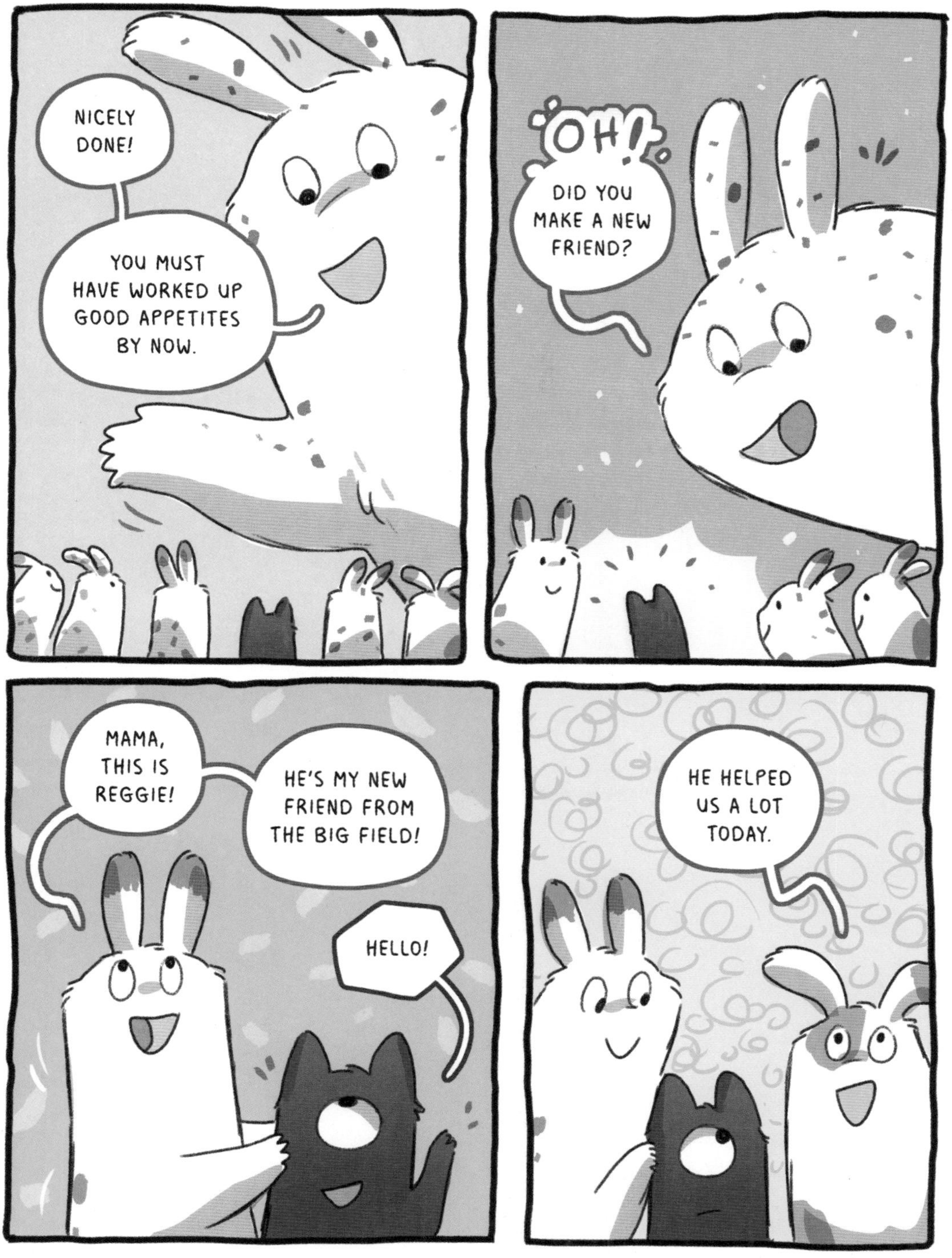
NICELY DONE!
YOU MUST HAVE WORKED UP GOOD APPETITES BY NOW.
OH!
DID YOU MAKE A NEW FRIEND?
MAMA, THIS IS REGGIE!
HE'S MY NEW FRIEND FROM THE BIG FIELD!
HELLO!
HE HELPED US A LOT TODAY.

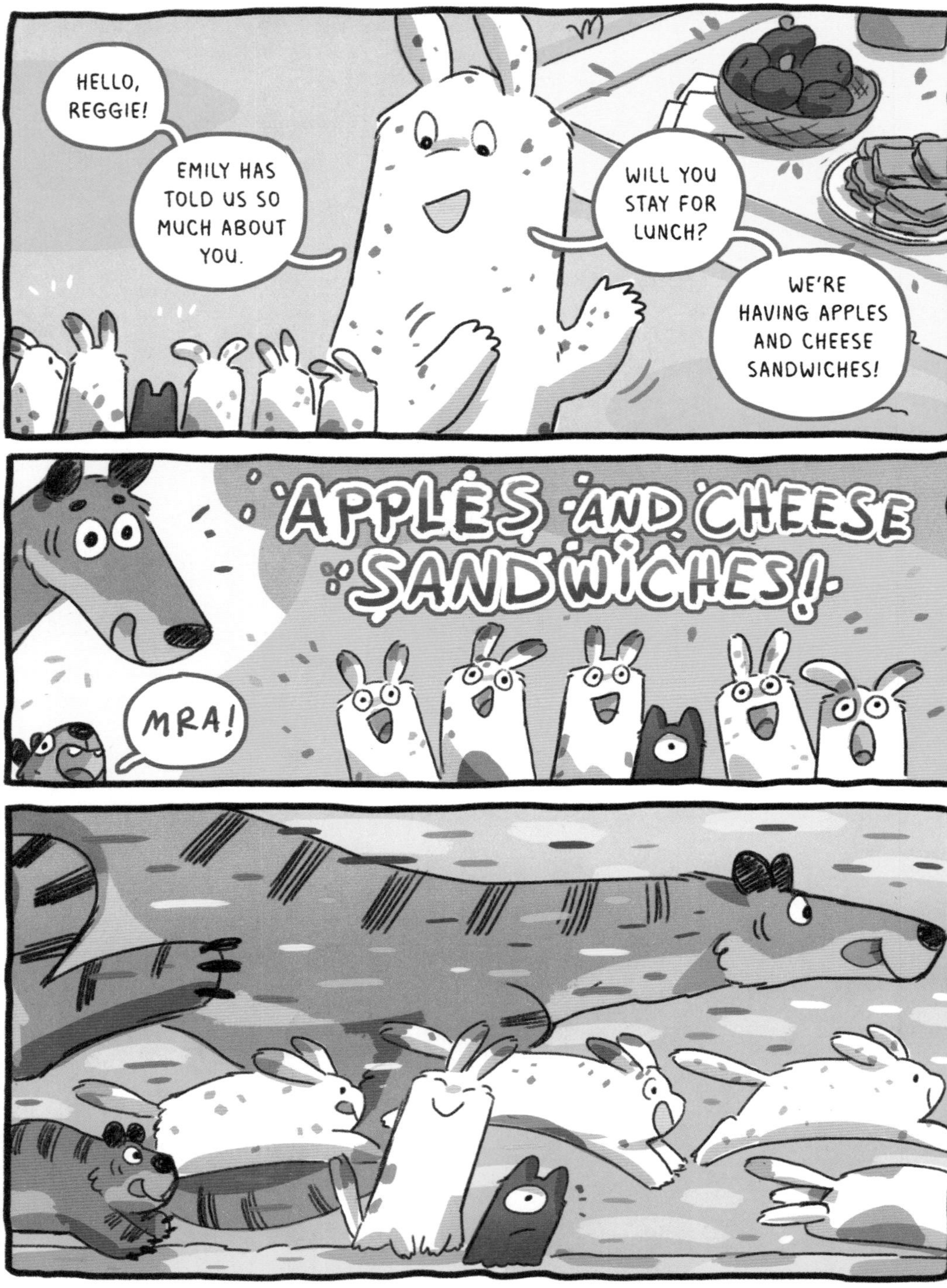
HELLO, REGGIE!
EMILY HAS TOLD US SO MUCH ABOUT YOU.
WILL YOU STAY FOR LUNCH?
WE'RE HAVING APPLES AND CHEESE SANDWICHES!
APPLES AND CHEESE SANDWICHES!
MRA!

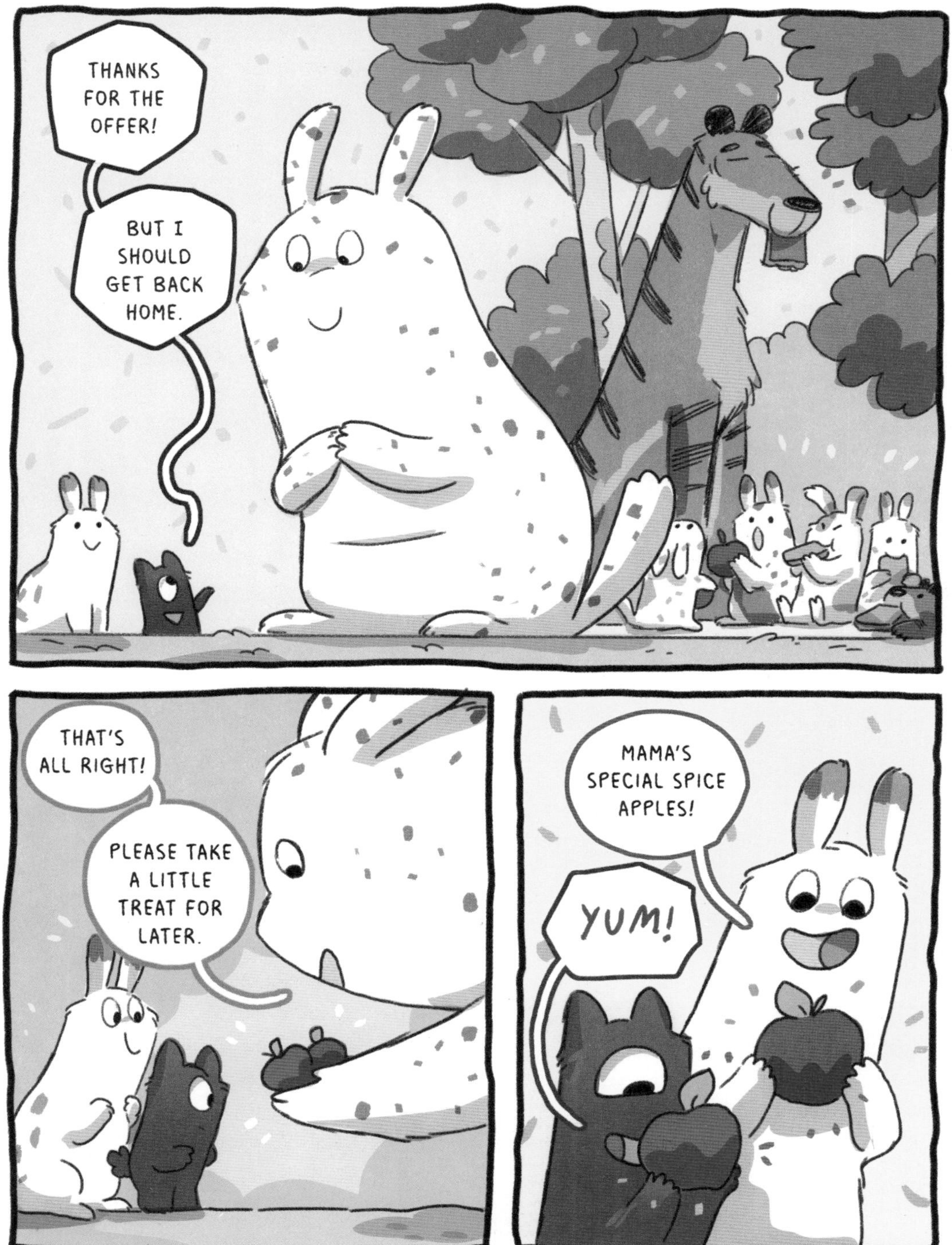
THANKS FOR THE OFFER!
BUT I SHOULD GET BACK HOME.
THAT'S ALL RIGHT!
PLEASE TAKE A LITTLE TREAT FOR LATER.
MAMA'S SPECIAL SPICE APPLES!
YUM!

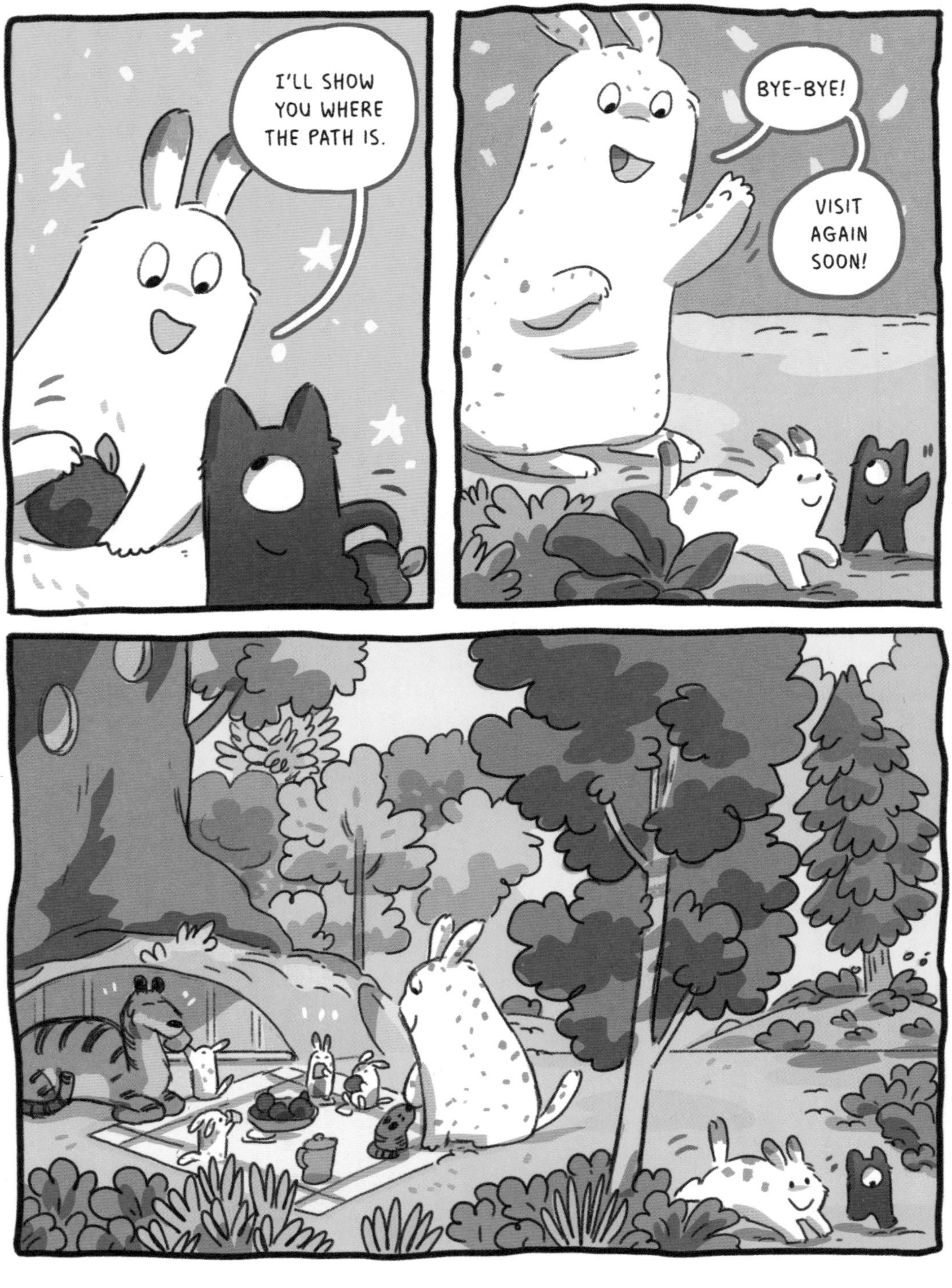
I'LL SHOW YOU WHERE THE PATH IS.
BYE-BYE!
VISIT AGAIN SOON!

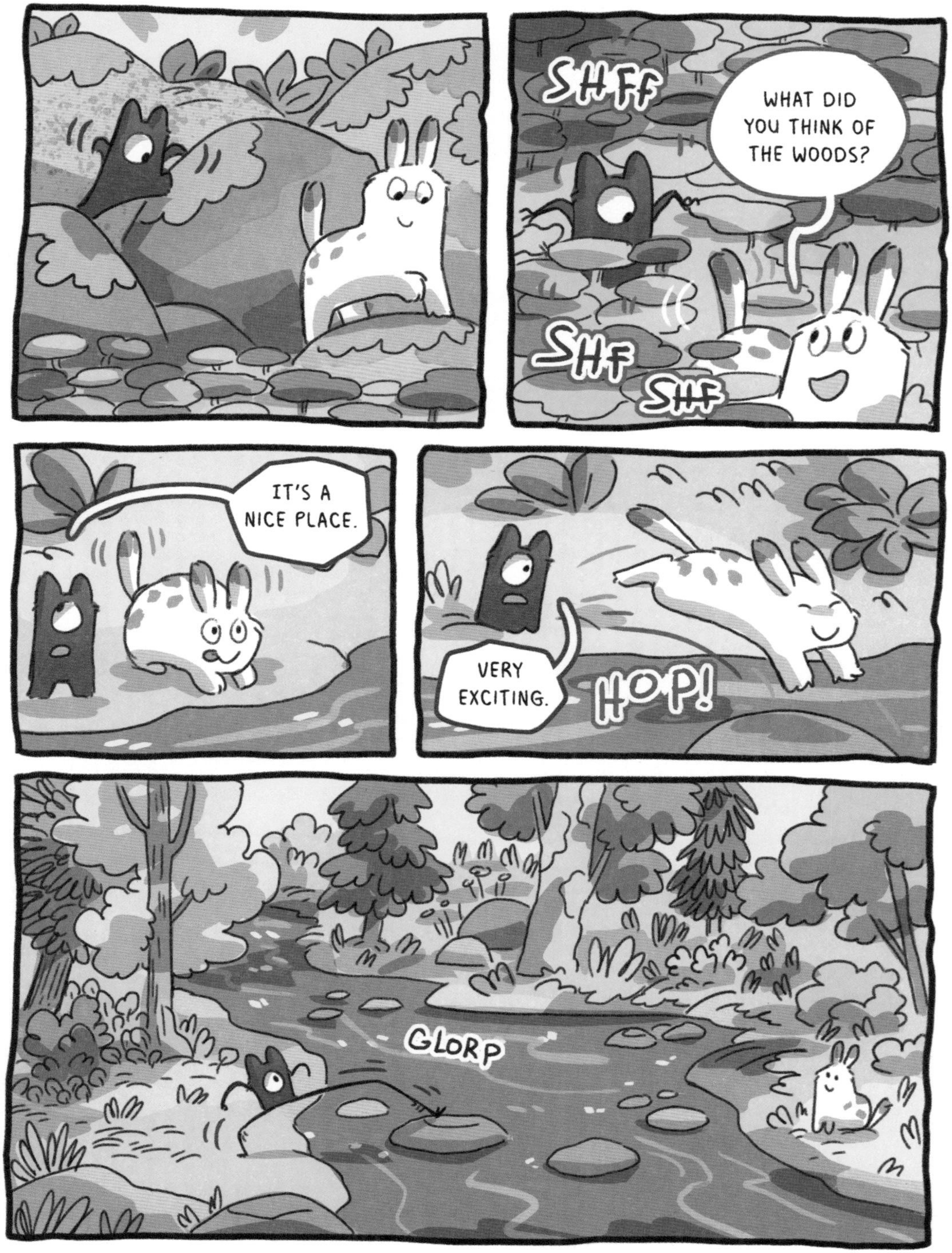
SHFF
WHAT DID YOU THINK OF THE WOODS?
SHF
SHF
IT'S A NICE PLACE.
VERY EXCITING.
HOP!
GLORP

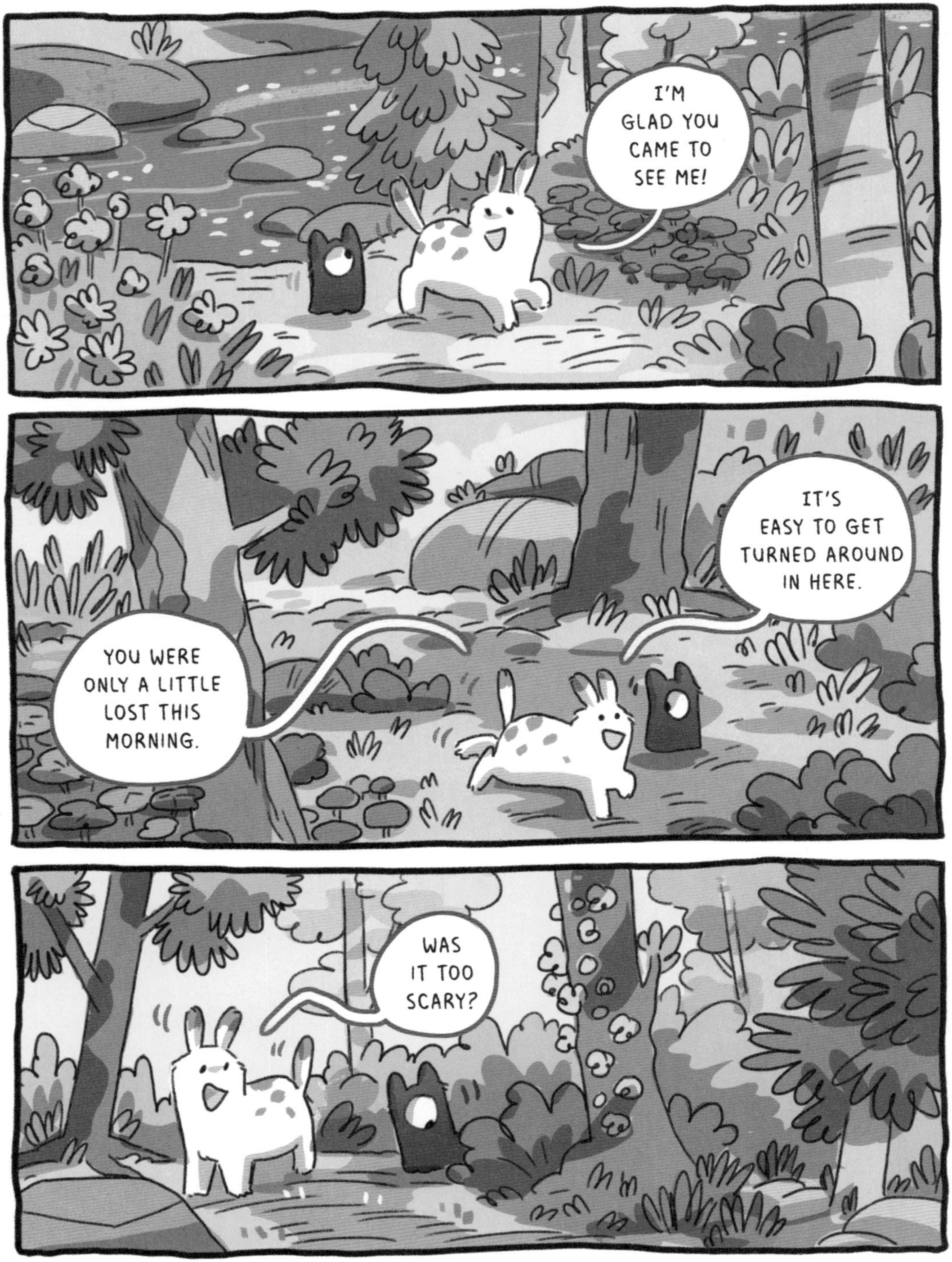
I'M GLAD YOU CAME TO SEE ME!
YOU WERE ONLY A LITTLE LOST THIS MORNING.
IT'S EASY TO GET TURNED AROUND IN HERE.
WAS IT TOO SCARY?

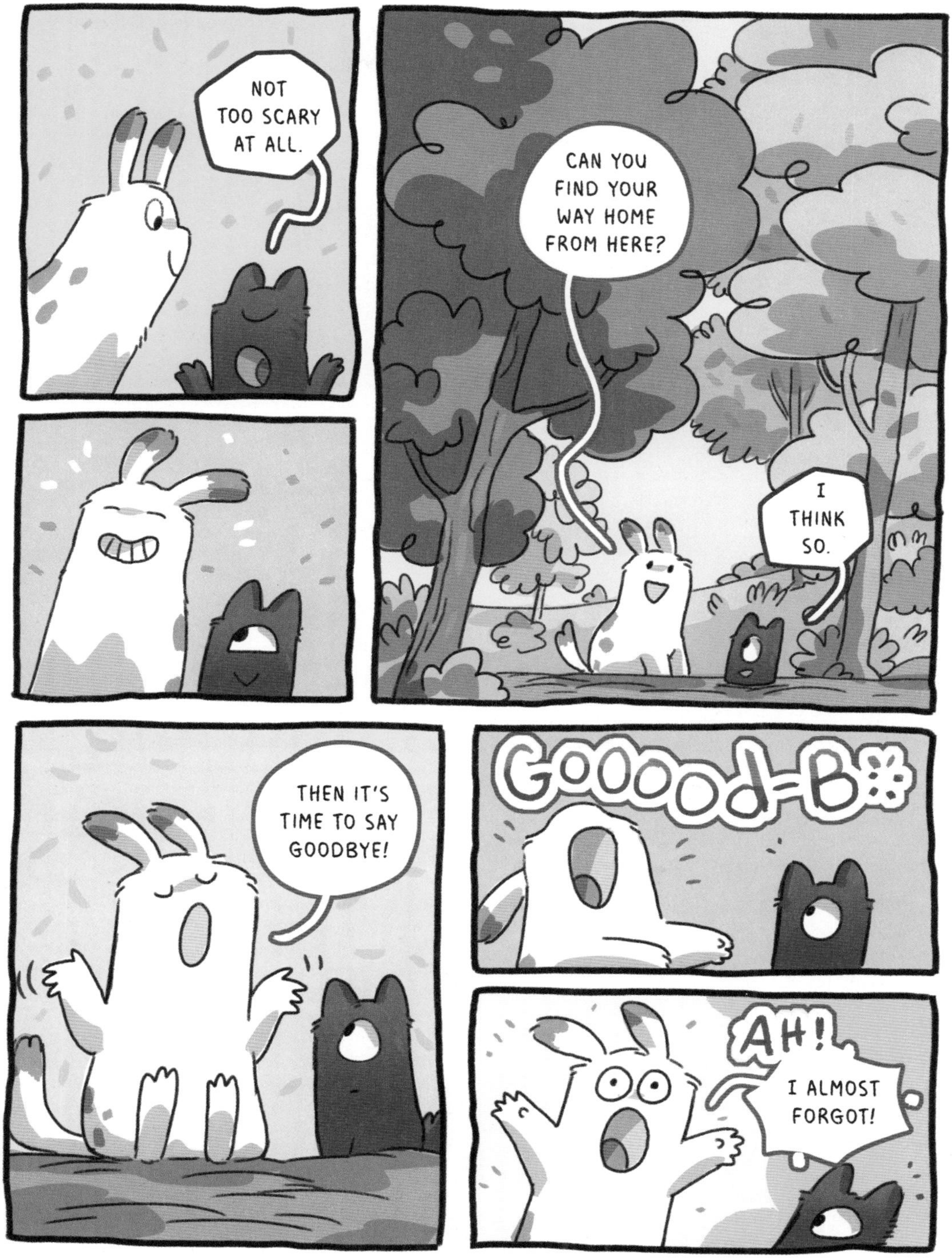
NOT TOO SCARY AT ALL.
CAN YOU FIND YOUR WAY HOME FROM HERE?
I THINK SO.
THEN IT'S TIME TO SAY GOODBYE!
GOOOOOD-B
AH!
I ALMOST FORGOT!

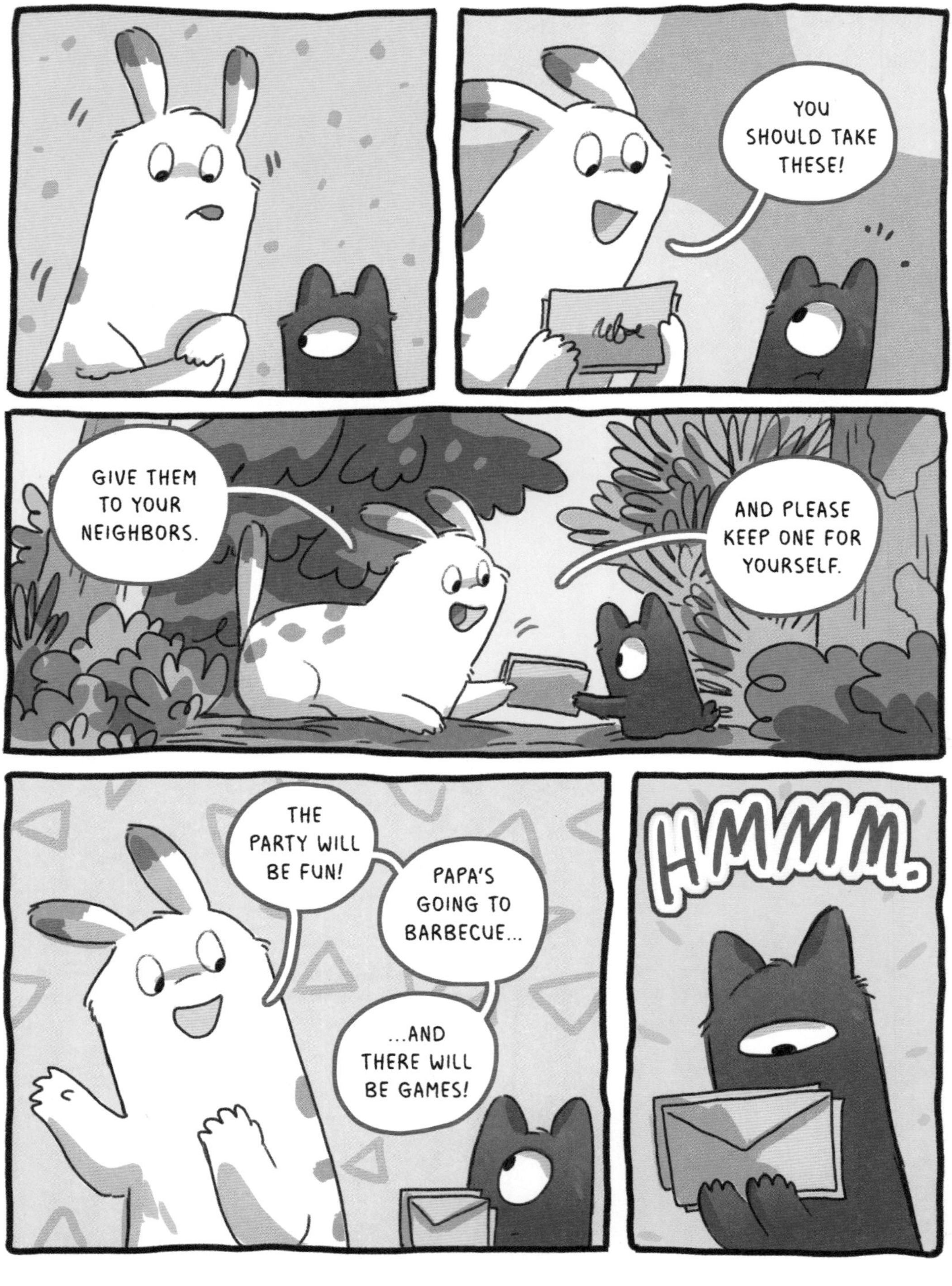
YOU SHOULD TAKE THESE!
GIVE THEM TO YOUR NEIGHBORS.
AND PLEASE KEEP ONE FOR YOURSELF.
THE PARTY WILL BE FUN!
PAPA'S GOING TO BARBECUE...
...AND THERE WILL BE GAMES!
HMMM.

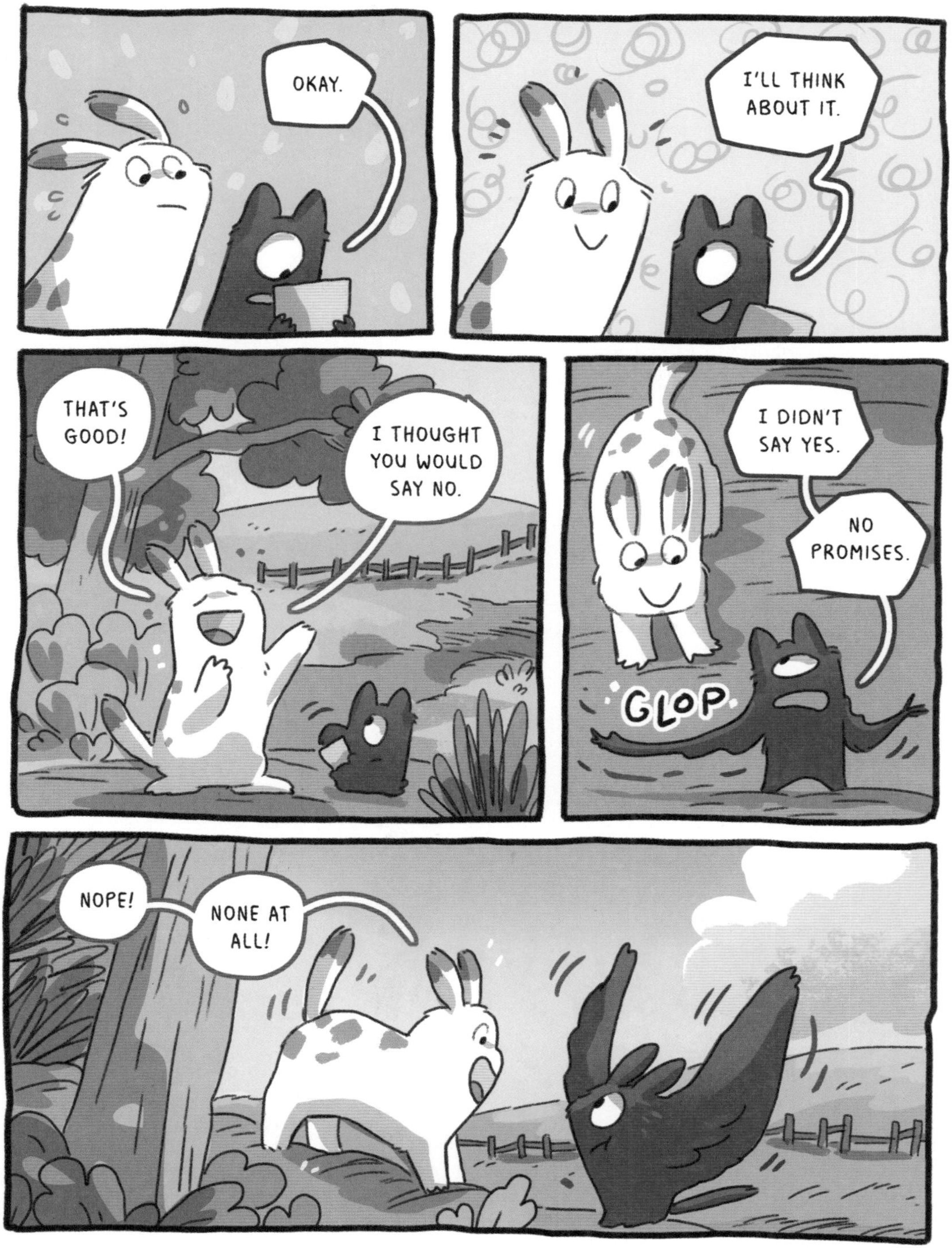
OKAY.
I'LL THINK ABOUT IT.
THAT'S GOOD!
I THOUGHT YOU WOULD SAY NO.
I DIDN'T SAY YES.
NO PROMISES.
GLOP
NOPE!
NONE AT ALL!

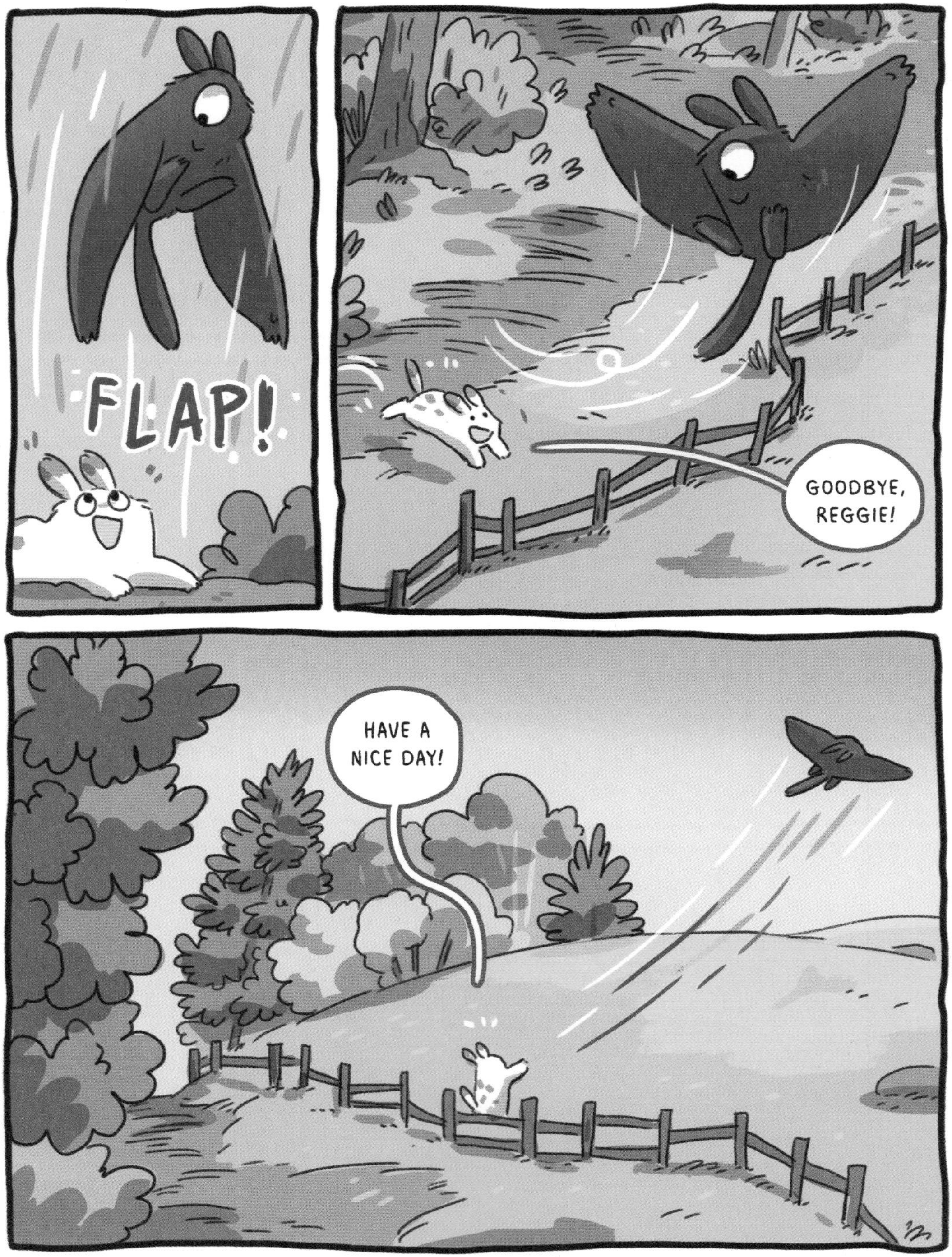
FLAP!
GOODBYE, REGGIE!
HAVE A NICE DAY!

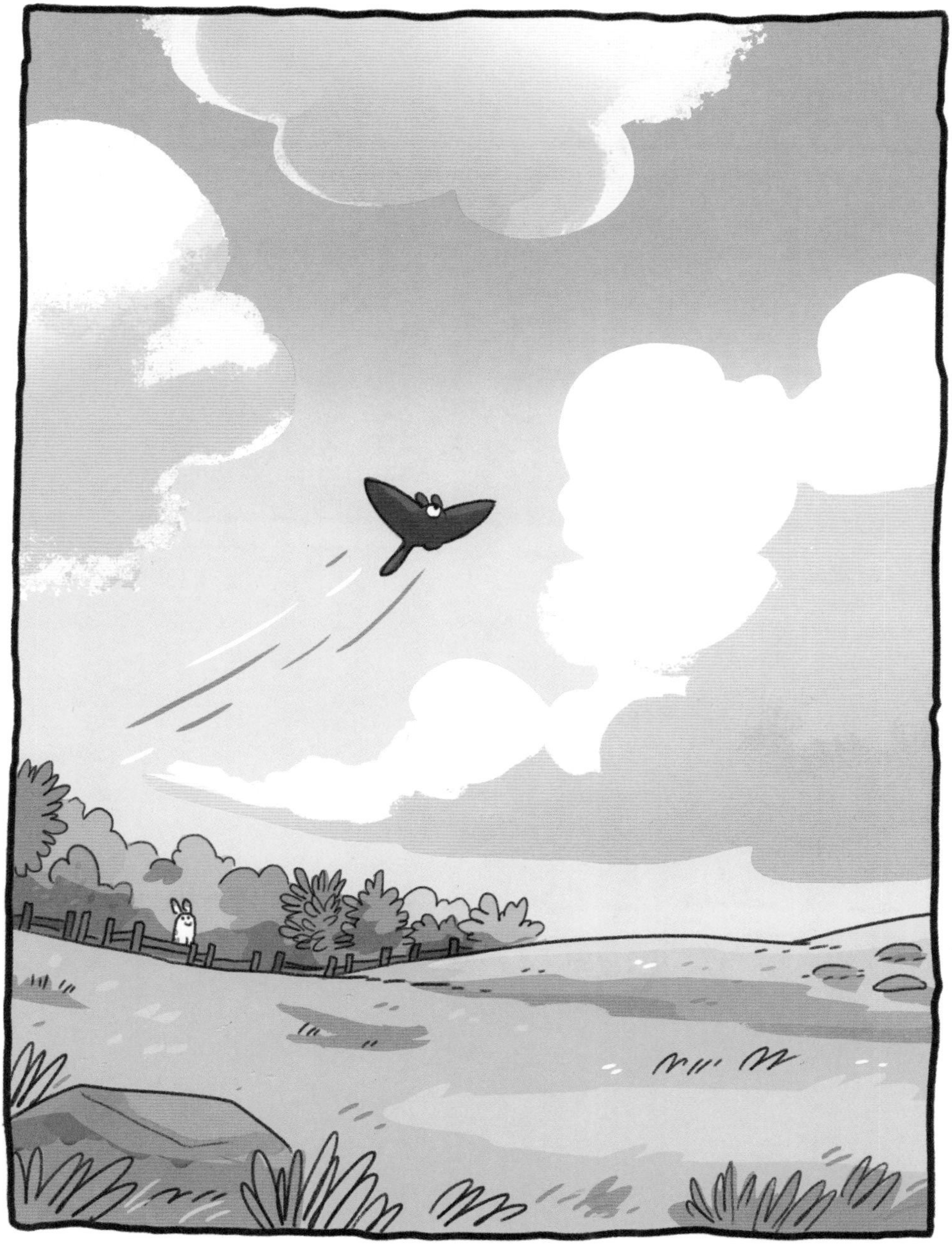

CHAPTER 4

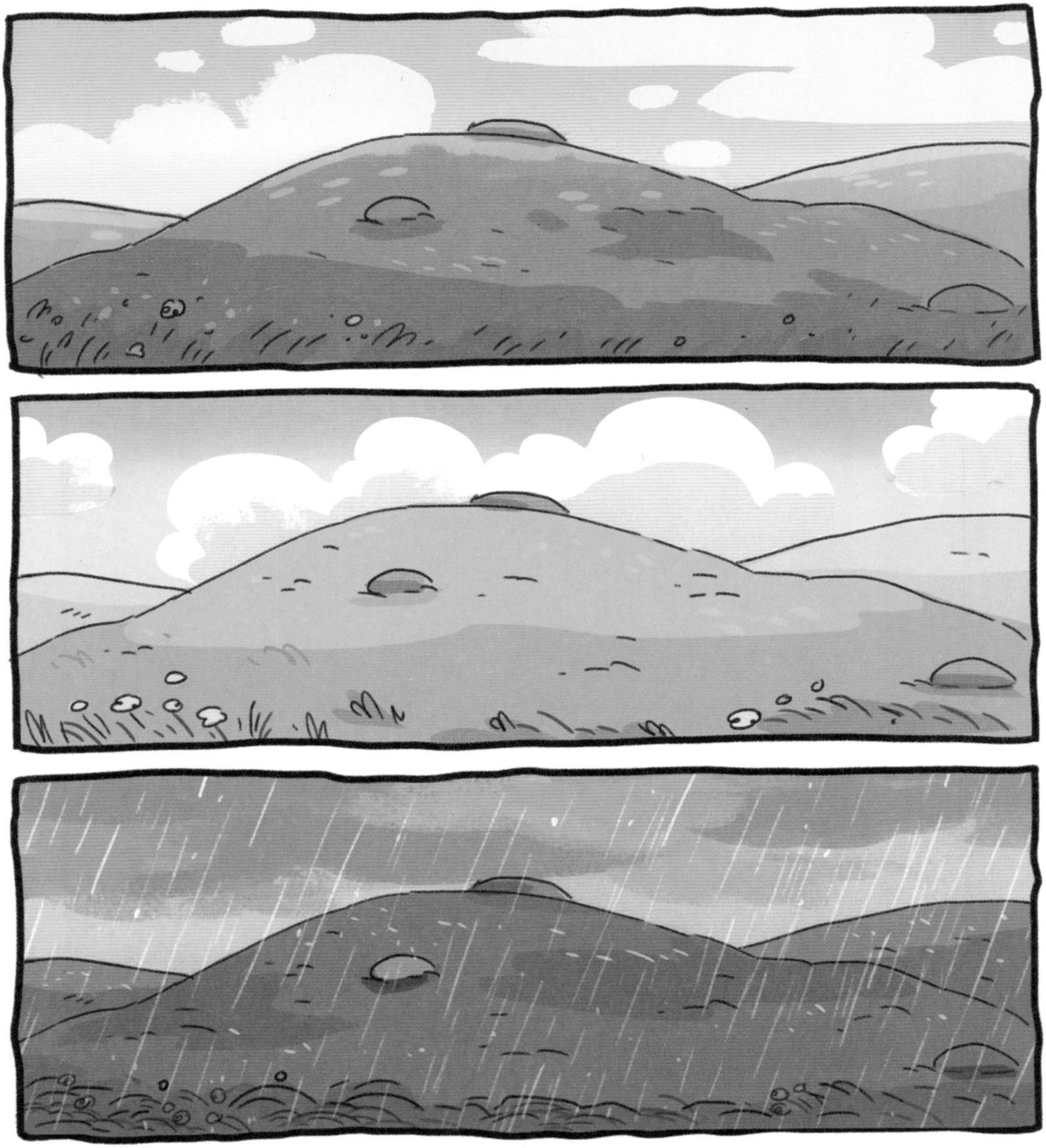

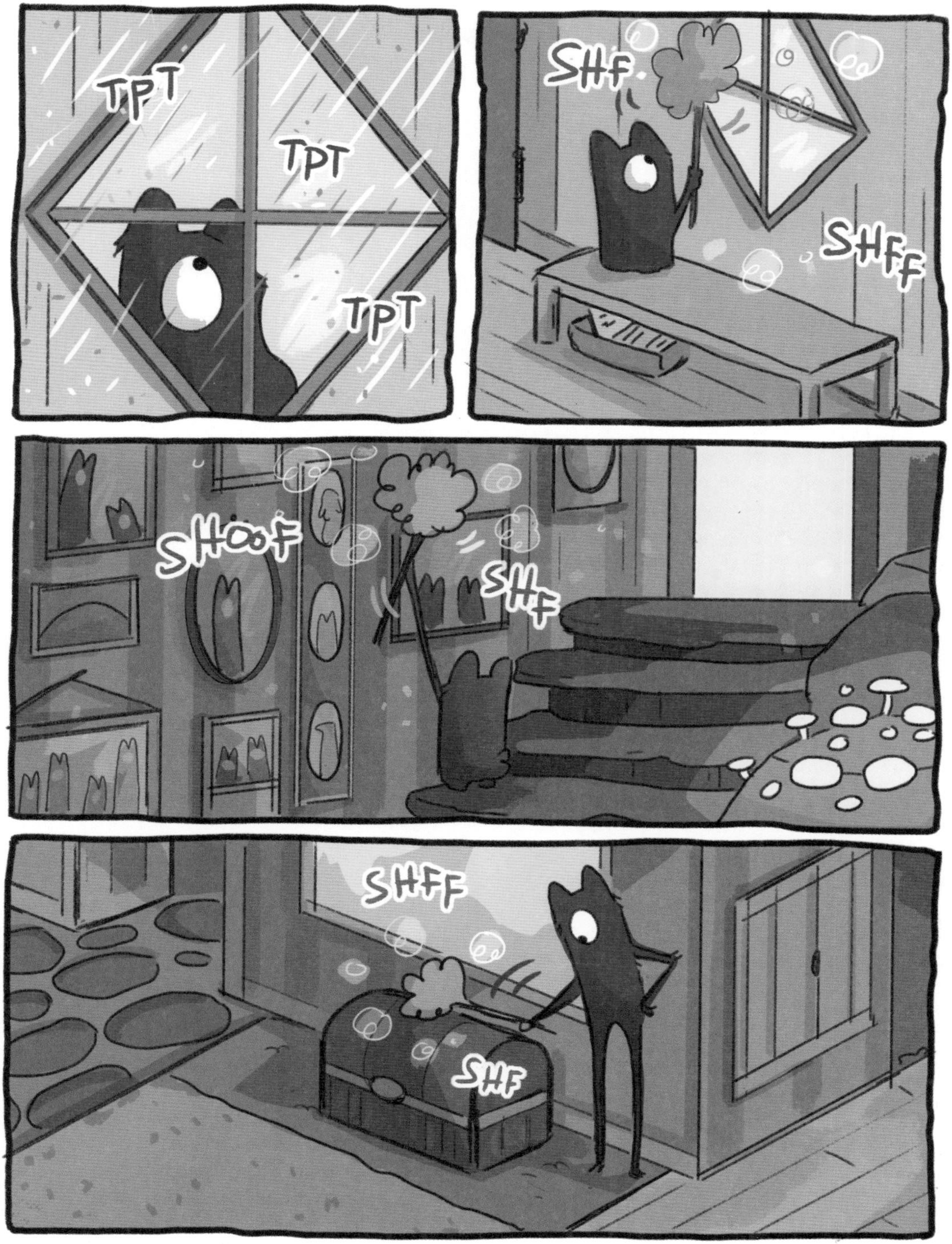
TPT
TPT
TPT
SHF
SHFF
SHOOF
SHF
SHFF
SHF

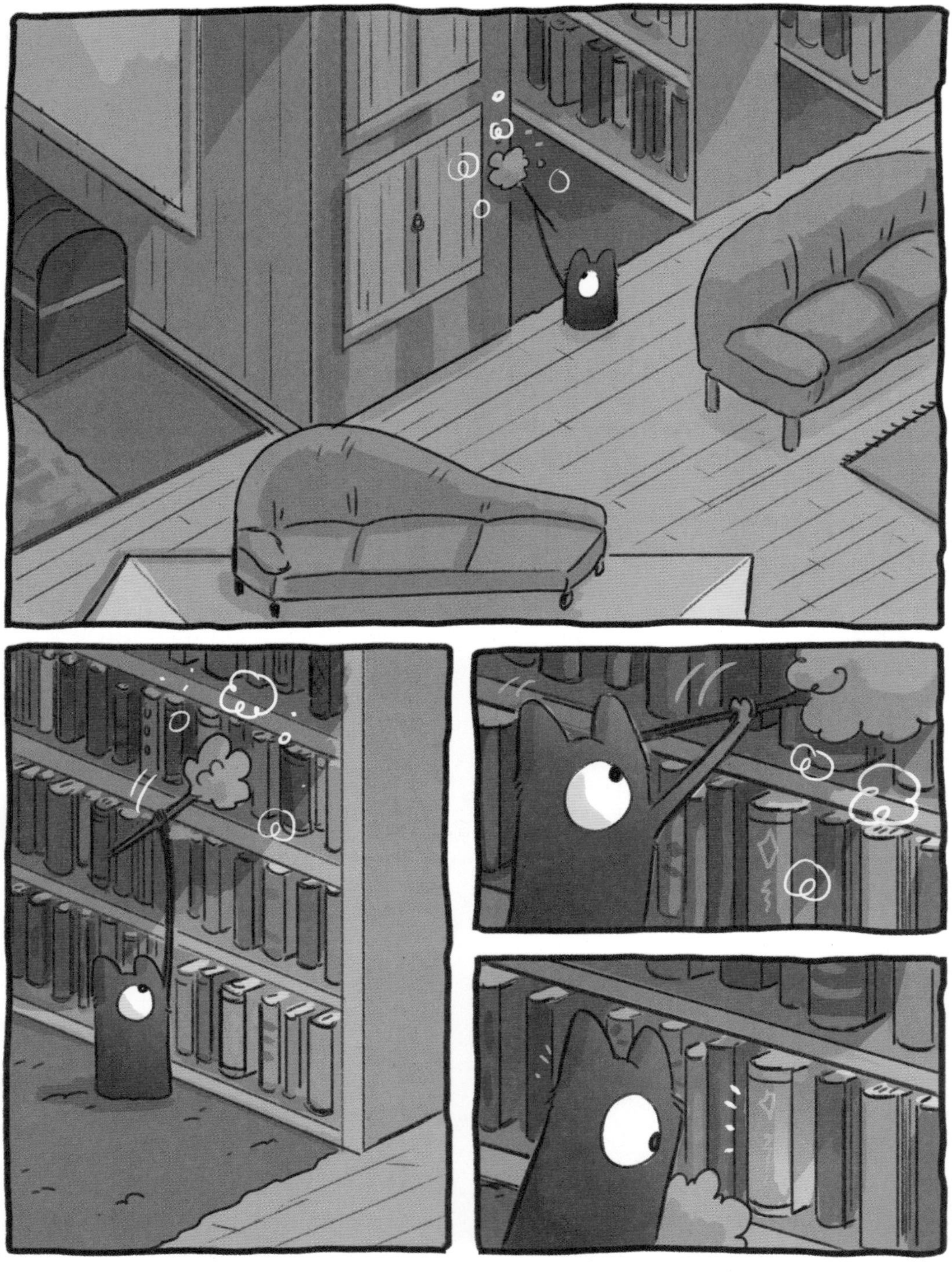

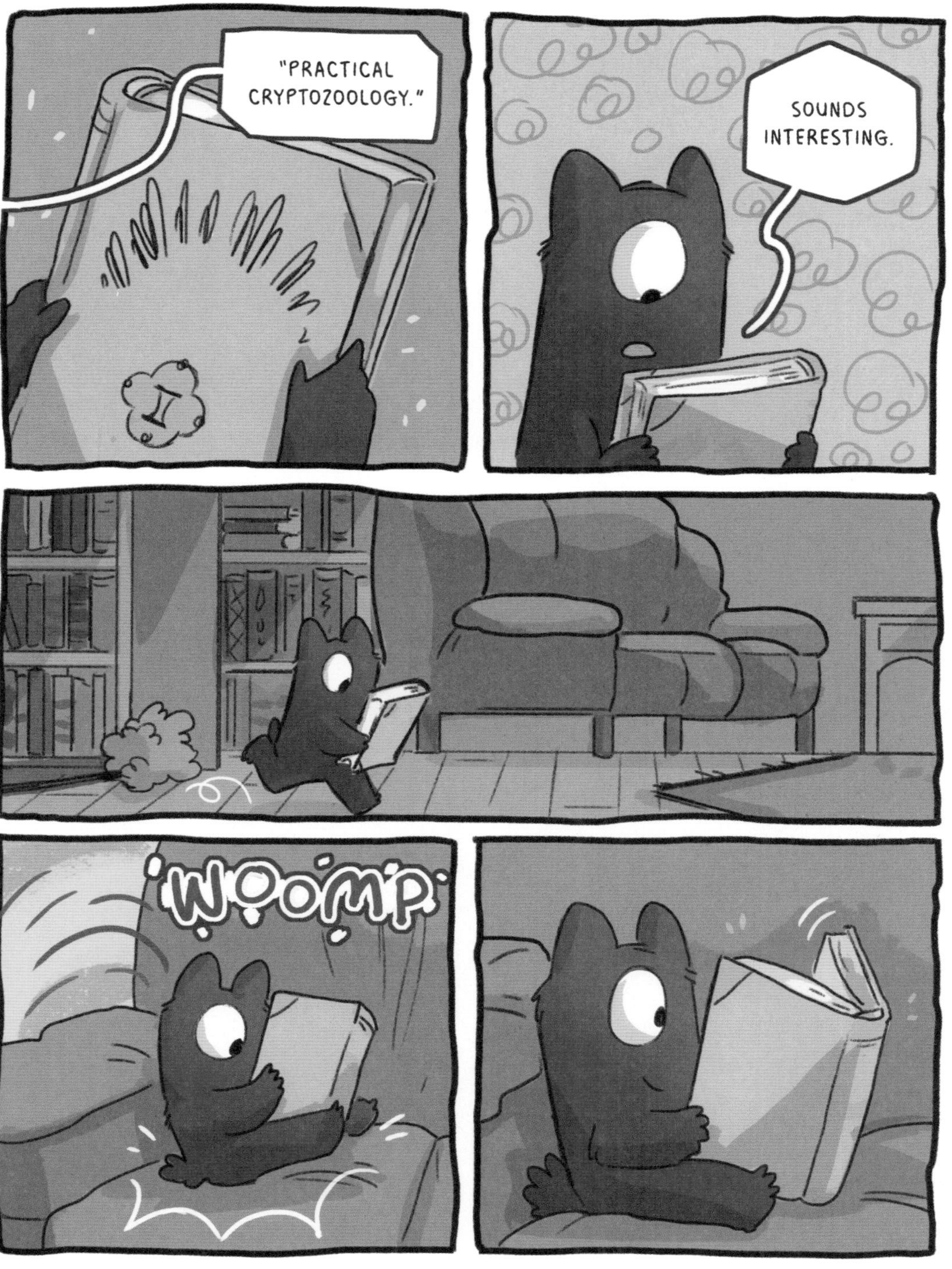
"PRACTICAL CRYPTOZOOLOGY."
SOUNDS INTERESTING.
WOOMP

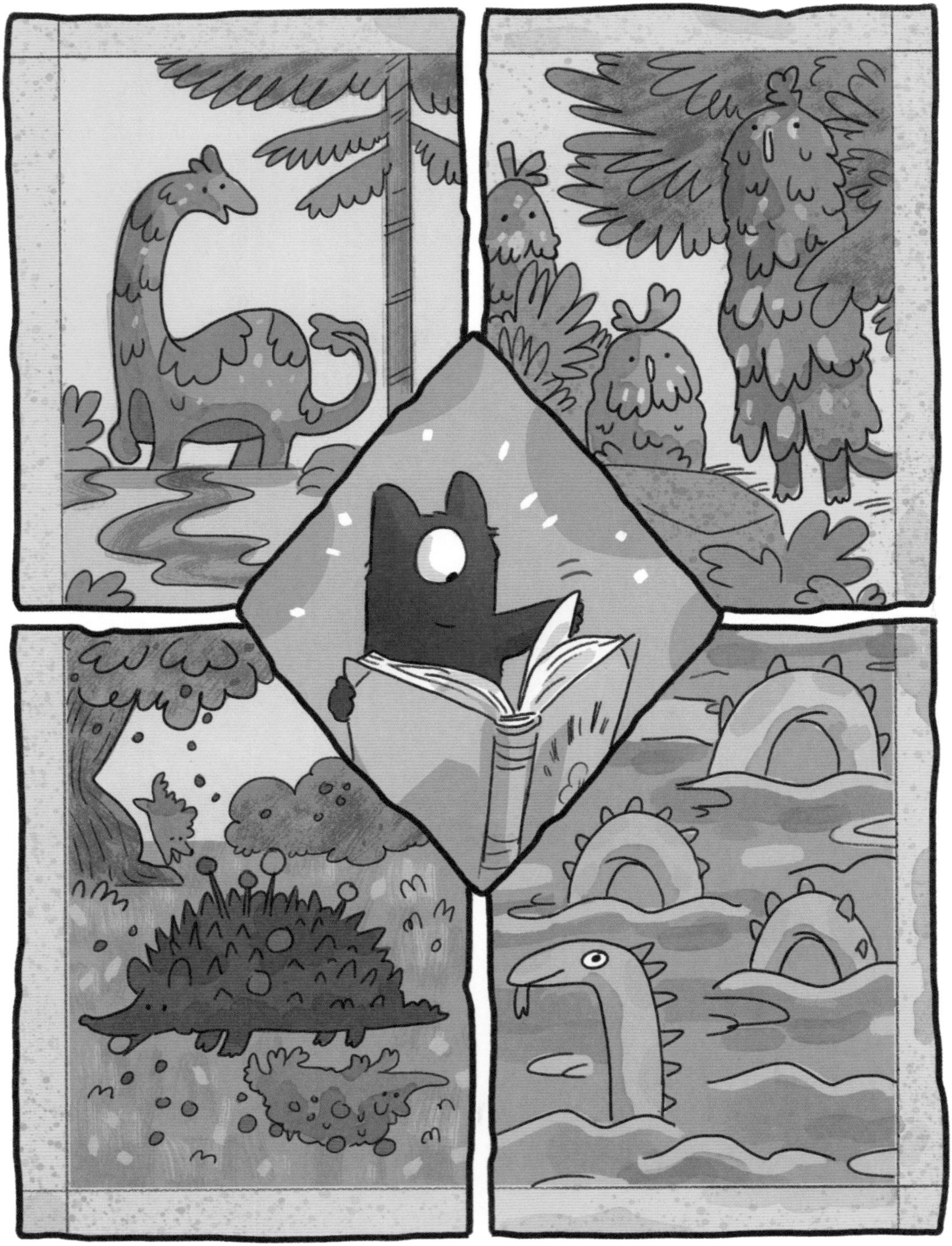

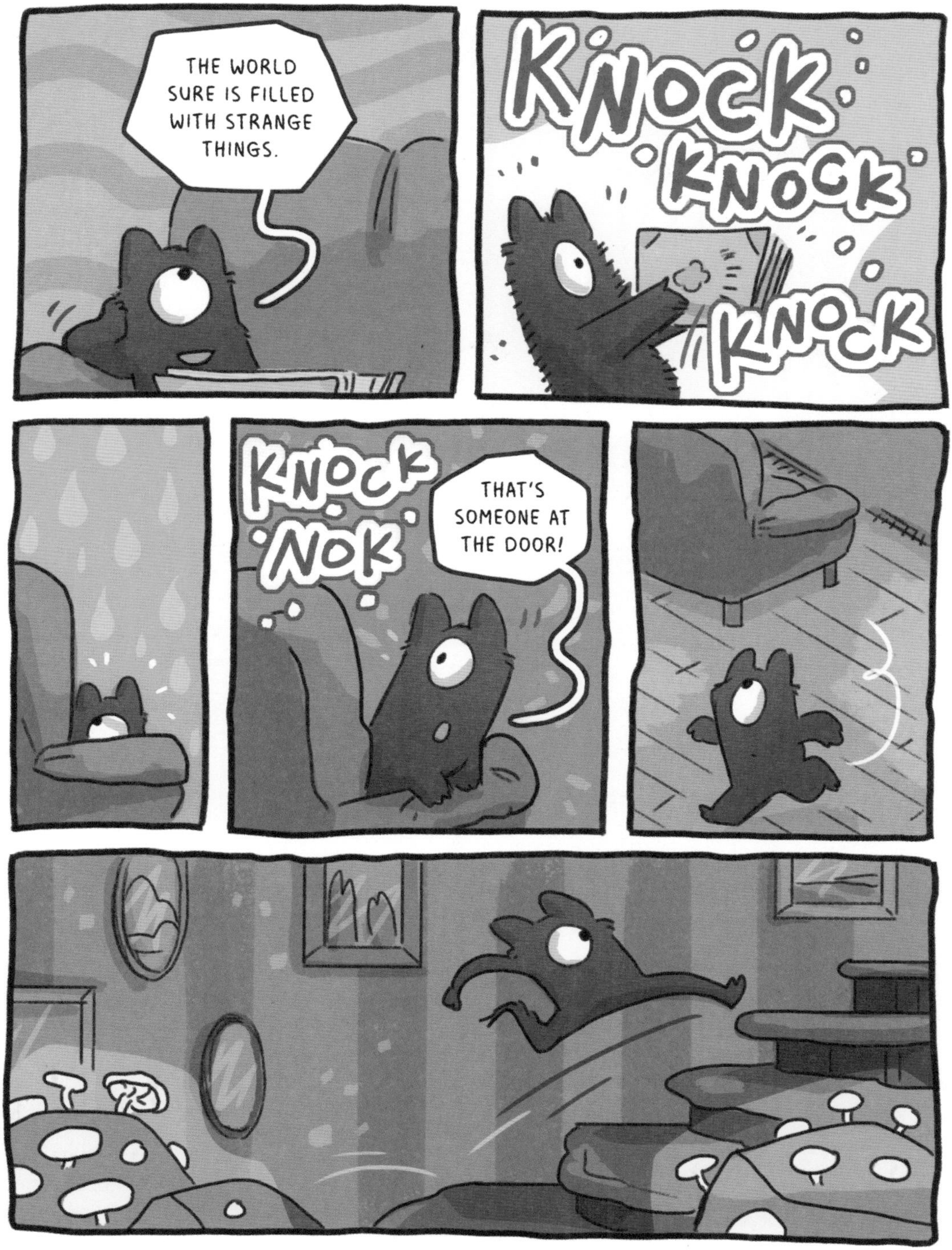
THE WORLD SURE IS FILLED WITH STRANGE THINGS.
KNOCK KNOCK KNOCK
KNOCK NOK
THAT'S SOMEONE AT THE DOOR!

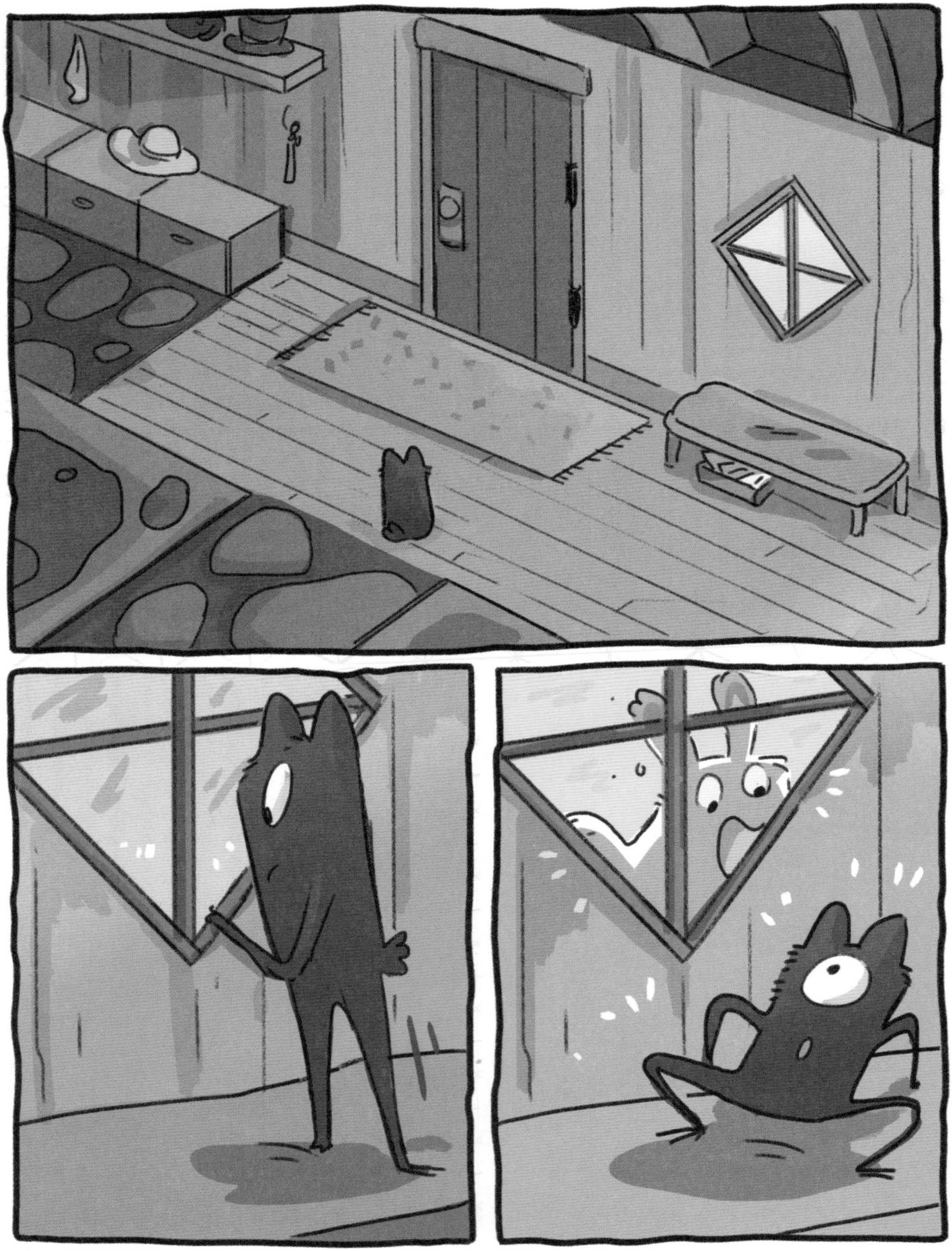

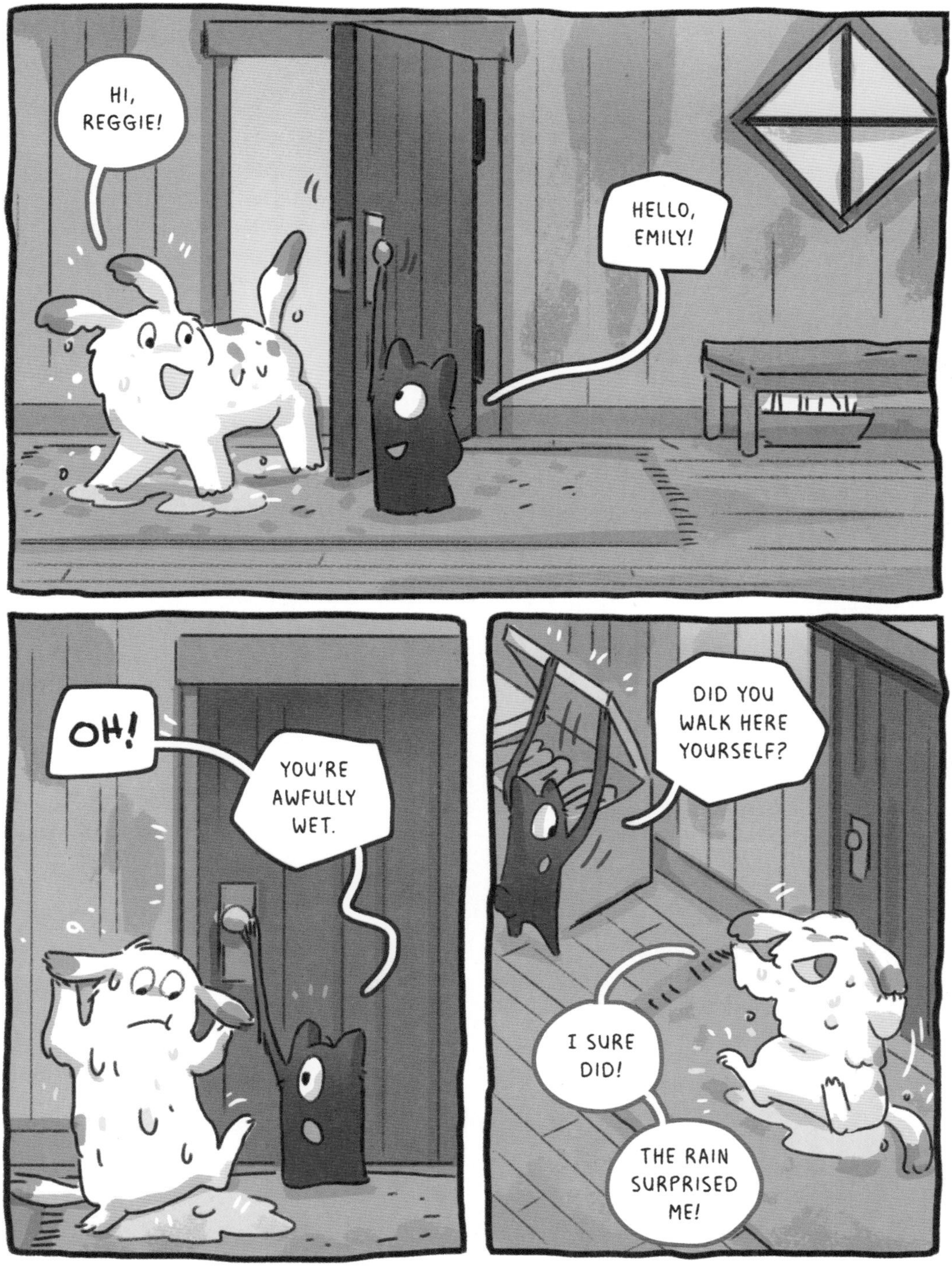
HI, REGGIE!
HELLO, EMILY!
OH!
YOU'RE AWFULLY WET.
DID YOU WALK HERE YOURSELF?
I SURE DID!
THE RAIN SURPRISED ME!

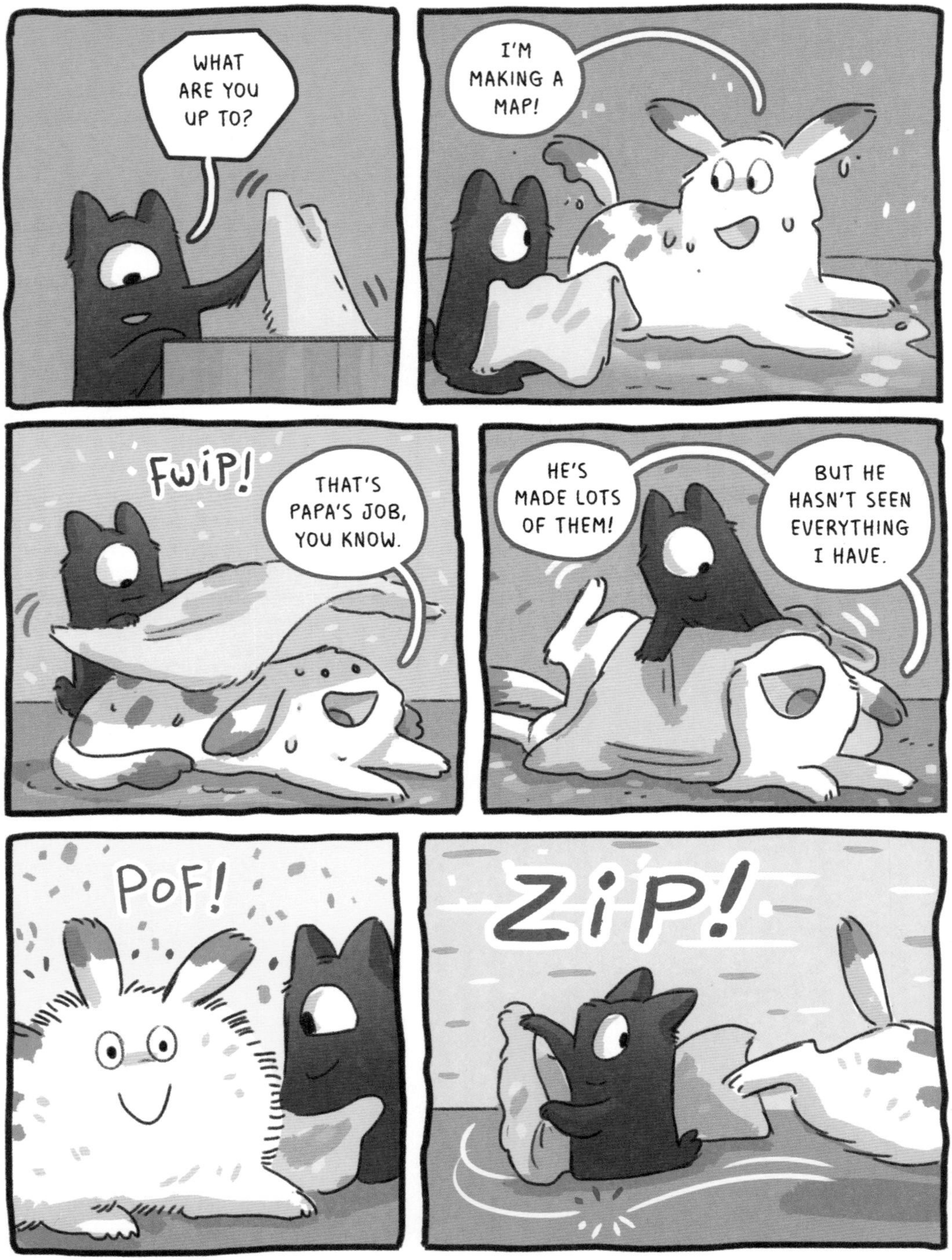
WHAT ARE YOU UP TO?
I'M MAKING A MAP!
FWIP!
THAT'S PAPA'S JOB, YOU KNOW.
HE'S MADE LOTS OF THEM!
BUT HE HASN'T SEEN EVERYTHING I HAVE.
POF!
ZIP!

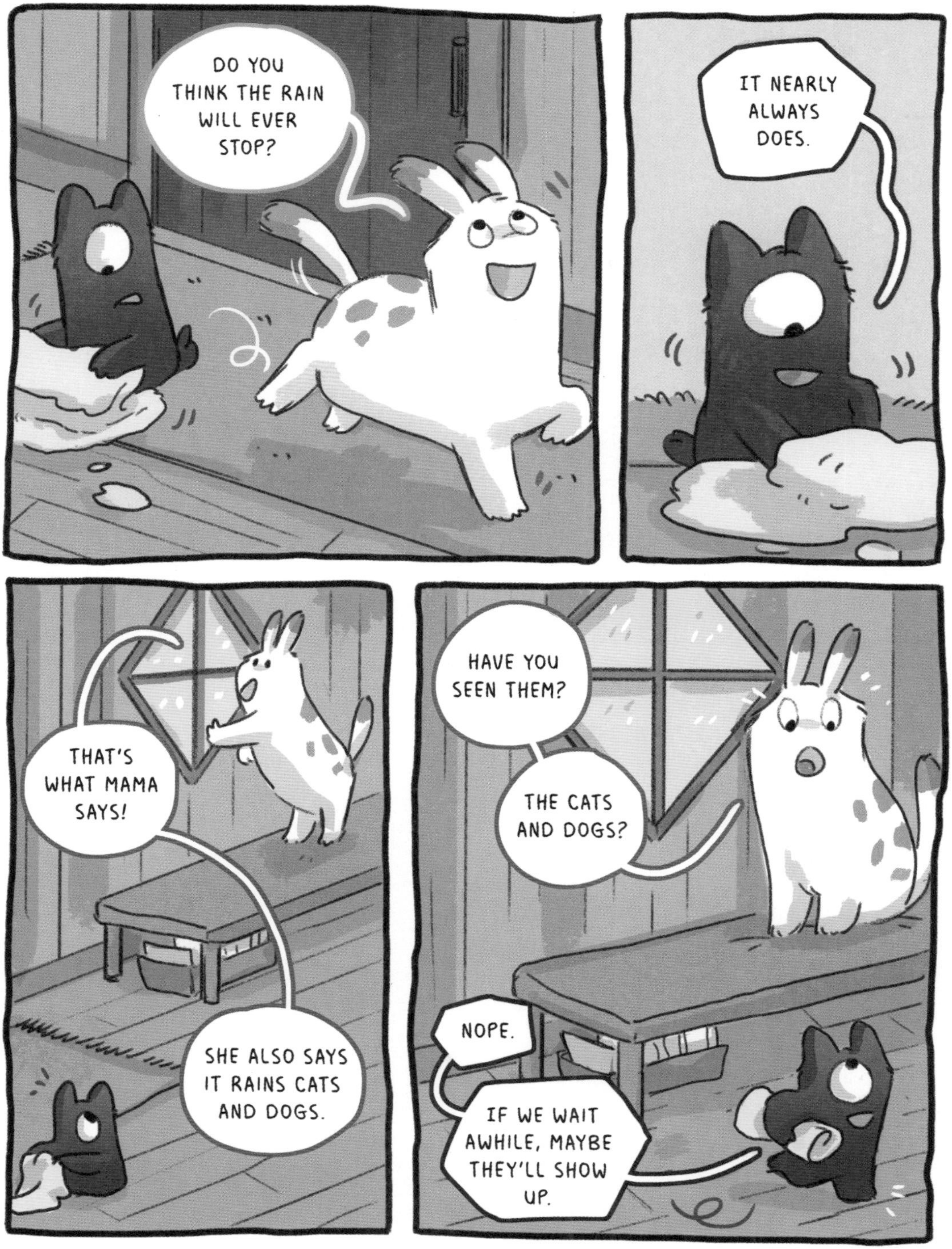
DO YOU THINK THE RAIN WILL EVER STOP?
IT NEARLY ALWAYS DOES.
THAT'S WHAT MAMA SAYS!
SHE ALSO SAYS IT RAINS CATS AND DOGS.
HAVE YOU SEEN THEM?
THE CATS AND DOGS?
NOPE.
IF WE WAIT AWHILE, MAYBE THEY'LL SHOW UP.

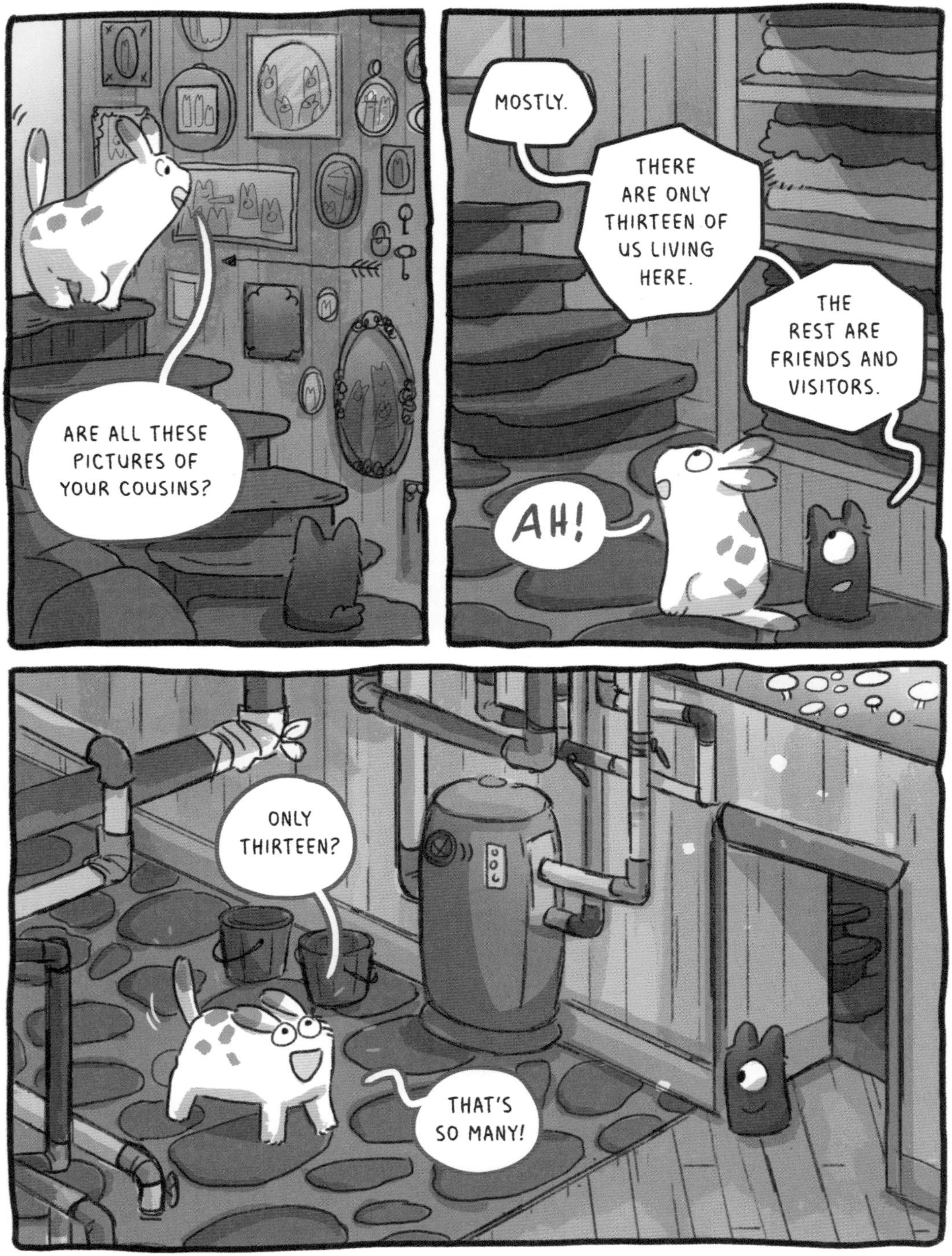
ARE ALL THESE PICTURES OF YOUR COUSINS?
MOSTLY.
THERE ARE ONLY THIRTEEN OF US LIVING HERE.
THE REST ARE FRIENDS AND VISITORS.
AH!
ONLY THIRTEEN?
THAT'S SO MANY!

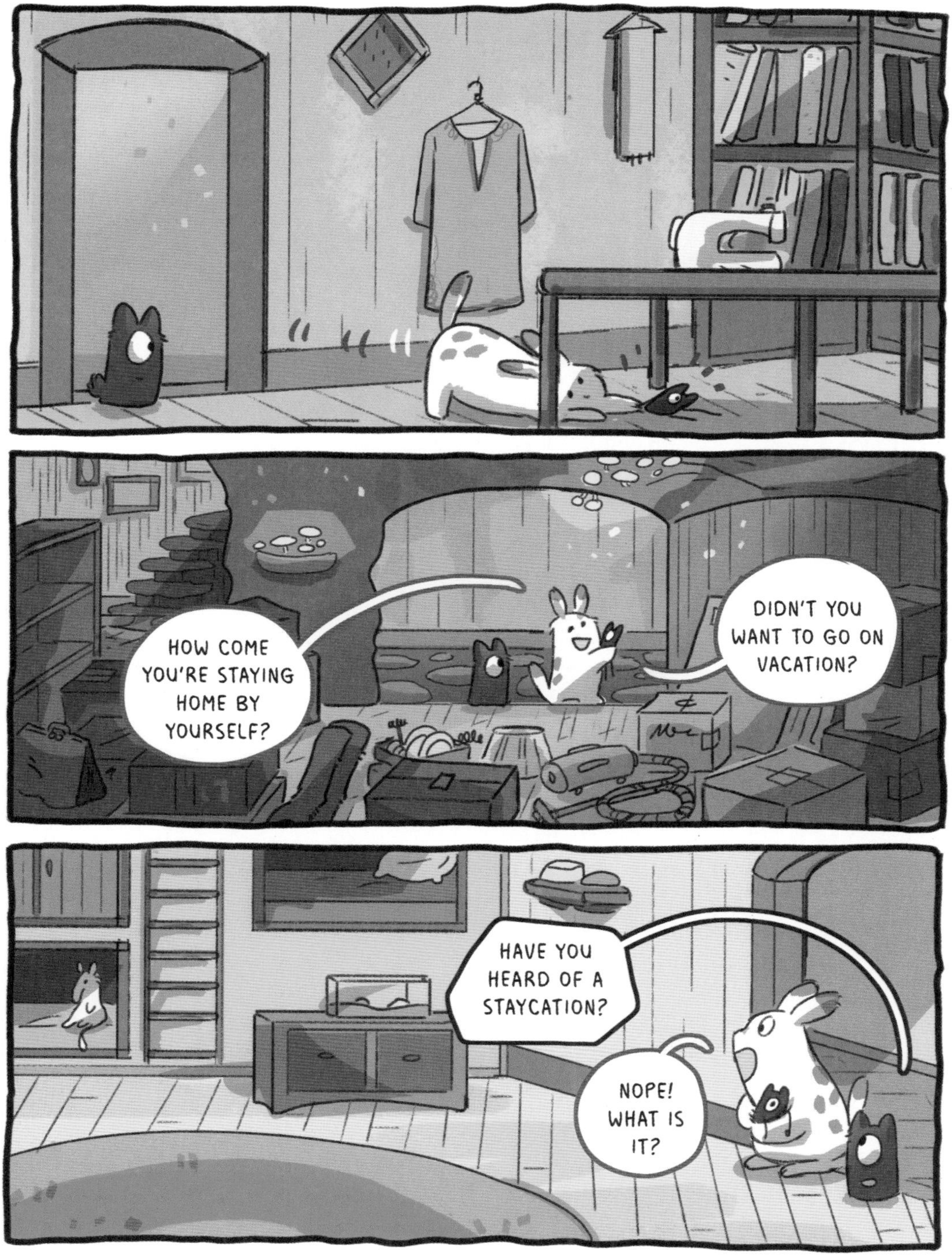
HOW COME YOU'RE STAYING HOME BY YOURSELF?
DIDN'T YOU WANT TO GO ON VACATION?
HAVE YOU HEARD OF A STAYCATION?
NOPE! WHAT IS IT?

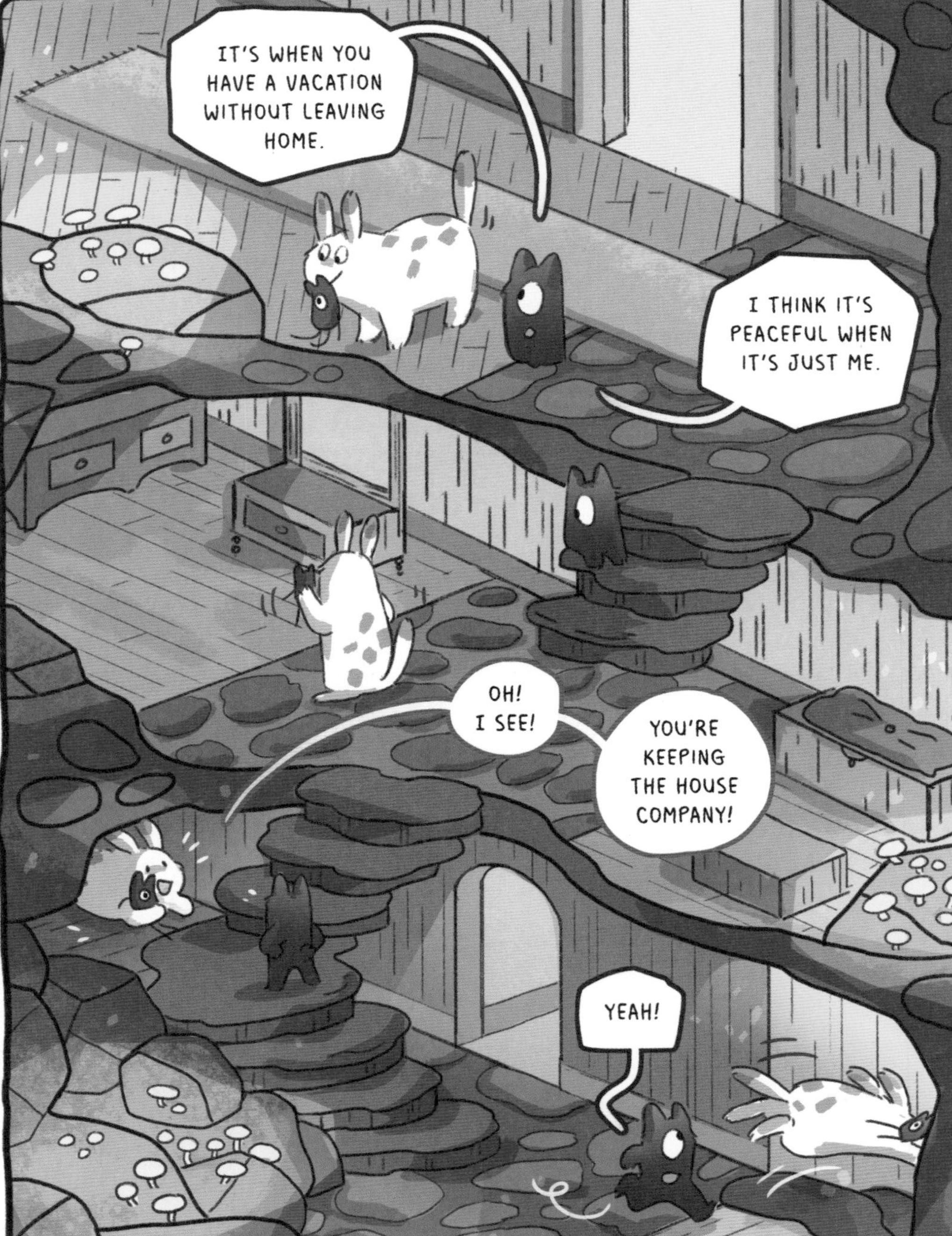
IT'S WHEN YOU HAVE A VACATION WITHOUT LEAVING HOME.
I THINK IT'S PEACEFUL WHEN IT'S JUST ME.
OH! I SEE!
YOU'RE KEEPING THE HOUSE COMPANY!
YEAH!

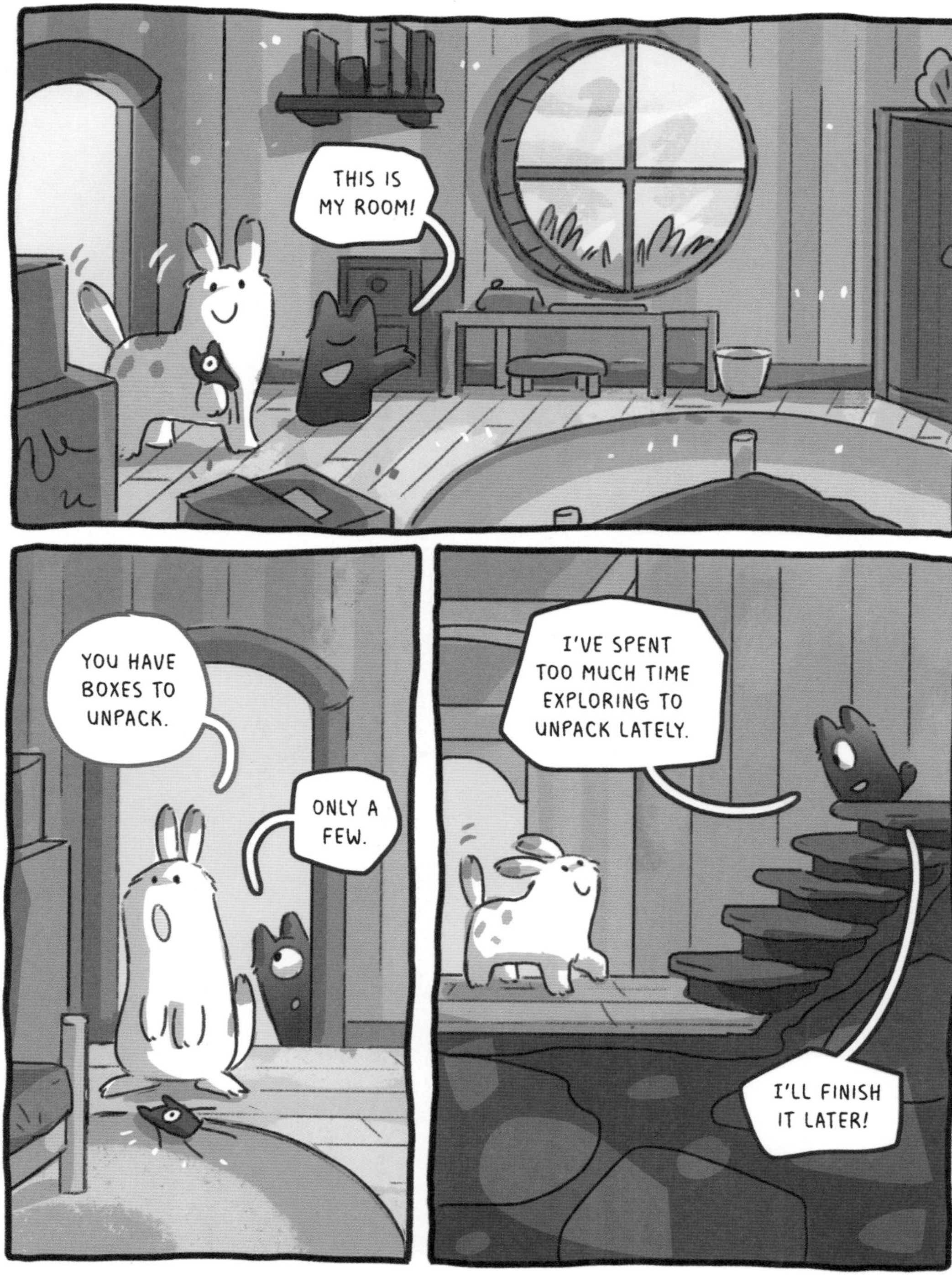
THIS IS MY ROOM!
YOU HAVE BOXES TO UNPACK.
ONLY A FEW.
I'VE SPENT TOO MUCH TIME EXPLORING TO UNPACK LATELY.
I'LL FINISH IT LATER!

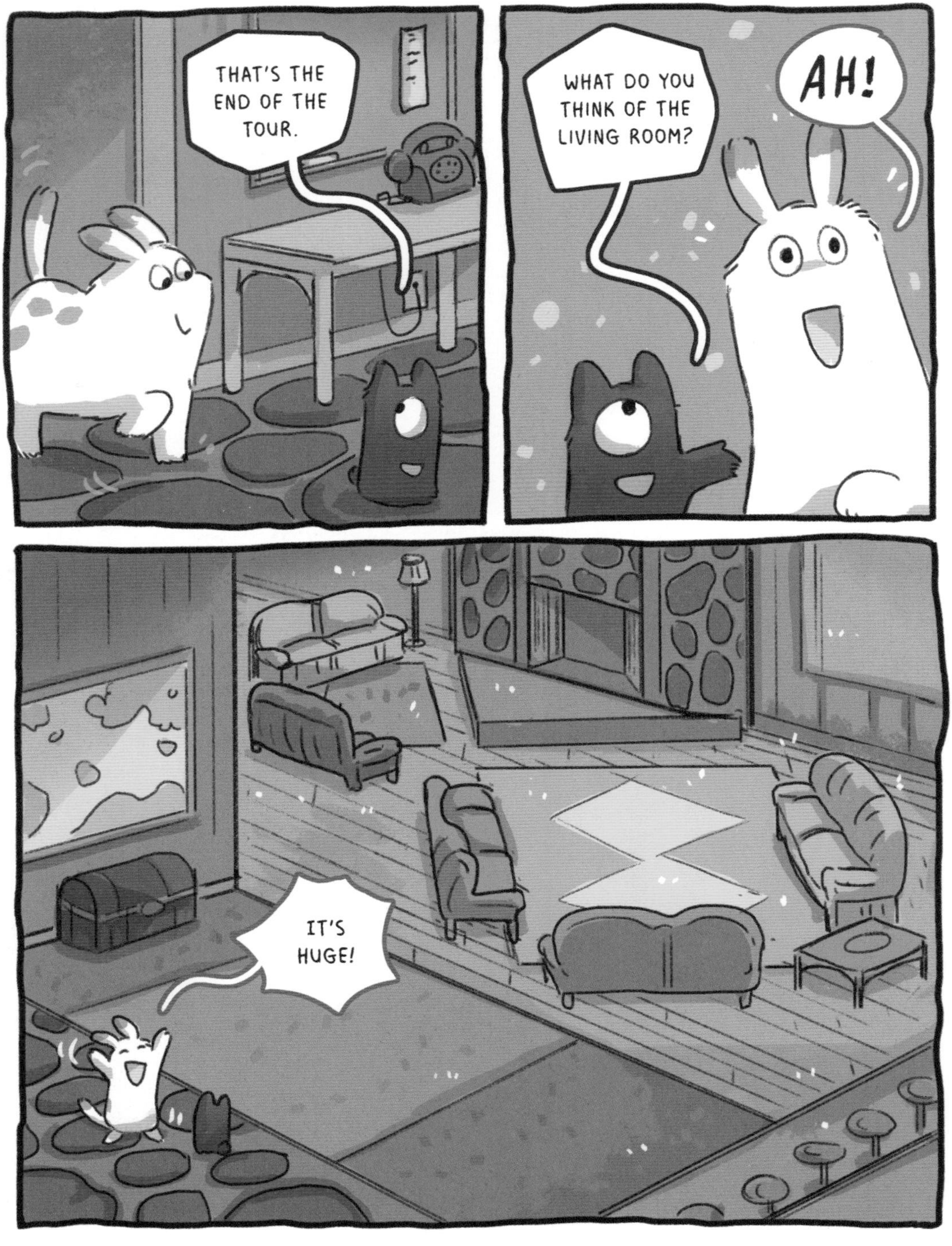
THAT'S THE END OF THE TOUR.
WHAT DO YOU THINK OF THE LIVING ROOM?
AH!
IT'S HUGE!

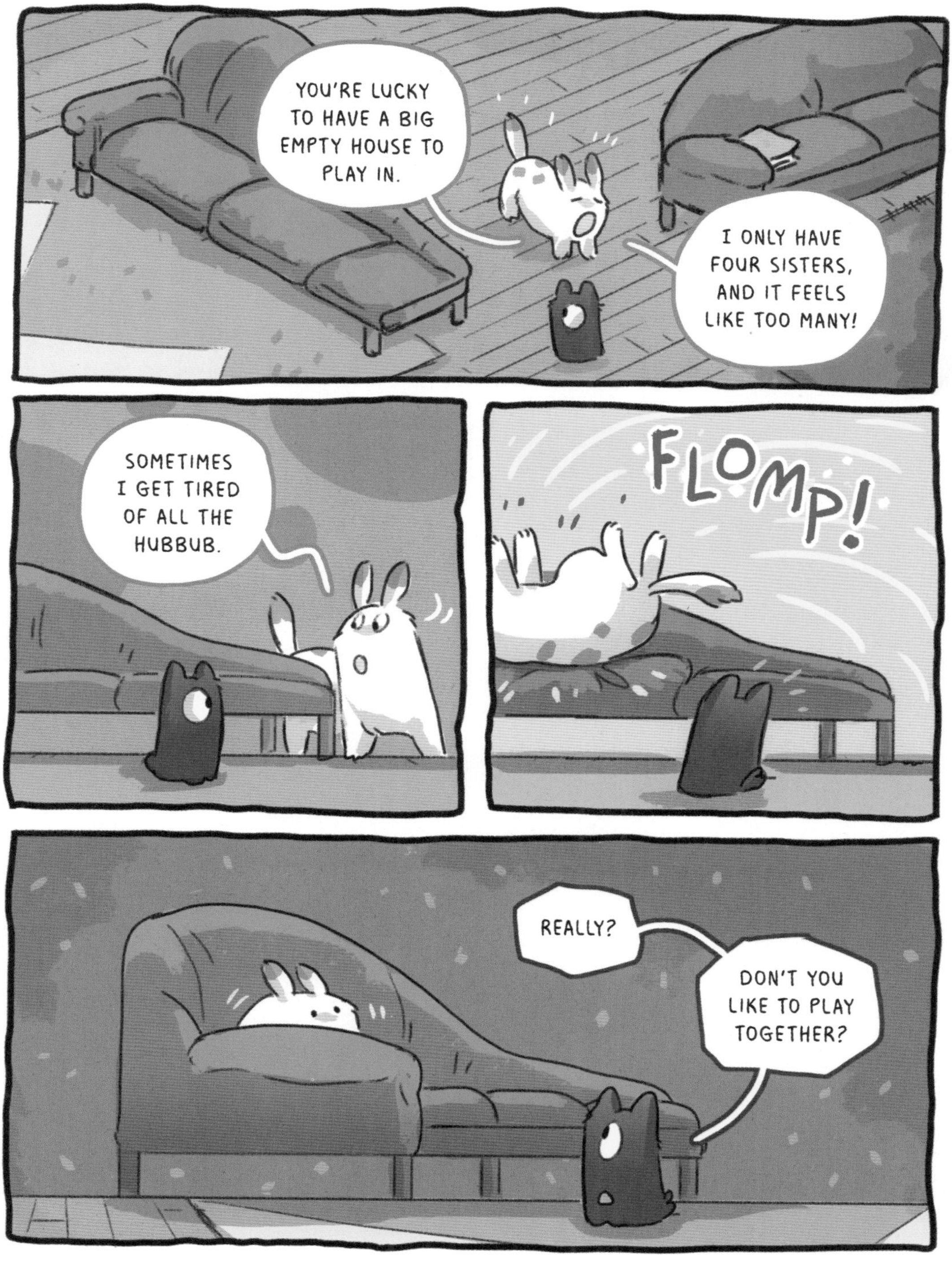

YOU'RE LUCKY TO HAVE A BIG EMPTY HOUSE TO PLAY IN.
I ONLY HAVE FOUR SISTERS, AND IT FEELS LIKE TOO MANY!
SOMETIMES I GET TIRED OF ALL THE HUBBUB.
FLOMP!
REALLY?
DON'T YOU LIKE TO PLAY TOGETHER?

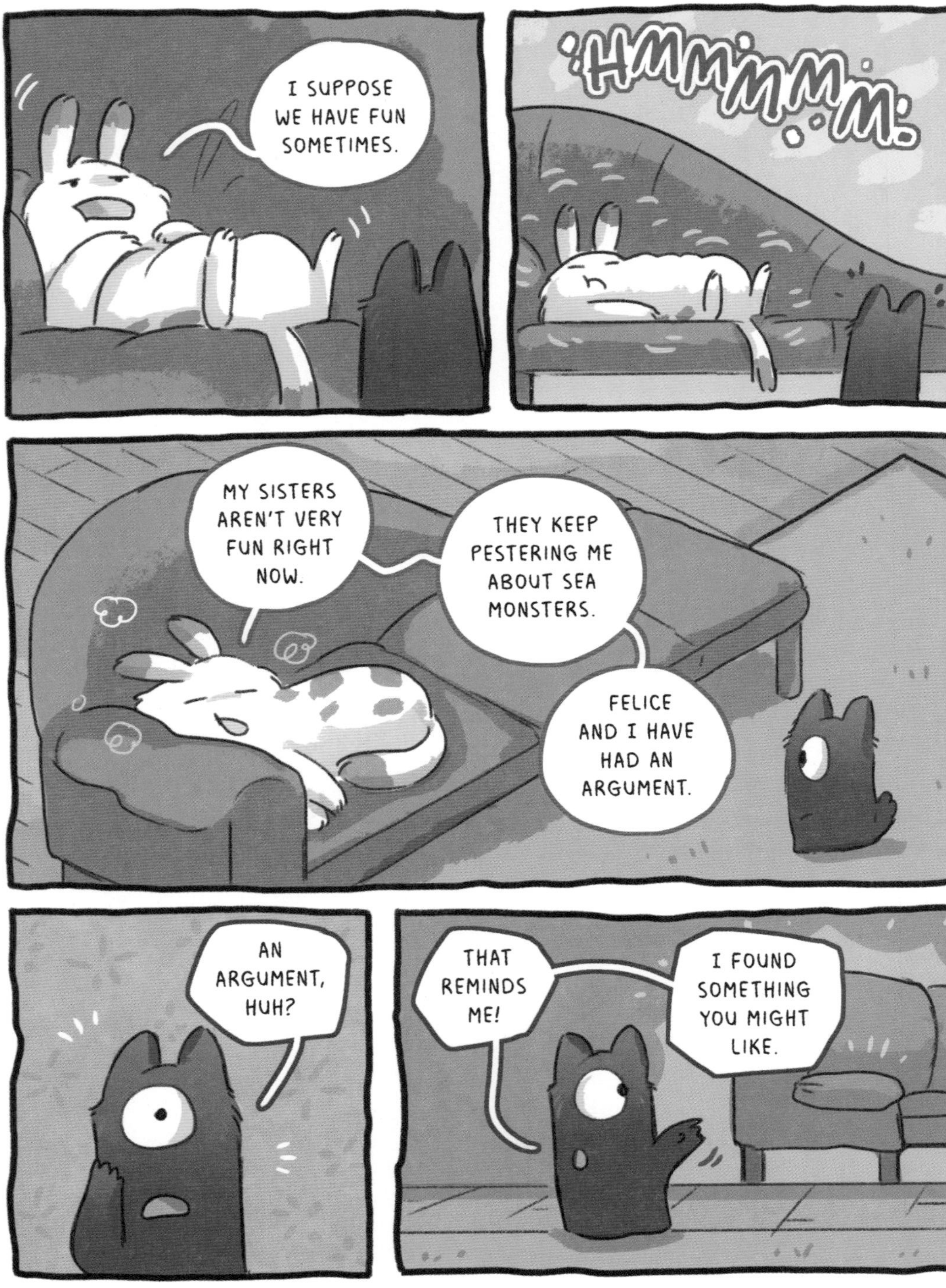
I SUPPOSE WE HAVE FUN SOMETIMES.
HMMMMMM
MY SISTERS AREN'T VERY FUN RIGHT NOW.
THEY KEEP PESTERING ME ABOUT SEA MONSTERS.
FELICE AND I HAVE HAD AN ARGUMENT.
AN ARGUMENT, HUH?
THAT REMINDS ME!
I FOUND SOMETHING YOU MIGHT LIKE.

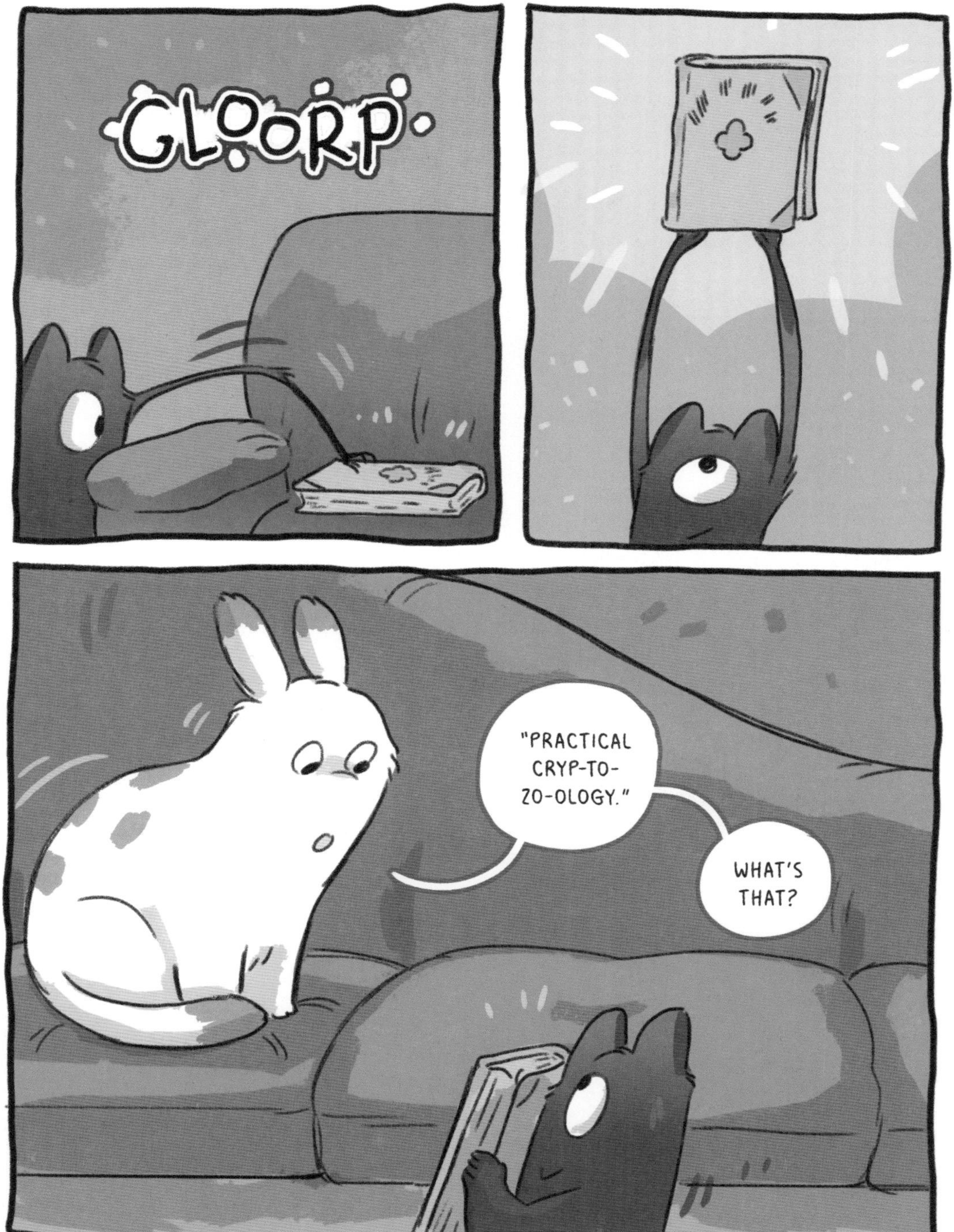
GLOORP
"PRACTICAL CRYP-TO-ZO-OLOGY."
WHAT'S THAT?

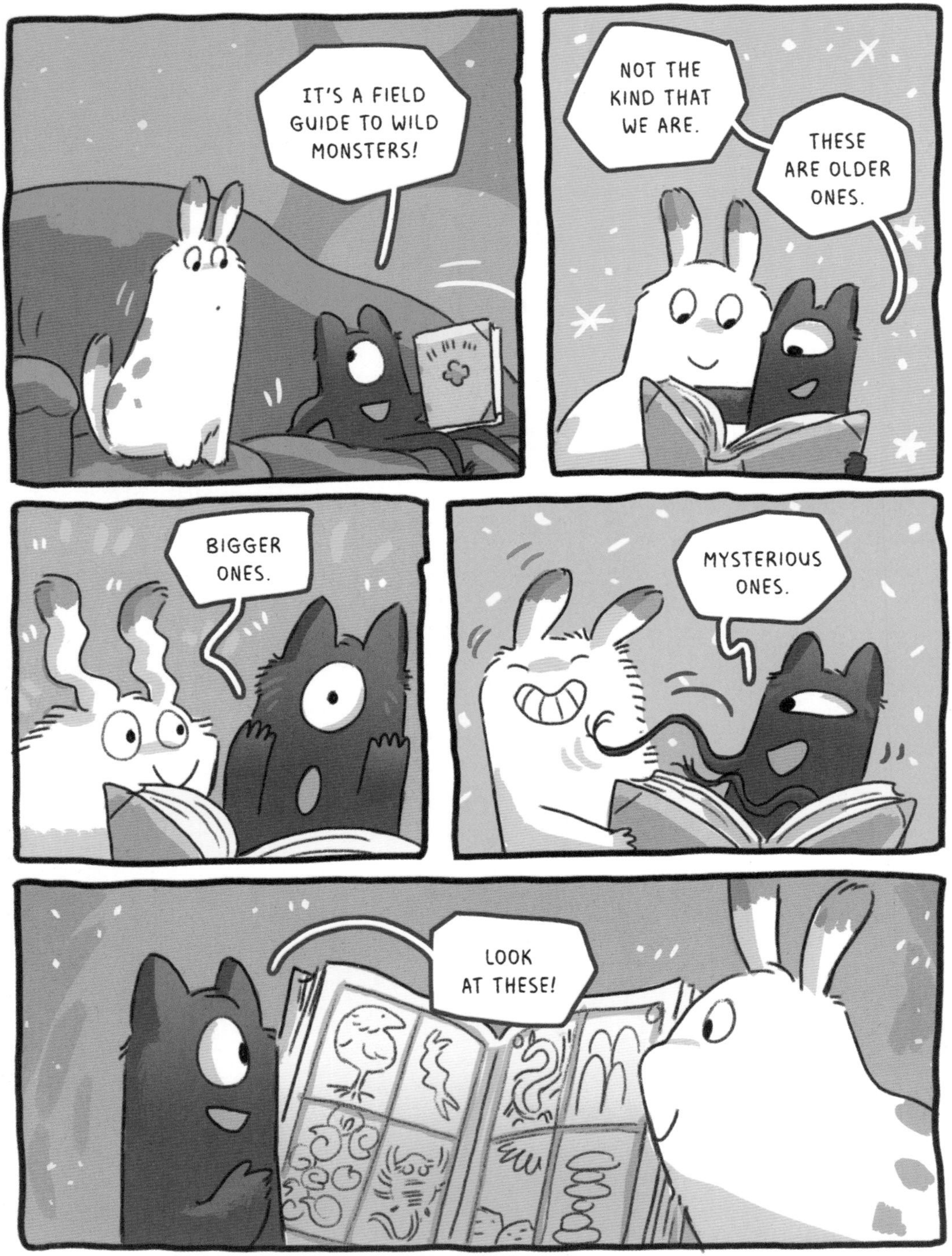
IT'S A FIELD GUIDE TO WILD MONSTERS!
NOT THE KIND THAT WE ARE.
THESE ARE OLDER ONES.
BIGGER ONES.
MYSTERIOUS ONES.
LOOK AT THESE!

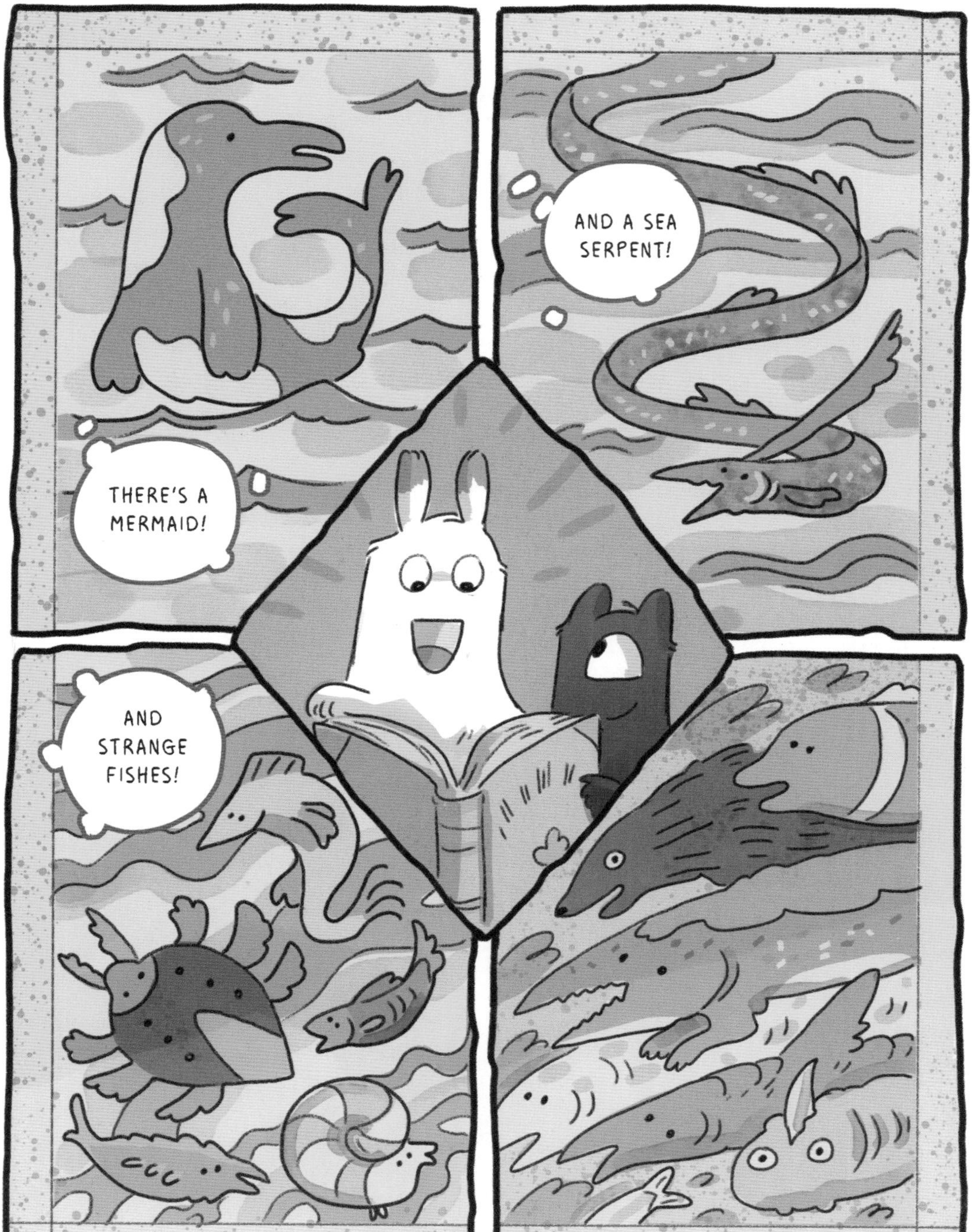
THERE'S A MERMAID!
AND A SEA SERPENT!
AND STRANGE FISHES!

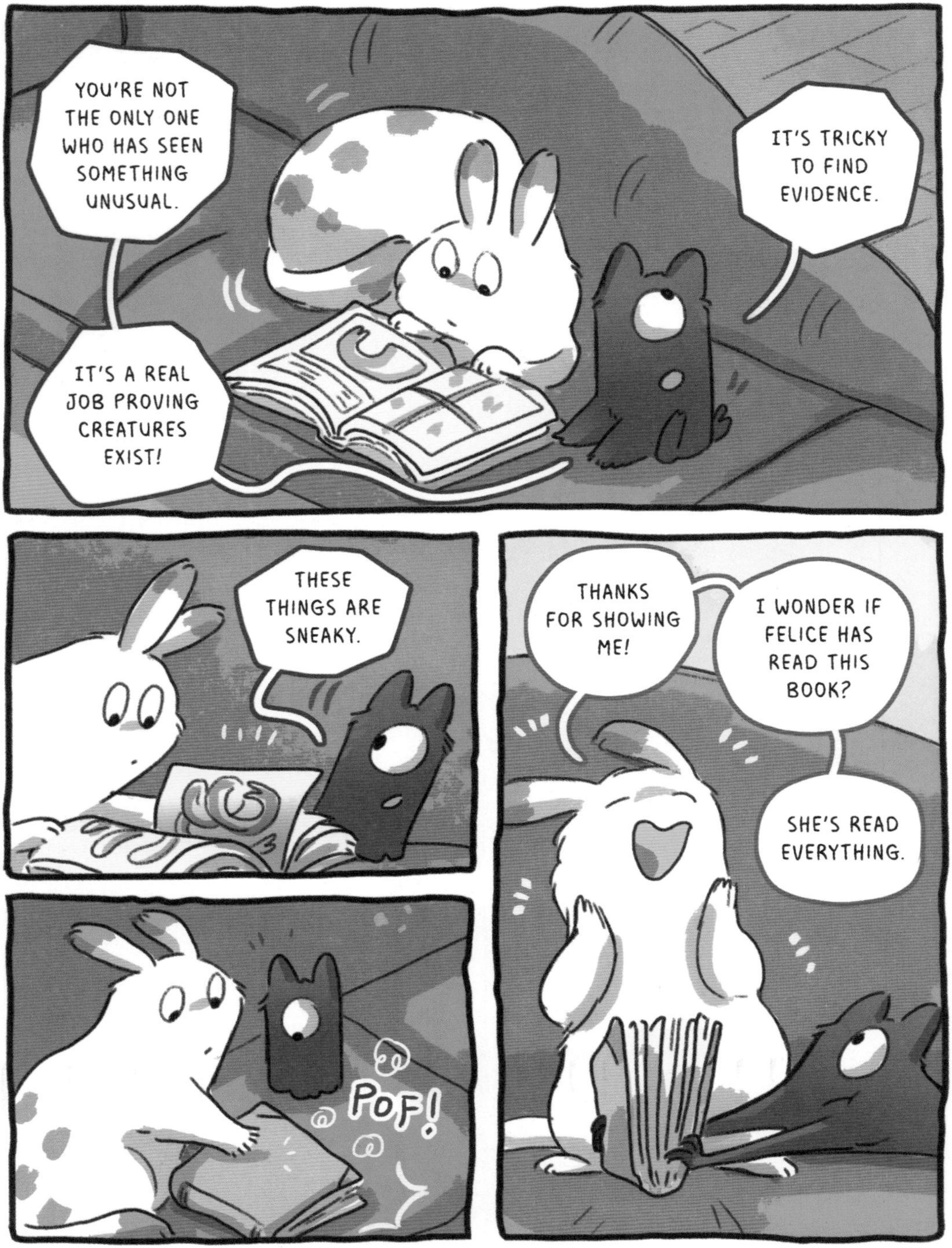
YOU'RE NOT THE ONLY ONE WHO HAS SEEN SOMETHING UNUSUAL.
IT'S A REAL JOB PROVING CREATURES EXIST!
IT'S TRICKY TO FIND EVIDENCE.
THESE THINGS ARE SNEAKY.
POF!
THANKS FOR SHOWING ME!
I WONDER IF FELICE HAS READ THIS BOOK?
SHE'S READ EVERYTHING.

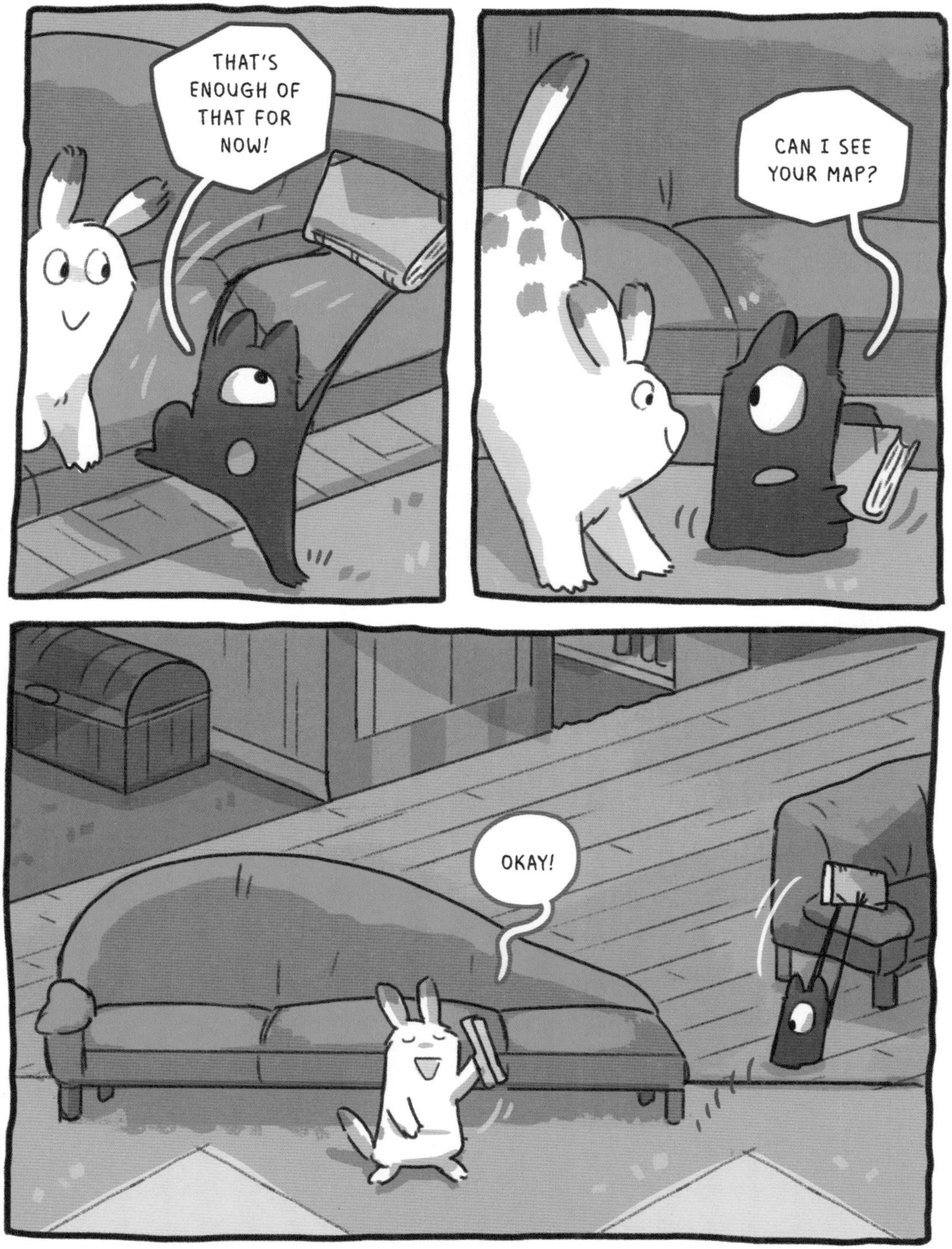
THAT'S ENOUGH OF THAT FOR NOW!
CAN I SEE YOUR MAP?
OKAY!

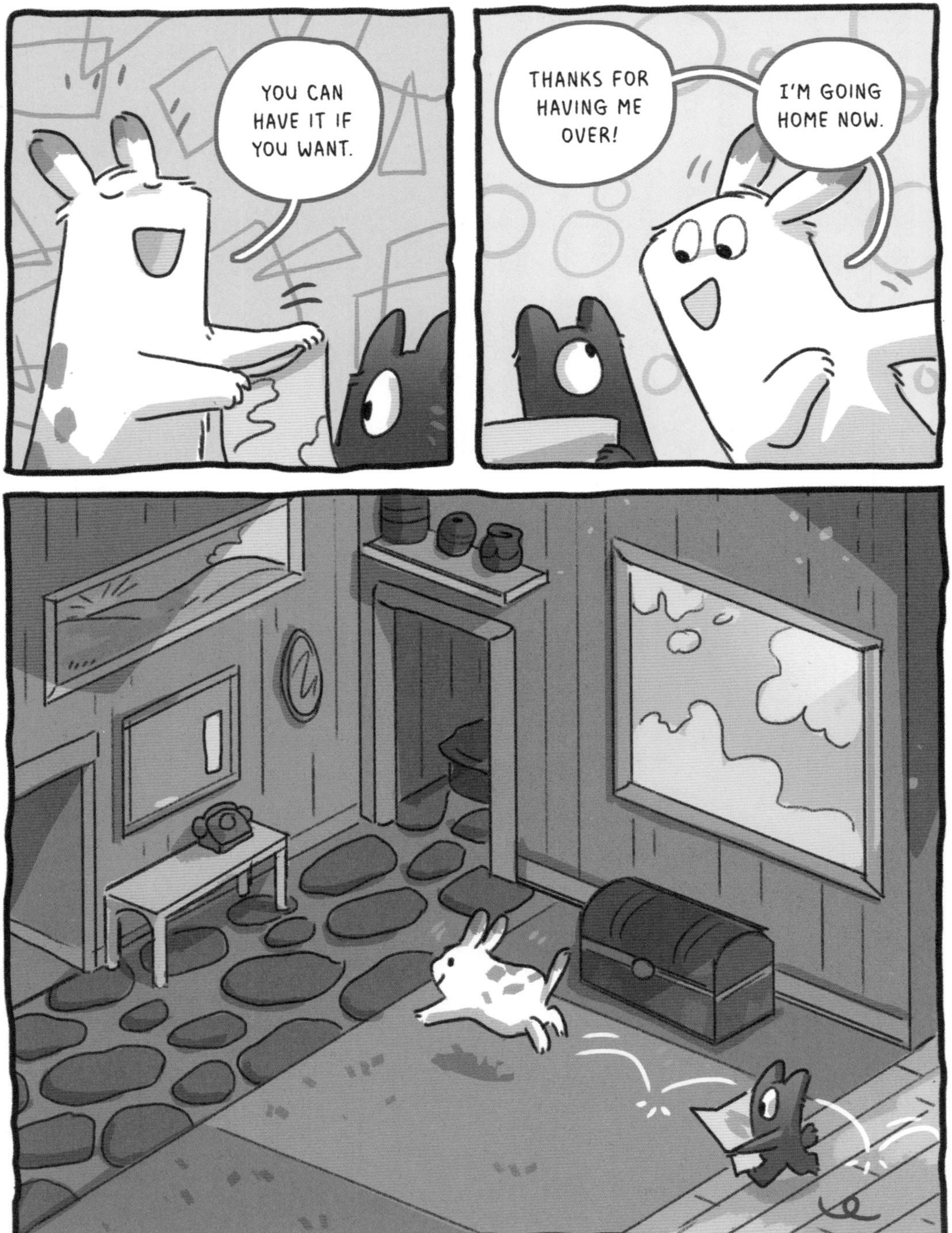
YOU CAN HAVE IT IF YOU WANT.
THANKS FOR HAVING ME OVER!
I'M GOING HOME NOW.

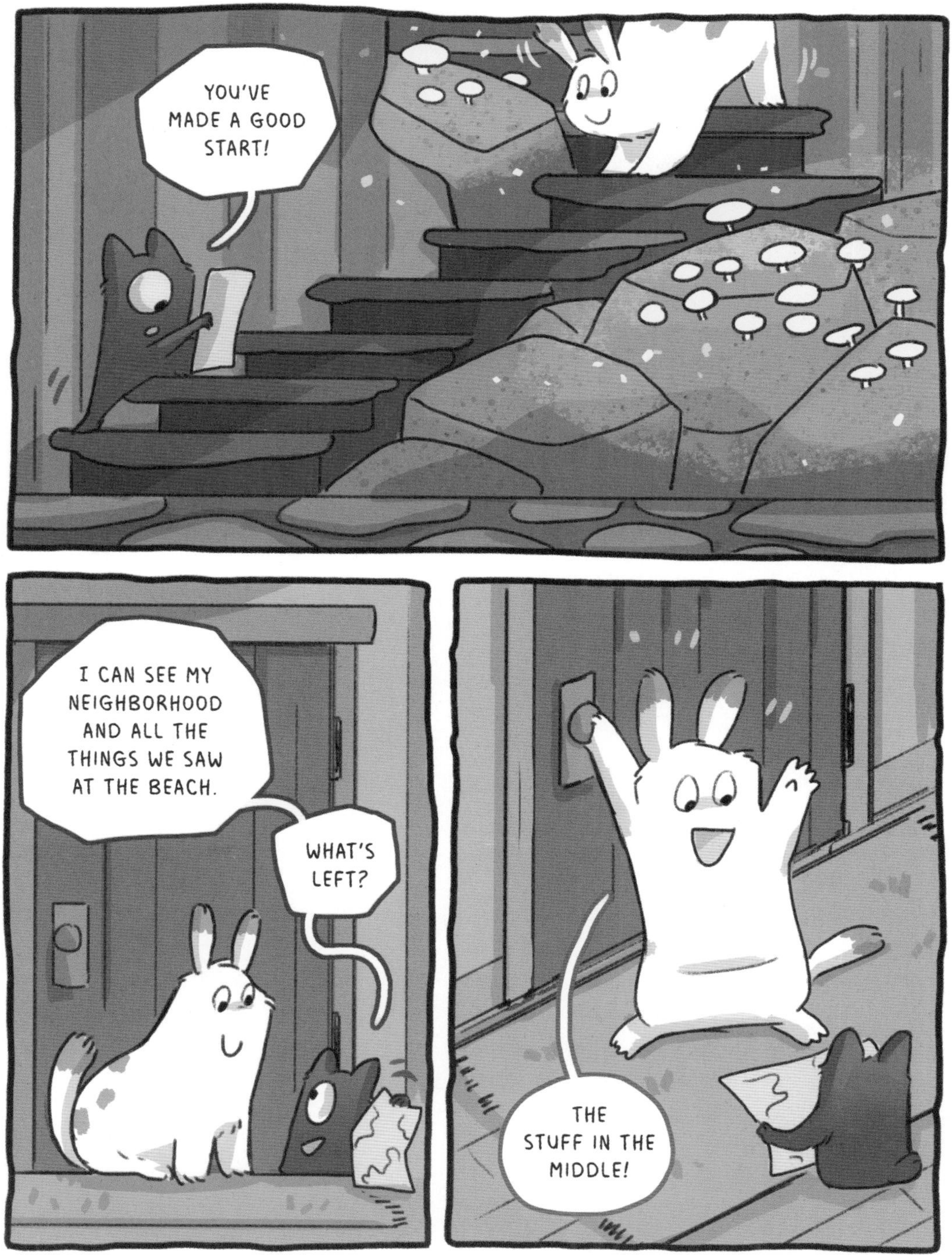
YOU'VE MADE A GOOD START!
I CAN SEE MY NEIGHBORHOOD AND ALL THE THINGS WE SAW AT THE BEACH.
WHAT'S LEFT?
THE STUFF IN THE MIDDLE!

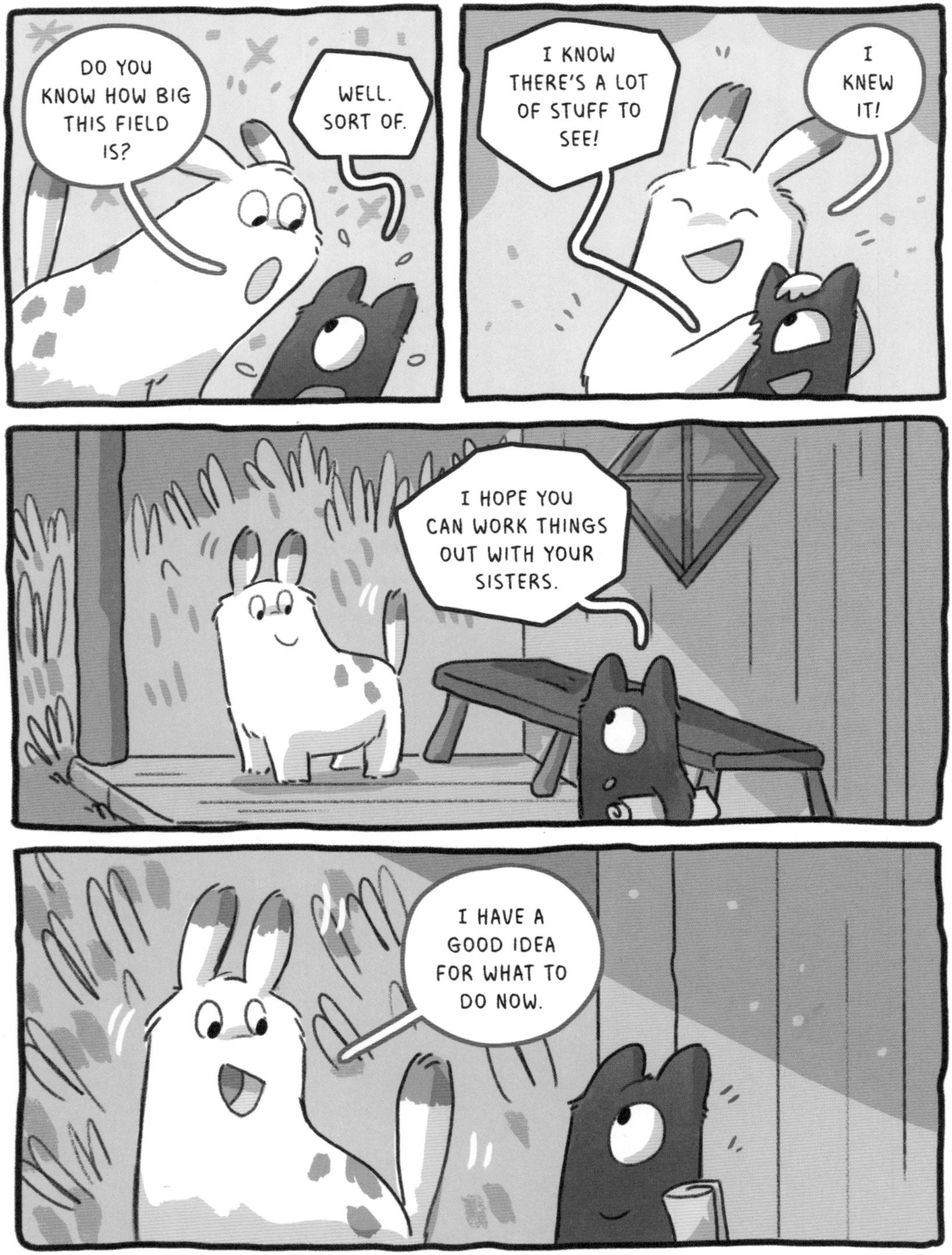
DO YOU KNOW HOW BIG THIS FIELD IS?
WELL. SORT OF.
I KNOW THERE'S A LOT OF STUFF TO SEE!
I KNEW IT!
I HOPE YOU CAN WORK THINGS OUT WITH YOUR SISTERS.
I HAVE A GOOD IDEA FOR WHAT TO DO NOW.

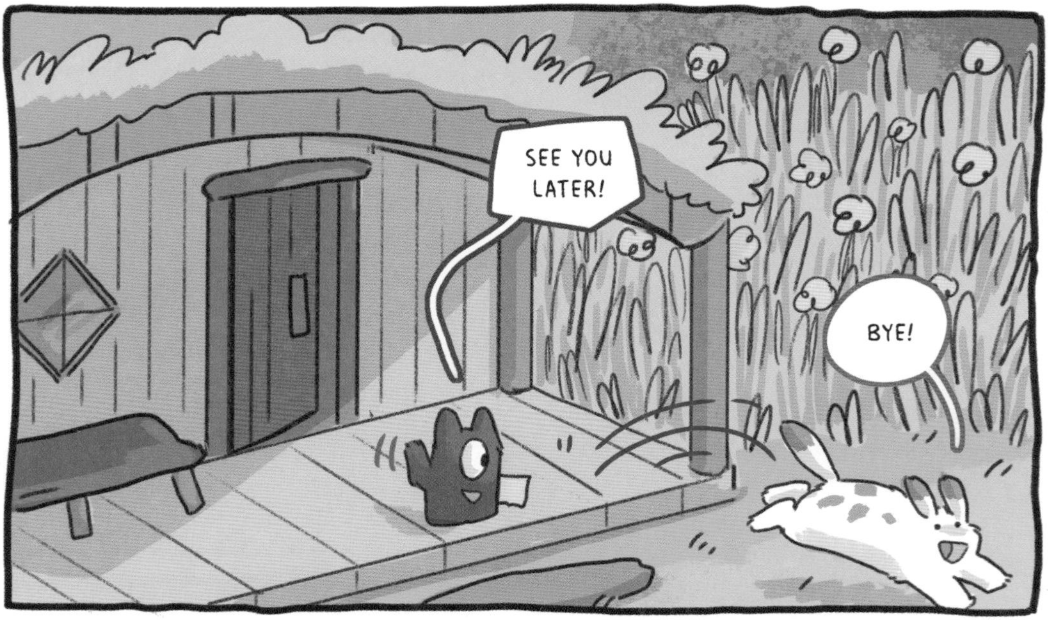
SEE YOU LATER!
BYE!

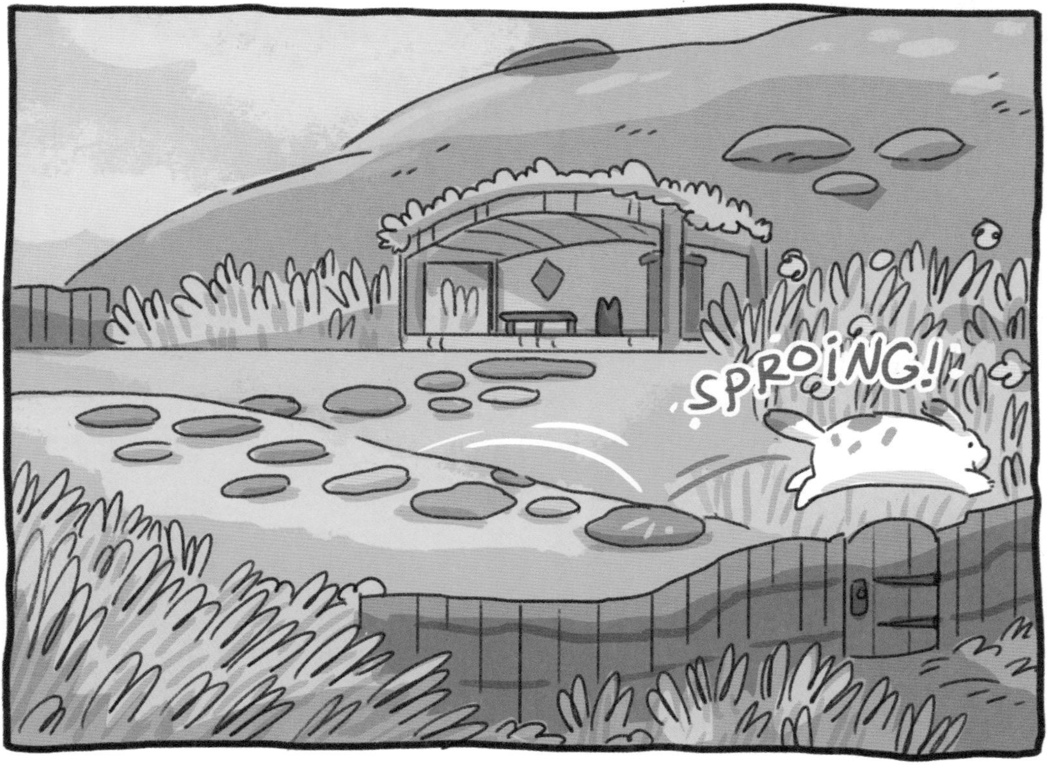
SPROING!

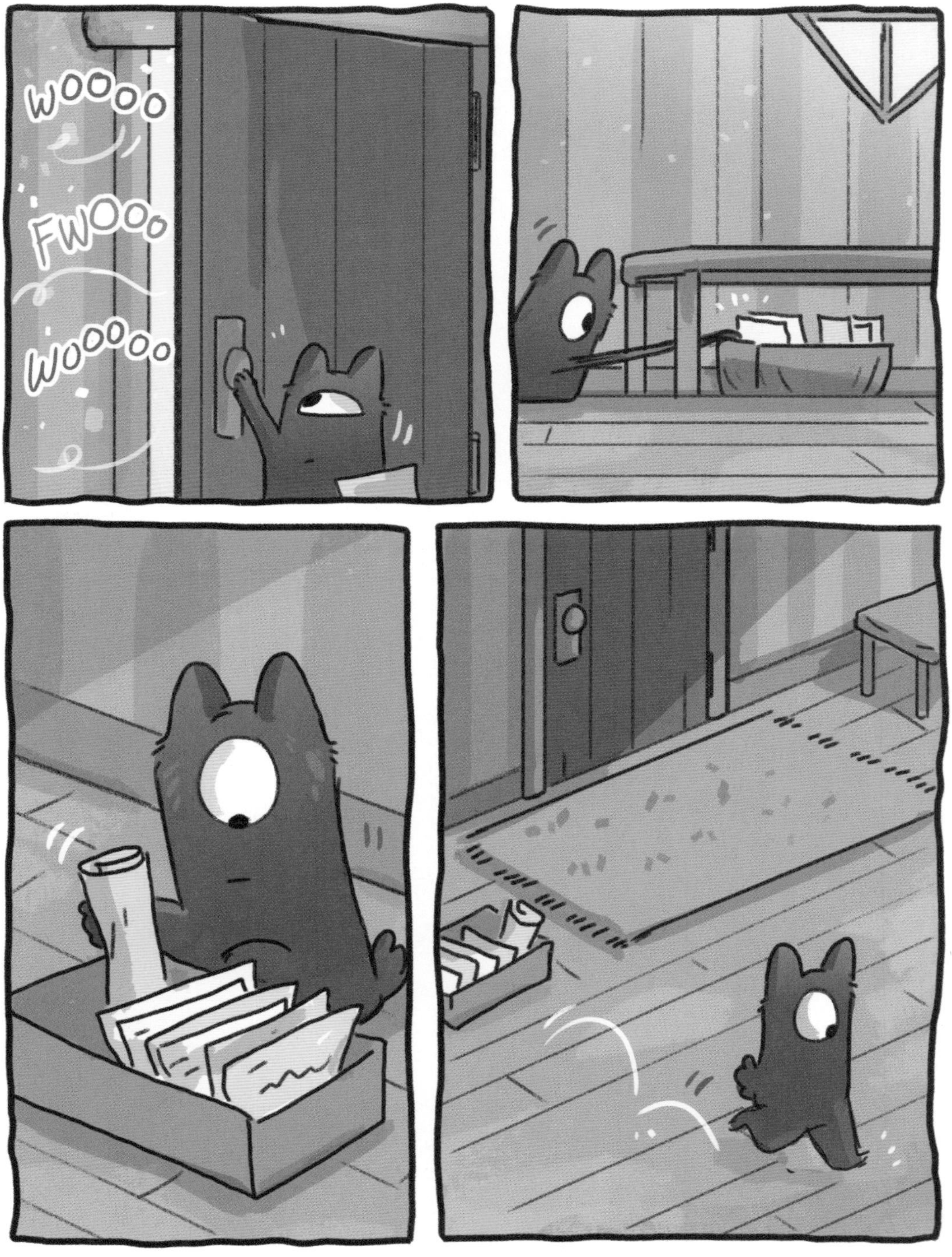
WOOOOO
FWOOoo
WOOOOOO

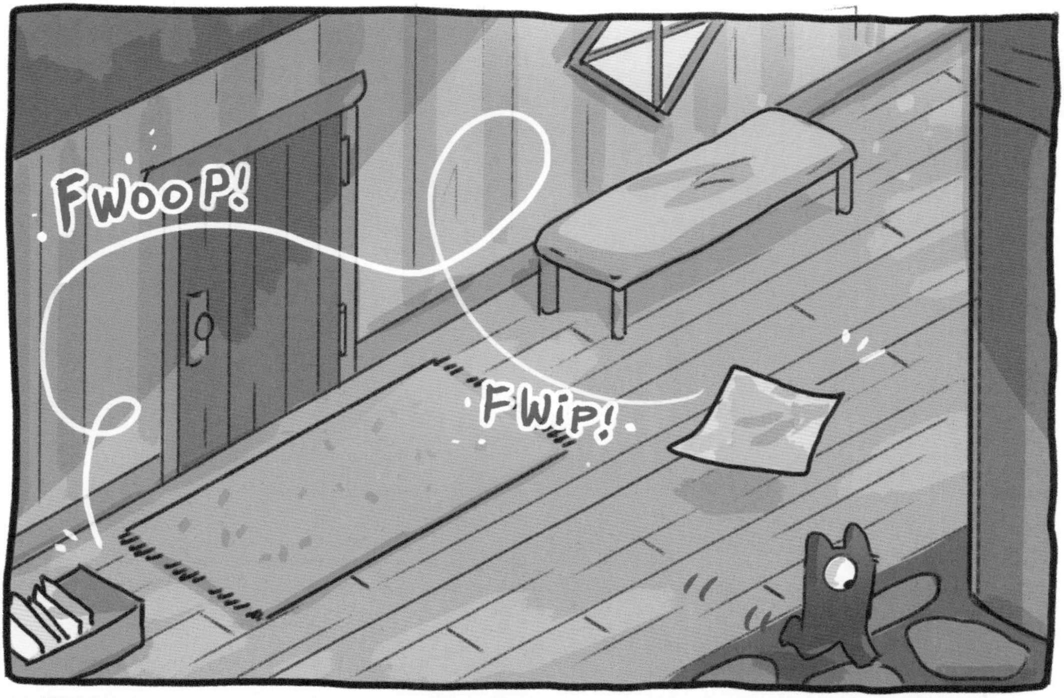
FWOOP!
FWIP!

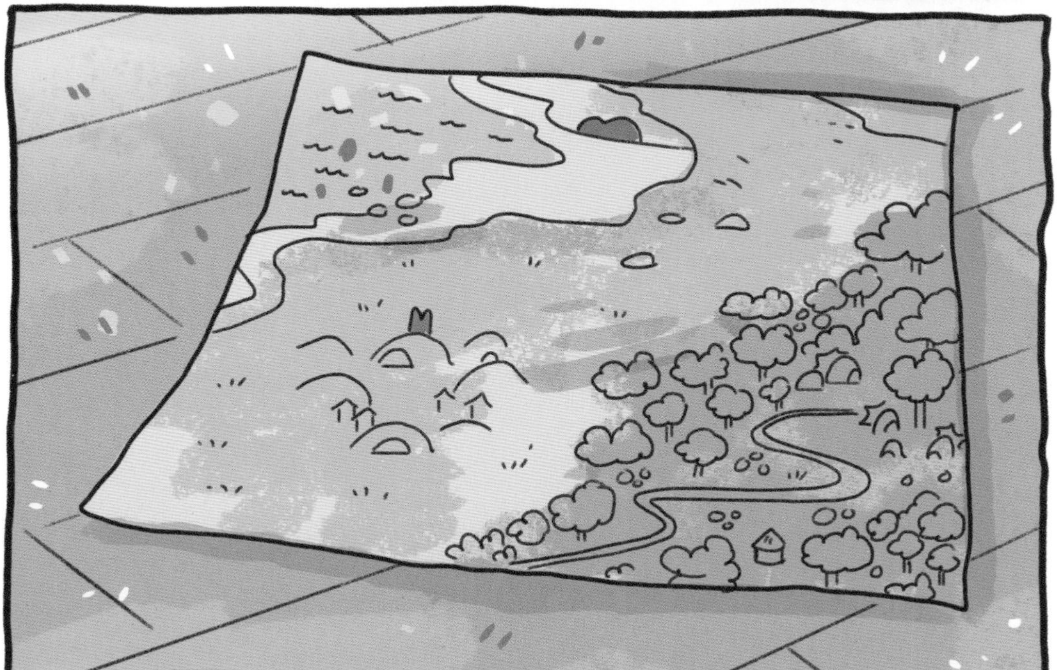

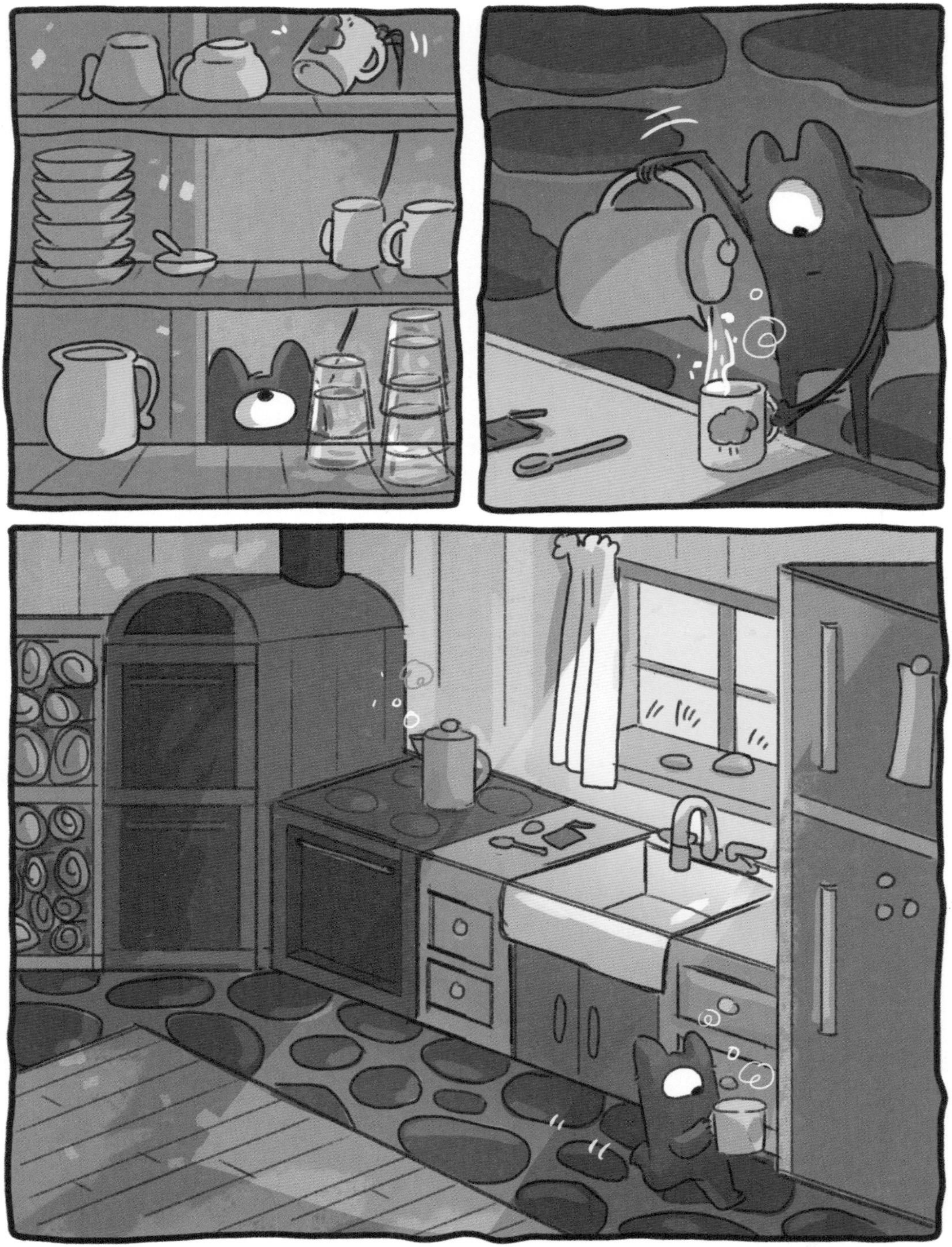

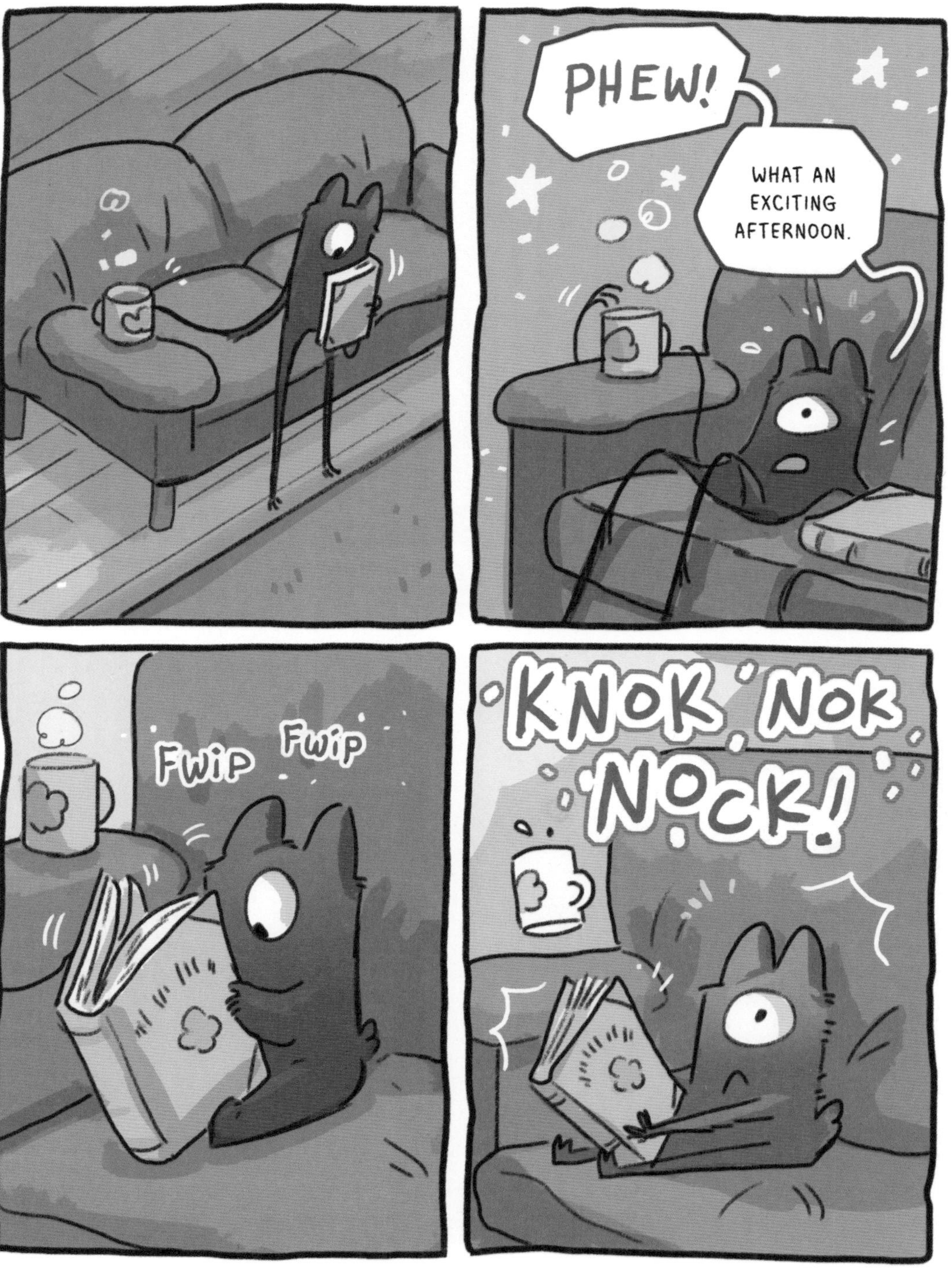
PHEW!
WHAT AN EXCITING AFTERNOON.
Fwip Fwip
KNOK NOK NOCK!

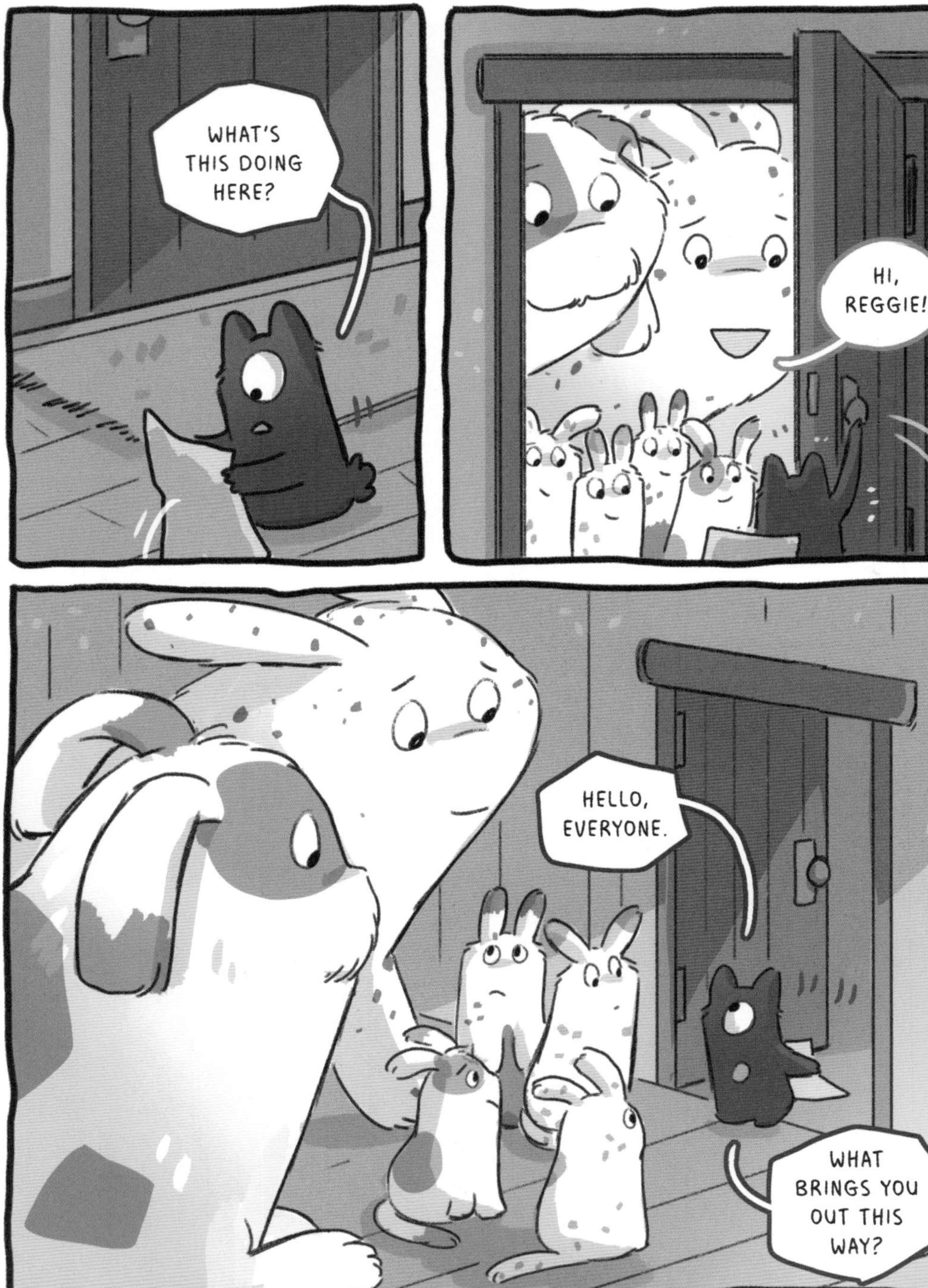
WHAT'S THIS DOING HERE?
HI, REGGIE!
HELLO, EVERYONE.
WHAT BRINGS YOU OUT THIS WAY?

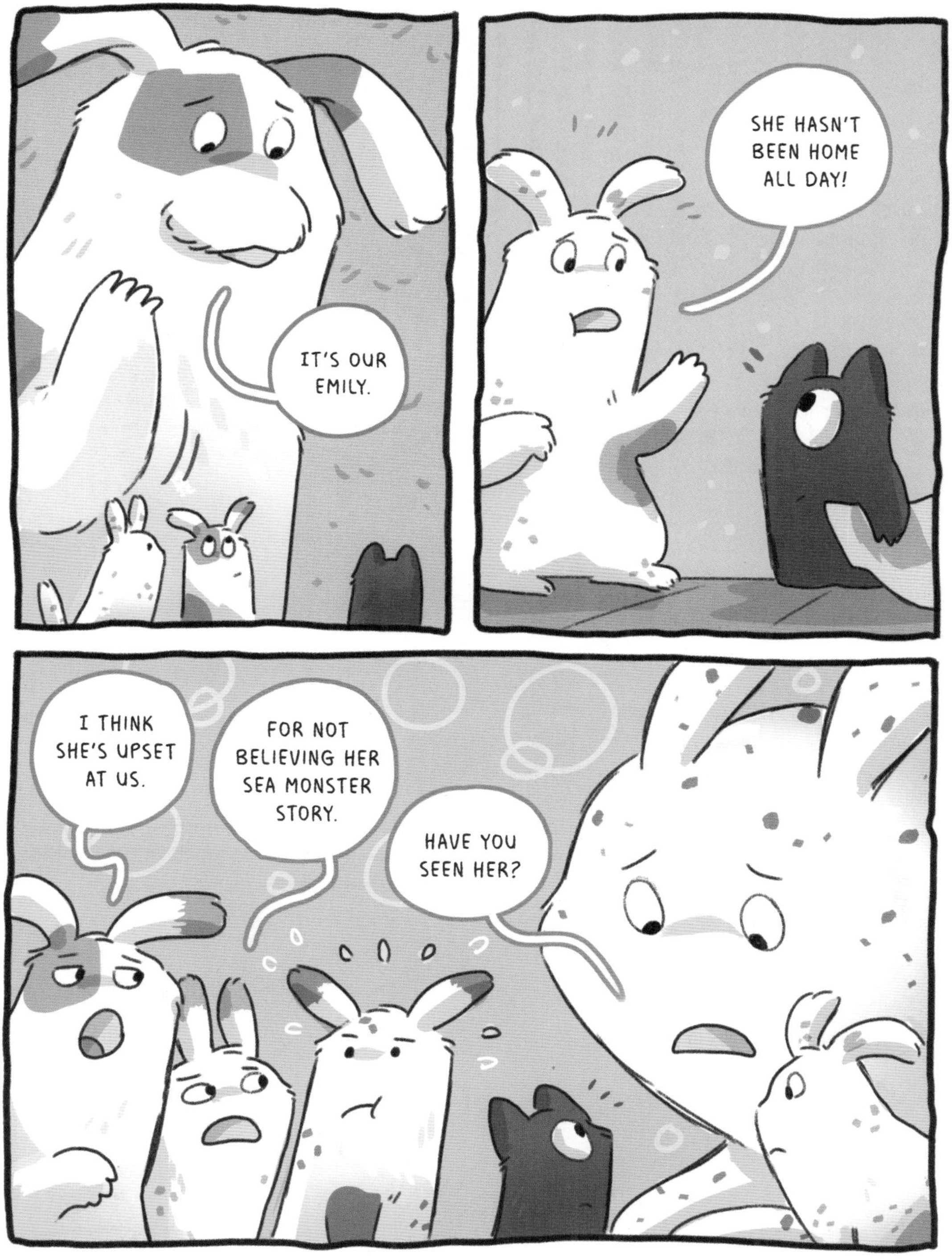
IT'S OUR EMILY.
SHE HASN'T BEEN HOME ALL DAY!
I THINK SHE'S UPSET AT US.
FOR NOT BELIEVING HER SEA MONSTER STORY.
HAVE YOU SEEN HER?

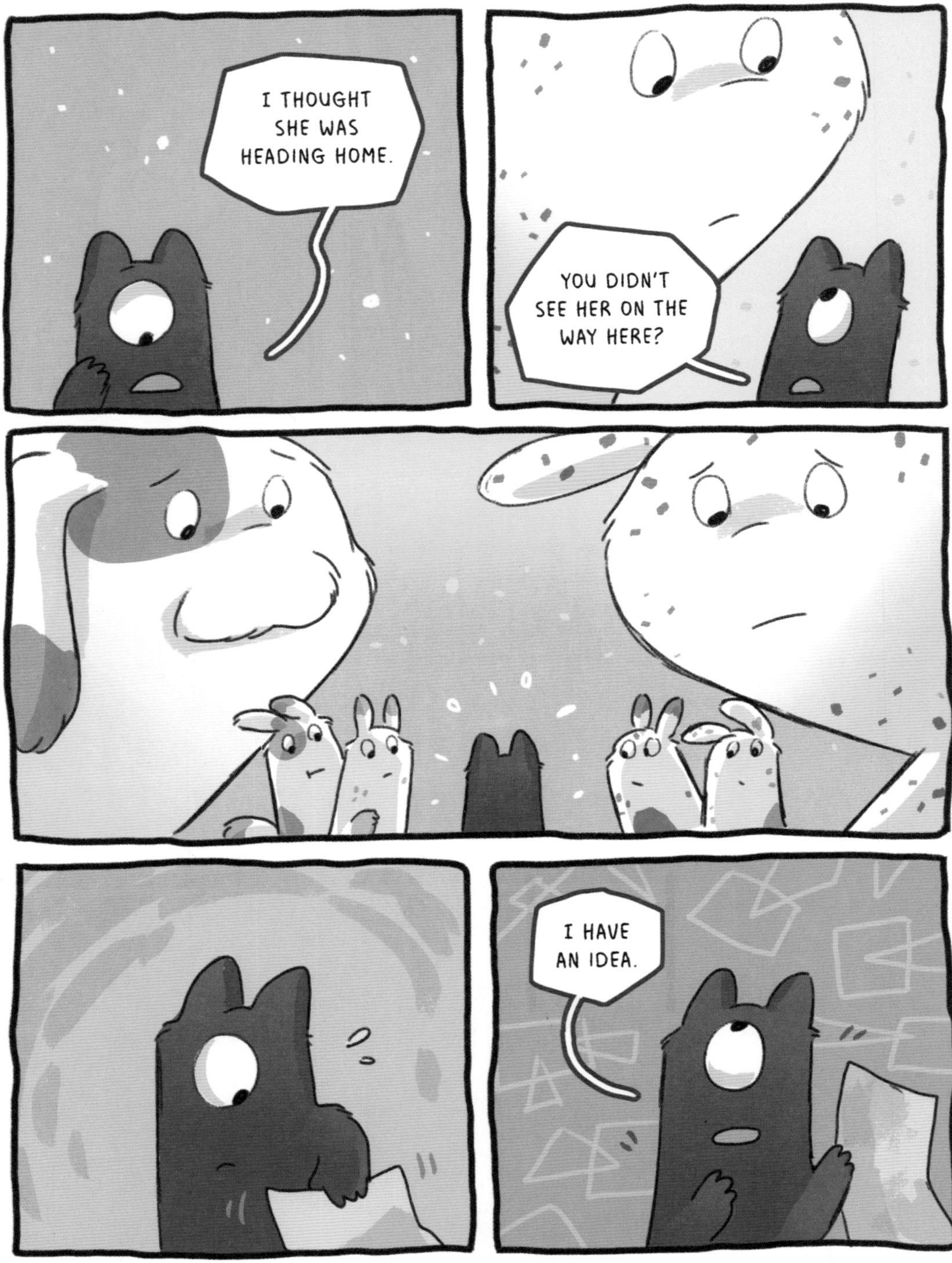
I THOUGHT SHE WAS HEADING HOME.
YOU DIDN'T SEE HER ON THE WAY HERE?
I HAVE AN IDEA.

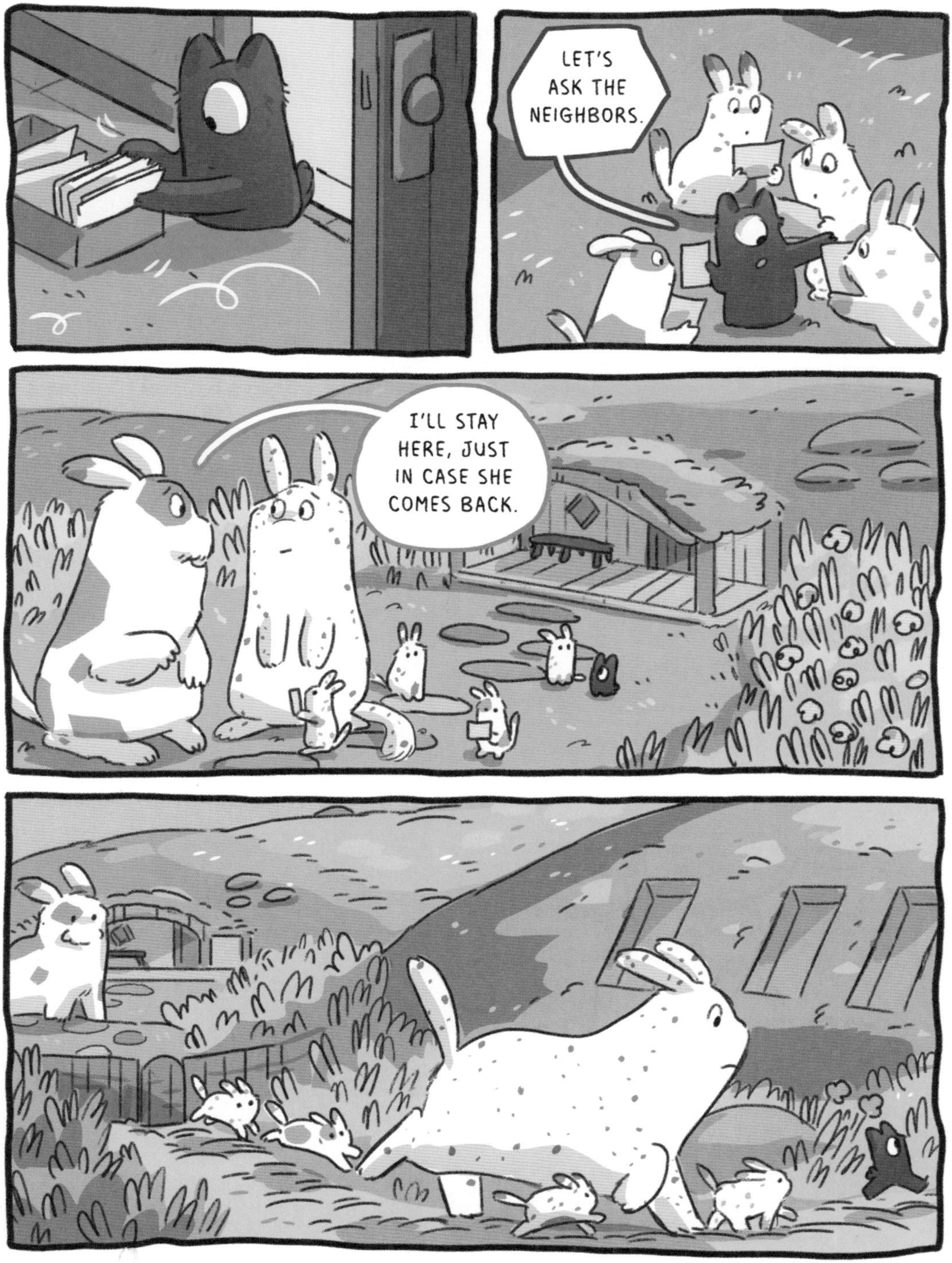
LET'S ASK THE NEIGHBORS.
I'LL STAY HERE, JUST IN CASE SHE COMES BACK.

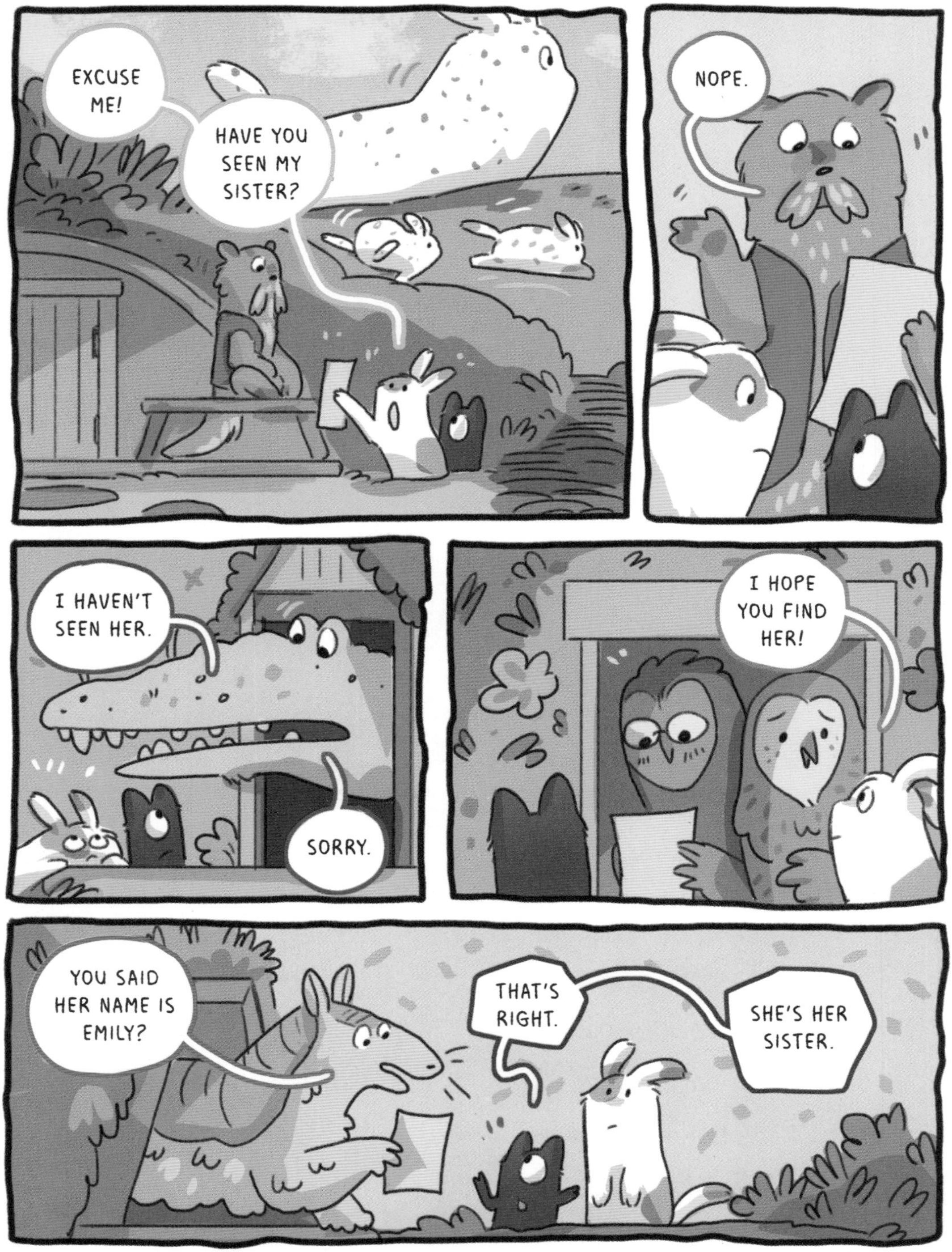
EXCUSE ME!
HAVE YOU SEEN MY SISTER?
NOPE.
I HAVEN'T SEEN HER.
SORRY.
I HOPE YOU FIND HER!
YOU SAID HER NAME IS EMILY?
THAT'S RIGHT.
SHE'S HER SISTER.

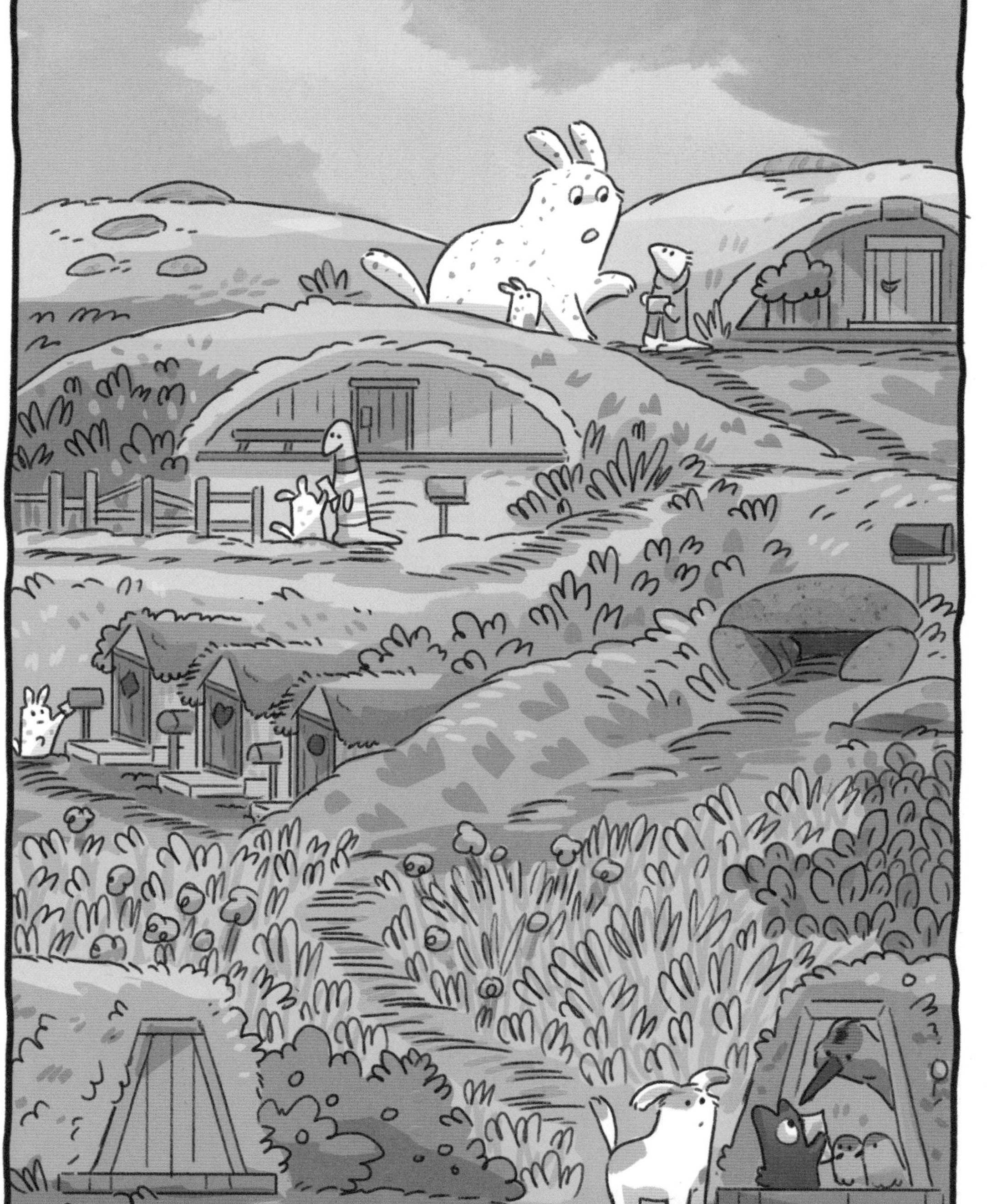

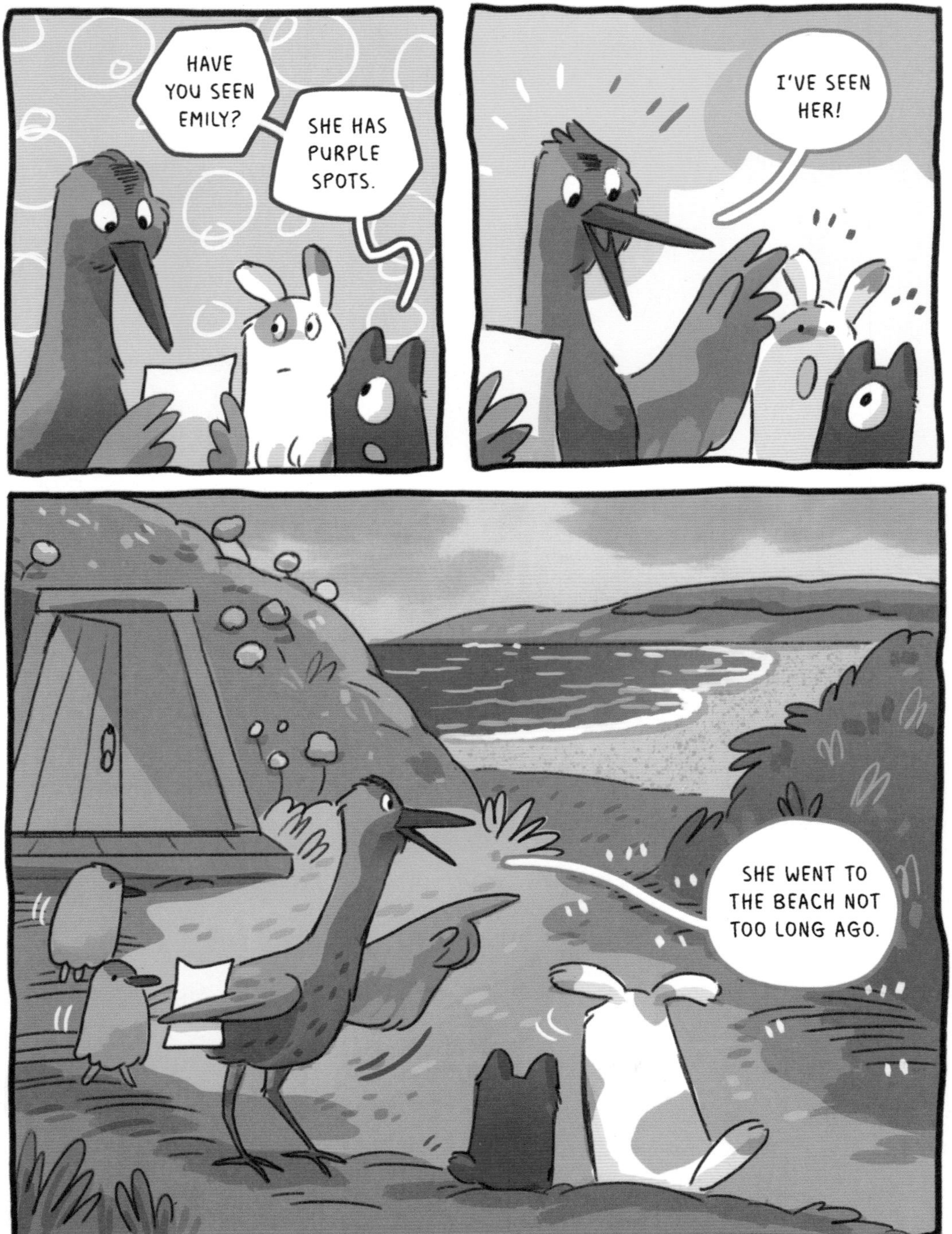
HAVE YOU SEEN EMILY?
SHE HAS PURPLE SPOTS.
I'VE SEEN HER!
SHE WENT TO THE BEACH NOT TOO LONG AGO.

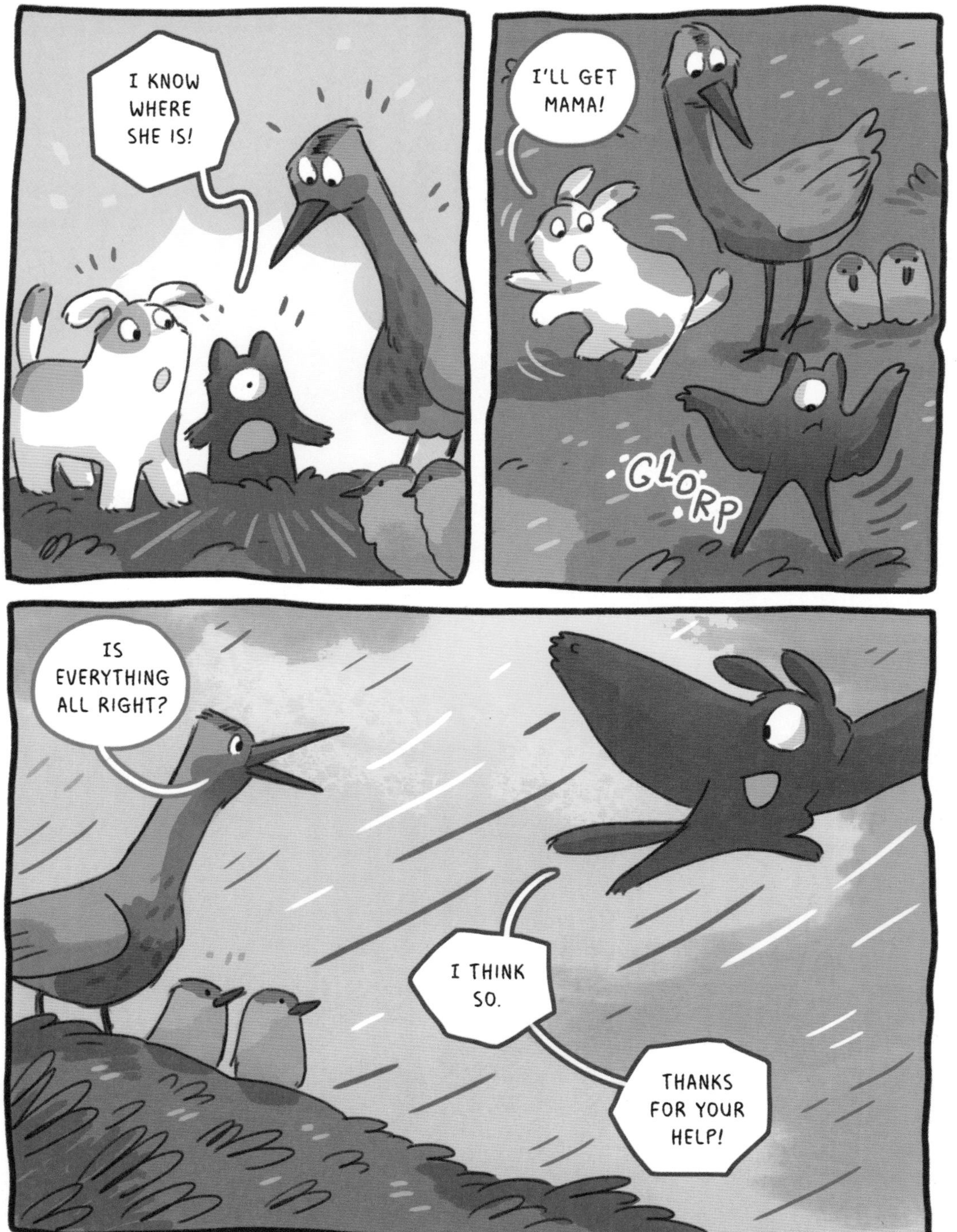
I KNOW WHERE SHE IS!
I'LL GET MAMA!
GLORP
IS EVERYTHING ALL RIGHT?
I THINK SO.
THANKS FOR YOUR HELP!

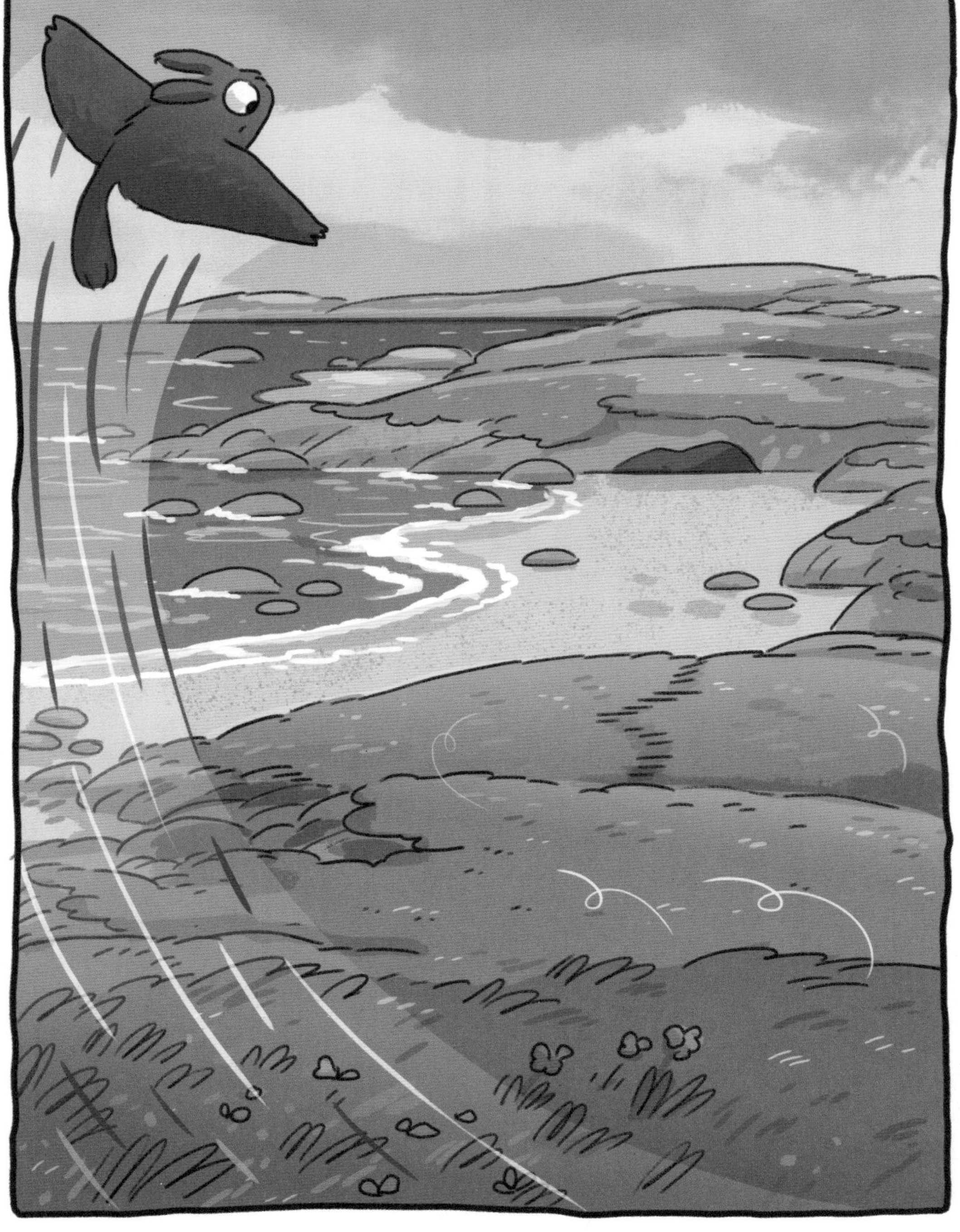

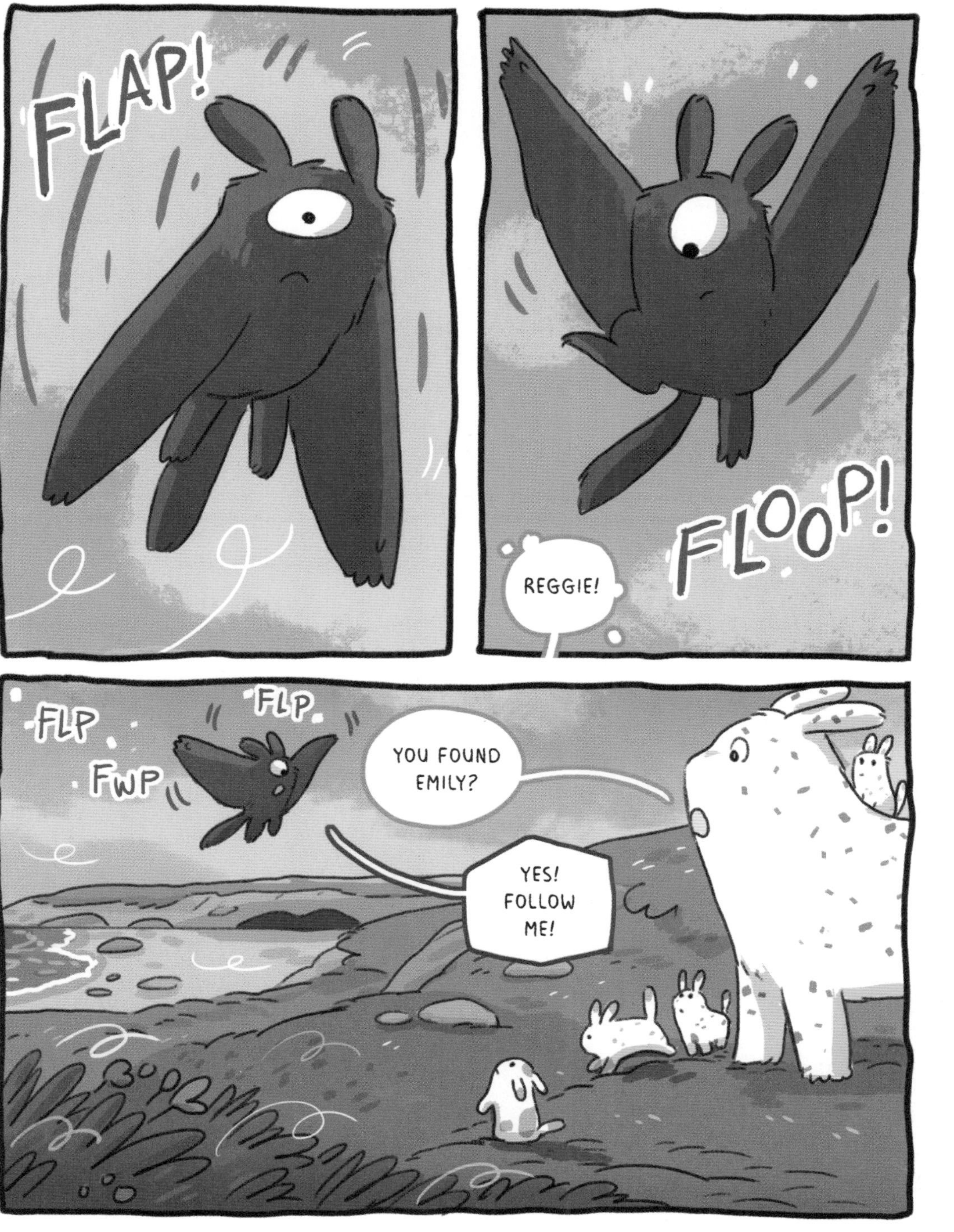
FLAP!
FLOOP!
REGGIE!
FLP
FLP
FWP
YOU FOUND EMILY?
YES! FOLLOW ME!

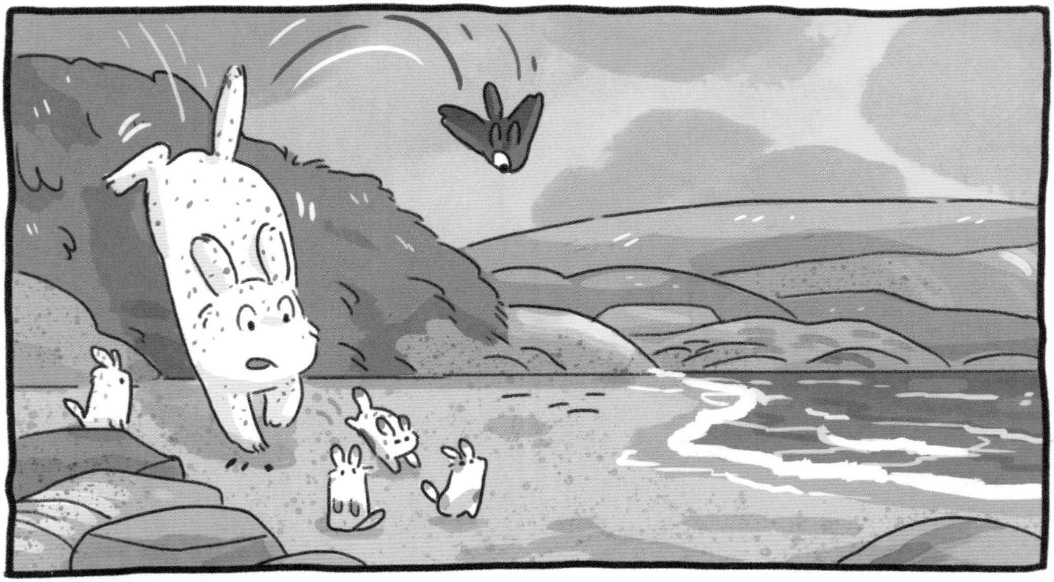

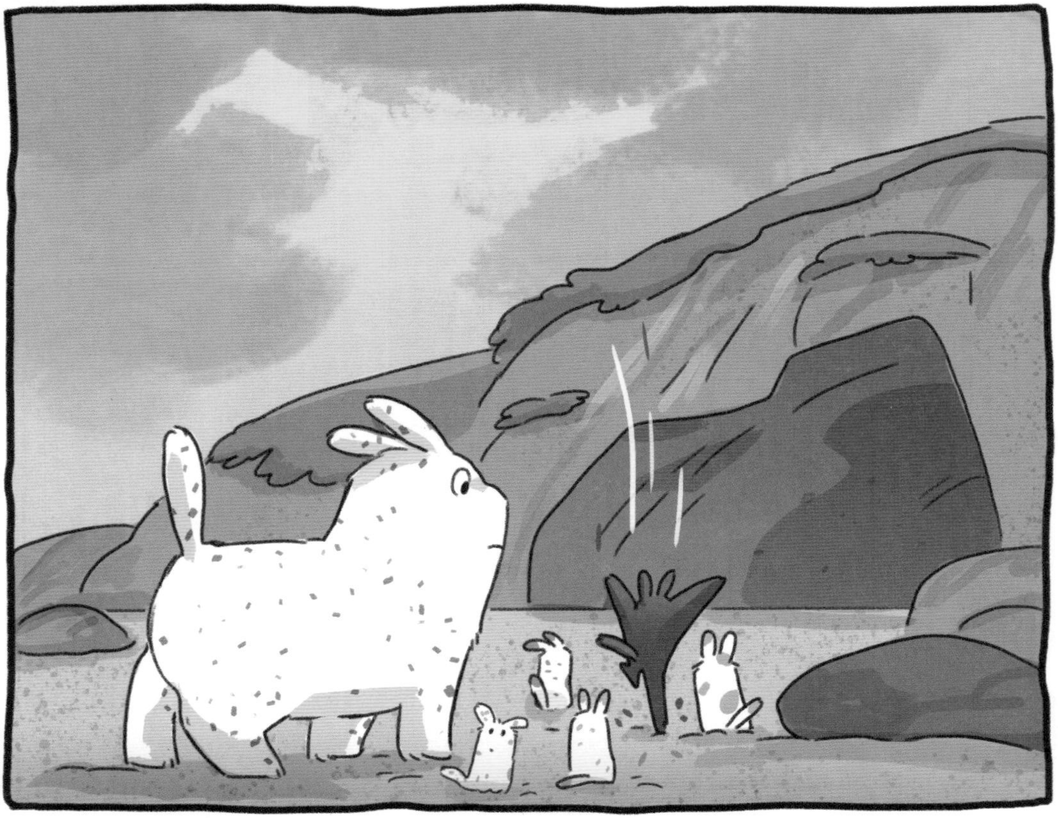

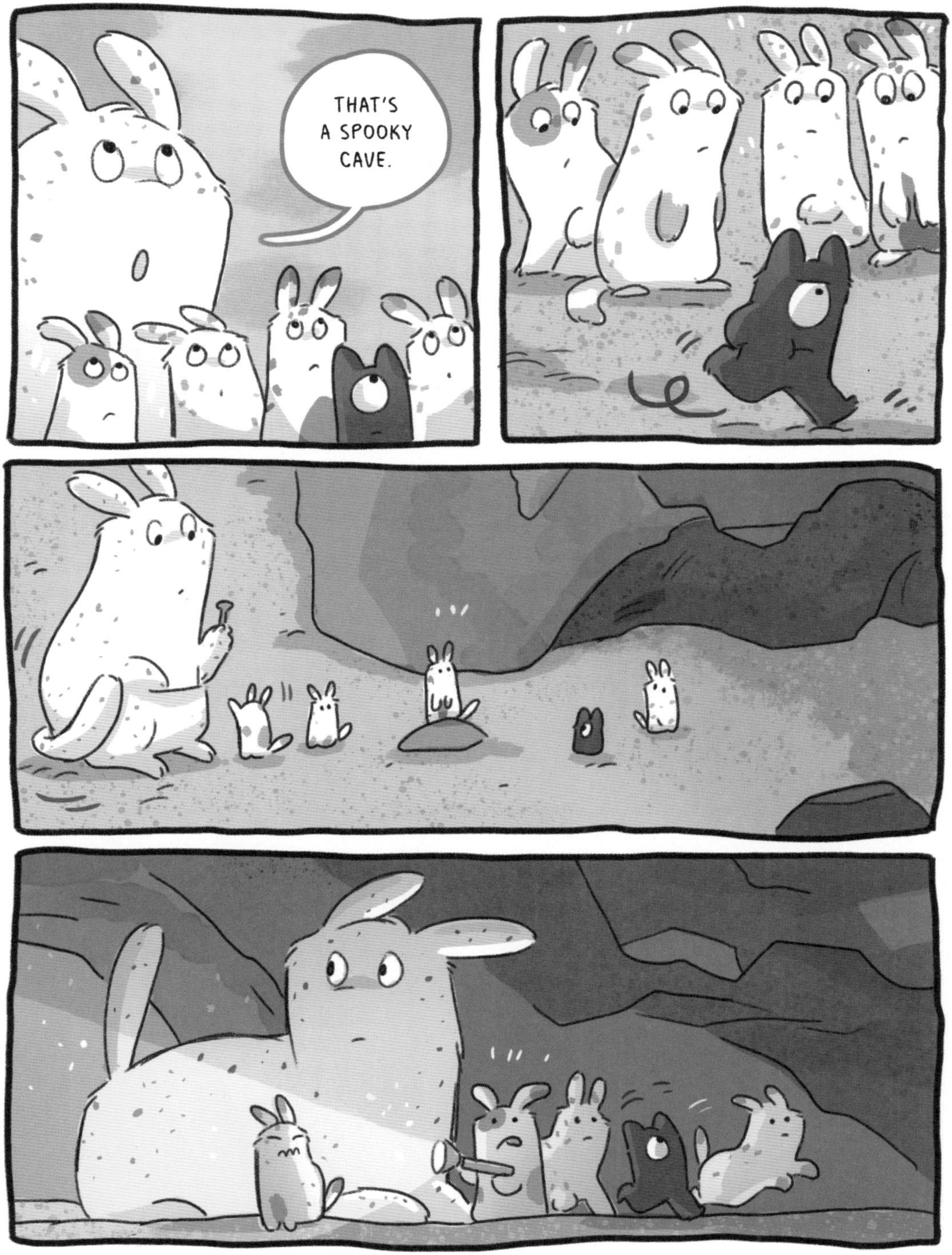
THAT'S A SPOOKY CAVE.

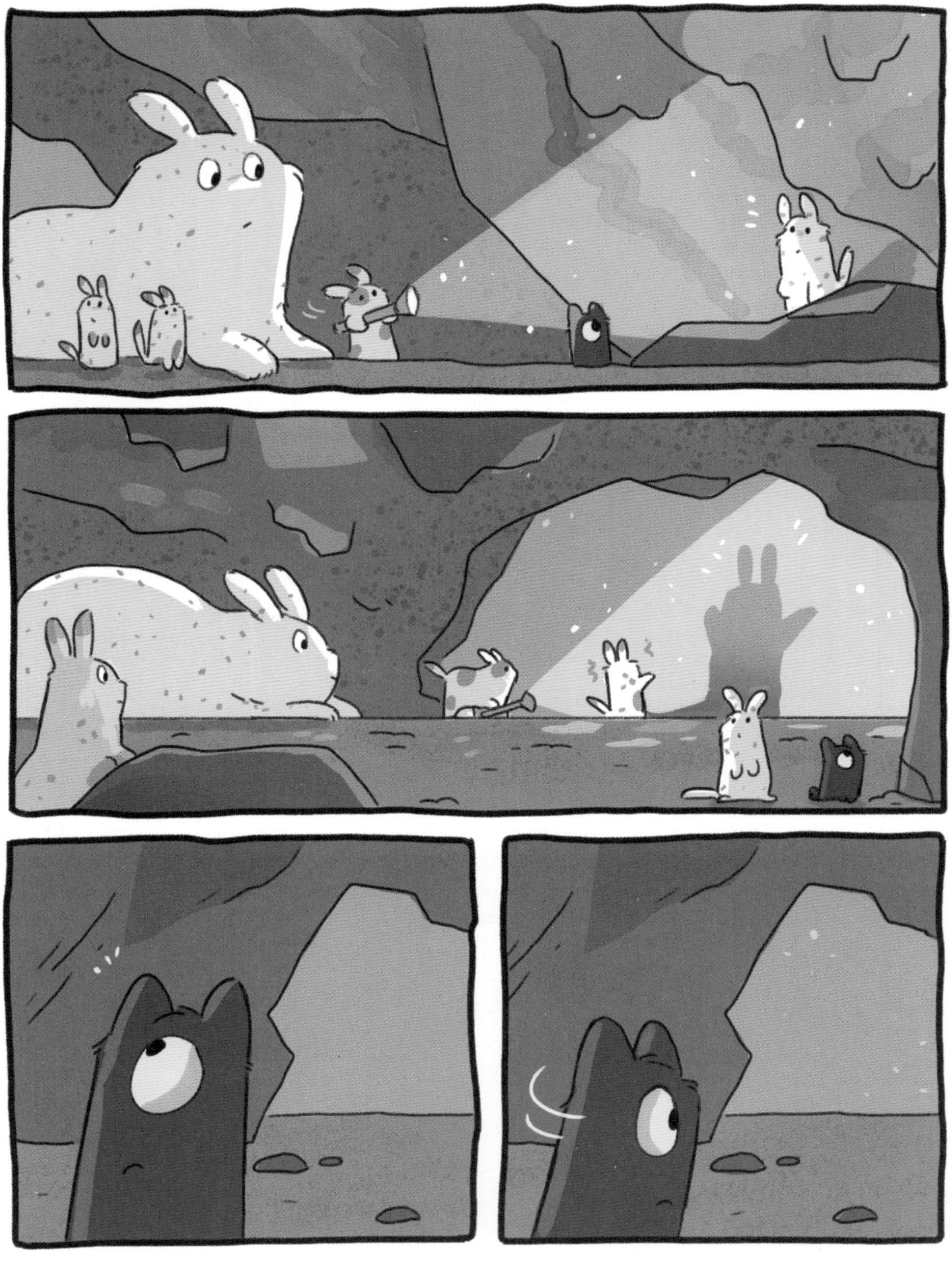

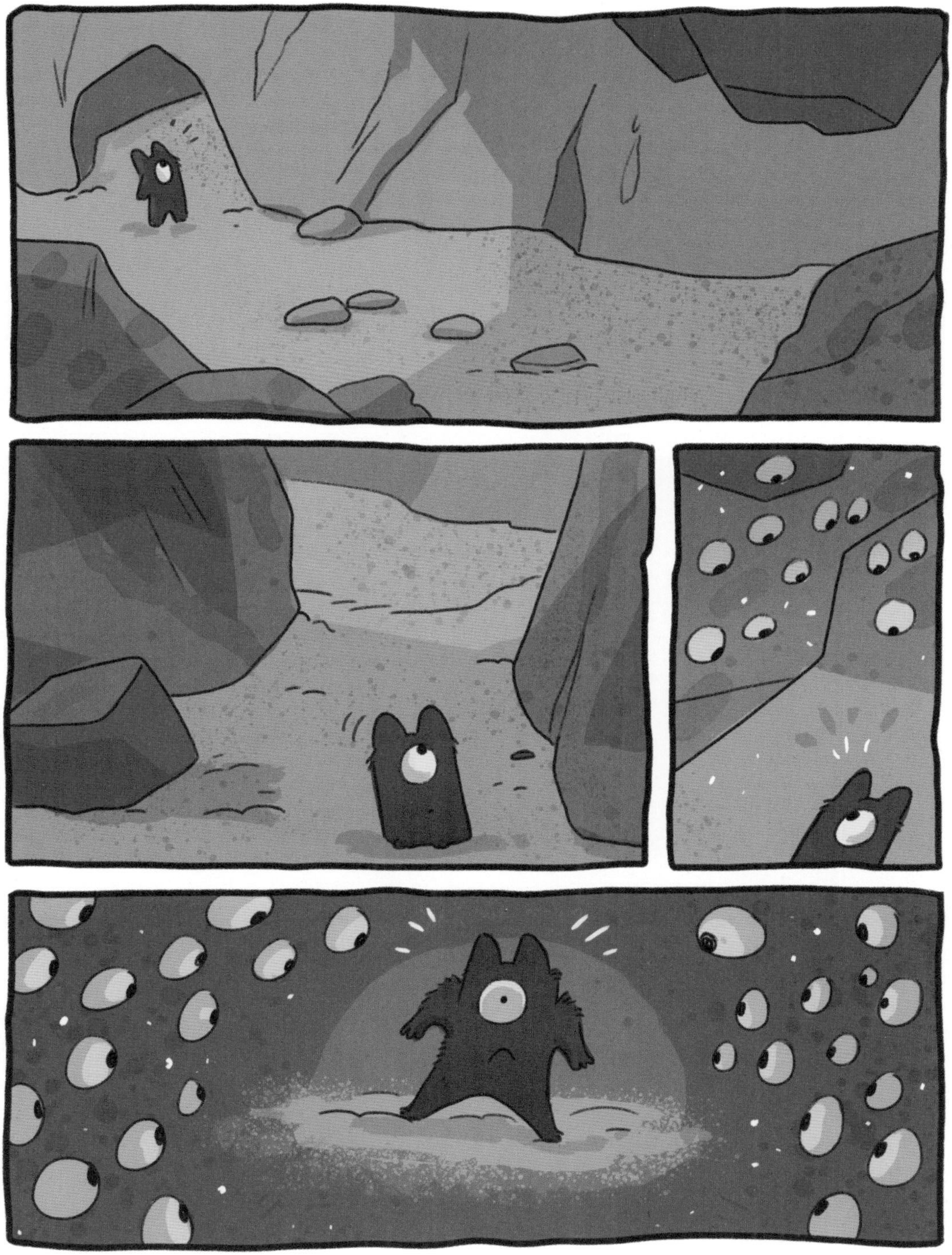

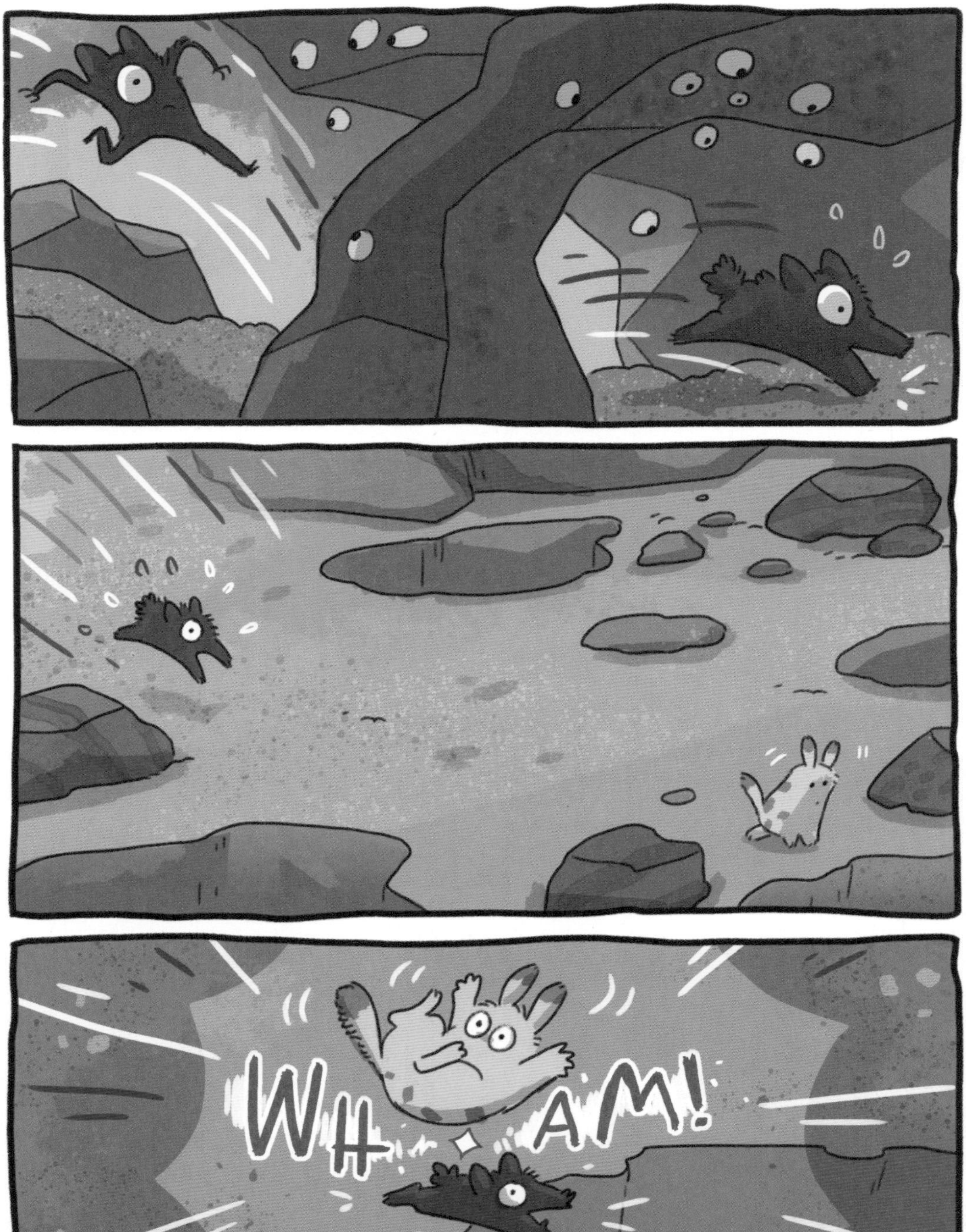
WH AM!

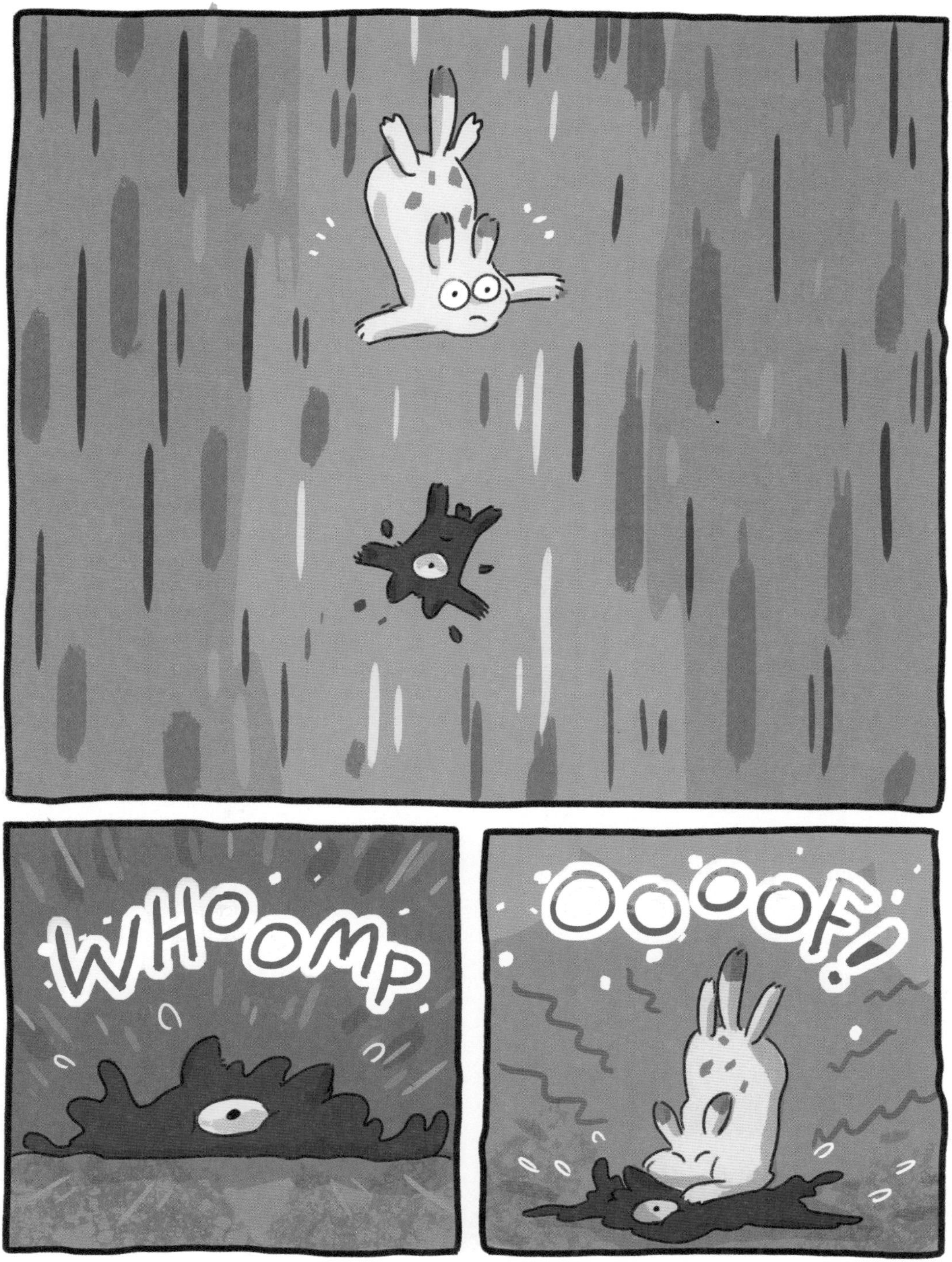
WHOOMP
OOOOF!

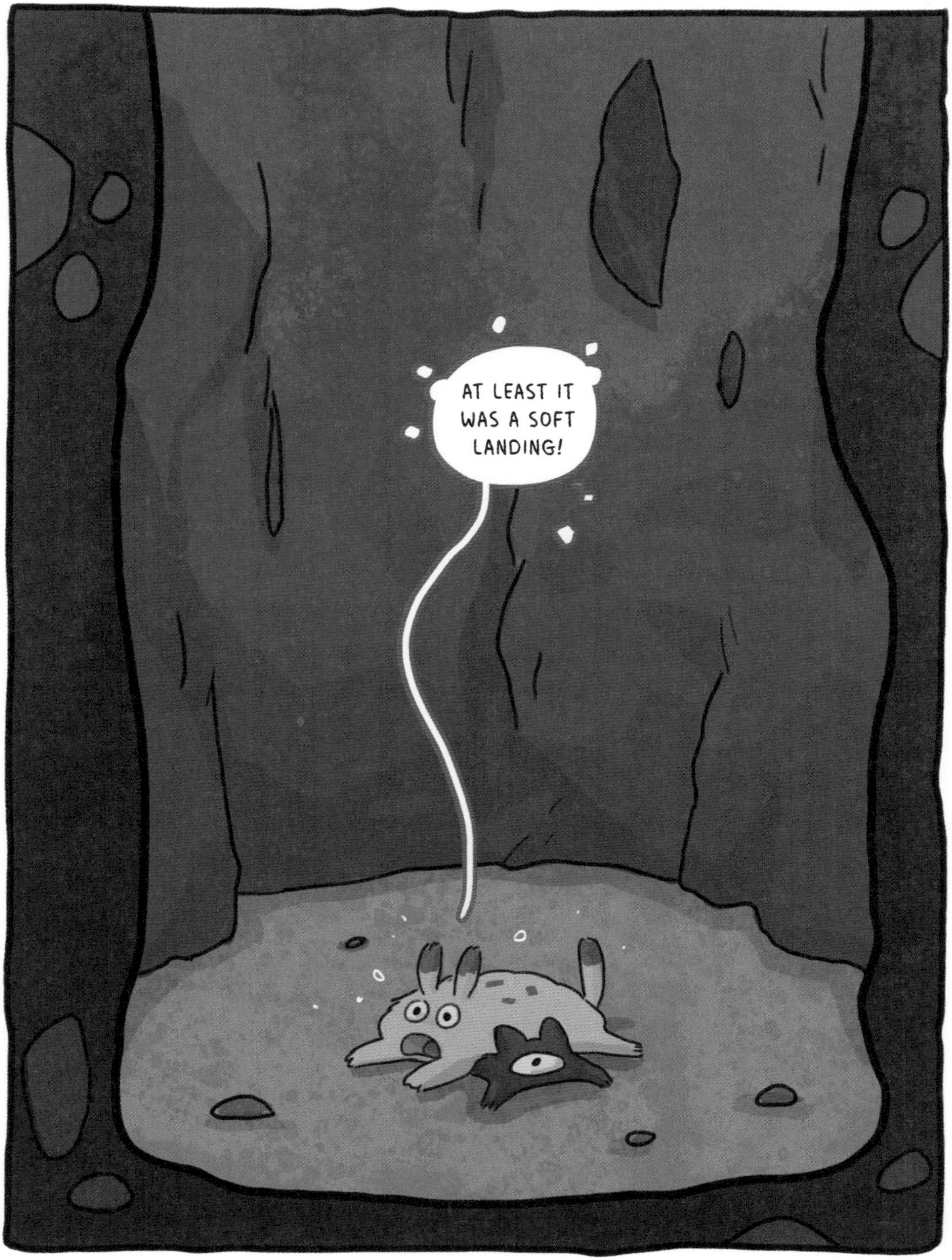
AT LEAST IT WAS A SOFT LANDING!

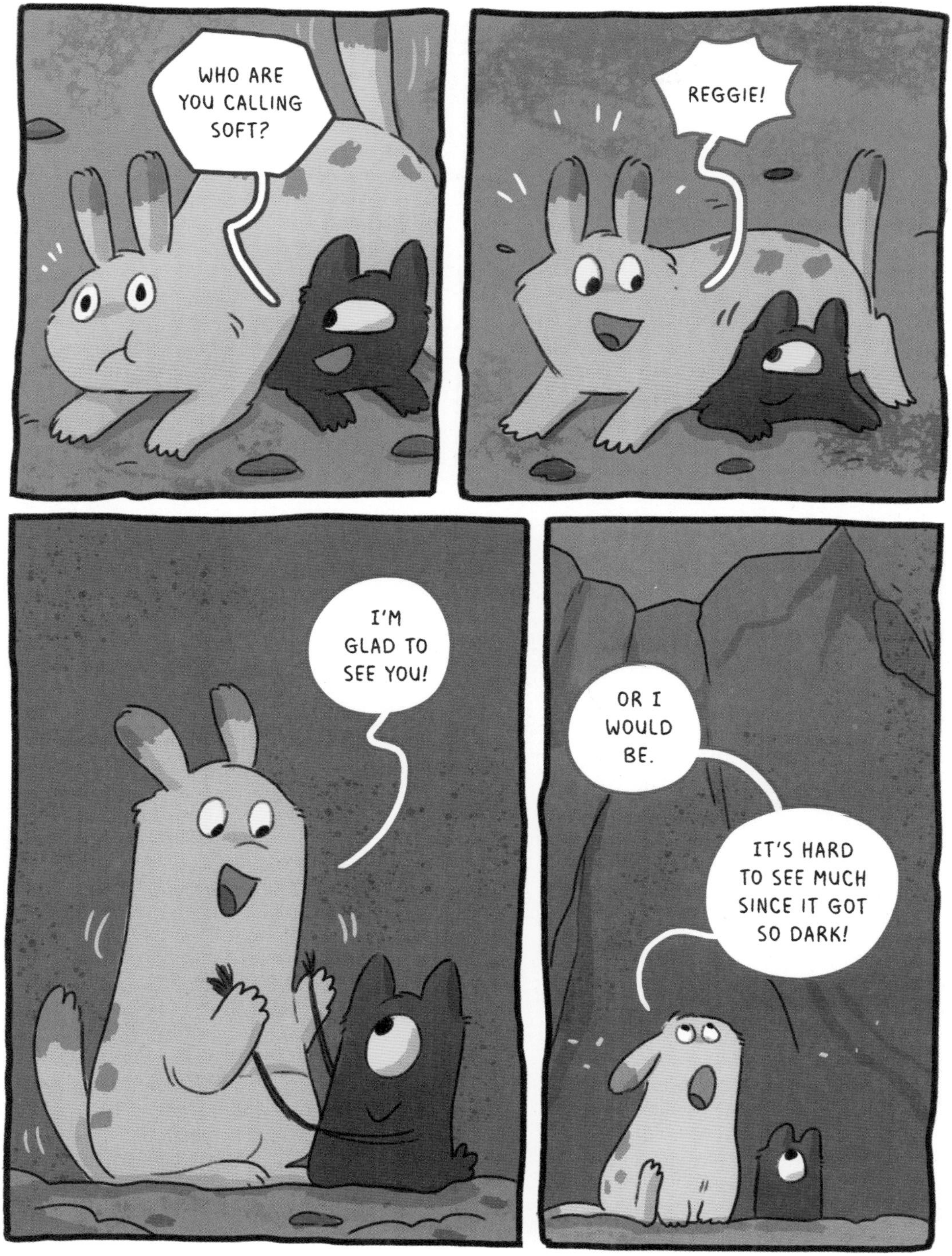
WHO ARE YOU CALLING SOFT?
REGGIE!
I'M GLAD TO SEE YOU!
OR I WOULD BE.
IT'S HARD TO SEE MUCH SINCE IT GOT SO DARK!

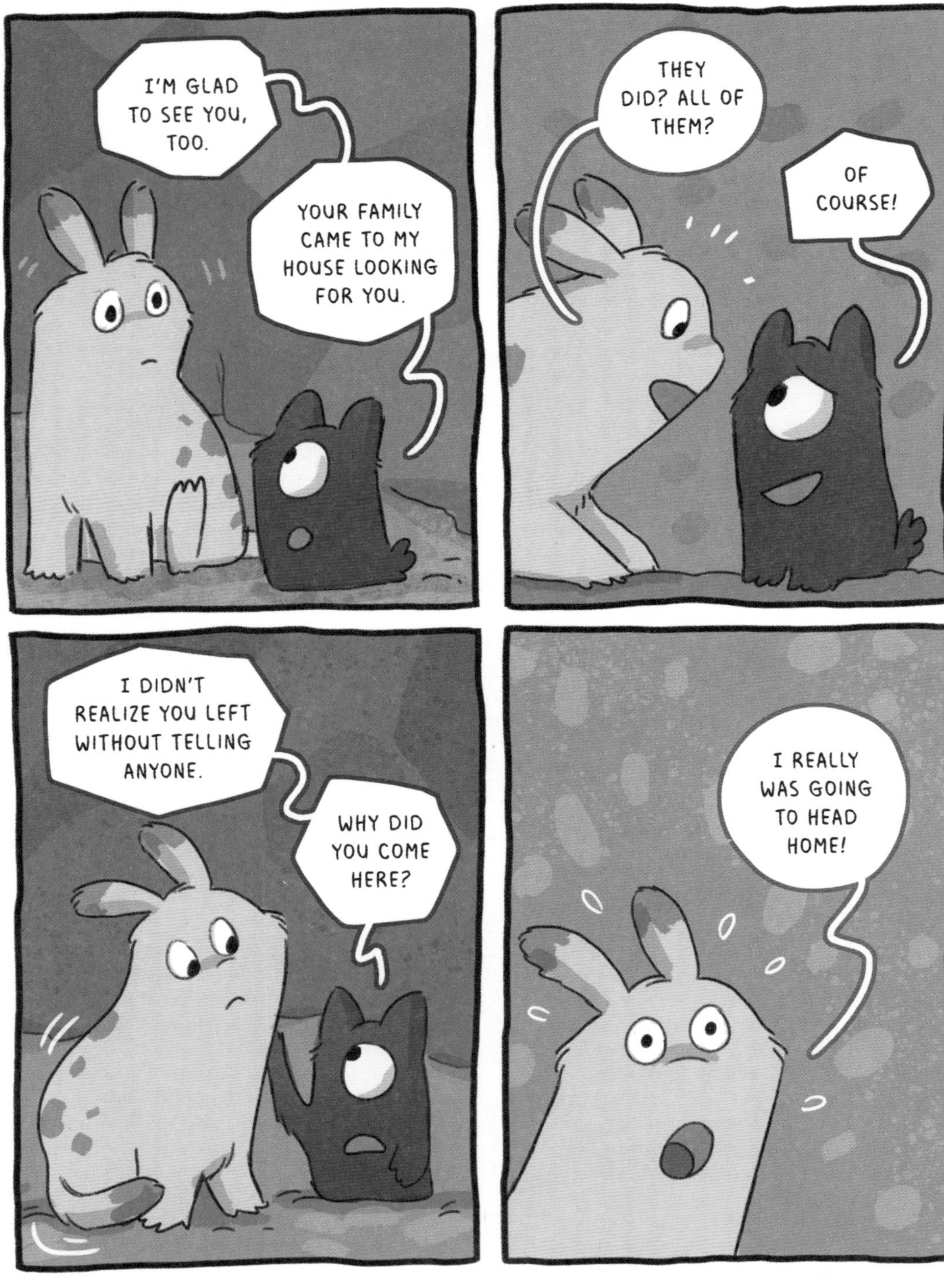
I'M GLAD TO SEE YOU, TOO.
YOUR FAMILY CAME TO MY HOUSE LOOKING FOR YOU.
THEY DID? ALL OF THEM?
OF COURSE!
I DIDN'T REALIZE YOU LEFT WITHOUT TELLING ANYONE.
WHY DID YOU COME HERE?
I REALLY WAS GOING TO HEAD HOME!

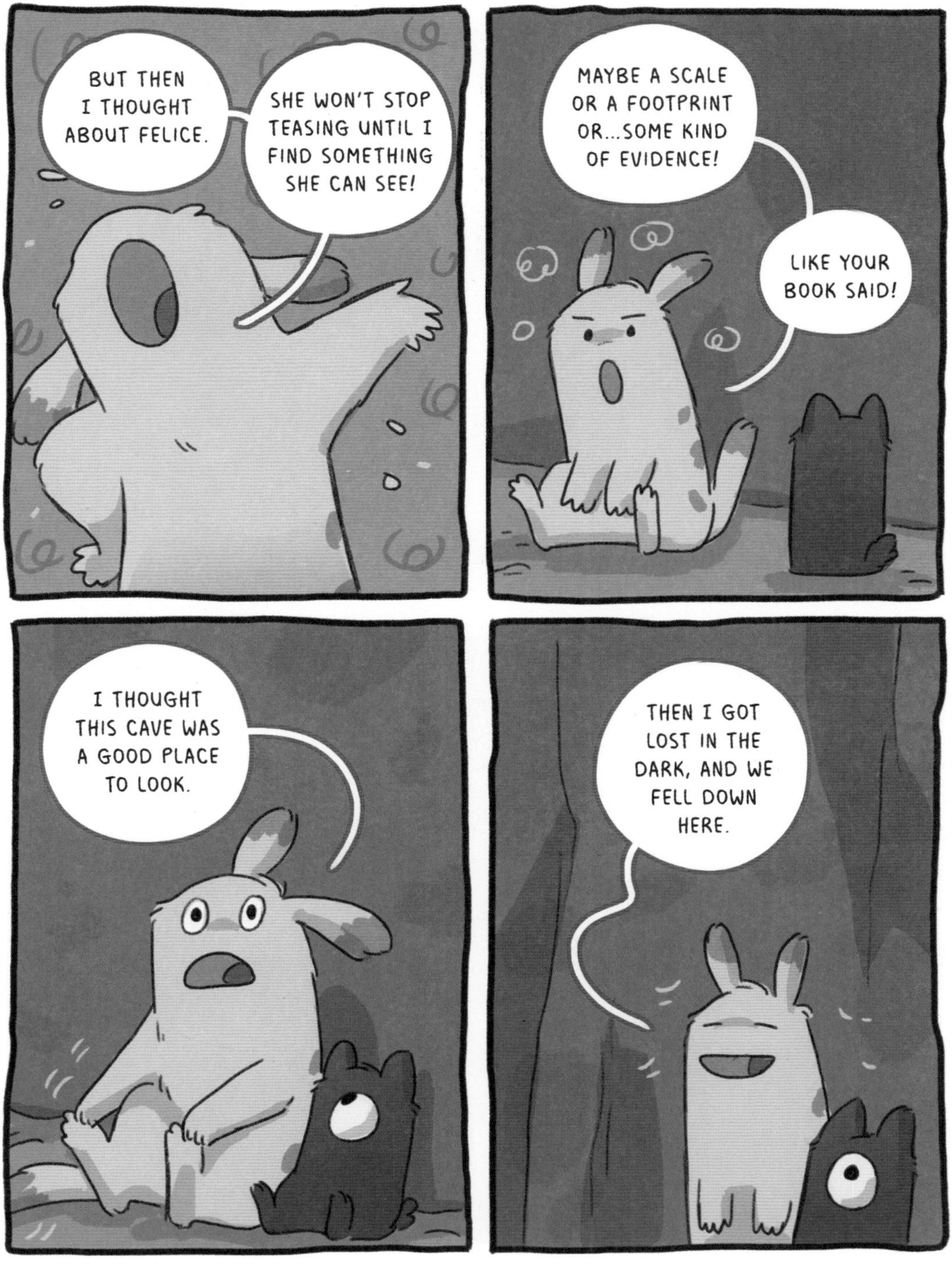
BUT THEN I THOUGHT ABOUT FELICE.
SHE WON'T STOP TEASING UNTIL I FIND SOMETHING SHE CAN SEE!
MAYBE A SCALE OR A FOOTPRINT OR...SOME KIND OF EVIDENCE!
LIKE YOUR BOOK SAID!
I THOUGHT THIS CAVE WAS A GOOD PLACE TO LOOK.
THEN I GOT LOST IN THE DARK, AND WE FELL DOWN HERE.

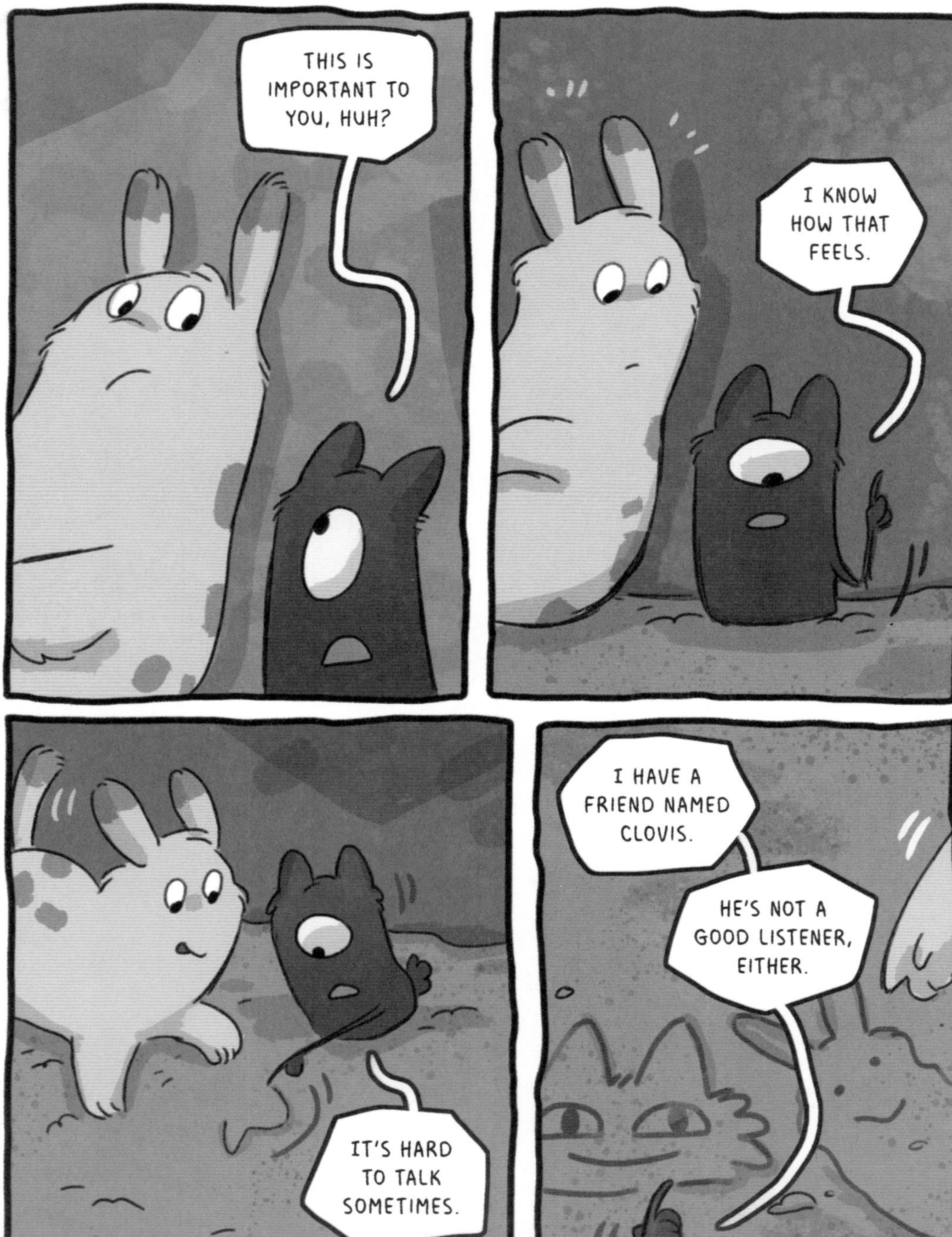
THIS IS IMPORTANT TO YOU, HUH?
I KNOW HOW THAT FEELS.
IT'S HARD TO TALK SOMETIMES.
I HAVE A FRIEND NAMED CLOVIS.
HE'S NOT A GOOD LISTENER, EITHER.

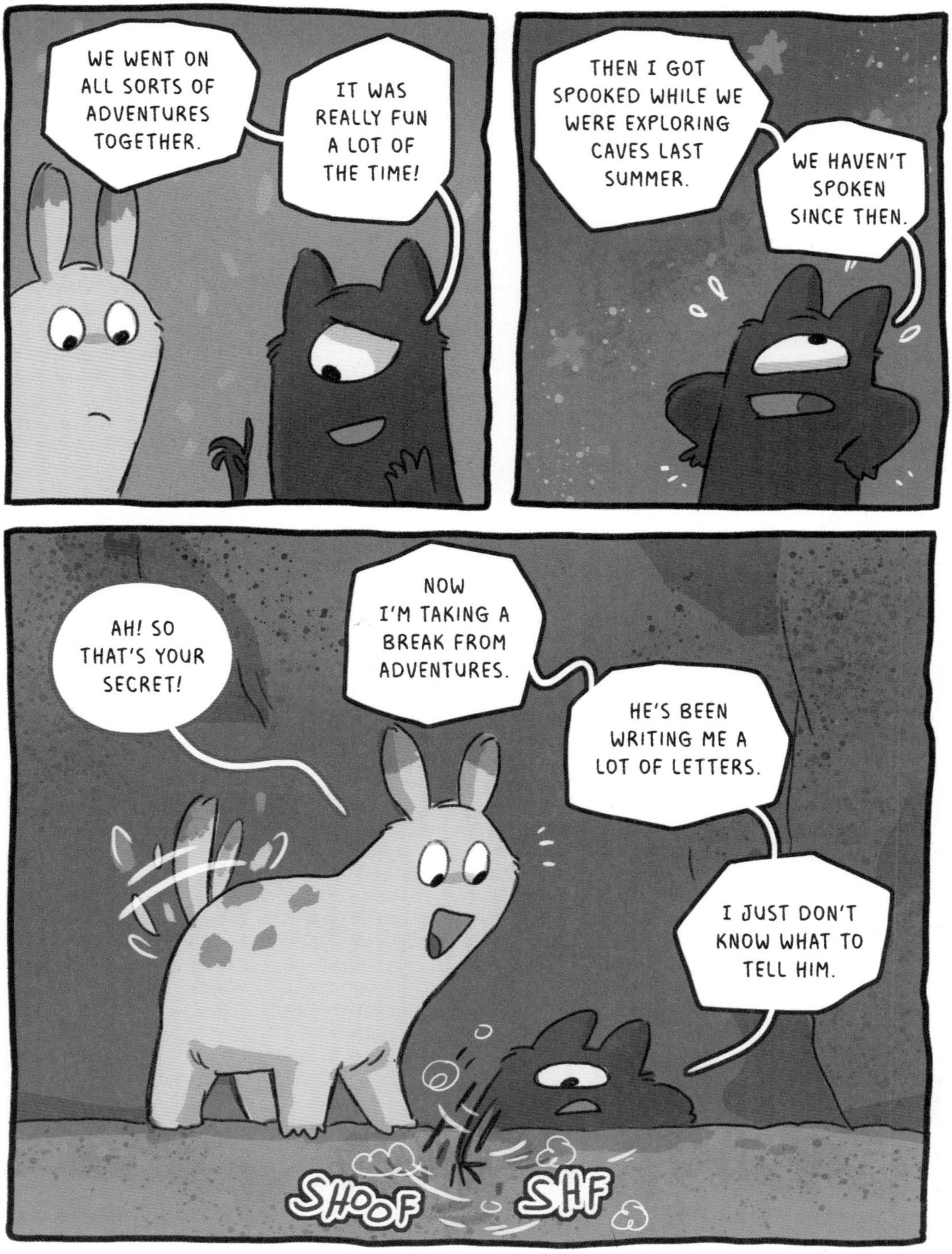
WE WENT ON ALL SORTS OF ADVENTURES TOGETHER.
IT WAS REALLY FUN A LOT OF THE TIME!
THEN I GOT SPOOKED WHILE WE WERE EXPLORING CAVES LAST SUMMER.
WE HAVEN'T SPOKEN SINCE THEN.
AH! SO THAT'S YOUR SECRET!
NOW I'M TAKING A BREAK FROM ADVENTURES.
HE'S BEEN WRITING ME A LOT OF LETTERS.
I JUST DON'T KNOW WHAT TO TELL HIM.
SHOOF
SHF

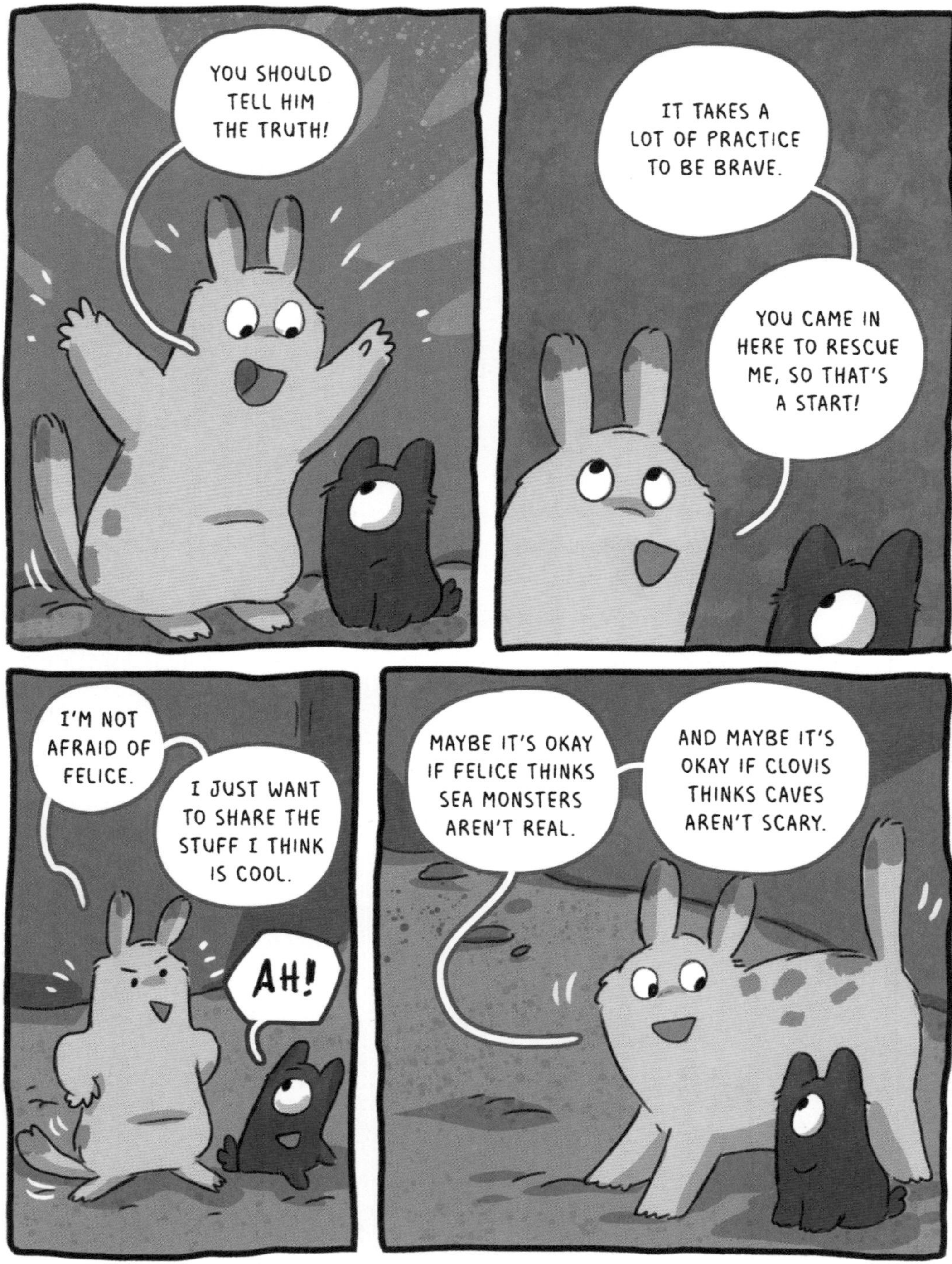

YOU SHOULD TELL HIM THE TRUTH!
IT TAKES A LOT OF PRACTICE TO BE BRAVE.
YOU CAME IN HERE TO RESCUE ME, SO THAT'S A START!
I'M NOT AFRAID OF FELICE.
I JUST WANT TO SHARE THE STUFF I THINK IS COOL.
AH!
MAYBE IT'S OKAY IF FELICE THINKS SEA MONSTERS AREN'T REAL.
AND MAYBE IT'S OKAY IF CLOVIS THINKS CAVES AREN'T SCARY.

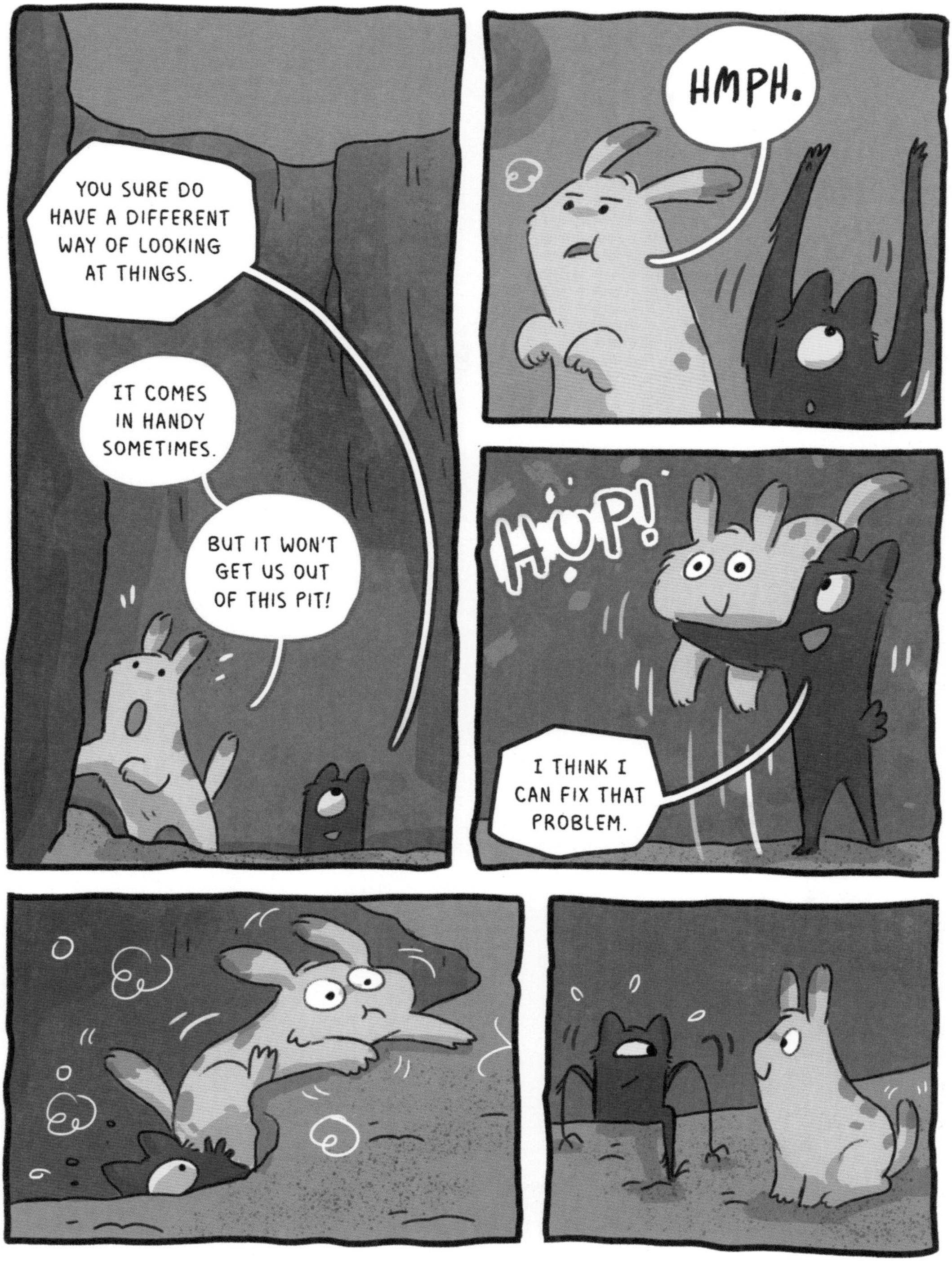
YOU SURE DO HAVE A DIFFERENT WAY OF LOOKING AT THINGS.
IT COMES IN HANDY SOMETIMES.
BUT IT WON'T GET US OUT OF THIS PIT!
HMPH.
HUP!
I THINK I CAN FIX THAT PROBLEM.

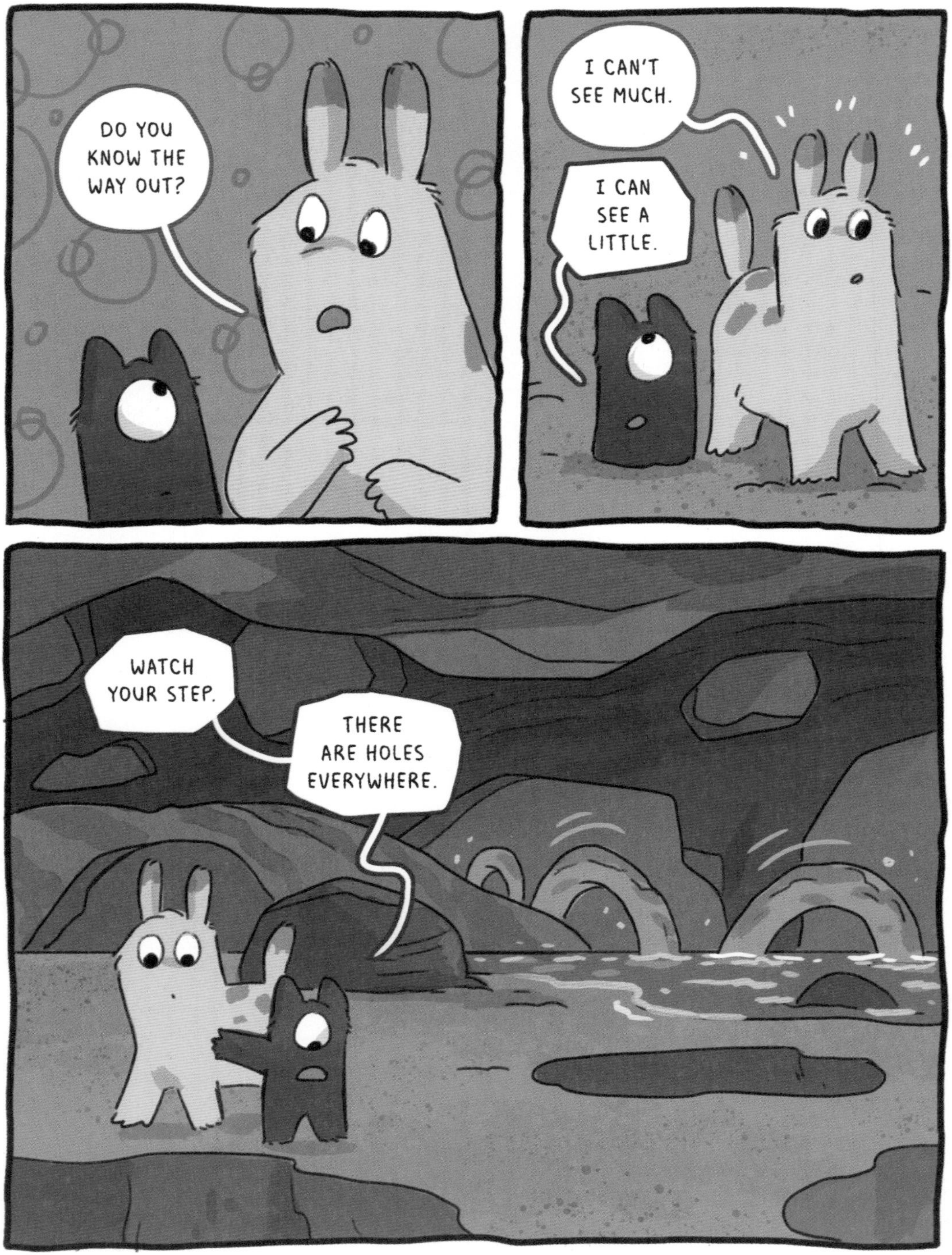
DO YOU KNOW THE WAY OUT?
I CAN'T SEE MUCH.
I CAN SEE A LITTLE.
WATCH YOUR STEP.
THERE ARE HOLES EVERYWHERE.

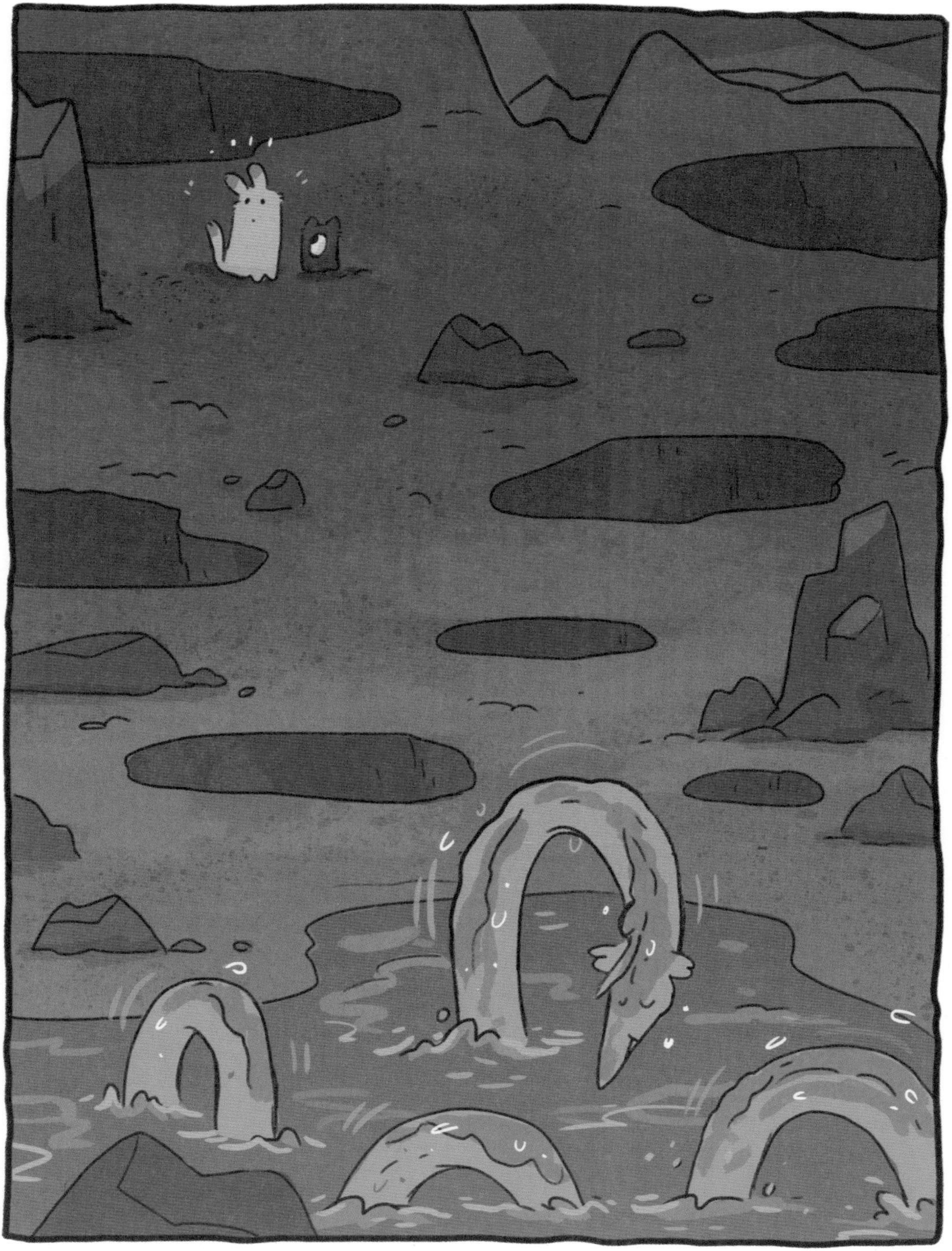

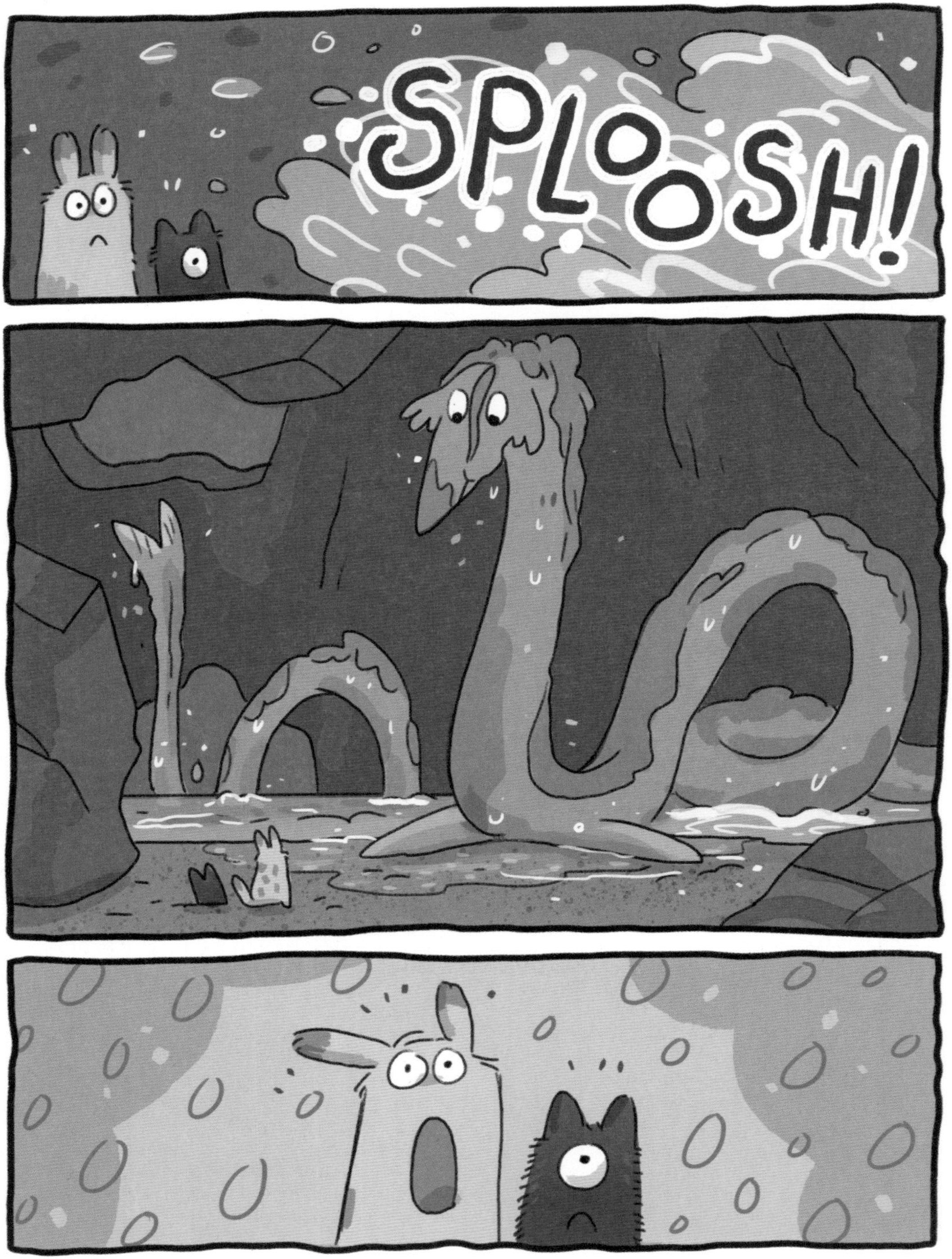
SPLOOSH!

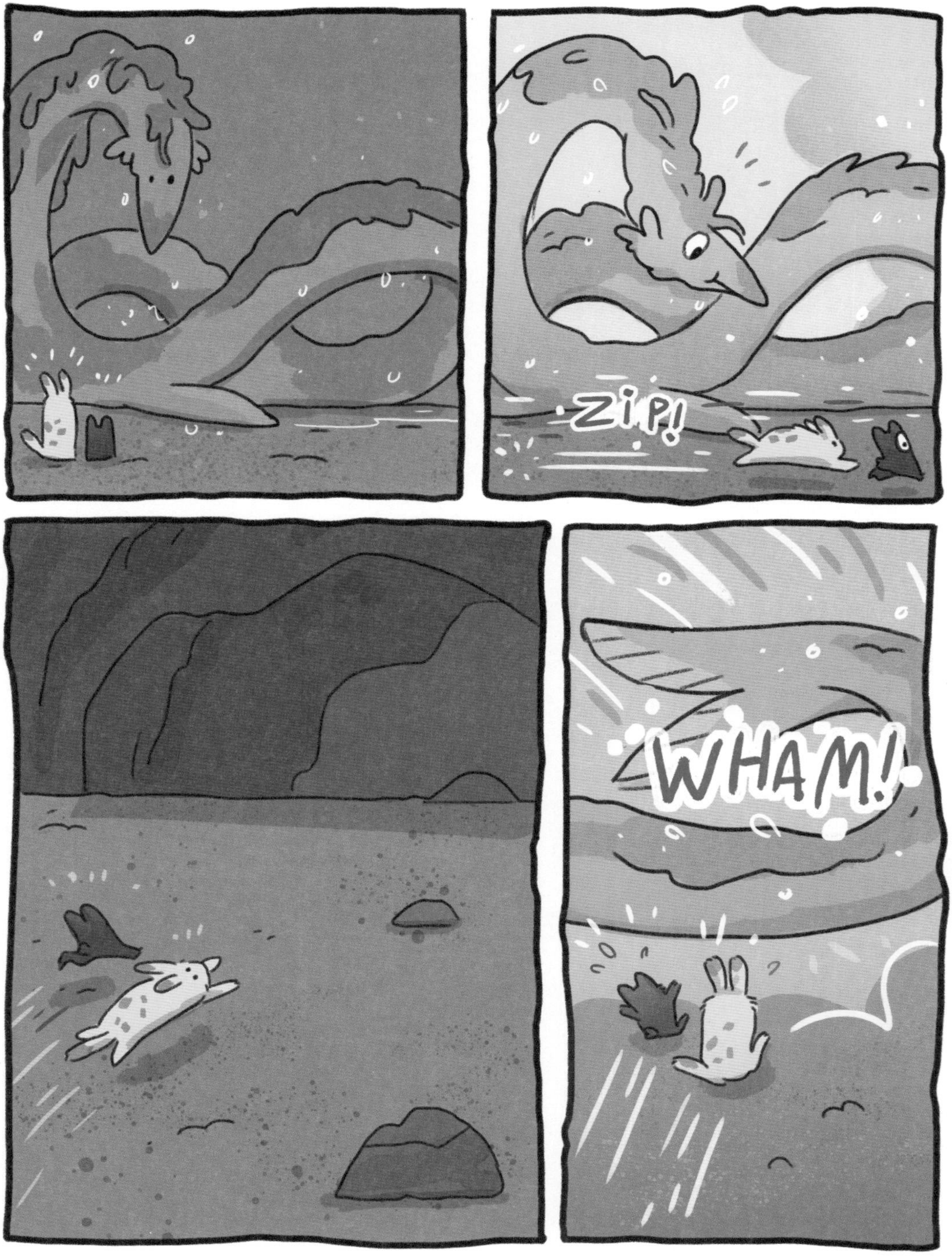
ZIP!
WHAM!

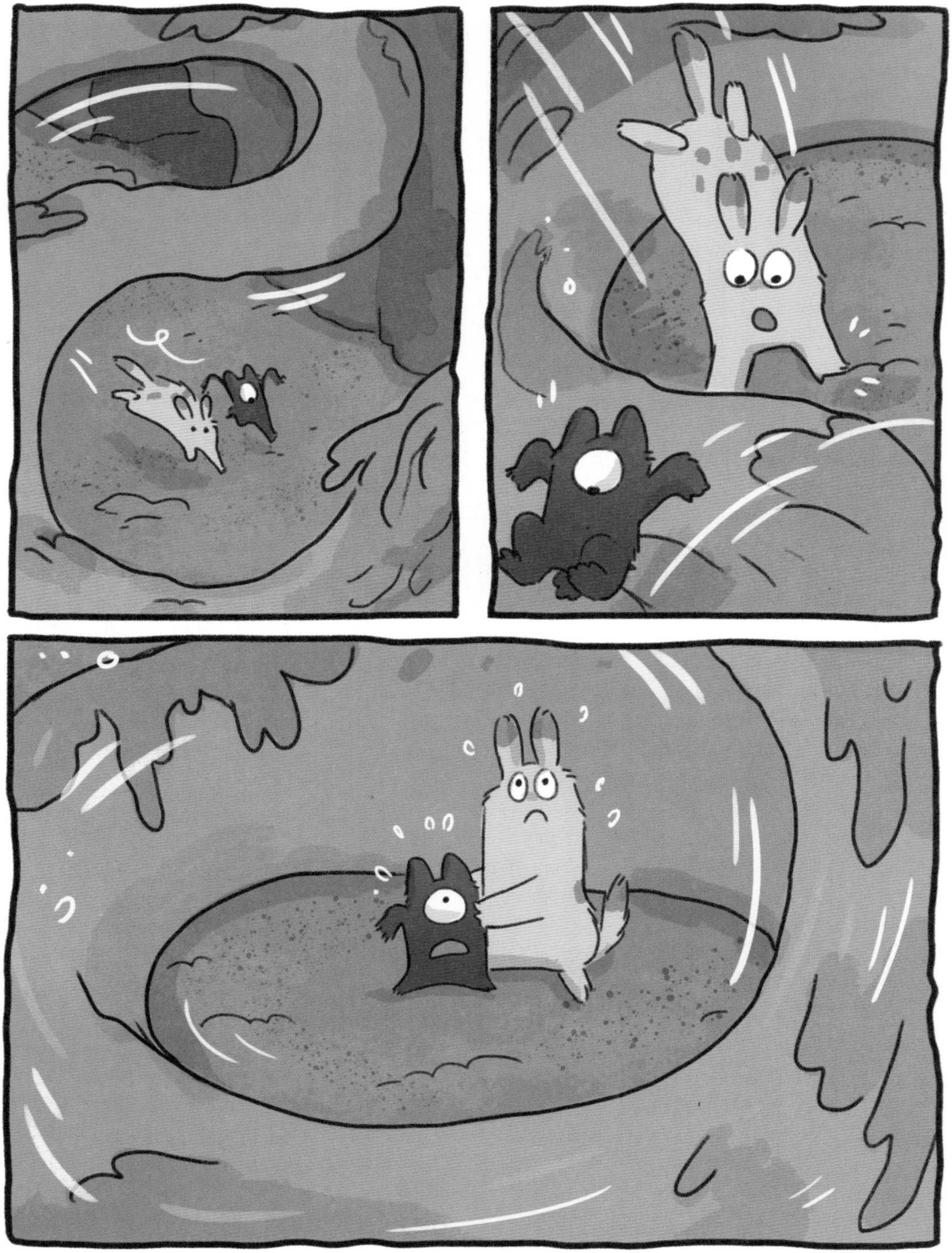

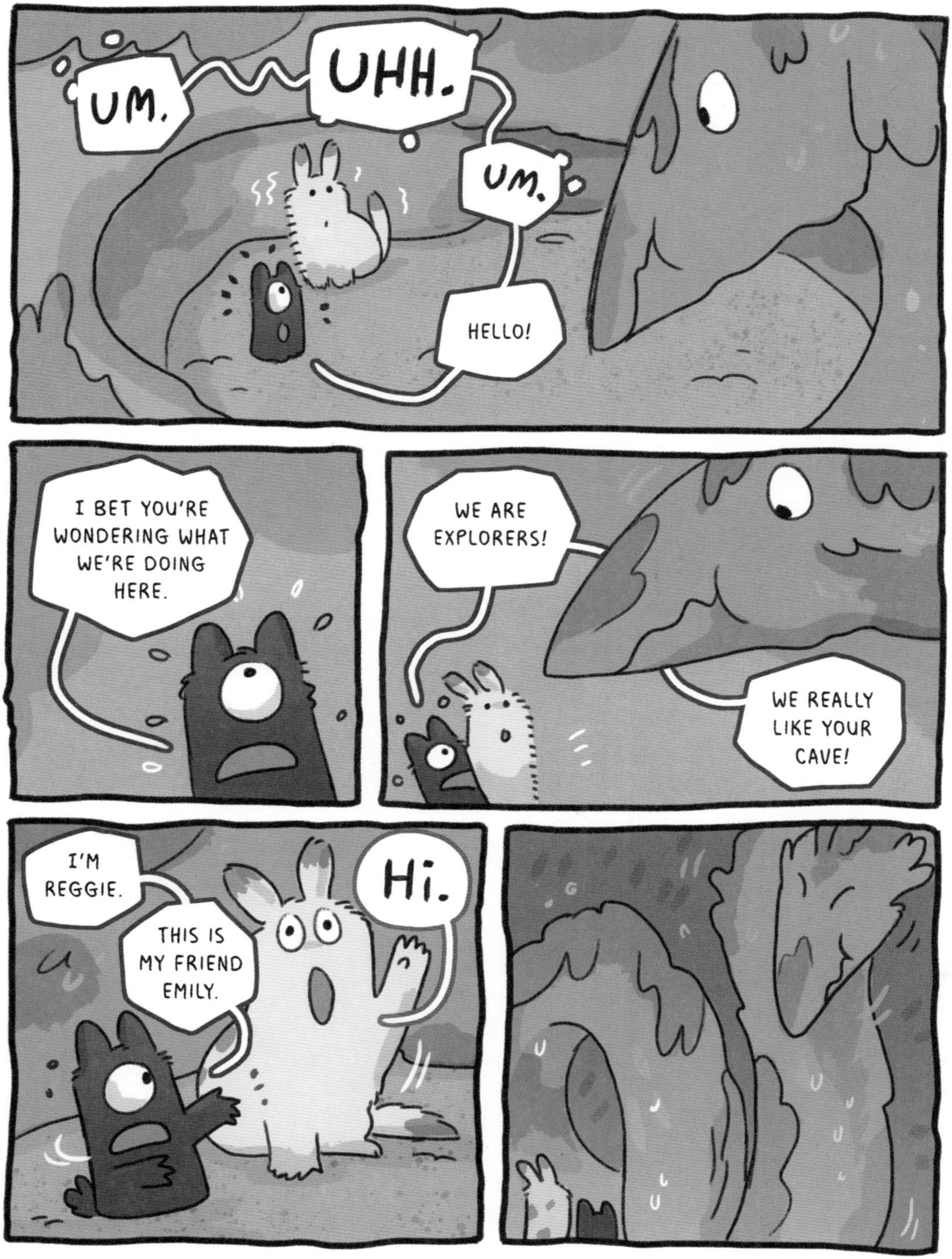
UM.
UHH.
UM.
HELLO!
I BET YOU'RE WONDERING WHAT WE'RE DOING HERE.
WE ARE EXPLORERS!
WE REALLY LIKE YOUR CAVE!
I'M REGGIE.
THIS IS MY FRIEND EMILY.
Hi.

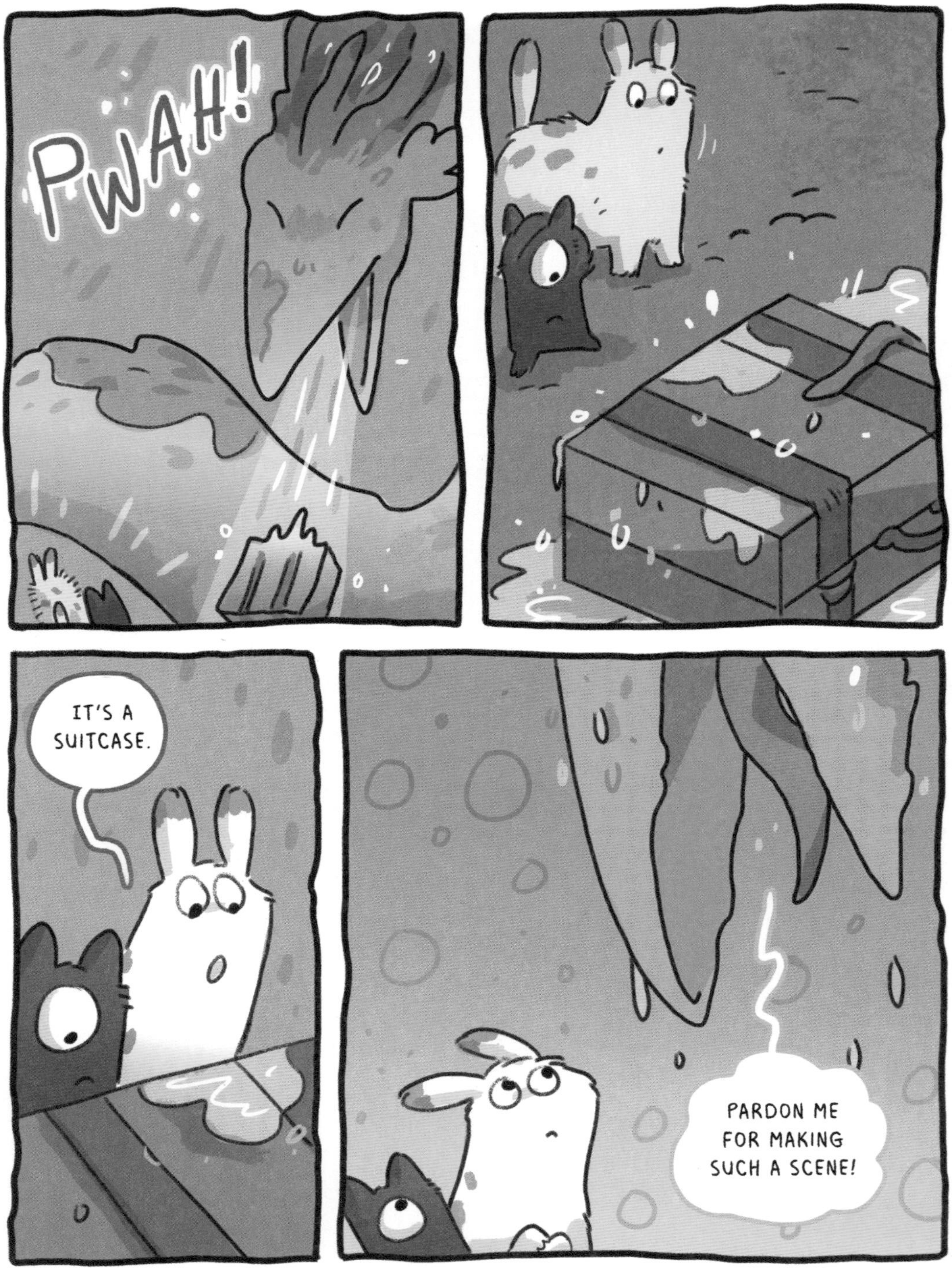
PWAH!
IT'S A SUITCASE.
PARDON ME FOR MAKING SUCH A SCENE!

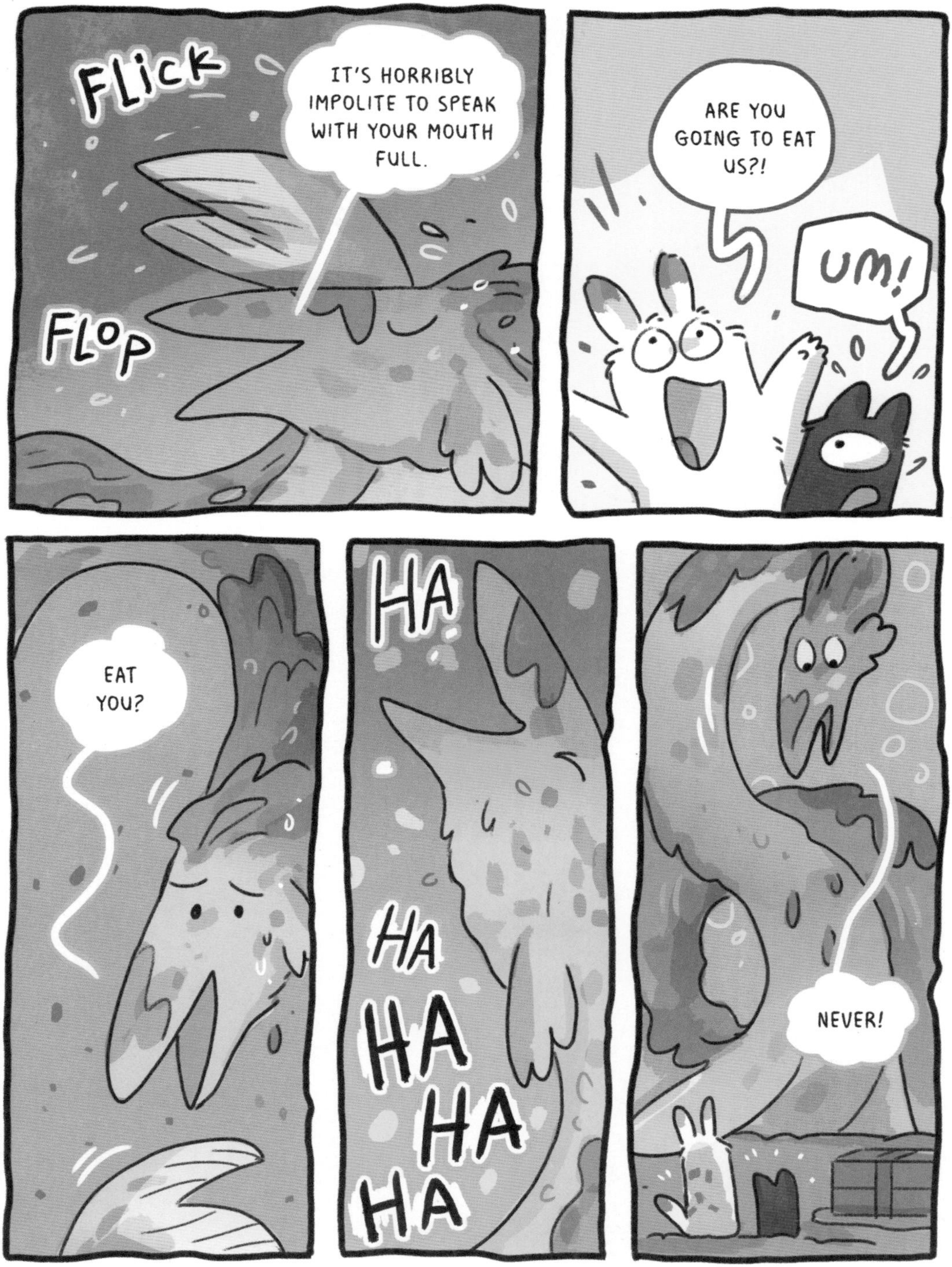
FLICK
IT'S HORRIBLY IMPOLITE TO SPEAK WITH YOUR MOUTH FULL.
FLOP
ARE YOU GOING TO EAT US?!
UM!
EAT YOU?
HA
HA
HA
HA
HA
NEVER!

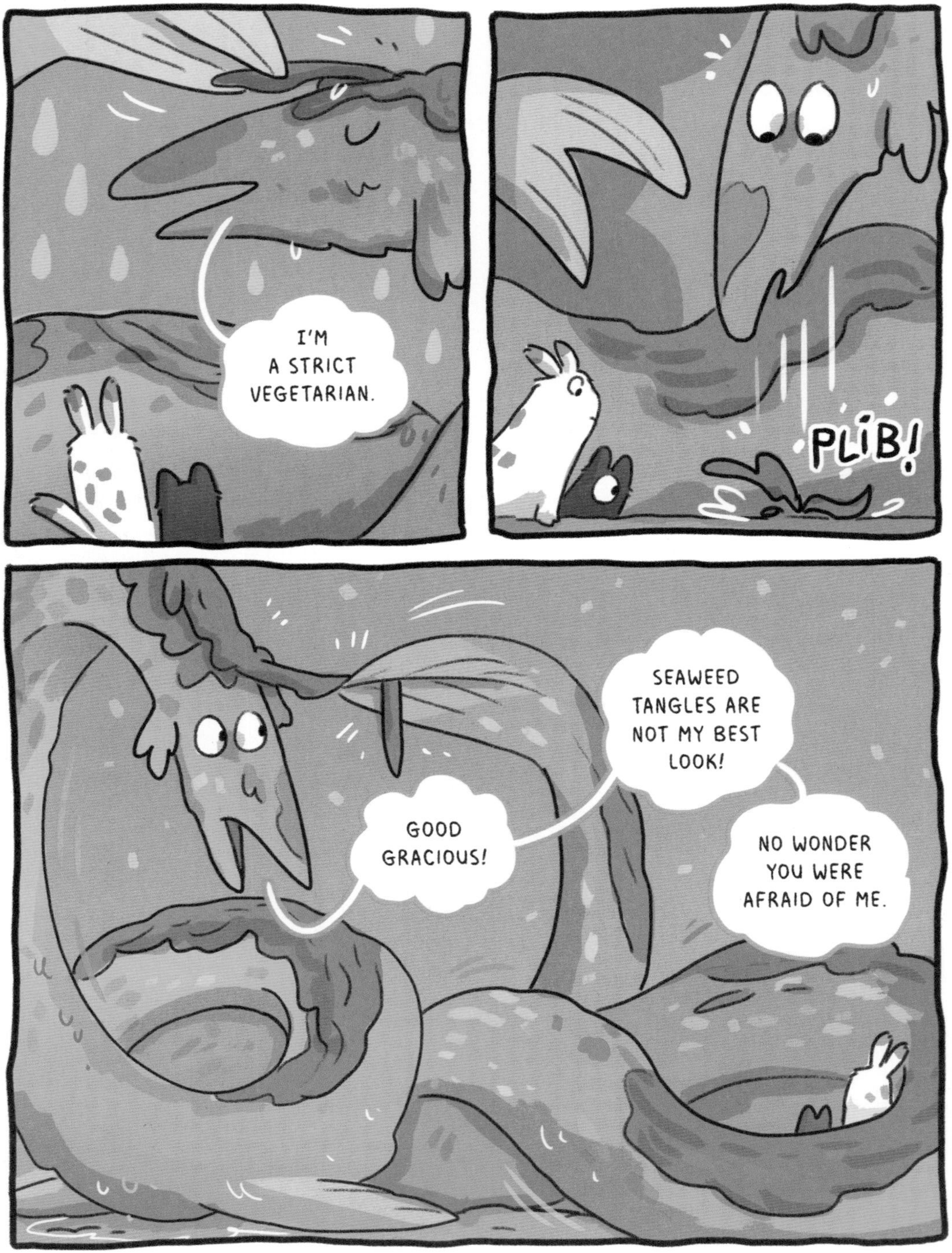
I'M A STRICT VEGETARIAN.
PLIB!
GOOD GRACIOUS!
SEAWEED TANGLES ARE NOT MY BEST LOOK!
NO WONDER YOU WERE AFRAID OF ME.

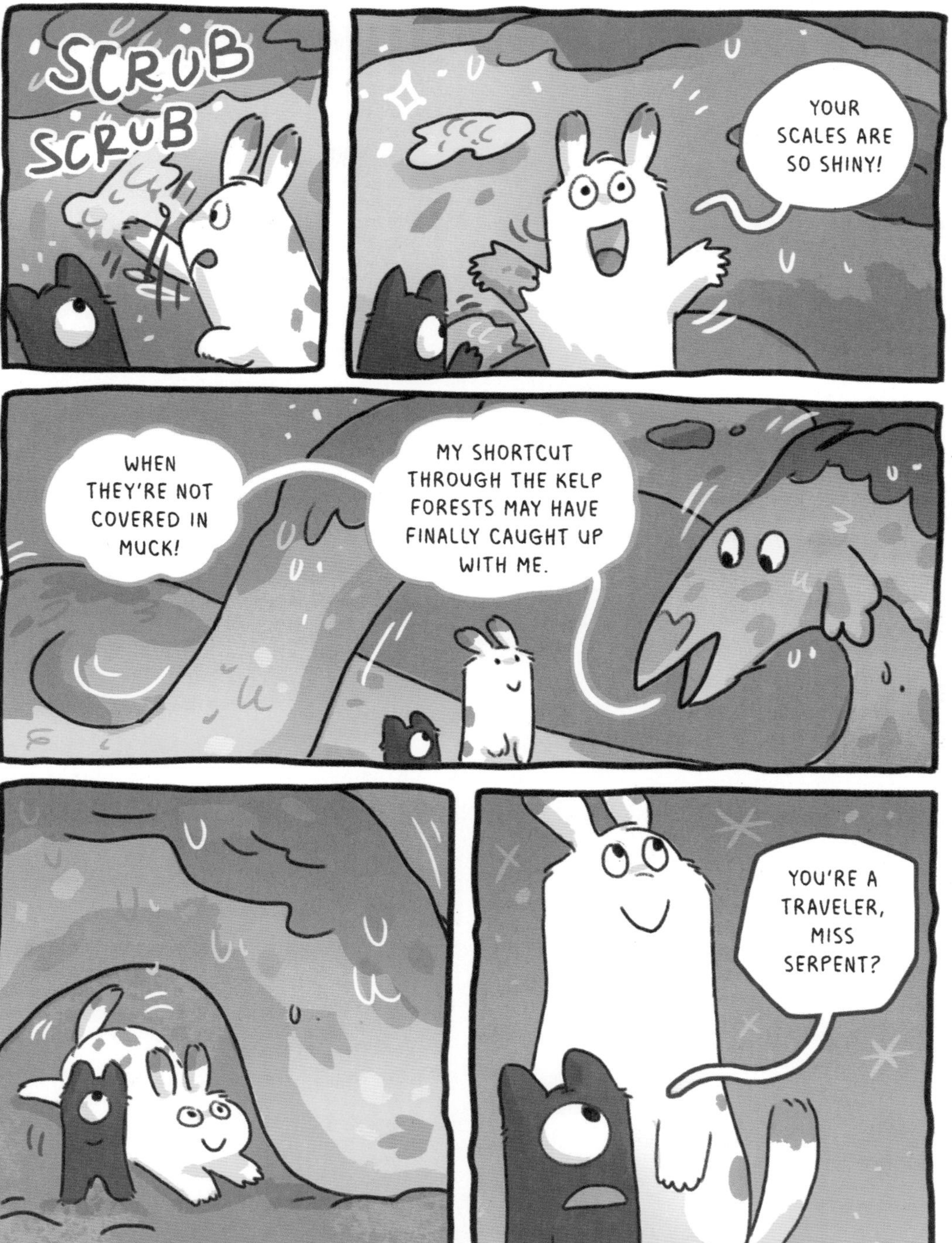
SCRUB
SCRUB
YOUR SCALES ARE SO SHINY!
WHEN THEY'RE NOT COVERED IN MUCK!
MY SHORTCUT THROUGH THE KELP FORESTS MAY HAVE FINALLY CAUGHT UP WITH ME.
YOU'RE A TRAVELER, MISS SERPENT?

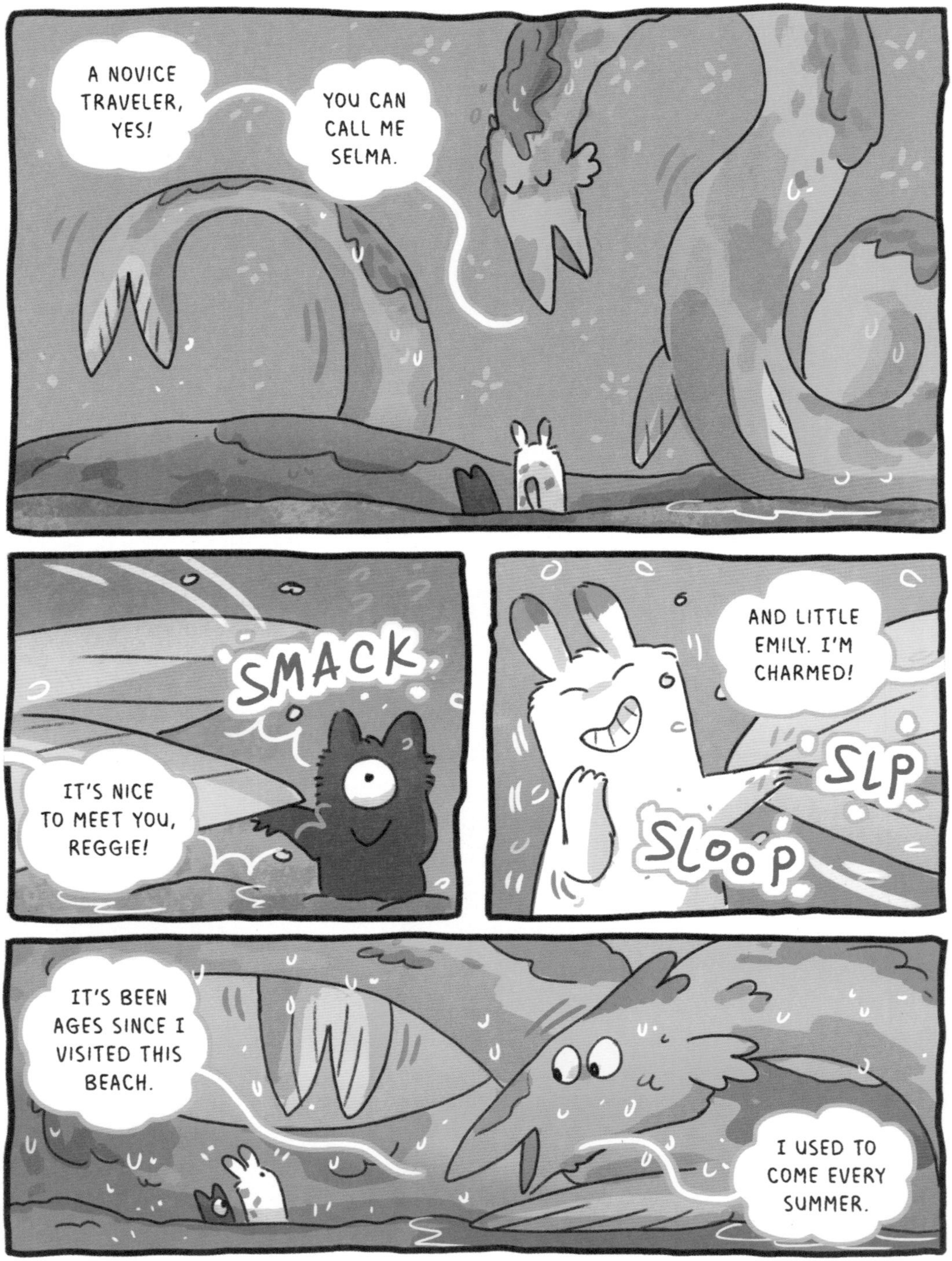
A NOVICE TRAVELER, YES!
YOU CAN CALL ME SELMA.
SMACK
IT'S NICE TO MEET YOU, REGGIE!
AND LITTLE EMILY. I'M CHARMED!
SLP
SLOOP
IT'S BEEN AGES SINCE I VISITED THIS BEACH.
I USED TO COME EVERY SUMMER.

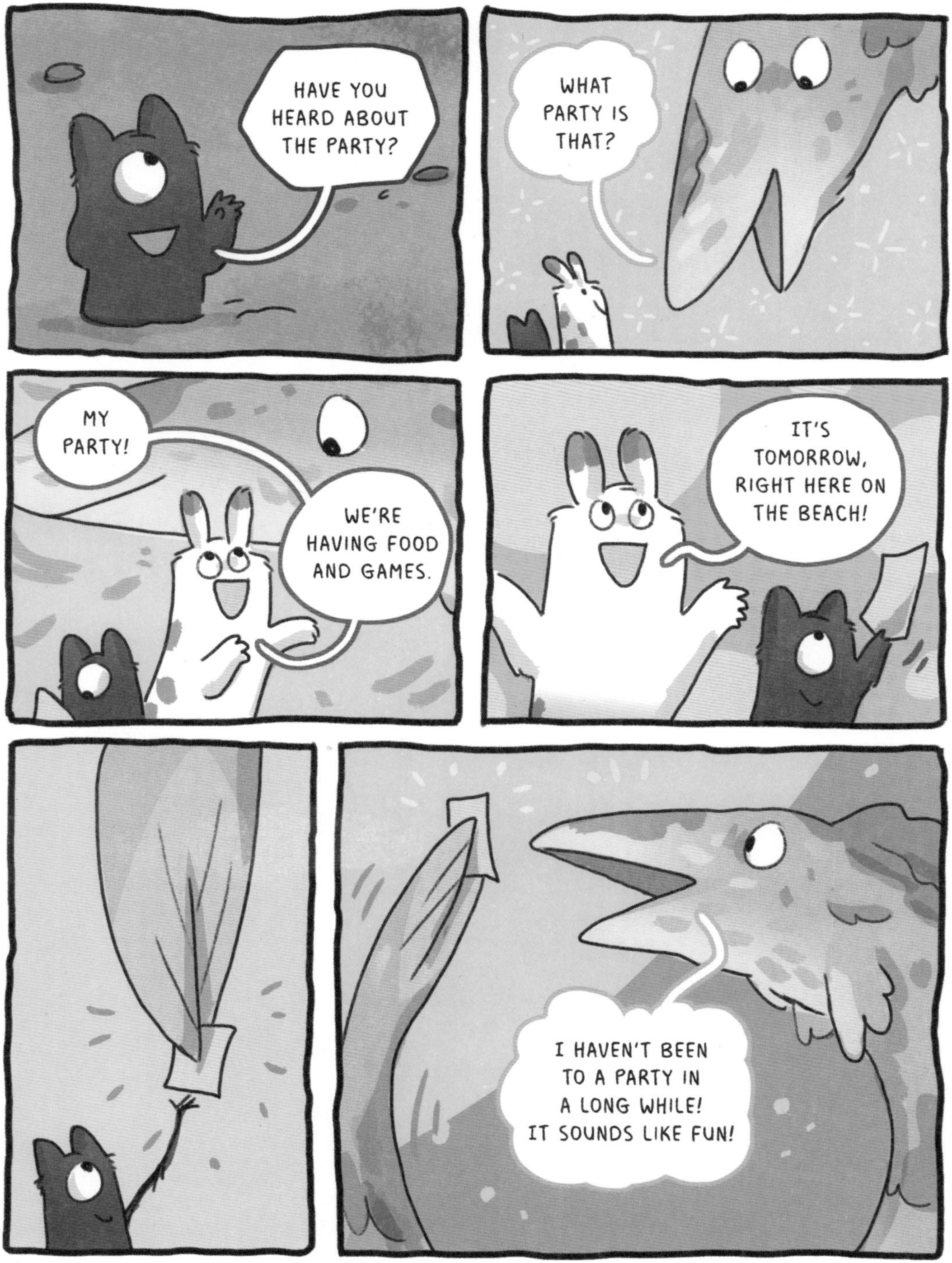
HAVE YOU HEARD ABOUT THE PARTY?
WHAT PARTY IS THAT?
MY PARTY!
WE'RE HAVING FOOD AND GAMES.
IT'S TOMORROW, RIGHT HERE ON THE BEACH!
I HAVEN'T BEEN TO A PARTY IN A LONG WHILE! IT SOUNDS LIKE FUN!

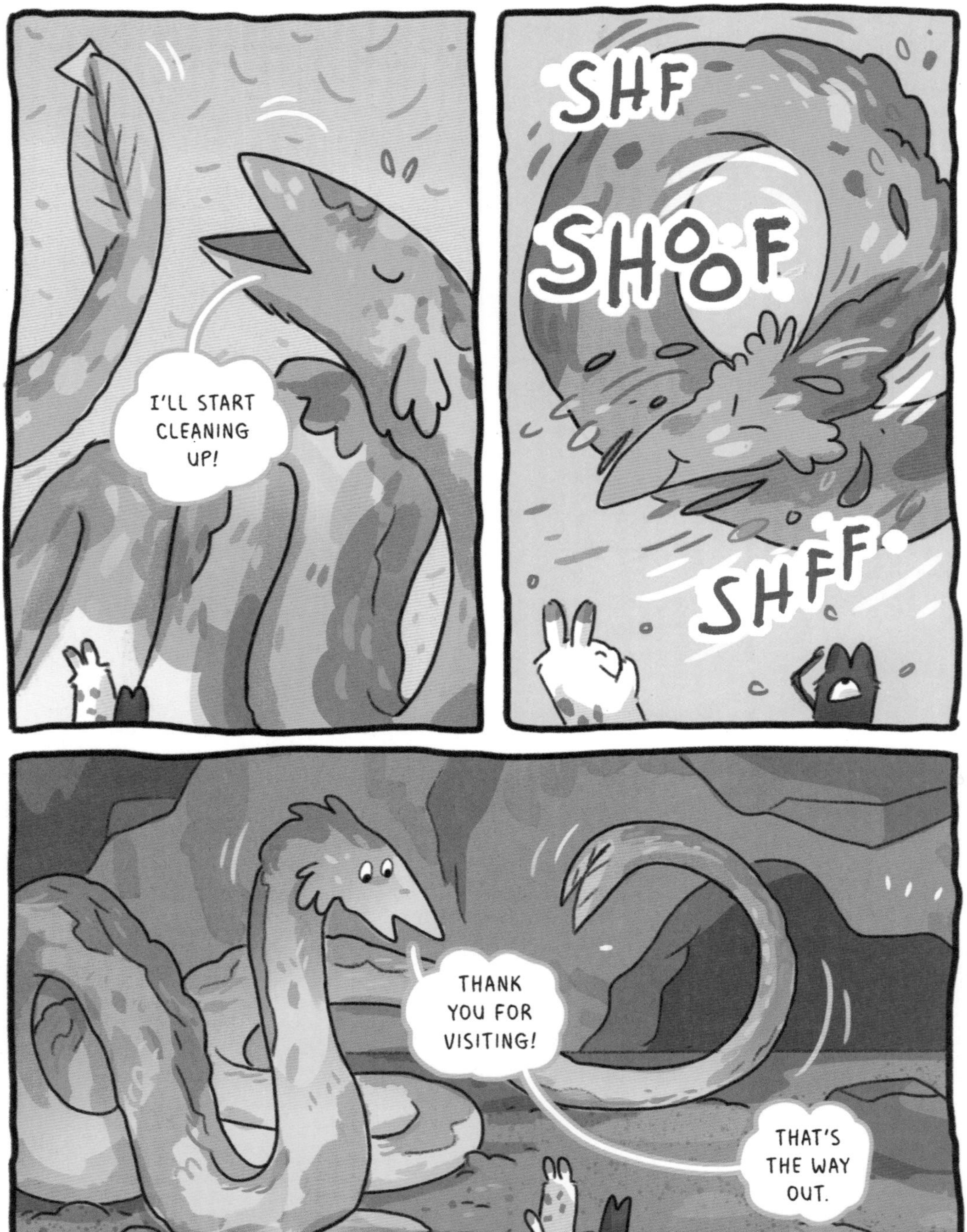
I'LL START CLEANING UP!
SHF
SHOOF
SHFF
THANK YOU FOR VISITING!
THAT'S THE WAY OUT.

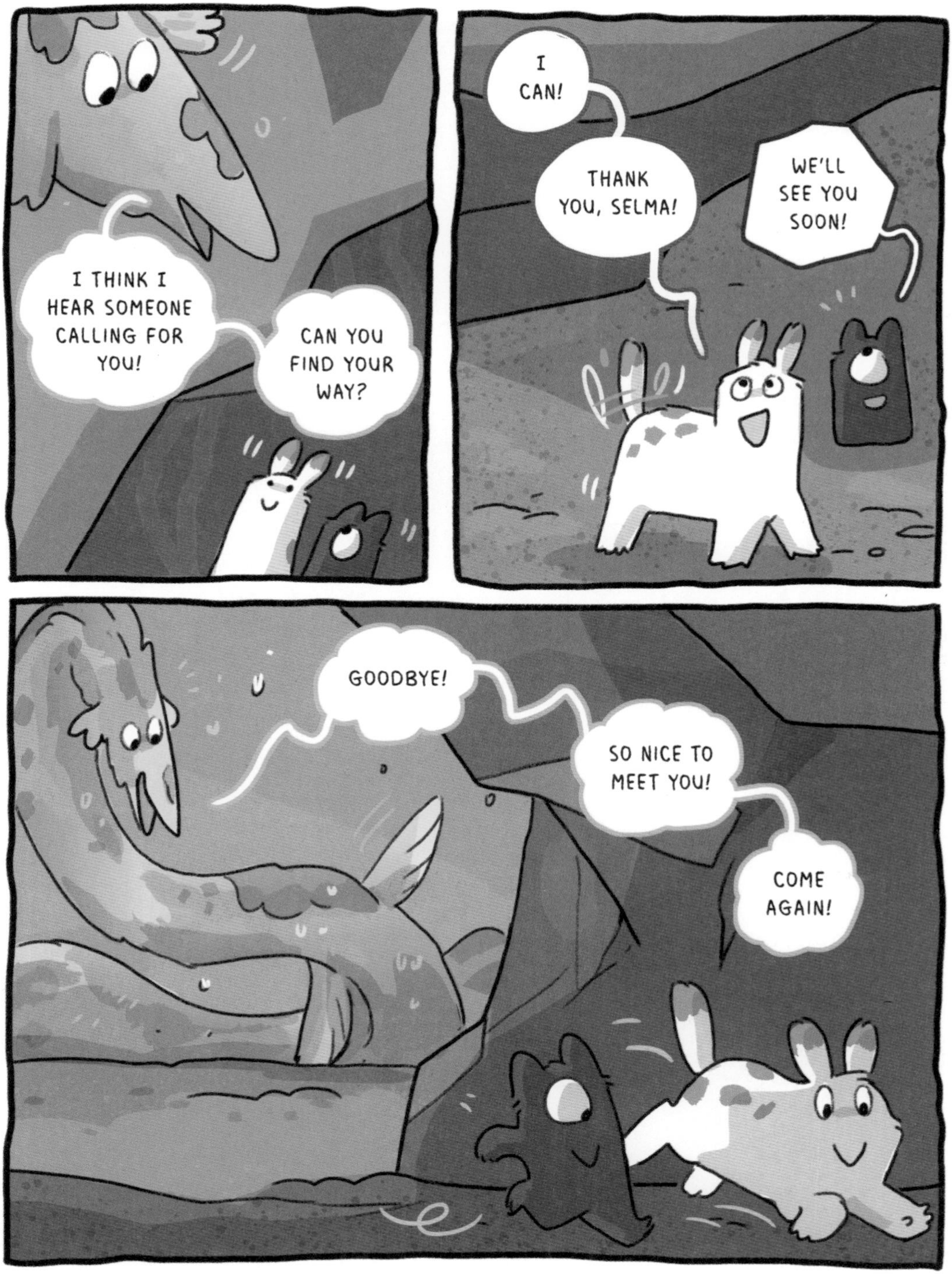
I THINK I HEAR SOMEONE CALLING FOR YOU!
CAN YOU FIND YOUR WAY?
I CAN!
THANK YOU, SELMA!
WE'LL SEE YOU SOON!
GOODBYE!
SO NICE TO MEET YOU!
COME AGAIN!

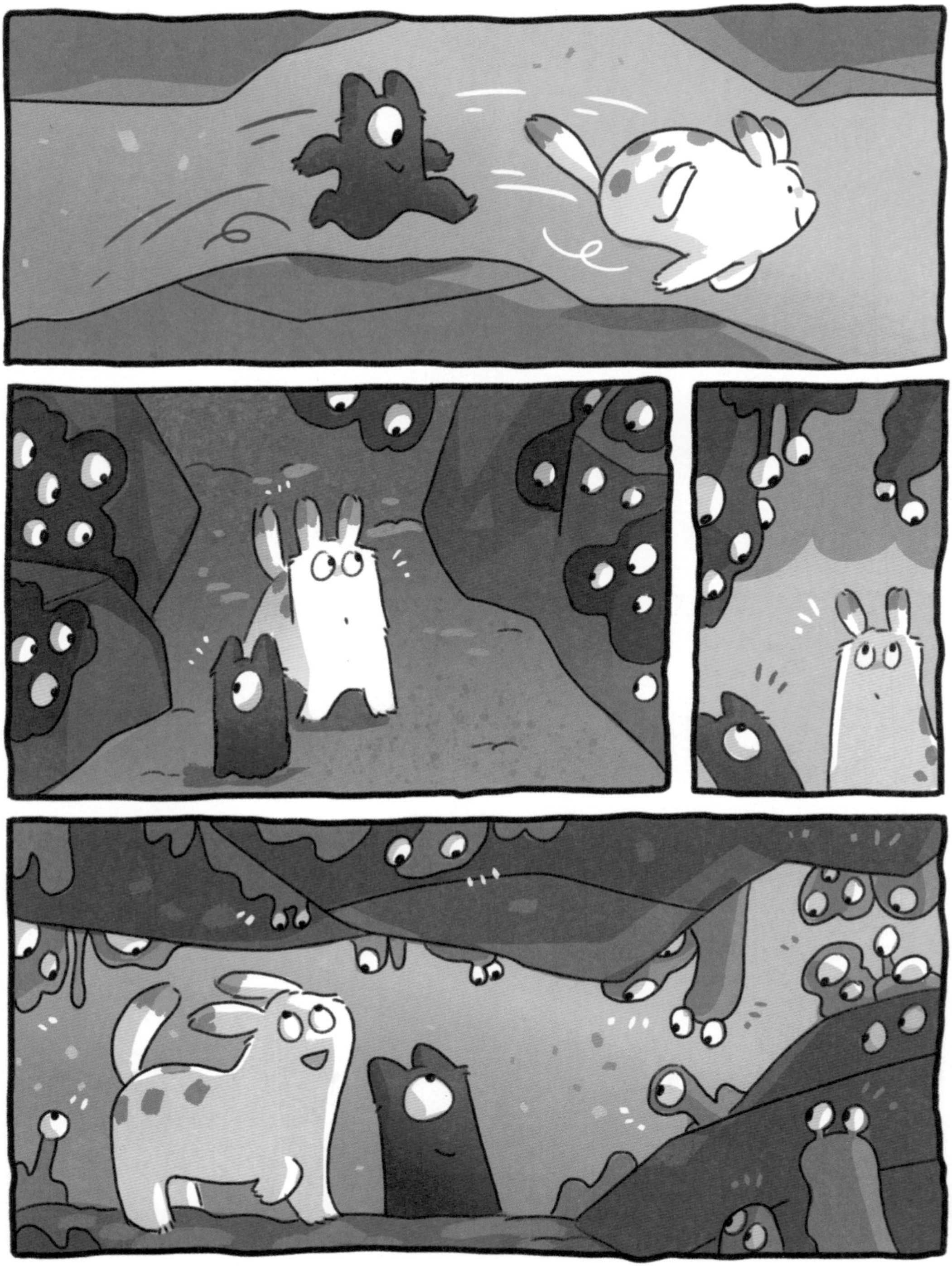

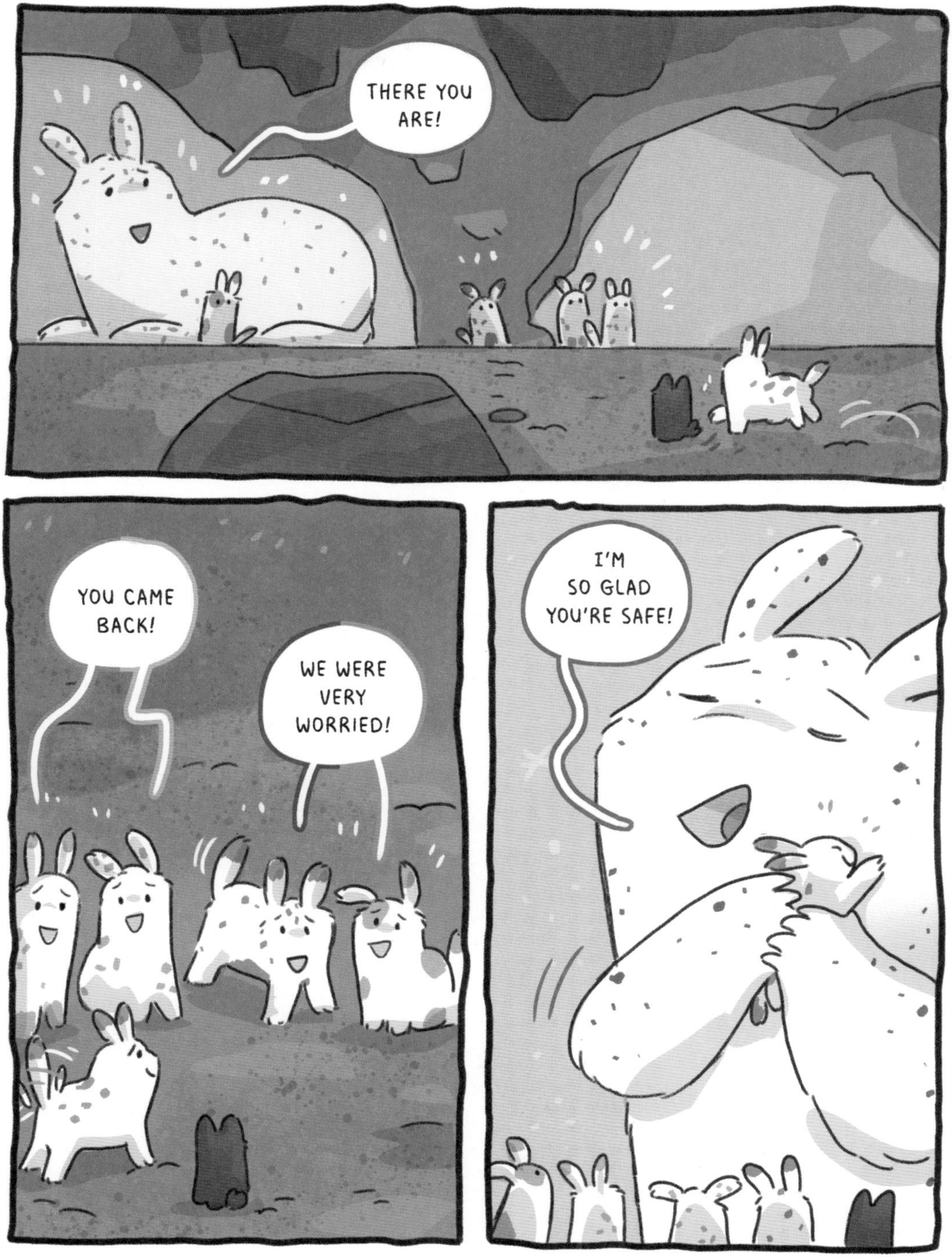
THERE YOU ARE!
YOU CAME BACK!
WE WERE VERY WORRIED!
I'M SO GLAD YOU'RE SAFE!

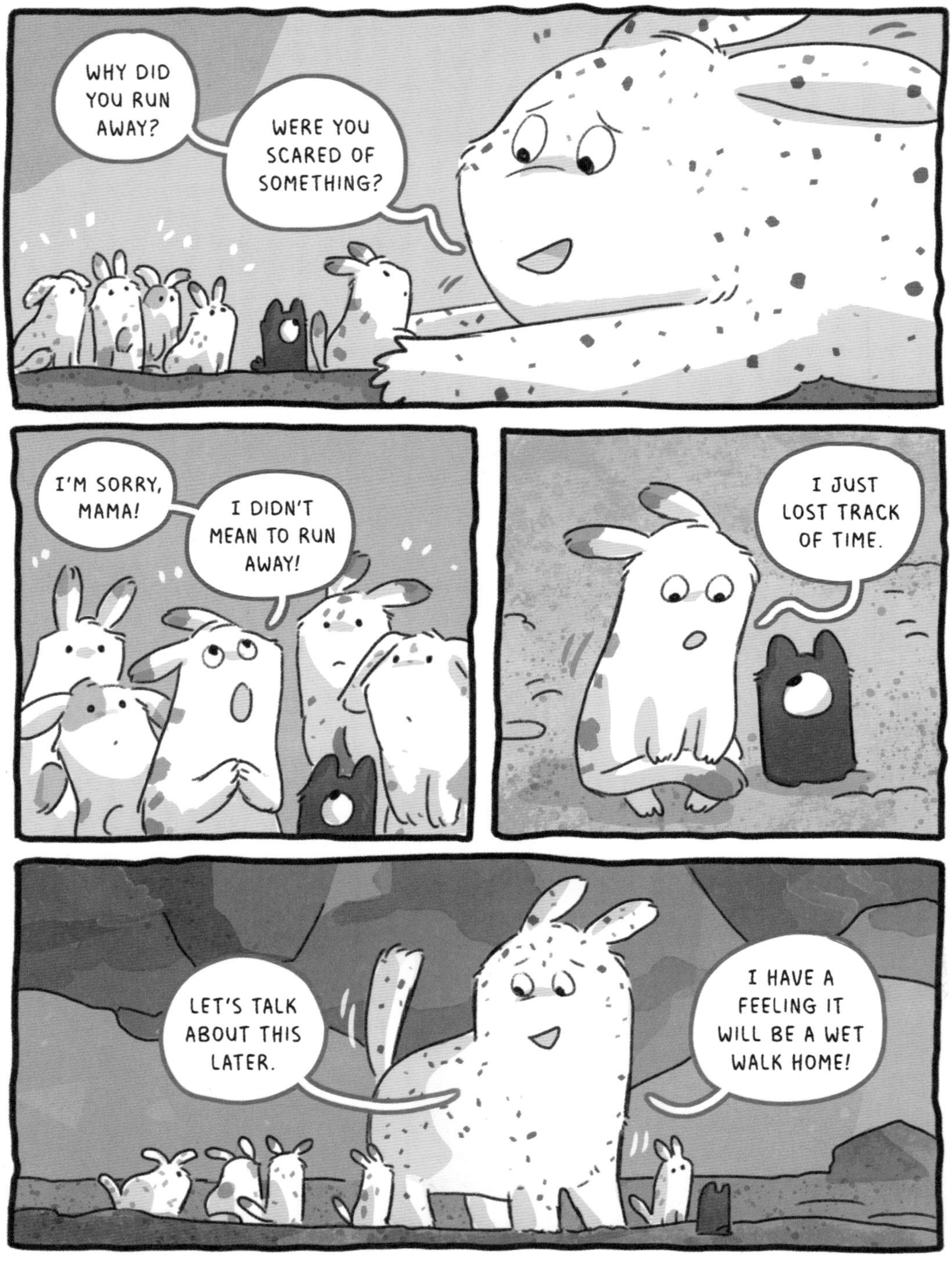

WHY DID YOU RUN AWAY?
WERE YOU SCARED OF SOMETHING?
I'M SORRY, MAMA!
I DIDN'T MEAN TO RUN AWAY!
I JUST LOST TRACK OF TIME.
LET'S TALK ABOUT THIS LATER.
I HAVE A FEELING IT WILL BE A WET WALK HOME!

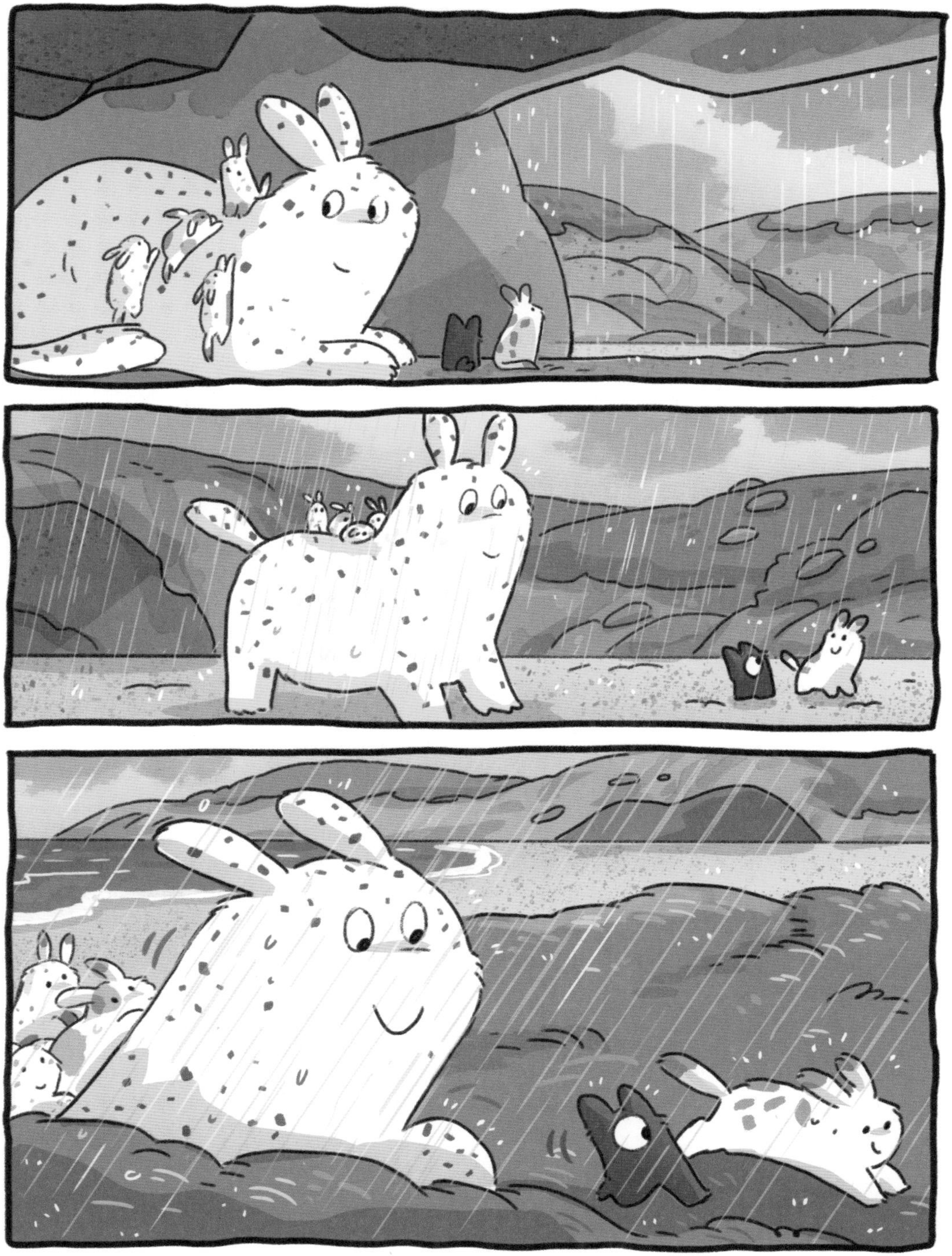

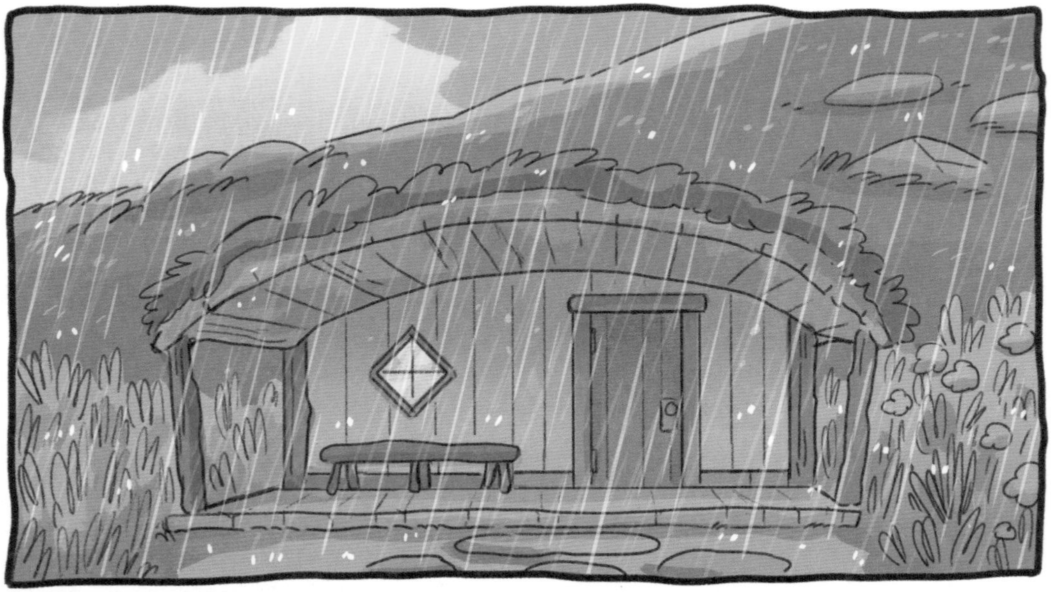

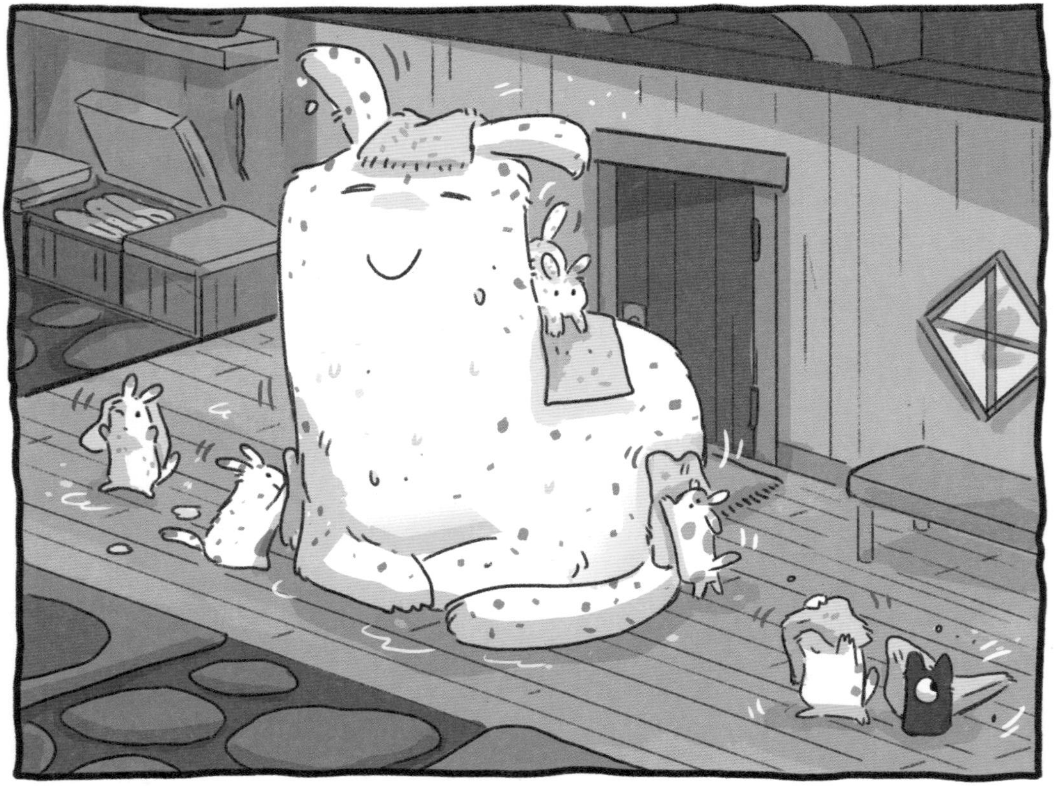

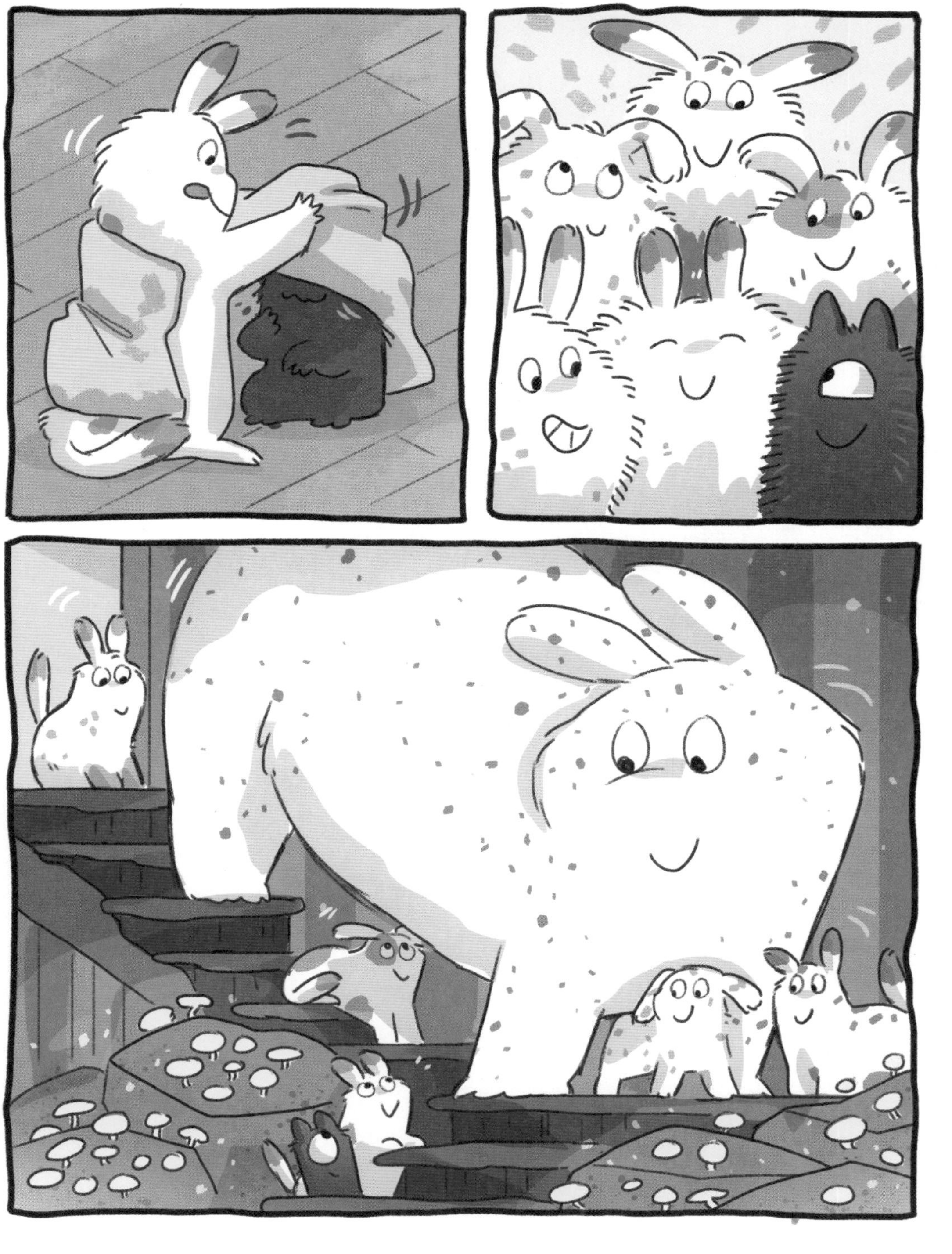

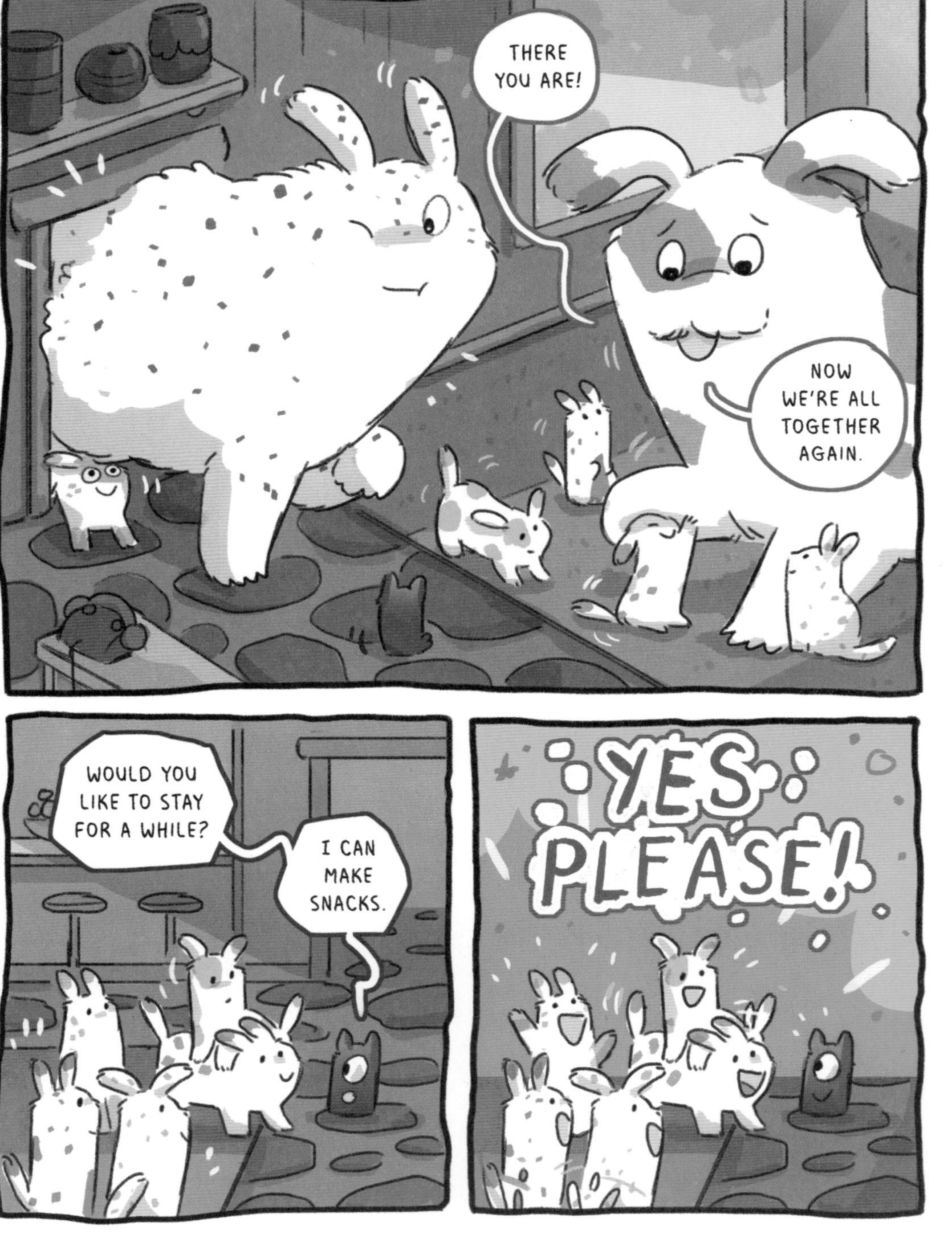
THERE YOU ARE!
NOW WE'RE ALL TOGETHER AGAIN.
WOULD YOU LIKE TO STAY FOR A WHILE?
I CAN MAKE SNACKS.
YES PLEASE!

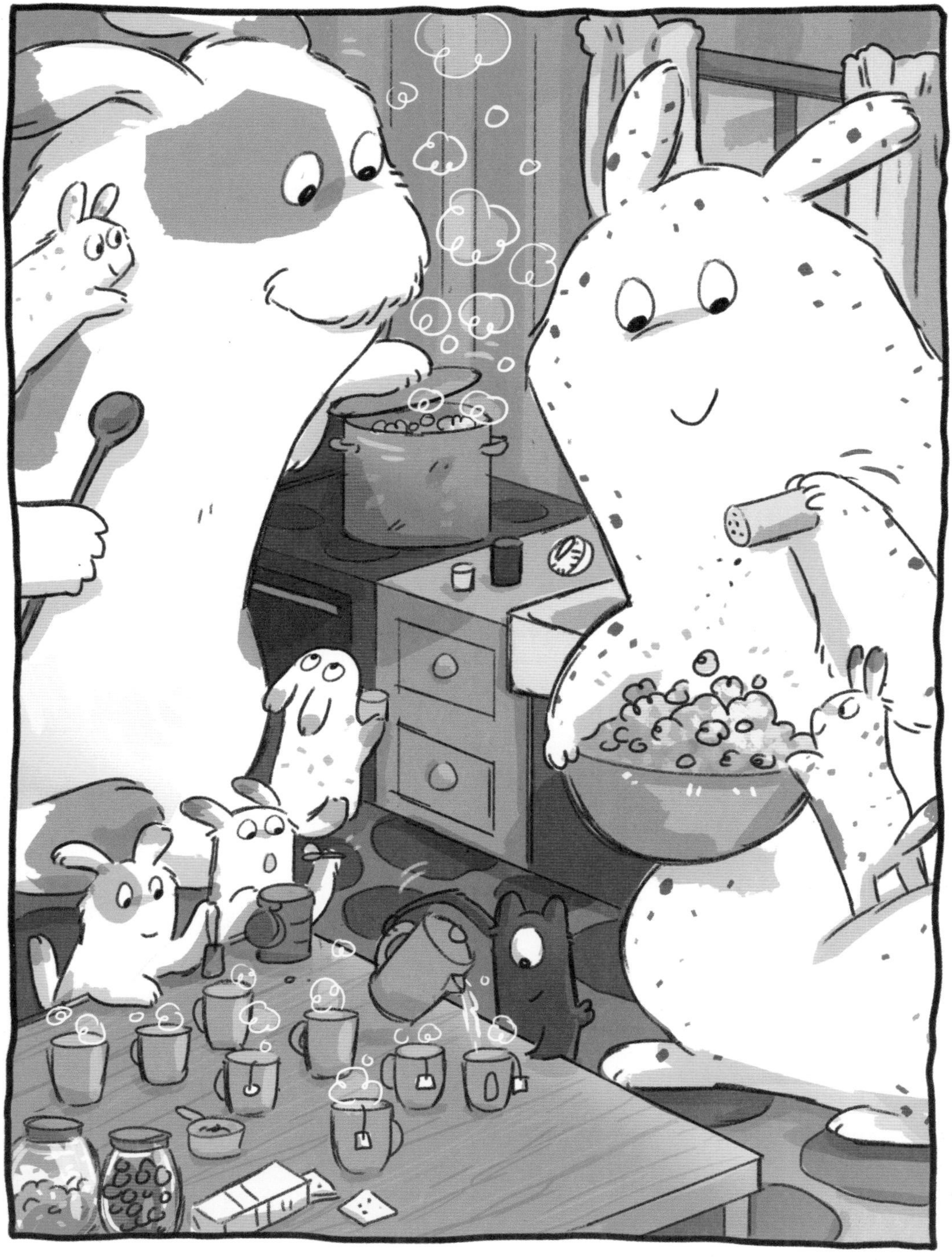

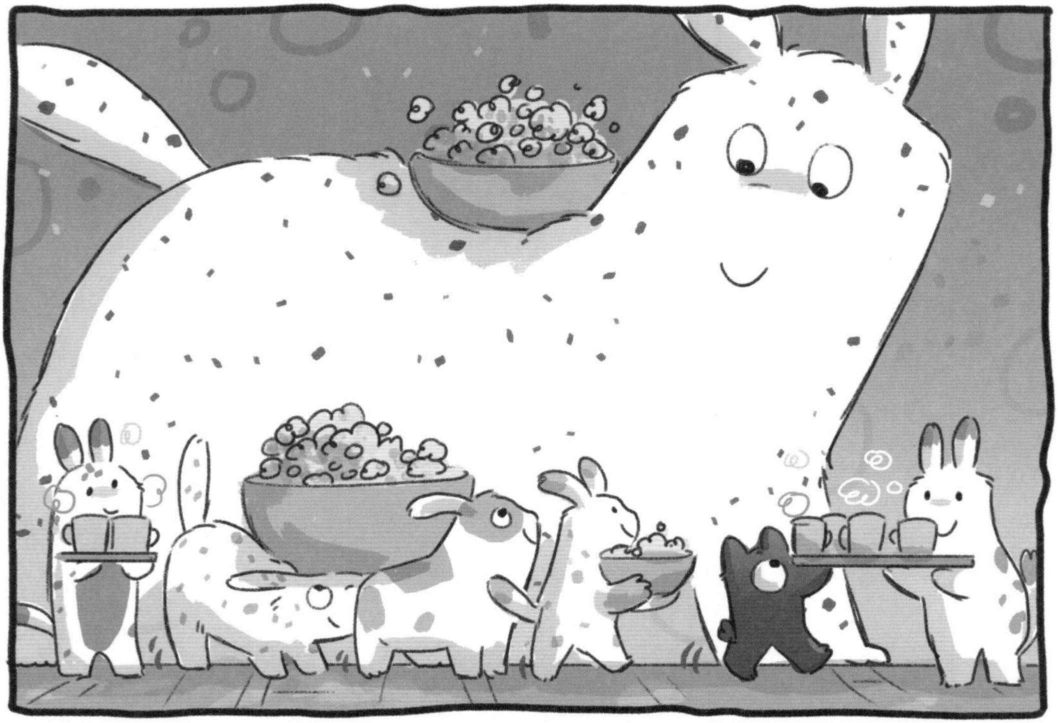

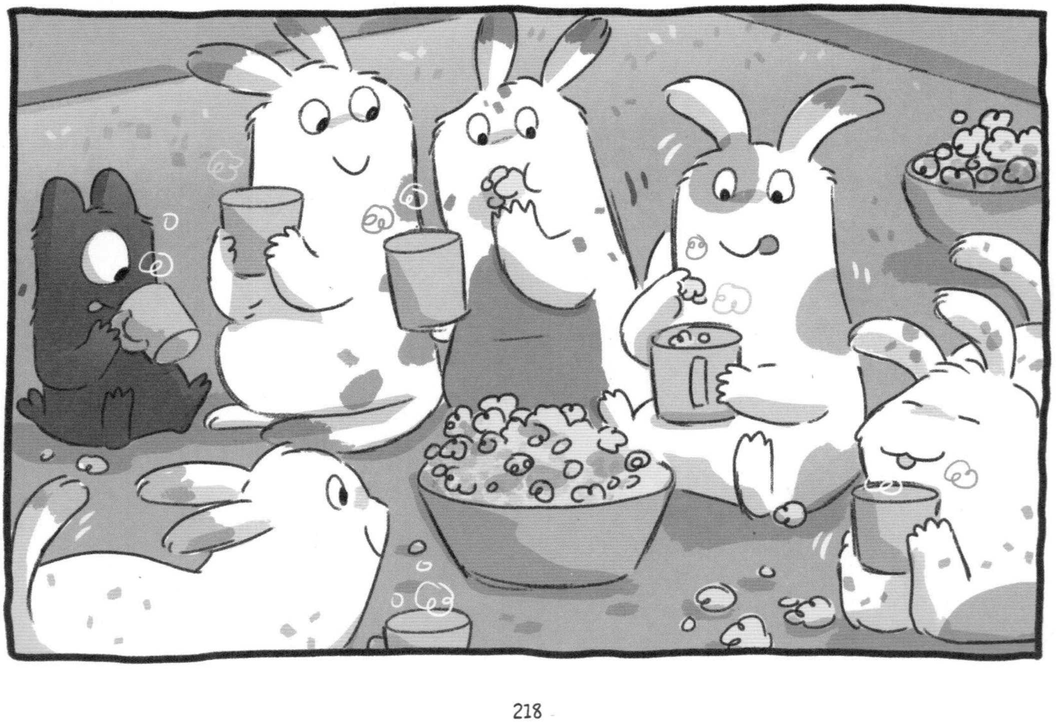

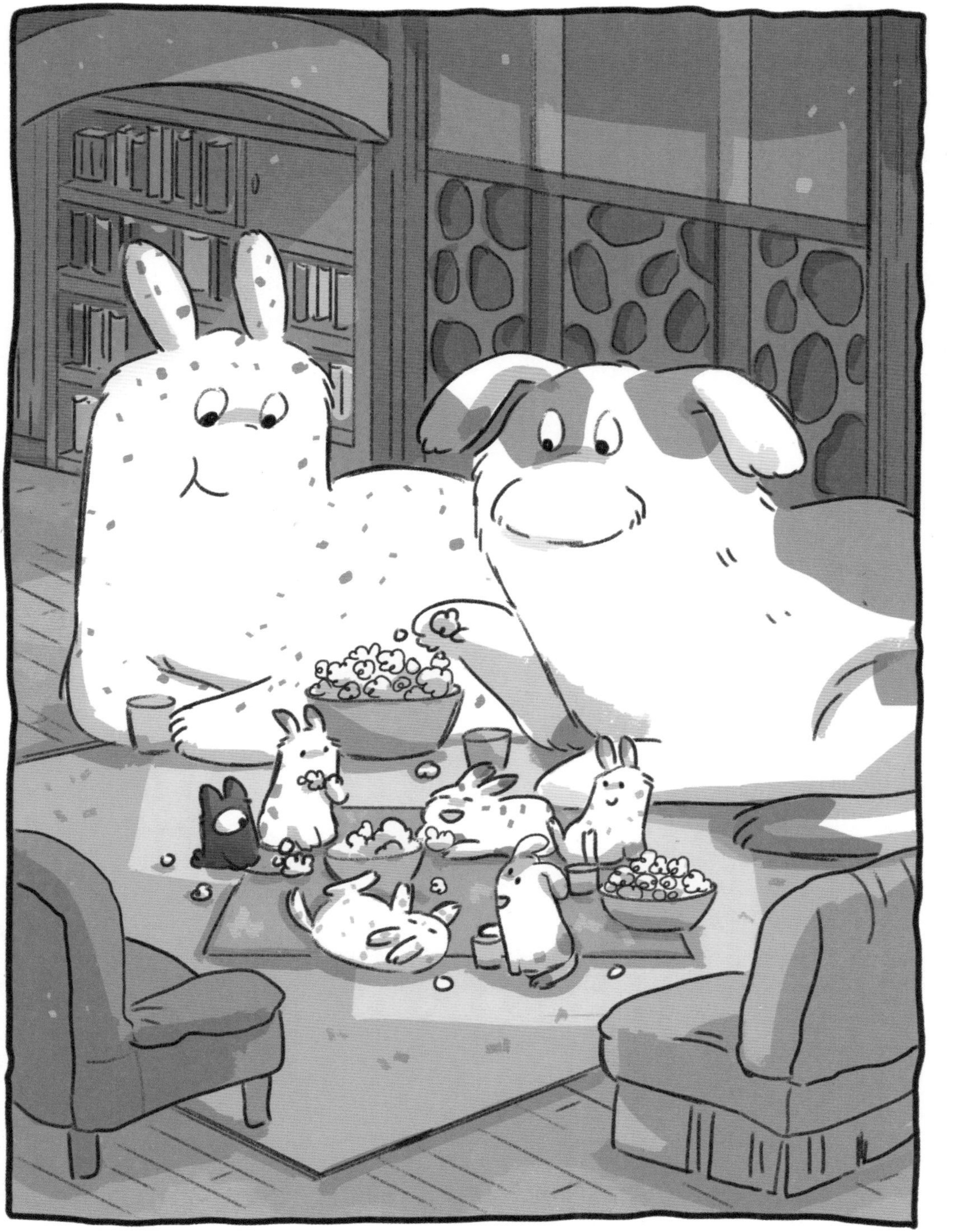

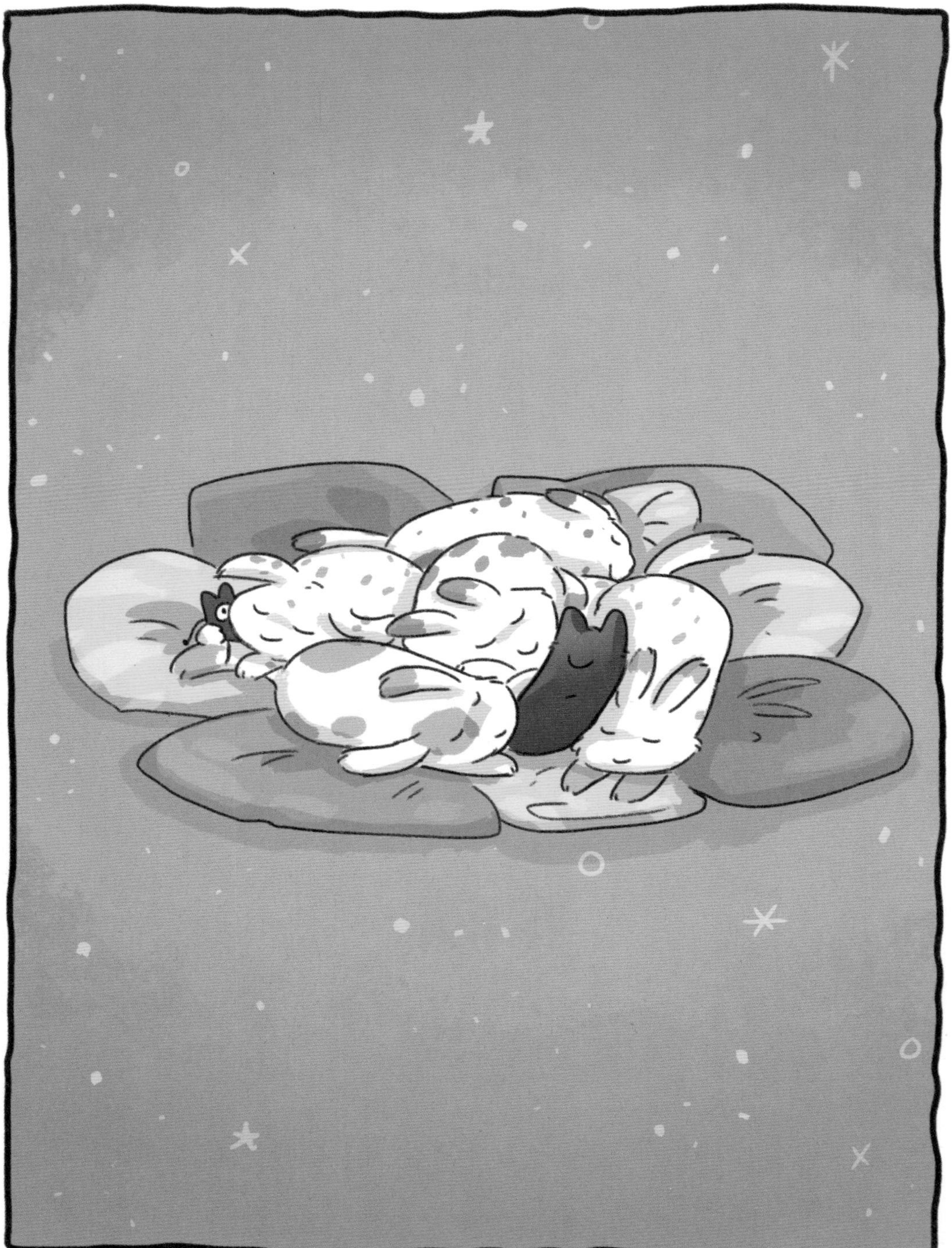

Chapter 5

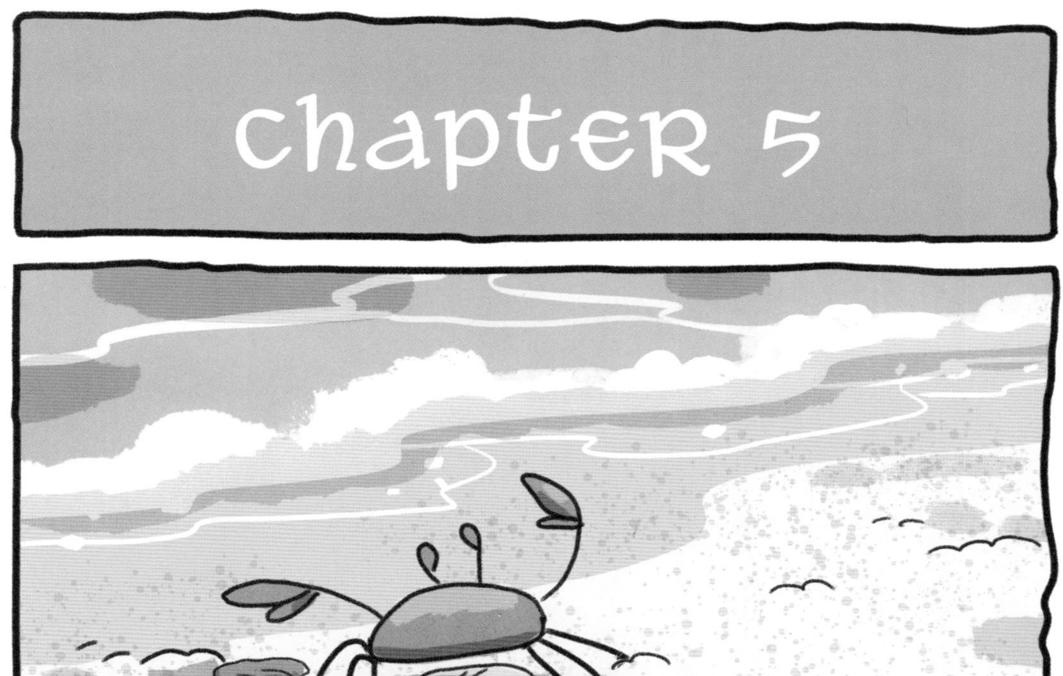

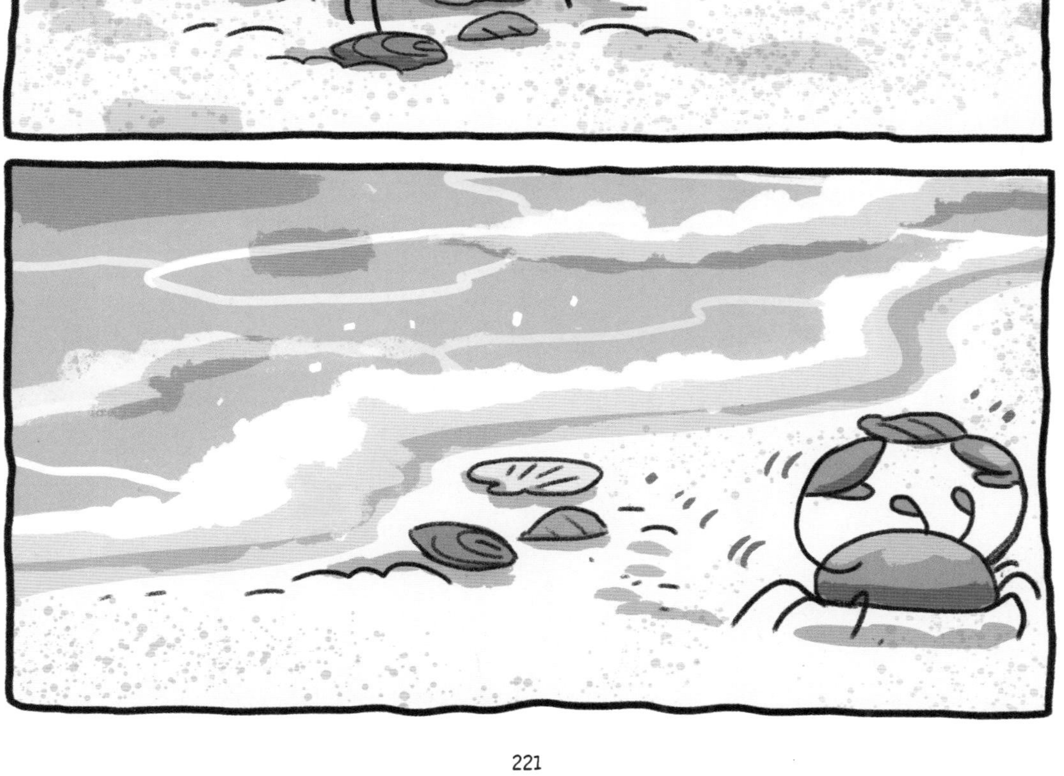

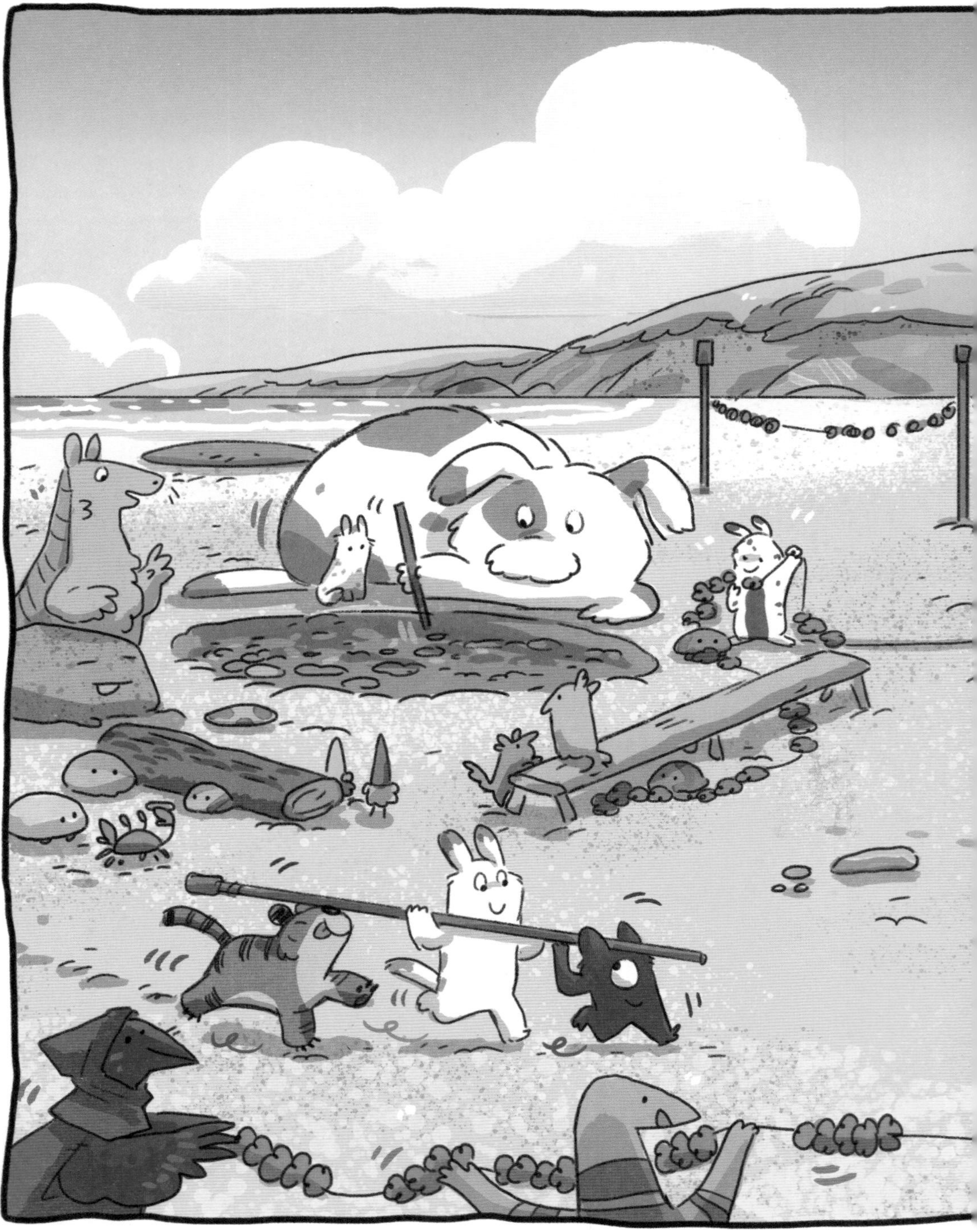

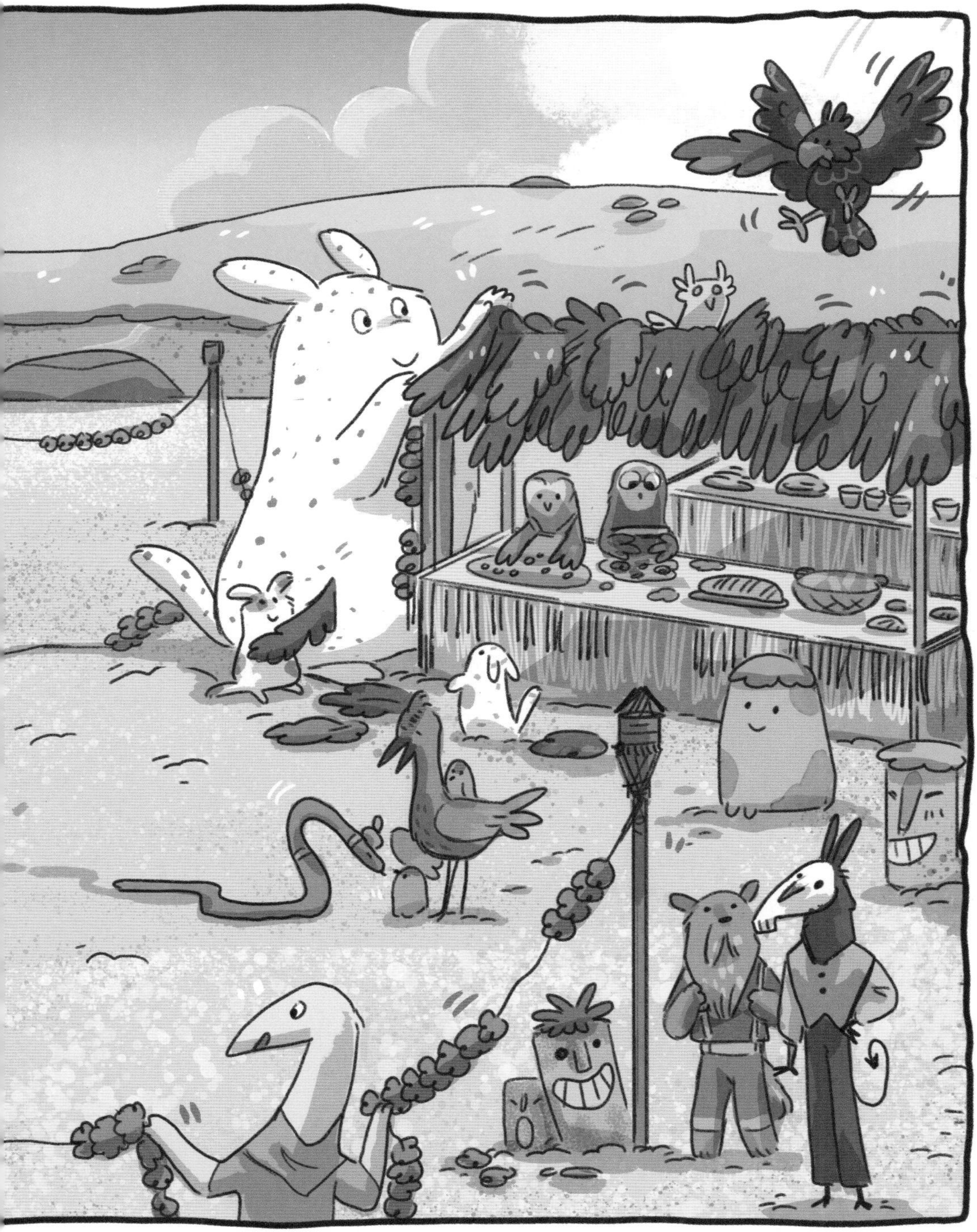

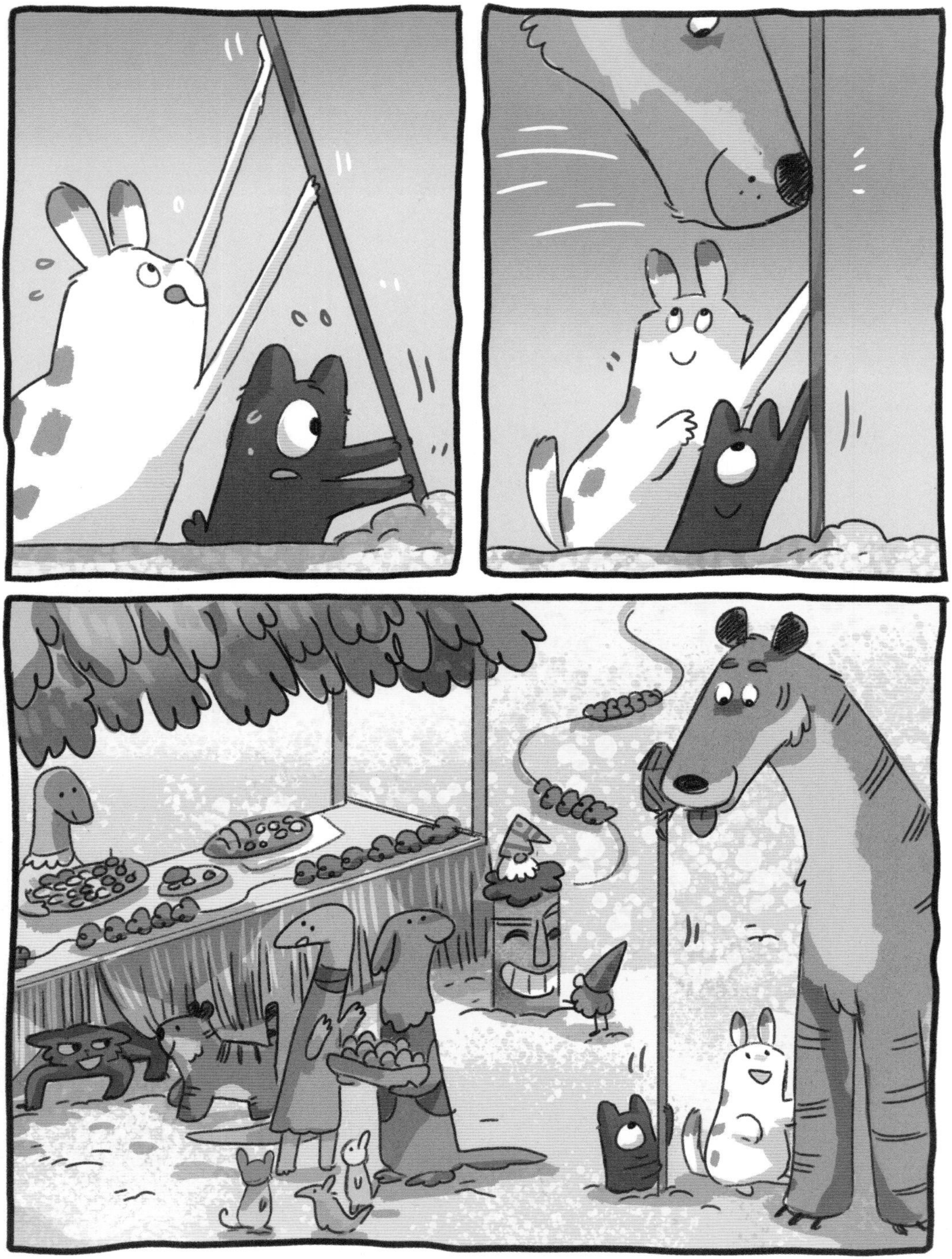

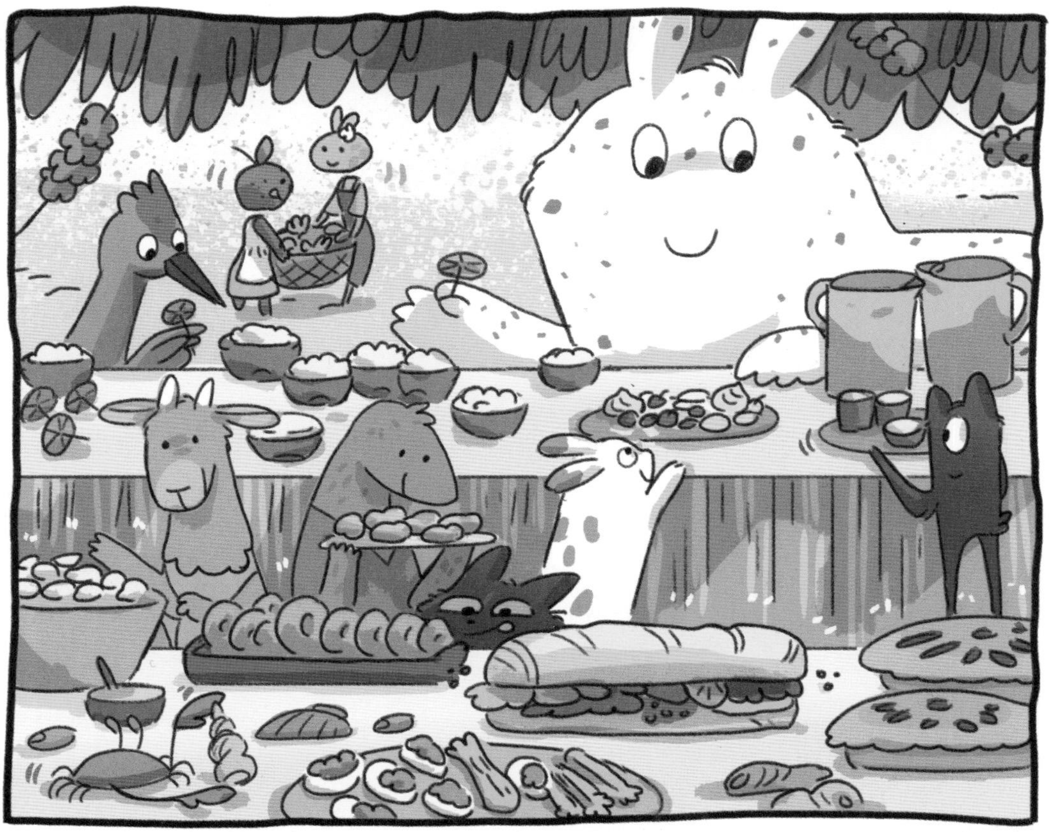

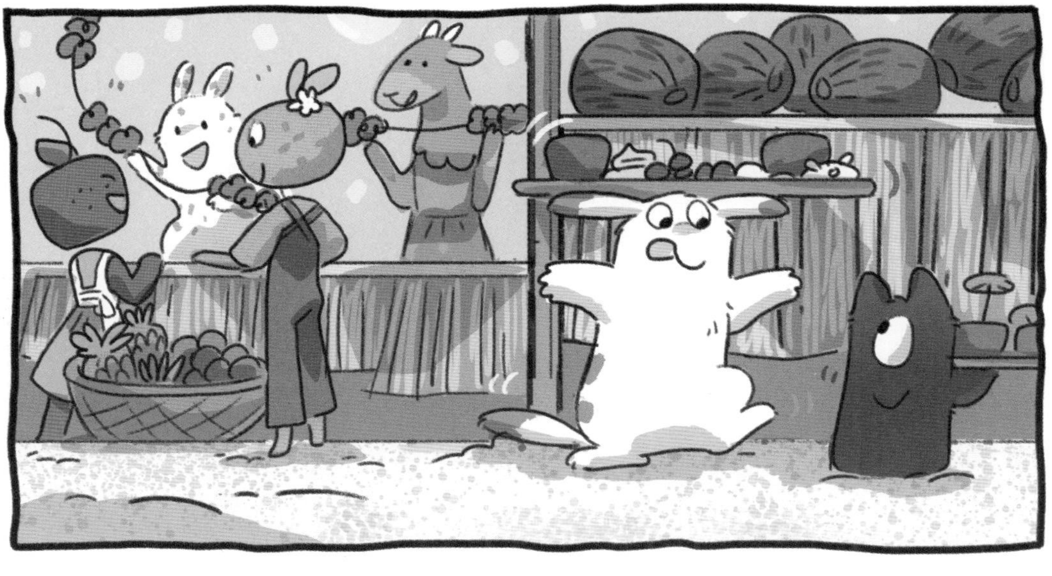

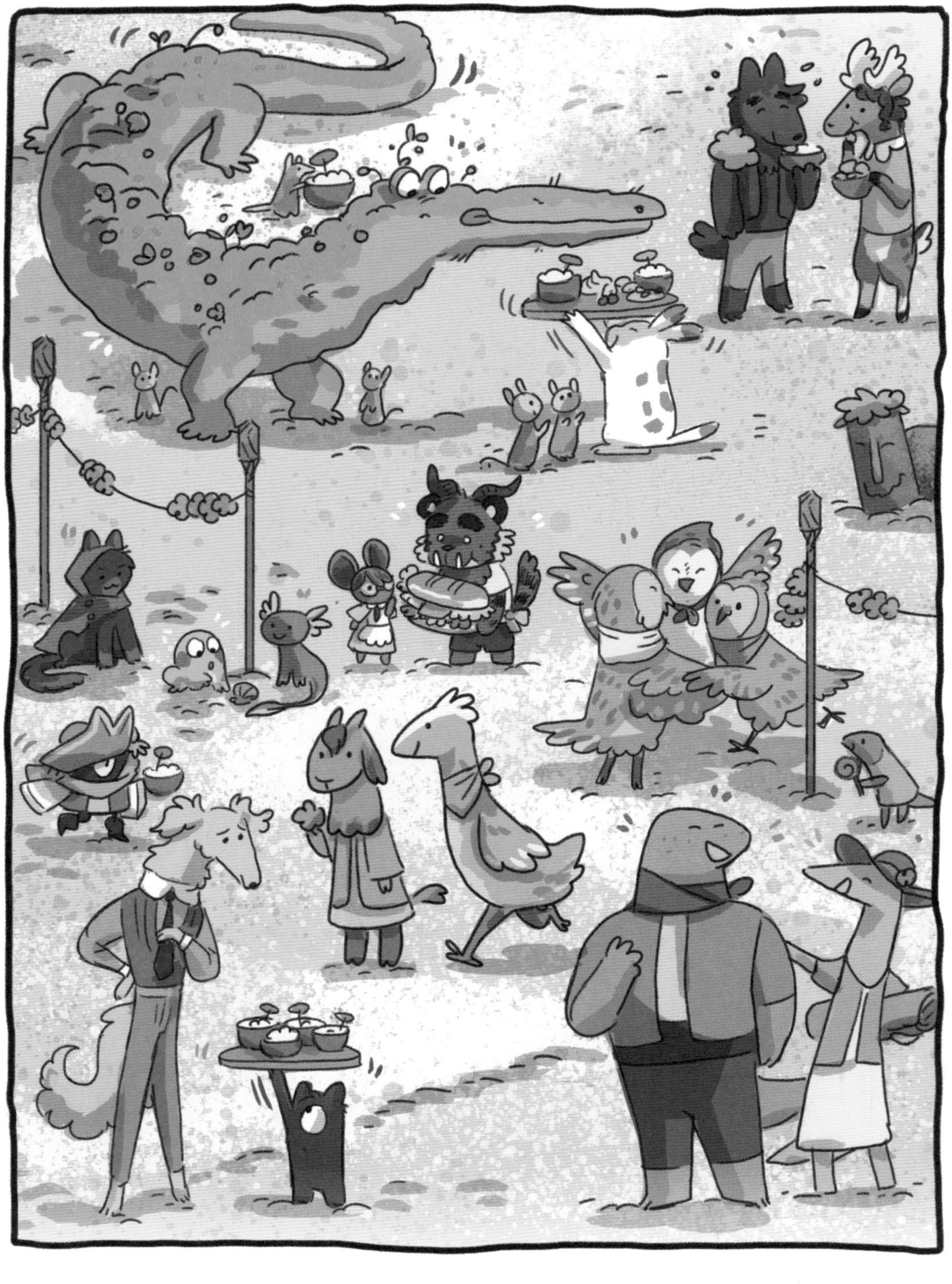

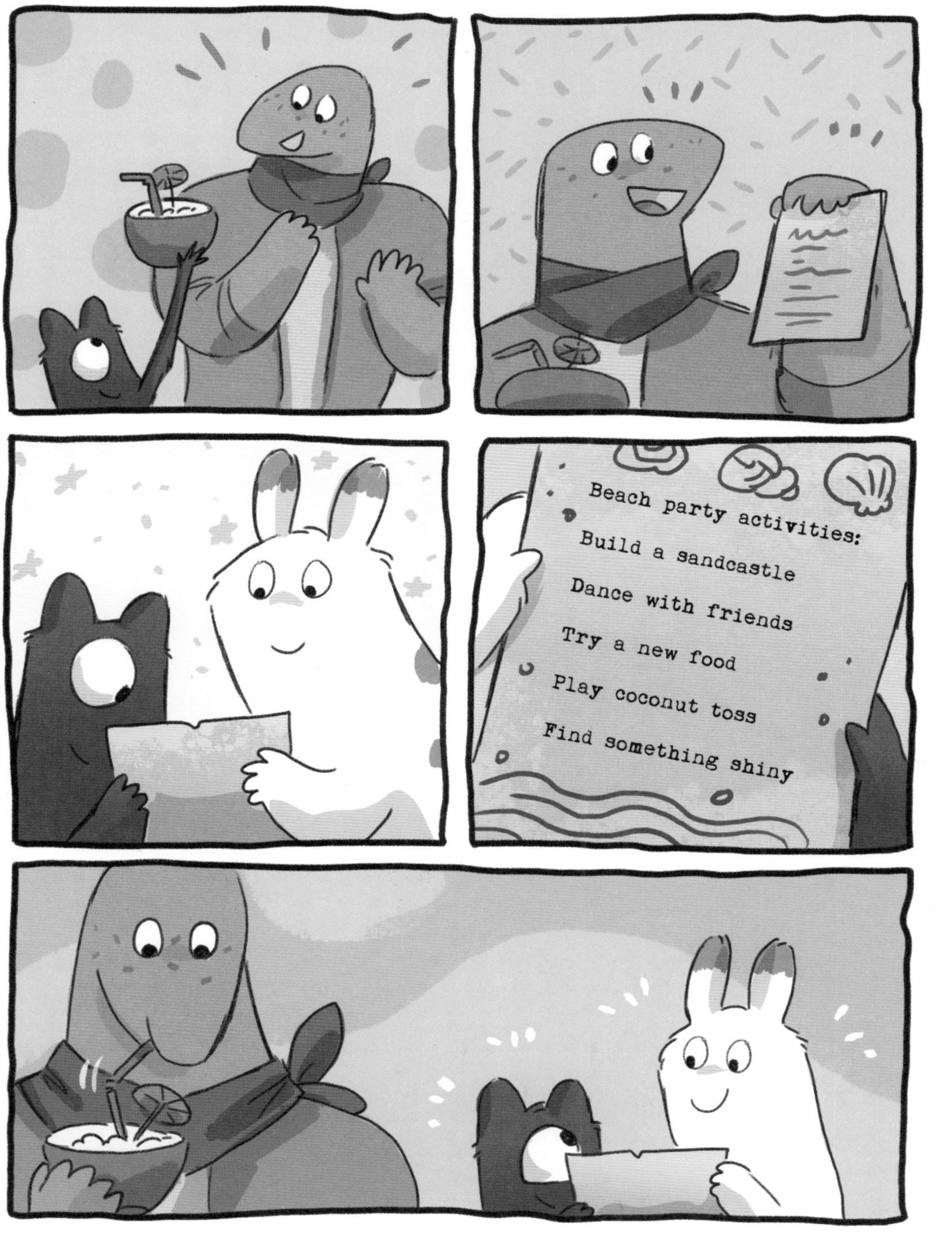
Beach party activities:
Build a sandcastle
Dance with friends
Try a new food
Play coconut toss
Find something shiny

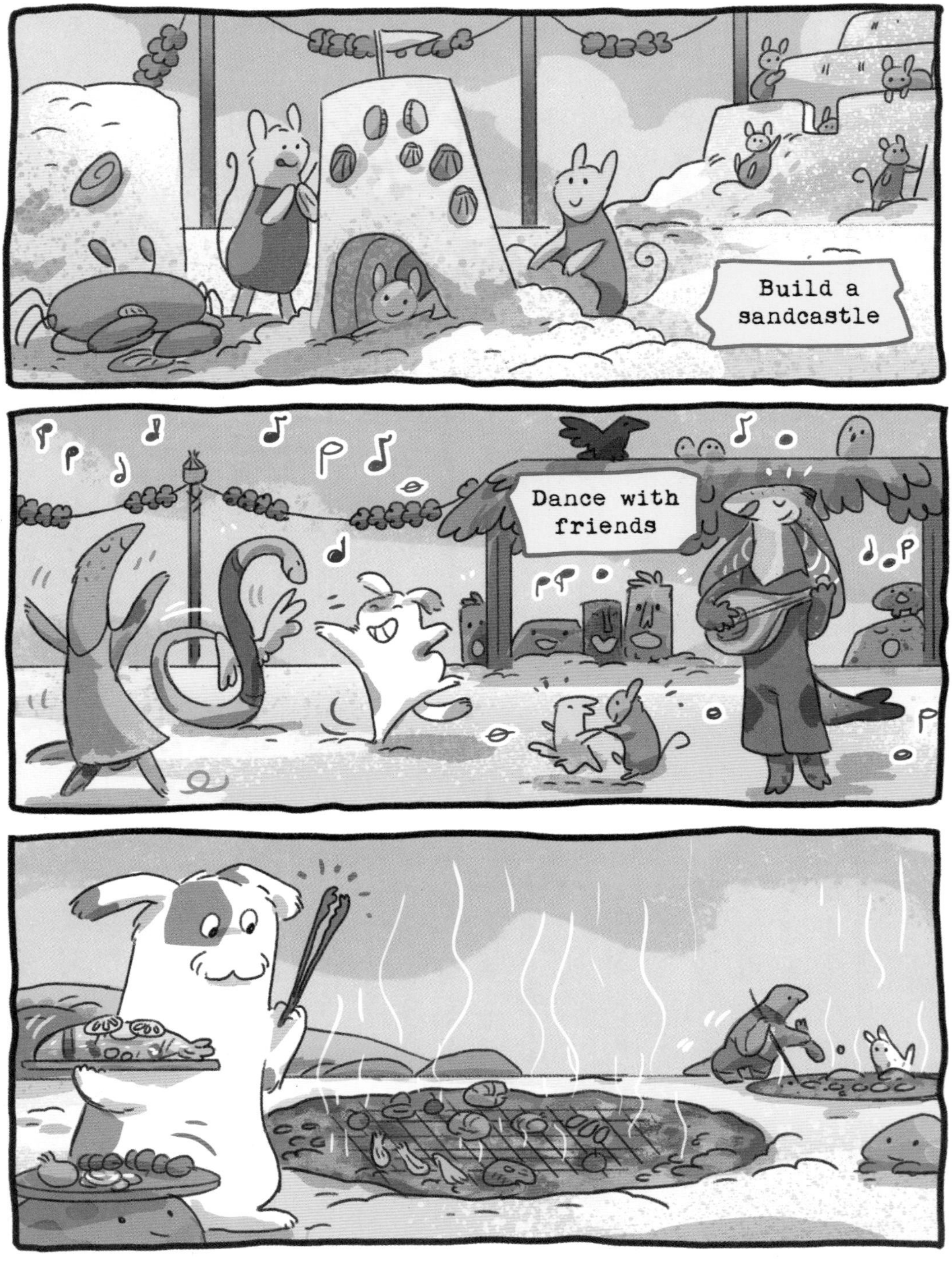
Build a sandcastle
Dance with friends

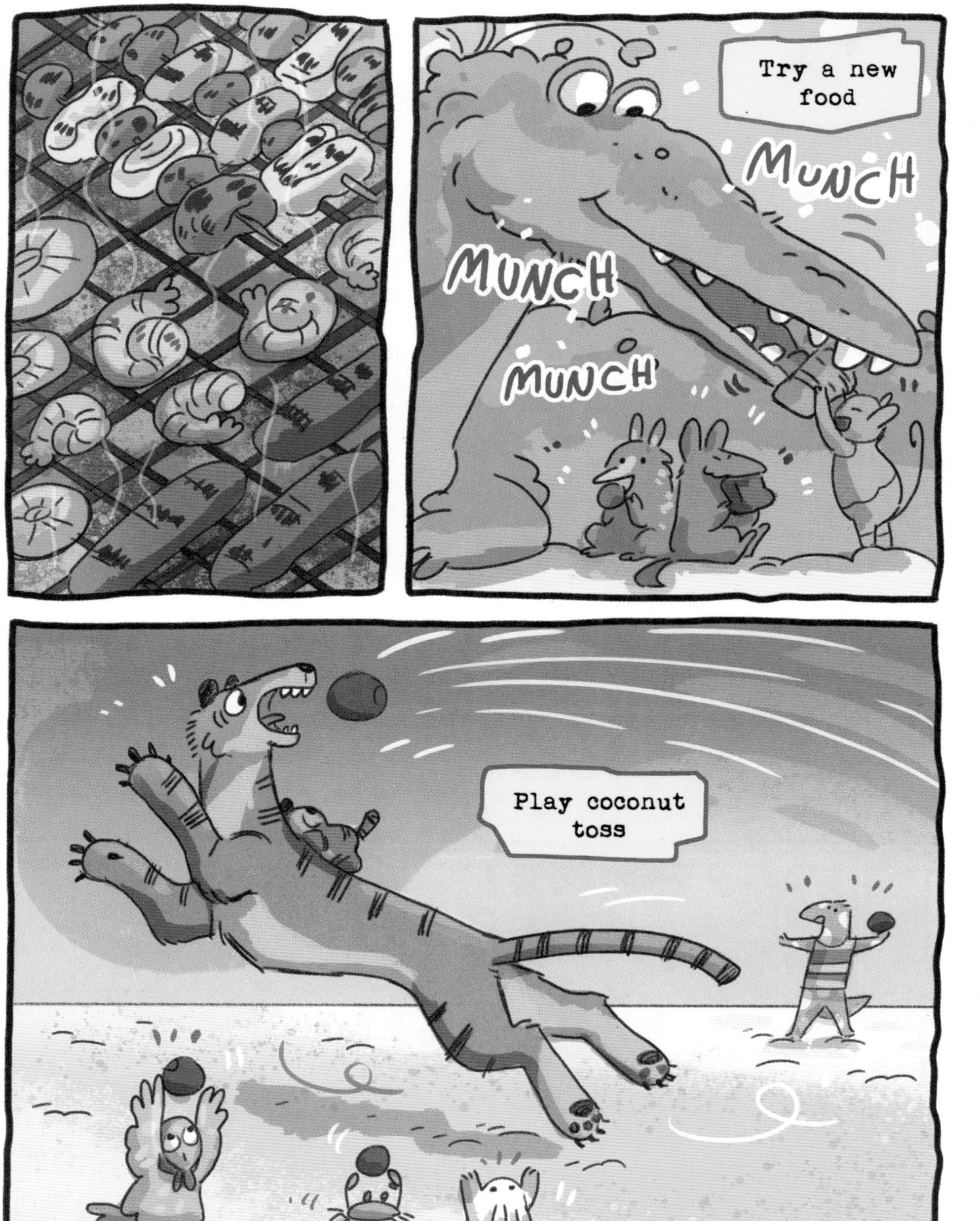
Try a new food
MUNCH
MUNCH
MUNCH
Play coconut toss

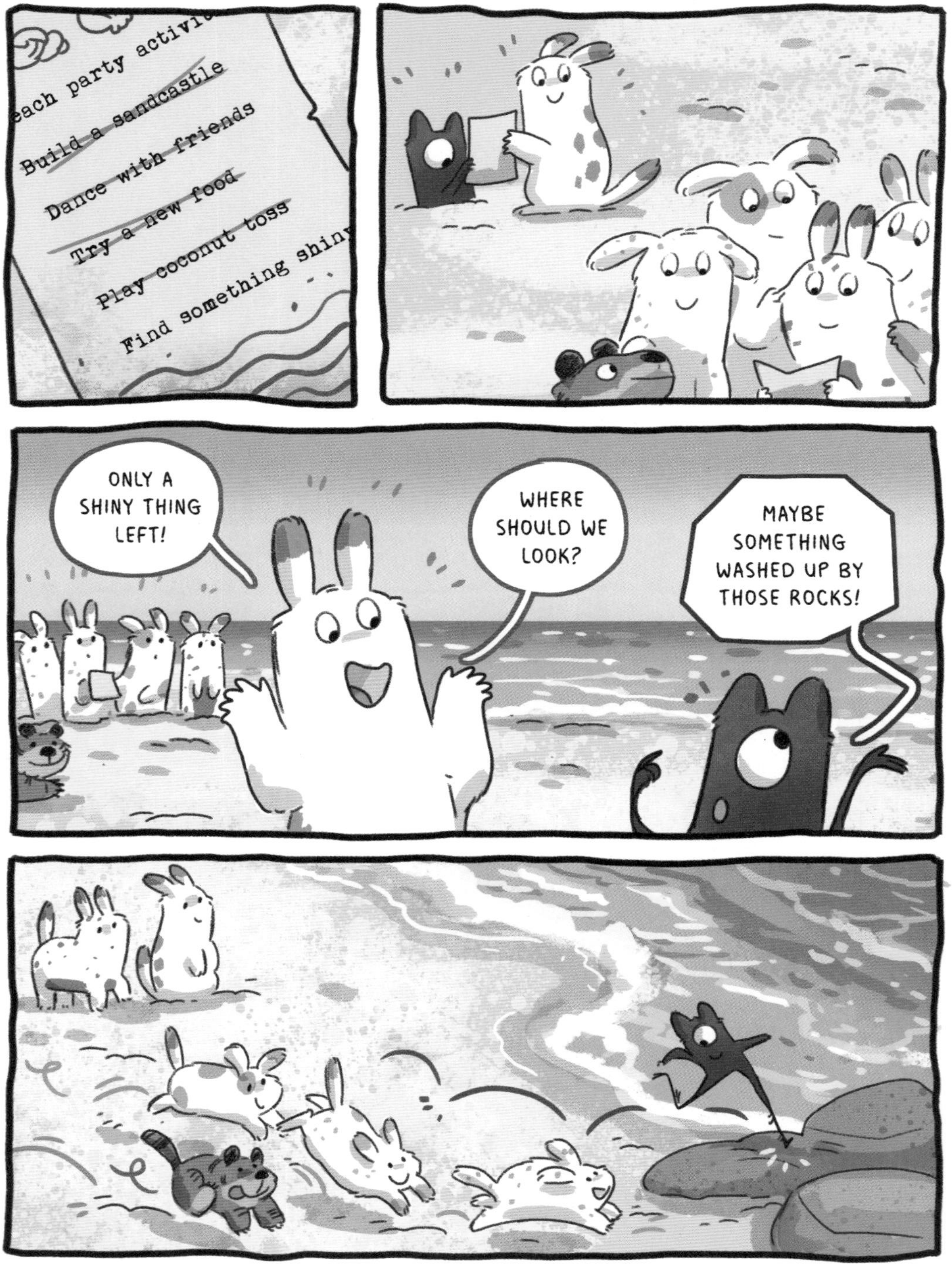
each party activi
Build a sandcastle
Dance with friends
Try a new food
Play coconut toss
Find something shiny
ONLY A SHINY THING LEFT!
WHERE SHOULD WE LOOK?
MAYBE SOMETHING WASHED UP BY THOSE ROCKS!

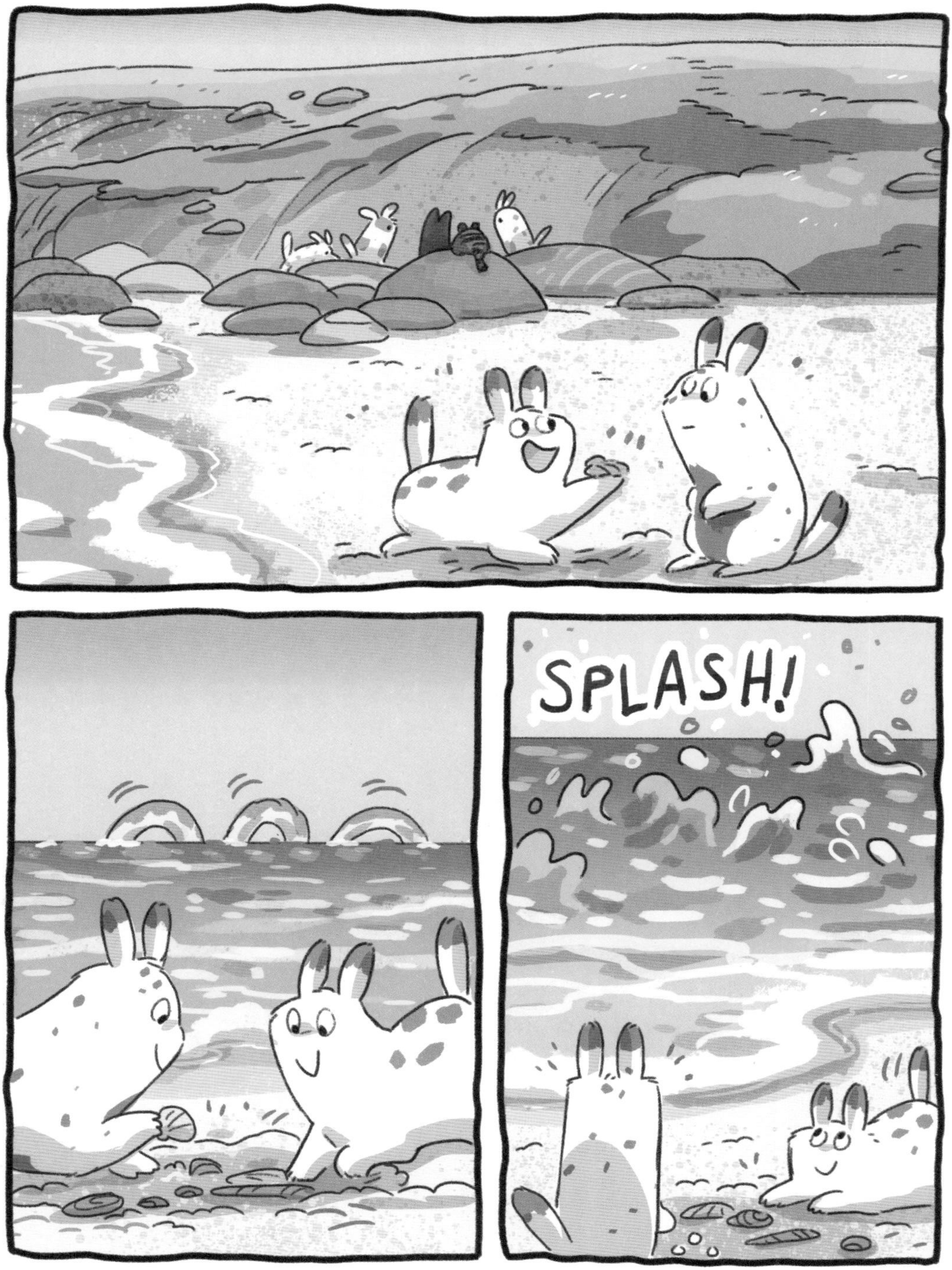
SPLASH!

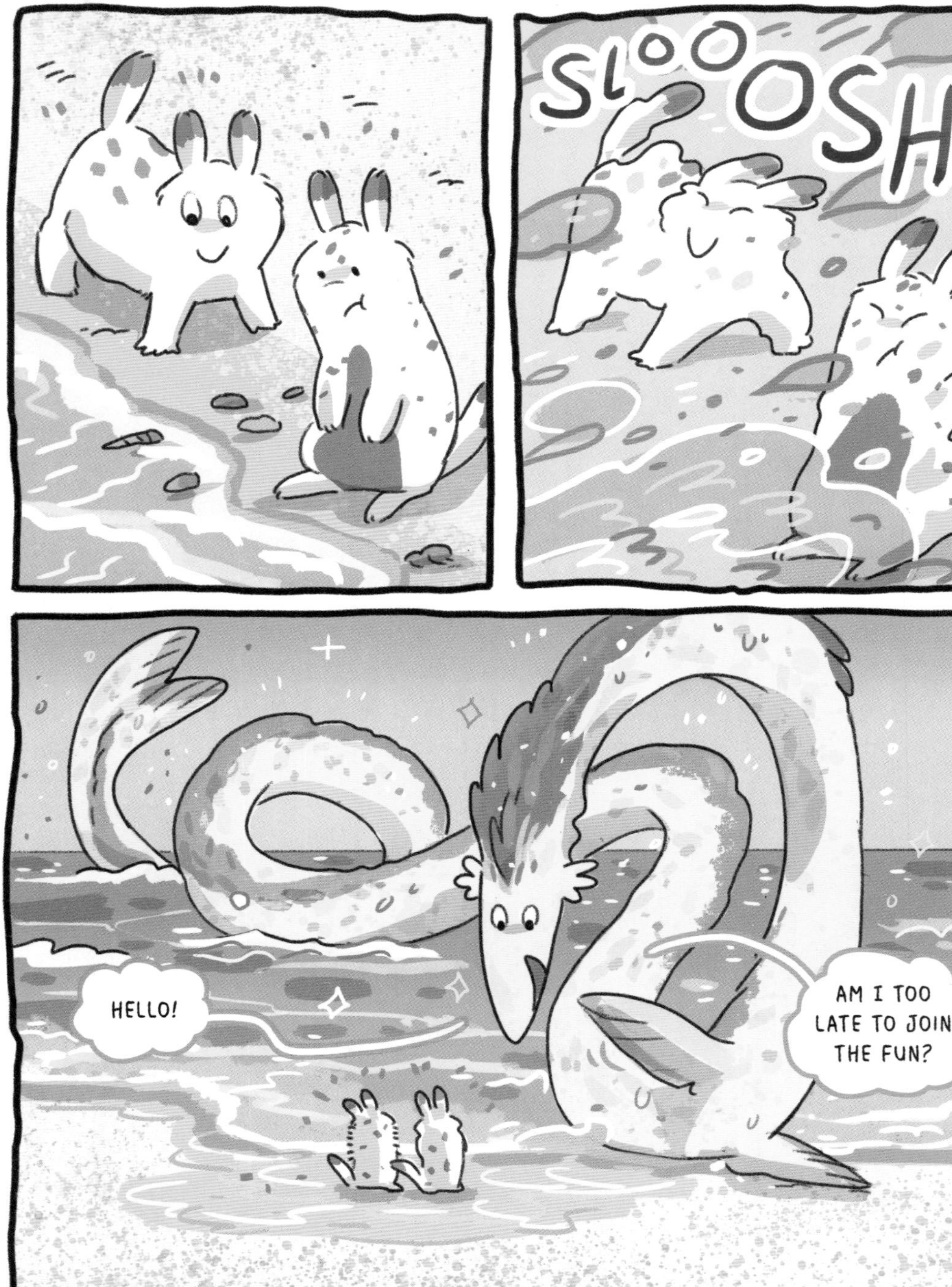
SLOOOSH
HELLO!
AM I TOO LATE TO JOIN THE FUN?

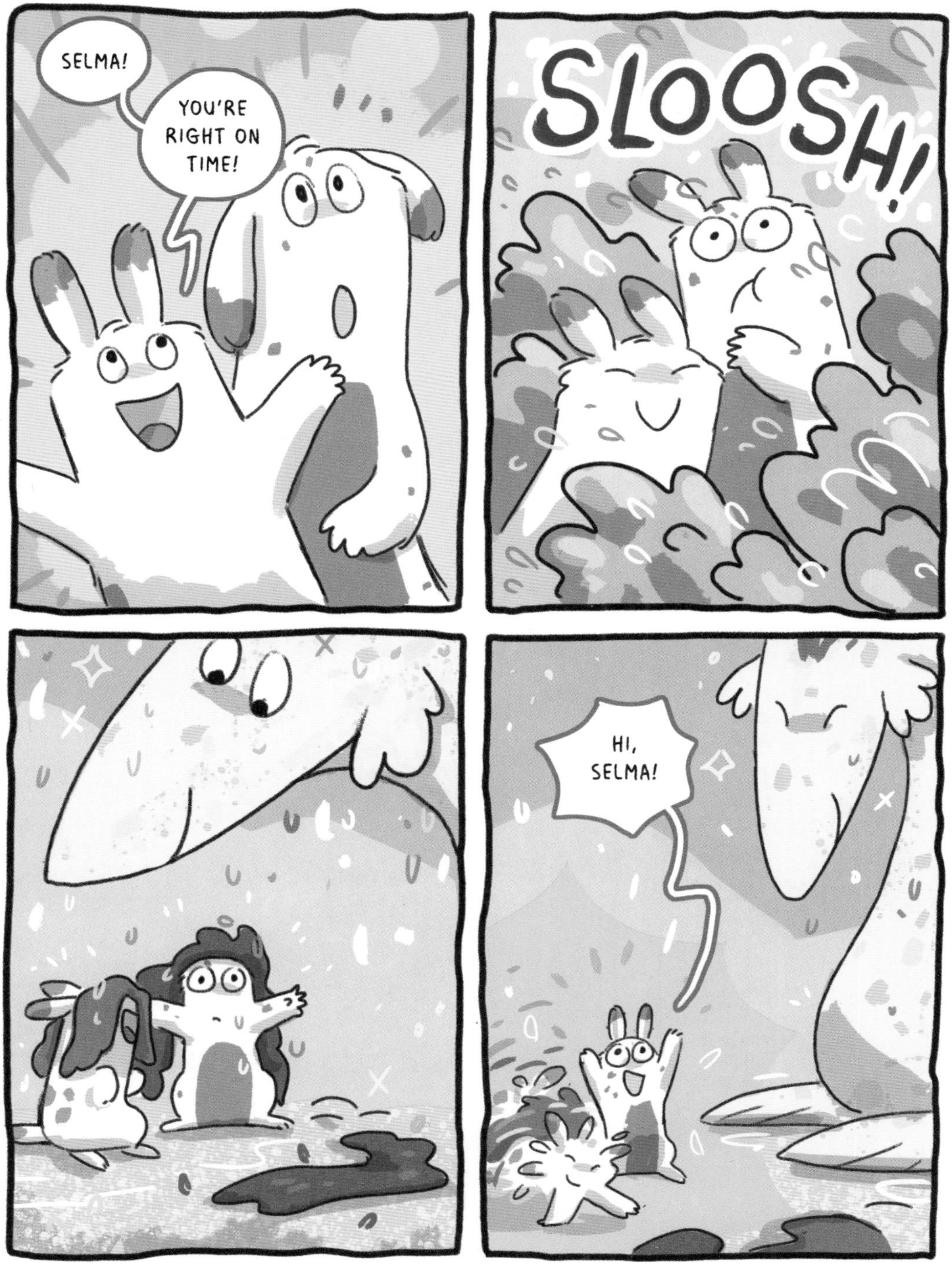
SELMA!
YOU'RE RIGHT ON TIME!
SLOOSH!
HI, SELMA!

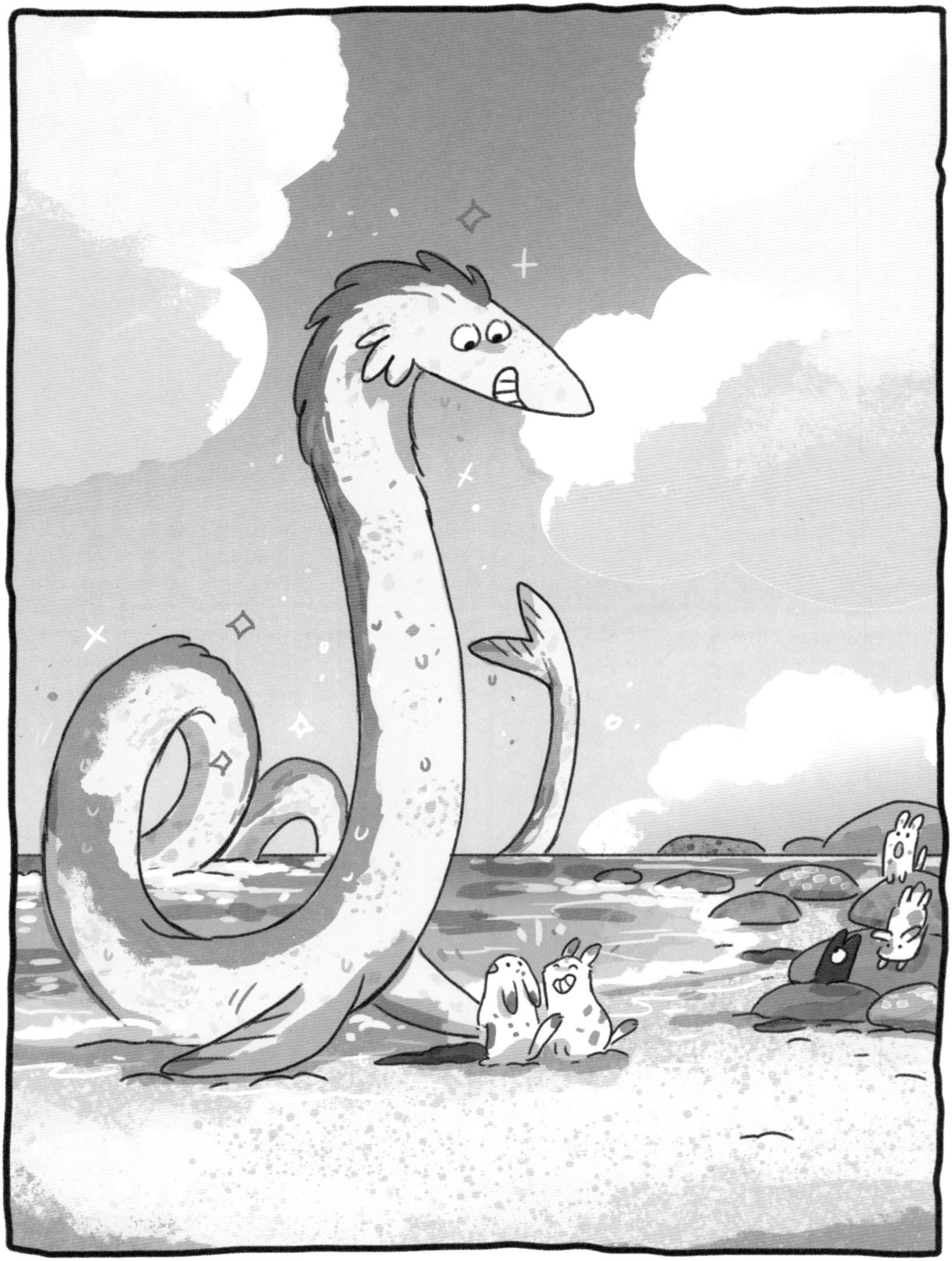

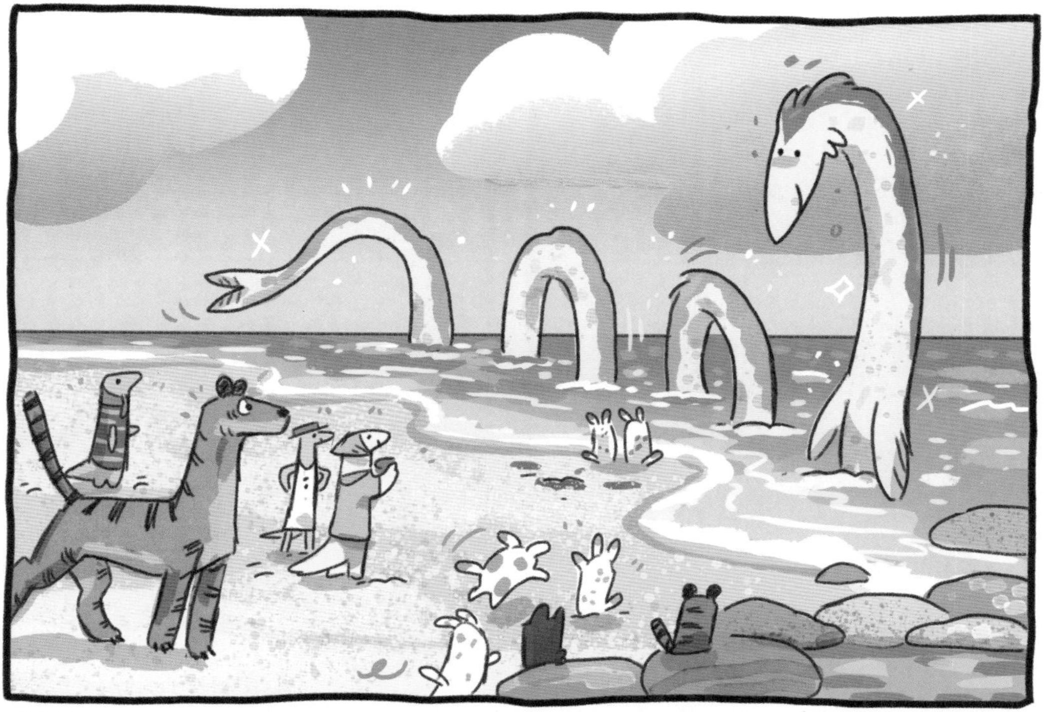

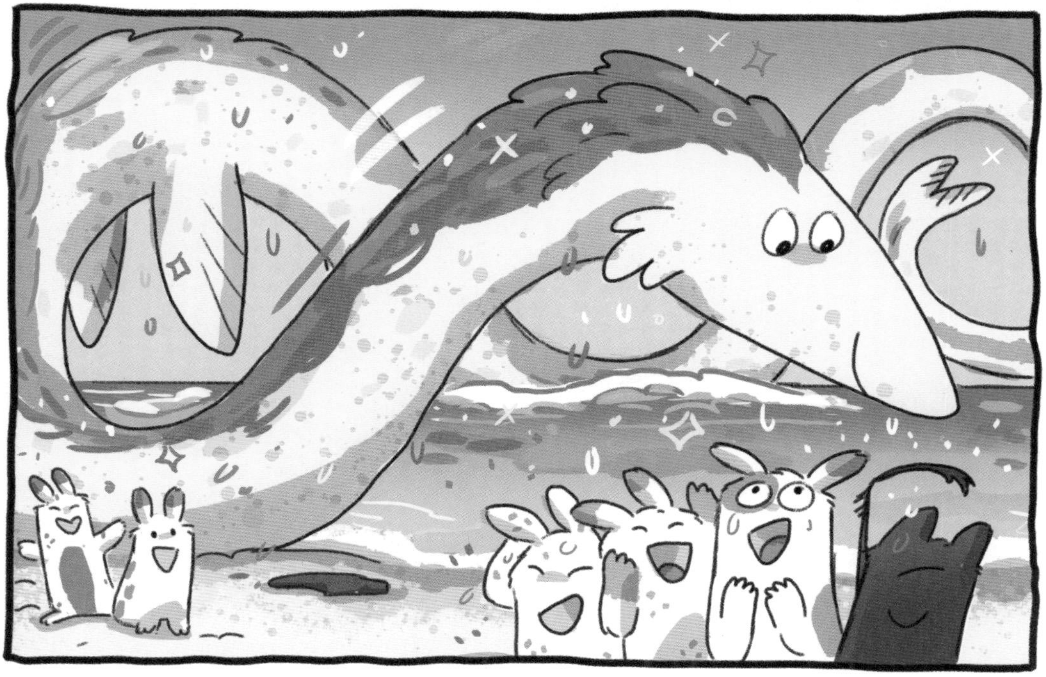

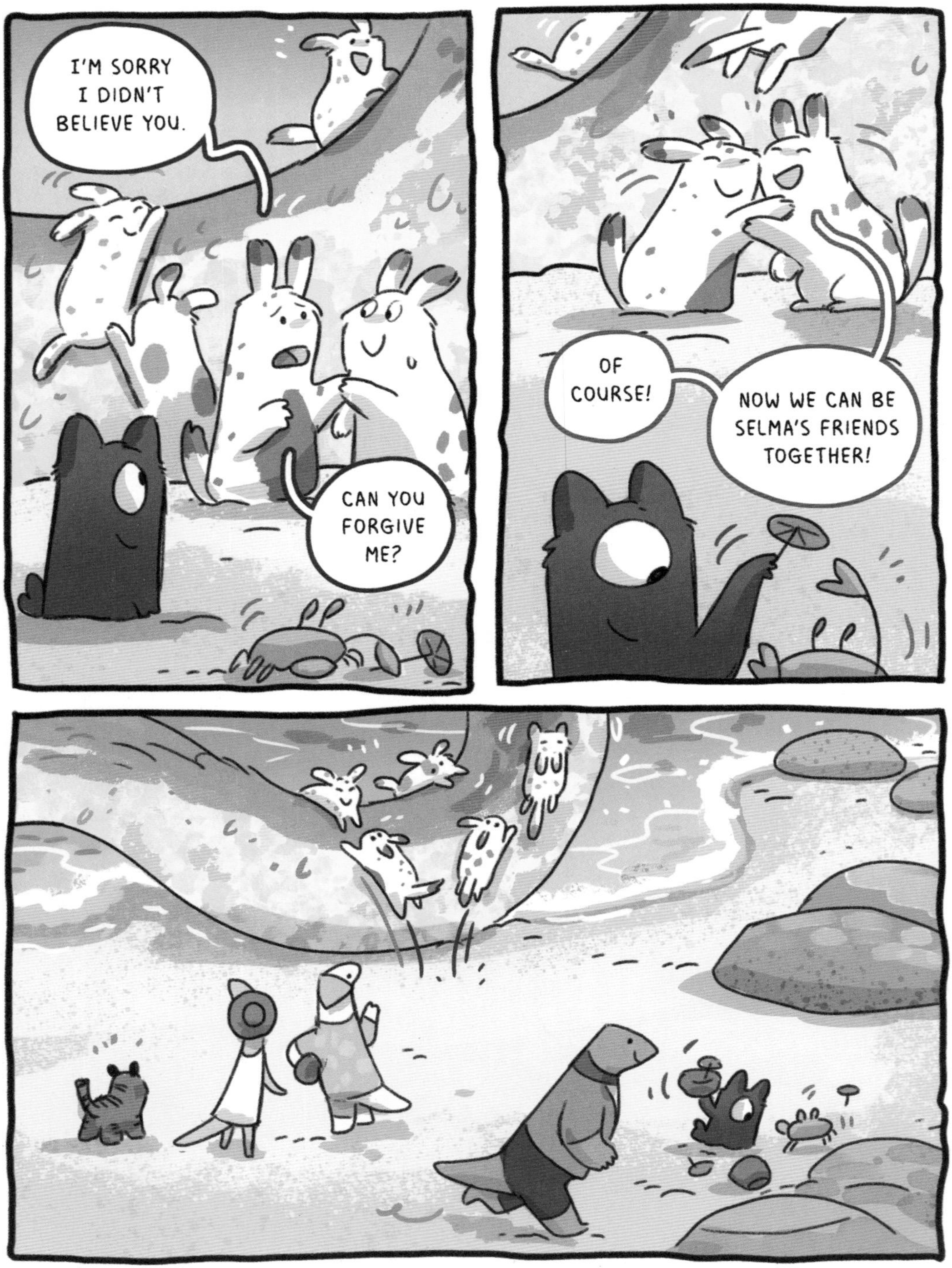
I'M SORRY I DIDN'T BELIEVE YOU.
CAN YOU FORGIVE ME?
OF COURSE!
NOW WE CAN BE SELMA'S FRIENDS TOGETHER!

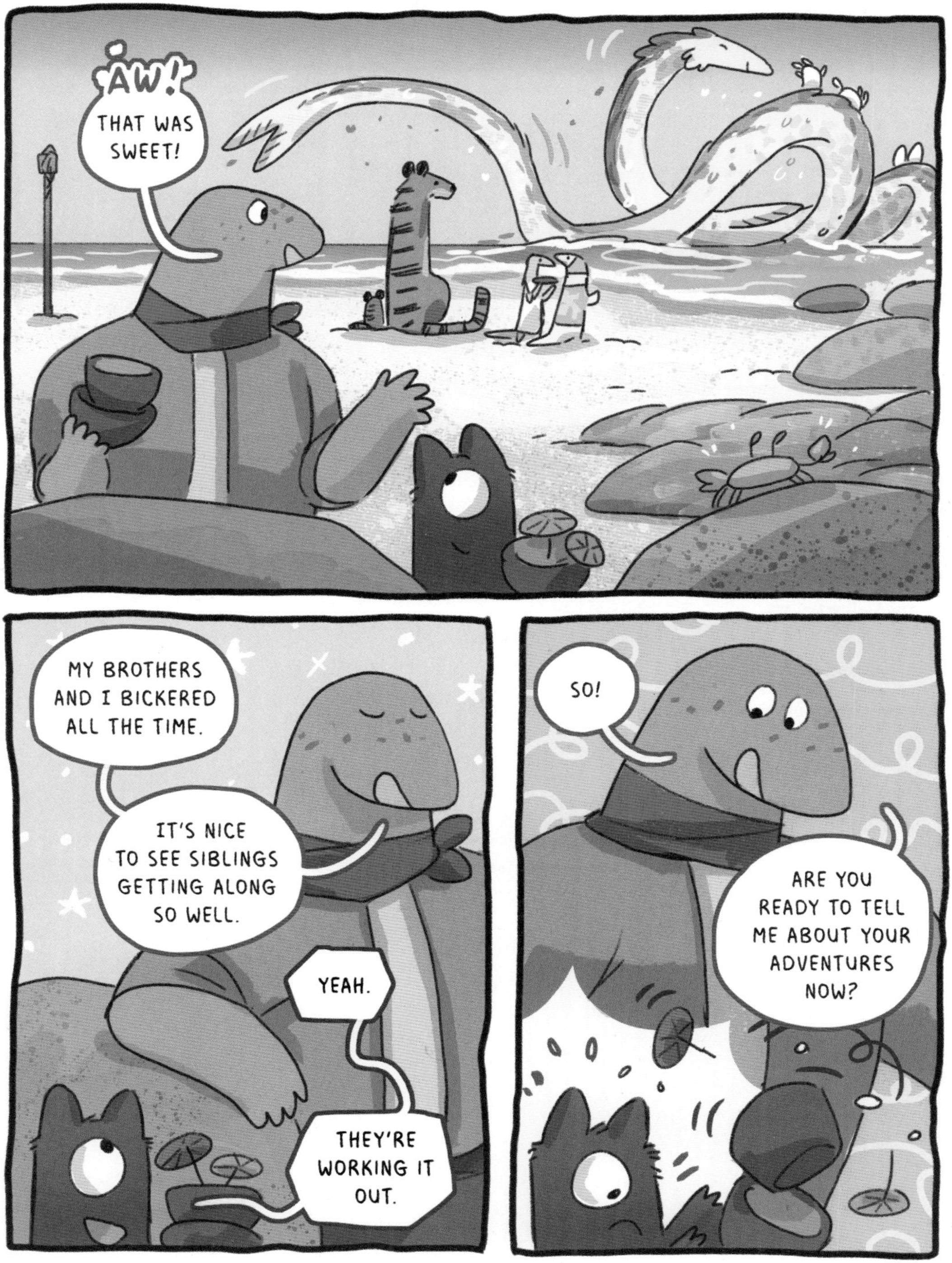
AW!
THAT WAS SWEET!
MY BROTHERS AND I BICKERED ALL THE TIME.
IT'S NICE TO SEE SIBLINGS GETTING ALONG SO WELL.
YEAH.
THEY'RE WORKING IT OUT.
SO!
ARE YOU READY TO TELL ME ABOUT YOUR ADVENTURES NOW?

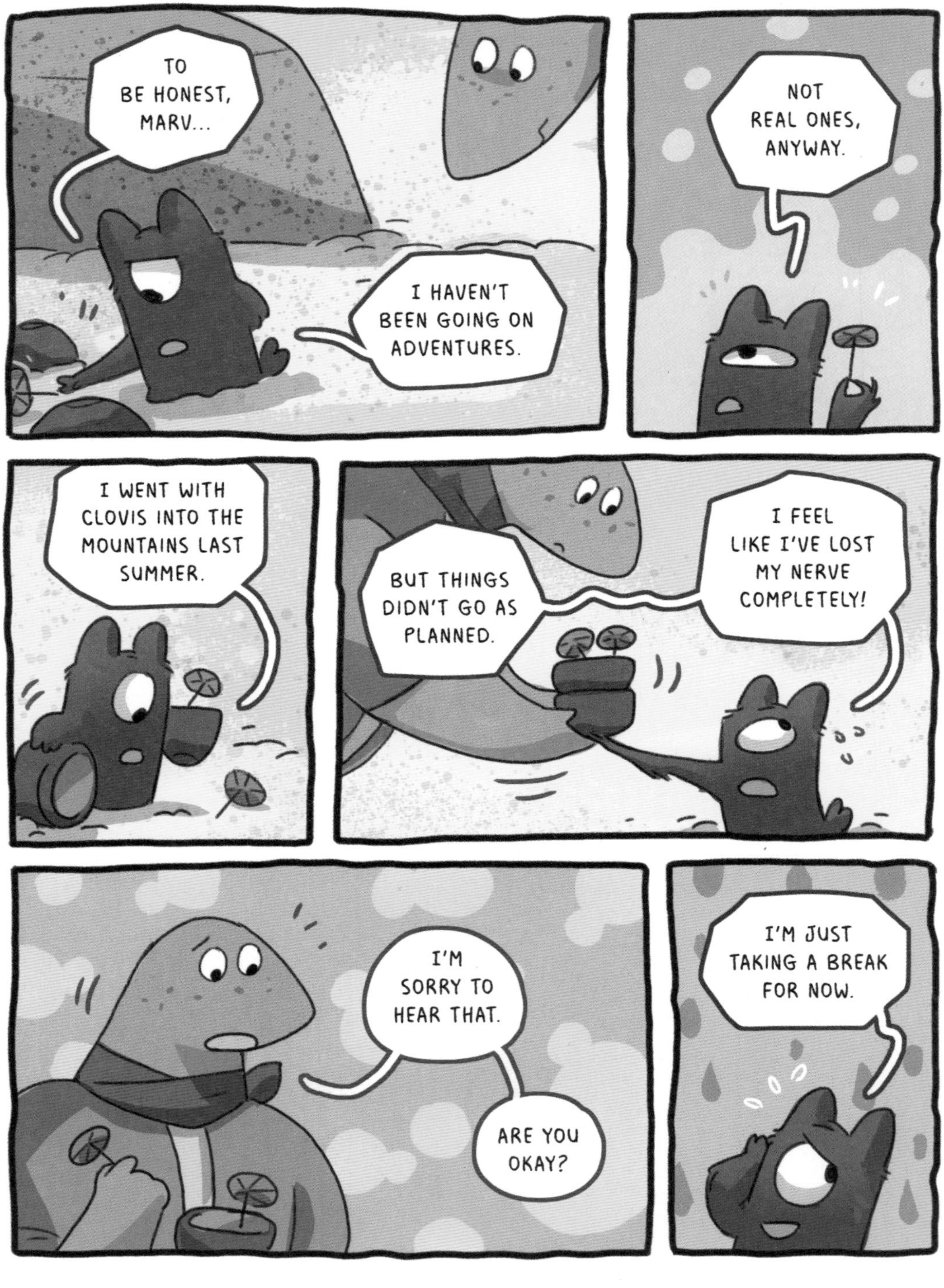
TO BE HONEST, MARV...
I HAVEN'T BEEN GOING ON ADVENTURES.
NOT REAL ONES, ANYWAY.
I WENT WITH CLOVIS INTO THE MOUNTAINS LAST SUMMER.
BUT THINGS DIDN'T GO AS PLANNED.
I FEEL LIKE I'VE LOST MY NERVE COMPLETELY!
I'M SORRY TO HEAR THAT.
ARE YOU OKAY?
I'M JUST TAKING A BREAK FOR NOW.

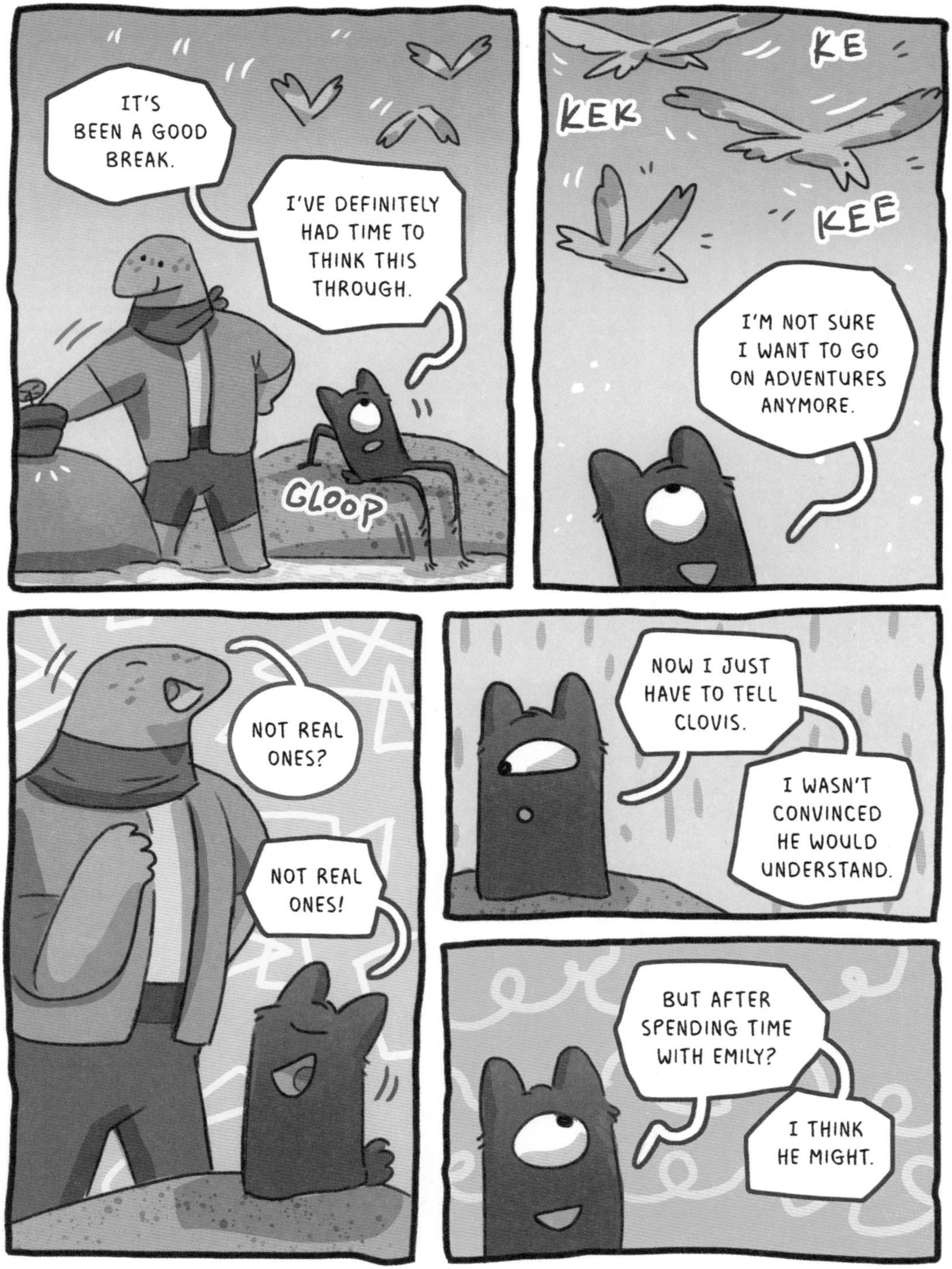

IT'S BEEN A GOOD BREAK.
I'VE DEFINITELY HAD TIME TO THINK THIS THROUGH.
GLOOP
KE
KEK
KEE
I'M NOT SURE I WANT TO GO ON ADVENTURES ANYMORE.
NOT REAL ONES?
NOT REAL ONES!
NOW I JUST HAVE TO TELL CLOVIS.
I WASN'T CONVINCED HE WOULD UNDERSTAND.
BUT AFTER SPENDING TIME WITH EMILY?
I THINK HE MIGHT.

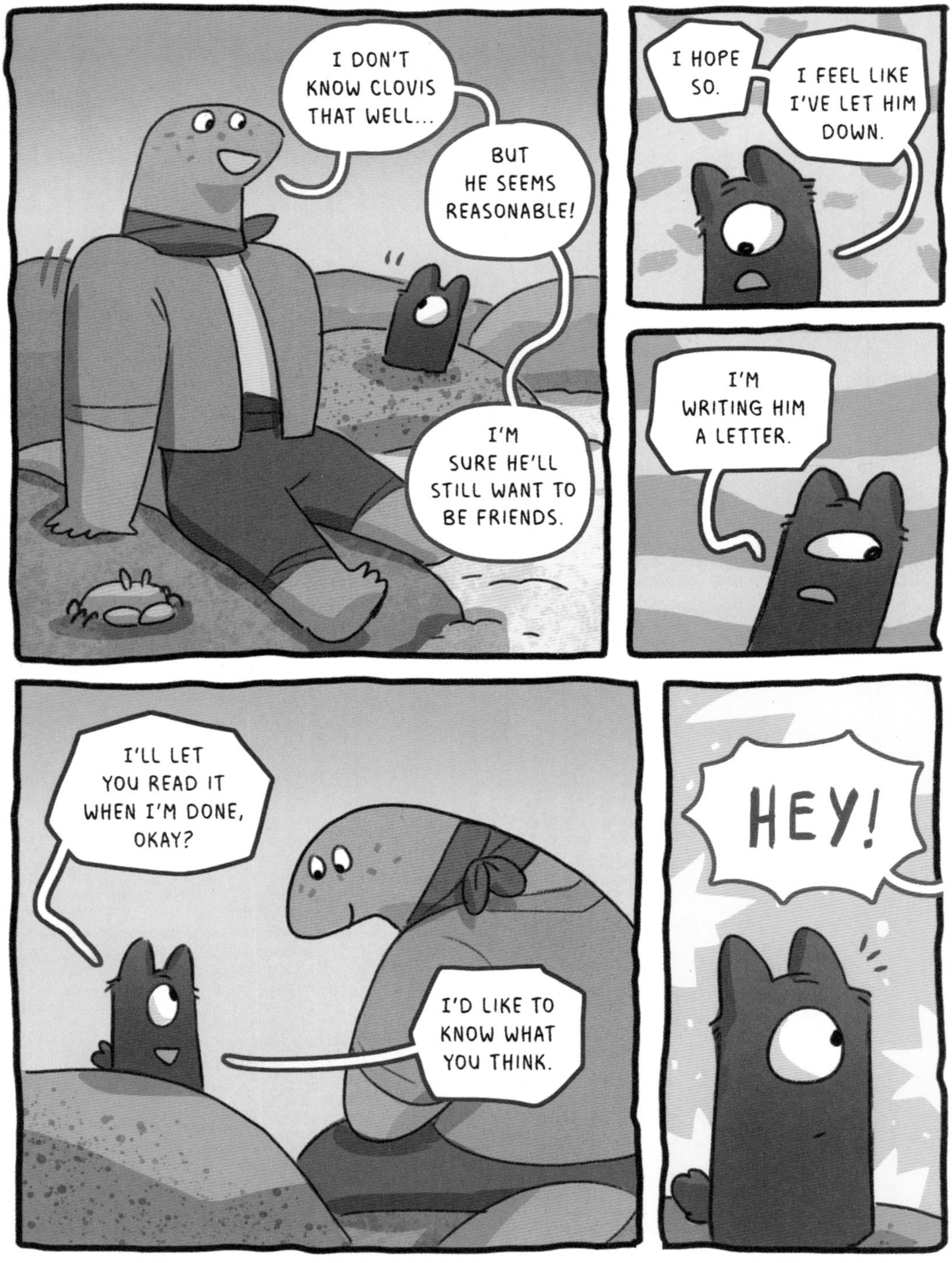
I DON'T KNOW CLOVIS THAT WELL...
BUT HE SEEMS REASONABLE!
I'M SURE HE'LL STILL WANT TO BE FRIENDS.
I HOPE SO.
I FEEL LIKE I'VE LET HIM DOWN.
I'M WRITING HIM A LETTER.
I'LL LET YOU READ IT WHEN I'M DONE, OKAY?
I'D LIKE TO KNOW WHAT YOU THINK.
HEY!

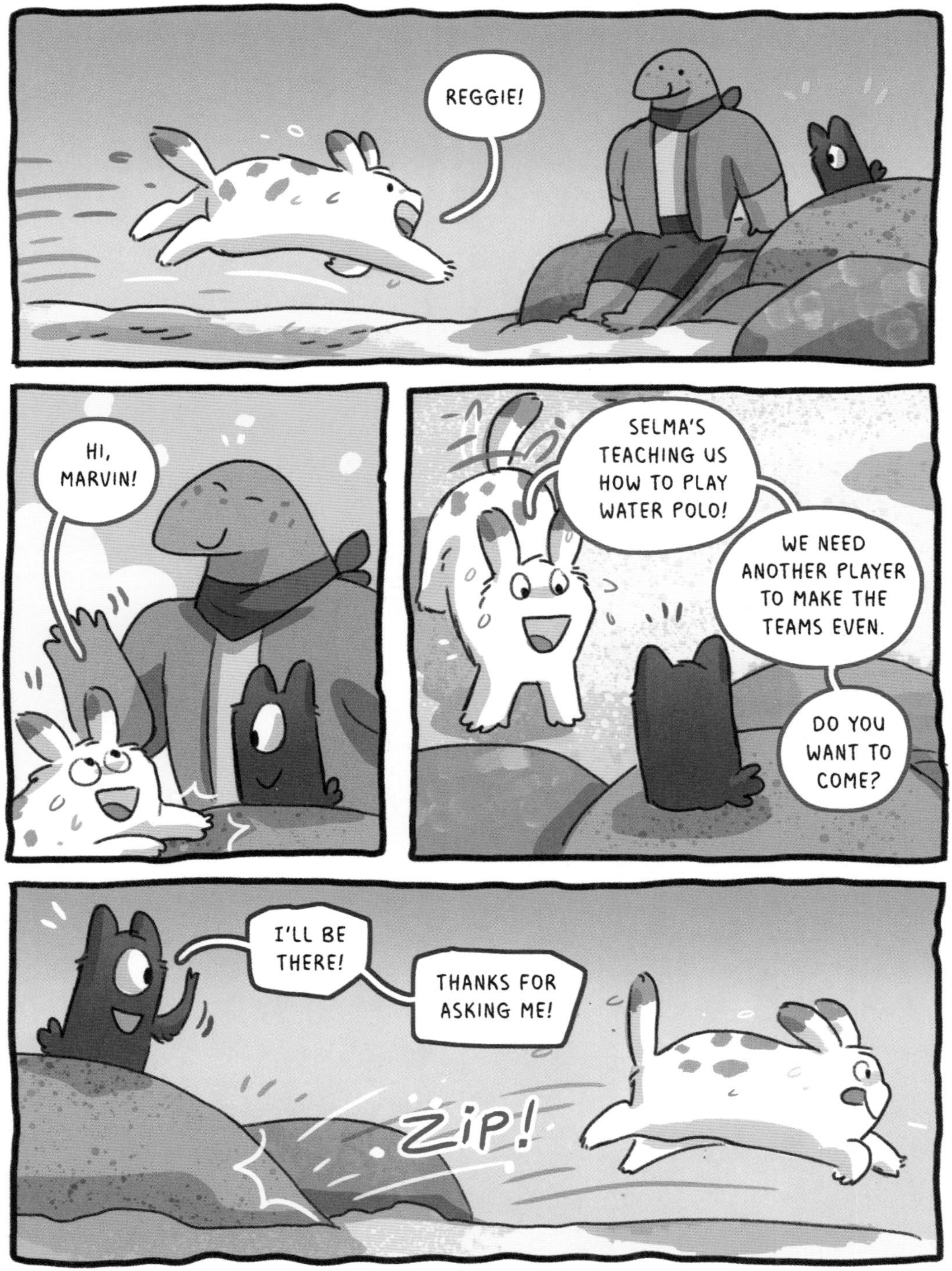
REGGIE!
HI, MARVIN!
SELMA'S TEACHING US HOW TO PLAY WATER POLO!
WE NEED ANOTHER PLAYER TO MAKE THE TEAMS EVEN.
DO YOU WANT TO COME?
I'LL BE THERE!
THANKS FOR ASKING ME!
ZIP!

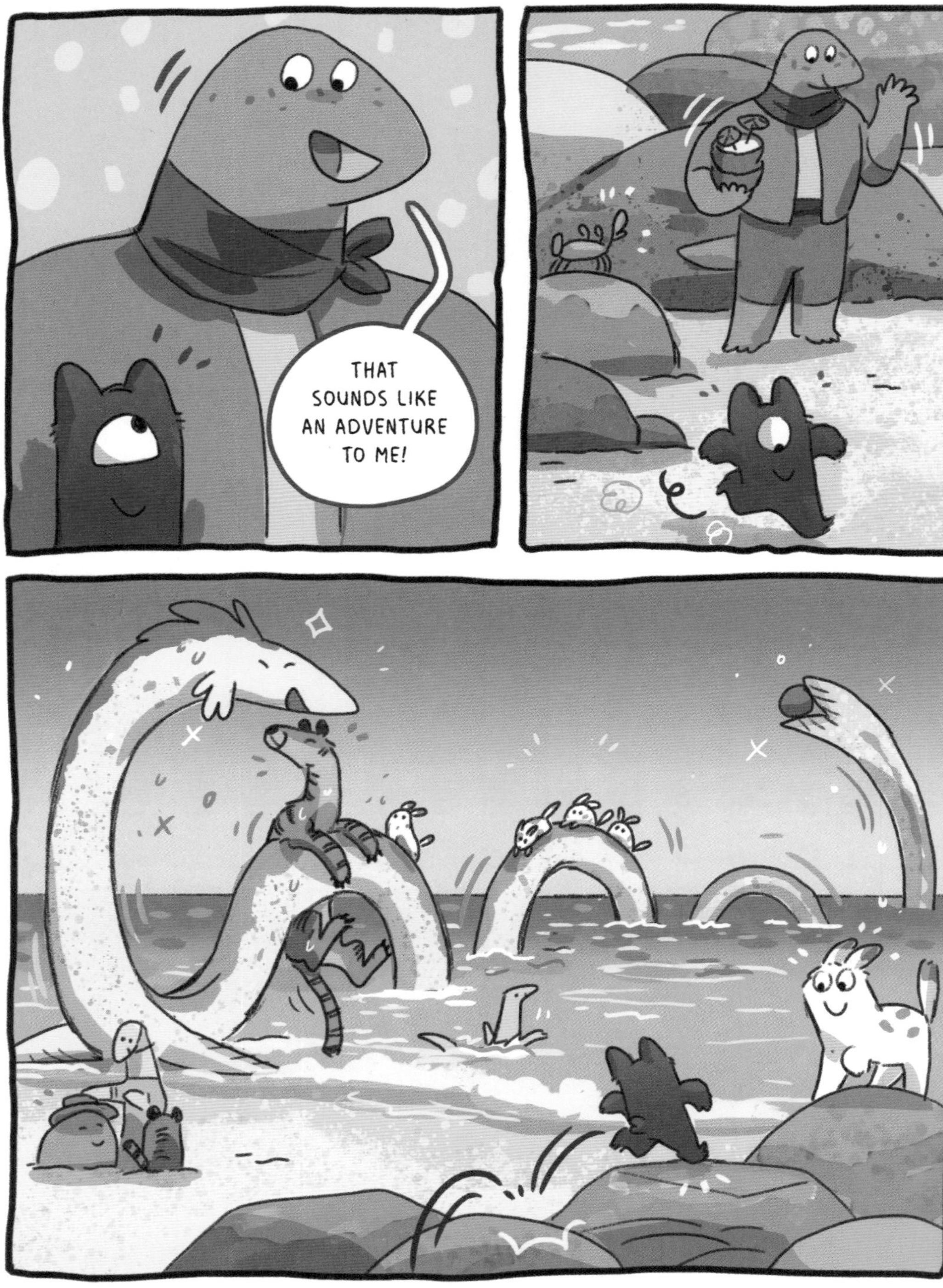
THAT SOUNDS LIKE AN ADVENTURE TO ME!

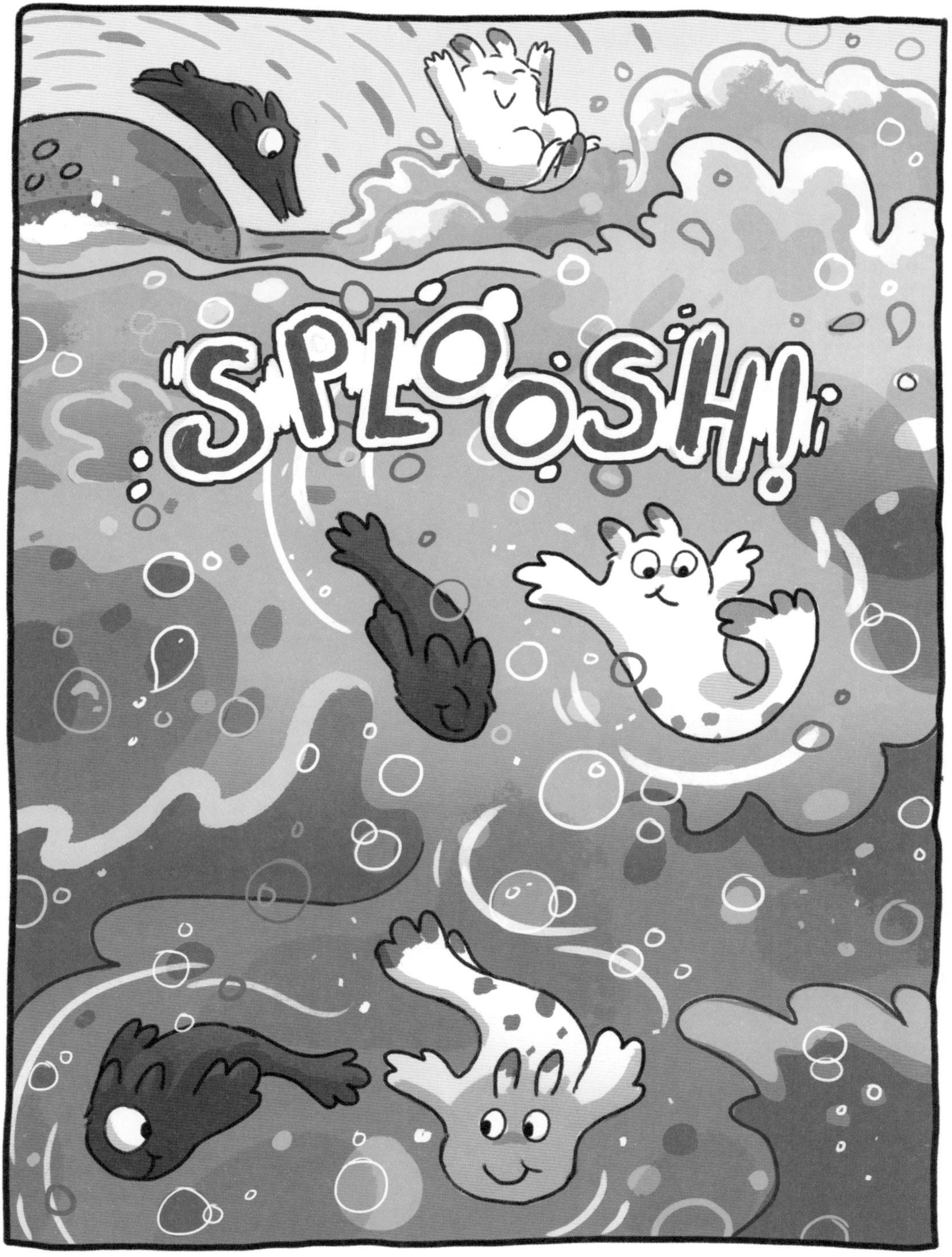
SPLOOSH!

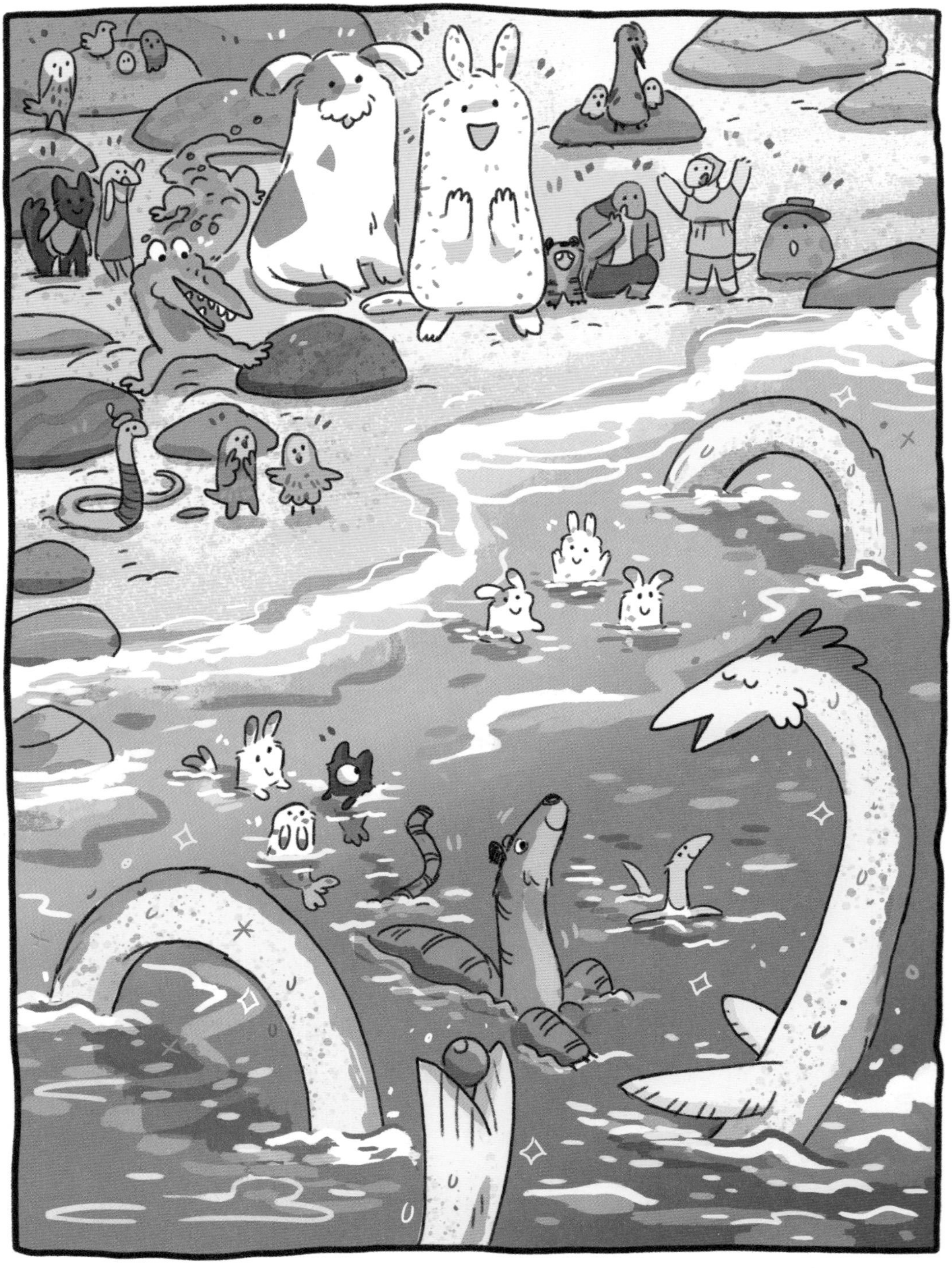

chapter 6

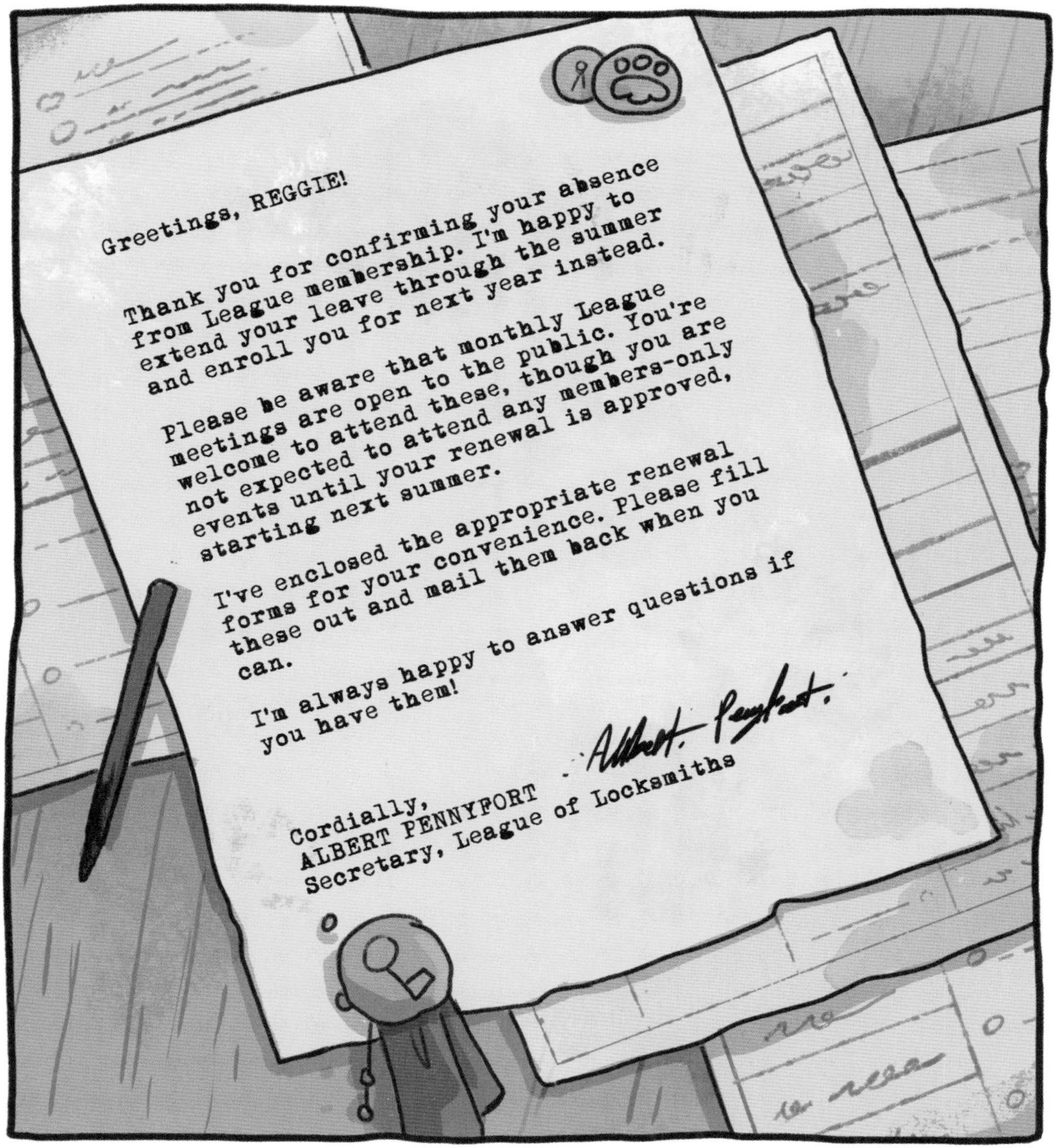
Greetings, REGGIE!
Thank you for confirming your absence from League membership. I'm happy to extend your leave through the summer and enroll you for next year instead.
Please be aware that monthly League meetings are open to the public. You're welcome to attend these, though you are not expected to attend any members-only events until your renewal is approved, starting next summer.
I've enclosed the appropriate renewal forms for your convenience. Please fill these out and mail them back when you can.
I'm always happy to answer questions if you have them!
Albert Pennyfort
Cordially,
ALBERT PENNYFORT
Secretary, League of Locksmiths

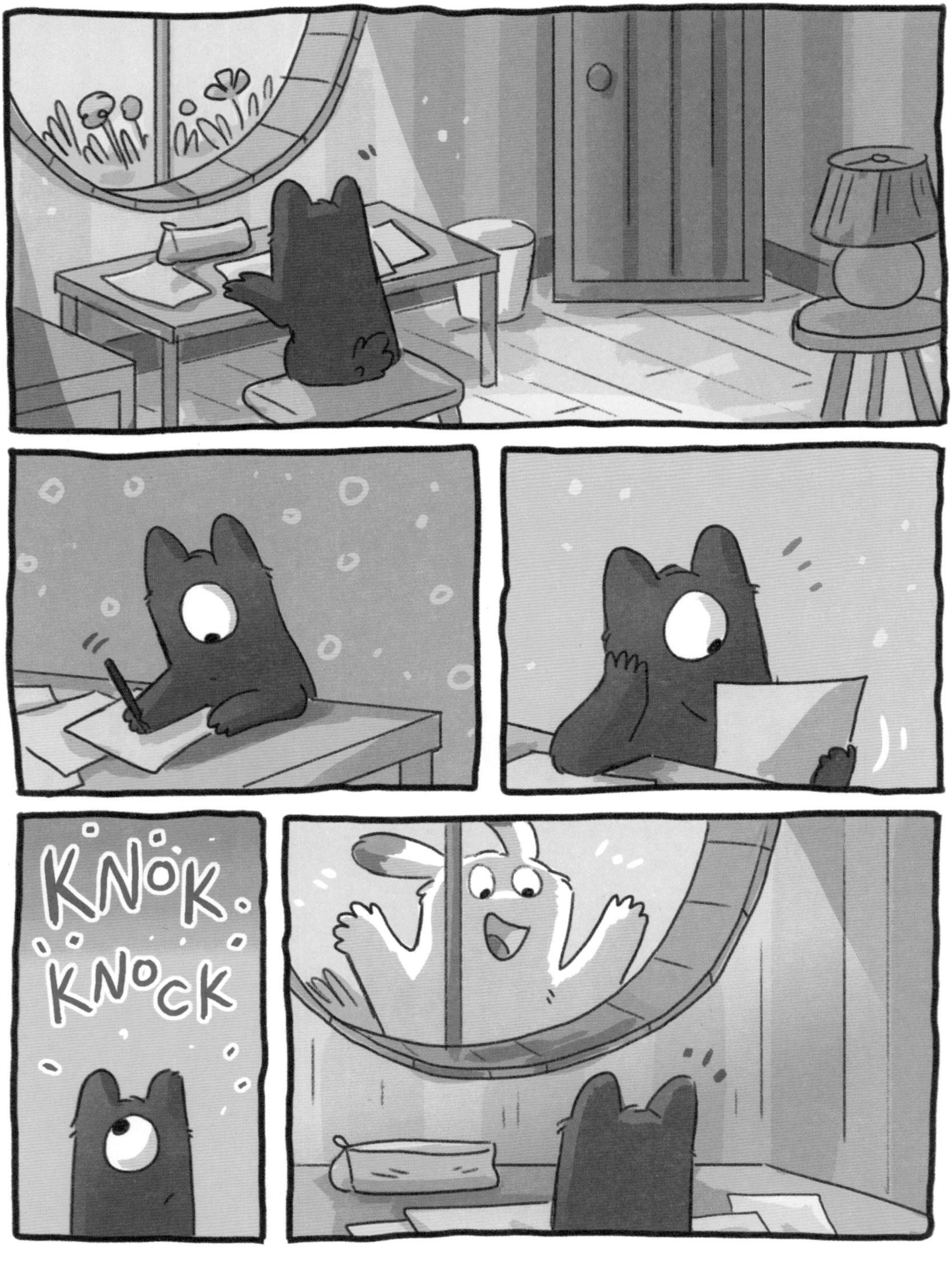
KNOK
KNOCK

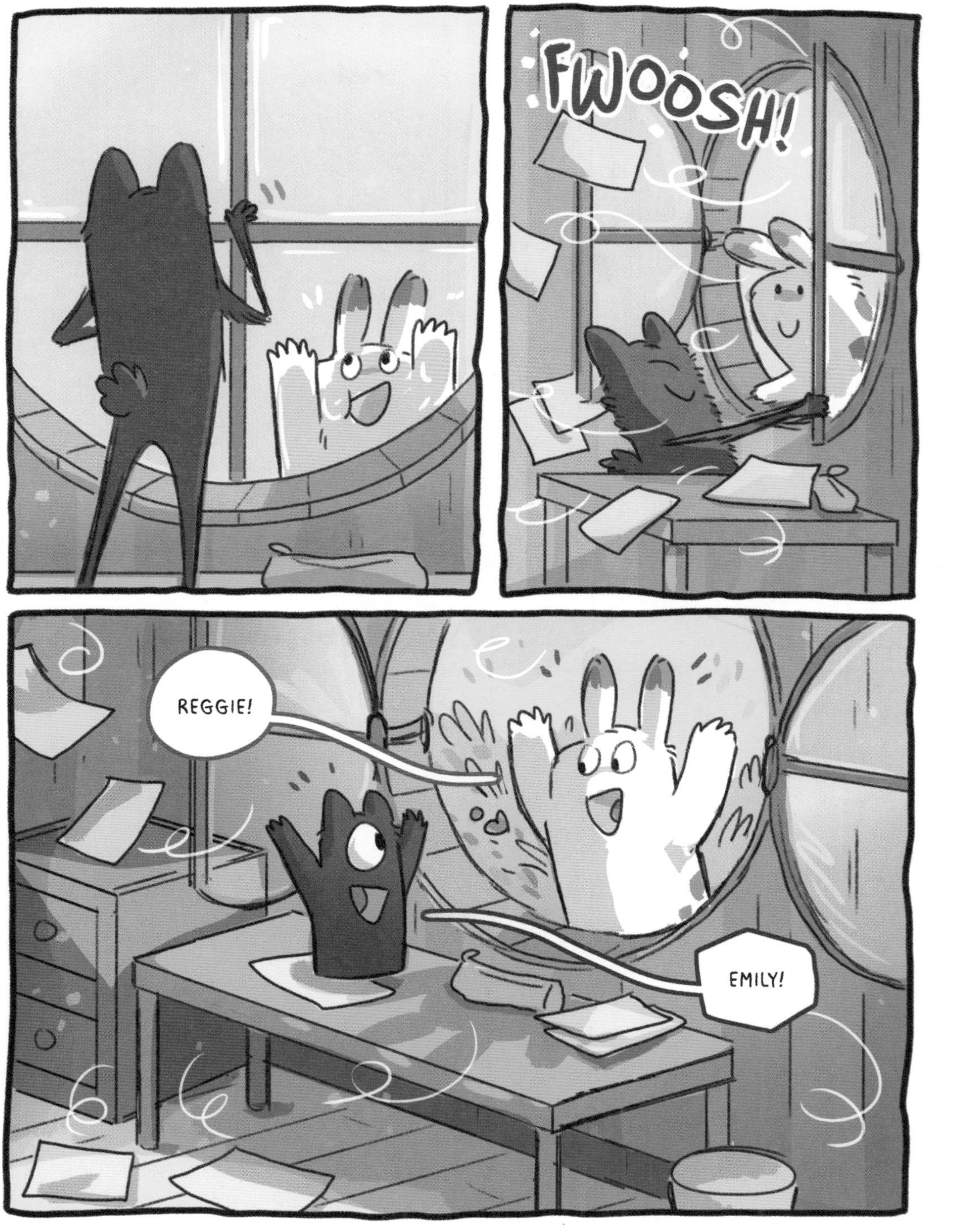
FWOOSH!
REGGIE!
EMILY!

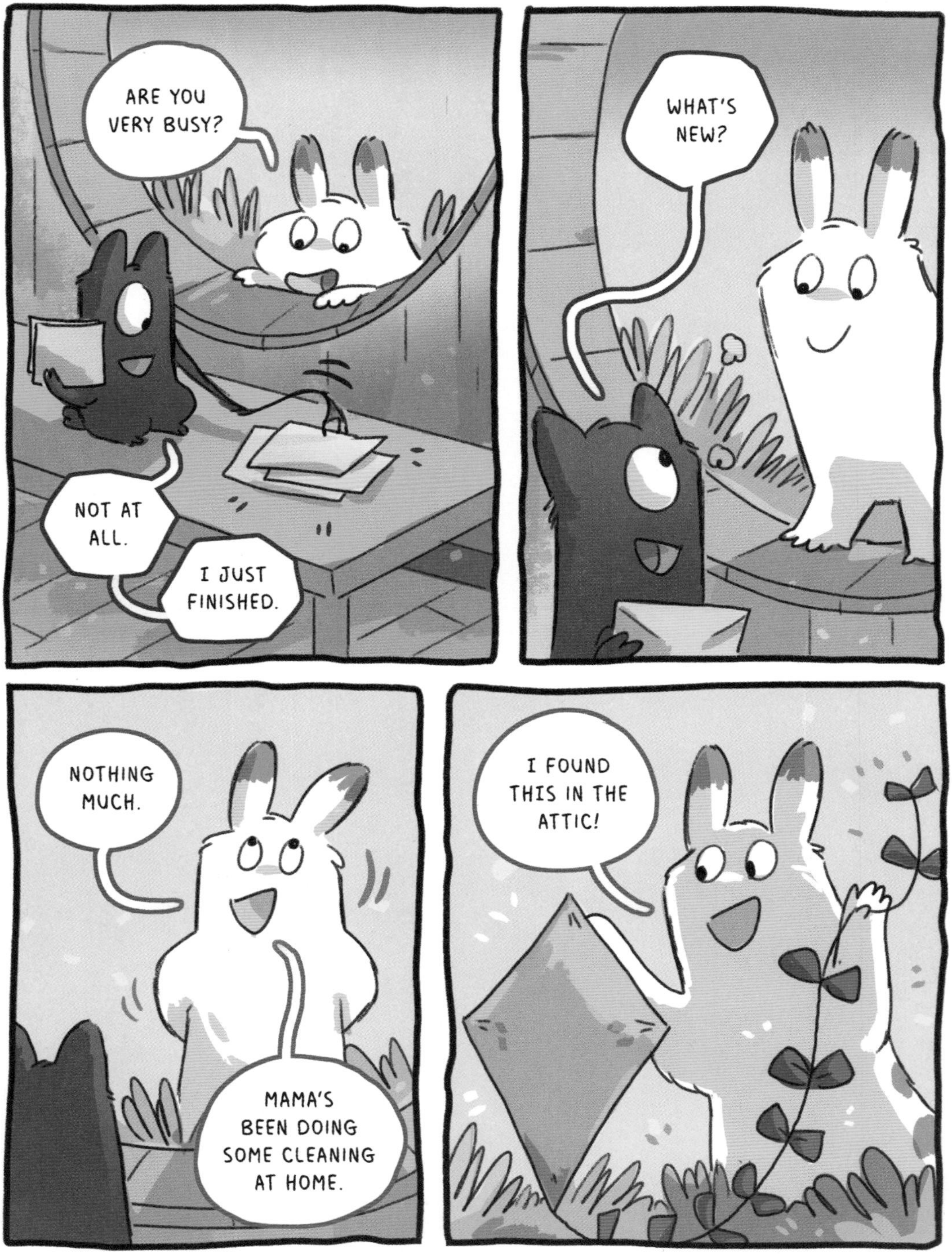
ARE YOU VERY BUSY?
NOT AT ALL.
I JUST FINISHED.
WHAT'S NEW?
NOTHING MUCH.
MAMA'S BEEN DOING SOME CLEANING AT HOME.
I FOUND THIS IN THE ATTIC!

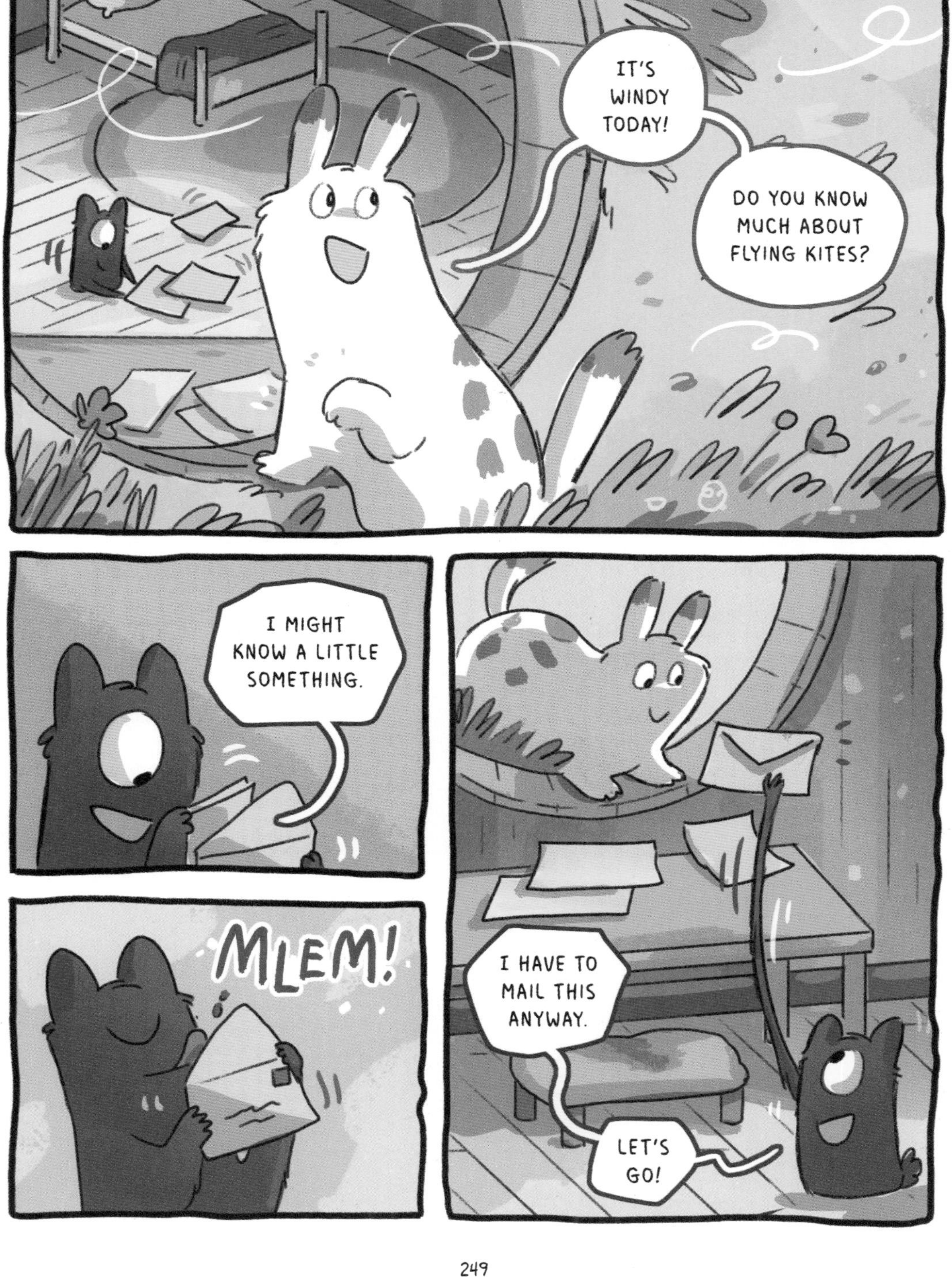
IT'S WINDY TODAY!
DO YOU KNOW MUCH ABOUT FLYING KITES?
I MIGHT KNOW A LITTLE SOMETHING.
MLEM!
I HAVE TO MAIL THIS ANYWAY.
LET'S GO!

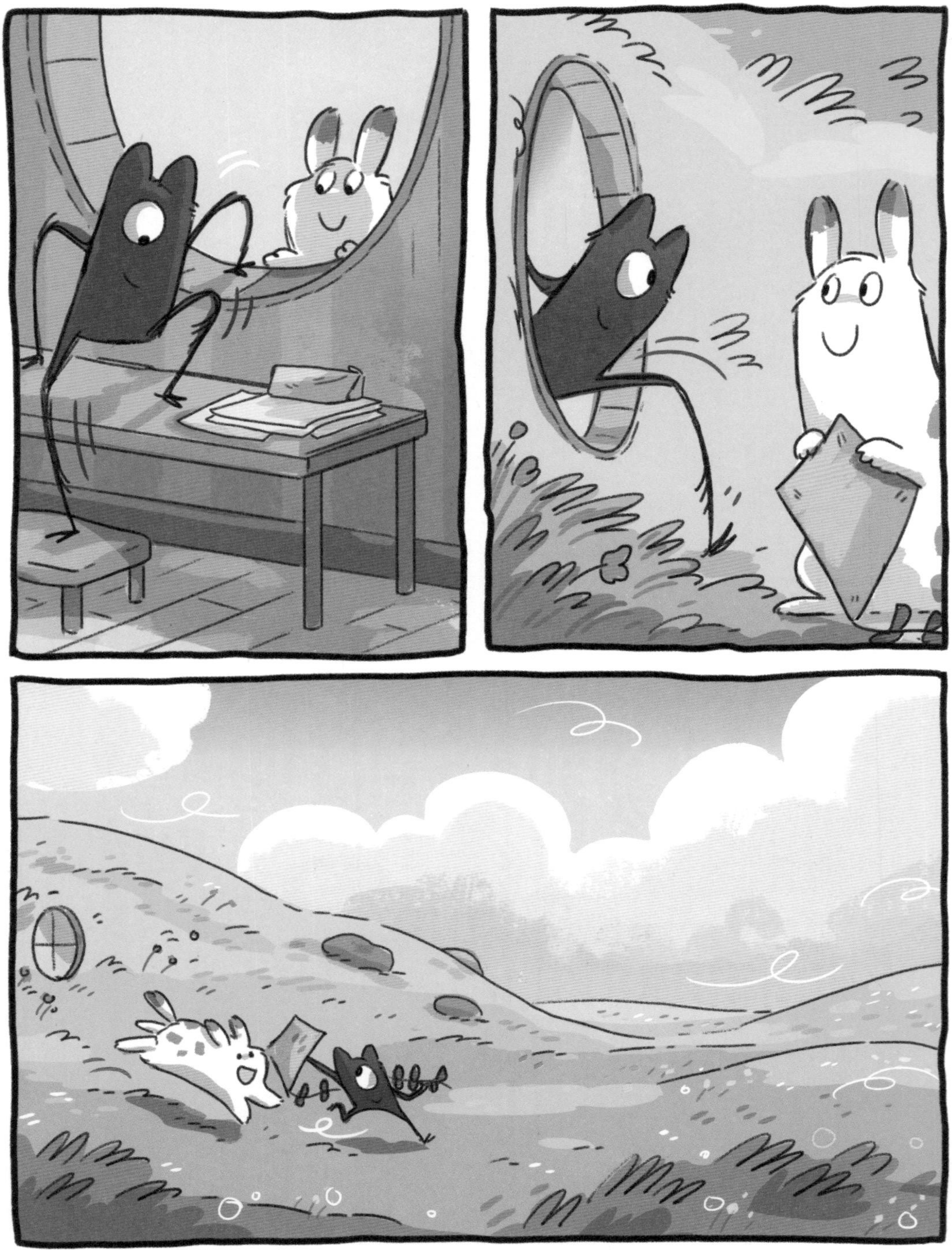

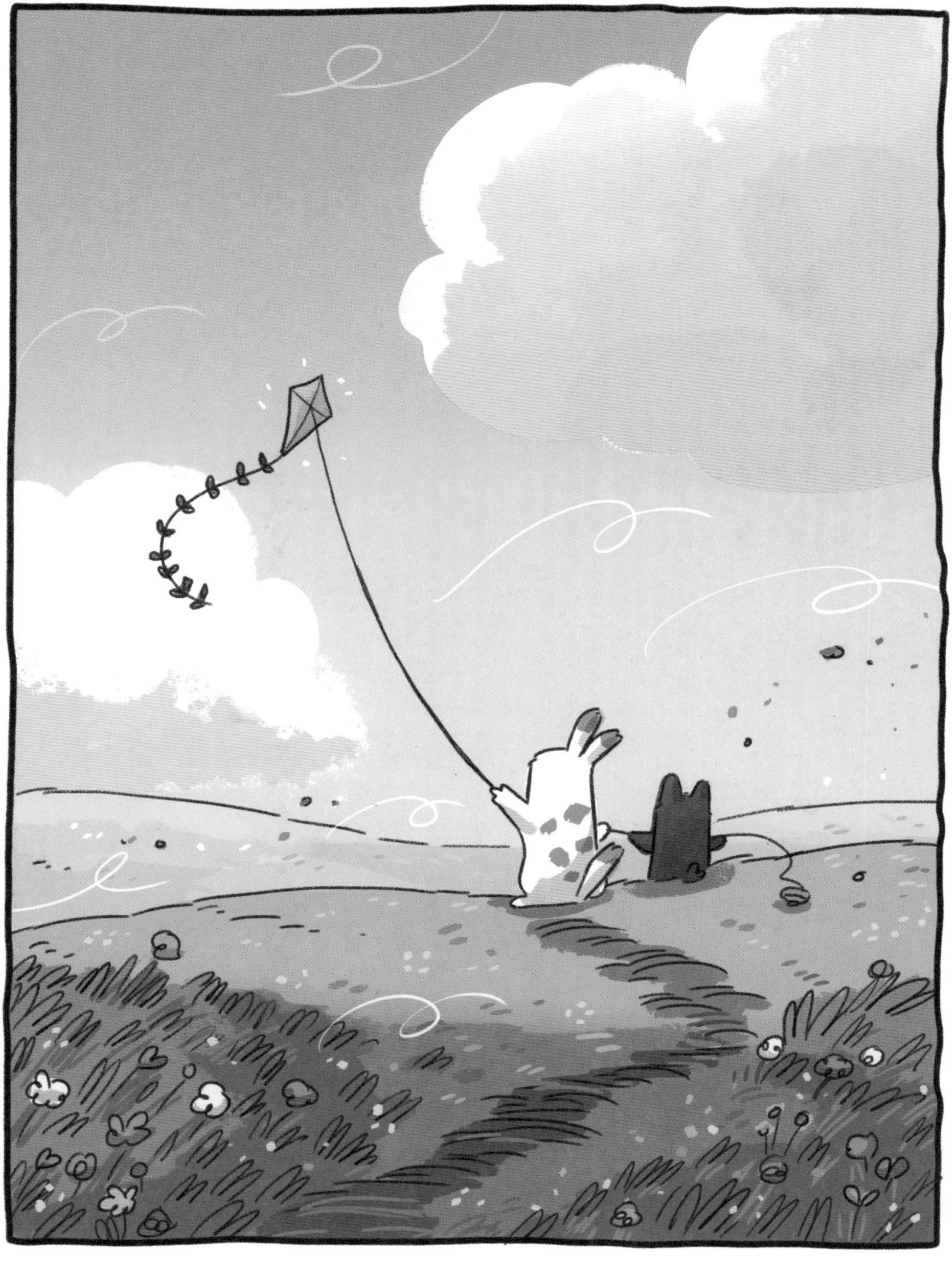

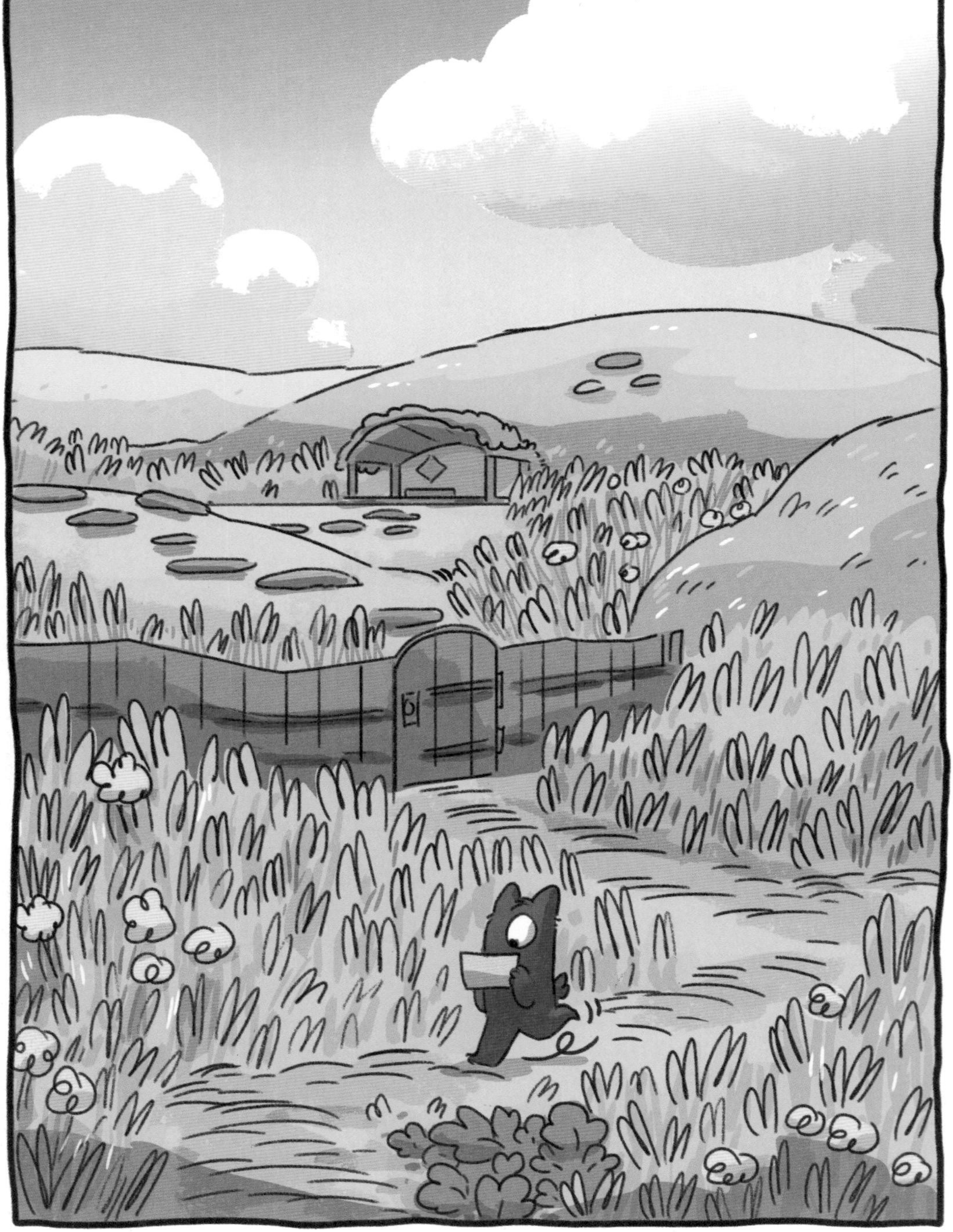

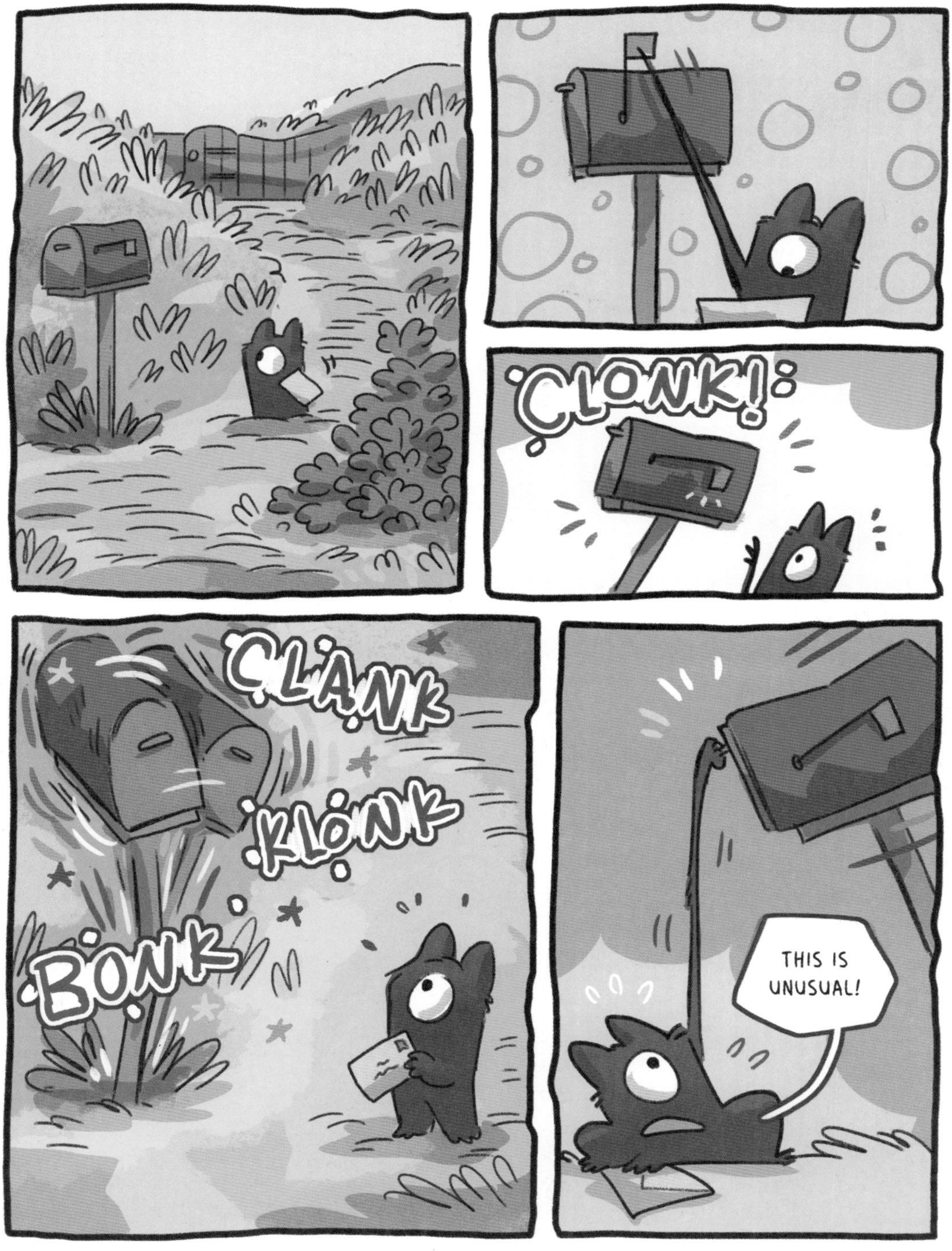
CLONK!
CLANK
KLONK
BONK
THIS IS UNUSUAL!

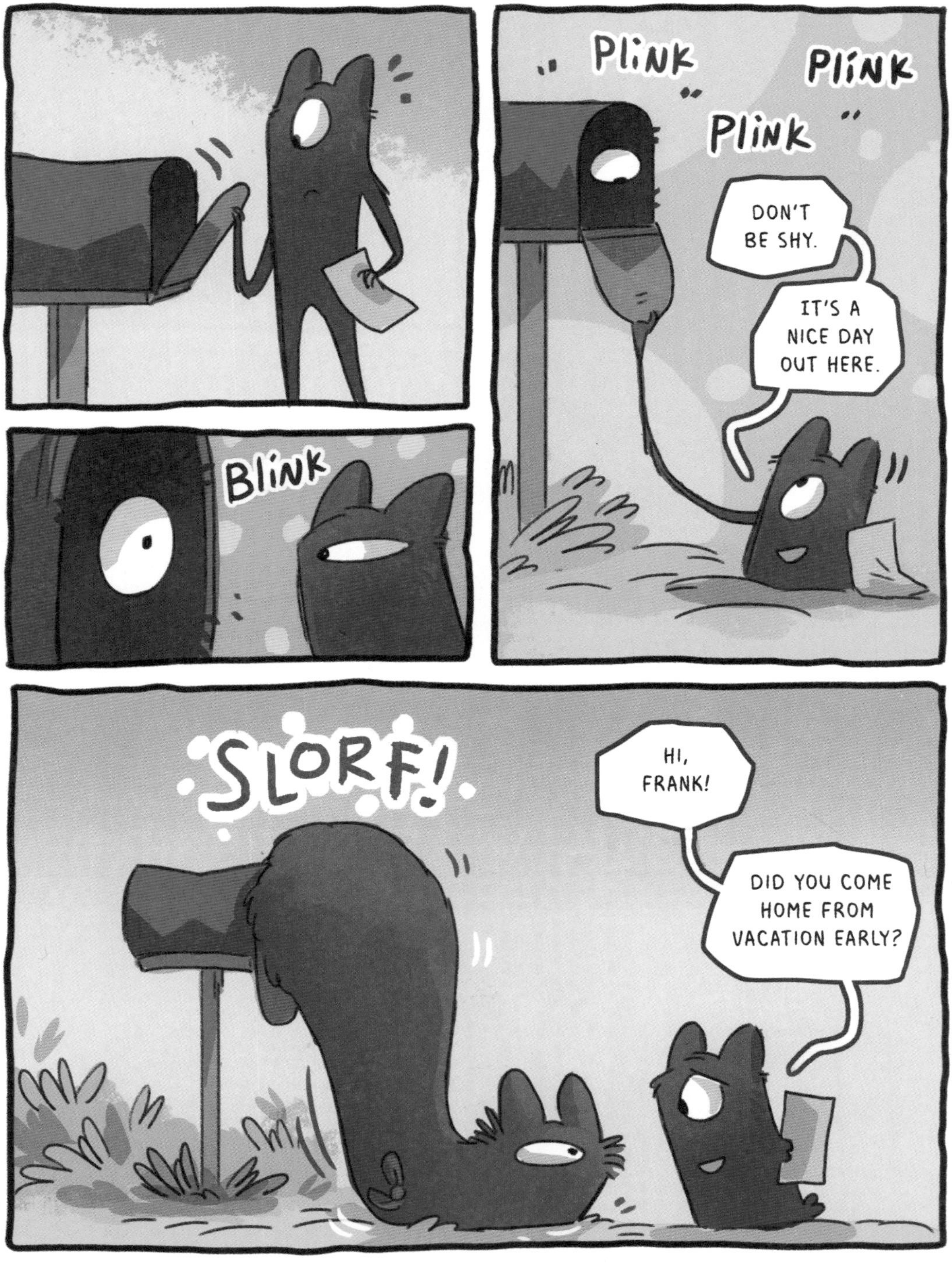
PLINK
PLINK
PLINK
DON'T BE SHY.
IT'S A NICE DAY OUT HERE.
BLINK
SLORF!
HI, FRANK!
DID YOU COME HOME FROM VACATION EARLY?

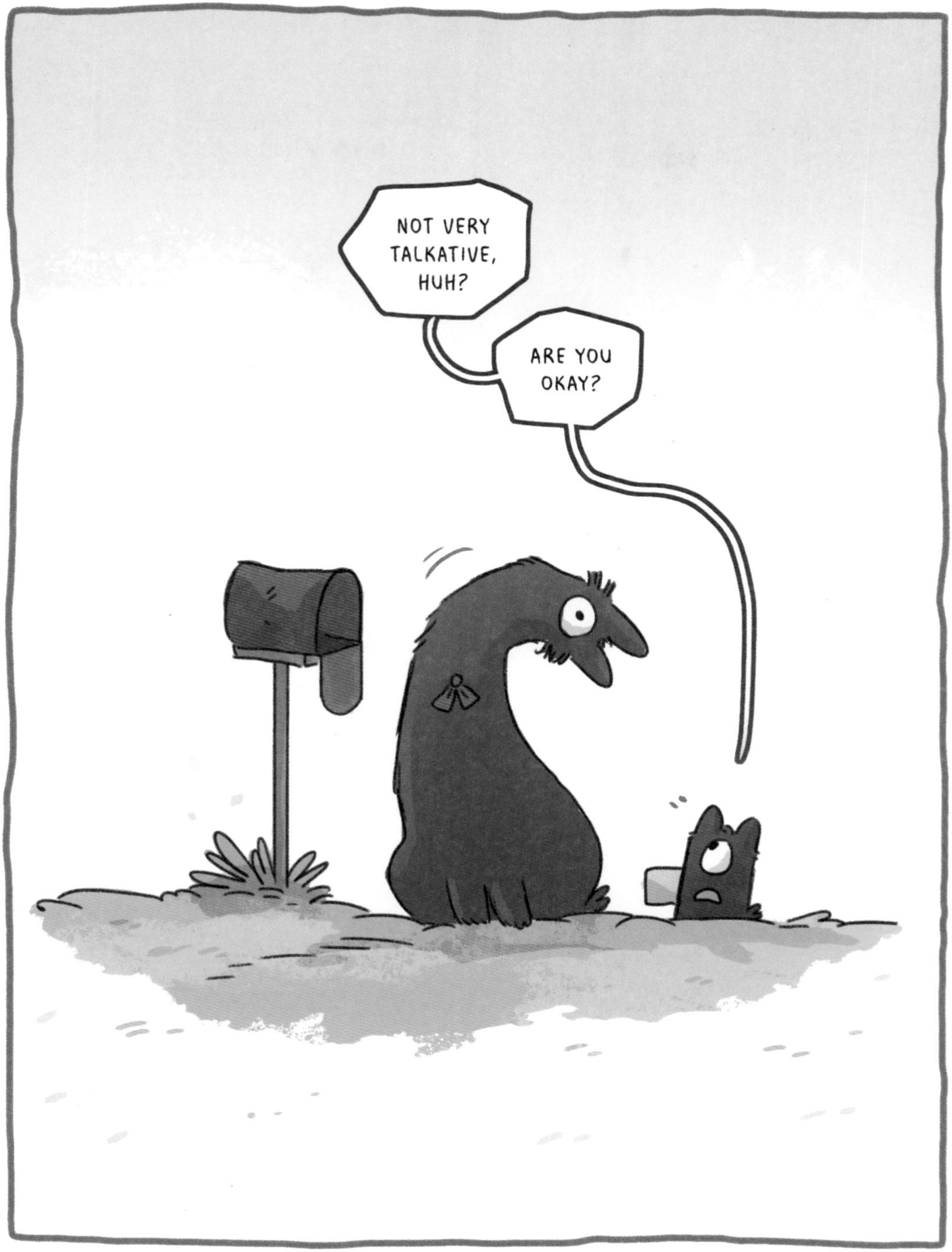
NOT VERY TALKATIVE, HUH?
ARE YOU OKAY?

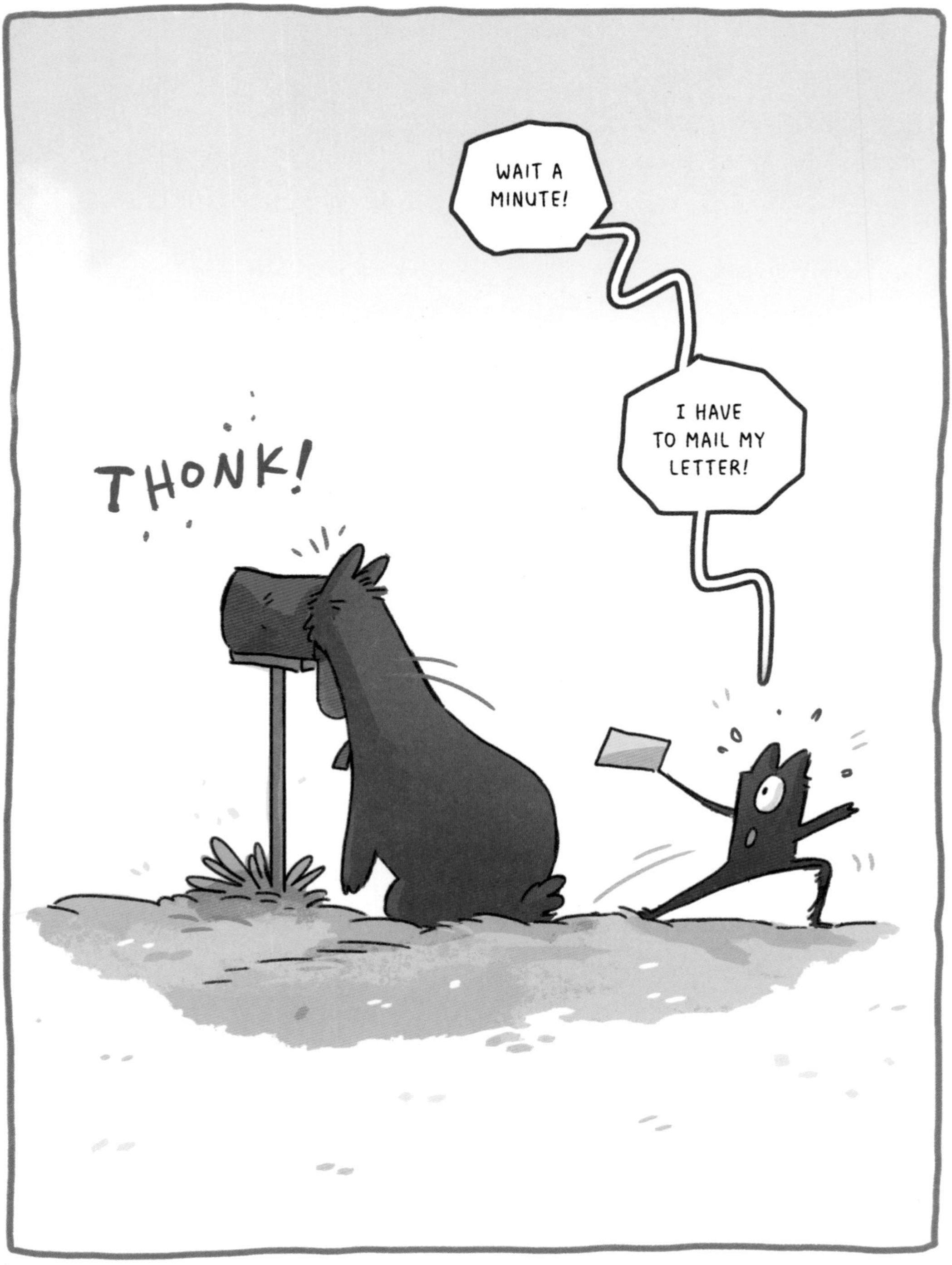
WAIT A MINUTE!
I HAVE TO MAIL MY LETTER!
THONK!

ACKNOWLEDGMENTS

A GINORMOUS THANK-YOU TO WHITNEY, GINA, AND PATRICK FOR HELPING MAKE **MONSTER FRIENDS** LOOK AMAZING! I'LL TAKE CREDIT FOR THE WRITING AND DRAWING, BUT Y'ALL PUT A POLISH ON THIS STORY WITH A SENSIBILITY I NEVER COULD HAVE MANAGED ON MY OWN.

MUCH THANKS ALSO TO MY LOVELY, SUPPORTIVE, AND VERY PATIENT FAMILY. EACH OF YOU HAS INSPIRED ME TO WRITE WITH THE VIBRANCY OF LIVED EXPERIENCE.

LASTLY, A ROARING THANK-YOU TO MY SMALL AND SUPPORTIVE SQUAD OF ONLINE FRIENDS. YOUR ENCOURAGEMENT AND COUNSEL MEANS THE WORLD TO ME.

AUTHOR'S NOTE

Original Character: An original character (OC) is a character that does not come from an existing copyright. In other words, it is a new fictional character.

REGGIE AND EMILY ARE SOME OF MY VERY EARLY ORIGINAL CHARACTERS. I'M SURE "OCs" ARE A STRANGE CONCEPT IF YOU DON'T WRITE STORIES ON THE REGULAR; BUT FOR ME, I CAN'T IMAGINE WHAT IT'S LIKE NOT TO BE CONSTANTLY MULLING OVER THE FICTIONAL LIVES OF IMAGINARY CHARACTERS. IT IS A CHANCE TO EXPLORE PROBLEM-SOLVING THROUGH SOMEONE ELSE'S EYES AND THE PUREST FORM OF PLAY.

IN **MONSTER FRIENDS** REGGIE AND EMILY BOTH STUMBLE THROUGH CHALLENGES THAT REQUIRE REFLECTION. REGGIE STRUGGLES WITH A FEAR OF CAVES AND DREADS EXPLAINING HIMSELF TO HIS MORE ADVENTUROUS FRIENDS. EMILY BURSTS WITH EXUBERANCE, MAKING TROUBLE WITH A PRAGMATIC SISTER IN HER EAGERNESS TO SHARE A SECRET. WHILE REGGIE'S PROBLEMS EXIST SOMEWHAT OFF-CAMERA, GIVING HIM THE LUXURY OF DISTANCE, EMILY IS CONFRONTED DAILY WITH HER SISTERS' CHILDISH ARGUMENTS, AND MAKES HER OWN SPACE BY SEPARATING HERSELF (DANGEROUSLY!) FROM THE PROTECTION OF HER FAMILY. A BIG PART OF MY WRITING PROCESS IS TO ASK MYSELF QUESTIONS ABOUT INTENT AND STRUCTURE. EVEN THOUGH THE STORY IS FINISHED, I WONDER HOW DIFFERENTLY THINGS WOULD HAVE UNFOLDED IF ANY ELEMENT HAD CHANGED SLIGHTLY. . . . AND THIS IS WHERE MY FAVORITE QUESTION COMES INTO PLAY: **WHAT IF THINGS WERE DIFFERENT?**

WHAT IF, INSTEAD OF EMILY, REGGIE HAD SEEN THE SEA MONSTER? DO YOU THINK HE WOULD HAVE TOLD EMILY? WOULD SHE HAVE BELIEVED HIM? AND **WHAT IF** REGGIE AND EMILY SWAPPED PERSONALITIES AT ANY POINT IN THE STORY? WOULD THE TONE HAVE CHANGED IF REGGIE HAD ASKED EMILY TO PLAY INSTEAD? I'M SURE YOU CAN IMAGINE ALTERNATE ENDINGS FROM EVEN THESE SMALL CHANGES . . . BUT THEN THAT'S WHAT OTHER OCs ARE FOR! I ENCOURAGE YOU, DEAR READER, TO THINK OF QUESTIONS FOR YOURSELF, AND ANSWER THEM YOUR OWN WAY THROUGH YOUR OWN ORIGINAL CHARACTERS. MAY YOU SURPRISE YOURSELF WITH THE ENDLESS POSSIBILITIES!

THE LITTLE CREATURES IN **MONSTER FRIENDS** HAVE BEEN THE SUBJECTS OF MY PERSONAL WORK FOR THE PAST TWENTY YEARS. SOMEWHAT UNINTENTIONALLY, REGGIE AND EMILY HAVE BECOME A SHORTHAND FOR WORKING THROUGH CONFLICT AND FINDING RESOLUTION. I'M NOT SURE THEY ALWAYS SOLVE THEIR PROBLEMS THE BEST WAY . . . BUT THEN WE'RE ALL LEARNING TOGETHER, AREN'T WE?

KAETI VANDORN IS AN AUTHOR, ILLUSTRATOR, AND CARTOONIST WHO LOVES DRAWING COLORFUL LANDSCAPES AND ADORABLE MONSTERS. SHE SPENT HER CHILDHOOD CHASING FIREFLIES IN KANSAS, THEN BEING CHASED BY MOSQUITOES IN ALASKA. SHE NOW LIVES WITH HER FAMILY ON A HILLTOP FARM IN VERMONT, WHERE SHE STAYS INDOORS MOST OF THE TIME TO AVOID ALLERGIES AND THE TERRIFYING INSECTS OUTDOORS. (ALSO, THAT BIG GUY, SASQUATCH.)

SHE HAS A DEGREE IN ILLUSTRATION FROM THE ACADEMY OF ART UNIVERSITY, WHICH SHE ACHIEVED THROUGH ONLINE CORRESPONDENCE. HER CASUAL INTERESTS LIE IN BOTANY AND HERPETOLOGY; IF SHE WEREN'T AN ARTIST (AND SO WARY OF BUGS), SHE WOULD PROBABLY BE A NATURALIST, STUDYING THE BIZARRE AND WONDERFUL CREATURES OF THE WORLD.

KAETI HAS HAD HER DRAWINGS FEATURED IN ART BOOKS, INDIE ZINES, AND GALLERY SHOWS HOSTED ACROSS THE UNITED STATES. SHE HAS ALSO DESIGNED ALBUM COVERS FOR THE MUSICAL ARTIST NANOBII.

KAETI HAS SELF-PUBLISHED COMICS ONLINE SINCE 2014. **MONSTER FRIENDS** WAS DEVELOPED FROM HER WEBCOMIC **CALL OF THE SENTINEL,** WHICH UPDATED BOTH WEEKLY AND MONTHLY FROM 2014 TO 2017. THE STORY HAS BEEN REWORKED AS A GRAPHIC NOVEL, TAKING ON A QUICKER PACE AND BRIGHTER TONE FOR YOUNG AUDIENCES. SHE IS ALSO THE CREATOR OF **CRABAPPLE TROUBLE,** A STORY ABOUT A CRABAPPLE-HEADED GIRL STRUGGLING WITH HER WORRIES.

PROTEIDAES.TUMBLR.COM
@PROTEIDAES

  # LET'S DRAW MONSTERS!

IF YOU WANT TO DRAW YOUR OWN MONSTER FRIENDS, YOU SHOULD GET TO KNOW SOME BASIC SHAPES!

WE CAN USE MANY SHAPE COMBINATIONS TO MAKE A MONSTER FEEL FUNNY, SCARY, OR FRIENDLY.

 GUMDROPS ARE AN ESPECIALLY GREAT SHAPE FOR FRIENDLY MONSTERS.

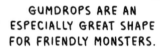 ## SHAPE DESIGN

THINK CAREFULLY ABOUT THE TYPE OF PERSONALITY YOU WANT YOUR MONSTERS TO HAVE, AND PICK SHAPES THAT WILL HELP YOU TELL THEIR STORIES.

ROUNDED SHAPES CAN MAKE A MONSTER FEEL VERY SOFT, SQUISHY, AND STRETCHY.

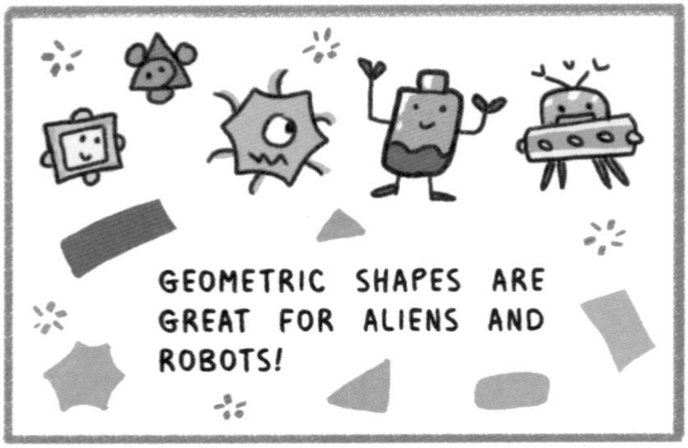
GEOMETRIC SHAPES ARE GREAT FOR ALIENS AND ROBOTS!

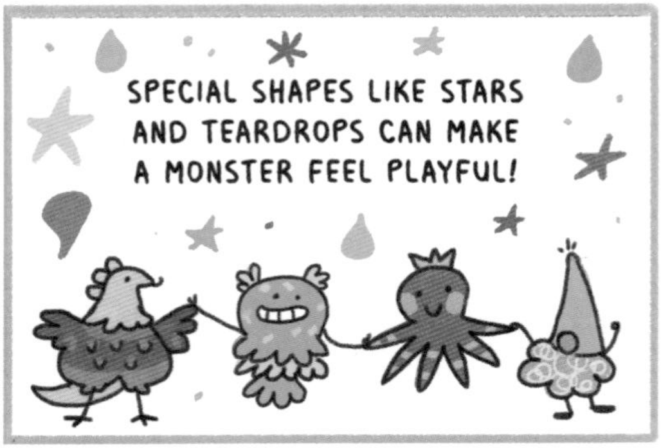
SPECIAL SHAPES LIKE STARS AND TEARDROPS CAN MAKE A MONSTER FEEL PLAYFUL!

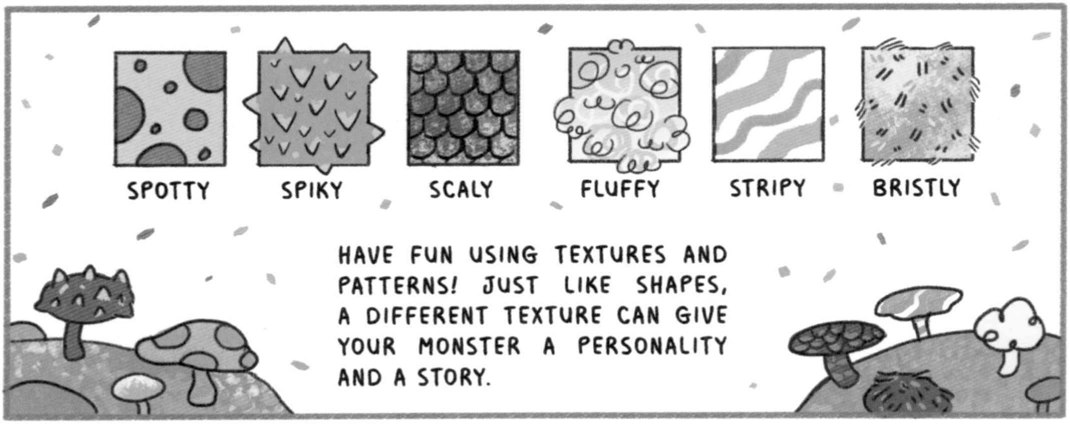
SPOTTY
SPIKY
SCALY
FLUFFY
STRIPY
BRISTLY
HAVE FUN USING TEXTURES AND PATTERNS! JUST LIKE SHAPES, A DIFFERENT TEXTURE CAN GIVE YOUR MONSTER A PERSONALITY AND A STORY.

THESE BOXDOGS ALL HAVE VERY DIFFERENT KINDS OF FUR.

THE PATTERNS AND TEXTURES YOU CHOOSE CAN INFORM WHERE A MONSTER LIVES AND HOW A MONSTER PLAYS.

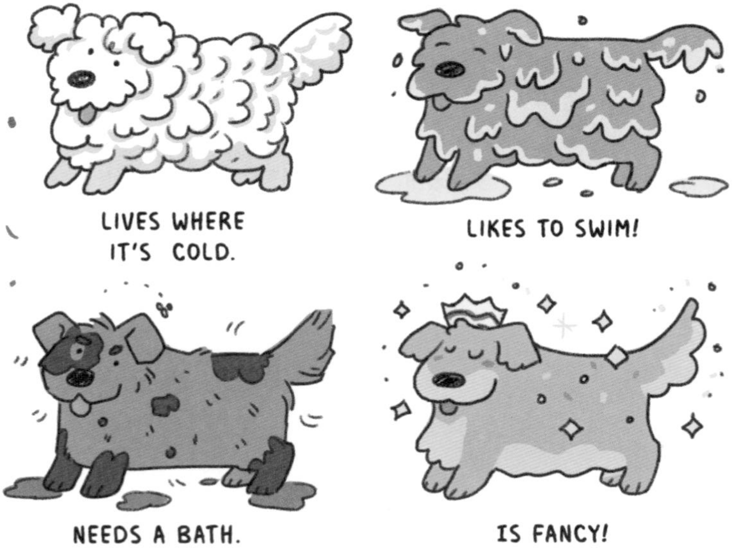
LIVES WHERE IT'S COLD.
LIKES TO SWIM!
NEEDS A BATH.
IS FANCY!

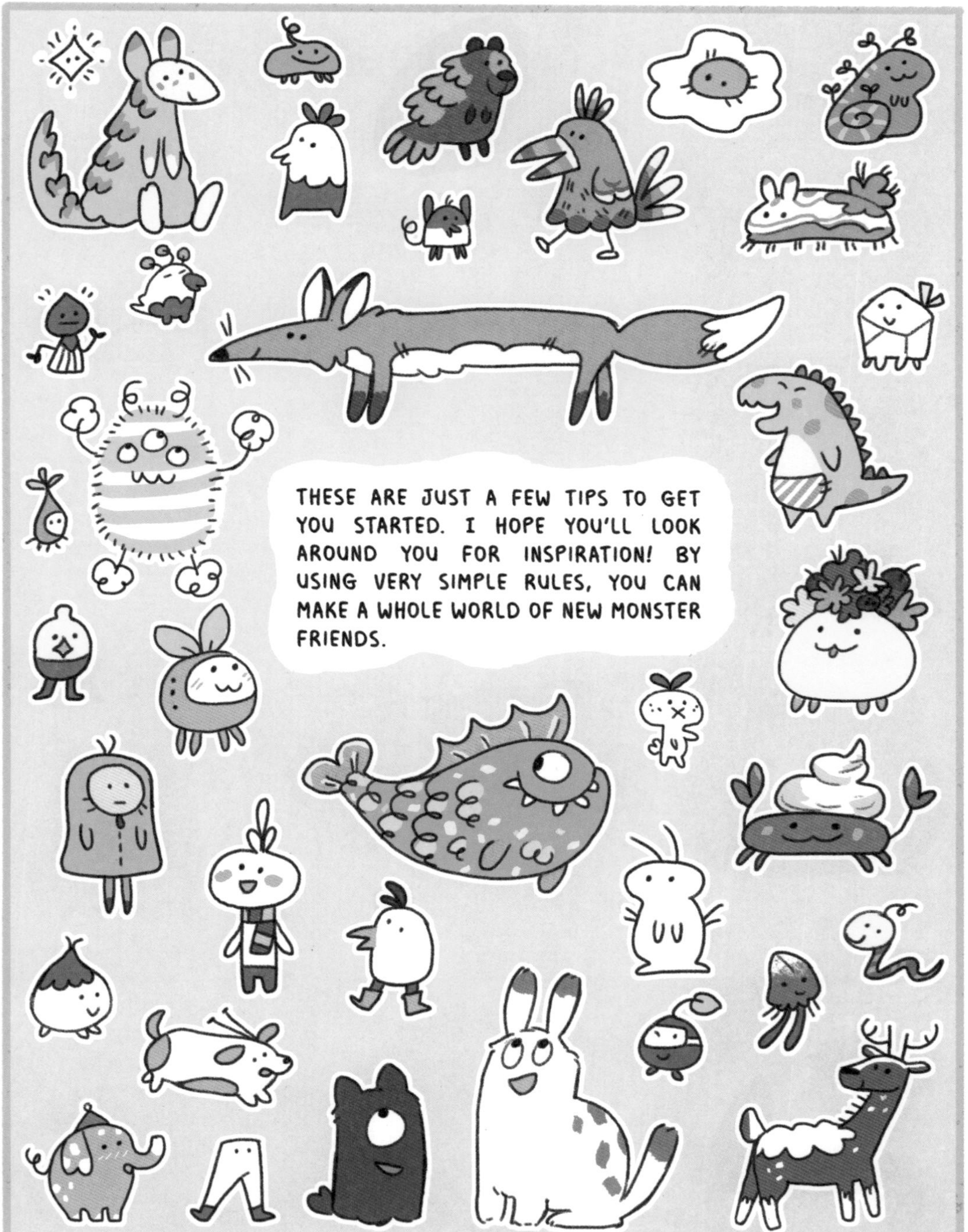
THESE ARE JUST A FEW TIPS TO GET YOU STARTED. I HOPE YOU'LL LOOK AROUND YOU FOR INSPIRATION! BY USING VERY SIMPLE RULES, YOU CAN MAKE A WHOLE WORLD OF NEW MONSTER FRIENDS.

LET'S DRAW REGGIE!

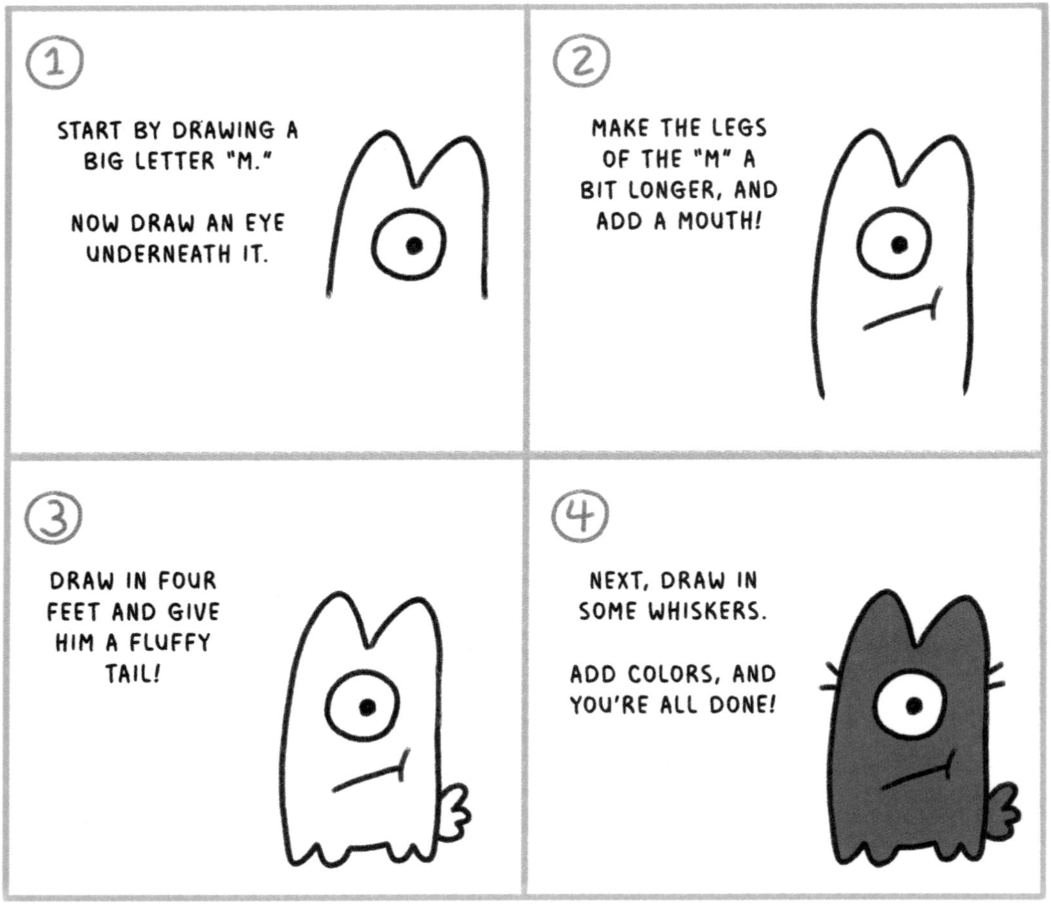
1
START BY DRAWING A BIG LETTER "M."
NOW DRAW AN EYE UNDERNEATH IT.
2
MAKE THE LEGS OF THE "M" A BIT LONGER, AND ADD A MOUTH!
3
DRAW IN FOUR FEET AND GIVE HIM A FLUFFY TAIL!
4
NEXT, DRAW IN SOME WHISKERS.
ADD COLORS, AND YOU'RE ALL DONE!

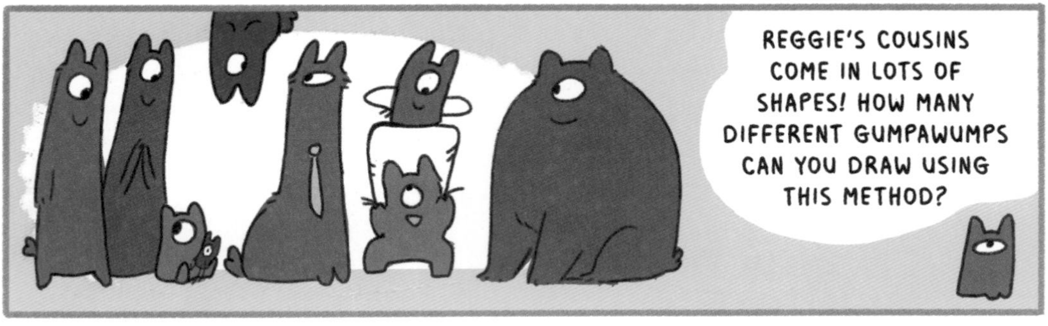
REGGIE'S COUSINS COME IN LOTS OF SHAPES! HOW MANY DIFFERENT GUMPAWUMPS CAN YOU DRAW USING THIS METHOD?

LET'S DRAW EMILY!

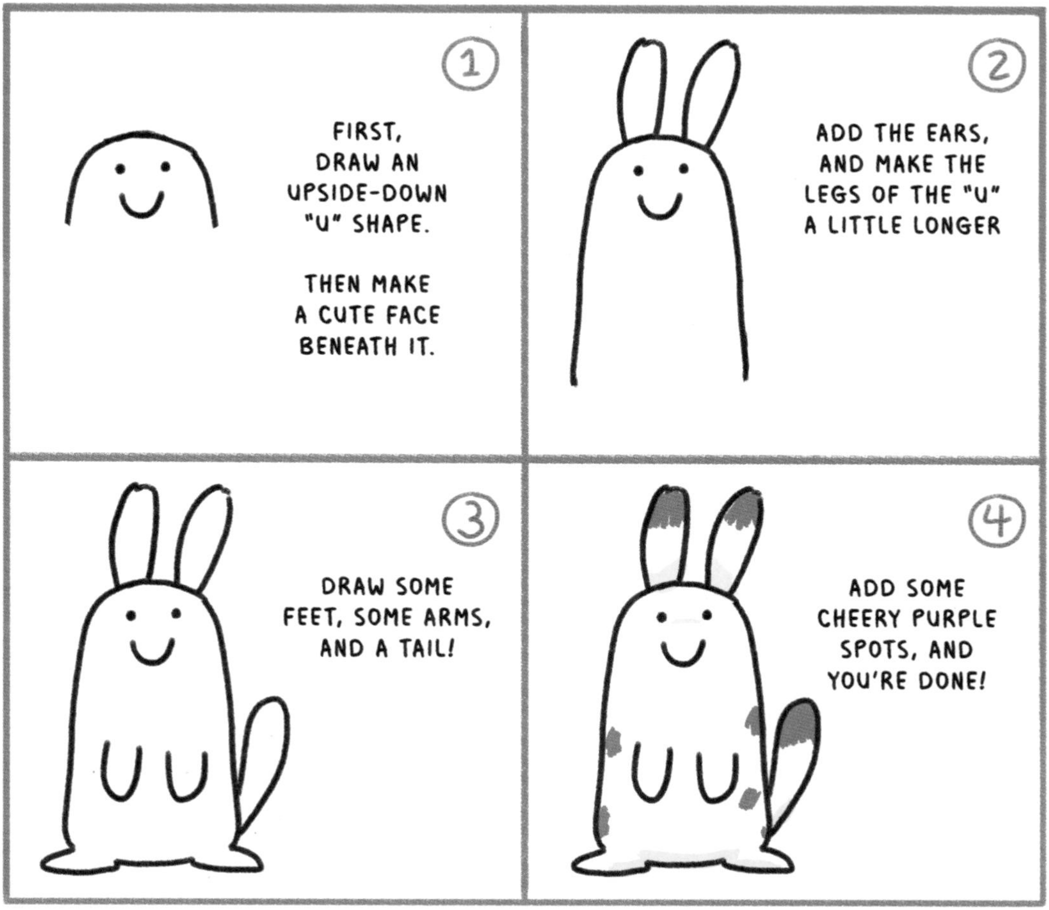

1
FIRST, DRAW AN UPSIDE-DOWN "U" SHAPE.
THEN MAKE A CUTE FACE BENEATH IT.
2
ADD THE EARS, AND MAKE THE LEGS OF THE "U" A LITTLE LONGER
3
DRAW SOME FEET, SOME ARMS, AND A TAIL!
4
ADD SOME CHEERY PURPLE SPOTS, AND YOU'RE DONE!

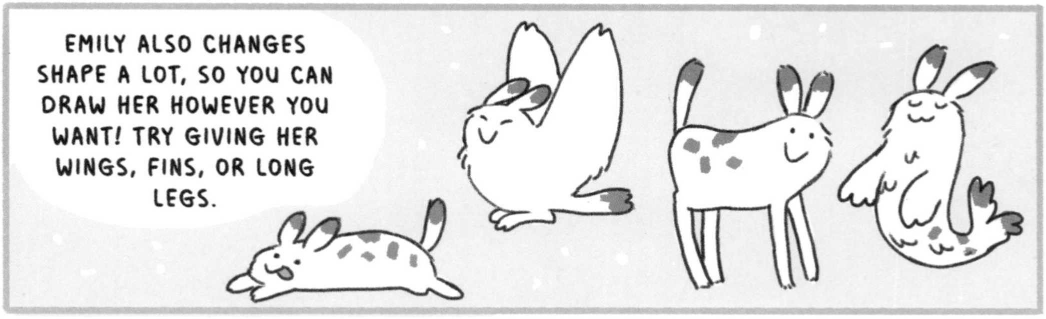

EMILY ALSO CHANGES SHAPE A LOT, SO YOU CAN DRAW HER HOWEVER YOU WANT! TRY GIVING HER WINGS, FINS, OR LONG LEGS.

AWESOME COMICS!
AWESOME KIDS!

Introduce your youngest reader to comics with

RH GRAPHIC

@RHKidsGraphic   A graphic novel on every bookshelf